"Dominick Birdsey is an epic hero
and his story an inspiring,
darkly comic tale of redemption—
a late twentieth-century *Les Miserables.*"
Glamour

"Stocked with a cast of fully developed,
unforgettable characters . . . *I Know This Much Is True* . . .
may be even better than his first."
San Francisco Examiner

"Mythic, powerful, and magical . . .
irresistibly absorbing . . . entertainment of a high order,
forceful and energetic, convincing and memorable . . ."
Memphis Commercial Appeal

"A magnum opus . . .
Lamb has crafted an engrossing tale, full of all
the pain, angst, and uncertainty of modern life. . . ."
Orlando Sentinel

"Terrific . . . long and satisfying . . .
[a] generous, big-hearted book . . .
[It] is Everyman's story, a mythic quest,
the story of a creation of a self. . . .
Wally Lamb is a master. . . ."
New Orleans Times-Picayune

"Exceptional . . .
Fine work, relentless in its effect."
Library Journal

"Lamb has written another winner."

Providence Journal-Bulletin

"It is a rare book that earns its blurbs.
Yet Wally Lamb's novel, *I Know This Much Is True*, is just as 'deeply moving and thoroughly satisfying' as the promotional prose claims. . . . A solid achievement . . . it powerfully conveys challenges that life brings, the difficulties that human beings must shoulder."

Baltimore Sun

"An epic, momentous journey . . .
A worthy successor to Lamb's hugely successful first novel *She's Come Undone* . . ."

Columbus Dispatch

"Relevant . . . immensely gratifying . . .
a moving and unforgettable novel."

Chattanooga Free Press

"An amazingly ambitious book . . .
an epic in every sense . . . a first-person narrative that sweeps you up on the first page, and is never less than enthralling."

Denver Rocky Mountain News

"Lamb is a writer's writer. . . .
I Know This Much Is True is prose written as well as good poetry, with each word and image necessary to the whole. A work of astonishing craftsmanship, structural symmetry, and literary self-awareness, its staggering emotional power comes from fearless exploration of universal truths."

St. Louis Post-Dispatch

"Very moving . . .
Every page is filled with good writing and great storytelling, and it ends far too soon. . . . With wit, incredible insight, and palpable emotions, Lamb brings this universal story of brotherly love, Oedipal conflicts, and mythic struggles to life. . . . Do not miss this book."

Richmond Times-Dispatch

"Worth every moment invested in reading it."

Chattanooga Times

"Sparkling . . .
much too good to put down . . .
the author has taken a giant leap with this story."

San Antonio Express-News

Books by
Wally Lamb

Fiction

I KNOW THIS MUCH IS TRUE
SHE'S COME UNDONE

Nonfiction

ALWAYS BEGIN WHERE YOU ARE:
THEMES IN POETRY AND SONG

COULDN'T KEEP IT TO MYSELF:
TESTIMONIES FROM OUR IMPRISONED SISTERS
(*with Women of the York Correctional Institution*)

I KNOW THIS MUCH IS TRUE

A NOVEL

WALLY LAMB

ReganBooks

HarperTorch
An Imprint of Harper Collins*Publishers*

Portions of *I Know This Much Is True*, some in slightly or substantially different versions, have appeared in the following publications: *Image: A Journal of the Arts and Religion*, *Missouri Review*, *Northeast Magazine*, and *USA Weekend*.

HARPERTORCH
An Imprint of HarperCollins*Publishers*
10 East 53rd Street
New York, New York 10022-5299

ISBN: 0-06-109764-0

First HarperTorch paperback printing: December 2003
First ReganBooks/Perennial trade paperback printing: May 1999
First ReganBooks/Perennial trade special printing: October 1998
First ReganBooks hardcover printing: June 1998

Printed in the United States of America

Visit HarperTorch on the World Wide Web at www.harpercollins.com

10 9 8 7 6 5 4

This book is for my father and my sons

In ways I don't fully understand, this story is connected to the lives and deaths of the following: Christopher Biase, Elizabeth Cobb, Randy Deglin, Samantha Deglin, Kathy Levesque, Nicholas Spano, and Patrick Vitagliano. I hope that, in some small way, the novel honors both their memory and the devotion and strength of the loved ones they had to leave.

Acknowledgments

I am deeply grateful to Linda Chester, my literary agent and friend, and to her associate, Laurie Fox, who shares equal billing. Glinda and Dorothy in one agency: how lucky can a writer get?

I am indebted to Judith Regan, my publisher and *paisana,* for her loyalty, her patient trust, and her passionate response to my work. *Grazie,* Judith.

The following writer-compadres offered invaluable critical reaction to this novel in its many stages, and I am grateful for and humbled by the generosity of their collective response. They are: Bruce Cohen, Deborah DeFord, Joan Joffe Hall, Rick Hornung, Leslie Johnson, Terese Karmel, Ann Z. Leventhal, Pam Lewis, David Morse, Bessy Reyna, Wanda Rickerby, Ellen Zahl, and Feenie Ziner.

A novel this size is both a big, shaggy beast and a complex process requiring faith, luck, moral support, and knowledge far beyond what its author brings to it. I bow deeply to the following, each of whom—in a variety of ways—helped me to find, tell, and publish this story (and, in two cases, to retrieve it from hard-drive never-never land): Elliott Beard, Andre Becker, Bernice Bennett, Lary Bloom, Cathy Bochain, Aileen Boyle, Angelica Canales, Lawrence Carver, Lynn Castelli, Steve Courtney, Tracy Dene, Barbara Dombrowski, David Dunnack, John Ekizian, Sharon Garthwait, Douglas Hood, Gary Jaffe, Susan Kosko, Ken Lamothe, Linda Lamothe, Doreen Louie, Peter Mayock, Susan McDonough, Alice McGee, Joseph Mills, Joseph Montebello, Bob Parzych, Maryann Petyak, Pam Pfeifer, Pit Pinegar, Nancy Potter, Joanna Pulcini, Jenny Romero, Allyson Salazar, Ron Sands, Maureen Shea, Dolores Simon, Suzy Staubach, Nick Stevens, Christine Tanigawa, David Teplica, Denise Tyburski, Patrick Vitagliano Jr., Oprah Winfrey, Patricia Wolf, Shirley Woodka, Genevieve Young, the morning crew at the Sugar Shack Bakery, and my students at the Norwich Free Academy and the University of Connecticut.

I am indebted to Rita Regan, who helped me with copyediting and advice about all things Sicilian, and to Mary Ann Hall, who put Gabrielle D'Annunzio's *Tales of My Native Town* into my hands.

Special thanks to Ethel Mantzaris for long-standing friendship and faithful support.

Finally, I feel gratitude beyond what I can articulate to Christine Lamb, my life partner and love, who makes my writing life possible.

I acknowledge and honor the following teachers, from elementary through graduate school, each of whom encouraged excellence and nurtured creativity: Frances Heneault, Violet Shugrue, Katherine Farrell, Leona Comstock, Elizabeth Winters, Lenora Chapman, Miriam Sexton, Richard Bilda, Victor Ferry, Dorothy Cramer, Mildred Clegg, Mary English, Lois Taylor, Irene Rose, Daniel O'Neill, Dorothy Williams, James Williams, Alexander Medlicott, Alan Driscoll, Gabriel Herring, Frances Leta, Wayne Diederich, Joan Joffe Hall, Gordon Weaver, and Gladys Swan.

I was fortunate to have the support of the following writer-friendly institutions and organizations during the writing of this novel: the Norwich Free Academy, the Willimantic, Connecticut, Public Library, the Homer D. Babbidge Library, the University of Connecticut, and the Connecticut Commission on the Arts.

This novel would not have come into existence without the generous support and validation of the National Endowment for the Arts.

one

On the afternoon of October 12, 1990, my twin brother Thomas entered the Three Rivers, Connecticut Public Library, retreated to one of the rear study carrels, and prayed to God the sacrifice he was about to commit would be deemed acceptable. Mrs. Theresa Fenneck, the children's librarian, was officially in charge that day because the head librarian was at an all-day meeting in Hartford. She approached my brother and told him he'd have to keep his voice down or else leave the library. She could hear him all the way up at the front desk. There were other patrons to consider. If he wanted to pray, she told him, he should go to a church, not the library.

Thomas and I had spent several hours together the day before. Our Sunday afternoon ritual dictated that I sign him out of the state hospital's Settle Building, treat him to lunch, visit our stepfather or take him for a drive, and then return him to the hospital before suppertime. At a back booth at Friendly's, I'd sat across from my brother, breathing in his secondary smoke and leafing for the umpteenth time through his scrapbook of clippings on the Persian Gulf crisis. He'd been collecting them since August as evidence that Armageddon was at hand—that the final battle between good and evil was about to be triggered. "America's been living on borrowed time all these years, Dominick," he told me. "Playing the world's whore, wallowing in our greed. Now we're going to pay the price."

He was oblivious of my drumming fingers on the tabletop. "Not to change the subject," I said, "but how's the coffee business?" Ever since eight milligrams of Haldol per day had quieted Thomas's voices, he had managed a small morning concession in the patients' lounge—coffee and cigarettes and newspapers dispensed from a metal cart more rickety than his emotional state. Like so many of the patients there, he indulged in caffeine and nicotine, but it was the newspapers that had become Thomas's most potent addiction.

"How can we kill people for the sake of cheap oil? How can we justify *that*?" His hands flapped as he talked; his palms were grimy from newsprint ink. Those dirty hands should have warned me—should have tipped me off. "How are we going to prevent God's vengeance if we have that little respect for human life?"

Our waitress approached—a high school kid wearing two buttons: "Hi, I'm Kristin" and "Patience, please. I'm a trainee." She asked us if we wanted to start out with some cheese sticks or a bowl of soup.

"You can't worship both God *and* money, Kristin," Thomas told her. "America's going to vomit up its own blood."

About a month later—after President Bush had declared that "a line has been drawn in the sand" and conflict might be inevitable—Mrs. Fenneck showed up at my front door. She had sought me out—had researched where I lived via the city directory, then ridden out of the blue to Joy's and my condo and rung the bell. She pointed to her husband, parked at the curb and waiting for her in their blue Dodge Shadow. She identified herself as the librarian who'd called 911.

"Your brother was always neat and clean," she told me. "You can't say that about all of them. But you have to be firm with these people. All day long, day in, day out, the state hospital van just drops them downtown and leaves them. They have nowhere to go, nothing to do. The stores don't want them—business is bad enough, for pity's sake. So they come to the library and sit." Her pale green eyes jerked repeatedly away from my face as she spoke. Thomas and I are *identical* twins, not fraternal—one fertilized egg that split in half and went off in two directions. Mrs. Fenneck couldn't look at me because she was looking at Thomas.

It was cold, I remember, and I invited her into the foyer, no further. For two weeks I'd been channel-flipping through the Desert Shield updates, swallowing back the anger and guilt my brother's act had left me with, and hanging up in the ears of reporters and TV types—all those bloodsuckers trying to book and bag next week's freak show. I didn't offer to take Mrs. Fenneck's coat. I stood there, arms crossed, fists tucked into my armpits. Whatever this was, I needed it to be over.

She said she wanted me to understand what librarians put up with these days. Once upon a time it had been a pleasant job—she liked people, after all. But now libraries were at the mercy of every derelict and homeless person in the area. People who cared nothing about books or information. People who only wanted to sit and vegetate or run to the toilet every five minutes. And now with AIDS and drugs and such. The other day they'd found a dirty syringe jammed behind the paper towel dispenser in the men's restroom. In her opinion, the whole country was like a chest of drawers that had been pulled out and dumped onto the floor.

I'd answered the door barefoot. My feet were cold. "What do you *want*?" I asked her. "Why did you come here?"

She'd come, she said, because she hadn't had any appetite or a decent night's sleep since my brother did it. Not that *she* was responsible, she pointed out. Clearly, Thomas had planned the whole thing in advance and would have done it whether she'd said anything to him or not. A dozen people or more had told her they'd seen him walking around town, muttering about the war with that one fist of his up in the air, as if it was stuck in that position. She'd noticed it herself, it always looked so curious. "He'd come inside and sit all afternoon in the periodical section, arguing with the newspapers," she said. "Then, after a while, he'd quiet down. Just stare out the window and sigh, with his arm bent at the elbow, his hand making that fist. But who'd have taken it for a *sign*? Who in their right mind would have put two and two together and guessed he was planning to do *that*?"

No one, I said. None of us had.

Mrs. Fenneck said she had worked for many years at the main desk before becoming the children's librarian and remembered my mother, God rest her soul. "She was a reader. Mysteries and romances, as I recall. Quiet, always very pleasant. And neat as a pin. It's a blessing she didn't live to see *this,* poor thing. Not that dying from cancer is any picnic, either." She said she'd had a sister who died of cancer, too, and a niece who was battling it now. "If you ask me," she said, "one of these days they're going to get to the bottom of why there's so much of it now and the answer's going to be computers."

If she had kept yapping, I might have burst into tears. Might have cold-cocked her. "Mrs. Fenneck!" I said.

All right, she said, she would just ask me point-blank: did my father or I hold her responsible in any way for what had happened?

"You?" I asked. "Why you?"

"Because I spoke crossly to him just before he did it."

It was *myself* I held responsible—for having tuned out all that babble about Islam and Armageddon, for not having called the doctors and bugged them about his medication. And then, for having gone to the emergency room and made what was probably the wrong decision. That Sunday at Friendly's, he'd ordered only a glass of water. "I'm fasting," he'd said, and I'd purposely asked nothing, ignored those dirty hands of his, ordered myself a cheeseburger and fries.

I told Mrs. Fenneck she wasn't responsible.

Then, would I be willing to put it in writing? That it had nothing to do with her? It was her husband's idea, she said. If I could just write it down on a piece of paper, then maybe she could get a decent night's sleep, eat a little of her dinner. Maybe she could have a minute's worth of peace.

Our eyes met and held. This time she didn't look away. "I'm afraid," she said.

I told her to wait there.

In the kitchen, I grabbed a pen and one of those Post-it notepads that Joy lifts from work and keeps by our phone. (She takes more than we'll ever use. The other day I shoved my hands into the pockets of her winter coat looking for change for the paperboy and found dozens of those little pads. *Dozens.*) My hand shook as I wrote down the statement that gave Mrs. Fenneck what she wanted: food, sleep, legal absolution. I didn't do it out of mercy. I did it because I needed her to shut her mouth. To get her the fuck out of my foyer. And because I was afraid, too. Afraid for my brother. Afraid to be his other half.

I went back to the front hall and reached toward Mrs. Fenneck, stuck the yellow note to her coat lapel. She flinched when I did it, and that involuntary response of hers satisfied me in some small, cheap way. I never claimed I was lovable. Never said I *wasn't* a son of a bitch.

I know what I know about what happened in the library on October 12, 1990, from what Thomas told me and from the newspaper stories that ran alongside the news about Operation Desert Shield. After Mrs. Fenneck's reprimand by the study carrel, Thomas resumed his praying in silence, reciting over and over Saint Matthew's gospel, chapter 5, verses 29 and 30: *"And if thy right eye offend thee, pluck it out and cast it from thee . . . and if thy right hand offend thee, cut it off and cast it from thee: For it is profitable for thee that one of thy members should perish and not that thy whole body should be cast into hell."* Thomas removed from his sweatshirt jacket the ceremonial Gurkha knife our stepfather had brought back as a souvenir from World War II. Until the afternoon before, it had hung sheathed and forgotten on an upstairs bedroom wall at the house where my brother and I grew up.

The orthopedic surgeon who later treated my brother was amazed at his determination; the severity of the pain, he said, should have aborted his mission midway. With his left hand, Thomas enacted each of the steps he'd rehearsed in his mind. Slicing at the point of his right wrist, he crunched through the bone, amputating his hand cleanly with the sharp knife. With a loud grunt, he flung the severed hand halfway across the library floor. Then he reached into his wound and yanked at the spurting ulna and radial artery, pinching and twisting it closed as best he could. He raised his arm in the air to slow the bleeding.

When the other people in the library realized—or thought they realized—what had just happened, there was chaos. Some ran for the door; two women hid in the stacks, fearing that the crazy man would attack them next. Mrs. Fenneck crouched behind the front desk and called 911. By then, Thomas had risen, teetering, from the study carrel and staggered to a nearby table where he sat, sighing deeply but otherwise quiet. The knife lay inside the carrel where he'd left it. Thomas went into shock.

There was blood, of course, though not as much as there might have been had Thomas not had the know-how and the presence of mind to stanch its flow. (As a kid, he'd earned advanced first-aid badges and certificates long after I'd declared the Boy Scouts an organization for assholes.) When it was clearer that Thomas meant harm to no one but himself, Mrs. Fenneck rose from behind the library desk and ordered the custodian to cover the hand with a newspaper. The EMTs and the police arrived simultaneously. The med techs hastily treated my brother, strapped him to a stretcher, and packed the hand in an ice-filled plastic bag that someone had run and gotten from the staff lounge refrigerator.

In the emergency room, my brother regained consciousness and was emphatic in his refusal of any surgical attempt to reattach the hand. Our stepfather, Ray, was away and unreachable. I was up on the scaffolding, power-washing a three-story Victorian on Gillette Street, when the cruiser pulled up in front, blue lights flashing. I arrived at the hospital during the middle of Thomas's argument with the surgeon who'd been called in and, as my brother's rational next of kin, was given the decision of whether or not the surgery should proceed. "We'll knock him out good, tranq him up the ying-yang when he comes out of it," the doctor promised. He was a young guy with TV news reporter hair—thirty years old, if that. He spoke in a normal tone, not even so much as a conspiratorial whisper.

"And I'll just rip it off again," my brother warned. "Do you think a few stitches are going to keep me from doing what I have to do? I have a pact with the Lord God Almighty."

"We can restrain him for the first several days if we have to," the doctor continued. "Give the nerves a chance to regenerate."

"There's only one savior in this universe, Doctor," Thomas shouted. "And *you're* not it!"

The surgeon and Thomas both turned to me. I said I needed a second to think about things, to get my head clear. I left the room and started down the corridor.

"Well, don't think for too long," the surgeon called after me. "It's only a fifty-fifty thing at *this* point, and the longer we wait, the worse the odds."

Blood banged inside my head. I loved my brother. I hated him. There was no solution to who he was. No getting back who he had been.

By the time I reached the dead end of that corridor, the only arguments I'd come up with were *stupid* arguments: Could he still pray without two hands to fold? Still pour coffee? Flick his Bic? Down the hall I heard him shouting. "It was a *religious* act! A *sacrifice*! Why should *you* have control over *me*?"

Control: that was the hot button that pushed me to my decision. Suddenly, that gel-haired surgeon was our stepfather and every other bully and power broker that Thomas had ever suffered. You tell him, Thomas, I thought. You fight for your fucking rights!

I walked back up the corridor and told the doctor no.

"No?" he said. He was already scrubbed and dressed. He stared at me in disbelief. *"No?"*

In the operating room, the surgeon instead removed a sheet of skin from my brother's upper thigh and fashioned it into a flaplike graft that covered his butchered wrist. The procedure took four hours. By the time it was over, several newspaper reporters and TV research assistants had already called my home and talked to Joy.

Over the next several days, narcotics dripped through a catheter and into my brother's spine to ease his pain. Antibiotics and antipsychotics were injected into his rump to fight infection and lessen his combativeness. An "approved" visitors' list kept the media away from him, but Thomas explained impatiently, unswervingly, to everyone else—police detectives, shrinks, nurses, orderlies—that he had had no intention of killing himself. He wanted only to make a public statement that would wake up America, help us all to see what he'd seen, know what he knew: that our country had to give up its wicked greed and follow a more spiritual course if we were to survive, if we were to avoid stumbling amongst the corpses of our own slaughtered children. He had been a doubting Thomas, he said, but he was Simon Peter now—the rock upon which God's new order would be built. He'd been blessed, he said, with the gift and the burden of prophecy. If people would only listen, he could lead the way.

He repeated all this to me the night before his release and recommitment to the Three Rivers State Hospital, his on-and-off home since 1970. "Sometimes I wonder why I have to be the one to do all this, Dominick," he said, sighing. "Why it's all on my shoulders. It's hard."

I didn't respond to him. Couldn't speak at all. Couldn't look at his self-mutilation—not even the clean, bandaged version of it. Instead, I looked at my own rough, stained housepainter's hands. Watched the left one clutch the right at the wrist. They seemed more like puppets than hands. I had no feeling in either.

two

One Saturday morning when my brother and I were ten, our family television set spontaneously combusted.

Thomas and I had spent most of that morning lolling around in our pajamas, watching cartoons and ignoring our mother's orders to go upstairs, take our baths, and put on our dungarees. We were supposed to help her outside with the window washing. Whenever Ray gave an order, my brother and I snapped to attention, but our stepfather was duck hunting that weekend with his friend Eddie Banas. Obeying Ma was optional.

She was outside looking in when it happened—standing in the geranium bed on a stool so she could reach the parlor windows. Her hair was in pincurls. Her coat pockets were stuffed with paper towels. As she Windexed and wiped the glass, her circular strokes gave the illusion that she was waving in at us. "We better get out there and help," Thomas said. "What if she tells Ray?"

"She won't tell," I said. "She never tells."

It was true. However angry we could make our mother, she would never have fed us to the five-foot-six-inch sleeping giant who snoozed upstairs weekdays in the spare room, rose to his alarm clock at three-thirty each afternoon, and built submarines at night. Electric Boat, third shift. At our house, you tiptoed and whispered during the day and became free each evening at nine-thirty when Eddie Banas, Ray's fellow third-shifter, pulled into the driveway and honked. I would wait for the sound of that horn. Hunger for it. With it came a loosening of limbs, a relaxation in the chest and hands, the ability to breathe deeply again. Some nights, my brother and I celebrated the slamming of Eddie's truck door by jumping in the dark on our mattresses. Freedom from Ray turned our beds into trampolines.

"Hey, look," Thomas said, staring with puzzlement at the television.

"What?"

Then I saw it, too: a thin curl of smoke rising from the back of the set. *The Howdy Doody Show* was on, I remember. Clarabel the Clown was chasing someone with his seltzer bottle. The picture and sound went dead. Flames whooshed up the parlor wall.

I thought the Russians had done it—that Khrushchev had dropped the bomb at last. If the unthinkable ever happened, Ray had lectured us at the dinner table, the submarine base and Electric Boat were guaranteed targets. We'd feel the jolt nine miles up the road in Three Rivers. Fires would ignite everywhere. Then the worst of it: the meltdown. People's hands and legs and faces would melt like cheese.

"Duck and cover!" I yelled to my brother.

Thomas and I fell to the floor in the protective position the civil defense lady had made us practice at school. There was an explosion over by the television, a confusion of thick black smoke. The room rained glass.

The noise and smoke brought Ma, screaming, inside. Her shoes crunched glass as she ran toward us. She picked up Thomas in her arms and told me to climb onto her back.

"We can't go outside!" I shouted. "Fallout!"

"It's not the bomb!" she shouted back. "It's the TV!"

Outside, Ma ordered Thomas and me to run across the street and tell the Anthonys to call the fire department. While Mr. Anthony made the call, Mrs. Anthony brushed glass bits off the tops of our crewcuts with her whisk broom.

We spat soot-flecked phlegm. By the time we returned to the front sidewalk, Ma was missing.

"Where's your mother?" Mr. Anthony shouted. "She didn't go back in there, did she? Jesus, Mary, and Joseph!"

Thomas began to cry. Then Mrs. Anthony and I were crying, too. "Hurry *up*!" my brother shrieked to the distant sound of the fire siren. Through the parlor windows, I could see the flames shrivel our lace curtains.

A minute or so later, Ma emerged from the burning house, sobbing, clutching something against her chest. One of her pockets was ablaze from the paper towels; her coat was smoking.

Mr. Anthony yanked off Ma's coat and stomped on it. Fire trucks rounded the corner, sirens blaring. Neighbors hurried out of their houses to cluster and stare.

Ma stank. The fire had sizzled her eyebrows and given her a sooty face. When she reached out to pull Thomas and me to her body, several loose photographs spilled to the ground. That's when I realized why she'd gone back into the house: to rescue her photo album from its keeping place in the bottom drawer of the china closet.

"It's all right now," she kept saying. "It's all right, it's all right." And, for Ma, it *was* all right. The house her father had built would be saved. Her twins were within arm's reach. Her picture album had been rescued. Just last week, I dreamt my mother—dead from breast cancer since 1987—was standing at the picture window at Joy's and my condominium, looking in at me and mouthing that long-ago promise. "It's all right, it's all right, it's all right."

Sometime during Ma's endless opening and closing of that overstuffed photo album she loved so much, the two brass pins that attached the front and back covers first bent, then broke, causing most of the book's black construction paper pages to loosen and detach. The book had been broken for years when, in October of 1986, Ma herself was opened and closed on a surgical table at Yale–New Haven Hospital. After several months' worth of feeling tired and run down and contending with a cold that never quite went away, she had fingered a lump in her left breast. "No bigger than a pencil eraser," she told me over the phone. "But Lena Anthony thinks I should go to the doctor, so I'm going."

My mother's breast was removed. A week later, she was told that the cancer had metastasized—spread to her bone and lymph nodes. With luck and aggressive treatment, the oncologist told her, she could probably live another six to nine months.

My stepfather, my brother, and I struggled independently with our feelings about Ma's illness and pain—her death sentence. Each of us fumbled, in our own way, to make things up to her. Thomas set to work in the arts and crafts room down at the state hospital's Settle Building. While Ma lay in the hospital being scanned and probed and plied with cancer-killing poisons, he spent hours assembling and gluing and shellacking something called a "hodgepodge collage"—a busy arrangement of nuts, washers, buttons, macaroni, and dried peas that declared: GOD = LOVE! Between hospital stays, Ma hung it on the kitchen wall where its hundreds of glued doodads seemed to pulsate like something alive—an organism under a microscope, molecules bouncing around in a science movie. It unnerved me to look at that thing.

My stepfather decided he would fix, once and for all, Ma's broken scrapbook. He took the album from the china closet and brought it out to the garage. There he jerry-rigged a solution, reinforcing the broken binding with strips of custom-cut aluminum sheeting and small metal bolts. "She's all set now," Ray told me when he showed me the rebound book. He held it at arm's length and opened it face down to the floor, flapping the covers back and forth as if they were the wings of a captured duck.

My own project for my dying mother was the most costly and ambitious. I would remodel her pink 1950s-era kitchen, Sheetrocking the cracked plaster walls, replacing the creaky cabinets with modern units, and installing a center island with built-in oven and cooktop. I conceived the idea, I think, to show Ma that I loved her best of all. Or that I was the most grateful of the three of us for all she'd endured on our behalf. Or that I was the sorriest that fate had given her first a volatile husband and then a schizophrenic son and then tapped her on the shoulder and handed her the "big C." What I proved, instead, was that I was the deepest in denial. If I was going to go to the trouble and expense of giving her a new kitchen, then she'd better live long enough to appreciate it.

I arrived with my toolbox at the old brick duplex early one Saturday morning, less than a week after her discharge from the hospital. Ray officially disapproved of the project and left in a huff when I got there. Looking pale and walking cautiously, Ma forced a smile and began carrying her canisters and knickknacks out of the kitchen to temporary storage. She watched from the pantry doorway as I committed my first act of renovation, tamping my flatbar with a hammer and wedging it between the wainscoting and the wall. Ma's hand was a fist at her mouth, tapping, tapping against her lip.

With the crack and groan of nails letting go their hold, the four-foot-wide piece of wainscoting was pried loose from the wall, revealing plaster and lath and an exposed joist where someone had written notes and calculations. "Look," I said, wanting to show her what I guessed was her father's handwriting. But when I turned around, I realized I was addressing the empty pantry.

I was thirty-six at the time, unhappily divorced for less than a year. Sometimes in the middle of the night, I'd still reach for Dessa, and her empty side of the bed would startle me awake. We'd been together for sixteen years.

I found my mother sitting in the front parlor, trying to hide her tears. The newly repaired photo album was in her lap.

"What's the matter?"

She shook her head, tapped her lip. "I don't know, Dominick. You go ahead. It's just that with everything that's happening right now . . ."

"You don't *want* a new kitchen?" I asked. The question came out like a threat.

"Honey, it's not that I don't appreciate it." She patted the sofa cushion next to her. "Come here. Sit down."

Still standing, I reminded her that she'd complained for decades about her lack of counter space. I described the new stoves I'd seen at Kitchen Depot—the ones where the burners are one continuous flat surface, a cinch for cleaning. I sounded just like the saleswoman who'd led me around from one showroom miracle to the next.

Ma said that she knew a new kitchen would be great, but that maybe what she really needed right now was for things to stay settled.

I sat. Sighed, defeated.

"If you want to give me something," she said, "give me something small."

"Okay, fine," I huffed. "I'll just make you one of those collage things like Thomas's. Except mine will say LIFE SUCKS. Or JESUS CHRIST'S A SON OF A BITCH." My mother was a religious woman. I might as well have taken my flatbar and poked at her incision.

"Don't be bitter, honey," she said.

Suddenly, out of nowhere, I was crying—tears and strangled little barks that convulsed from the back of my throat. "I'm scared," I said.

"What are you scared of, Dominick? Tell me."

"I don't know," I said. "I'm scared for you." But it was myself I was scared for. Closing in on forty, I was wifeless, childless. Now I'd be motherless, too. Left with my crazy brother and Ray.

She reached over and rubbed my arm. "Well, honey," she said, "it's scary. But I accept it because it's what God wants for me."

"What God wants," I repeated, with a little snort of contempt. I dragged my sleeve across my eyes, cleared my throat.

"Give me something little," she repeated. "You remember that time last spring when you came over and said, 'Hey, Ma, get in the car and I'll buy you a hot fudge sundae'? *That's* the kind of thing I'd like. Just come visit. Look at my album with me."

Tucked in the inside front cover pocket of my mother's scrapbook are two pictures of Thomas and me, scissored four decades earlier from the *Three Rivers Daily Record.* The folded newsprint, stained brown with age, feels as light and brittle as dead skin. In the first photo, we're wrinkled newborns, our diapered bodies curved toward each other like opening and closing parentheses. IDENTICAL TWINS RING OUT OLD, RING IN NEW, the caption claims and goes on to explain that Thomas and Dominick Tempesta were born at the Daniel P. Shanley Memorial Hospital on December 31, 1949, and January 1, 1950, respectively—six minutes apart and in two different years. (The article makes no mention of our father and says only that our unnamed mother is "doing fine." We were bastards; our births would have been discreetly ignored by the newspaper had we not been the New Year's babies.) "Little Thomas arrived first, at 11:57 P.M.," the article explains. "His brother Dominick followed at 12:03 A.M. Between them, they straddle the first and second halves of the twentieth century!"

In the second newspaper photo, taken on January 24, 1954, my brother and I have become Thomas and Dominick Birdsey. We wear matching sailor hats and woolen pea jackets and salute the readers of the *Daily Record*. Mamie Eisenhower squats between us, one mink-coated arm wrapped around each of our waists. Mrs. Eisenhower, in her short bangs and flowered hat, beams directly at the camera. Thomas and I, age four, wear twin looks of bewildered obedience. This picture is captioned FIRST LADY GETS A TWO-GUN SALUTE.

The President's wife was in Groton, Connecticut, that winter day to break champagne against the USS *Nautilus*, America's first nuclear-powered submarine. Our family stood in the crowd below the dignitaries' platform, ticket-holding guests by virtue of our new stepfather's job as a pipe fitter for Electric Boat. EB and the Navy were partners in the building of the *Nautilus*, America's best hope for containing Communism.

According to my mother, it had been cold and foggy the morning of the launch and then, just before the submarine's christening, the sun had burned through and lit up the celebration. Ma had prayed to Saint Anne for good weather and saw this sudden clearing as a small miracle, a further sign of what everybody knew already: that Heaven was on our side, was *against* the godless Communists who wanted to conquer the world and blow America to smithereens.

"It was the proudest day of my life, Dominick," she told me that morning when I started, then halted, the renovation of her kitchen and sat, instead, and looked. "Seeing you two boys with the President's wife. I remember it like it was yesterday. Mamie and some admiral's wife were up there on the VIP platform, waving down to the crowd, and I said to your father, 'Look, Ray. She's pointing right at the boys!' He said, 'Oh, go on. They're just putting on a show.' But I could tell she was looking at you two. It used to happen all the time. People get such a kick out of twins. You boys were always special."

Her happy remembrance of that long-ago day strengthened her voice, animated her gestures. The past, the old pictures, the sudden brilliance of the morning sun through the front windows: the mix made her joyful and took away, I think, a little of her pain.

"And then, next thing you know, the four of us were following some Secret Service men to the Officers' Club lounge. Ray took it in stride, of course, but I was scared skinny. I thought we were in trouble for something. Come to find out, we were following Mrs. Eisenhower's orders. She wanted her picture taken with my two boys!

"They treated us like big shots, too. Your father had a cocktail with Admiral Rickover and some of the other big brass. They asked him all about his service record. Then a waiter brought you and your brother orange sodas in frosted glasses almost as tall as you two were. I was scared one of you was going to spill soda all over Mamie."

"What did you and she have to drink?" I kidded her. "Couple of boilermakers?"

"Oh, honey, I didn't take a thing. I was a nervous wreck, standing that close to her. She ordered a Manhattan, I remember, and had some liver pâté on a cracker. She was nice—very down to earth. She asked me if I'd sewn the little sailor suits you and Thomas were wearing. She told me she knitted some still when she and the President traveled, but she'd never had a talent for sewing. When she stooped down to have her picture taken with you two boys, she told you she had a grandson just a little older than you. *David* Eisenhower is who she was talking about. Julie Nixon's husband. *Camp* David."

Ma shook her head and smiled, in disbelief still. Then she pulled a Kleenex from the sleeve of her bathrobe and dabbed at her eyes. "Your grandfather just wouldn't have believed it," she said. "First he comes to this country with holes in his pockets, and then, the next thing you know, his two little grandsons are hobnobbing with the First Lady of the United States of America. Papa would have gotten a big kick out of that. He would have been proud as a peacock."

Papa.

Domenico Onofrio Tempesta—my maternal grandfather, my namesake—is as prominent in my mother's photo album as he was in her life of service to him. He died during the summer of 1949, oblivious of the fact that the unmarried thirty-three-year-old daughter who kept his house—his only child—was pregnant with twins. Growing up, my brother and I knew Papa as a stern-faced paragon of accomplishment, the subject of a few dozen sepia-tinted photographs, the star of a hundred anecdotes. Each of the stories Ma told us about Papa reinforced the message that *he* was the boss, that *he* ruled the roost, that what *he* said went.

He had emigrated to America from Sicily in 1901 and gotten ahead because he was shrewd with his money and unafraid of hard work, lucky for us! He'd bought a half-acre lot from a farmer's widow and thus become the first Italian immigrant to own property in Three Rivers, Connecticut. Papa had put the roof over our heads, had built "with his own two hands" the brick Victorian duplex on Hollyhock Avenue where we'd lived as kids—where my mother had lived all her life. Papa had had a will of iron and a stubborn streak—just the traits he needed to raise a young daughter "all by his lonesome." If we thought *Ray* was strict, we should have seen Papa! Once when Ma was a girl, she was bellyaching about having to eat fried eggs for supper. Papa let her go on and on and then, without saying a word, reached over and pushed her face down in her plate. "I came up with egg yolk dripping off my hair and the tip of my nose and even my eyelashes. I was crying to beat the band. After that night, I just ate my eggs and shut up about it!"

Another time, when Ma was a teenager working at the Rexall store, Papa found her secret package of cigarettes and marched himself right down to the drugstore where he made her eat one of her own Pall Malls. Right in front of the customers and her boss, Mr. Chase. And Claude Sminkey, the soda jerk she had such an awful crush on. After he left, Ma ran outside and had to throw up at the curb with people walking by and watching. She had to quit her job, she was so ashamed of herself. But she never smoked again—never even liked the smell of cigarettes after that. Papa had fixed *her* wagon, all right. She had defied him and then lived to regret it. The last thing Papa wanted was a sneak living under his own roof.

Sometime during our visit with the photo album that morning, my mother told me to wait there. She had something she wanted to get. With a soft sigh of pain, she was on her feet and heading for the front stairs.

"Ma, whatever it is, let *me* get it for you," I called out.

"That's okay, honey," she called back down the stairs. "I know right where it is."

I flipped quickly through the pages as I waited—made my family a jerky, imperfect movie. It struck me that my mother had compiled mostly a book of her father, Thomas, and me. Others make appearances: Ray, Dessa, the Anthonys from across the street, the Tusia sisters from next door. But my grandfather, my brother, and I are the stars of my mother's book. Ma herself, camera-shy and self-conscious about her cleft lip, appears only twice in the family album. In the first picture, she's one of a line of dour-faced schoolchildren posed on the front step of St. Mary of Jesus Christ Grammar School. (A couple of years ago, the parish sold that dilapidated old schoolhouse to a developer from Massachusetts who converted it into apartments. I bid on the inside painting, but Paint Plus came in under me.) In the second photograph, Ma looks about nine or ten. She stands beside her lanky father on the front porch of the house on Hollyhock Avenue, wearing a sacklike dress and a sober look that matches Papa's. In both of these photos, my mother holds a loose fist to her face to cover her defective mouth.

It was a gesture she had apparently learned early and practiced all her life: the hiding of her cleft lip with her right fist—her perpetual apology to the world for a birth defect over which she'd had no control. The lip, split just to the left of her front teeth, exposed a half-inch gash of gum and gave the illusion that she was sneering. But Ma never sneered. She apologized. She put her fist to her mouth for store clerks and door-to-door salesmen, for mailmen and teachers on parents' visiting day, for neighbors, for her husband, and even, sometimes, for herself when she sat in the parlor watching TV, her image reflected on the screen.

She had made reference to her harelip only once, a day in 1964 when she sat across from me in an optometrist's office. A month earlier, my ninth-grade algebra teacher had caught me squinting at the blackboard and called to advise my mother to get my eyes tested. But I'd balked. Glasses were for brains, for losers and finky kids. I was furious because Thomas had developed no twin case of myopia—no identical need to wear stupid faggy glasses like me. *He* was the jerk, the brownnoser at school. *He* should be the nearsighted one. If she made me get glasses, I told her, I just wouldn't wear them.

But Ma had talked to Ray, and Ray had issued one of his supper table ultimatums. So I'd gone to Dr. Wisdo's office, acted my surliest, and flunked the freaking wall chart. Now, two weeks later, my black plastic frames were being fitted to my face in a fluorescent-lit room with too many mirrors.

"Well, I think they make you look handsome, Dominick," Ma offered. "Distinguished. He looks like a young Ray Milland. Doesn't he, Doctor?"

Dr. Wisdo didn't like me because of my bad attitude during the first visit. "Well," he mumbled reluctantly, "now that you mention it."

This all occurred during the fever of puberty and Beatlemania. The summer before, at the basketball courts at Fitz Field, a kid named Billy Grillo had shown me and Marty Overturf a stack of rain-wrinkled paperbacks he'd found out in the woods in a plastic bag: *Sensuous Sisters, Lusty Days & Lusty Nights, The Technician of Ecstasy*. I'd swiped a couple of those mildewed books and taken them out past the picnic tables where I read page after faded page, simultaneously drawn to and repelled by the things men did to women, the things women did to themselves and each other.

It flabbergasted me, for instance, that a man might put his dick inside a woman's mouth and have her "hungrily gulp down his creamy nectar." That a woman might cram a glass bottle up between another woman's legs and that this would make both "scream and undulate with pleasure." I'd gone home from basketball that day, flopped onto my bed and fallen asleep, awakening in the middle of my first wet dream. Shortly after that, the Beatles appeared on *Ed Sullivan*. Behind the locked bathroom door, I began combing my bangs forward and beating off to my dirty fantasies about all those girls who screamed for the Beatles—what those same girls would do to me, what they'd let me do to them. So the last person I wanted to look like was Ray Milland, one of my mother's old fart movie stars.

"Could you just shut up, please?" I told Ma, right in front of Dr. Wisdo.

"Hey, hey, hey, come on now. Enough is enough," Dr. Wisdo protested. "What kind of boy says 'Shut up' to his own mother?"

Ma put her fist to her mouth and told the doctor it was all right. I was just upset. This wasn't the way I really was.

As if *she* knew the way I really was, I thought to myself, smiling inwardly.

Dr. Wisdo told me he had to leave the room for a few minutes, and by the time he got back, he hoped I would have apologized to my poor mother.

Neither of us said anything for a minute or more. I just sat there, smirking defiantly at her, triumphant and miserable. Then Ma took me by complete surprise. "You think *glasses* are bad," she said. "You should try having what I have. At least you can take your glasses off."

I knew immediately what she meant—her harelip—but her abrupt reference to it hit me like a snowball in the eye. Of all the forbidden subjects in our house, the two *most* forbidden were the identification of Thomas's and my biological father and our mother's disfigurement. We had never asked about either—had somehow been raised not to ask and had honored the near-sacredness of the silence. Now Ma herself was breaking one of the two cardinal rules. I looked away, shocked, embarrassed, but Ma wouldn't stop talking.

"One time," she said, "a boy in my class, a mean boy named Harold Kettlety, started calling me 'Rabbit Face.' I hadn't done anything to him. Not a thing. I never bothered anyone at all—I was scared of my own shadow. He just thought up that name one day and decided it was funny. 'Hello there, Rabbit Face,' he used to whisper to me across the aisle. After a while, some of the other boys took it up, too. They used to chase me at recess and call me 'Rabbit Face.' "

I sat there, pumping my leg up and down, wanting her to stop—wanting Harold Kettlety to still be a kid so I could find him and rip his fucking face off for him.

"And so I told the teacher, and she sent me to the principal. Mother Agnes, her name was. She was a stern thing." Ma's fingers twisted her pocketbook strap as she spoke. "She told me to stop making a mountain out of a molehill. I was making things worse, she said, by calling it to everyone's attention. I should just ignore it. . . . Then more boys got on the bandwagon, even boys from other grades. It got so bad, I used to get the dry heaves before school every morning. You didn't stay home sick in our house unless you had something like the measles or the chicken pox. That's the last thing Papa would have stood for—me home all day long just because some stinker was calling me a name."

I needed her to stop. Needed not to hear the pain in her voice—to see the way she was twisting that pocketbook strap. If she kept talking, she might break down and tell me everything. "I don't see how any of this sob story stuff has anything to do with me," I said. "Are you planning to get to the point before I die of old age?"

She shut up after that, silenced, I guess, by the fact that her own son had joined forces with Harold Kettlety. On the drive home from the optometrist's, I chose to sit in the backseat and not speak to her. Somewhere en route, I drew my new glasses from their brown plastic clip-to-your-pocket case, rubbed the lenses with the silicone-impregnated cleaning cloth, and slipped them on. I looked out the window, privately dazzled by a world more sharp and clear than I remembered. I said nothing about this, spoke no apologies, offered no concessions.

"Ma's *crying* downstairs," Thomas informed me later, up in our bedroom. I was lifting weights, shirt off, glasses on.

"So what am *I* supposed to do about it?" I said. "Hold a snot rag to her nose?"

"Just try being decent to her," he said. "She's your *mother,* Dominick. Sometimes you treat her like s-h-i-t."

I stared at myself in our bedroom mirror as I lifted the weights, studying the muscle definition I'd begun to acquire and which I could now see clearly, thanks to my glasses. "Why don't you *say* the word instead of spelling it," I smirked. "Go ahead. Say 'shit.' Give yourself a thrill."

He'd been changing out of his school clothes as we spoke. Now he stood there, hands on his hips, wearing just his underpants, his socks, and one of those fake-turtleneck dickey things that were popular with all the goody-goody kids at our school. Thomas had them in four or five different colors. God, I hated those dickeys of his.

I looked at the two of us, side by side, in the mirror. Next to me, Thomas was a scrawny joke. Mr. Pep Squad Captain. Mr. Goody-Goody Boy.

"I *mean* it, Dominick," he said. "You better treat her right or I'll say something to Ray. I *will*. Don't think I wouldn't."

Which was bullshit and we both knew it.

I grabbed my barbell wrench, banged extra weights onto the bar, lifted them. Fink. Pansy Ass Dickey Boy. "Oh, geez, I'm nervous," I told him. "I'm so scared, I'll probably shit my p-a-n-t-s."

He stood there, just like Ma, his look of indignation melting into forgiveness. "Just cool it, is all I'm saying, Dominick," he said. "Oh, by the way, I like your glasses."

When Ma came back down the stairs on that day of failed kitchen renovation, she was carrying a gray metal strongbox. I put down the picture album, stood, and walked toward her. "Here, honey," she said. "This is for you. Phew, kind of heavy."

"Ma, I *told* you I'd get it." I took it from her. "What's in it, anyways?"

"Open it and see," she said.

She had masking-taped the key to the side of the box; I kidded her about it—told her it was a good thing she didn't work for Fort Knox. She watched my fingers peel the key free, put it in the lock, and turn. In anticipation of my opening the strongbox, she didn't even seem to hear my teasing.

Inside the box was a large manila envelope curled around a small coverless dictionary and held in place with an elastic band that broke as soon as I touched it. The envelope held a thick sheaf of paper—a manuscript of some kind. The first ten or fifteen pages were typewritten—originals and carbon copies. The rest had been written in longhand—a scrawling, ornate script in blue fountain-pen ink. "It's Italian, right?" I asked. "What is it?"

"It's my father's life story," she said. "He dictated it the summer he died."

As I fanned through the thing, its mildewy aroma went up my nose. "Dictated it to who?" I asked her. "You?"

"Oh, gosh, no," she said. Did I remember the Mastronunzios from church? Tootsie and Ida Mastronunzio? My mother was always doing that: assuming that my mental database of all the Italians in Three Rivers was as extensive as hers was.

"Uh-uh," I said.

Sure I did, she insisted. They drove that big white car to Mass? Ida worked at the dry cleaner's? Walked with a little bit of a limp? Well, anyway, Tootsie had a cousin who came over from Italy right after the war. Angelo Nardi, his name was. He'd been a courtroom stenographer in Palermo. "He was a handsome fella, too—very dashing. He was looking for work."

Her father had been saying for years how, someday, he was going to sit down and tell the story of his life for the benefit of *siciliani*. He thought boys and young men back in the Old Country would want to read about how one of their own had come to America and made good. Gotten ahead in life. Papa thought it might inspire them to do likewise. So when he met Tootsie's cousin one day over at the Italian Club, he came up with a big idea. He would tell Angelo his story—have Angelo write it all down as he spoke and then type it up on the typewriter.

The project had begun as something of an extravaganza, according to my mother. "Careful with his money" his whole life, Papa now spared no expense at first on his inspirational autobiography. He cleared some of the furniture out of the parlor and rented a typewriter for Angelo. "Things were hunky-dory for the first couple of days," Ma said. "But after that, there were problems."

Papa decided he could not tell his story as freely with Angelo in the room—that he would be able to remember things better if he was by himself. "So the next thing you know, he was on the telephone with a bunch of office equipment companies—making all these long-distance calls, which I could hardly believe he was doing, Dominick, because he'd never even call his cousins down in Brooklyn to wish them a Merry Christmas or a Happy Easter. *They* always had to call *us* every year because Papa didn't want to waste his money. But for that project of his, he called all over creation. He ended up renting this Dictaphone machine from some place all the way down in Bridgeport." Ma shook her head, wonder-struck still. "Jeepers, you should have seen that contraption when it got here! I almost fell over the day they lugged that thing into the house."

Two machines sat on rolling carts, she said—one for the person dictating, the other for the stenographer who would turn the recorded sounds first into squiggles and then into typewritten words. They set it up in the front parlor and moved Angelo's typewriter into the spare room. "Poor Angelo," Ma said. "I don't think he knew what he was getting himself into."

Neither Angelo nor Papa could figure out how to run the Dictaphone at first, Ma said. They tried and tried. That whole day, Papa swore a blue streak! He finally made Angelo take the bus down to Bridgeport so that he could learn how to operate the foolish thing. "And here the poor guy could just barely speak English, Dominick. He'd just gotten over here from the Old Country. But anyway, when he came back again, he knew how to run it—how to make everything work.

"Every morning, Angelo would set things up—get everything ready—and then he'd have to leave Papa alone. That was the rule. Papa got so he wouldn't dictate a word of it until he was alone. Angelo used to come out in the kitchen and wait. So I got to know him a little. He was a nice man, Dominick, and so *handsome*. I'd make him coffee and we'd talk about this and that—his life back in Palermo, his family. I used to help him a little with his English. He was smart, too; you'd explain something to him and he'd pick it up just like that. You could just tell he was going places."

The Dictaphone had red plastic belts, Ma said; that was what the voice was recorded on, if she remembered right. Papa would stay in there for two or three hours at a time and then, when he was finished, he'd call Angelo and Angelo would have to go running. He'd wheel the cart into the back room where the typewriter was. Listen to whatever was recorded on the belts and take it down in shorthand. Then he'd type it up. "But my father hated the sound of typewriting, see? He didn't want that clickety-clacking all over the house after he'd finished his end of things for the day. All that remembering made him cranky."

"I don't get it," I said. "Why didn't he just dictate it to him directly?"

"I don't know. He was just nervous, I guess." She reached over and touched the manuscript—passed her fingers across her father's words. She herself didn't dare to go anywhere near that parlor when Papa was speaking into the Dictaphone, she said. He was so serious about it. He probably would have shot her on sight!

Ma told me that the complicated system her father had devised—stenographer, Dictaphone, private rooms for dictator and dictatee—had worked for about a week and then that, too, had fallen apart. First of all, there had been a misunderstanding about the rental price for the recording equipment. Papa had thought he was paying eight dollars per week to rent the Dictaphone but then learned that he was being charged eight dollars a *day. Forty* dollars a week! "So he told the rental company where they could go, and he and Angelo wheeled the carts onto the front porch. Those machines were parked out there for two whole days before someone drove up from Bridgeport and picked them up. I was a nervous wreck with those contraptions just sitting out there. I couldn't even sleep. What if it had rained? What if someone had come along and snitched them?

"But anyway, Papa went back to dictating his story directly to Angelo. But that didn't go any better than it had the first time. Things got worse and worse. Papa started accusing Angelo of poking around in his business—asking him to clear up this thing or that thing when Papa had told him exactly as much as he wanted to tell him and nothing more. Oh, he could be a stubborn son of a gun, my father. He started accusing poor Angelo of changing around some of the things that he had said—of deliberately trying to portray my father in a bad light. Angelo got fed up, the poor guy. The two of them started fighting like cats and dogs."

Somewhere in the middle of July, Papa fired Angelo, my mother said. Then, after a few days, he cooled down and rehired him. But the day after Angelo came back, Papa fired him all over again. When he tried to rehire him a second time, Angelo refused to come back again. "He moved away pretty soon after that," she said. "Out west to the Chicago area. He wrote me one letter and I wrote back and then that was that. But after all that business with Angelo and the Dictaphone and everything—all that rigmarole—Papa finally just went up to the backyard and wrote the rest of his story himself. He worked on it all the rest of that summer. He'd climb up the back stairs every morning, right after breakfast, unless it was raining or he didn't feel well. He'd sit up there at his little metal table with his paper and his fountain pen. Writing away, all by his lonesome."

I leafed again through the musty manuscript—those pages and pages of foreign words. "You ever read it?" I asked her.

She shook her head. We lost eye contact.

"Why not?"

"Oh, I don't know, Dominick. I peeked at it a couple of times, I guess. But I just never felt right about it. My Italian's too rusty. You forget a lot of it if you don't use it."

We sat there, side by side on the couch, neither of us speaking. In less than a year, I thought, she'll be dead.

"It's funny, though," she said. "It was kind of out of character for Papa to do something like that. Write things down. He'd always been so private about everything. Sometimes I'd ask him about the Old Country—about his mother and father or the village where he'd grown up—and he'd say, oh, he didn't even remember that stuff anymore. Or he'd tell me

Sicilians kept their eyes open and their mouths shut. . . . But then, that summer: he hired Angelo, rented that contraption. . . . Some mornings I'd hear him crying up there. Up in the backyard. Or speaking out loud—kind of arguing with himself about something. Papa had had a lot of tragedy in his life, see? Both his brothers who he came over here with had died young. And his wife. All he had was me, really. It was just the two of us."

The first page of the manuscript was hand-lettered in blue fountain-pen ink, lots of flourishes and curlicues. "I can read his name," I said. "What does the rest say?"

"Let's see. It says, 'The History of Domenico Onofrio Tempesta, a Great Man from . . .' *Umile? Umile?* Humble! . . . 'The History of Domenico Onofrio Tempesta, a Great Man from Humble Beginnings.' "

I had to smile. "He had a pretty good idea of himself, didn't he?"

Her eyes brimmed with tears. "He was a wonderful man, Dominick."

"Yeah, right. As long as you ate your eggs. And your cigarettes."

Ma stroked the small, coverless dictionary. "I've been meaning to give you this stuff for a long time, honey," she said. "You take it with you when you go. It's for Thomas, too, if he ever wants to look at it, but I wanted to give it to you, especially, because you were the one who always used to ask about Papa."

"I was?"

She nodded. "When you were little. See this dictionary? This is the one he used right after he came over from the Old Country—the one he learned his English from."

I opened the tattered book. Its onionskin pages were stained with grease from his fingers. On one page, I covered his thumbprint with my thumb and considered for the first time that Papa might have been more than just old pictures—old, repeated stories.

I took my mother into the kitchen and showed her the pencil marks written onto the joist. "Yup, that's his writing!" she said. "I'll be a son of a gun. Look at that! It almost brings him right back again."

I reached out and rubbed her shoulder, the cloth of her bathrobe, the skin and bone. "You know what I think?" I said. "I think you should translate that story of his."

Ma shook her head. "Oh, honey, I can't. I told you, I've forgotten more Italian than I remember. I never learned it that good to begin with. It was confusing. Sometimes he'd speak the Italian he'd learned in school—up in the North—and sometimes he'd speak Sicilian. I used to get them mixed up. . . . And anyway, it's like I said. I just don't think he wanted me to read it. Whenever I'd go out into the yard to hang the clothes or bring him a cold drink, he'd get so mad at me. Shout at me, shoo me away. 'Stay out of my business!' he'd say. I'm telling you, he was a regular J. Edgar Hoover about that project of his."

"But, Ma, he's *dead,*" I reminded her. "He's been dead for almost forty years."

She stopped, was quiet. She seemed lost in thought.

"What?" I said. "What are you thinking about?"

"Oh, nothing, really. I was just remembering the day he died. He was all alone out there, all by himself when he had that stroke." She drew her Kleenex from her sleeve. Wiped her eyes. "That same morning, while he was eating his breakfast, he told me he was almost done with it. It took me back a little—him giving me a progress report like that—because up until then, he had never said one word to me about it. Not directly, I mean. . . . And so I asked him, I said, 'What are you going to do with it, Papa, once you're finished?' I thought he was going to start writing away to some publishers back in Italy. Try to get it made into a book like he'd said. But you know what he told me? He said maybe he'd just throw it into the ash barrel and put a match to it. Burn the whole thing up once he was finished writing it. It just wasn't the answer I was expecting. After all that trouble he'd gone to to get it down. . . . I heard him sobbing up there a couple of times that last morning—really wailing one time. It was terrible. And I *wanted* to go up to him, Dominick, but I thought it would have made him mad if I did. Made things worse. He'd been so private about it.

"And then, later on, when I went out there with his lunch, there he was. Slumped over, his head on the table. These pages were all over the place: stuck in the hedges, stuck against the chicken coop. They'd blown all over the yard.

"And so I ran back down inside and called the police. And the priest. Your grandfather wasn't a churchgoer—he had a kind of a grudge against St. Mary's for some reason—but I figured, well, I'd call the priest anyway. . . . It was awful, Dominick. I was so scared. I was shaking like a leaf. And here I was, carrying your brother and you. . . ."

I reached over. Put my arm around her.

"After I made those two phone calls, I just went back out there and waited. Went back up the stairs. I stood there, about ten or twelve feet away from him, watching him. I knew he was dead, but I kept watching him, hoping maybe I'd see him blink or yawn. Hoping and praying that I was mistaken. But I knew I wasn't. He hadn't moved a muscle." She passed her hand again over Papa's manuscript. "And so I went around the yard, picking up this thing. It was all I could think of to do for him, Dominick. Pick up the pages of his history."

The room filled up with silence. The sun had shifted—had cast us both in shadow.

"Well, anyway," she said. "That was a long time ago."

Before I left, I tapped the wainscoting back into place, covering once again Domenico's notes and calculations. I walked out the door and down the front porch steps, balancing my toolbox, the strongbox, and several foil-wrapped packages of frozen leftovers. ("I worry about you in that apartment all by yourself, honey. Your face looks too thin. I can tell you're not eating the way you should. Here, take these.") At the door of the truck, I heard her calling and went back up the steps.

"You forgot this," she said. I put my hand out, palm up, and she opened her fist. The strongbox key fell into my hand. "*La chiave,*" she said.

"Come again?"

"*La chiave.* Your key. The word for it just came back to me."

"*La chiave,*" I repeated, and dropped the key into my pocket.

That night, I awoke from a sound sleep with the idea: the perfect gift for my dying mother. It was so simple and right that its obviousness had eluded me until 2:00 A.M. I'd have her father's life story translated, printed, and bound for her to read.

I drove up to the university and found the Department of Romance Languages office tucked into the top floor of a stone building dwarfed by two massive, leafless beech trees. The secretary drew up a list of possibilities for me to try. After an hour's worth of false leads and locked doors, I walked the narrow steps to a half-landing and knocked at the office door of Nedra Frank, the last person on my list.

She looked about forty, but it's hard to tell with those hair-yanked-back, glasses-on-a-chain types. As she leafed through my grandfather's pages, I checked out her breasts (nice ones), the mole on her neck, her gnawed-down cuticles. She shared the office with another grad student; her sloppy desk and his neat one were a study in opposites.

"Some of this is written in standard Italian," she said. "And some of it's . . . it looks like peasant Sicilian. What was he—schizo or something?"

Okay, bitch, thanks anyway. Give it the fuck back to me and I'll be on my way.

"I'm a scholar," she said, looking up. She handed me back the manuscript. "What you're asking me to do is roughly the same as trying to commission a serious artist to paint you something that goes with the sofa and drapes."

"Oh," I said. "Okay." Already, I'd begun backing out of her low-ceilinged office—a glorified closet, really, and not all that glorified.

She sighed. "Let me see it again." I handed it back and she scanned several pages, frowning. "The typed pages are single-spaced," she said. "That's twice as much work."

"Yeah, well . . ."

"The penmanship's legible, at least. . . . I could do the handwritten material for eight dollars a page. I'd have to charge sixteen for the typed ones. More on the ones where explanatory footnotes were necessary."

"How much more?"

"Oh, let's say five dollars per footnote. I mean, fair is fair, right? If I'm actually *generating* text instead of just translating and interpreting, I should be paid more. Shouldn't I?"

I nodded. Did the math in my head. Somewhere between

eight hundred and a thousand bucks *without* the footnotes. More than I thought it would be, but a lot less than a kitchen renovation. "Are you saying you'll do it then?"

She sighed, kept me waiting for several seconds. "All right," she finally said. "To be perfectly honest, I have no interest in the project, but I need money for my car. Can you believe it? A year and a half old and the tranny's already got problems."

It struck me funny: this Marian the Librarian using gearhead lingo. "Why are you smiling?" she asked.

I shrugged. "No reason, really. What kind of car is it?"

"A Yugo," she said. "I suppose *that's* funny, too?"

Nedra Frank told me she wanted four hundred dollars up front and estimated the translation would take her a month or two to complete, given her schedule, which she described as "oppressive." Her detachment annoyed me; she had looked twice at her wall clock as I spoke of my grandfather's accomplishments, my mother's lymphoma. I wrote her a check, worrying that she might summarize or skip pages—shortchange me in spite of what she was charging. I left her office feeling vulnerable—subject to her abbreviations and interpretations, her sourpuss way of seeing the world. Still, the project was under way.

I called her several times over the next few weeks, wanting to check her progress or to see if she had any questions. But all I ever got was an unanswered ring.

Whenever my mother underwent her chemotherapy and radiation treatments at Yale–New Haven, Ray drove her down there, kept her company, ate his meals in the cafeteria downstairs, and catnapped in the chair beside her bed. By early evening, he'd get back on the road, driving north on I-95 in time for his shift at Electric Boat. When I suggested that maybe he was taking on too much, he shrugged and asked me what the hell else he was supposed to do.

Did he want to talk about it?

What was there to talk about?

Was there anything I could do for him?

I should worry about my mother, not him. He could take care of himself.

I tried to make it down to New Haven two or three times a week. I brought Thomas with me when I could, usually on Sundays. It was hard to gauge how well or poorly Thomas was handling Ma's dying. As was usually the case with him, the pendulum swung irregularly. Sometimes he seemed resigned and accepting. "It's God's will," he'd sigh, echoing Ma herself. "We have to be strong for each other." Sometimes he'd sob and pound his fists on my dashboard. At other times, he was pumped up with hope. "I *know* she's going to beat this thing," he told me one afternoon over the phone. "I'm praying every day to Saint Agatha."

"Saint who?" I said, immediately sorry I'd asked.

"Saint Agatha," he repeated. "The patron saint invoked against fire and volcanoes and cancer." He rambled on and on about his stupid saint: a virgin whose jilted suitor had had her breasts severed, her body burned at the stake. Agatha had stopped the eruption of a volcano, had died a Bride of Christ, blah blah blah.

One morning at 6:00 A.M., Thomas woke me up with the theory that the Special K our mother ate for breakfast every day had been deliberately impregnated with carcinogens. The Kellogg's Cereal Company was secretly owned by the Soviets, he said. "They target the relatives of the people they're *really* after. I'm on their hit list because I do God's bidding." Now that he was on to them, he said, he was considering exposing Kellogg's—rubbing it right in their corporate face. He would probably end up as *Time* magazine's Man of the Year and have to go into hiding. Stalkers followed famous people. Look what had happened to poor John Lennon. Did I remember the song "Instant Karma"? John had written it specifically for him, to encourage him to do good in the world after he'd gone. "Listen!" my brother said. "It's so obvious, it's pathetic!" He broke out into a combination of song and shouting.

Instant karma's gonna get you—gonna look you right in the FACE
You better recognize your BROTHER and join the HUMAN RACE!

* * *

One Sunday afternoon when Thomas and I drove down to visit Ma, her bed was empty. We found her in the solarium, illuminated by a column of sun coming through the skylight, sitting by herself among clusters of other people's visitors. By then, the chemo had stained her skin and turned her hair to duck fluff—had given her, once again, the singed look she'd had that day she emerged from the burning parlor on Hollyhock Avenue. Somehow, bald and shrunken in her quilted pink robe, she looked beautiful to me.

Thomas sat slumped and uncommunicative through that whole visit. He had wanted me to stop at McDonald's on the way down and I'd told him no—that maybe we could go there on the ride back. In the solarium, he pouted and stared trancelike at the TV and ignored Ma's questions and efforts at conversation. He refused to take off his coat. He wouldn't stop checking his watch.

I was angry by the time we left, angrier still when, during the drive home, he interrupted my speech about his selfishness to ask if we were still going to McDonald's. "Don't you get it, asshole?" I shouted. "Don't you even come up for air when your own goddamned mother's dying?" He undid his seatbelt and climbed over the front seat. Squatting on the backseat floor, he assumed a modified version of the old duck-and-cover.

I pulled the car into the breakdown lane, threw her into neutral, and told him to get the fuck back in front—that I was sick and tired of *his* bullshit, fed up with *his* crap on top of everything else I was trying to juggle. When he refused to get up, I yanked him up and out of the car. He pulled free and bolted, running across the interstate without even looking. Horns wailed, cars swerved wildly. Don't ask me how he made it across. And by the time I got across the highway myself, Thomas had disappeared. I ran, panic-stricken, through woods and yards, imagining the ugly thump of impact, Thomas ripped in half, his blood splattered all over the road.

I found him lying in the tall grass at the side of the highway about a quarter of a mile up from where the car was. His eyes were closed, his mouth smiling up at the sun. When I helped him up, the grass was dented in the shape of his body. Like a visual aid at a crime scene. Like one of those angels he and I used to make in new snow. . . . Back in the car, I gripped the wheel to steady my hands and tried not to hear and see those cars that had swerved out of his way. In Madison, I pulled into a McDonald's and got him a large fries, a Quarter Pounder with cheese, a strawberry shake. If he was not exactly happy for the rest of the trip, he was at least quiet and full.

That evening, Nedra Frank picked up on the first ring.

"I know you're busy," I said. I told her what Ray had just called and told me: that my mother's condition had gotten worse.

"I'm working on it right now, as a matter of fact," she said. "I've decided to leave some of the Italian words and phrases intact to give you some sense of the music."

"The music?"

"Italian is such a musical language. I didn't want to translate the manuscript to death. But you'll recognize the words I've left untouched—either contextually or phonetically. Or both. And some of the proverbs he uses are virtually untranslatable. I've left them in whole but provided parenthetical notations—approximations. Now, I'm preserving very little of the Sicilian, on the assumption that one *weeds* the garden. Right?"

"Yeah," I said. "Whatever. It's the *English* I'm more interested in, anyway." She sure didn't have a whole lot of use for Sicily. "So . . . what's he like?" I asked.

There was a pause. "What's he *like*?"

"Yeah. I mean, you know the guy better than I do at this point. I'm just curious. Do you like him?"

"A translator's position should be an objective one. An emotional reaction might get in the way of—"

The day had been brutal. I had no patience with her scholarly detachment. "Well, just this once, treat yourself to an emotional reaction," I said. "For my sake."

There was dead air on the other end for the next several seconds. Then I got what I had asked for. "I don't like him, actually, no. Far from it. He's pompous, misogynistic. He's horrible, really."

Now the silence was coming from my end.

"You *see*?" she said. "Now you're offended. I *knew* I shouldn't have relinquished my objectivity."

"I'm not offended," I said. "I'm just impatient. I just want it to get done before she's too sick to enjoy it."

"Well, I'm doing the best I can. I told you about my schedule. And anyway, I think you'd better read it first before you decide to share it with her. If I were you, I wouldn't talk it up just yet."

Now her lack of objectivity *was* pissing me off. What right did she have to tell me what I should or shouldn't do? Screw you, I wanted to tell her. You're just the translator.

Ma's third round of chemo made her too sick to eat. In February, she landed back in the hospital weighing in at ninety-four pounds and looking like an ad for famine relief. By then, I'd stopped bringing Thomas to see her. The incident on the highway had scared me shitless, had kept me up more nights than one.

"This may jab a little going in, sweetie pie," the nurse said, her intravenous needle poised in front of my mother's pale face.

Ma managed a nod, a weak smile.

"I'm having a little trouble locating a good vein on you. Let's try it again, okay? You ready, sweetheart?"

The insertion was a failure. The next one, too. "I'm going to try one more time," she said. "And if that doesn't work, I'm going to have to call my supervisor."

"Jesus fucking Christ," I mumbled. Walked over to the window.

The nurse turned toward me, red-faced. "Would you rather step outside until we're finished?" she said.

"No," I said. "I'd rather you stopped treating her like she's a friggin' pincushion. And as long as you're asking, I'd just as soon you stop calling her 'honey' and 'sweetie pie' like we're all on fucking *Sesame Street* or something."

Ma began to cry—over my behavior, not her own pain. I've got this talent for making bad situations worse. "Later, Ma," I said, grabbing my jacket. "I'll call you."

Late that same afternoon, I was standing at the picture window in my apartment, watching unpredicted snow fall, when Nedra Frank pulled up unexpectedly in her orange Yugo, hopping the curb and coming to a sliding stop. She'd parked half on the sidewalk, half in the road.

"Come in, come in," I said. She was wearing a down vest, sweatshirt, denim skirt, sneakers—clothes I never would have predicted. She carried a bulging briefcase.

"So it's finished?"

"What?" Her eyes followed mine to the briefcase. "Oh, *no,*" she said. "This is my doctoral thesis. The apartment house where I live was broken into last week, so I'm carrying this wherever I go. But I'm working on your project. It's coming along." She asked me nothing about my mother's condition.

"How did you know where I live?" I asked.

"Why? Is it a deep, dark secret or something?"

"No, I just—"

"From your check. I copied your address down before I cashed it. In case I had to get ahold of you. Then I was just out for a drive—I've been so stressed out lately—and I just happened to pass by your street sign and I remembered it. Hillyndale Drive. It's such an unusual spelling. Was someone trying to be quaint or something? *Faux* British?"

I shrugged, jingled the change in my pockets. "Couldn't tell you," I said.

"I'd been meaning to call you anyway. About the manuscript. Your grandfather used a lot of proverbs—country sayings—and they don't lend themselves to translation. I thought I'd just leave them as is and then paraphrase them in the endnotes. If that's okay. I mean, it's your money."

Hadn't we already had this conversation once? She was just out for a drive, my ass. "That would be fine," I said.

I offered her a beer; she accepted.

"So why are you stressed out?" I said.

For one thing, she said, the two undergraduate classes they made her teach were certifiably "brain-dead." They didn't want to learn anything; they just wanted A's. And for another thing, her department chair was threatened by her knowledge of Dante, which was superior to his. And for a third thing, her office mate had disgusting personal habits. He flossed his teeth right there at his desk. Manicured his fingernails with a nail clipper that sent everything flying over to her side. Just that day she had found two fingernails on her desk blotter, after she had *told* him. . . . She was sick to death of academic men, she said—sucking, forever, on the breast of the university so that they wouldn't have to get on with real life. "What do *you* do for a living?"

"I paint houses," I said.

"A *housepainter*!" she groaned, flopping down on my couch. *"Perfect!"*

She finished her beer, said yes to another. When I came back in with it, she was over at my bookcase, cocking her head diagonally to read the spines. "Garcia Marquez, Styron, Solzhenitsyn," she said. "I must say, Mr. Housepainter, I'm impressed."

"Yeah," I said. "You'd think a dumb fuck like me would be reading—what?—Mickey Spillane? *Hustler?*"

"Or this," she said. She took my boxed James M. Cain trilogy from the shelf, waving it like a damning piece of evidence. She walked over to the picture window. "Is this snow supposed to amount to anything? I never follow the forecast."

"It *wasn't* forecast," I said. "Let's see what they're saying." I clicked on the little weather radio I keep in the bookcase. The staticky announcer said three to five inches. Oh, great, I thought. Snowed in with this supercilious bitch. Just what I needed.

Nedra picked up the weather radio, looked at it front and back, clicked it on and off. "So you're a real fan of weather?" she said.

"I'm not a *fan* of it," I said. "But you need to know what it's going to be doing out there when you're in the painting business. *In* season. You have to stay on top of it."

"You have to stay on top," she repeated. "God, you men are all alike." She laughed—a fingernails-down-the-blackboard kind of shriek—asked *me* if *I* wanted a beer. If I was planning to feed her or just get her drunk and then push her back out in the snow.

I told her I didn't have much of anything, unless she liked chicken broth or Honey Nut Cheerios.

"We could order a pizza," she said.

"All right."

"I'm a vegetarian, though. If *that* changes anything."

The kid from Domino's arrived two beers later. I'd ordered a large mushroom and olive, but ours was the last stop before his shift ended, he said, and all he had left in his vinyl warmer bag was two medium pepperonis. "I'm sure it's my retarded manager's fault, not yours," he said. Snowflakes lit on the fur collar of his jacket, on the brim of his dorky Domino's hat. "Here," he said. "Free of charge. I'm quitting anyways."

When I closed the door and turned around again, I saw my quilt draped around Nedra Frank's shoulders. Which meant she'd been in my bedroom.

At the kitchen table, she picked off all the pepperoni slices and stacked them like poker chips, then blotted the tops of the pizzas with paper towels. We opened a second six-pack.

It must have been a Thursday night because later *Cheers* was on—a show Nedra said offended her politically because all the women characters were either bimbos or bitches. She'd come late to feminism, she said, after having been daddy's little girl, then a majorette in high school, then a slave to a chauvinist husband and a Dutch colonial on Lornadale Road. "I had to go into therapy for three years just to give myself permission to get my Ph.D.," she said. "Take *this*!" She aimed the remote control at Ted Danson, deadening the TV.

"My wife was in *Ms.* magazine once," I said. "She and her friend Jocelyn."

"You have a *wife*?"

"My *ex*-wife, I meant. She and this friend of hers organized day care for women welders down at Electric Boat. Then they got the honchos down there to put into writing a policy about on-the-job harassment from the male workers. It was a year or two after EB started hiring women to work in the shipyard."

"You were married to a *welder*?" she asked, a smirk on her face.

"Her friend was a welder. Dessa ran the day care center. 'Kids, Unlimited!' it was called. Exclamation mark at the end."

"Fascinating," Nedra said. Except she didn't sound too

fascinated. She was attacking that pizza like the shark in *Jaws*. "My ex-husband's a psychiatrist," she said. "He's an administrator down at the state hospital."

I almost told her about Thomas, but didn't want to encourage any wow-what-a-small-world connections between the two of us. Besides, she'd made that crack about my grandfather being "schizo." I kept hoping she'd leave before those bald tires of hers closed out leaving as one of her options. It frosted me a little that she'd just gone into my room and taken the quilt. Who knew what kind of liberties she was taking with my grandfather's story? What *else* she was weeding out of that thing besides his "peasant Sicilian"?

"Todd's crazier than the inmates, though," Nedra said. "Vicious, too. It was sort of like being married to the Marquis de Sade, except that it was all pain, no pleasure."

"Oh," I said. "Todd de Sade."

That screechy laugh again. I turned the TV back on. "God," I said. "*L.A. Law*'s on already. It must be after ten. I can drive you back in my truck if you don't want to chance it in this snow. It's four-wheel drive."

"You tell time by the television shows?" she said. "Amazing." I let her keep assuming what she assumed: that I was just some uneducated goober she could use to get herself through a lonely evening. Back when I was teaching high school, I never would have called a class "brain-dead."

"So do you want me to? Drive you home?"

"Oh, I get it," she said. "You're the big four-wheel-drive hero and I'm the damsel in distress, right? Thanks but no thanks."

She lifted my quilt off her shoulders and tossed it on the sofa. "Let's listen to some music," she said. Before I could say yes or no, she hit the power switch on my tuner and went searching for a station. I'd have pegged her for a classical music type, but she settled on Tina Turner: *What's love got to do, got to do with it?*

She turned around and smiled. "Hello, there, Mr. Housepainter." She walked over to me. Kissed me. Took my hands in hers and put them against her hips. Her tongue flicked around inside my mouth.

"Is this a turn-on, Mr. Housepainter?" she whispered.

"Am I making you feel good?" I couldn't tell if she was being daddy's little girl or a majorette or what. I pretended I was kissing Dessa, but she was thicker than Dessa, damp to the touch no matter *where* I touched. I hadn't been with a woman since the divorce—had imagined it happening pretty differently. Had imagined being more a part of the decision process, for one thing. I found Nedra a little scary, to tell the truth. The last thing I needed in my life was another nutcase. I wanted my wife.

"Um, this is very nice," I said, "but sort of unexpected. I'm not sure I'm really ready for—"

"I have one," she said. "Relax. Touch me."

She slid my hand down to her butt, placed my other hand up under her sweatshirt. Then suddenly, right in the middle of kissing her, I started laughing. A few little nervous burps of laughter at first that I tried to swallow back. Then worse: full-throttle, out-of-control stuff—the kind of laughing that turns into a coughing attack.

She stood there, smiling, humiliated. "What's so funny?" she kept asking. *"What?"*

I couldn't answer her. Couldn't stop laughing.

Nedra headed for the bathroom. She stayed in there for a good fifteen minutes, long enough for me to begin to wonder if a person could commit suicide by overdosing on Nyquil, by cutting her wrists with a nail clipper. She emerged, red-eyed. Without a word, she went for her coat and briefcase. I told her I'd just been nervous—that I was still getting over things. That I was really, really sorry.

"Sorry for what?" she said. "For getting your kicks by degrading women? Don't apologize. You're born to the breed."

"Hey, look," I said. "I didn't—"

"Oh, please! Not another word! I *beg* of you!"

At the door, she stopped. "Maybe I should call your ex-wife," she said. "We could commiserate about sexual harassment." She pronounced it in that alternative way—William Henry *Harass*ment.

"Hey, wait a minute. *You* put the moves on *me*. How did *I* harass *you*?"

"What's her number, anyway? Maybe I'll call her. Maybe she and I can have our picture in *Ms.* magazine."

"Hey, listen. All I ever contracted you for was an overpriced translation. The rest of this was your idea. Leave my wife out of it."

"Overpriced? *Overpriced?* That work is painstaking, you bastard! You unappreciative—!" Instead of finishing her sentence, she swung her briefcase at me, whacked me in the leg with her freaking twenty-pound doctoral thesis.

She slammed the door behind her and I yanked it open again—scooped up some snow, packed it, and let it fly. It thunked against her Yugo.

She gave me the finger, then got into her car and revved up for takeoff. Oblivious of the road conditions, she gunned it all the way down the street, slipping and sliding and nearly front-ending a honking city plow.

"Your lights!" I kept yelling at her. "Put on your lights!"

By March, the oncology team at Yale had begun to sound like snake oil salesmen. Ma was in near-constant pain; what little comfort she was getting was coming from an old Polish priest and the hospice volunteers. Painting season had begun, jump-started by an early spring that I couldn't afford not to take advantage of. It was mid-April before I got the time and the stomach to drive back to the university and walk the steps up to Nedra Frank's little cubicle. Finished or not, I wanted my grandfather's story back.

Nedra's office buddy told me she'd withdrawn from the degree program. "Personal reasons," he said, rolling his eyes. Her desk was a clean slate, the bulletin board behind her stripped to bare cork.

"But she's got something of mine," I protested. "Something important. How can I get ahold of her?"

He shrugged.

The head of the department shrugged, too.

The head of humanities told me she would attempt to locate Ms. Frank and share my concerns, but that she couldn't promise I'd be contacted. The agreement we had made was between the two of us, she reminded me; it had nothing whatsoever to do with the university. Under no circumstances could she release Nedra Frank's forwarding address.

* * *

My mother slipped out of consciousness on May 1, 1987. Ray and I kept a vigil through the night, watching her labored, ragged breathing and thwarting, until the very end, her continual attempts to pull the oxygen mask from her mouth. "There's a strong possibility that someone in a coma can hear and understand," the hospice worker had told us the evening before. "If it feels right to you, you might want to give her permission to go." It *hadn't* felt right to Ray; he'd balked at such an idea. But ten minutes before she expired, while Ray was down the hall in the men's room, I leaned close to my mother's ear and whispered, "I love you, Ma. Don't worry. I'll take care of him. You can go now."

Her death was different from the melodramatic versions I'd imagined during those final months. She never got to read her father's history. She never sat up in her deathbed and revealed the name of the man with whom she'd conceived my brother and me. From early childhood, I had formed theories about who our "real" father was: Buffalo Bob; Vic Morrow from *Combat;* my seventh-grade shop teacher, Mr. Nettleson; Mr. Anthony from across the street. By the time of Ma's death, my suspicions had fallen on Angelo Nardi, the dashing, displaced courtroom stenographer who had been hired to transcribe my grandfather's life story. But that, too, was just a theory. I told myself it didn't really matter.

After the hospital paperwork had been gotten through, Ray and I drove to the funeral parlor to make final arrangements, then drove back to Hollyhock Avenue and drank Ray's good Scotch. The old photo album was out, sitting there on the dining room table. I couldn't open it up—couldn't look inside the thing—but on impulse, I took it with me when we went down to the hospital to tell my brother the news.

Tears welled up in Thomas's eyes when he heard, but there was no scene—no difficult overreaction, as I'd imagined. Dreaded. When Ray asked Thomas if he had any questions, he had two. Had she suffered at the end? Could Thomas have his GOD = LOVE! collage back now?

Ray left after half an hour or so, but I stayed behind. If Thomas was going to have a delayed bad reaction, I told myself, then I wanted to be there to help him through it. But that wasn't entirely true. I stayed there because I needed to—needed on the morning of our mother's death to be with my twin, my other half, no matter who he had become, no matter where my life—our lives—were careening.

"I'm sorry, Thomas," I said.

"It's not your fault," he said. "You didn't give her the cancer. God gave it to her." With grim relief, I noted that he was no longer blaming the Kellogg's Cereal Company.

"I mean, I'm sorry for blowing up at you. That time we visited her? In the car on the way home? I shouldn't have lost my cool like that. I should have been more patient."

He shrugged, bit at a fingernail. "That's okay. You didn't mean it."

"Yeah, I *did*. I meant it at the time. That's *always* my problem. I let stuff eat away and eat away inside of me and then—bam!—it just explodes. I do it with you, I did it with Ma, with Dessa. Why do you think she left me? Because of my anger, that's why."

"You're like our old TV," Thomas sighed.

"What?"

"You're like our old TV. The one that exploded. One minute we were watching a show and the next minute—ka-boom!"

"Ka-boom," I repeated, softly. For a minute or more, neither of us spoke.

"Do you remember when she came running out of the house that day?" Thomas finally said. He reached over and grabbed the photo album, touched its leather cover. "She was holding this."

I nodded. "Her coat was smoking. The fire had burned off her eyebrows."

"She looked just like Agatha."

"Who?"

"Agatha. The saint I prayed to while Ma was sick." He got up and took his dog-eared book from the bottom drawer of his nightstand. *Lives of the Martyred Saints*. Flipped through the lurid color paintings of bizarre suffering: the faithful, besieged by hideous demons; afflicted martyrs gazing Heavenward, bleeding from gaping Technicolor wounds. He found Agatha's full-page illustration and held it up. Dressed in a nun's habit, she stood serene amidst chaos, holding a tray that bore two women's breasts. Behind her, a volcano erupted. Snakes fell out of the sky. Her body was outlined in orange flame.

Thomas shuddered twice and began to cry.

"It's all right," I said. "It's all right. It's all right." I reached back for the scrapbook. Opened it. We looked in silence, together.

When Ray had repaired my mother's broken book, he'd made no effort to restore the loose pages to their proper chronological order. The result was a book of anachronisms: Instamatic snapshots from the sixties opposite turn-of-the-century studio portraits; time shuffled up and bolted. Here were Thomas and I in front of the Unisphere at the 1964 World's Fair; Ray in his Navy uniform; Papa in a greased handlebar mustache, arm in arm with his young bride who, later, would drown at Rosemark's Pond. Though my grandfather had died several months before Thomas and I were born, in Ma's book we met him face-to-face. Stupidly, carelessly, I had lost Domenico's dictated story, but my mother had entered the fire and rescued his image.

Thomas unfolded the old newspaper clipping of the two of us in our sailor suits, saluting the camera and flanking Mamie Eisenhower. Despite my sadness, I had to smile at those two bewildered faces.

Thomas told me he had no recollection whatsoever of that day when the *Nautilus,* America's first nuclear submarine, eased down the greased ways and into the Thames River to help save the world from Communism. As for me, my memories are fragments—sounds and sensations that may have more to do with my mother's retelling of the story than with any electrical firings in my own brain. What I seem to recall is this: the crack of the water as the flag-draped submarine hits the river, the prickle of orange soda bubbles against my lip, the tickle of Mamie's mink.

three

When you're the sane brother of a schizophrenic identical twin, the tricky thing about saving yourself is the blood it leaves on your hands—the little inconvenience of the look-alike corpse at your feet. And if you're into both survival of the fittest *and* being your brother's keeper—if you've promised your dying mother—then say so long to sleep and hello to the middle of the night. Grab a book or a beer. Get used to Letterman's gap-toothed smile of the absurd, or the view of the bedroom ceiling, or the indifference of random selection. Take it from a godless insomniac. Take it from the *un*-crazy twin—the guy who beat the biochemical rap.

Five days after my brother's sacrifice in the public library, Dr. Ellis Moore, the surgeon who had grafted the flap over Thomas's wound, declared him out of the woods infection-wise and stable enough to be released. That same day, Dr. Moore filed a Physician's Emergency Certificate with the judge of probate, stating in writing that he found Thomas to be "dangerous to himself and/or others." This set into motion a mandatory fifteen-day observation period at the Three Rivers State Hospital complex. At the end of those fifteen days, one of three things would happen to my brother: he would be freed to face the breach of peace and assault charges that had been brought against him; he could commit himself voluntarily to the hospital for further treatment; or, if the treatment team evaluating Thomas felt that his release might be harmful to himself or to the community, he could be held involuntarily at the state hospital for a period of six months to a year, by order of the probate court.

By the time the paperwork was signed and the police escorts had arrived for the transfer, it was after 8:00 P.M. They put one of those Texas belts around Thomas's waist, then handcuffed him, taking care to snap on the left cuff six inches or so above his stump. When they locked the cuffs to the belt, it had the effect of making my brother slump forward in a posture of surrender. While an aide was getting Thomas into a wheelchair, I pulled the cops aside. "Hey, look. This handcuff stuff is totally unnecessary," I told them. "Can't you let the guy have a little dignity while he's being wheeled out of here?"

The younger cop was short and brawny. The other was tall and tired and baggy-looking. "It's standard procedure," the older guy shrugged, not unsympathetically.

"He's potentially violent," the younger cop added.

"No, he isn't," I said. "He was trying to *stop* a war. He's *non*violent." I followed the guy's eyes down to my brother's missing hand.

"It's procedure," the older cop repeated.

Thomas led the parade out of the hospital, the aide pushing his wheelchair down the hall, the two cops and me pulling up the rear. Everyone walking toward us risked sneaky little glances at my brother's restraints. I was holding Thomas's stuff for him: a get-well plant from my ex-wife, duffel bag, toiletry bag, his Bible.

The trip across town from Shanley Memorial to the state hospital is about five or six miles. Thomas asked me to ride in the cruiser with him; I could tell he was scared. At first, the younger cop hassled me about going with them, but then the older guy said I could. They made me ride shotgun up front. The older cop rode in back with Thomas.

At first nobody said anything. In between squawks from the police radio, the AM station was giving updates on Operation Desert Shield. "If you ask me," the cop in back said, "Bush ought to show that crazy Hussein who's boss the same way Reagan showed 'em down in Grenada. Flex some muscle. Nip it in the bud."

"That was Carter's whole problem with those tent-heads in Iran," the younger guy agreed. "He made the U.S. look like a bunch of wimps."

Thomas had been given some kind of Valium cocktail for the road, but I was afraid their talk would rile him. I hunched toward the driver and mumbled a request that he change the subject. He gave no response except for a pissy look, but he did shut up.

Riding through downtown, we passed the McDonald's on Crescent Street where Thomas had worked briefly and the boarded-up Loew's Poli movie house where, once upon a time, my brother and I had shaken hands with Roy Rogers and Dale Evans during the town's three-hundredth anniversary celebration. We passed over the Sachem River Bridge. Passed Constantine Motors, the car dealership my ex-in-laws own. Passed the public library.

"Dominick?" Thomas called up to the front.

"Hmm?"

"How much longer?"

"We're about halfway."

Three Rivers State Hospital is on the southern border of town, a left turn off the John Mason Parkway, the four-lane state highway that runs to the Connecticut shoreline. Once part of the hunting and fishing grounds of the Wequonnoc Indians, the sprawling hospital property is bordered behind by the Sachem River, on the north by the town fairgrounds, and on the south by the sacred burial grounds of the Wequonnocs. Back in the summer of '69, Thomas and I mowed and trimmed that little Indian graveyard. We were seasonal employees, home from our freshman year at college. By then, Thomas's illness had already started flirting with him in little ways I couldn't or didn't want to see. Nine months later, there'd be no avoiding it: March of 1970 was when Thomas's brain dropped him to his knees.

It was hard to believe over twenty years had gone by between that crazy summer and this ride in the police cruiser. I'd graduated from college, taught high school history for a while, and then started my painting business. Ma had died, and the baby. Dessa had left me; I'd hooked up with Joy. Now here I was, after all that water under the bridge, still riding back with my brother to the state hospital. There'd been two decades' worth of shifting diagnoses, new medications, exchangeable state-appointed shrinks. We'd long since given up on miracles for Thomas, settling instead for reasonable intervals between the bad spells and ugly episodes. Seventy-seven and '78 were good years, I remember. That's when they decided Thomas wasn't manic-depressive after all, took him off lithium, and started him on Stelazine instead. Then Dr. Bradbury retired and Thomas's new guy, that fucking little Dr. Schooner, decided that if six milligrams of Stelazine a day was good for my brother, eighteen milligrams a day would be even better. I can still feel that little quack's tweed coat lapels in my fists the day I went down to see Thomas and found him sitting there paralyzed and glassy-eyed, his tongue sticking out of his mouth, his shirt front sopping with drool. Schooner had *meant* to check in on my brother, he told me after I let him go, but it had been so busy. He'd had to cover for another doctor; his in-laws were in town. One of the nurses told me they'd called that slimeball and left messages about Thomas all weekend long.

There was a pretty good stretch in the early eighties. Dr. Filyaw started Thomas on Haldol in 1983. My brother began doing so well that they transferred him to a group home and got him that maintenance job at McDonald's. (Thomas had me photocopy his first paycheck before we cashed it, I remember. He kept it framed on his bedroom wall at the group home, along with a ten-dollar bill that somebody stole later on to buy cigarettes.) Thomas even had himself a girlfriend back then, this bride-of-Frankenstein chick named Nadine. Nadine was a holy roller like him but not nuts in any official way. Not *categorized* as crazy. They met in a Bible study group. She was in her midforties, a good ten years older than he was at the time. Don't ask me how they squared it with God and their holy roller group, but my brother and Nadine were doing it. I should know. I'm the guy who had to buy Thomas his Trojans. It was Nadine who convinced him that if his faith was strong enough, he didn't have to rely on medication—that what God wanted from him was a test of faith.

It's tempting to delude yourself when your screwed-up brother becomes gainfully employed and starts acting less screwed up for a while. You begin to take sanity for granted—convince yourself that optimism's in order. Thomas had a girlfriend and a job and was living semi-independently. If the signs were there, I guess I overlooked them. Let down my guard. Big mistake.

Nobody except Thomas and Nadine knew he'd stopped taking his Haldol. Or that he'd begun to wear a ring of aluminum foil around his head every night when he went to bed because it somehow let God's voice through but scrambled the messages of his enemies. My brother: the human radio receiver pulling in the Jesus frequency. Mr. Tinfoil Head. I mean, it's not funny, but it is. If I didn't laugh about it sometimes, I'd be down in the bughouse in the bed next to his.

The new drive-thru window at McDonald's had been installed only about a week or two before Thomas cracked. Later on, he blamed his assistant manager, who had balked that morning when Thomas showed up for work wearing his aluminum foil hat. Thomas had tried to explain to the guy that Communist agents were ridiculing him through the outside speaker—calling to him as he emptied the garbage or swept the parking lot, encouraging him to go inside and eat the rat poison in the utility closet. By the time the police got there, Thomas, wielding his floor polisher, had already knocked off Ronald McDonald's life-sized fiberglass head and wasted the restaurant's brand-new drive-thru speaker. The cops found him sobbing away behind the Dumpster, bees hovering all around him. Thomas had to check out of the group home, of course—check back into the hospital. About a month after that, he got a postcard of the Grand Ole Opry from Nadine and Chuckie, this other high-on-Jesus buddy of theirs. Chuckie and Nadine had eloped, were honeymooning in Tennessee. I was worried the news from Nadine was going to set Thomas back further, but he took it like a stoic and held no grudges.

* * *

"Read me something from my Bible, Dominick," Thomas ordered me now in the cruiser, midway between Shanley Memorial and the hospital. He'd been making demands for four days: get him this, check on that. Ordering instead of asking, the way he always did when he was in bad shape. I turned around and looked back at him. The lights from a passing car illuminated his face. Despite the Valium, his eyes looked clear, hungry for something. "Read to me from the Book of Psalms," he said.

The binding on Thomas's Bible is broken, its loose pages nearly translucent from finger oil. The whole thing's held together with rubber bands. "The Book of Psalms?" I said. I pulled off the elastics, flipped through the tissuey pages. "Where are they at?"

"In the middle. Between the Book of Job and the Book of Proverbs. Read me the Twenty-sixth Psalm."

In the confusion at the library five days earlier, my brother's Bible had been left behind, then scooped up by the police detectives assigned to the case. Later, in the recovery room, Thomas had bubbled up from the anesthetic calling for it. He called for it all the next day, too. Clamored for it. A substitute wouldn't do—it had to be *his* Bible—the one Ma had given him for his confirmation back when we were in sixth grade. (She'd given us each one, but mine was long gone. Gone where is anyone's guess.) After several hours of listening to his bellyaching, I'd finally gone down to police headquarters and told the guy behind the glass that we needed that Bible over at the hospital a lot more than they needed it at the station. I'd repeated my request to his supervisor, then to *that* guy's supervisor. It was Jerry Martineau, the deputy chief, who finally cut through all the "official police investigation" bullshit and ended the impasse. Martineau and I had played hoops together in high school. Well, to be accurate, we'd mostly kept each other company on the bench while the hotshots played. Jerry was the comedian type—the kind of kid that could get you laughing so hard, you couldn't breathe. He did this imitation of Jerry Lewis from *The Nutty Professor* that still makes me crack a smile when I think of it. Martineau could do anybody: Elmer Fudd, President Kennedy, Maxwell Smart. One time, our coach, Coach Kaminski, walked into the locker room and caught Jerry imitating *him.* Martineau was doing laps for about the next three months.

"Here you go, Dominick," he said when he slipped my brother's blood-splattered Bible from a plastic bag labeled "official police evidence" and handed it to me. "Keep the faith, man."

I looked into Jerry's eyes for the joke—the mimicry—but there was none. That's when I remembered that his father had committed suicide when we were in high school—had gone out to the woods one afternoon and blown out his brains. The whole team went to the wake together, I remember—sat slumped in those cushioned chairs, our knees pushed against the seats in front of us, our big feet tapping the carpeted floor a mile a minute. Martineau's old man had been a cop, too.

The Lord is my light and my salvation; whom should I fear? I read now to my brother, squinting in the dim light of streetlamps. *The Lord is my life's refuge; of whom should I be afraid?* The driver reached over and turned off the radio. Even the dispatcher back at the station shut up. *When evildoers come at me to devour my flesh, my foes and my enemies themselves stumble and fall. . . . Though war be waged upon me, even then will I trust.*

I felt my chest tighten. Tasted acid in my throat as I read the words. If Thomas hadn't latched onto that Bible voodoo—that "if your right hand sinneth, then cut it off" crap—then none of this would have happened. We wouldn't be taking this ride. My phone at home wouldn't be ringing off the wall with calls from reporters and religious crackpots. "You know, Thomas," I told him, clearing my throat, "I can hardly see what's on the page here. I'm going to go blind if I keep reading this."

"Please," he said. "Just a little more. I like hearing your voice say the words."

I could hear him whispering along with me as I read. *Hear, O Lord, the sound of my call; have pity on me, and answer me. . . . Though my father and mother forsake me, yet will the Lord receive me.*

"How's Ray?" Thomas asked, out of the blue.

"Ray? He's okay, I guess. He's fine."

"Is he mad at me?"

"Mad? No, he's not mad." It embarrassed me to have him ask about our stepfather in front of those two cops.

"He hasn't come to see me."

"Oh, well . . . he just got home. From fishing."

"Today?"

"Yesterday. Well, day before yesterday, I guess it was. This week's been so screwed up, I can't even keep the days straight."

"Screwed up because of me?" Thomas asked.

My fingers tap-tapped against the open Bible. "They've probably got Ray working overtime or something," I said. "He'll come see you. He'll probably stop in this weekend down at the other place."

"He's mad at me, isn't he?"

I could feel myself blush when the cop next to me looked over for my answer. "Nah," I said. "He's . . . he's just worried. He's not mad."

Three days earlier, when Ray had gotten back from his fishing trip, I'd driven over to Hollyhock Avenue to tell him the news. He was out in the garage cleaning his gear when I pulled my pickup into the driveway. He started telling me all about these largemouth bass he and his buddy had caught. "So you haven't heard, have you?" I asked.

"Heard what?" I looked away from the fear in his eyes. He'd been caught with his guard down, same as me.

He didn't say much when I told him. He just stood there and listened, his face going gray while I delivered the particulars: that Thomas had used Ray's ceremonial knife from World War II to do it—had gone over to the house, taken it off Ray and Ma's bedroom wall, even sharpened the damn thing on the grinding stone out in the garage. I told Ray what the doctor had said: that the complete severance had been nearly "superhuman," given the obstruction of the wrist bone and the amount of pain he must have had to endure—that Thomas's determination was, in a way, remarkable. I told Ray I was the one who'd decided not to have them attempt a reattachment.

Even for a spit-and-polish ex-Navy man, my stepfather seemed that afternoon to take extraordinary care to put all his gleaming fishing paraphernalia back in its proper order. Back inside the house, he scrubbed his hands with Boraxo at the kitchen sink, then went upstairs to shower and change his clothes so that we could go to the hospital.

"Jesus God," I heard him groan to himself up there. Heard him blow his nose once, twice. Then, again, "Jesus. Jesus."

We rode over to Shanley Memorial in my pickup, Ray reading the two-day-old front-page story in the *Daily Record* while I drove. A veteran of both World War II and Korea, Ray was angry with the article's mention of Thomas's act as a sacrifice to end the standstill over Kuwait. "The kid's crazy—doesn't even know what the hell he's doing—and they're playing it up like he's some goddamned antiwar protester." Alongside the story, the paper had run my brother's twenty-two-year-old high school yearbook picture: long hair, muttonchop sideburns, peace sign pinned to his sports jacket lapel. Back during Vietnam, Ray had maintained that all draft dodgers should be taken somewhere and shot.

"But it *was* an antiwar statement, Ray," I said. "That was his whole point: he thought if he cut off his hand, Hussein and Bush would both stop and notice. Come to their senses. He thought he could short-circuit a war. It was heroic, in its own goofy way."

"Heroic?" Ray said. He rolled down the window, spat, rolled it back up again. *"Heroic?* I've seen heroics, buddy boy. I've been there. Don't you sit there and tell me this stunt he pulled was *heroic!"*

As a kid, I had had a recurring fantasy in which my biological father was Sky King, the adventuresome pilot on Saturday morning TV. After the worst times, the loudest shouting, I'd sometimes circle around the backyard, my arms swooping wildly at passing planes. Sky would spot me, I imagined—make an emergency landing, having located us at last: his long-lost wife, his twin sons. He'd help Ma and Thomas and me into the *Songbird,* then make Ray pay—punch him a couple of good ones, buzz him all the way down our street to make him sorry for the way he bullied us. The four of us would fly away. Later, somewhere around the time I began to sprout armpit hair and lift weights down in the cellar, I gave up on heroes and took to buzzing Ray myself, goading him in small ways—stepping, usually, *on* the line but not quite *over* it. I was still afraid of his anger but saw, now, how he punished weakness—pounced on it. Out of self-preservation, I hid my fear. Smirked at the dinner table, answered him in grudging single syllables, and learned how to look him back in the eye. Because Ray was a bully, I showed him as often as possible that Thomas was the weaker brother. Fed him Thomas to save myself.

When I pulled into the parking lot at Shanley Memorial, I put the brake on and kept the engine running. Ray got out of the truck. I just sat there, immobile, my legs as heavy as lead. I looked up at the sound of his Navy ring click-clicking against the glass.

"Aren't you coming?" he asked me.

I rolled down the window. "You know what?" I said. "I felt the truck pulling a little while I was driving over here. I think one of the front tires is soft. I'm just going to go to the gas station and have them check it out."

He scowled, glanced quickly at the tires. "I didn't feel any pull," he said.

"It won't take long. He's in room 210 West. I'll see you up there."

I watched him pass through the revolving door. Watched visitors and delivery men and a vendor in a Patriots jacket selling hot dogs from a cart. Punched the radio buttons, settling finally for a duet: Willie Nelson's croon and Dylan's nasal twang, together.

There's a big aching hole in my chest now where my heart was
And a hole in the sky where God used to be

I don't know how long I sat there.

I was just about to throw her in reverse and get the hell out of there—drive somewhere, anywhere—when my ex-wife rolled past me in her van and pulled in three spaces away. GOOD EARTH POTTERS it says on the side. It's *his* van, I guess, not hers. From time to time, I've seen the two of them, Dessa and her live-in boyfriend, driving around town in that truck. Dessa runs a day care place. *He's* the potter.

She got out of the truck holding a pot of chrysanthemums and one of those silver balloon things. The wind had picked up and that balloon was bobbing around like crazy. When I saw her, I was glad I'd put her name on the "approved visitors" list. I figured she might come. Dessa had always been good to my brother.

She was wearing jeans and a purple turtleneck and this short little jacket. She looked more like thirty than forty. She looked better than ever. She walked right past my truck without seeing me. It wasn't until after she'd passed through the revolving door that I realized I'd been holding my breath.

Danny Mixx, the boyfriend's name is. Don't ask me what kind of a name Mixx is, or what nationality. He's sort of the ex-hippie type: bib overalls, red hair that he wears in a braid that goes halfway down his back. I saw him in two braids once. . . . If you ask me, they're a mismatch. He's successful, I guess, not that I know anything about pottery. He's won awards and shit. A while back, they did a story about him in *Connecticut* magazine. Dessa was in one of the pictures—in the background. Dessa's sister Angie told me about it when I ran into her in the parking lot at ShopRite, and I went back in and bought a copy. That magazine hung around our house for over a month. *See this woman?* I kept imagining myself telling Joy. *That's her. She's why I hold back. This is who's between us.* I looked at that picture of Dessa so many times that, after a while, the magazine opened to it automatically. Then, one day, it was gone. Thrown out with the trash. Recycled.

They live out on Route 162, Dessa and him—the old Troger farm, about half a mile past Shea's apple orchard. You should see that house: it's all peeling to shit, mildew problem on the north side. The place is practically crying out for a power-washing and a couple coats of paint, but I guess they have other priorities. The other day, while I was putting gas in the truck, I caught myself in the middle of this fantasy where Dessa hires me to paint that house and, right in the middle of my work, she waves me down from the ladder and we go inside and make love. She tells me she still loves me, that she's made a mistake. . . . By the time that little pipe dream was over, I had pumped myself nineteen dollars' worth of gas, which was a little complicated because all I had in my wallet at the time was a ten-dollar bill and no credit card.

Dan the Man converted their barn into a studio and built his own wood-fired kiln out in the field next to it. I kept track of his progress. When they first moved there, I used to find all kinds of excuses to drive out onto 162, which, all it is is the slow way to Hewett City. More masochism than curiosity, I guess—me doing that. One time, he was out there in just his cutoffs, painting their mailbox these jazzy psychedelic pinks and blues and yellows. "Constantine/Mixx," it said the next time I drove by. Blue skies and puffy clouds and a sun with a face on it: happily-ever-after painted onto a mailbox. I hadn't known she'd gone back to her maiden name. Reading that mailbox hurt somewhere in the vicinity of a swift kick to the groin.

Dessa had parked just three spaces away. I cut the engine, got out of the truck, and went over to that van. Inside on the dashboard was a pair of women's sunglasses, an Indigo Girls cassette, and a grungy-looking coffee mug with the Three Stooges on the side. "Nyuk nyuk nyuk," it said. The guy's a prize-winning potter in *Connecticut* magazine and she has to drink her coffee out of *that* thing? Sadie, Dessa's black Lab, was asleep in the sun on the passenger's seat.

"Hey, girl," I said, rapping on the window. "Hey, Sadie."

I'd given that crazy dog to Dessa for Christmas—when? '79, maybe? '80? As a pup, she'd chewed everything in sight, including our coffee table legs and half my socks and underwear and even the hose of my brand-new compressor. Goofus, I called her. She used to drive me crazy. Now, roused from sleep, she looked up at me with milky eyes. Her black face was flecked with gray. "What's up, Goofus?" I said to her through the glass. No recognition whatsoever.

By the time Dessa came out again, I was back in my

truck. At first, I wasn't going to say anything, but then I rolled down my window. "Hey!" I gave the horn a little tap. It made her jump.

"Dominick," her lips said. She smiled.

When I got out of the truck, she took my hands in hers and squeezed them. Came a step closer and gave me a hug. I placed my hand on the small of her back, tentative and unsure. We'd been together sixteen years—sixteen *years,* man—and there I was, touching her as awkward as a kid at a school dance.

"How you doing?" I said. Her curly black hair was pulled back, one or two wiry gray strands boinging in the breeze. Being that close to her was pain and pleasure both.

"I'm okay," she said. "But, God, Dominick—how are *you* doing?"

I blew out a breath, nodded at the hospital's upper windows. "About as well as you'd expect, I guess. Especially now that he's become Freak of the Week."

She pressed her lips together, shook her head. "It was on the news again all day yesterday," she said. "They just won't let it rest, will they?"

"Guy from the *Enquirer* called last night. Offered us three hundred bucks for a recent picture of him, a thousand for one of him without the hand."

"Inquiring minds want to know," she said, smiling sadly.

"Inquiring minds can go fuck themselves." She reached out and touched my arm.

"He seemed pretty good just now, though, Dominick. Considering. Better than I expected. Thanks for putting my name on the visitors' list."

I shrugged. Looked away. "No problem," I said. "I just thought if you *wanted* to see him . . ."

"We had a nice little chat, and then he said he was tired. He seemed pretty peaceful."

"It's the Haldol," I said.

"So how's Ray doing with all this?"

I shrugged. "You probably know better than I do." She gave me a quizzical look.

Sadie was up and slobbering against the driver's side window. "I see this sorry excuse for a dog is still among the living," I said. When Dessa unlocked the door, I reached in and patted Sadie's belly the way she used to like. "So how's Dan the Man?"

We lost eye contact on that one, but she answered me like he and I were old buddies. "Fine. Busy. It gets a little crazy for him from now until after Christmas. He just got back from Santa Fe. Took the top prize in a big juried show there."

"Santa Fe, huh? You go out there with him?"

She shook her head. "The Museum of American Folk Art? In New York? They just took two of his pieces." She reached up and rubbed her knuckles against my cheek. "God, you look exhausted, Dominick. Are you sleeping?"

I shrugged. "Enough. It's just hard, you know?"

"You know who I keep thinking about through all this?" she said. "Your mother. The way she used to worry so much about him. This would have really clobbered her."

I stroked Sadie's back, scratched under her chin. "Yup. She would have had to say a couple billion novenas over this one," I said.

Dessa reached out and fingered the sleeve of my jacket. She was always like that—tactile. Joy's different—not a toucher unless we're fucking or she's looking to get fucked. Then her hands are everywhere. But Dessa's touch is different. Something I had and lost.

"And the thing is, he *meant* well," she said. "He wanted to stop a war from happening. How can someone cause so much pain when all he wants to do is help out the world?"

I didn't answer her. There *was* no answer. The last thing I wanted to do was tear up like this right in front of her.

"Well," she said.

"Hey, thanks again for coming. You didn't have to, you know. You're not under any obligation."

"I *wanted* to come, Dominick. I *love* your brother. You know that."

It overwhelmed me, her saying that. I couldn't help it. I leaned over and tried to kiss her. She turned her head away. My lips hit her eyebrow, the bone underneath.

She climbed up into the van, gunned it a little more than necessary, and backed out of the parking space. Braked.

Gave me a thumbs-up. I stood there, watching her drive off. Masochistic or not, I can't stop loving her. I'm going to love Dessa forever.

The hospital lobby was decorated for Halloween: Hallmark witches and black and orange crepe-paper streamers, a pumpkin on the desk where you get the visitor's passes. "Birdsey," I told the woman. "Thomas Birdsey. Second floor."

"Birdsey," she repeated, typing the name into her computer. "Are you a relative?"

"Brother," I said. She and I had gone through this same little ballet the past three days. I'm the identical twin of the guy who lopped his freakin' hand off, I felt like screaming at her. The psycho you been reading about and hearing about on TV and squawking about with all your blue-haired friends. Just give me the freakin' visitor's pass.

"Here you go," she said.

"Thanks."

"You're welcome entirely."

Fuck *you,* lady.

Thomas was sleeping. Ray wasn't there. The balloon Dessa had brought him bobbed around in the air current coming out of the baseboard. "You've got a friend," it said. The little card was signed, "Love, Dessa and Danny." Her handwriting *and* his. Cute.

Neither the nurse nor the aides had seen Ray, they said. So where the fuck was he? I waited for ten minutes, then left.

Back downstairs, I was a step or two off the elevator when someone called my name. Ray. He sat slumped in a waiting room chair. He looked small, lost in his coat.

"What's the matter?" I said.

"Nothing's the matter. How's the tire?"

"It's okay," I said. "You see him? You been up there?"

He looked around to see if anyone was listening. Shook his head.

"Why not?"

His voice was a croak. "I don't know. I got halfway up there and then I just changed my mind, that's all. Come on. Let's get out of here. Don't make a federal case out of it."

He stood up and walked toward the door. "Did you see Dessa?" I asked. "She was just here, visiting him."

"I saw her," he said. "She didn't see me."

We were almost out the door when I noticed he was still holding the visitor's pass. "Your pass," I said. "You forgot to hand in your pass."

"The hell with it," he said, stuffing it into his jacket pocket.

Halfway home, Ray regained his composure—became Mr. Tough Guy again. "You know what the trouble always was with that kid?" he said. "It was all that namby-pamby stuff. . . . All that 'Thomas my little bunny rabbit' stuff she used to say to him all the time. With you, it was different. You went your own way. You could handle yourself. . . . Jesus, I remember the two of you out on the ballfield in Little League. You two guys were like night and day. Jesus, that kid was pitiful out there on that field, even for the farm system."

I shook my head a little but kept my mouth shut. That was Ray's theory? That Thomas had cut off his hand because he sucked at baseball? Where did you even *begin* with Ray?

"If she'd have just let me raise him the way he *should* have been raised, instead of running interference for him all the time, maybe he never would have landed down below in the first place. 'It's a tough world,' I used to tell her. 'He's got to be toughened up.' "

"Hey, Ray," I said. "He's a paranoid schizophrenic because of his biochemistry and the frontal lobes of his brain and all that shit Dr. Reynolds went over with us that time. It wasn't Ma's fault. It wasn't anybody's fault."

"I'm not *saying* it was her fault," he snapped. "She was a good woman. She did her best by both of you two, and don't you forget it!"

And you're a hypocrite and a bully and a horse's ass, I wanted to snap back. Wanted to pull over to the side of the road and yank him right out of the goddamned truck and speed away. Because if anyone had fucked up Thomas when he was a kid, it was Ray. These days they called Ray's kind of "toughening up" child abuse.

We rode the next couple of miles in silence.

"Want one?" he said. We were stopped for a red light on

Boswell Avenue. His shaking hand held out an open roll of Life Savers, butterscotch. He'd probably sucked a million of those things since he gave up cigarettes. That had really gotten me: how *he* was the one who'd smoked like a chimney all those years and *she* was the one who died of cancer.

"No thanks," I said.

"You sure?"

"Yup." Neither of us spoke for the rest of the way back. When I pulled up in front of the house, he asked me if I wanted to come in, have a sandwich with him.

"No thanks," I said again. "I've got to get to work."

"Where?"

"That big Victorian on Gillette Street. Professor's house."

"Still?"

"Yeah, *still.* That goddamned place has more gingerbread on it than a bakery. I ought to have my head examined for taking that job at the end of the season." Not to mention that it had rained four days last week. Not to mention that my goddamned brother had complicated things just a little bit.

"You want some help with it? I can give you some time tomorrow. Thursday, too, if you want. I don't go back to work until Friday."

Ray's help was the last thing I needed. The only other time he'd helped me, he'd spent more time giving unsolicited advice than painting. Telling me how to run my own business. "I'll get it done," I said.

Maybe I wouldn't even go over to Gillette Street that afternoon. Maybe I'd just go home and smoke a joint, watch CNN. Find out if either Bush or Saddam Insane had fired the first shot. *Not* answer the phone. . . . That morning at breakfast, Joy and I had fought about whether or not to disconnect the damn thing. I'd accused her of getting off on all the attention—talking with all those media assholes.

"Well, screw you, Dominick!" she'd fired back. "You think this is easy on *me*? You think I like everyone looking at me weird because I happen to be living with his brother?"

"Hey, how'd you like to get the looks *I'm* getting?" I said. "How'd you like to *be* his brother? His friggin' look-alike?" The two of us stood there, shouting at each other. Having a pity contest. You think Dessa would have ever pulled that shit? You think Joy would have ever gotten her ass over to the hospital and visited him like Dess had done?

Ray got out of the truck and walked toward the house. I backed down the driveway. Braked. "Hey?" I called. "You okay?" He stopped in his tracks. Nodded. "Don't talk to any of those reporters or TV jerks if they call. Or if they come over here. Just tell 'em, 'No comment.' "

Ray spat on the grass. "Any of those clowns come around here, I'll take a baseball bat to them." He probably would, too. Fuckin' Ray.

I backed onto the road and threw her into first. "Hey!" he called. He was walking toward the truck. I rolled down the window and braced myself.

"Just answer me one thing," he said. "Why didn't you let them at least *try* to put his hand back on? Now he's got a physical disability on top of a mental one. How come you didn't have them at least *try*?"

I'd been flogging myself with the same question for the past two days. But it pissed me off—*him* asking it. A little late for fatherly concern, wasn't it?

"For one thing, they were only giving the reattachment a fifty-fifty chance," I said. "If it *didn't* work, it would have just sat there, dead, sewn to his wrist. And for another thing . . . for another thing. . . . You didn't *hear* him, Ray. It was the first time in twenty years he was in charge of something. And so I couldn't. . . . I mean, okay, you're right—it *doesn't* make him a hero." I looked up from the steering wheel. Looked him in the eye—that trick I'd taught myself way back when. "It was *his* hand, Ray. . . . It was *his* choice."

He stood there, hands in his pockets. Half a minute or more went by.

"You know what the funny thing is?" he said. "I never even bought that goddamned knife. I won it in a card game from this guy in my outfit. Big, beefy Swede, came from Minnesota. I can see him plain as the nose on your face, but I been trying all afternoon to think what that guy's name was. Isn't that something? My kid cuts his hand off with that knife, and I can't even remember the guy's name I won the damn thing from."

"My kid." It struck me that he said that. Claimed Thomas.

* * *

That night, Joy brought home Chinese food as an apology. I sat there, eating without really tasting it. "How is it?" she asked me.

"It's great," I said. "Great."

Later, in bed, she rolled over to my side and started getting friendly. "Dominick?" she said. "I'm sorry about this morning. I just want things to get back to normal." She rubbed her leg against my leg, flicked her finger in and out of the waistband on my underpants. Got me interested with her hands. I just lay there, letting her do me without doing anything back.

She got on top and put me inside of her. Put my hand, my fingers, where she wanted them. I was just going through the motions at first—performing a service. Then I started thinking about Dessa out there in the hospital parking lot, in her jeans and little jacket. I was making love to Dessa . . .

Joy came quickly—intensely. Her orgasm felt like a relief, a burden lifted off my shoulders. I was almost there myself, almost ready, when I just stopped. I didn't mean to. I just started thinking of things: the way the state hospital corridors smell like dead farts and cigarettes, and the way Dan the Man had painted that happily-ever-after mailbox out there for them, and the picture I'd conjured up for Ray to get myself off the hook: Thomas's severed hand, stitched to his wrist like dead gray meat.

I went soft on her. Slipped out. Nudged her off me and rolled away.

"Hey, you?" she said. Her hand curled around my shoulder.

"Hey me what?"

She grabbed my earlobe, pulled it a little. "It's okay. No biggie."

"Now there's a compliment," I said.

She jabbed me one. "You know what I mean."

Yanking up the covers, I turned further away from her—swung my hand up for the light switch. "God, I'm whipped," I said. But a few minutes later, it was *her* breathing that was soft and regular.

I couldn't sleep at all that night. Spent hour after hour

staring up at the void that, in the daytime, was nothing but our goddamned bedroom ceiling.

"Finish, Dominick," Thomas said. "Finish the psalm."

I felt, rather than saw, the cop look over at me. I opened my brother's Bible. *Give me not up to the wishes of my foes,* I read, *for false witnesses have risen up against me, and such as breathe out violence. I believe that I shall see the bounty of the Lord in the land of the living. Wait for the Lord with courage; be stouthearted, and wait for the Lord.*

The police cruiser took the familiar turn off the parkway, the cop waved to the security guard, and eased over the speed bump. We rode by the boarded-up Dix Building. Coasted past Tweed, Libby, Payne. . . . Someone had told me once that back during the state hospital's heyday, those brick monstrosities had housed over four thousand patients. Now, the inpatient population was down to around two hundred. Decay and downsizing had closed every building but Settle and Hatch.

"Hey, you just passed it," I told the cop when the cruiser rolled past the Settle Building. "Turn back."

He looked in the rearview mirror, exchanged a look with his partner. "He's not going to Settle," the other one said.

"What do you mean, he's not going to Settle? That's where he always goes. He runs the news rack at Settle. He runs the coffee cart."

"We don't know anything about the coffee cart," the escort said. "All we know is our orders say to take him to Hatch."

"Oh no, not Hatch!" Thomas groaned. He pulled and struggled against the restraints they'd put on him; his resistance rocked the cruiser. "Oh, God, Dominick! Help me! Oh no! Oh no! Oh no!"

four

The maximum-security Hatch Forensic Institute, located at the rear of the Three Rivers State Hospital grounds, is a squat concrete-and-steel building surrounded by chain link and razor wire. Hatch houses most of the front-page boys: thc vct from Mystic who mistook his family for the Viet Cong, the kid at Wesleyan who brought his .22-caliber semiautomatic to class. But Hatch is also the end of the line for a lot of less sexy psychos: drug fry-outs, shopping mall nuisances, manic-depressive alcoholics—your basic disturbing-the-peace-type wackos with no place else to go. Occasionally, someone actually gets better down at Hatch. Gets released. But that tends to happen *in spite of* things. For most of the patients there, the door swings only one way, which is just fine with the town of Three Rivers. Most people around here are less interested in rehabilitation than they are in warehousing the spooks and kooks—keeping the Boston Strangler and the Son of Sam off the streets, keeping Norman Bates locked up at the Hatch Hotel.

There's never been an escape from Hatch. Circular in shape, the place is divided into four independent units, each with its own security station. The outside wall of the building is windowless; the inside windows look onto a small, circular courtyard—the hub of the wheel, so to speak. There are some picnic tables out there and a rusted basketball hoop that pretty much gets ignored because most of the guys are fat and sluggish from Thorazine. Unit by unit, twice a day, patients whose submissiveness has won them the privilege can enter that concrete-floored courtyard for a twenty-minute hit of fresh air and nicotine.

I've heard motormouths on the radio and on the barstool next to me complain that the insanity plea is one of the things that's wrong with this country—that we let rapists and killers get away with murder by letting them hide out at "country clubs" like Hatch. Well, guess again, folks. I've been there. Walked out with the stink of the place still on my clothes and my brother's screaming still in my ears. If there's a hell worse than Hatch Forensic Institute, then God must be one vengeful motherfucker.

The cruiser's blue lights winked on and off. The cop who was driving us stopped at Hatch's front gate and handed a guard some paperwork. "It was a *sacrifice*!" Thomas kept shouting. "It was a *sacrifice*!"

I turned around and told him to take it easy—that I'd get the whole thing straightened out and get him back to Settle that night. But I only half-believed that myself. The steel grid between the front and back seats of the cruiser—between my brother and me—was beginning to feel like a preview of coming attractions.

There was a whirring sound. The gate glided open and clunked to a stop, and the cruiser eased past, over a speed bump, and around the building. We came to a halt at a double door marked "Patients Receiving—Unit Two." A red light above the door flashed. We sat and waited with the motor running.

"What law did I break?" my brother blurted out. "Who did I hurt?"

The answer to the last question was as obvious as the bandaged stump on the end of his arm, but how did that make him a criminal? It *had* to be a mistake, I told myself. It made no sense. But as I sat there staring ahead at those double doors, that winking light, I felt a yank in my chest—

one of those fight-or-flight rushes. "Hey," I said, turning to the cop next to me. "What's your name?"

The question surprised him. "My name? Mercado. Sergeant Mercado."

"All right, look, Mercado. Just do me a favor, will you? Just bring him over to the Settle Building for five minutes. I know the night people there. They can call his doctor and get this sorted out. Because this whole thing is a big mistake."

"You're tampering with an agreement between God and me!" Thomas warned. "The Lord God Almighty has commanded me to prevent an unholy war!"

Mercado looked straight ahead. "No can do," the cop in back answered for him. "They'd have our ass in a sling if we ignored signed orders."

"No, they won't," I said. I turned around to look at the guy. His face and Thomas's were crisscrossed by that metal screen that divided us. "They'll be *glad* that you straightened out the mix-up before any shit hit the fan. They'll be *grateful.*"

"I run the news rack at Settle!" Thomas pleaded. "I run the coffee cart!"

"Hey, I can sympathize with you," Mercado told me. "I got brothers myself. But the thing is, we can't just—"

"No, don't!" I said, interrupting him. I was wired, pumped on sheer desperation. "Just think about it for a second before you let some knee-jerk police response come out of your mouth. All I'm asking you to do is be a human being instead of a cop for five minutes, okay? All I'm asking is that you throw this thing in reverse and drive—what?—one-sixteenth of a mile over to Settle. You don't even have to leave the hospital grounds, Mercado. One-sixteenth of a mile, man. Five minutes, tops. That's all I'm asking."

Mercado looked in the rearview mirror. "What do you think, Al? We could just—"

"Uh-uh," from the backseat. "No way, José. No can do."

"Then *you* get up tomorrow morning at five-thirty and start the coffee!" Thomas shouted. "*You* make sure there's enough change in the change box and that nobody buys Mrs. Semel's Drake's cakes. *You* make sure none of the other doctors get Dr. Ahamed's *Wall Street Journal*!"

Mercado and I looked at each other. "You got brothers?" I said. "How many?"

"Four."

"Come on, man," I whispered. "Follow your gut. Five minutes."

Reflected in the flashing light over the "Patients Receiving" door, Mercado's face turned red, not red, red. I saw the hesitation in his eyes, the struggle. That's when I blew it. I reached over to touch his arm—make some human contact with the guy—and he freaked. Batted my hand away so hard that it hit the windshield.

"Keep your hands to yourself!" he said. "Understand?" His own hand was down at his holster, a shield over the butt of his gun. "That's the *last* thing you want to do is grab an armed officer. Understand? You could end up *real* sorry next time you did that."

I looked out the side window. Took a deep breath. Gave it up.

A uniformed guard unlocked the double doors and motioned us inside. Mercado got out and opened the back door, easing my brother out of the cruiser. "Watch your head now," he said. "Watch your head."

A part of me wanted to stay right there inside that cruiser: to secure my status as the *un*crazy twin, the one who *wasn't* going into that place. I'm not talking about major abandonment, just five seconds' worth of hesitation. But I admit it. I hesitated.

"Here," the older cop said when I got out of the cruiser. He handed me Thomas's duffel bag. I was already holding his Bible.

Thomas stood, hunched over a little from his restraints. He told the older cop he had to go to the bathroom. Was there a bathroom inside that he could use? He'd had to go most of the way there.

His leg chains rattled with each small step he took toward the building. I had a bitter taste in my mouth and a dull, thudding feeling in the pit of my stomach. It was like I'd swallowed those chains or something. What was going on? Why were they doing this?

The guard let my brother and the two escorts through but

stopped me at the door. "Who are you?" he said. He was one of those short, gung-ho types. Late twenties, early thirties, maybe. Robocop.

"I'm his brother," I said. As if he couldn't tell. As if he couldn't see that by looking at our faces.

He and Mercado exchanged a look. "Mr. Birdsey was visiting the patient when we arrived for the escort," Mercado said. "The patient requested that he accompany us."

"We thought it might make him less combative," the other cop added.

"He's *not* combative," I said. "He's never hurt anyone in his whole life."

Robocop looked down at my brother's stump, then back at me.

"Look, this is just a screwup by some secretary or something," I said. "He should be over at Settle. He's in the outpatient program over there. He always checks in at Settle after an episode. One call to his doctor and we can get this whole thing straightened out. But he's not combative. God, he's about as combative as Bambi."

"I run the coffee cart at Settle," Thomas added. "They need me there first thing in the morning."

Robocop told me I could enter the building and accompany my brother during the initial part of the admitting process, but that I couldn't go with him into the ward itself—couldn't go any further than the security station. Any calls to the doctor would have to be made in the morning.

Whatever you say, asshole, I thought to myself. A foot in the door was some kind of progress. Once I got inside, I could talk to somebody on the medical staff.

Robocop led us down a short corridor: halogen lighting, yellow cinder-block walls. Hatch has a singular smell to it—nothing like the stink over at Settle. Something else. Something sweet and putrid: bad food at the back of the refrigerator. Human rot, I guess. Human decay.

Another guard joined us when we got to the metal detector. He had a gut hanging off the front of him, a puffy pink alcoholic face. He reeked of cologne.

The police escorts unlocked Thomas's restraints and took them off. Thomas mentioned again that he had to go to the toilet. Mercado frisked him and walked him through the metal detector.

"Did you hear him?" I said. "He has to take a leak."

"What's this?" the fat guard asked me. His chin pointed down at the stuff I was carrying: Thomas's duffel bag, his Bible.

"His personal stuff," I said.

"Like what?"

"Like *personal* stuff: wallet, toothpaste, comb."

Fatso took the bag and the Bible away from me. Unzipped the bag and poked around. He was one of those guys who breathes through his nose so that you can hear what work every single breath is for him. He dumped everything out onto a conveyor belt: foot powder, a Bic pen, a tin button that said "Jesus Is the Reason for the Season," a pair of wingtip shoes with a clip-on necktie coiled inside one of them. It was pathetic: Thomas's shitty life laid out there like a bunch of groceries at Stop & Shop. Fatso flipped a switch and the belt rolled. Everything passed through one of those X-ray machines like they have at the airport. Big surprise: no hidden daggers, no pipe bomb sewn into the duffel bag lining.

"You're going to have to be padded, too," Robocop told me.

"Padded? What's padded?" I was thinking padded cell.

"Frisked," Mercado said.

"Frisk me then," I told Mercado, leaning myself against the wall the way they'd made my brother do it. "Go ahead. Be my guest."

But it was Robocop who did it: a little rougher, a little more thorough in the privacy zones than he needed to be—just in case I didn't get who was the big man around there. I would have said something to him—asked him while he was feeling me up if he enjoyed his work—but I was in no position to throw darts. Not yet. Not if I was going to get Thomas out of there that night.

Just when I thought he was done humiliating me, Robocop had me walk through the metal detector. The thing beeped and whistled and he had me fork over my key ring. I passed the second time, but Robocop told me I'd have to pick up my keys on my way out of there because of the little jackknife I keep on the ring. Like I was going to sneak in there and jackknife all the inmates free. What bullshit.

Robocop told the escorts to put the cuffs back on my brother.

"Why's *that* necessary?" I said. "I'm telling you, you're wasting your time. He's taking a U-turn out of here as soon as we get ahold of his doctor. Why does he have to be restrained?"

He looked at me without answering, his face as blank as the cinder block. Fatso told Thomas his personal items would be cataloged and stored at the security station. That he'd get state issue for his toiletries. That all reading material would have to be approved first by his doctor or the unit lead.

"Where's my Bible!" Thomas said. "I want my Bible."

"All reading material has to be approved first by his doctor or the unit lead," Fatso repeated.

"He can't have a *Bible*?" I said. "You guys even have to approve the goddamned word of God?"

Robocop came forward, close enough so that I could see a chicken pox scar, smell the Juicy Fruit in his mouth. "This is a maximum-security facility, sir," he said. "There are regulations and procedures. If you have a problem with that, then let us know so you can wait outside instead of accompanying your brother through the rest of the preliminary admit."

We glared at each other for a couple of seconds. "I'm not saying I have a problem with it," I said. "All I'm saying is that it's a waste of time admitting him. Because as soon as you talk to his doctor, he's going to tell you this is a mistake."

"This way, sir," he said.

The security station was around the next corner. Behind the tinted window glass were two more guards, a bank of black-and-white security TVs, an open cabinet with rows of keys and cuffs and Texas belts. Next to the station on one side was a conference room and a couple of offices. On the other side was a john, a utility closet, more offices. The hallway on both sides was blocked off by double-locked steel doors.

"You got a phone in there?" I asked, nodding toward the security station. "Just tell one of those guys to call Dr. Willis Ehlers and see if Thomas Birdsey is supposed to be here. Call him at home. You guys must have a directory for the doctors, right? Go ahead. He won't mind."

"Dr. Ehlers doesn't treat patients at Hatch," Fatso said. "He's not on staff here."

"Fine! That's my point!" I said. "His patients are over at Settle. Which is exactly where my brother belongs."

Robocop leafed through some paperwork clipped to a clipboard. "According to this, he's been reassigned," he said.

"What do you mean, 'reassigned'? Reassigned by who?"

"I'm not free to give you that information, sir," he said. "Either his new doctor will notify you or you can make an appointment and talk to the social worker assigned to his case."

"Excuse me," Thomas said, addressing Robocop. "Do you happen to know a Dr. Ahamed, the assistant superintendent of this entire hospital complex?"

"Thomas," I said, "just keep your shirt on. Let me handle this. All right?"

"Dr. Ahamed?" Robocop said. "Yeah, I know who he is. Why?"

Thomas's chin was thrust forward. His whole body was shaking. "Because you're going to be in big trouble tomorrow morning if Dr. Ahamed goes to his office and doesn't find his *Wall Street Journal* and his corn muffin!" He was shouting now, shuddering. "I wouldn't want to be you when he finds out who's holding me here against my will!"

Fatso waved "come here" fingers at one of the guards behind the glass.

"Take it easy, take it easy," I told Thomas. I reminded him that he'd lost track of time—that he'd been away from the coffee cart for five days already while he was recuperating at Shanley. "And anyway, I'm sure those two helpers of yours are holding down the fort," I said. "What are their names again? I forget."

"Bruce and Barbara!" he shouted. "You think *they* can handle things without me there! That's a laugh!" Only he wasn't laughing; he was sobbing.

"Everything copacetic out here?" the third guard asked, approaching us.

"Jesus! Jesus!" my brother cried. Fear flashed on his face, and then there was a splattering sound on the concrete floor. Thomas was pissing himself.

Fatso went to call maintenance.

"I'm sorry, Dominick," Thomas said. "I couldn't help it." A dark, wet stain covered the front of his pants.

I told him it was okay. That it happens. That it was no big deal. Then I turned to Robocop. "Here's the bottom line," I said. "I'm not leaving until I get him out of here and he's getting out *tonight,* understand? So someone had better call the goddamned doctor."

Behind the window, Fatso spoke into a phone. "Call my brother's doctor!" I shouted in at him. "Dr. Willis Ehlers! Please!"

Robocop told me to keep my voice down. "The doctors are only called in after hours when there's an emergency," he told me.

"This *is* an emergency," I said, waving my thumb in the direction of my brother. "This is an emergency in the making. The poor guy isn't even allowed to take a leak and you think I'm *leaving* him here with *you* fucking Nazis?"

I saw the muscles in his jaw tighten. Saw him look at the other guard. "Sir," the new guard said, "the patients' relatives don't determine what constitutes an emergency. The medical staff does."

I told myself to calm down—that busting Robocop's jaw was a luxury my brother couldn't afford. I'd probably already sabotaged things with that Nazi comment. "All right," I said. "Let me just speak to a nurse then. There's got to be a head nurse on duty, right?"

"The nurses at Hatch have no contact with family members, sir," the other guard said. "It's policy. If you have questions or concerns, you should call tomorrow and make an appointment with the social worker assigned to your brother's case."

"They just called from the unit," Fatso said. "We ready to rock 'n' roll?"

Robocop nodded. "Tell them to come and get him. We

can finish admittance down in the ward. I've about had it with the Doublemint Twin here."

Fatso talked into his radio. Thomas started mumbling scripture.

"Mr. Birdsey, he's going to be admitted to the unit now," Mercado said. "Come on. We have to go."

"But nobody's listening!" I said. "This whole thing is just some administrative screwup or something. He belongs at Settle."

"Look, bud," the older escort said. "He may belong at Settle, but he sure in hell isn't going there tonight. Maybe that's where he's going first thing tomorrow, but I can guarantee you that tonight he's staying here."

"Come on, Mr. Birdsey," Mercado said to me. "You can't do anything until tomorrow. We'll give you a ride back to Shanley. You parked in the big lot or the one in back?"

"I'm not going anywhere until we get this thing straightened out!" I said. When he grabbed me by the arm, I yanked it back.

"They're nailing me to the cross!" Thomas shouted.

I ran over to Robocop. "How about that social worker? Is that social worker here?" My heart was pumping like a jackhammer.

"No, sir, she is not here. Only the unit nurses and the FTSs are here after regular hours."

"What are they? What are the FTSs?"

"Forensic Treatment Specialists," Fatso answered. He winked at the older of the two escorts. "When I started working here, we called 'em 'bughouse aides.' Nowadays everybody's got a fancy title. Looky here, for instance."

He pointed to a guy approaching with a bucket and mop. I knew him: Ralph Drinkwater. "Ralphie here used to be a janitor. Now we call him an 'operations engineer.' Right, Ralphie?" Ignoring him, as impassive as ever, Ralph began to mop up my brother's urine.

The escort's chuckle put Fatso in a good mood. "She *is* here tonight, though, Steve," he told Robocop. "She came in to catch up on some of her paperwork. I checked her in when you were on dinner break."

"Who?" I said. "Who's here?"

"Ms. Sheffer."

"Who's that? Who's Ms. Sheffer?"

"The social worker for Unit Two."

"The social worker's here? Let me speak to her then!"

"You can't," Robocop said. "It's after hours. You'll have to make an appointment like everyone else."

The steel doors opened. Two aides approached. This was getting more and more surreal. "Hey, how you doing, Ralph?" I said. "Listen, talk some sense into . . ." He looked right through me.

"Come on, Mr. Birdsey," Mercado said. "We've got to get going."

"Then go then!" I told him. "I'm not going anywhere until I see the social worker!" I turned toward the aides. "Don't touch him! You just . . . just don't even *touch* him!"

An office door opened; a head poked out from behind it. "Does somebody need to see me?"

"Not tonight!" Robocop shouted. "He can make an appointment. It can wait."

"Is that the social worker? Are you the social worker who—"

"Tomorrow!" Robocop shouted at her. "Close your door! We got a situation here!"

"Dominick!" Thomas screamed. The aides had taken hold of him, one guy on each side.

"Get your hands off of him!" I shouted. Robocop and Mercado and his partner held me back. Fatso and the other guard came running. "Get your fucking hands off of me, you fucking Nazi goons!" I bucked and struggled to get free.

"Close that door!" Robocop yelled.

In the middle of the scuffle, I saw the social worker's door close. Saw the aides unlock the steel doors and hustle my brother into the ward. "They're nailing me to the cross, Dominick!" Thomas screamed. "They're nailing me to the cross!"

The doors slammed shut behind them.

Robocop wrenched my arm back, slammed me up against the wall. "This one's crazier than the other one, for Christ's sake," he said.

"Take your motherfucking hands off me!" I screamed,

spitting and straining and trying to pull away. Mercado and Fatso and the other escort held me back. The third guard came running out from behind the glass office. Robocop leaned his knee in toward my groin—no pain, just the promise of it. Just the pressure.

"You get off on this or something?" I said. "Feeling guys up while you're frisking them? Give you a cheap thrill, does it?"

He kneed me.

One hard, quick jerk that dropped me to the floor. I think I blacked out for a minute, and when I came back, it took me a while to realize that the moaning and heaving I heard was coming from me, not my brother. The pain is something I can't even try to describe.

That's when I knew what Thomas was up against. That's when I felt it for myself: the spike against flesh, the hammer's piercing thud.

five

1958

Thomas and I are going to the movies with Ma—the Back-to-School Festival of Fun. We're on the city bus. I get to pull the stop cord when we get to the five-and-ten because Thomas did it last time. The bus won't stop at the show, only the five-and-ten.

We have the *nice* bus driver today—the one who says, "Hey, whaddaya got in there?" and pulls candy out of your ears. Last time we came downtown, we got the grouchy driver with no thumb. Ma thinks maybe he lost it in the war or in a machine. She told me not to look at it if I was afraid of it, but I did look. I couldn't help it. I didn't want to but I did.

Here's the five-and-ten. Ma lifts me up and I pull the cord. "See you later, alligator!" the bus driver says when we get off. Ma smiles and puts her hand to her mouth, and Thomas says nothing. From the safety of the sidewalk, I yell, "After a while, crocodile!" The driver laughs. He makes his fingers into a "V" and slaps the bus doors shut.

We walk over to the show. There's a line at the ticket booth. The kids right in front of us are big kids. Wiseguys. "Well, next time, bring your birth certificate then!" the ticket lady yells. It's the crippled lady. Sometimes she works inside at the candy counter and sometimes she sells the tickets. Her and this other lady switch around. Ma says the crippled lady got polio before they had polio shots. Maybe that's why she's always crabby.

Inside, a bulgy-eyed man rips our tickets and gives Thomas and me our free back-to-school pencil boxes. With his pen, he makes an X on the back of our hands. "One to a customer," he tells Ma. "I mark them so I can tell if some kid tries to pull a fast one."

I want to go all the way down in front, but Ma says no, it will hurt our eyes. She makes us stop halfway. Here's how we're sitting: first Thomas, then Ma, then me on the end. "Now, don't open your pencil boxes," Ma says.

The man in charge is called the husher. He has a uniform and a flashlight, and he's very, very tall. His job is to yell at kids when they put their feet on the seats in front of them. If they answer him back, he shines his flashlight right in their face.

They show cartoons first: Daffy Duck, Sylvester and Tweety, Road Runner. *Beep-beep! Beep-beep!* On the radio, they said they were showing ten cartoons, but they don't. They show eight. I'm only on my eighth finger when the Three Stooges come on.

Ma doesn't like the Three Stooges. When Moe pokes his fingers in Larry's eyes, Ma leans over and whispers, "Don't you ever try anything like that now." Her voice in my ear tickles—makes me scrunch up my shoulder. In this one, the Three Stooges are bakers. They just finished decorating this fancy cake for a snotty rich lady, and she's yelling at them. Then Larry slips and falls back against Curly and Curly bumps into the rich lady and she falls right into the cake! All three of us laugh—Thomas and Ma and me. From this side, you can't even tell my mother has a funny lip. You can only tell from Thomas's side.

There are lots of bad kids here with no mothers or fathers. They're talking loud and fooling around instead of watching the movie. *"I tawt I taw a puddy cat!"* one kid keeps yelling out, even though the cartoons are over. Every time he yells it, other kids laugh. Some boys in front have flattened their popcorn boxes and they're throwing them up in the air. The boxes make shadows on the screen.

"Can we get some popcorn?" I whisper to Ma.

"No," she whispers back.

"Why not?"

"Just watch the movie."

Thomas taps Ma's arm and I lean over to listen. "Ma, I'm thinking about her again," he says. "What should I do?"

"Think about something else," she says. "Watch the movie."

Thomas means Miss Higgins. In just one more week, we'll be third-graders and Miss Higgins will be our new teacher. She's the meanest teacher in our whole school. All summer long, Thomas has been getting stomachaches thinking about her.

Thomas opens his pencil box even though we're not supposed to. He starts chewing on one of his brand-new pencils like it's corn on the cob. The last time Ray caught Thomas putting stuff in his mouth, he said, "One of these days I'm going to get a roll of EB green tape and tape up your hands. See if *that* cures you! See how you like *them* apples!"

I open my pencil box, too. If Thomas can, then so can I. I bend and bend my eraser to see how far I can bend it, and it boings out of my hand and into the dark.

"See!" Ma says. "What did I tell you?"

She says I can't look for it under the seats because it's too filthy down there and because it would be like trying to find a needle in a haystack. One time when Ma was a little girl, she went to the show and saw a rat under her seat. It was at a different movie theater than this one. They tore it down. People used to call it the "scratch house" because the seats had fleas.

Down in front, someone yells a naughty word. Another kid screams. *Ping!* Something hits the back of my seat.

"Hey! Cut it out down there!" a voice yells. I look back. It's not the husher. It's Bulgy Eyes, the man who gave us our pencil boxes. Ma says those bad kids better behave because he sounds like he really means business. She says Bulgy Eyes is the boss even though the husher is bigger. Now Thomas has his eraser in his mouth. He's sucking on it. *Slurp, slurp, slurp.* "What are you doing that for?" I say. He says he's cleaning it. Which is stupid. It's already clean. It's brand new.

The Three Stooges are over and Francis the Talking Mule

comes on. *Francis Goes to West Point*. Ma says West Point's a school. . . . You know what? Last year, at our school, a dog snuck in. He came running into our classroom during spelling and knocked over the easel. All the kids were laughing and saying, "Here, boy! Here, boy!" and Miss Henault made us flip our spelling papers over and put our heads on our desks to calm down. That dog came right up our row. He was tan and white and had a smiley face, and he smelled a little like a sewer. He had a collar on, though, so he must have belonged to somebody. When Mr. Grymkowski pulled him out of our room, he was choking him and that dog made a noise like *gak-gak-gak*.

Ping! Ping! Ma says don't turn around or we might get hit in the eye. She says someone should complain to the manager before someone gets hurt. *Ping!* We're cowboys. Bad guys are shooting at us.

My new favorite cowboy show is *The Rifleman*. I used to like *Cheyenne* the best, but now I like *The Rifleman*. Lucas McCain can fire his rifle in three-tenths of a second. Plus he's nice to his son, Mark McCain. Lucas has to raise Mark all on his own because his wife died. Ray says Lucas McCain used to play baseball before he became a cowboy. For the Chicago Cubs. "He couldn't hit the ball, and now he can't act, either, and he's probably a goddamned millionaire," Ray said. If you say "damn," it's a venial sin, but if you say "goddamn," then it's a mortal sin. That's what the nun told us in catechism. She said every time you sin, it makes a little dirty mark on your soul, and people like Khrushchev and Jayne Mansfield have jet-black souls.

I'm not really paying attention to this movie. I'm watching those bad kids instead—the ones up in front. Popcorn boxes swoop in the dark like bats. Someone yells another bad word. The "P" word. Piss. . . . Sometimes bats come out on our street when it's getting dark. They look like birds but they're not. They trick you. *Ping!*

"Piss on you, too!" some kid shouts.

A girl laughs a shrieky laugh.

"I tawt I taw a puddy cat!"

The lights come on even though the movie's still playing. "Hey!" everyone starts going. "Hey!" Then the movie stops.

Bulgy Eyes and the husher walk down the aisle and up on the stage, and Bulgy Eyes starts yelling at us. Ma's scared. Her hand taps against her mouth like it does when Ray yells. With the lights on, I can see the bad kids better. I see Lonnie Peck and Ralph Drinkwater from our school. Last summer, Lonnie spit on the playground instructor and got kicked off playground for a whole week. He used to come anyway and stand outside and spit at us through the fence. We were supposed to just ignore him. Penny Ann Drinkwater's up in front, too, sitting by herself. Her and Ralph are twins, like Thomas and me, but Penny Ann stayed back. Ralph's going to be in fourth, but she's going to be in our class. She has to have Miss Higgins *twice.* Penny Ann's a big baby. She cries every single recess. The Drinkwaters and us are the only twins in our whole school. They're colored kids.

Up on the stage, Bulgy Eyes points his thumb at the husher. "You see this guy here? From now on, him and me are going to be looking for troublemakers. And when we find 'em, we're going to kick 'em out and not give 'em their money back. *And* call their fathers. Understand?"

"Good," Ma whispers from behind her hand. "It serves them right."

Now everyone's real quiet. Just sitting there. The lights go off. The movie starts up. Bulgy Eyes and the husher walk up and down the aisles. All the bad kids are being good.

Thomas pulls on Ma's sleeve again. He says he can't help it—he's thinking about Miss Higgins so much, he has the runs. He wants Ma to go to the bathroom with him, not me. "Can you stay here by yourself?" Ma asks me. I say yes, and Ma goes up the aisle with Thomas. I hold his pencil box.

Slide it open.

His pencil is rough and bumpy where he chewed it. His eraser's all wet. If Ray *does* tape up Thomas's hands, he should do it while it's still summer vacation because how could Thomas do his work? He'd get in trouble with Miss Higgins right off the bat. I bend Thomas's eraser way, way back. It goes flying. It was an accident. Cross my heart and hope to die.

We're not supposed to say that: cross my heart and hope to die. The nun says it's the exact same thing as swearing. I didn't say it, though. I just thought it.

Ray swears when he gets mad at Ma. One time he yanked her arm and gave her a black-and-blue mark, and I got so mad I drew a picture of him with big giant daggers in his head. Then I ripped it up. At first, Ray wasn't going to let us come to the movies today because movies are nothing but a waste of money. Then he changed his mind. One time, a long long time ago, he came with us to the show—with Ma and me and Thomas. It was on Sunday afternoon. The night before, he and Ma had a big fight and Ray made Ma cry. Then, the next morning, he was nice. He went to Mass with us and we ate at a restaurant and then we came to the movies. We saw *The Wizard of Oz.* Thomas spoiled it, though. Him and his stupid crying. Thomas always wrecks things.

They come back from the bathroom. "Push over, push over," Ma says. Now Thomas is sitting next to me. He has a box of Good & Plentys. It's for both of us to share, Ma says, but Thomas gets to hold it because the last time we went to the show and I held the popcorn, I kept stuffing it in my mouth instead of eating it nice so that Thomas wouldn't get as much. "Take two at a time," Thomas tells me, holding out the Good & Plenty box. "That's the rule." I tell him okay, but I take more than two every single time. One time, I put two fingers down real deep and get five. Thomas doesn't even realize it. You can always trick Thomas. It's easy. He doesn't even know his stupid eraser's missing.

Here's what Thomas was crying about that time we saw *The Wizard of Oz:* those flying monkeys. The ones who work for the Wicked Witch and swoop down and kidnap Dorothy. Thomas was crying so hard that I started crying, too. At first, I didn't even think they were scary, but then I did. Ray took us out in the lobby and yelled at us and said we were wrecking our mother's whole nice day. The candy counter lady kept looking at us. That crippled lady. Ray said if we didn't stop acting like two little scaredy-girls, he was going to take us to a store and buy us dresses. "Suzie and Betty Pinkus, the little scaredy-girls," he said. That was when we were little—first-graders. If I saw those flying monkeys now, I'd just laugh because they'd be so fake.

Last year at recess, the third-graders used to sing this song:

First grade, babies!
Second grade, dumb!
Third grade, angels!
Fourth grade, bums!

This year, *we* can sing it. Thomas and me. Because we're big. By the way, my muscles are bigger than Thomas's.

Now *I* have to go to the bathroom. "Well, why didn't you go before when your brother went?" Ma leans past Thomas and whispers. Her mouth is so close to my ear, she gets spit in it. I tell her I didn't have to go until just now. It's okay, I say. I'm big. I can go by myself. So she lets me. Thomas holds my pencil box because I held his.

I begin walking up the long, long aisle. At first, I'm a little afraid, but then I'm not. *Ping!* It misses. They better watch out. I'm Mark McCain. My father's The Rifleman.

I like being out here in the lobby all by myself. At the soda machine, a man is buying his little boy a grape soda. I stop to watch the cup drop down, the streams of soda and syrup. "Boy, I'm thirsty," I say out loud. The boy looks at me, but the man doesn't.

Downstairs, in the room outside the lavatory, they have ashtrays with sand in them. There's cigarette butts poking out of the sand. I play with them a little—the cigarette butts are bulldozers. I make bulldozer sounds.

Guess who's in the bathroom? The husher. He's leaning against the wall, smoking a cigarette and blowing smoke rings. Cigarette smoke swirls around his head. His mouth is a smoke-ring factory.

"I could have worked at the First National this summer," he says. I'm the only one in there, but he's watching himself in the mirror. I can't tell if he's talking to me. If he can even see me. Maybe I'm invisible. "But then I didn't because he said he might let me run the projector. Only he hasn't. Not once." He makes another smoke ring—a big fat one. A smoke doughnut. He sticks his tongue out and pokes it in the middle. Follows it as it floats away.

"Guess what my mother saw one time in the show?" I say. "A rat." I didn't plan on talking. It just came out.

"Big deal," he says, still looking at himself smoking. "We

see 'em all the time in here. They come up from the river." He has big red pimples on his forehead. "What do you think I cleaned off the top of the candy counter this morning? Rat crap, that's what. We set traps. You can hear 'em going off in the basement—right during the movie sometimes. *Snap!* The springs are set so tight, it breaks their frickin' backs." He chucks his cigarette in one of the toilets, and it makes a little sound like *tsst.*

"If you find an eraser on the floor later, it's mine," I say.

He looks right at me for the first time but doesn't say anything. Then he leaves. I have this whole huge bathroom to myself.

The urinals have big white pills at the bottom that smell like Christmas trees when you pee on them. When you *piss* on them. I say it out loud: "Piss on this!" Saying it—hearing the bad word echo in this shiny bathroom—gives me a little shiver. My hand shakes, wobbling the pee coming out. Now *my* soul has a dirty mark.

The bathroom door bangs open. Oh, no. It's Ralph Drinkwater and Lonnie Peck. I zip up quick. "Hey, kid?" Lonnie goes. "Want some money?"

I tell him no and he grabs my wrist. I can see the X's that Bulgy Eyes made on his hand and my hand. "Come on. For real. Hold your hand out flat."

I know it's a trick—he's probably going to spit on it—but I do it. Lonnie grabs me by the wrist and jerks my hand up—makes me slap myself in the face. "Why you hitting yourself, kid? Huh?" he laughs. He does it again. Again. "Why you hitting yourself?" It doesn't really hurt that much. It stings a little. I try to yank my hand away, but Lonnie's bigger than me. *Way* bigger. How's a third-grader supposed to fight someone in fifth grade who stayed back about fifty times?

"Hey, watch this!" Ralph goes. He rushes down the line of urinals, flushing. Turns all the sinks on full blast. Behind the wall, the pipes rattle and shake. Lonnie lets me go and starts pulling paper towels out of the paper towel holder. "Welcome to the fun house!" he screams.

I run. Out the door, past the ashtrays, up the stairs, through the lobby. Bulgy Eyes is leaning against the candy counter. "No running!" he goes.

When I get back to my seat, Ma stands up and lets me in. I don't say anything about Lonnie and Ralph. About the husher or those rats. I sit in my seat Indian-style so no rats will walk on my feet. My heart is beating so hard I can feel it, and my face feels hot where I was slapping myself.

"Like my earrings?" Thomas says.

He's taken his protractor and my protractor out of our pencil boxes and hung them on his ears. I yank mine back. "Ow!" he goes. He pokes me and I poke him back.

"Watch the movie!" Ma begs. "It's *funny*!"

But it isn't funny. It's stupid. Francis the Talking Mule is marching in a parade. Big deal. "How come you were wearing earrings?" I whisper to Thomas. "Because you're a stupid little girlie?"

He elbows me; I elbow him back. "That's enough, now, Dominick," Ma leans over and whispers. "You be nice to your brother."

"Say it, don't spray it," I tell her, right out loud. "You're getting spit in my ear."

If Ray was here, he'd wallop me one.

After the show, we walk back to the five-and-ten. We're early for the bus. Ma says we can walk around inside but not buy anything. If we have time and we're good, she might buy us an ice cream soda.

We enter the store, walk past the nuts and candies behind the glass case. Past the books, the comic rack, the toys. The five-and-ten has creaky floors. And a ceiling fan that goes *thwocka-thwocka-thwocka*. And a gypsy in a glass case that gives you your fortune for a penny. It comes out on a little card. The gypsy's fake, but the cat on her shoulder is real. A real, dead stuffed cat.

"See that fan up there?" I ask Thomas. "If a real tall guy came walking by, that fan would chop his head right off."

"No it wouldn't."

"Yes it would."

Ma is looking at some paintings: clowns, mountains, two horses running through a river. An orange paper sign—GIANT ART SALE—moves in the breeze the fan makes. "Boys, look at this one," Ma says.

She holds up a holy picture—Jesus floating in the sky. The Father and the Holy Ghost are up at the top, looking down at him. At the bottom, shepherds and other guys are hugging each other and looking up.

"Watch!" Ma says. She taps her finger against Jesus' chest. When she moves the painting, you can see Jesus' heart on fire. When she moves it back, it's gone. It's like magic. We make her do it over and over.

"Should I buy one of these?" Ma says.

"Yes!" we say. "Buy one!"

"Maybe next payday," she says. "Come on. I'll get you two your ice cream sodas." When we pass the ceiling fan, Thomas asks Ma if it could chop off a tall guy's head, and she says, "Oh, Thomas, what a thing to say."

Thomas can't finish his ice cream soda because he starts thinking about Miss Higgins again, so I finish mine and his. "You know what I bet will happen?" Ma says. "I bet I'll come back on Thursday and all those paintings will be sold already."

When we get up to go, she says, "Well, gee whiskers, if someone had treated me to ice cream and a movie when I was a little girl, I would have said, 'Thank you.' "

"Thank you!" we say, exactly together. Sometimes I know what Thomas is going to say even before he says it. Ma will go, "What do you want for a sandwich, Thomas?" and I'll go to myself, baloney and cheese. And then he'll say, "Baloney and cheese, please." I wonder if the Drinkwater twins can do that, too. I bet they can't. They're stupid. Penny Ann must be, anyway, if she's staying back.

On our way out to the bus stop, we stop at the paintings again. Ma picks up the Jesus painting and points to the label on the bottom of the frame. "Who can read this?" she asks.

" *'He is . . . ,'* " Thomas says, then stops, stuck.

" *'He is risen,'* " I say. " *'We are saved.'* "

"That's right, Dominick," Ma says. "Very good. Do you think I should just splurge and buy this?"

She doesn't ask Thomas. Just me. "Buy it," I say, like I'm the boss.

Ma takes crumpled-up money out of her change purse. The cash register lady wraps the painting in brown paper and asks Thomas and me if we are good boys at home. We say yes, and she gives us each a peppermint. We go outside and wait for the bus.

Ma rests the painting on the side of the building while we wait. We look and look and look, but that stupid bus won't come. Ma says if it doesn't come soon, supper will be late and Ray will get mad. She hopes he won't get mad about the painting.

Ray is not our real father. That's why we call him Ray. We don't know who our real father is. I don't know if Ma knows. I think he is very, very, very tall. I think he could beat up Ray. Our new painting is tall, but I'm taller.

Thomas says, "Look, Dominick. Communion!" He opens his mouth to show me the peppermint stuck to his tongue, but it slides off and falls on the sidewalk. Ma says it's too dirty to put back in his mouth. Thomas cries. The bus comes.

Oh, no! It's the grouchy bus driver with his stupid missing thumb. "Move to the back!" he says. "Come on. We haven't got all day! Move to the back!"

The bus is crowded. We have to go way, way back. Ma tells Thomas and me to sit together on one of the long bench seats and she sits across the aisle, facing us. She puts her new painting in front of her. It's resting on her knees.

Then the scary man gets on the bus (the man I would see and dream about my whole life after). He comes down the aisle toward us. He has crazy hair and whiskers and a big lump on his forehead. He's mumbling to himself. His coat's dirty. He squeezes into a small space next to my mother.

I don't like looking at this man—don't want to look at him—but I can't help it. Ma shakes her head at me, which means, "Don't stare." But the man keeps staring at Thomas and me. He says something naughty—something about seeing "goddamned double." Then he laughs. I know this man has a very, very, very dirty soul. I can tell Thomas is going to cry. I'm not even looking at Thomas, but I can tell.

The bus starts to move. Now the man is staring at Ma. Leaning toward her. He starts sniffing her like he's a dog. Ma leans away from him as best she can. Her hand is up against her lip. Her other hand is holding the painting. Thomas starts to cry.

Someone will help us, I tell myself. But none of the other people on the bus pay attention to the man. His hand moves out of his jacket pocket. Moves over to our new painting and then behind it where my mother's legs are. Ma's hand against her mouth is shaking. Her other hand holds the painting tight.

She says *nothing*—does *nothing*—and I'm scared and mad and my whole head is boiling hot. . . .

At the next stop, Ma jumps up, hurrying Thomas and me up the aisle, banging the edges of the painting against things as she leaves.

"Yes, thank you!" she says when the bus driver asks if everything's all right. We hurry down the steep, skinny stairs. The doors slap shut behind us. The bus jerks forward.

Then it stops again. The doors open.

The scary man is on the sidewalk, too.

Is he going to hurt us? Is he trying to steal our new painting? We run. Thomas's pencil box has slid open and everything's falling out. "Don't stop!" Ma screams. "Don't look back!"

But I *do* look back, and every time I do, the scary man is further away. Finally he just stops on the sidewalk and shouts something at us—something I can hear but not understand.

By the time we get home, my feet burn from all our running. All three of us are crying. Ma runs through the house, locking all the doors and windows and pulling down the shades. Then she sits on one of the dining room chairs and cries with her whole body. She cries so hard that she shakes the table and rattles the dishes in the china closet. Thomas and I stop our own crying to stare.

"Don't tell your father what happened, now," she says later, after she can speak again. "If he says, 'How was the movie?' you just say, 'Good.' If he gets wind of what happened, he won't let us go to the movies anymore. That man wasn't really bad. He just didn't know any better. He was just crazy."

Upstairs in her and Ray's bedroom, Ma kneels on the bed and tap-taps a nail in the wall. Hangs the new picture. She promises Thomas she'll get him another pencil box to replace the other one. "A *nice* one," she says. "A better one than those junky things they gave out at the show."

I'm tired now. I feel like crying. Why should Thomas get a nice pencil box when I have a junky one with no eraser? I thought this was going to be a good day, but it isn't. Today is my worst, worst day.

"Who knows what might have happened today," Ma says, "if Jesus hadn't been there to protect us from that crazy man?" She sighs, stepping back to admire the new painting. I look, too. Jesus looks back, his arms extended toward us. When I move my head back and forth, his flaming heart blinks on and off.

"Someday," Ma says, "I'm going to have Father LaFlamme come over and bless this painting. Bless our whole family. Our entire house."

That night at supper, Ray catches Thomas chewing on his sleeve.

"Okay! That's it!" he says.

Ray stands up and draws his belt from his pants. Loops it. Snaps it against the table. I think about those rats at the show, running through the dark basement, tripping the traps. *Snap!* Ray's belt goes. *Snap!*

"Come on, now, Ray," Ma says.

He jabs his finger at her. "*You* can just keep out of it, Suzie Q!" he says. "If you didn't namby-pamby him all the time, he wouldn't be like this!" He throws the belt down. Goes down to the cellar. Comes back upstairs with a roll of tape. "Am-scray!" he says, turning to me.

Out in the backyard, I can hear Thomas crying and choking and trying to breathe the way that dog tried to breathe when Mr. Grymkowski was pulling his collar. "I'm sorry, Ray!" Thomas keeps moaning. "Don't tape my hands up, please! I'm sorry! I forgot! I'm sorry."

Mosquitoes are out. Two bats crisscross the streetlight. An airplane's red lights blink on and off in the sky.

In *The Wizard of Oz,* the Wicked Witch melts and the spell is broken and those flying monkeys turn nice. They weren't even monkeys; they were men.

Our real father could be anyone.

The Rifleman.

Or that nice bus driver who finds candy in our ears.

Or even this pilot up in the sky. I run around and around and around the backyard, waving and flapping my arms so he can find us—Thomas and Ma and me.

Our real father could be anyone in the whole wide world.

Anyone but Ray.

six

Hi Dominick,

Thad & I are off to mixology class, we're learning cream drinks tonite! Guess who called? CONNIE CHUNG!!

She wants to interview your brother. (Details later!)

If you have one of my Lean Cuisines for supper, could you not eat the vegetable lasagna. Thanks!

Love, Joy

P.S. Call Henry Rood!!! (That guy's a pain!)

I read the note without really reading it. My brain wouldn't stop flashing sights and sounds from Hatch: Thomas's leg chains, his shabby Bible going through that X-ray machine. I walked around the condo, yanking down blinds, putting on lights. Passing the TV, I turned it on for the relief of the squawking.

In the bedroom, I eased myself out of my jeans and into a pair of sweats. If I felt sore now, I was probably going to feel a hell of a lot worse tomorrow. The first thing I was going to do was get my brother out of that snake pit. Then I was going to get a lawyer and sue their asses off: the state of Connecticut, the hospital, that fucking guard who'd kneed me. I'd have that son of a bitch hanging by *his* balls before I was through. So what if I'd gotten a little out of control? So fucking what?

I went back in the kitchen for a beer. Did we still have those Tylenol with codeine left over from her root canal? Where had I seen those things? Not in the medicine cabinet, of course. Not with Joy's "system." Keeps aspirin in the phone book drawer, peanut butter in the fridge. "Where's the vacuum cleaner bags?" I asked her the other day when I was cleaning out her car for her.

"Under the couch," she says, like that was the most logical place in the world.

The answering machine had . . . six, seven, eight blinks. Fuck. I hit the button.

Beep. "This is Henry Rood, 67 Gillette Street, and this is my *fourth* call in three days." I clamped my eyes shut and saw that peeling three-story Victorian headache of his. Saw Rood and his wife with their little his-and-hers potbellies, their rosy alcoholic faces. "I'd like to know when *in hell* you're going to get back to work over here, if that's not too much to ask. If at all possible, I would like to be able to look out my office window by the time the snow flies and *not* see your scaffolding!"

Before the snow flies: that was cute. Well, not tomorrow, Henry. There was no way in hell I was going to be climbing up and down ladders for the next twenty-four to forty-eight hours. I was going to be down at Hatch, figuring out how to spring my brother. Shit, I'd hire a fucking helicopter if I had to. Get him out of there like they did in that Charles Bronson movie the other night on HBO. . . .

Beep. A hang-up. A freebie.

Beep. Somebody at the something-something *Examiner* wanting to interview Thomas. When hell freezes over, pal. Order yourself a cream drink. Get in line behind Connie Chung.

Beep. Did I have *this* one right? Some guy from New York wanted to be my brother's *booking agent*? I closed my eyes, leaned my forehead against the kitchen cabinet. Reached out and hit the stop button without looking. Shit, man, when was this whole thing going to end?

There were four cans of Lite in the refrigerator. Sixteen-ouncers. After I'd specifically told her *not* to get Lite beer. She was going to make a great bartender, the way she listened. I grabbed the beers by the plastic ring anyway. Yanked one, popped the top, chugged a third of the can nonstop.

I looked through the cupboard, the freezer. Fished through Joy's Lean Cuisines. Considered the turkey tetrazzini. With the portions they gave you, eating those things was like foreplay. Plus you had to wait around for twenty minutes. There were a couple of hot dogs in there—left over from the Ice Age from the looks of them. A can of Chunky clam chowder in the cabinet—New England chowder, naturally, because I'd told her I liked Manhattan.

I hit the message button again. *Beep.* "Ray Birdsey. 3:30 P.M. 867-0359."

Real considerate, Ray. You never can tell when I'm going to go prematurely senile and forget the family phone number. I told myself I *should* call him back. Let him know about the mix-up—about having to leave Thomas at Hatch. He was his stepfather, wasn't he?

Beep. "This call is for Joy? From Jackie at A New You?" I picked up my beer again and drank. "Just wanted to let you know that the cocktail dress you were interested in is here now. We're open every day till five-thirty. Thanks!"

If she was running up her charges again, she could forget about me bailing her out. What had we been invited to that she needed a new cocktail dress, anyway? I stopped the tape, took another swig.

I closed my eyes and saw Robocop again: ice-blue eyes, acne scars. What had he said? "This one's crazier than the brother." I opened up the soup and poured it into a pan. Threw in the dogs. Canned soup and hot dogs for supper. And where's the woman of the house? Over at the community college learning how to mix cream drinks. Poor Ma was probably rolling over in her grave.

God, my testicles were killing me. Where *were* those codeine pills, anyway? I'd seen them someplace. . . . Okay,

I admitted it: I'd acted like a jerk down there. Saw now that I should have played it calm and cool. Story of my life: acting like a hothead, *especially* when it came to Thomas. But did that give the bastard the right to knee me in the nuts? What I should probably do was get back in the truck and drive over to the emergency room at Shanley. Have them examine me. Get it documented in case I decided to sue. I *should* sue, too—go after that guy personally with some shark of a lawyer. Knee him back, in the bank account. I had witnesses, up to and including that social worker who'd poked her head out the door. Only there was no way in hell I was going back to any hospital tonight. I popped another beer. Went looking for those pills of Joy's.

They were in the medicine cabinet after all, behind her Oil of Olay. She gets logical every once in a while. Has a temporary bout of organization. I washed down a couple of pills with the beer. "Caution: may cause drowsiness." Shit, man, let it happen. Let *this* day end. . . . Ever since Thomas cut off his hand, I hadn't slept for shit. Had woken up like clockwork every night at two-thirty. Gotten out of bed and sat there on the couch in my skivvies, channel-flipping past Sy Sperling and *Hawaii Five-O* and that muscle guy who claims a flat stomach's the way to happily-ever-after. . . . When I closed the medicine cabinet, I saw Thomas's face in the mirror.

Had they at least given him something to zonk him out down there? Was he at least sleeping through this nightmare? If anyone hurt him, they were going to have to answer to me. They were going to have to *cry* for mercy.

Back in the kitchen, I reread Joy's note: cream drinks, Connie Chung. Good God. I balled up the note, shot it toward the garbage. Bricked it.

It figured, didn't it? The one night I could have really used a little moral support and she's out at bartender school with her little gay boyfriend. Thad the massage therapist. The Duchess. I'd started calling him that when we went over to him and his boyfriend's house for dinner and he made those duchess potato things. Joy hates it when I call him that: the Duchess. "You're homophobic," she said the other night. Which I don't really consider myself. My opinion is, they can do anything they want with each other as long as they don't invite *me* to the party. . . . Homophobic. Where'd she get *her* psychology degree from? Geraldo Rivera Community College?

This was Joy's big plan: she was going to learn bartending and then moonlight until she paid off the rest of her MasterCard. Back in '87, after her second marriage busted up, she'd gone on a nine-month charging spree. Shopped till she dropped. She still owed $8,000, down from $12,500 since I loaned her a thousand and the collection agency started attaching her pay down at the health club.

That's where I met Joy—down at Hardbodies. It was after Ma died. After Nedra Frank hijacked my grandfather's life story and disappeared. Dessa and I had been history for about a year and a half by then, and it *still* hurt like hell. Leo was the one who kept bugging me to join up at Hardbodies with him; they were running one of those two-for-one "buddy membership" specials. I kept telling him I didn't have the time or the interest to join a gym, but he wore me down. Talked me into it. Fucking Leo, man: Mr. Car Salesman. Mr. Bullshitter. He could talk a Tahitian into buying snow tires.

We go way back, Leo and me—all the way back to 1966: summer school remedial algebra. He's my ex-brother-in-law, too—married to Dessa's sister, Angie. I was best man at Leo and Angie's wedding, and he was best man at Dessa's and mine. They got married three months after we did. It was your basic shotgun situation: Angie was three months pregnant. She lost it, though. Miscarried while they were on their honeymoon in Aruba. God, if that kid had lived, it'd be what? Seventeen by now? Eighteen? Everyone thought it was an accident—Angie's pregnancy—but come to find out, she did it on purpose. Leo told me a while back, after they ended up in marriage counseling. She just came out with it one session: that she'd wanted to get married because her big sister was getting married. When she dropped that little bombshell, Leo was *pissed*!

She's good people, Angie, but she's always been jealous of Dessa. Always looking over her shoulder to see what Dessa has, who loves Dessa better than they love her. When the four of us were newlyweds—Leo and Angie, Dessa and me—we used to hang out together all the time. Go to the beach together, go to each other's apartments and play cards. It got a little intense, though. All that unspoken competition. If Dessa hung baskets on our kitchen wall, Angie had to go home and hang some on hers. If we got a sleep-sofa, Angie and Leo would suddenly need a sleep-sofa. Angie finally got the upper hand when she had Shannon. Dessa and I had been trying for years to have a kid. Had been to two fertility specialists—put up with one humiliation after another. It's funny, when you think about it, though: of the two couples, Dessa and I were the ones everyone predicted would last. Us included. "They're never going to make it," we used to say about Leo and Angie. They'd fight all the time, right in front of you. In front of Dessa and Angie's *parents,* even. One time, we were all over there for dinner and Angie started chucking dinner rolls across the table at Leo. He'd said she was fat or something, I can't remember. Easter, it was. Greek Easter.

The reason Leo wanted me to join the health club with him was because he'd auditioned for this new sports drink commercial down in New York, made the first cut, and then gotten stiffed. (Twenty years out of acting school, nine years selling cars, and he's *still* waiting for his big break in show biz. You want to say to him, "Wake up, Leo! It didn't happen!") When he pressed the casting director about why he didn't get the part, she told him that he was the right age—they were targeting baby boomers—but that they were looking for somebody with a "better bod." Leo *had* begun to put on a few pounds around the middle; even I'd noticed it, and I don't usually notice shit like that. It practically killed him when he heard that, though. She might as well have stuck a dagger in his heart. "Look at this, Birdseed," he'd say, pinching a little of his spare tire. "A knit shirt, man. That's the acid test." He wouldn't drop it. It was like he was facing his immortality or something. Leo's more vain about his appearance than any woman I know. Always has been. Which is kind of funny, because Angie never bothers with makeup or dresses or any of that stuff. Lives in jeans and sweatshirts: what you see is what you get.

I actually started *liking* it down at Hardbodies, though. Not the weight machines or the exercise bikes or any of that shit. There aren't enough hours in the day as it is and I'm going to waste time riding a bike to nowhere? What *I* liked was the racquetball. Smashing those little blue balls against four walls felt good to me in a way nothing else had for a long time. Felt therapeutic, I guess. Racquetball spends you, you know? Sweats the piss and vinegar right out of you. Those little rubber balls can be anybody.

I met Joy the first day, right when Leo and I walked in the front door. Joy's the membership coordinator—the one who gives you the tour, then signs you up and takes the photos for your ID card. "Okay, there, good-looking," she said, from behind the camera. "Smile!" Said it to *me,* not Leo, who's never passed by a mirror he hasn't fallen in love with. "I'll laminate you guys and you can pick these up at the desk after your game," Joy told us after she took our ID pictures.

"Or," Leo said, leaning over the desk, "we can skip the game and you can just laminate us."

She shut him down cold just by the way she looked at him. *Iced* the guy.

"You know, Leo," I told him as we headed toward the locker room that day, "you're like in a time warp or something. Women these days *hate* that kind of talk."

"Bullshit," Leo said. "You mark my words, Birdseed. That one would screw anything." He held up the handle of his racquetball racquet. "She'd screw this. She'd screw *you,* for Christ's sake!"

That first day, she was wearing one of those ass-hugging pink Lycra things and a pink sweatshirt knotted around her shoulders. *Okay, good-looking. Smile!* That one little comment was like a life raft tossed to a drowning man.

I asked her out two or three visits later; I'd just beaten Leo and some other guy three games in a row in this round robin thing we were playing. I was feeling a little cocky, I guess. Leo dared me to and I just did it. It wasn't until after she'd said yes that the cold sweat crept over me. For one thing, Joy's a very good-looking woman—short, blond, in great shape from all those machines at the club. For another thing, she's fifteen years younger than I am. Joy was born in

1965. The year Sandy Koufax pitched his perfect game against the Cubs. The year *after* the Mustang came out. Joy's *mother's* only five years older than I am. Nancy. Now *there's* a trip. On her fifth husband: Mr. and Mrs. Homeopathy. They're always sending us yeast and extracts in the mail, which we keep for a while to be polite and then flush down the toilet. Joy's last "stepfather" was a junkie.

It turned out better than I expected, though—Joy's and my first date. It went great. I picked her up at work and we drove down to Ocean Beach. There was a full moon out; the sky was clear. We played Skee-ball, ate soft ice cream. Danced on the boardwalk to the music of these goofy father-and-son Elvis impersonators. The son was dressed all in black—young Elvis. The father was fat, white-jumpsuit Elvis. End-of-the-road Elvis, which, at Joy's age, is the only Elvis she remembers. They took turns: first the son would do "Heartbreak Hotel," and then the father would do "Hunka Hunka Burning Love." It went back and forth. Everyone was dancing and singing along, and every guy there was checking out Joy. I don't know, it just felt like I was back from the dead or something. Felt like: okay, Life After Dessa. This is doable after all.

I cut up the hot dogs and poured the soup in a bowl. Invented a new recipe: Clam & Hot Dog Chowder. I found some saltines that were so stale they were almost bendable. You say to her, "Joy, just twist the wrapper on the end so they'll stay good," and she stands there, looks at you like she's from some other planet. Which, in some ways, it almost seems like. It's the age difference. We both try and tell ourselves it doesn't matter, but it does. How couldn't it?

Here's what Ray said when I told him we were living together: "Jesus God Almighty, she's only twenty-three years old and she's gone through two husbands already?" I hadn't made any big announcement or anything—hadn't sent him a notice that she'd moved her leotards into my dresser, her futon and wicker furniture into the living room. Ray just called one morning and wanted to know who the "chippy" was who was answering the phone at 8:00 A.M., so I told him. And that was his response. Not "Gee, I'd like to meet her." Or, "Well, it's time you moved on." Just, "Twenty-three years old and she's already gone through two husbands?" See, Ray was always crazy about Dessa. Used to call her his "little sweetie" and stuff like that. He could even get, I don't know, *playful* with Dessa. He treated her a lot nicer than he ever treated Ma. It would never bother me much when we went over there, but then later on it would. Dessa used to always say how "needy" Ray was, how "on the surface" his insecurities were. She was always declawing him for me—analyzing him to the point where my stepfather seemed almost sympathetic, which I hated. "Hey, you didn't have to grow up with the guy," I used to remind her. "He's a lot more mellow now than he used to be." Ray's always assumed that Dessa's and my divorce was 100 percent *my* fault. *My* failure. That his "little sweetie" was blameless. Even though *she* left *me*. Even though *I* was the one who wanted to try and work things out. The only one of the two of us who'd *meant* "for better or worse."

It was great for a while, though—Joy and me. She's from Anaheim, California. She'd been out here almost three years but hadn't really seen that much. We used to travel on weekends—up to the Cape, over to Newport, down to New York. For a while, the only sex we had was in motels. Joy had a studio apartment and a roommate, so that didn't work. And, I guess this was stupid, but I just didn't want to do her on Dessa's and my old bed. I finally drove that thing over to Goodwill and bought a brand-new mattress and box spring. It was pretty wild, though—all that motel sex with Joy. It was like a drug or something. Here she was fifteen years younger and she was teaching *me* things.

Leo says it's a trend: that younger women are much sluttier than women our age. He and I were driving home from Fenway when we had that particular conversation, I remember. New York had just humiliated the Sox. "I didn't say she was slutty," I corrected him. "I said she was uninhibited."

He laughed out loud. "Slutty. Uninhibited. Same difference, Birdseed." We'd just stopped at the drive-thru at Burger King and were cruising along the Mass Pike, me driving, naturally. Leo's stuffing his face and talking about blow jobs: women who like it versus women who are doing you a big favor; women who swallow versus women who won't. He wanted to know which category Joy was in.

"What do you mean, what 'category'?"

"Is she a swallower or a nonswallower?"

I told him it was none of his goddamned business.

"Which means she's a nonswallower, right?" he said.

"Which means it's none of your business," I said. "Fat boy."

That shut him up. His jaw stopped moving. His Whopper dropped back onto the paper in his lap. "What'd you just call me?" he said.

"Fat boy."

"That's what I thought you said." He crammed his food back in the bag and threw it down on the floor. Stared out the side window. Didn't say anything for the next five or six exits. Fucking Leo, man. I mean, the guy had to go to a therapist because he was turning forty.

I put my dirty dishes in the sink without rinsing them. Fuck it, let Joy do them tomorrow. What's that called? Passive-aggressive? I opened the last of the beers.

Call Ray back, call Ray back, I kept telling myself. Maybe *he* knew why they'd switched doctors on Thomas. Why they'd switched him to Hatch. Maybe Ray had talked to Dr. Ehlers. Doubtful, though. Ehlers almost always called me, not Ray. I closed my eyes. Heard my brother's "*Jesus! Jesus!*" Saw the wet stain spreading on the front of his pants. . . . I could have gotten my head blown off in that cruiser when I'd reached out to grab Mercado's arm and he'd gone for his gun. Cowboy. Cops were all cowboys—that's why most of them got into it in the first place. *This one's crazier than the brother. . . .*

I picked up the phone, intending to dial Ray's number. Dialed Leo's instead.

It's not that Leo's a great listener or anything. Far from it. But at least he knows the complete deal with Thomas—the whole sordid history. . . . The summer we were all nineteen? When Leo and Thomas and I were on a city work crew together? That's when Thomas started falling apart at the seams. Thomas and me, Leo, Ralph Drinkwater. It was weird, come to think of it. I hadn't seen Drinkwater for years and years and then, bam—there he is at Hatch, with a mop and a bucket. It was like one of those crazy guest appearances people make in your dreams. . . .

Leo always asks about Thomas; I'll give him that much. Goes to see him every once in a while down at Settle. He even stopped in at Shanley Memorial after Thomas's accident, but they wouldn't let him go up because I hadn't thought to put him on the list.

Angie answered the phone. She said Leo was in New York, auditioning for something. She puts up with it—all those jaunts to New York when he should be going to work and getting home at a decent hour and helping her out with the kids. It's sad, in a way. Not all of those "auditions" of Leo's are auditions.

"How's your brother, Dominick?" Angie said.

Not so good, I said. I told her about Hatch.

"Oh, my God," she said.

"Police escort, leg chains," I said. "Like he's Lee Harvey Oswald instead of my stupid, screwed-up brother."

"Oh, my God," she said again.

"Tell Dessa, will you?" I said. "That he's down there?"

"Okay. Sure. She and Danny went camping for a few days, but I'll let her know when she gets back."

I twisted the phone cord around my hand. Cinched it, cut off the blood. She's been living with the guy for two years and she can't go camping with him? Because it bothers *me*? "How are the kids?" I said.

"They're great, Dominick. Great. Amber just won the fire prevention poster contest. Just for her school, not for the whole district."

"Yeah? That's cool. Tell her congratulations."

"Shannon's got a walkathon coming up for soccer. You want to sponsor her?"

"Sure," I said. "Put me down for ten bucks." Shannon's already in high school—a freshman. She was about six when Leo and that "hostess with the mostest" down in Lyme got caught with their pants down. Amber's nine. The post–marriage-counseling baby.

"Okay, Dominick. Thanks. Hey, you should come over for dinner sometime." There was a pause. "Both of you."

Come over *sometime:* one of those noninvitations.

"Yeah, thanks," I said. "We will. Once things calm down with my brother." Which was going to be when? Never? It was a nonrefusal for a noninvitation.

"I'll tell Leo you called," she said. "You want him to call you back if he gets in before eleven or so?"

"Nah, that's okay. I'll get ahold of him tomorrow. What's he auditioning for?"

"Some movie. I don't know much about it. You hang in there, now, okay?"

"Okay."

"Hey, Dominick?"

"Hmm?"

"You're a good brother. You know that?"

How stupid is this? She tells me that and I start crying. Have to hang up the phone. Oh, great, I thought to myself. Just what we need: the *other* Birdsey brother cracking up. The identical twin cruising into the breakdown lane. Both of us down there.

The real estate booklets were in our bedroom, on my pillow—a Post-it note stuck to the cover: "Dominick, what do you think of these???" She gets those things every week: *The Realty Shopper, Gallery of Homes*. I'm starting to recognize the smiling face of every goddamned realtor-*bandito* in eastern Connecticut. Joy puts stick-on notes all over the ads she wants me to look at. It's an ongoing pipe dream is what it is—her doing that. She still owes eight thousand bucks, and with what I've got saved, I could probably just about swing a down payment on a doghouse. I don't know; we might not even stay together. I go back and forth on that one.

Joy's got liabilities. Things you can't see right off the bat, when you're staring at her assets. Her bad credit rating, for one—her whole attitude about money. The second month we were living together—after it dawned on me that she didn't have a clue when it came to finances—I had to sit her down and show her how to do a budget. It wasn't that she was stupid, she said; it was just that no one before me had ever taken the time, made the effort on her behalf. Both her husbands had always paid all the bills, which was why she'd gotten so messed up with plastic. After we had her output and input mapped out, I took all her credit cards out of her wallet, laid them end to end on the kitchen table. Handed her the scissors. "Here," I said. "Cut." Which she did.

Another of Joy's liabilities surfaced three or four months after that. She was out that night—shopping up at the Pavilions. Leo was over at the house. We were watching the NBA championship, I remember—the final game where Worthy and the Lakers took it away from the Pistons. The phone rings and it's Joy, talking so low I couldn't even understand her at first. She was at the Manchester police station—that much I got. At first, I thought she'd been in an accident, but that wasn't it. They'd caught her shoplifting.

Stealing fancy underwear at Victoria's Secret. She'd just gotten arrested for petty larceny. It was weird, man. I stood there, not quite getting it, part of me still watching the game.

Before I drove up and got her, I made Leo promise not to say anything to Angie. I didn't want it getting back to Dessa that my girlfriend had just gotten arrested. Leo said he'd drive up there with me, but I said no.

After Joy and I got back to the condo that night, it was true confession time. She told me she'd been stealing on and off since high school. That she *liked* doing it. This was only the third time she'd ever gotten caught—the first time here on the East Coast. She started going through our drawers and closets, throwing stuff onto our bed that she'd fingered: perfume, jewelry, silk scarves, even a coat—a goddamned winter coat. She was acting weird about it—charged up or something. She *liked* doing it and she *didn't* like doing it, she said. It was a little scary. We were both scared, I guess. But the thing was, she was a little cocky about it, too. Proud of herself—of that pile she'd made on the bed. She starts kissing me, pawing me all over the place. We ended up screwing right there in the middle of all that stolen merchandise—Joy on top and me on the bottom, this pair of stolen earrings digging into my back. She was hotter that night than I'd ever seen her. Like I said, it was weird.

The lawyer we hired got her off with community service: fifty hours helping out with girls' gymnastics at the Manchester YMCA. Joy never talked about any of the kids or anything when she came back. Just drove every Saturday morning to Manchester, put in her hours, and came home. She's funny that way—a little emotionally absent. A little indifferent. With schizophrenics, they call it flat affect. I mean, I think *I* felt worse about Joy getting arrested than she did.

She went to this psychologist for a while afterwards—after the big lingerie heist. The guy's name was Dr. Grork. She saw him until her insurance ran out. I'm not a big believer in shrinks—all that probing and prodding into my brother's potty training and puberty never did *him* any good. Not that I could see. Did harm, actually. Harmed Ma. I remember this one shrink right at the beginning—this old guy with hair in his nose—who tried to pin the rap for Thomas's illness on *her.* He told her the research suggested that mothers who couldn't love their sons enough sometimes kick-started manic-depressive disorder and/or schizophrenia. Which was pure horseshit. Ma gave the both of us everything she could and then some—*especially* Thomas. Her "little bunny rabbit." She lived and breathed for that kid, sometimes to the point where it got a little sickening. Where it was like, *Yoo-hoo. Hey, Ma? Remember* me*?* Believe me. I was there. Not loving him enough was *not* the problem.

But anyway, Joy and this Grork guy got to the bottom of things pretty quickly. The breakthrough came one day when he asked her to describe what she felt like when she stole and she told him she felt turned on. That she'd get wet when she did it—sometimes even play with herself in the car driving away. It embarrassed me when she'd go into it like that—come home from Dr. Grork's and tell me everything she'd just told him. One time, she said, she stole a purse at G. Fox, then got in the car and started rubbing the merchandise against herself while she was driving out of the parking lot. Began finger-fucking herself and came right there on the entrance ramp to I-84—it was so intense, she said, she almost rammed right into the back of a Jag. "Okay, okay," I told her. "That's enough. Spare me the details."

According to Dr. Grork, Joy's compulsion had to do with the fact that she'd been sexually abused when she was in junior high. By her mother's brother. Well, *half*-brother, I guess he was, technically. *Is.* He was stationed at the naval base in San Diego; he lived with them for a while. He was ten years older than Joy, in his early twenties when it started; she was thirteen. It wasn't rape or anything. Well, it was and it wasn't. Statutory rape, I guess. It had started as fooling around, Joy said—water fights, wrestling matches. Then one thing led to another. They were alone a lot, she said. After a while, she just stopped moving his hands away. Stopped telling him to stop. Joy's mother worked second shift.

It went on until "Unc" got transferred to Portsmouth, New Hampshire. Here's the sickest part: they kept it going for a while. Through the mail. He'd write her these dirty letters and enclose little pieces of himself: fingernail clippings, beard trimmings, even dead skin from a sunburn. It was *her* idea, she told me; she'd beg him to. She'd take them out of the envelope and eat them. Sit there chewing on the guy's fingernails. Then he got a girlfriend and stopped writing. Stopped answering her letters and accepting the charges when she'd call him collect after school. Then the new girlfriend got on the phone and told her off. Screamed bloody murder at her. That's when Joy started shoplifting. Dr. Grork said stealing made Joy feel powerless and powerful at the same time. The same as her uncle had. The same as her two husbands, too, I guess. Really, she'd just come home from those sessions with Dr. Grork and lay everything right out there, whether I wanted to hear it or not.

She was eighteen when she married the first guy. Ronnie. Graduates from high school and—bam!—elopes out in Las Vegas before the end of the summer. She's always talking about what a big mistake that was—how she'd gone right after graduation to Disneyland and had a job interview to be a cast member there. She'd make a perfect Cinderella, the woman told her. That's one of the big disappointments of Joy's life—that she never got to be Cinderella at Disneyland. That Ronnie guy was just a kid, too, I guess—twenty or twenty-one. That's how she came east: he was transferred to the sub base in Groton. They lived down in Navy housing on Gungywamp Road. I've painted houses there. It's depressing: house after house, all of them just the same. Joy and her *second* husband lived there, too—different house, same street. Dennis, the chief petty officer. She started sleeping with number two while number one was out at sea.

That's what I'd identify as Joy's third liability, I guess. Her *major* one. The fact that I can never quite trust her. Not 100 percent anyway. Not that she ever cheated on me—at least not that I know of. Just that she might. With some guy closer to her own age. That's how I picture it happening, anyway: Joy and some superficial asshole in his twenties—some idiot who isn't able to see beyond his own dick. There are plenty of those guys strutting their stuff down at Hardbodies, where she works. All those young guys with the gelled hair and the weight-lifting belts and the one earring. They're coming out of the woodwork at that place. It's like a fucking epidemic.

Which is not to say there's trouble between us in bed. We're still okay in that department, Joy and me. We're fine. It's not off the chart the way it was at first in those Ramadas and Best Westerns, but it's still pretty damn satisfactory. It's work sometimes, though. On my part. It's probably stress—my brother and the business and shit. Joy's always telling me to get down to the club and work out more. She's always trying to get me to get a massage from her buddy, the Duchess. "He's a genius," she told me once. "His fingers, his rhythm—you can feel him actually drawing the tension out of you."

"That's just what I'm afraid of," I said.

"Stop it," she said. "You're just being homophobic."

"Yeah, well," I told her, "whatever." That time we went over to their house for dinner? Thad and Aaron's house? . . . Aaron's somewhere around my age. They live over on Skyview Terrace in one of those glass-walled contemporaries that look out onto the river. Land of the big bucks out there, folks; land of the high-altitude tax brackets. Skyview Terrace used to be part of the old mill complex, and before that, it was part of the Wequonnoc reservation lands. We used to fish out there sometimes before they developed it—Leo and me, Thomas and me. You should see the views of the river, especially in early June when everything's just come out—the leaves on the trees and the mountain laurel. You look out there and you can almost believe in God.

Aaron's an architect. *He's* the one with the Porsche and the deed to the house. On the way over there that night, we had to stop at two package stores before we found this twenty-four-dollar bottle of special wine that Thad said would go perfectly with what he was making: scallops in cream sauce with those stupid duchess potatoes. The theory was that Aaron and I were supposed to have something in common because of our age and because we were both "in the building industry." I had to laugh at that one. An architect and a housepainter are both in the building industry the same way Roger Clemens and the guy who sells the Fenway franks are both part of the Red Sox organization. That dinner lasted forever. I sat there all night, drinking Danish beer and listening to Aaron talk about jazz fusion and mutual funds. Trying to be cool about all this gay art they had hanging up all over the place. Joy and Thad spent the whole night gossiping about people they knew from work. Joy says Thad wants to phase out his massage therapy and get into the catering business. Aaron will put up the money if it's what he really wants to do, Joy says, but first Thad has to learn the business: marketing and management courses, not just the fun stuff like mixology. Thad told Joy that when he opens his business, he wants her to be his bartender. Joy says she's never had a girlfriend she could trust as much as she trusts Thad. She says she can tell him things she can't even tell me. Which is sort of scary, because she tells me *plenty.* Miss Openness. Miss Finger Fucks Herself on Interstate I-84 and Eats Guys' Fingernails.

Joy has this idea that, once she gets all her debts paid off, we can start saving and buy a house and get married. Live in one of those places in the real estate books. "I'm fifteen years older than you," I told her one time. "I stopped believing in somewhere-over-the-rainbow a long time ago. I'm damaged goods."

"I'm damaged goods, too!" she said, cheerfully, like it was some happy coincidence—me and her discovering we had the same birthday or something. . . .

I changed my mind, did the dishes after all. Put away the pans. Passive-aggressive: what's the point?

Joy keeps her distance from Thomas; she's afraid of him,

I know that much. She was afraid of him *before* he cut off his hand—right from the beginning. When she first moved in with me, I used to bring him over to the house on Sunday afternoons. Dessa and I had always done that, and then, after the divorce, I'd kept it up. It was a pattern, a ritual. Joy didn't say anything about it one way or the other for a while. She was on her best behavior. Then one Sunday morning—we'd been together for about six months by then—she asked me out of the clear blue not to go get him.

"But he *always* comes over on Sunday," I said. "He *expects* me."

"Well, I just thought it would be nice for once to spend the whole Sunday alone—just you and me. Just call and tell him you're sick or something. Please?"

We were both naked together in the bathroom when she said it, I remember. We'd just had some pretty intense sex and I was about to grab a shower. Before Joy, I didn't even know they made women who liked that much of it.

"Just you and me," she repeated. She took my hand in her hand and slid my fingertips over her breasts, across her stomach, down to the stickiness we'd just made. Steam clouds rolled in the air around us. I'd already gotten the shower just the right temperature. "Please?" she said.

"But he *expects* me, Joy. He *waits* for me. Sits out in the solarium with his jacket zipped up."

She let go of my hand and put herself against me—reached up under my balls and stroked me there. Smiled. Watched me blink. Watched me swallow. Good sex with Dessa was something we'd taught each other, but Joy came into the thing we had already *knowing* what would drive me crazy. Same things that had driven her two husbands crazy, I guess. And her uncle.

"What about what *I* expect?" she said. "Doesn't that count for anything?" Her finger kept stroking. In another ten seconds, she'd get whatever she wanted.

I took her hand by the wrist and held it away from me. Stared at her. Waited.

"It's not . . . ," she said.

"It's not what?"

"It's not that I don't *like* him. I *do* like him, Dominick.

He's a nice guy, in his own weird way. But he scares me. The way he acts sometimes. The way he looks at me."

It was crap, what she was implying: that Thomas was eyeballing her. Lusting after her. I mean, most guys do. Joy's a very good-looking woman. She gets her share of ogling. But with all the medication he's taken over the years, my brother has about as much sex drive as a mannequin. "*How* does he look at you?" I said. "Give me the specifics."

"I don't know," she said. "It isn't even really that. He just kind of gives me the creeps."

"He gives *everybody* the creeps," I said. I was still squeezing her wrist. Squeezing it a little harder, even.

"Yeah, but . . . well, part of it—I'm just trying to be honest, okay, Dominick? Don't get mad, but . . . part of it is that you and he *look* so much alike. *That's* what's a little scary. Sometimes he seems like some weird version of *you.*"

I kept looking at her until she looked away. Then I let go of her hand and stepped into the shower.

"Hey, just forget it, okay?" she called in, over the hiss of the water. "Go ahead. Bring him over. I'll deal with it. It's my problem, not yours. I'm sorry, Dominick. Okay?"

Her hand reached past the plastic curtain and inside for my hand. I stood there and watched it move, searching, like the grope of a blind person. I refused to grab it, to take her small, perfect hand in some soggy gesture that gave her permission to feel that way—to say what she'd just said about him.

I wouldn't give her that. I couldn't. Which is probably, right there, why it's never going to work with her and me.

I picked up Thomas same as usual that day. Drove him all the way up to the Basketball Hall of Fame in Springfield, Mass., which he didn't give a crap about seeing. Took him out to eat at a Red Lobster on the way home, where he spilled melted butter all over himself. Got back purposely late. I gave Joy the silent treatment for the next couple of days—treated her so shabbily that I ended up rooting for her instead of me. She doesn't have it easy living with me. I know that. *You* try being the brother of a paranoid schizophrenic. See if it doesn't royally fuck up *your* life. *Your* relationships.

I stood there staring at the blinking message machine. Remembered the other phone messages—the ones I hadn't listened to yet. Hit the button.

Beep. "Good afternoon, Mr. Birdsey. This is Henry Rood again. It's five o'clock, sir—the end of the workday." (He was slurring his words, had jumped the gun on cocktail hour again.) "Not that *your* workday ever began, Mr. Birdsey. At least not here it didn't. I'm still waiting for you to return one of the five calls I've made to you now. I'm marking them down—all my attempts to communicate with you. I have a little pad here. Maybe I should just call the Better Business Bureau instead."

"Maybe you should just blow it out your ass," I told the machine. I'd get to his freakin' house when I got to it.

Beep. "Uh, yeah, hello. My name is Lisa Sheffer. I'm trying to reach Dominick Birdsey? In regard to *Thomas* Birdsey? Your brother?"

Here we go again, I thought. What illustrious organization are you with, honey? *Hard Copy*? *Geraldo?*

"I'm a social worker at Hatch Forensic Institute and I've been assigned to him, or he's been assigned to me, or whatever. . . . I know you were pretty upset tonight when you came in with him, and I just thought you might want to talk to me? Have me walk you through the procedures down here or whatever? You can give me a call if you want to. I'm going to be in my office until about ten o'clock tonight." I looked up at the clock. Fuck! It was twenty after ten. "Or, you can call me tomorrow. Relax, now. Okay? Okay."

End of message. Shit! If I had just listened to the whole goddamned tape as soon as I got home. . . .

But the voice spoke again.

"I, um, I just talked to him. We just had a nice talk. He's okay. He's fine, under the circumstances. *Really.* I know you had a bad . . . sometimes some of the guards here can get a little . . . well, he's okay. Your brother. Inside the unit, it's not like, you know, a torture chamber or anything. It's really a pretty humane place, for the most part. I just thought it might help if you knew that after what happened tonight. Okay? . . . They've got him on one-to-one observation in a room right across from the nurses' station. Which is *good,* right? And the nurse who's on tonight is super. I know her. . . . So, anyway, just relax. And like I said, call me if you want to. So, uh . . . well, no. That's it, I guess. Bye."

I tried calling her back. Maybe she'd stayed later than she'd planned. But there was no answer.

I went into the living room and stood there, channel-flipping. Lisa Sheffer: at least *she* sounded somewhat human. I paced. Went into the bathroom and popped another of Joy's pills. The codeine was either working or it wasn't working—I wasn't sure. I was still sore down there below the belt, but it was like, who gives a shit? Which I guess meant that it was working. . . .

I woke up from a dream where I was apologizing to Connie Chung for something. Begging her to forgive me. To give me the key so that I could unlock my brother. *"La chiave,"* she said. "Say it. *La chiave.*"

When I opened my eyes, Joy was sitting on the couch next to me. "Hi," she said.

"Hi. . . . What's up?"

She ran her fingers through my hair. "He looks like a little boy when he first wakes up, doesn't he?" she said. At first, I didn't know who she was talking to, or if I was still dreaming or what. Then I saw him. The Duchess. He was sitting across the room on her overstuffed futon, smiling at me. They both had drinks in their hands. Cream drinks.

"How are you?" Joy said.

"I'm all right," I said. "I'm good."

"Good," she said. She put her hand to my face. Stroked my cheek with her shoplifter's fingers. They were damp from her drink. Damp and cold.

seven

Thomas and I meander along the edge of the pond, stopping whenever we see flat stones. Skimming stones. Thomas stoops. He's found a good one. "Watch this," he says, and lets it fly. The stone hops the water's surface six, seven, eight . . .

A sound distracts me—a chattering noise—a monkey! It's high up on a branch in the big tree behind us, partly visible and partly hidden by the fluttering silver bottoms of leaves. "Dominick!" Thomas says. "Watch!" He hurls another stone. Eight, nine, ten, eleven. . . . I look back up in the tree. Now the monkey is an old woman. She sits, cackling, scrutinizing us. . . . *Beep! Beep! Beep! Beep!*

"Yeah, wait a minute, wait a minute," I grumbled at the clock radio. My hand flailed, found the button. Silence. Lying there, half-awake, half-asleep, I suddenly remembered the night before: Thomas in leg chains, the sound of his screaming as they led him into the locked ward. His being at Hatch dropped onto my back like an anvil.

The bedroom was cold. Should have started the furnace by now. I reached down and grabbed the blanket, pulled it up to my neck.

Was he already awake down there? Maybe he and I were

waking up at the same exact second. We'd had that telepathy thing off and on our whole lives—had shared each other's life in ways that only twins can. Answering each other's questions, sometimes before the other one even asked. That time in seventh grade when I broke my arm in gym class and Thomas felt the pain on the other side of the school. Or that summer Ray rented the cottage at Oxoboxo Lake—that game Thomas and I used to play where we'd psyche each other out: jump off the dock and see if we'd both thought of the same kind of dive to do. . . . The week before, even. I mean, hey, I didn't know he was over at the library, lopping his hand off because of Kuwait, but I knew *something* was wrong. I'd been agitated all that morning—dropped a can of paint, something I never do. And when that cruiser was coming down Gillette Street, riding toward the Roods' house, the first thing I thought was: *Thomas.*

I heard the shower stop, the curtain swish open. The clock said 5:55. She does that all the time on her early days, the mornings when she teaches aerobics: gets up before the alarm and then forgets to shut the damn thing off. . . . When Joy and I were first going out, I used to go down there and take that class. The "A.M. Executive Stretch," it's called. She gives you a good workout—makes it worth the effort. It was the locker room afterwards I couldn't take. All these suit-and-tie types hooking their socks back up to their garters and speculating about Joy's cup size, about what kind of a workout she gave in bed. They didn't know I was the boyfriend—didn't know me from a hole in the wall. When I finally called one of them on it—this pencil-necked insurance honcho who was worse than the others—he complained to the manager about me. Joy said maybe it would be better if I didn't come to that class. It's part of the con down there, see? Guys are *supposed* to fantasize about the instructors. It's good for business.

I sat up in bed and swung my legs onto the floor. Oh, man, I was sore. There was no way I was going to paint today. I was probably going to have to take Ray up on his offer—have him give me a hand with Rood's house, no matter what it cost me, sanity-wise. Now I wished I'd called Ray the night before to tell him about Thomas. About Hatch.

I made a mental list: Call Ray. Call Rood. Call Thomas's doctor. Call that social worker. What was her name? Lisa something. A real rookie from the sound of her message on the machine, but at least she was a starting point. I'd find out who her superior was and cut to the chase. Talk to the biggest mucky-muck I could find down there. I wanted to have some answers by the time I saw my brother. Wanted to be able to say to Thomas, okay, look, here's the deal: we're getting you out of here by such-and-such.

The bathroom door opened, steam clouds chasing Joy out like an entourage. It's no wonder the ceiling in there's a mildew factory. "Leave the door *open* if you're going to run the water so hot," I tell her. She says she can't because of that stupid movie *Psycho*.

Psychos: that's who they'd thrown my brother in with down there. A bunch of violent psychopaths. If Thomas had so much as a mark on him by the time I got him out of there, I'd sue their asses off. Make them pay in spades.

Joy touched my shoulder when she walked by me. Took off her towel. I liked watching her get ready like this, first thing in the morning. Before the phone rang. Before either of us opened our mouths and blew it. She liked me watching her, too. The morning performance. The reverse striptease. Dessa was always kind of shy about getting dressed around me—used to always hustle into her clothes over near our closet. Joy's the opposite.

She squirted cream onto her hand and began rubbing her neck, her breasts, the insides of her legs. Joy's pubic hair's this neat, perfect triangle. Light brown, silky to the touch, not coarse like Dessa's. She gets it bikini-waxed down at the health club. They have the world's shittiest medical plan down there—no prescription rider, no dental plan—but you can get unlimited time in the tanning booths. Get your bush trimmed for free. I watched her shimmy into her leotard—the zebra stripe one with that black thong thing to make sure your eye travels down to the right place. Sore balls or not, I was starting to come to attention. I'm like a dog around Joy. She can just walk into the room. . . .

That's what they count on down at that club where she works: that guys are dogs. That everyone's just their bodies.

Joy's taken these seminars in something called "client maximization," which is corporate-talk for "screw the customer." Take that zebra-striped leotard, for instance: they make the employees wear the same stuff they sell in that little overpriced boutique of theirs. Here's the theory: some fat chick goes in there, coughs up forty or fifty bucks for one of those leotard-and-thong numbers, and comes out of the locker room thinking she looks like Joy. Client maximization: give me a break. You know who owns the Hardbodies chain? United Foods.

"Hi," Joy said.

"Hi."

"How you feeling?"

I shrugged. "I guess I'll live."

I got up and hobbled toward the bathroom. That goddamned guard had me walking bowlegged.

Jesus, it was like the rain forest in there—walls dripping, mirror and window fogged up. "Are you working today, Dominick?" she called in.

"Can't. I've gotta go down there and get this thing about my brother straightened out." I started the shower, dropped out of my underwear. There was a maroon bruise on the inside of my thigh. My scrotum was swollen. Black and purple and blue.

"No way in hell I'd be able to get up and down that scaffolding over on Gillette Street," I called out to her.

"Is Gillette Street Henry Rood's house?" she said.

"Yup. How'd you guess?"

"He was so nasty yesterday when he called. I was like, excuse me, but *I'm* not painting your house. Don't yell at *me*."

"You told him that?"

"No. But I *felt* like it."

"Good," I said. "Next time, do it. Give him hell."

The warm water soothed me. Maybe that's what I should do: stay in the shower all day. Brother? What brother? . . . As I stood there, my dream came back to me—the one I'd woken up to. Me and him up at . . . Rosemark's Pond, I guess it was. Monkeys and old ladies up in the trees? Shit, man, I didn't even *want* to know what that meant. . . . He'd always been a good stone skimmer, my brother. He'd always been better at that than me.

When I opened the shower curtain, Joy was standing in front of our vanity, putting on eye makeup. "Look at this," I said, showing her my war wounds from the night before.

"Oh, my God. . . . Hey, Dominick?"

"What?"

"I was just wondering. What about Connie Chung?"

"What about her?"

"What should I tell her when she calls back? About the interview? She needs to know one way or the other. I had to give her my work number in case she can't get ahold of you."

"Tell her no," I said. Joy stood there, not getting it.

"Okay, fine," she finally said. "It's your decision. I just . . ."

"You just what?"

"Well, I just think maybe you should talk to her first. They're doing this special? On people's reactions to Operation Desert Shield?"

"He had a reaction, all right," I said. "His reaction got him locked up in a maximum-security prison. 'Good evening, this is Connie Chung, coming to you live among the psychopaths.' That ought to be great for the ratings."

"Just hear what she has to say before you decide. She was nice, Dominick. She sounded real sympathetic."

I shook my head. "Yeah, right."

"No, really. She *was*. Thad thought so, too."

"Thad? What the fuck does *he* have to do with it?"

"Nothing. He was here when she called, that's all. He answered the phone. When I got off, we were both like, 'Oh, my God, we were just talking to Connie Chung from TV.' "

"Yeah, big whoop," I said. "Look, from now on, I don't want that jerk answering our phone."

She let that one go. She was still stuck on Connie Chung. "Really, Dominick. Just talk to her. She was real sweet."

"She was 'real sweet' because she wanted something from you. Believe me, Joy, Connie Chung's not your new best friend."

She pivoted around and glared at me. "I *know* she's not

my new best friend, okay?" she said. "I'm not stupid, whether you think I am or not."

"Look," I said. "I just don't want . . . I've just got one or two other things that I'm trying to deal with right now, and I don't—"

"You know what *I* wish sometimes?" she said. "I wish that you'd take care of *me* the way you take care of *him*. Because that would be a real nice surprise sometime, Dominick: being taken care of a little by my own boyfriend. But that's never going to happen, is it? Because *I'm* not crazy."

Forgetting my injury, I flopped back down on the bed. Waited out the pain. "Don't *do* this, Joy, okay?" I said. "Not right now. Just don't. . . . First of all, I *don't* think you're stupid. I *know* this is hard for you. It's hard for all of us. But it's nonnegotiable—me looking out for him. Okay? It's just something I have to do."

"Fine," she said. "Do it then. Go for it, Dominick." She walked out of the room.

It was funny, in a way—funny-ironic: an interview with Connie Chung. A national audience. It was exactly what Thomas had been looking for. Exactly why he'd hacked off his hand in the first place. He thought he could stop a war from happening if he could just get everyone's attention. Once people heard what he had to say, he'd told me, he would find his flock. His ministry. And he probably *would*, too, knowing how many lunatics there were out there. I could see it now: the Church of St. Thomas Birdsey. The Holy Order of Amputees for Peace. It would be "dangerous," though, Thomas told me. Saving the entire world would *really* put him on Satan's shit list.

Joy came back into the bedroom. Started towel-drying her hair. "Hey, some store left a message on the machine for you," I said. "The cocktail dress you ordered is in."

Her not saying anything made her seem guilty of something. I couldn't see her face.

"So what do you need a cocktail dress for?" I said.

She shook out her hair, poked at it with her fingers. Joy's got one of those *au naturel* hairdos. I watched her eyes in the mirror. No guilty expression. No expression at all. That deadpan of hers was probably the reason she'd been such a good shoplifter.

"You hear me?"

"What?"

"I said, what do you need a new cocktail dress for?"

"I *don't* need a new cocktail dress," she said. "Why would I need a new cocktail dress when we never go anywhere?"

I let that one fly by. Knew better than to strike at the remark. We were both fly-fishing this morning. She went over to the closet. Started putting on her warm-up suit, available at the Hardbodies boutique, no doubt.

"So why'd you order it then?"

She wouldn't look at me. We find the defendant guilty of something. Of what?

"I just wanted to see how it looked on me. Okay, Dominick? You can do that, you know. Order something in your size. Take it home and try it on, and then bring it back. It's not against the law."

"I'm not saying it is. But isn't it kind of a waste of everyone's time if you know you're not going to buy it anyway?"

She answered me by not answering. By walking into the kitchen.

It hurt to put on underwear. Jeans? Forget it. I found those drawstring pants she'd gotten me a while back and put them on—those jazzy things with the skulls and crossbones all over them. I'd never really worn those stupid things. Not out, anyway. At least they were nice and loose. . . . I could probably have that guard's job if I wanted to pursue it. If I wanted to check in with a doctor and a lawyer. Which I didn't have either the time or the energy for—not with everything else that was going on. Fuck it.

Joy was painting her toenails at the kitchen table. I hate when she does that: puts her feet up right where we eat. It wouldn't occur to her in a hundred years to grab a sponge afterwards.

"Nice pants," she said. Smart-mouthed it.

"Well, *you* got them for me. Didn't you?"

"Yeah, back when they were in style."

I put some coffee on. I'd given up caffeine the year before—felt better, slept better. Then I'd started up again—back in the summertime, when all that Kuwait stuff had started. It was all Thomas would talk about: those Biblical prophesies that were going to come true, all that Armageddon crap. That's a pattern with Thomas when he's starting to spiral down—he latches on to one thing and he won't let go. Won't give it a rest. *Perseveration,* the doctors call it. . . . A while back it was abortion. Then it was the hostages and the Ayatollah. Now it's the Persian Gulf. You want to scream at him, "Just shut up!" But he won't shut up. He can't. He perseverates. . . .

Joy's and the Duchess's cream drink glasses were still in the sink from the night before. She does that all the time—leaves things soaking in the sink until I break down and wash them. I'll promise myself I'm not going to do it this time and then I'll do it. It's just easier than letting it torture me. The broiler pan's the worst. She'd let that broiler pan sit and soak till Judgment Day.

I leaned against the counter and read the headlines while I waited for the coffee. I didn't know if Joy was speaking to me or not. Didn't pursue it, either. Who gave a fuck? OIL PRICES CLOSE AT RECORD HIGH AS U.S.-IRAQ SHOWDOWN LOOMS. . . . WEQUONNOC TRIBE GRANTED FEDERAL RECOGNITION. . . . DAVID SOUTER WINS SENATE APPROVAL.

"Oh, great," I said aloud. "Just what this country needs: Barney Fife sitting on the Supreme Court."

"Who?" Joy says.

"Barney Fife. Don Knotts."

"Oh," she said. "You mean Mr. Furley?"

"Mr. Furley?"

"On *Three's Company.* Jack's landlord. After the Ropers left." I stood there, looking at her. Looked back at the newspaper. Joy and me: we were like two people trying to communicate from opposite rims of the Grand Canyon.

The coffeemaker gurgled its grand finale. I went over and poured myself a cup. Joy doesn't usually read the paper because she says it's too depressing. She doesn't drink coffee, either. She has the exact same thing for breakfast every morning: herb tea, vitamins, and a frosted strawberry Pop Tart. Go figure.

IVANA TRUMP FILES FOR DIVORCE. . . . IS COMMUNISM FAILING? . . . REDS CAN'T COMBAT BREAM'S TWO-RUN HOMER. Oh, man, I would *love* to see Pittsburgh make it to the Series. Love to see it come down to the Pirates versus the Sox—Doug Drabek going against Clemens. Leo had a connection in the box office up at Fenway. Maybe if Boston made it back to the Series, we could go up there and scream our freakin' heads off the way we used to. . . .

I caught myself: Thomas was locked up in a maximum-security psych hospital and here I was, worrying about baseball playoffs. Thinking about the freakin' Red Sox instead of my own goddamned brother.

"So what does Ray say?" Joy asked.

"About what?"

She capped the nail polish bottle. Fanned her toes with a grocery store circular. "About him being transferred to Hatch."

Him: that was what she always called my brother. Not Thomas. *Him*. In the five days he was lying over there at Shanley Memorial after he cut off his hand, she didn't bother to go see him once. It had never even come up as a possibility. Even Ray had done better than that. Even Ray had at least made it as far as the visitors' lounge. "He doesn't say *anything* about it," I said. "Because I haven't told him yet."

"Well, call him, Dominick," she said. "It doesn't have to be all on your shoulders all the time. He's his *father*."

"He's his *step*father," I said.

"That doesn't mean he shouldn't share some of the burden. You don't have to be the big hero all the time. You take on too much."

"The big hero": that was a joke. When was the last time some asshole guard kneed Superman in the gonads? "I'm not *trying* to be the big hero," I said. "It's just that—it's just . . . hey, forget it, okay? It's a little too complicated for 6:00 A.M."

"No, *tell* me," she said. "*Talk* about it, Dominick. Complicated how?" She was just sitting there, looking at me. Actually listening for a change.

"I don't know," I said. "I've *always* been the one who had

to look out for him. Not that I ever signed up for the job, *believe* me. . . . The year I went away to college? That was supposed to be my big chance. My big run for freedom. . . . Except it didn't exactly work out that way."

"Why not?"

"Oh, my mother . . ."

I followed Joy's eyes down to my hands. Realized I'd been sitting there, shredding the package her Pop Tart had come in. That I'd made a little pile of foil strips without even noticing. "Shit," I said, laughing. "Get help from Ray? Ray was one of the guys I had to keep him safe *from*."

"What do you mean?"

"Nothing. All that's ancient history. . . . Ray could be brutal with Thomas sometimes. I mean, he took aim at me plenty of times, too, but I never got blasted as bad as Thomas did."

"Why not?"

"I don't *know* why not. Because I made all-stars in Little League and Thomas quit in the middle of the season? Because I used to hang around and watch Ray change the oil in his car? I could never figure out why he used to go gunning for him. He just *did*."

"Maybe that's why Thomas got so messed up," she said.

"Because of Ray? Uh-uh. It's not that simple. I used to think that, too, though: that all the shit he took from Ray was what made him crack up. I used to *like* thinking it, actually: making Ray the big villain, wishing he was dead. But it wasn't that simple. I mean, hey, it's not like Ray ever *helped* the situation much. But he didn't cause Thomas's illness. His brain caused it. It's biological. Chemical. Remember?"

"Did he used to hit him?" she asked.

"Hit Thomas? Yeah, sometimes. We both got batted around from time to time. My mother, too. Not *that* much. Ray was more of a screamer than a hitter. Telling us what human garbage we were. Telling Ma how she'd still be hanging out there in the wind with her two little bastards if he hadn't come along and married her. This one time . . . this one time, I remember . . . see, Thomas would get nervous and chew on things? Pencils, napkins, the sleeves on his shirts. Half the time, he wouldn't even realize he was doing it. And Ray . . . and Ray . . . it used to drive him apeshit. He turned it into this huge deal—used to practically stalk the poor kid, waiting for him to put something else in his mouth. So one night, we're eating supper and . . . and Thomas forgets. Starts chewing on his shirt. Ray goes down in the cellar and he comes back up with a roll of duct tape and he duct-tapes Thomas's hands. Covers up his fingers so that he can't chew on them. He had to wear the tape for, I don't know, a couple of days, at least. . . . It's funny, the things you remember: I can still see Thomas with his head down in his plate, eating his meals like a fucking dog. Can still hear his whimpering, all goddamned day long."

Joy reached over. Covered my hand with hers. "That's so awful," she said.

"This other time? Ray punished us both by pouring rice out of the box and making us kneel on it. On the kitchen floor. I can't even remember what the 'crime' was. Just the punishment. . . . It seemed silly, you know? Kneeling on rice. Big deal. But after about five minutes, it wasn't so funny anymore. It *hurt.* I got to get up after about fifteen minutes because I hadn't cried, but Ray made Thomas stay down there on his knees because he was crying. Bawling his head off. That was the biggest sin you could commit, as far as Ray was concerned. Letting the enemy see you cry."

"And your mother used to just let him get away with it?"

"Ma? Ma was more scared of Ray than we were. More scared than I was, anyway. I was the only one of the three of us that would stand up to him. Stick my neck out. I guess, in a way, that was what saved me from the worst of it."

It felt strange, actually: having Joy's full attention like that. Letting my guard down. It was like going over to that emergency room after all and pulling down my underwear and saying, "Here. Look. Here's what that Nazi guard down there did to me. Take a look." . . . Robocop, Ray: I was forty years old and *still* watching out for bullies.

I walked over to the window, looked out. There'd been a frost, first of the season. All the leaves were changing. "It's just not worth dredging up, Joy," I said. "It's all ancient history. . . . I better shut up or you're going to be late."

She got up and came up behind me. Put her arms around

me and leaned her forehead against my shoulder. "Hey," she said.

"Hey, what?"

"I'm sorry."

"Sorry for what?"

"That Ray was so mean. That you have to go through all this with your brother."

I gave a little snort. "Don't feel sorry for me. *Thomas* is the one who's locked up down there. Not me."

She kept holding me. Held on tighter, as a matter of fact. Held on for over a minute.

After she left, I poured myself more coffee. Leafed through the rest of the paper. Maybe I'd give up caffeine again, once this stuff with Thomas was settled. Once I had pain-in-the-ass Rood's house finished. Start jogging again, maybe. Take Joy on a trip. We could make it work, the two of us, if only we . . . if only . . .

I went back to the window. Watched all those dying leaves flapping outside in the wind. Came up with all kinds of arguments to give her—all kinds of reasons why I *had* to keep running interference for Thomas.

I *know* you need to be taken care of, Joy, but guys kill each other in places like Hatch. He never *could* defend himself. It'd be like throwing a rabbit to the wolves.

It's *different* when you're a twin, Joy. It's complicated.

I promised Ma.

eight

1968–69

When my brother and I graduated from Three Rivers' John F. Kennedy High School in June of 1968, we received a joint present from our mother. She had Scotch-taped a three-quarter-inch aluminum key to the inside of each of our graduation cards and written identical inscriptions. "Congratulations! Love, Ma and Ray. Proceed to the front hall closet."

Inside the closet, Thomas and I found a portable Royal typewriter in a dark blue carrying case, lockable and unlockable with either of our duplicate keys. We brought the typewriter into the living room, put it on the coffee table, and unlocked the case. Thomas, who had taken a typing class at JFK, rolled a piece of paper into the machine and tried a test sentence: *Now is the time for all good men to come to the aid of their country*. I typed one, too: *Thomas Birdsey is an asshole*. Ma said, all right, all right, that was enough of that kind of stuff. She gave us each a kiss.

Ma hadn't bought the typewriter; she'd redeemed it. For years, she had been saving S&H green stamps in hopes of cashing them in for a chiming grandfather clock, handcrafted in Germany and obtainable for 275 books. Ma had wanted that grandfather clock so badly that she visited it from time to time at the redemption store on Bath Avenue, just to hear its tone and stroke the polished wood. She was more than halfway to her goal—had accumulated nearly 150 books of green stamps—when she revised her plan and got us the typewriter instead. Our success, she told us, was more important than some silly clock.

By "our success," I think Ma meant our safety. The year before, a neighbor of ours, Billy Covington, had been killed in Vietnam—shot down during a bombing raid near Haiphong. As a kid, Billy had walked to our house after school because his father had left the family and his mother worked downtown. Four years older than Thomas and me, he was unbeatable at tag and baseball and his favorite game, Superman. He owned Superman pajamas, I remember, and would pack them in his school bag and change into them before we played, completing his costume with one of our bath towels, which Ma would safety-pin around his neck. Billy would begin each episode of our play with an imitation of the TV show opening: *"Faster than a speeding bullet! More powerful than a locomotive!"* But if Billy seemed invincible as the Man of Steel, he was pitiable afterwards. "Poor Billy," Ma would sometimes sigh as we watched him walk down our front steps, hand in hand with Mrs. Covington. "He doesn't *have* a nice daddy like you boys do. *His* father left Billy and his mother high and dry."

Years later, Billy Covington was our paperboy—a lanky near-man of fourteen or fifteen whose voice alternated between baritone and donkey's bray and who, from the street, could land a folded *Daily Record* at the base of our cement flowerpot with deadly accuracy. By the time Thomas and I entered high school ourselves, Billy had graduated and enlisted in the Air Force and become irrelevant. At his military funeral, I thought nothing about the meaning of Billy Covington's life and death or the waste of the Vietnam War or even the implications for my brother and me. I focused, instead, on Billy's fiancée, whose breasts shook tantalizingly as she sobbed, and on his black GTO (386 cubes, 415 horses). Maybe his mother would want to sell his "goat" dirt cheap so she could forget about him and get on with her life, I remember calculating in the very presence of Billy's flag-draped silver casket.

Although Billy Covington's death failed to move me at age sixteen, it clobbered my mother. "Goddamn this war," she said in the car on the way back from the memorial service. "Goddamn this war to hell." In the backseat, Thomas and I looked at each other, jolted. We had never before heard Ma use God's name in vain. More shocking, still, was the fact that she'd said it right in front of Ray, who had fought in both World War II and Korea and thought all antiwar protesters should be put against the wall and shot. Ma moped for days afterward. She found an old snapshot of Billy and bought a frame and put the picture on her chest of drawers along with the studio portraits of Thomas and me and her framed photos of her father and Ray. She said novenas on behalf of Billy's departed soul. Her eyes teared over whenever she saw Mrs. Covington walking zombielike past our house. I remember feeling slightly annoyed by what I perceived as Ma's mournful overreaction. It was only years later—well after the trouble with Thomas had begun—that I came to understand my mother's strong reaction to Billy Covington's death: four years our senior, Billy had been, all his life, a sort of living "preview of coming attractions" for her two boys. If Superman could be shot down from the sky, then so could his younger sidekicks. Vietnam could kill us. College would keep us safe.

Ray hadn't really signed our graduation cards with love and congratulations. Our stepfather had, in fact, opposed the idea of college educations for Thomas and me. For one thing, he said, he and Ma couldn't afford twin tuition bills. He should know, not her. *He* was the one who paid the bills and managed their savings. She had no idea what they could or couldn't afford. For another thing, from what he read and heard down at the shipyard, half the teachers at those colleges were Communists. And half the kids were on drugs. If he ever caught either of us messing with that kind of junk, he'd knock us into the day after tomorrow. He couldn't for the life of him see why two able-bodied young men out of high school couldn't *work* for a living. Or enter the Navy the way he had done. There were worse things in life than a military career. It was the draftees they were sending to Vietnam; enlisted men had choices. Or, if we didn't want that, maybe he could get us in down at Electric Boat as apprentice pipe fitters or electricians or welders. Some of those jobs carried deferments. Building submarines might not be a fancy college-boy job, but it "backed the attack." It put meat and potatoes on the table, didn't it?

"But that's not the point, Ray," my mother said one night at supper.

"What do you mean it's not the point?" His fist banged against the tabletop hard enough to make the dishes jump. "I'll tell you what the point is. The point is, Tweedledum and Tweedledee here have been living high off the hog all their lives. The two of them know nothing but take, take, take, and I'm getting goddamned fed up with it." He got up and slammed out of the house. When he came back, he was speaking single syllables to Thomas and me but nothing at all to Ma. He gave her the silent treatment for days.

After that, there were arguments and tears behind my mother and Ray's bedroom door. Ma threatened to go to work if she had to in order to get us the money for school, and when Ray told her no one would hire her, she called his bluff and filled out an application for a maid's job down at Howard Johnson's. She was petrified at the thought of working outside the home—afraid of taking orders from a boss and making mistakes, scared that she might have to make small talk with strangers who would look at her funny because of her cleft lip. Howard Johnson's called her for an interview and offered her the job that same afternoon. She was to start the following Monday.

On the morning of her first day of work, Ma stood at the stove cooking breakfast in her uniform, distracted, her hands shaking visibly. From his seat at the table, Ray taunted and bullied her. People were pigs. There was no telling *what* they'd leave behind for her to clean up. A while back, he'd read a story in the *Bridgeport Herald* about a maid who'd found an aborted baby wrapped up in bloody sheets. Ma clunked his dish of eggs down in front of him. "All right, Ray. That's enough," she said. "I'll clean up whatever I have to. These boys are going to school and that's that." Only then—when the threat of a working wife stood before him in a yellow acetate uniform—did my stepfather agree to cough up four thousand dollars for Thomas's and my college educations and allow my mother to stay home. No wife of *his* was going to clean toilets for strangers. No wife of *his* was going to do nigger work.

Relieved to be spared the outside world, Ma was nevertheless ashamed not to show up at her new job. She made *me* drive down to Howard Johnson's and surrender her uniform on a wire hanger. The man at the desk made a joke about it. Holding up the uniform, he called into the empty collar. "Hello, Connie? Yoo-hoo? Anybody home?" I made no objection on my mother's behalf. I might have even smiled at the joke. But I was so pissed off that when I got outside, I kicked the tire of Ray's Fairlane, hard enough to break my toe. It was Ray I was kicking, not the tire or the stupid fuck of a desk clerk. With Ray's four thousand dollars and our student loans and the money we made from our part-time jobs, Thomas and I now had the funds to go to school. But he had made Ma beg for that money—had taken his usual pound of flesh and then some. Over the years, he had taken so much of her that it was a wonder she *wasn't* an empty uniform.

As a high school senior, I had hungered for a clean break from my entire family—a reprieve from Ray's bullying and Ma's overindulgence and from the lifelong game of "me and my shadow" I had played with Thomas. My grades and SATs were decent, and my guidance counselor had helped me envision how I might turn my work as a YMCA swimming instructor—a job I loved and was good at—into a career in teaching. Duke University had rejected me, but I'd been accepted at New York University and the University of Connecticut. Thomas had applied only to UConn and been accepted. At first, he didn't know what he wanted to be, but then he said he wanted to be a teacher, too.

When cost made it impossible for me to distance myself from my brother, I lobbied hard for separate dorms, separate roommates at UConn. It was time for each of us to become our own person, I told Thomas. It was the perfect opportunity for both of us to make the break. But Thomas resisted the idea of my cutting free, offering a number of reasons why separation was a big mistake. By summertime, his main argument centered on our joint ownership of that typewriter.

"But it's *portable*!" I kept screaming in exasperation. "I'll *deliver* it to you when you need it."

"It's just as much mine as it is yours," he shot back. "Why should I have to wait around for someone to deliver a typewriter I already half-own?"

"Keep it in *your* room then!"

Sensing Thomas's gathering panic about our separation, Ma appeared out of the blue one afternoon at the YMCA pool while I was working. At the time, I had a crush on the head pool instructor, a woman in her twenties named Anne Generous who was married to a sailor. At night, in the dark, I'd sometimes lie in my top bunk and pull down my underpants, pretending to pull down Anne Generous's black one-piece bathing suit with its YMCA insignia. I'd imagine her swimsuit-trapped breasts popping free, Anne Generous fondling one in each hand like a woman in a dirty magazine. I'd stroke those long, wet legs of hers as I lay there stroking my own boner and let go inside of Anne Generous the stuff that spilled onto my chest and belly. Below, in the bottom bunk, my brother slept unstained.

Innocent of our nighttime flings, Anne Generous told me one afternoon at the pool that I was a sweetie pie but too shy for my own good. She kept goading me to ask out a fellow instructor named Patty Katz. Patty was a junior at our school. She was cheerful and patient with kids and had purple acne on her back and a swimsuit that was always getting stuck in the crack of her ass. "Patty's *crazy* about you, Dominick," Anne confided. "She thinks you're the greatest."

When Ma showed up that day at the Y pool, Anne Generous and Patty both shook her hand and said they were pleased to meet her. They directed the kids to the other side of the pool so that my mother and I could have some privacy. Ma told me that she was sorry to bother me at work but that she really needed to speak to me about Thomas when Thomas wasn't around. The two of them had had a little talk, she said. He was nervous about being away from home; living with me would make him feel more secure. And he was upset about the typewriter. She told me she just wanted everything to go right. It *would* be easier if the typewriter stayed put in one room, wouldn't it?

I stood there, saying nothing, watching the tears in her eyes.

"I know he gets under your skin sometimes. But could you just do *me* a favor and be his roommate? He's just feeling a little unsure of himself, that's all. He's never had your self-confidence, Dominick. Things have always been harder for him than they've been for you. You know that."

"Things have been *plenty* hard for me," I said. "Growing up in *our* house."

Ma looked away. She said she knew one thing: that deep down, no matter how it seemed, our stepfather loved us very, very much. Ignoring my snort, she said that all Thomas needed was a little boost.

"And what about what *I* need, Ma?" I said. "What about *that*?"

She had interrupted a game of water tag when she'd arrived, and now several kids drifted back to our side of the pool and began calling my name. One of the boys cannonballed into the water and accidentally splashed my mother. I swore out loud at him, I remember, and everyone just stopped—treaded water and stared. From the middle of the pool, Anne Generous looked at me with a mixture of pity and disapproval.

"All right, fine," I told Ma. "You win. I'll room with him. Now would you please get out of here, for cripe's sakes, before you get me fired? Your skirt's sopping wet. You're embarrassing me."

After work that day, I stayed in the pool, swimming laps and sputtering curses and arguments into the chlorine. I hated my brother almost as much as I hated Ray. If I gave in, I'd never get free of him. *Never.* I swam until my eyes burned and my head ached—until my arms and legs were leaden.

When I got out of the Y, Patty Katz beeped at me from the front seat of her parents' station wagon. She knew I was upset, she said. She was a good listener. *Her* mother drove *her* crazy, too. Why didn't I let her buy me an ice cream?

When we got to the Dairy Queen, Patty got out of the car and got my cone so that I could sit and sulk. I studied her as she waited in line. With her hair dry and her clothes on, she wasn't that bad. She was passable. She got back in the car and handed me my ice cream and an inch-thick stack of napkins. "What am I, a slob or something?" I said, and she blushed and apologized and said *she* was the slob—she was a klutz and a half.

On the long drive we took, Patty told me she thought that I was right to insist on a new roommate and that I should stick to my guns. She said she knew who Thomas was but didn't really know him; they'd been in a study hall together, that was all. She said she could tell us apart with absolutely no problem: I was cool and my brother was a little on the finky side, no offense. A lot of people at school thought that about us. I'd be surprised.

We ended up on a dirt road out by the Falls, with the station wagon's backseat flopped down and my tongue down Patty's throat and her hand on my crank. She was eager to please but inexperienced, yanking away as if she'd gotten hold of a cow's udder. "Faster, *faster,*" I whispered, and guided her, my hand over her hand. When she got it about right, I closed my eyes and came to the wet inside of Anne Generous's mouth, to my hands on Anne Generous's breasts, to Anne Generous's hurried stroking.

I cleaned myself off with the Dairy Queen napkins. Patty Katz said she had never done anything like this before. It wasn't that she regretted it. She wasn't sure how she felt. Her voice, her crying, were like the sounds of a girl in some other car. I got up, got zipped, got out of the car for a walk.

When Patty dropped me off at my house, she said she thought she loved me. I thanked her for the ice cream and told her I'd call her the next day—a promise I doubted I'd deliver on, even as I was making it. After she drove away, I stood there in the front yard, looking up at the light behind the shade in Ma and Ray's bedroom. It was after midnight: Ma was up there worrying. It wasn't as if she ever asked for much, I reminded myself. Or *got* much, either, for that matter—from Ray or from my brother and me. I had put up with Thomas for seventeen years at that point. What was one more friggin' year?

I *didn't* call Patty Katz that next day. And the following week, when I suggested that she and I go for another drive out by the Falls, she told me she'd rather go to a movie or go bowling or do something with other people. Did I know Ronnie Strong from school? He and her girlfriend Margie were going out. Maybe we could double. Yeah, maybe, I told her. But I didn't want to date Patty; I only wanted to screw her. So I was cool to her for the rest of the week and got a little chillier each week after that. Anne Generous, too, had lost some of her allure. She had large feet for a woman her size. She could be bossy. By the middle of August, I was hardly speaking to either of them.

But here's the funny thing: after the big stink Thomas had made about that typewriter, he hardly touched the damn thing all during our freshman year. Hardly ever cracked the books, either. He'd been a pretty conscientious student in high school—had worked harder for his B's and B-minuses than I'd worked for my A's. But at UConn, Thomas couldn't sit still long enough to study. He claimed he was too distracted. The dorm was too noisy. His professors were impersonal. Our room was too hot; it bothered his sinuses and made him sleepy whenever he tried to read. He was always walking out to the fire escape for gulps of air, or squirting Super Anahist up his nose, or talking about how miserable he was—how much he hated all the jerks and losers and skanky girls who went to our stupid school. Instead of studying, he watched TV in the lounge, drank instant coffee all day long (we had an illegal hot plate), then stayed up half the night and slept through his morning classes. He resisted making friends and resented the friendships I made with some of the other guys on our floor—Mitch O'Brien and Bill Moynihan and this senior named Al Menza who was always looking for a game of pinochle or pitch. Thomas would get a bug up his ass if someone just knocked on the door or asked to borrow something of mine or wanted me to play some pickup basketball. "Am I *invisible* or something?" he'd huff. Or mimic. "Is Dominick here? Where's Dominick? *Everyone* loves Dominick the Wonder Boy!"

"Hey, if you want to play some hoops, then just come out on the court and start *playing,*" I told him. "What do you expect, an engraved invitation?"

"No, I *don't,* Dominick. All I expect is that my own brother isn't going to stab me in the back."

"How's my playing a game of basketball stabbing you in the back?" I asked, exasperated.

He sighed and flopped facedown on his bed. "If you don't know, Dominick, then just forget it."

One afternoon, Menza asked me in the middle of a pitch game what was "with" my brother. Instantly, I felt the cards bend in my hand. Felt my face get hot. "What do you mean, what's 'with' him?" I said.

"I don't know. He's a little off kilter or something, isn't he? You don't see him all day long and then you get up in the middle of the night to take a leak and there he is, wandering around the halls like Lurch from *The Addams Family*."

The other guys laughed. O'Brien was one of them. I forget who else was playing with us. O'Brien said he'd gotten up one night and seen Thomas running laps around our dorm. After midnight, this was. The middle of the frickin' *night*. I said nothing, stared hard at my cards, and when I finally looked up, all three guys were looking at me. "Jesus Christ, Birdsey, you're blushing like a virgin on her wedding night," Menza said. "Someone pop your cherry or something?"

I threw my cards down on the bed and got up, walked toward the door. "Hey, where you going?" Menza protested. "We're in the middle of a game?"

"You win," I said. "All of you. I fucking forfeit."

For the rest of that afternoon, those guys blasted "The Monster Mash" nonstop on Moynihan's stereo. Put the speaker in the doorway and filled up the hallway with the sound of that friggin' song. Sang the *Addams Family* theme when Thomas and I went downstairs to supper, complete with finger-snapping. It passed; that kind of ball-busting usually does. But the nickname they'd given Thomas stuck. From that afternoon on, he was "Lurch" to all the guys in Crandall Hall.

When I wasn't arguing with Thomas or defending him in some half-assed way, I was spending my time with my face in the books or slumped in front of our Royal typewriter, hunting-and-pecking my way through some paper that was almost due. The noises I made while I was studying became an issue: the clacking of the typewriter keys, the squeak of the highlighter across the page, even the crinkling of cellophane if I got myself a snack from the machine in the basement. I began studying in the library as much as possible. I hated the sight of Thomas's scowling face, the squirt-squirt of his nose spray, and those faraway sighs of his in the dark in the middle of the night. He was going to flunk out if he didn't wake up—break Ma's heart and make Ray hit the roof. He could end up getting his head blown off in Nam. But I was goddamned if I was going to *make* him study—if I was going to throw him over my shoulder and *carry* him to his classes.

Somewhere near the end of second semester, Thomas got notification from the freshman dean about his academics. The letter advised my brother to make an appointment with his office as soon as possible. Instead, Thomas began a frenzy of makeup work. "I can pull this off, Dominick," he told me. "What are you looking at me like that for? I *can*." He went to professors' offices and pleaded for extensions and incompletes. He kept our hot-plate coils glowing orange and threw cup after cup of coffee down his throat. A kid on the second floor sold him some speed so that he could cram night and day for his upcoming exams. He was popping No-Doz like they were M&Ms. Thomas put so much shit into his system that he burst blood vessels in both his eyes.

One afternoon I came back to our room and found him sobbing on my bed. "Don't be mad at me, Dominick," he kept repeating. "Just don't be mad. Please." It was the way Thomas had begged Ray when we were kids—when Thomas had triggered one of Ray's rampages.

Our whole room was pulled apart; there were papers and shit all over the floor. Over on my desk was a screwdriver and a rock and a hammer and our typewriter. The case had been cracked up the middle, a six-inch piece broken right off.

I told him he'd better fucking explain what was going on.

"Okay, okay," he said. "Just don't be mad at me."

He had finally written an overdue English paper, he told me, and then had gone to type it and not been able to find his key. He'd waited and waited and waited for me—he never knew where I was anymore. He might as well not even *have* a roommate. After a while, he'd panicked, convincing himself that I'd taken the key and hidden it from him because I wanted him to fail. I *wanted* him to flunk out. Why did I even lock the stupid typewriter, anyway? Why did it always have to be locked?

"Because guys in this dorm steal," I said.

"Then they'd steal the whole thing!" he sobbed. "It's *portable*!"

When the lock on the typewriter case wouldn't give, no matter what he tried, Thomas had gone outside and gotten the rock and busted it open. It had seemed like the best thing to do until he did it. Then, right after that, he remembered where he'd hidden the key at the beginning of the semester: in his extra soap dish up on the top shelf, the one he never used. Would I please, *please* just type his paper for him? He'd straighten out, buy a new case for the typewriter. The paper was due at 9:00 o'clock the next morning. He couldn't type because his hands wouldn't stop shaking. He was too nervous to concentrate. The "w" and the "s" on our typewriter weren't working now, but he'd gone down to O'Brien's room and O'Brien said we could borrow his typewriter. The paper itself had come out pretty good, he thought. But his English teacher wouldn't give an inch. If he got it there at 9:01, she probably wouldn't even accept it. She was out to get him.

I could have whaled into him for what he'd done—for what he had failed to do all year long. But as angry as I was, I felt scared, too—scared of those blotches of blood in his eyes and the tremors in his hands, the revved-up way he was talking.

I got him calmed down. Heated him a can of soup. Yeah, I'd type the stupid paper, I told him. I had him lie down and told him to not say one friggin' word about the noise O'Brien's typewriter was making. I began.

It was an essay about the theme of alienation in modern literature—a patchwork of *Cliff Notes* and bullshit that contained no specifics and made hardly any sense. Its rambling sentences went off in a dozen different directions and never came back; the handwriting was almost unrecognizable as Thomas's. That paper scared me more, even, than his behavior. But I typed what he'd written, fixing up things here and there and hoping against hope that his teacher would find something coherent in what he'd put together.

He was asleep before I finished the first page. He slept through the night and at 8:45 the next morning was still sleeping. I walked across campus and handed his teacher the late paper. Assuming I was Thomas, she gave me a dirty look and said she hoped I had learned a lesson about personal management. Maybe in the future, I wouldn't be so quick to inconvenience people.

I wouldn't, I said. I definitely wouldn't.

When I got back to our dorm, I stood, bewildered, before our broken typewriter case—passed my finger over its sharp, smashed edge. Turned and stood there, studying my brother as he slept, mouth agape, his eyes shifting behind the lids.

At the end of second semester, the university put my brother on academic probation.

nine

"Come in, come in," she said, standing up from her computer. "I'm Lisa Sheffer."

Flat-top haircut, *Star Trek* sweatshirt, little earrings all the way up one ear: whatever I'd expected, *she* wasn't it. Five-one, five-two at the most. She probably didn't weigh a hundred pounds soaking wet.

"Dominick Birdsey," I said. She had a handshake like a vise grip. I thanked her for her message the night before and started rambling about my brother, telling her his history, about how his being there was a big mistake. Sheffer put her hand up, traffic cop style. "Could you just hold on a minute?" she said. "I need to enter some information about another patient before I forget. Have a seat. This should take like two seconds."

It was fair, I guess. We'd made a 10:00 appointment; the wall clock above her head said 9:51. My eyes bounced from that flat-top to the mounds of paperwork on her desk to a carved wooden bird with its head cocked to the side. Overhead, a fluorescent light buzzed like a mosquito.

"You get used to one program and the next thing you know the computer nerds up in Hartford change it on you," she said. "They have these workshops whenever they update the software, like they're doing you a favor. I go to the office manager, 'Excuse me? I've got a kid in after-school day care and an Escort that's already living on borrowed time. Why can't I just use the stuff I'm used to?' But no-*ooo.*"

The phone rang. "Uh-huh," she kept telling the person on the other end. "Uh-huh. Uh-huh." I got up and walked to the window—wired glass, two-foot square. Why would anyone want to work at this place?

Outside was a recreation area—a pitiful excuse for one, anyway. Couple of picnic tables chained to a cement floor, a rusty basketball hoop. A small group of patients was being herded out there, each guy squinting as he hit the sun. No sign of Thomas.

"So your real name's Domenico, right?" Sheffer said. She was off the phone, back at her computer.

"Only on paper," I said. "How'd you know that?"

She said she'd seen it somewhere in my brother's records.

I nodded—told her I'd been named after my grandfather. Had she seen our birth certificates or something? Thomas and me listed under Ma's maiden name?

"And your brother says you're a housepainter, right?"

"Yup." Jesus, was this appointment about Thomas or me?

"You give free estimates?"

"Uh . . . yeah. I do. So how about my brother?"

She clicked away a little more on her keyboard. Looked up. "Domenico was my grandfather's name, too," she said. "That's why it popped out at me. Domenico Parlapiano. How's that for a mouthful?"

I sat back down again, drumming my fingers against the sides of my chair. Impatience wasn't going to get me what I needed, I reminded myself. What Thomas needed. That stupid wooden bird of hers looked like it was staring right at me.

"So is Sheffer your married name?" I said.

She looked up at me. Shook her head. "My father's Jewish, my mother's Italian. Ever had spaghetti and matzo balls?" I just looked at her, no reaction. "I'm kidding, Domenico," she said. "It was a joke. Hey, you want a candy bar?"

"Candy?"

"Dollar a bar. Fund-raiser for my daughter's Midget

Football cheering squad." She stuck out her tongue, made a face. "I've got almond, peanut butter, and crunch."

I hadn't yet ruled out the possibility that she might have some say in Thomas's situation. "Yeah, all right. Sure. Almond, I guess." I stood up and fished out a buck.

I was still wearing those drawstring pants—those skull-and-crossbone things. I caught Sheffer smiling at them. "Cool pants," she said, and I looked away, embarrassed.

She reached into a desk drawer and handed me the candy bar. No wedding ring. Early thirties, I figured. "I'll be right with you, Domenico," she said. "Let me just shut my mouth and figure out one last thing and we'll be ready to roll."

"Dominick," I mumbled. "My name's Dominick."

There was a knock on the door. "Come in," she said. A janitor entered, emptied a wastebasket.

"Hey, Smitty," Sheffer said. "Do me a favor, will you? Throw this computer in the Dumpster for me. Simplify my life by about a thousand percent."

"You got it, Lisa!" he said. He looked over at me, smiling a little too eagerly. "Hello, there, sir," he said.

I nodded. Looked away.

"Hey, Lisa? You got any more of those candy bars?"

"You haven't paid me for the other ones yet, Smitty," Sheffer said. "You already owe me four dollars."

"Oh, okay. How much are they?"

"Dollar apiece. Same as the other days."

"Oh." He looked long-faced. Stood there, waiting. Sheffer let out a sigh.

"Okay, okay, here," she said, tossing him one. He was already eating his candy before he was out the door.

"It's a losing proposition trying to raise money at this place," Sheffer said, smiling. "These fund-raisers are going to bankrupt me."

I asked her how old her kid was.

"Jesse? She's seven. How about you? Any kids?"

Any kids? That casual question was always a sock in the gut. "No," I said. "No kids." The denial was easier than the truth: that we'd *had* a little girl, Dessa and me. Had had her and then lost her. She would have been seven now, too.

Outside the door, there was a commotion—someone with a high-pitched voice screaming about toilet paper. "I'm not saying that!" the voice said. "All I'm saying is, when I *defecate,* I like to pull my own toilet paper off the toilet paper roll instead of having someone standing there handing it to me. I don't need a valet, thank you very much. And don't tell me I wipe it on the walls because I *don't* wipe it on the walls."

Sheffer rolled her eyes. Got up and opened the door. "Excuse me, Ozzie, but would you keep it down, please? I have someone in my office and we're having a little—"

"Up yours, *Ms*. Sheffer!"

When I looked out there, the voice materialized as a middle-aged bald guy, gaunt and scabby, his hospital johnny hanging open in the back. An aide was with him—a white guy in dreadlocks. "I *told* him to keep his voice down, Lisa," he said.

"It's all right, Andy. Hey, Andy, you want to do me a favor? If you see Dr. Patel on the floor, would you tell her Thomas Birdsey's brother is here? Maybe she can stop down and meet him if she has a second."

"Sure thing," he said. "Come on, Ozzie. Let's go."

"Don't *touch* me!" Ozzie protested. "What do you think this is—the *petting zoo*?"

Sheffer shook her head and closed the door again. "Sorry. Things can get a little surreal around here," she said.

I got up and went back to that little window. Hard to believe: that Angela would be seven by now. This goofball social worker disarmed me a little with her candy bars, her spaghetti and matzo balls. Knocked me off center. The jury was still out on this one.

Outside in the courtyard, the inmates were lining up in front of a guy in a cowboy hat. One by one, he was lighting their smokes. This was recreation? Everyone just sitting on the picnic tables, wearing their army camouflage and smoking? The only exercise I saw was one skinny black guy, dribbling a basketball without taking any shots. Thunk, thunk, thunk: he looked completely stoned. Probably zoned out on Thorazine, I figured. And *he* was the active one.

"Hey, tell me something," I said. "How come half those

guys out there are wearing camouflage? Is that the hot fashion around this place?"

She stood up from her chair and looked out, cracked a smile. "Unit Four," she said. "About half the population on that ward are Vietnam casualties."

"That guy from Mystic's down here, right? The one who mistook his family for the Viet Cong?"

"I can't really discuss other cases," she said. "But not all of these vets have criminal records; a lot of them are just here because the VA hospitals are overcrowded and because so many other programs have gone down the tubes. Got to put them somewhere, right? Vietnam: the war that keeps on giving."

"And now we're gearing up for another one," I said.

She shook her head, disgusted. "They make it sound so noble, don't they? 'Operation Desert Shield.' It's like the whole country's decided to have selective amnesia. Yea, rah-rah, America! Here we go again."

Now her clock said 10:07. We were supposed to be seven minutes into my appointment and she was still hunting-and-pecking on her keyboard and treating me to her political opinions. "That's what my brother was trying to do in the library," I said. "Stop the war before it gets started." She looked over at me. Nodded.

Out in the courtyard, the guy in the cowboy hat was entertaining the troops. You could tell without a scorecard which patients were his pets and which ones weren't. "Who's the cowboy out there?" I said.

"Hmm?" She looked out. "Oh, that's Duane. He's one of the FTSs."

"One of the whats? Jesus, I couldn't keep all these initials straight."

"Forensic Treatment Specialists. One of the psych aides. He's quite a character."

"So what do you got, pyromaniacs at this place? Nobody can light their own cigarettes?"

She didn't answer. "Okay! Wait a minute. Here we go," she said. She turned to me, beaming. "I was trying to transfer data by hitting the 'shift' key instead of 'control.' That's what you had to do with the other program. Hit the 'shift' key. I *hate* computers, don't you? I mean, who invented them, anyway? Who's responsible? Alexander Graham Bell invented the telephone; we know that. Eli Whitney invented the cotton gin. Whoever invented the computer is probably afraid to show his face."

Outside, that basketball stopped thunking. The office was suddenly quiet. "So, anyway," I said. "About my brother?"

She nodded, shifted in her chair, opened his file. "Have a seat," she said.

She started talking hospital talk: Thomas had been admitted on a "fifteen-day paper." When the observation period was up, his case would go before probate and then most likely to the PSRB.

"Look," I told her. "I don't mean to be rude or anything—you're the first human being I've run into at this place—but number one, don't sit here talking initials at me, and number two, don't give me any 'fifteen-day paper' because I'm getting him out of here today."

"Hey, how about if you don't take that tone, okay?" she said. "Calm down."

"I'll calm down once this runaround's over with. All you need to do is get ahold of his doctor. Dr. Willis Ehlers. He'll verify that my brother doesn't belong here. That this is someone's screwup and he belongs over at Settle."

She shook her head. "Ehlers isn't his doctor anymore, Dominick. They've reassigned him."

"*Who's* reassigned him?"

She flipped through his papers. "Looks like it floated down from the gods. The state commissioner's office in Hartford."

She slid some papers across the desk, tapped her finger at some honcho's signature. "Why from Hartford?" I said. "What's Hartford got to do with it?"

"I can't say for sure. Don't quote me on this, but my guess is that your brother's a political appointee."

"What's that mean?"

She looked up at the ceiling. Puffed out her cheeks. "Shut up, Sheffer," she advised herself.

"No," I said. "Come on. Tell me."

"I don't know for sure, okay?" she said. "I haven't *heard* anything, through the grapevine *or* officially, so this is strictly theory, okay? But usually when Hartford gets involved in something like this, it's about damage control. We're fairly autonomous out here otherwise. My guess is that it's Jimmy Lane fallout. I'm not 100 percent positive, but I'm pretty sure. But like I said, don't quote me."

I didn't know what the hell she was talking about.

"It's not all bad news, though," she said. "His new psychiatrist is Dr. Chase—it could be worse—and his psychologist is Dr. Patel, which is *very* cool. I have a lot of respect for—"

"His doctor is Dr. *Ehlers,*" I said. "Ehlers has been treating my brother for the past four years—successfully, for the most part."

"Successfully?" she said. "He cut off his hand, Domenico."

"Because he stopped taking his medication, that's why," I snapped. I wasn't taking any crap from this scrawny little—. "Okay, maybe Ehlers *should* have been on top of it. But I should have been, too. We *all* missed it. We were *all* asleep at the wheel."

"This is none of my business," she said. "But I can see already that you take an awful lot of this on yourself. Compared to most patients' siblings, I mean. What is that, a twin thing?"

"Never mind about me," I said. "All I'm saying is that Ehlers has been better than most of them—has been consistent, anyway. Thomas feels safe with him. Comfortable. So I don't *care* what anyone in Hartford wants. Just have this Dr. Chase or this Dr. . . . ?"

"Dr. Patel."

"Have this Dr. Patel guy call up Ehlers so that I can get him out of here."

"Dr. Patel's a woman," she said.

I closed my eyes. "Okay, fine, whatever," I said. "That's irrelevant."

"I'm just telling you. She's Indian. Indian Indian, not American Indian."

I slapped my hand down on her desk. "Hey, what is it with this place?" I said. "Why doesn't anyone listen? It's a *mistake.* I don't give a rat's ass if Dr. Patel is from Mars or if she's a man or a woman or a friggin' three-headed extraterrestrial, okay? My brother's getting stuck down at this sinkhole is someone's stupid bureaucratic *mistake.*"

She cocked her head just like that wooden bird on her desk. "Mistake how, Domenico?" she said. "Go ahead. I'm listening."

"Because he *always* goes to Settle after an episode. He's practically a *fixture* over there. He has a part-time *job* there."

She sat there, mute. Waiting.

"And because . . ."

"Yeah? Because what?"

"Because right about now he must be scared out of his mind, okay? Look, the guy has no defenses. Zip. Zero. And it's not a 'twin thing.' It's . . . I've just *always* had to run interference for Thomas, okay? Putting him in this place is like throwing a rabbit in with the wolves."

She took a deep breath—let it out slowly, audibly. "Coffee and newspapers, right?"

"What?"

"His job? He was telling me about it. We talked for over an hour last night."

"Listen to me," I said.

"Oh, I'm listening. It sounds like I'm listening to myself talk, actually. My *old* self."

"What's *that* supposed to mean?"

"Oh, nothing. Personal observation, that's all. It's irrelevant." I just sat there, trying to figure out what the fuck she was talking about. "I was in a nine-year relationship with a substance abuser, that's all. So I know all about running interference. Being someone else's main line of defense. I call it the Don Quixote complex. Makes you feel noble to defend the defenseless. Plus, it's a great avoidance tactic. You don't have to deal with your own stuff, right? But, listen, I'm way over the line here. I just thought I recognized a fellow Quixote, that's all. I'm sorry."

"Yeah, well, thanks for the free psychoanalysis," I said. "But this is about my brother, not me. Or *you.*"

"Ouch," she said. "Fair enough. Really—I'm sorry. Let me give it to you straight, *paisano.* They've placed your brother in a forensic hospital because he's seriously mentally ill *and* because he's committed a serious crime."

"What crime? What'd he do? Interrupt a couple of old ladies during their afternoon reading? Get a little blood on the library rug? Look, I know what he did was bizarre. He gets totally fucked up when he's not taking his medication. I'm not saying otherwise. But what 'serious crime' did he commit?"

"Carrying a dangerous weapon."

"He wasn't . . . he used it on *himself*!"

"Well," she shrugged. "He counts. Right?"

We sat there, staring at each other—two gunslingers, each waiting for the other to make a move. "He gets . . . he gets these religious delusions," I said. "Thinks God's hand-picked him to save the world. . . . Hey, he's got *your* politics. Feels the same way you do about this Persian Gulf thing. . . . He wanted to *do* something—make some sort of big sacrifice that would wake up Saddam Hussein and Bush. He says God directed him through the Bible. . . . He's nuts, okay? He's *not* a criminal."

"And here's another way of looking at it," she said. "He was brandishing a knife in a public building. He needs to be locked up so that decent people can walk the streets."

"Brandishing? What do you mean, *brandishing*?"

Her hands flew into the air, palms outward. "Don't get defensive, *paisano*. I'm just playing devil's advocate here. I'm Mr. and Mrs. John Q. Public, reading about what happened in the paper. You see what I'm saying?"

"But he wasn't *brandishing* it. He wasn't threatening anybody. He was sitting in a study carrel, minding his own business. Look, I know the guy. I know him better than anyone. *I'm* probably more dangerous than he is."

She smiled. "Look. You know what your problem is? Can you calm down a minute and listen to something? You're making the assumption that this is the worst place in the world for him to be and that's not necessarily the case. And at any rate, there's nothing you can do about it, anyway. You're just going to have to take a leap of faith."

I sucked in a couple of deep breaths. Took a ten-second time-out. "You're a real company gal, aren't you?" I said.

She laughed so hard, she snorted. "I've been called a lot of things down here, Domenico, but never—"

"You are, though. You don't look the part, but you're walking the walk, talking the talk. You spout the party line just like the rest of them."

She shook her head. Kept smiling. "Now there's a low blow," she said.

"Hey, look—"

"No, *you* hey look. Let *me* have the floor for half a second. In the first place, *paisano,* I'm a woman, not a gal. Okay? If we're going to be working together on this, you're going to have to remember that distinction. 'Gal' sounds like someone's horse, which I'm not. All right? And in the second place—"

"Who's your supervisor?" I said.

She smiled, skimmed her hand across the top of her crewcut. "Why do you want to talk to my supervisor?"

"Because if I have to get someone with a little authority to pick up the phone and call his goddamned doctor, then that's what I have to do. I want him out of here *today.*"

Her face remained unperturbed. "My supervisor is Dr. Barry Farber."

"And where's he at?"

"Dr. Farber's at a conference in Florida. *She's* delivering a speech there." She smiled at the surprise on my face. "Gotcha again. Didn't I, Domenico? Funny thing about professional women these days, isn't it? The world is *crawling* with them."

"Who's *her* supervisor?" I said.

"That would be Dr. Leonard Lessard. One of yours."

"Hey, look," I said. "I'd appreciate it if you just cooled it on the sarcasm, okay? I've got one or two things I'm trying to deal with here without you—"

She tapped her finger again on the signature in front of me. "Dr. Lessard's the Deputy Commissioner for Clinical Services. He's the guy who ordered the transfer."

I stood up. Opened my mouth. Shut it again and sat back down.

"I tell you one thing," I said. "If my brother gets so much as a scratch while he's in this place—"

"He won't," she said. "I *promise* you. And you're right, he *is* scared. And I can see you're scared, too, which is probably why you're being so obnoxious. But I want to tell you something. Are you listening, now? Can you really listen to me here, Domenico?"

"Dominick," I told her again. "My name's Dominick."

"Dominick," she said. She sat there waiting.

"All right. I'm *listening*."

"You might be right," she said. "Your brother might very well do better over at Settle than here at Hatch. Security's tight here, by necessity; paranoiacs tend to have a hard time with all the watching and monitoring and security checks. But there's a misconception about this place—that it's the house of horror or the torture chamber or something. It's not. Are there problems on the wards? Sure there are. Every day. Does anyone really want to be here? Uh-uh. Club Med it isn't. But overall, the care is really pretty decent. Pretty humane."

I let go a laugh. "I don't want to burst your bubble or anything, but this place is so decent and humane that last night I got my gonads pushed back up into my gut by one of your hired goons. I got *real* humane treatment down here. You want to know why I'm wearing these stupid pants you were laughing at before? Because I'm black and blue and swollen. I can hardly walk because of one of the compassionate guards you got down at this place. And *I* didn't even get beyond the locked steel doors."

"I know, I know," she said. "I saw the tail end of that. I'm sorry. That shouldn't have happened, no matter how much of an asshole you were being. But just because one guard on the night shift thinks he's Rambo, that doesn't condemn this whole hospital. In the first place, the guards pretty much stay in the security areas unless there's a problem. They don't hang out in the wards; they have pretty limited contact with the patients, actually. And second, I *know* this place—especially Unit Two where your brother is. He's in the best unit here. I may sound like a 'company gal' when I say this, but the people in Unit Two really do care. I mean it. And, like I told you before, Dr. Patel's a real sweetheart. He's lucky to have—"

"Fine," I said. "Great. But it's a *mistake*."

"Hey, *paisano*," she said. "It's not a mistake. Let me walk you through it. Are you listening?"

"Yeah, I'm listening," I said. "Just don't talk in initials. And don't say stuff like, 'He was a political appointee,' or, 'Oh, it's Jimmy Lane fallout,' when I don't even know what you're goddamned talking about."

She reached over and grabbed the candy bar I'd bought. Peeled off the wrapper at one end. Broke me a piece and took one for herself. "Okay, let me spell it all out," she said. She glanced quickly at the intercom box on the wall. "Don't quote me on any of this," she said. "All right?"

She explained her theory first: that the order to transfer Thomas to Hatch had probably come down from Hartford as a result of all the publicity his self-mutilation had caused. "I knew he was in trouble the minute I saw he'd landed on the front page of the *Courant,*" she said. "And then, when it went national—when it started showing up in papers like *USA Today* . . ."

I told her about the *Enquirer, Inside Edition,* Connie Chung.

"Shit," she said. "The state hates that kind of negative publicity. You remember Jimmy Lane, don't you? The psych patient who strangled that college kid up on Avon Mountain?"

"In front of her girlfriends, right?"

She nodded. "God, what a horror show that was. I don't know if you remember this part of it, but Jimmy Lane was on a day pass from Westwood—on a hike with a supervised group—and he just wandered away from the rest of them. Just grabbed that poor kid. The guy had no history of violent behavior—nothing at all in his record to indicate that he might be anything but passive. He just snapped that day up there. That case set the department back years. Reinforced all the old stereotypes about the mentally ill—that they're all psychotic killers, lurking in the shadows. That no one's safe around them. It was a public relations nightmare. Remember all those letters to the editor? And the newspaper and TV editorials? I saw one bumper sticker: 'Electric Fry Jimmy Lane.' Good God, everyone in the state wanted blood. And when the insanity defense prevented a lynching, everyone wanted to lynch the system instead. And the system got pretty touchy about it. Pretty media-weary. See what I'm saying?"

"He's here, isn't he? Lane? Didn't he get sentenced to this place?"

She ignored the question. "NGRI—not guilty by reason of insanity—became a real political hot potato because of that case," she said. "So, to save face, the governor made some heads roll. He fired the commissioner. They retooled the entire department. And then, *voilà,* the PSRB was born."

"What's that? The PSRB? You mentioned them before."

"The Psychiatric Security Review Board," she said. "Very conservative and *very* media-conscious. They're powerful, too. They wield what amounts to sentencing power."

Since the Review Board came into power, Sheffer said, lawyers had begun backing away from the insanity plea, even when it was legitimate. Psychiatric patients with charges against them were being advised to go through the criminal justice system instead: bite the bullet, go to a state prison, do one-half or one-third of their sentence, and then get out because of overcrowding, or on good behavior. "If the PSRB gets ahold of someone on the insanity plea," Sheffer said, "they can keep him at Hatch indefinitely. Which they've tended to do. That's been the pattern so far."

"So what are you saying?" I asked her. "That they should arrest Thomas and send him to prison for what he did? That's ridiculous."

"I'm not saying that. Not at all. If he did prison time, the psychological treatment would be minimal—a Band-Aid approach, and that's only if he was lucky. And he *needs* treatment, Dominick. No doubt about it, your brother is a very sick man. But if it's not a criminal matter, then the Review Board are the ones who are going to decide when he gets out of here. And like I said, they tend to be conservative. And jittery about the media. It reads better, you know? Freddy Kruger's locked up and all's well. Come out, come out, wherever you are. Have you seen today's paper yet?"

Had I? I couldn't remember.

Her phone rang again. While she spoke to the person on the other end, she unfolded a copy of the *Daily Record,* thumbed to an inside page, and pointed:

COMMIT 3 RIVERS SELF-AMPUTEE
TO FORENSIC HOSPITAL

My stomach muscles clenched. Jesus Christ, I thought. Here we go again. At least he wasn't front-page news anymore. He was front-page second-section news. Maybe Thomas's fifteen minutes were almost up.

The article implied that if my brother hadn't gone into shock when he amputated his hand, he might have started hacking away at other people. It made him sound like the kind of psychopath who *did* belong at Hatch. It made a *case* for it. The reporter quoted some talking head from Hartford about public safety—about how patients' rights "coexisted" with the rights of the community to a safe environment, but that the latter was priority number one.

It was bullshit: Thomas as a public menace. I knew it and so did any doctor who'd ever worked with him. But I was beginning to get what the deal was. With Sheffer's help, the situation was beginning to clarify itself like one of those Polaroids that develops in the palm of your hand: my brother's being locked up at Hatch was about public relations. Order restored. They'd slammed the door on him, and now this Psychiatric Review Board was going to throw away the key. Okay, I sat there thinking. Now I've got it. Now, at least, I have a hand to play.

"I'm sorry, Dominick," Sheffer said, after she'd hung up the phone. "I know I'm throwing a lot at you here—a lot more than the state of Connecticut wants me to, actually."

"Who cares what the state of Connecticut wants?" I said.

"Well, for starters, *I* have to," she said. "Unless you're interested in supporting me and my daughter. Look, let me back up a little—tell you a little bit about the legality of what's already happened and what you can expect now. Okay?"

"Yeah," I said. "Okay."

Thomas had been admitted to Hatch on something called a Physician's Emergency Certificate, which the surgeon at Shanley Memorial had put into motion.

"That's the fifteen-day paper, right?"

"Right," she said. The hospital now had fifteen days to observe the patient—to determine over a two-week period if he was dangerous to himself or others. "The fifteen-day paper's airtight, Dominick," she said. "There's no way in hell you're getting your brother out of here today. It's out of your hands. Thomas is going to be here for fifteen court-ordered days, minimum."

"This sucks," I said. "This just *sucks.*" I got up, walked back over to the window. The patients in the rec area had gone inside. "There's no way to fight this fifteen-day thing?"

"There is, actually, but it's a long shot. A waste of time, probably. Your brother or you could request a 'probable cause' hearing. Then the hospital would have to *prove* that Thomas is dangerous to himself. But think about it: all a judge has to do is look down at his stump. There's the proof of probable cause, right? You want my advice?"

I was still looking out the window. "Go ahead," I said.

"Just ride out the fifteen days. Let us take care of him, observe him, see how well he starts coming around now that he's gotten back on his meds. This is probably going to be the safest place for him."

"Oh, yeah, right," I said. "In with a bunch of psychotics with violent histories."

"That's not fair, Dominick, and it's not accurate, either. There are all kinds of psychiatric patients here—not all of them violent by a long shot. Sooner or later you're going to have to face the fact that the person who's most dangerous to Thomas is Thomas. But he's on close watch. For the next forty-eight to seventy-two hours, there's going to be an aide within ten feet of him, twenty-four hours a day. If he's suicidal, someone's going to be there."

"He's *not* suicidal," I said.

"Well, all right, suppose he were."

"So then what?" I said. "What happens after the fifteen days?"

She said Unit Two's evaluation team would file a report with the probate judge. She'd have input into it. And Dr. Patel, and Dr. Chase, and the head nurse of the unit. The recommendation would be that he should be discharged, or transferred to another facility, or kept here under the jurisdiction of the Review Board.

"Okay, let's say the judge hands him over to this Review Board. What do *they* do?"

"They commit him."

"Where?"

"Here, I said. At Hatch."

"For how long?"

Her eyes fell away from mine. "For a year."

"A *year*!"

Her hands flew up in defense. "Don't kill the messenger, *paisano*. He'd be here for a year, and then his case would come up for annual review."

I sat there, slumped in the chair, my arms bracketed around my chest. "A year," I said again. "How the hell am I supposed to look him in the eye when I see him today and say, 'Okay, Thomas, here's the deal. They got you for the next 15 days and maybe for the 365 days after that'? How am I supposed to tell him that?"

"Dominick?" Sheffer said. "That's another thing."

"What is?"

"Visiting. You can't see him yet."

Visits were restricted, she said, because of the maximum-security status. Thomas and she would work up a list of potential visitors—up to five people. A security check would have to be run on everybody on the list. We'd have to wait until we were notified. It would take about two weeks to get clearance.

"*Two weeks?* In two weeks, he'll be out of here!"

She reminded me that that was not a given. Suggested I lower my voice a little.

"So you're saying that for two weeks, he just twists in the wind down here. He can't even see his own brother? Jesus, that's great. He probably *will* be suicidal by then."

She shrugged an apology. "There's nothing I can do about it," she said. "Except fill in the gaps as much as possible. Act as your liaison." She smiled. "Which I'll be very happy to do. You can call me whenever you want to. Whenever you *need* to. You guys can communicate through me until your clearance comes through."

I nodded, resigned. I felt suddenly, profoundly, sleepy.

She spent the rest of the time describing Thomas's surroundings, his daily routine: what the rooms were like, how they ran things at mealtimes, how patients had access to computers and arts and crafts and college extension programs. I couldn't really listen. In the past thirty-six hours, I'd spent all my anger and outrage. I was running on empty.

On our way out, we bumped into this Dr. Patel. Middle-aged woman: salt-and-pepper hair rolled into a bun, orange sari underneath her lab coat. "A pleasure," she said, extending her hand. Dr. Patel said she was in the "information-gathering stage" of her treatment of my brother. She'd call me after she'd read through all his records and she and Thomas had had two or three sessions. Perhaps I would be willing to share some personal insights that might augment his medical history?

Sheffer escorted me back toward the main entrance; it felt like I was sleepwalking. "I'll go in and see him right after you leave," she promised. "I'll tell him you were down here trying to visit him. Anything else you want me to tell him for you?"

"What?"

"You know something? You look like you need to get some serious sleep. I asked you if there was anything you wanted me to tell your brother for you."

"No, I guess not."

"You want me to tell him you love him?"

I looked at her. Looked away. "He knows I love him," I said.

Sheffer shook her head and sighed. "What is it with you guys and the 'L' word, anyway?" she said.

She was overstepping her ground again, but I was too tired to resist. "All right, fine," I said. "Tell him."

We shook hands. She told me to call her anytime. Asked me where I was headed.

"Where am I headed *now*?" I shrugged. "Home, I guess. I guess I'll just go home and disconnect the phone and crash. You're right. I haven't slept for shit."

"Oh," she said. She looked around, waved to the guard at the door, and spoke a little lower. "I thought maybe you were going to check things out at the doctor's."

"What for? You told me Ehlers isn't even his doctor anymore. That it's out of my hands."

"I didn't mean Dr. Ehlers," she said. "I meant a medical

doctor. Get those bruises of yours looked at. Have a few pictures taken while you're still swollen."

I looked at her, my face a question.

"In case, you know, you needed some documentation. A little leverage for later on. A bargaining tool with the state of Connecticut. . . . Of course, you didn't get that idea from a company gal like me. I'd *never* suggest something like that."

Halfway toward the entrance, I turned around to look. She was still standing there. A jowl-faced guard and a metal detector stood between us. "See you later, Mr. Birdsey," she called. Gave me a thumbs-up. *"Shalom! Arrivederci!"*

ten

1962

Thomas and I have been to three different states: Massachusetts, Rhode Island, and New Hampshire. *Four,* counting Connecticut.

The only place we've ever been to in New Hampshire is Massabesic Lake. Ray took us fishing there last year. We stayed overnight in a wooden cabin, and all night long, mosquitoes kept bugging us. We didn't catch any fish, either. Not one. The one thing I remember about that trip was this dead squirrel that someone had trapped inside a firebox. They'd put a bunch of rocks on top to keep him trapped in there. He was all huddled up in a corner, but you could tell he'd gone mental trying to get out. There was crusty black blood around his mouth and he stunk and bugs had eaten out his eyes. Ray lifted him out with a stick and flung him. He didn't land all the way in the woods; he landed right on the edge. Thomas wanted to bury him and have a funeral, but Ray told him to stop the sissy stuff. All the time we were there, you could see that dead squirrel right out in plain sight. Whenever anyone mentions New Hampshire, that squirrel is always what I think of. I bet I've thought about that squirrel a million times.

In less than half an hour, we'll be in a new state, New

York, because we're on our sixth-grade field trip to the Statue of Liberty and Radio City Music Hall. We're riding in a coach bus with cushioned seats and a bathroom in the back. We're still in Connecticut: Bridgeport. Eddie Otero says Bridgeport's close to the New York border. Otero has cousins who live in the Bronx, and this is the same way they go when they go to his cousins'. We've been riding almost two hours. I'm sitting in the way-way-back seat with Otero and Channy Harrington. Thomas is midway up the aisle. He got stuck sitting with Eugene Savitsky, this weird kid in our class who's fat and always talks about the planets and geology and weather. Mrs. Hanka let us pick our seatmates. Thomas and Channy both picked me, and I picked Channy. No one picked Eugene. At recess last week, Billy Moon asked Eugene to name five football teams and he couldn't name *any*. Not *one*.

My brother and I have been waiting for this trip a long time, but for different reasons. Thomas wants to see the Radio City Easter show. Ma went once; she said the religious part was so beautiful, it made her cry. It sounds boring to me; it sounds like church. I can't wait to get to New York because then I'll have visited four states and because I have spending money—thirty-seven dollars I earned from shoveling snow and walking Mrs. Pusateri's dog and helping Ray on weekends. Last weekend, Ray and I installed a tool cabinet in his truck. Ray let me do some of the drilling and tighten the screws. It's always me who Ray asks to help him, not Thomas. "Handy Andy" he calls me. He calls my brother "Charlie Ten Thumbs." Come to think of it, I was thinking about that squirrel up at Massabesic Lake when we were working on the tool cabinet, too—how a squirrel might get caught in there. Get trapped.

They show you a movie with the Easter show. The one we're seeing is *The Music Man*. Mrs. Hanka—we call her "Muriel Baby" behind her back—she saw *The Music Man* when it was a play instead of a movie. She brought in her record of all the songs and made us listen to it. Everybody was laughing because it was so corny. Eddie Otero started making pig snorts. Then three or four other kids started doing it. Muriel Baby got so hurt, she stopped the record and looked for a minute like she was going to cry. She told us that if she hadn't already bought the Radio City tickets, she'd cancel our whole trip. She gave us this big speech about how if we didn't care about anything, then she didn't care either. Then she did something weird. She turned off all the lights and went to the closet behind her desk and put on her coat. She just sat there. No social studies like we usually have. No nothing. Nobody said anything. All of us just sat there, nobody saying a word, until the intercom started calling the bus runs at 2:55. Like I said, it was weird. Creepy. The next day, everyone behaved, even Otero.

We might be able to go to a souvenir shop in Times Square if there's time. If it's the same one Marie Sexton from our class thinks it is, they have a whole aisle that's nothing but joke gifts: snapping packs of gum, whoopie cushions, ice cubes with flies inside, fake vomit. When I asked Ma how much I could spend on the trip, she told me to ask Ray. He said five dollars, but I've brought thirty-seven: a ten, a five, and twenty-two ones. I might spend just a little of it, or I might spend the whole thing if I feel like it. Why shouldn't I? It's my money, not his.

Last night when Ma was making our lunches for the trip, she told us that when we ride on the Staten Island ferry, we'll see the exact same view her father saw when he first came to this country in 1901: the harbor, the Statue of Liberty, the New York skyline. Ma's always talking about her father. Papa, Papa, blah blah blah. At first, she wasn't going to let us put our soda cans in the freezer overnight. "What if they explode?" she said, but I got her to give in. You can always get what you want from Ma if Ray's at work. Right now, the sodas are in our lunch bags, in the rack above our heads. I just checked mine. It's half-melted. By lunchtime, it'll be melted all the way but still cold. In other words, perfect. Channy Harrington did the same thing with his soda. It was his idea. He says kids always do that with their sodas out in California. Channy's father is one of the big bosses down at Electric Boat. When I visit over at Channy's house, Ray says I'm "hobnobbing." You can tell he likes me going over there, though. The Harringtons have a housekeeper and a built-in swimming pool and a baseball-pitching machine for Channy and his older brothers. You can put it on three different speeds. The fastest speed goes seventy miles an hour. Sometimes the housekeeper makes us after-school snacks: oatmeal cookies, potato chips with onion dip, peanut butter and Marshmallow Fluff sandwiches. Thomas has never been invited to Channy's house. He says he's sick of hearing all the time about that housekeeper and her stupid sandwiches and Channy's stupid pitching machine.

Eugene Savitsky is giving my brother a lecture on how things break the sound barrier. He's so jazzed up on the topic, you can hear him over everybody else. We're not just going *to* the Statue of Liberty; we're going *inside* it. They have stairs that go right to the top. Eddie Otero says he's going to climb down the nose and hang out there like he's the Statue of Liberty's booger. He would, too. Otero's insane.

Muriel Baby comes to the back of the bus and makes us stop singing "A Hundred Bottles of Beer on the Wall." It's inappropriate for us to be singing about alcohol on a school trip, she says. We should know better. While she's warmed up, she yells at Marty Overturf for eating his lunch already when it isn't even 9:15 in the morning yet. What does she care? It's his lunch, not hers.

Channy Harrington's the only boy in our class who already shaves. Every single girl in our school is in love with Channy, just about. Debbie Chase asked him to sit with her on the bus ride to New York, but Mrs. Hanka told her no boy-girl combinations. When Channy transferred to our school last November, he was automatically popular, even on the *first day.* He has swimming and basketball trophies from his old school on a shelf in his bedroom. Channy says everyone in California has outdoor swimming pools, even poor people. His older brother, Clay, plays baseball in college. He's being scouted by the Cardinals.

Now Eugene is blabbing away to my brother about the planets. Uranus this, Uranus that. Out of the blue, Otero yells, "Hey, Savitsky! Stop talking about your asshole!" The whole bus looks back at us and cracks up. Muriel Baby stands up from her seat at the front of the bus, scowls back in our direction, and then sits down again. The bus driver keeps staring at us in his rearview mirror. What's *he* looking at? His job is to drive the bus, not give us dirty looks. "That dipshit driver should take a picture," Channy says. "It'd last longer."

Our seats are right next to that little bathroom. Mostly it's the girls who have to use it. Otero and Channy and I say wiseguy things to them as they go in and out. "Don't fall in now. . . . Don't do anything in there we wouldn't do." We crack each other up. Channy's been to Radio City before. Twice. He says when they open the doors, we should rush to the front seats so that when the Rockettes do their high kicks, we can see some good "crotch shots." Even though it's Channy who says it, Susan Gillis turns around and gives *me* a dirty look, and I go, real snotty, "What are you looking at?" Susan's mother was supposed to be our chaperone for this trip, but she came down with the mumps. Now Susan's acting like *she's* the chaperone. "You better stop talking like that," she says.

"Like what?" I go.

"Like what you just said about the Rockettes."

"Make us," I say.

"You're already made and what a mess."

It's not like Mrs. Hanka's going to let us sit wherever we want to when we get to Radio City, anyway. She'll make us all sit together in the same row, like babies, and I bet you any amount of money she plops right down next to Otero. Last week we had the word *incorrigible* on our vocabulary list and Muriel Baby used Otero as an example.

I've been over to Channy's house three times. The last time I was there, he told me he once saw all these women who were stark naked. At a beach in California where people don't have to wear bathing suits if they don't want to. Channy kept talking about the women's "fur burgers." At first, I didn't know what he meant by fur burgers, but I kept my mouth shut. Later on, we snuck into his brother Trent's room and Channy showed me Trent's dirty magazines. That's when I got it—what fur burgers were. I'd never seen any women naked before, not even in pictures. I never even knew they had hair down there, like men. It was Channy's brother Clay who took Channy to that beach. Him and some of his friends from college. From his baseball team. Channy says California has lots of those kinds of beaches. He's always talking about how much better California is than Connecticut. He says in his old classroom, all the desks had little buttons on the side and, at the end of the day, you just pushed the button and the desks disappeared into the floor. I'm pretty sure that's a bunch of bull. Maybe that stuff about the beaches is, too. But maybe not. I haven't even been to four states yet. What do I know?

Thomas gets up from his seat, climbs over Eugene, and walks back toward us. Someone trips him accidentally on purpose and everyone laughs, Channy and Eddie Otero loudest of all. Thomas acts so retarded sometimes. I look out the window so that I don't have to look at him.

He opens the bathroom door. "Don't get any on you," Channy says.

"If Althea comes down here, I'll send her in for you," Otero promises. He means Althea Ebbs, this big fat girl in our class who has BO and cries all the time. Thomas doesn't answer them. I hear the bathroom door click shut. Hear him slide the bolt.

Five minutes go by and he's still in there. Then six or seven minutes. I heard him flush a long time ago. Marie Sexton and Bunny Borsa have both gotten out of their seats about a million times to see if the john's free. "Who's in there?" Bunny asks us.

"His brother," Otero says, jabbing his thumb at me. "He's taking a two-ton dump."

"Either that or he's pulling his pud," Channy jokes.

They laugh when Bunny calls us dirty pigs.

Then the door handle starts clicking back and forth like crazy. "Dominick?" It's Thomas. "Dominick?"

He's locked himself in there. He can't get out. I can hear the panic in his voice, in the frantic clicking of that door handle, the thump of his fists against the door. Channy and Otero are busting a gut.

Marie Sexton and Susan and I start calling instructions to Thomas, but he's either too scared or too spastic to follow them. "I'm going to get sick if I don't get out of here!" he warns. That makes Otero and Channy laugh even harder.

"Calm down," I keep telling him. "Keep your voice down. You're making it worse."

"It's stuck! It won't budge!"

Five or six other kids are standing there now; everyone's shouting orders at Thomas. Some of the girls are complaining that they really have to go. Mrs. Hanka starts down the aisle. In class, she likes my brother better than me. You can tell. Mr. Goody Two-shoes. Mr. Perfect. But now she's mad at him. "To the left! Push it to the left!" she shouts, in the exasperated voice she usually saves for Otero or Althea Ebbs.

I know it's serious when the driver pulls over to the side of the highway and stops the bus. "Sit down! Sit down!" he's yelling at everyone, elbowing his way down the aisle. I can't believe it: my stupid, retarded brother is wrecking our entire trip to New York City.

"*Together!* Move the handle and the bolt *together*!" the driver keeps screaming at the locked door. He takes off his uniform jacket and the back of his shirt is soaked in sweat. His face is the same color as rare roast beef. We've been on the side of the highway for fifteen minutes.

"Let . . . me . . . out . . . of . . . here!" Thomas keeps shouting. "Please! Please! LET ME OUT!" His body keeps making thudding noises against the door. My stomach feels like I'm on this elevator that's dropping way too fast. If I start crying in front of Channy and Otero, I don't care what anyone says. I'm changing schools.

"Twelve years I've been driving these things," the driver tells Mrs. Hanka. "And I bet I could count on one hand the number of times I forgot my tools." He says we'll have to get off at the next exit and get to a gas station. Maybe with a flatbar, he can jimmy the door open. Or maybe the gas station will have a drill he can use to unfreeze the bolts. If not, he'll have to call the bus company and have someone drive down with the right tools.

"Well, how long will that take?" Mrs. Hanka demands. "Our Radio City tickets are for the 2:30 P.M. show. We have to get on the ferry by 10:45 at the latest or we'll miss the Statue of Liberty."

"I don't know how long it'll take, lady," he says. "I can't give you any guarantees."

"I'm sorry, Dominick!" Thomas screams from behind the door. "I'm sorry!"

The bus gets off at the next exit and is crawling through traffic on some main street. Eugene Savitsky has gotten up and come to the back of the bus. He stands there, picking at his seat and staring at the locked bathroom door like it's a science problem. "Have him push the bolt the opposite way," he tells me. "Have him push it to the right instead of the left."

"It doesn't *go* to the right," someone says.

"But just tell him. Maybe he's mixed up."

"Push it to the right," I tell Thomas.

The bolt thunks. The door squeaks open.

Thomas emerges to the sound of hoots and applause. He's so pale, his skin looks blue. At first, he smiles. Then his face crumples up. He begins to cry.

I feel bad for him. And mad. And humiliated. Kids are looking at me, too, not just at Thomas. The Birdsey brothers: identical twin retards. I'd like to punch that smirk off of Channy Harrington's rich little stupid face. Bust Eddie Otero's big, fat Spic nose.

The bus driver turns around in an empty parking lot and heads back toward the interstate. Mrs. Hanka reassigns seats. Now Thomas and I sit together up front and Otero has to sit with Eugene Savitsky. Channy and Debbie Chase and Yvette Magritte are giggling together in the back.

For the rest of that whole, long day, Thomas acts really out of it. At the Statue of Liberty, he tells Mrs. Hanka he feels too scared to go up inside. She makes me stay down with him. Some guy in a uniform comes over and yells at me for chucking gravel into the water. After that, my brother and I sit on a wall, looking out at the harbor. "Just think," Thomas says, finally breaking the silence. "This is exactly what our grandfather saw the day he first came over from Italy."

"Would you do me a favor?" I tell him. "Would you just shut the fuck up?" I've never said "fuck" out loud before. Saying it feels good. I feel as mad, as mean, as Ray.

I spend all my money. At Radio City, I buy a three-dollar deluxe souvenir book that I don't even really want. At that novelty shop in Times Square—it *is* the same one Marie thought it was—I buy a back scratcher, a Roger Maris &

Mickey Mantle plaque, a rubber tarantula, a puddle of plastic vomit. At the restaurant on the way home, I order shrimp cocktail, a T-bone steak, and Dutch apple pie à la mode. Channy and Otero eat their hamburgers at a booth with Debbie and Yvette. I get stuck at a table with fat, stupid Eugene Savitsky and my stupid, ugly brother. Eugene orders liver and onions. All Thomas has is chicken noodle soup and saltines.

Channy's brother Trent gives Thomas and me a ride home. It had been arranged before—Channy's idea. Channy and Trent sit up front and Thomas and I sit in back. Channy doesn't say two words to either of us. He talks to his brother, turns the radio up loud, mentions something about someone they knew in stupid California. I know I'm never going over to Channy's house again—that the Harringtons' housekeeper has already made me the last of those peanut butter and fluff sandwiches with the crusts cut off. I've taken my last swing at those machine-hurled pitches.

"How was your trip?" Ma asks us when we get home.

"Pretty good," Thomas says. "I really liked the Easter show. It was nice." He says nothing about locking himself in the bathroom. I say nothing either.

"And how about you, Dominick?" Ma goes. "Did you have a good time?"

I've left my deluxe souvenir program on the bus. Someone has sat on my back scratcher and broken it. Of the thirty-seven dollars I brought with me, I have only eighty-three cents left. For a second or more, I'm on the verge of tears. Then I'm all right again. "It was boring," I tell my mother. "It stunk, just like everything always stinks."

That night, I dream I'm trapped in a small, dark cave in a woods I don't recognize. It's pitch dark. I bang and cry for help and when, at last, I discover a way out, I realize I've not been trapped in a cave after all, but inside the Statue of Liberty.

eleven

It was musical chairs and months-old *Newsweeks* at the medical clinic. In the hour I waited, I put up with the sneaky peeks and sidelong glances of everyone who wanted to check out that library lunatic's duplicate. One teenage girl out and out stared at my two hands. The receptionist who gave me the insurance forms to sign jerked her hand away when I reached for her pen. After my name was called, I cooled my jets in the examining room for another fifteen or twenty minutes. Then I told my story to Dr. Judy Yup.

Dr. Yup, whose smile never left her face during my ten-minute examination, pronounced me damaged and said she'd testify to the fact. She told me she'd studied a year abroad in China and had friends who'd been involved in Tiananmen Square. Her cousin, she said, had been in hiding in the southern provinces ever since.

"Well," I said, "you can't really compare one jerky guard to what happened over there."

"Why can't you?" she countered, the smile finally dropping off her face. "Oppression is oppression."

Dale, the nurse's aide who took the pictures of my injuries, treated me to a running monologue about the time he and his cousin got pulled over and roughed up by some state cops on their way home from an Aerosmith concert. "I wish I'd had the smarts to do what you're doing, man," he said. "We could have cashed in bigtime."

I didn't want to cash in. But a picture was forming in my head: my brother walking out the main door at Hatch, squinting into the sunshine. That social worker had been right, I guess; I *had* acted like an asshole down there the night before. Whatever came of this medical exam, Sheffer had stuck her neck out to suggest it. Thinking about her down there at Hatch, keeping an eye on my brother, gave me some relief. Relaxed me. Made me sleepy. When I got back in the truck, I just sat there, almost dozing off before I managed to put the key in the ignition and drive away.

From the clinic, I swung over to Henry Rood's house. Might as well get this one over with, too, I told myself. I'd finish power-washing that goddamned place over the weekend, try to have it scraped and primed by the middle of the following week. Maybe with Ray's help, I could get that three-story headache finished up by Halloween. I didn't want to push it beyond that. November temperatures were iffy for oil-based paint; you'd only have three or four hours of good midday sun, and that's if you were lucky. While I was at it, I'd tell Rood to cool it on the phone messages. I'd had enough of his harassment.

It had been cold that morning, but now the air was dry and warm, the temperature in the midseventies. Perfect painting weather. When I pulled up to the house on Gillette Street, Rood's wife Ruth was out on their front porch step, sunning herself. With her stringy black hair and her pasty complexion, she reminded me a little of Morticia Addams. Especially parked in front of that Victorian house of horrors of theirs. She smiled as I approached. "I *should* be inside grading papers," she said, "but here I am, celebrating Indian summer instead." Beside her, a portable radio was broadcasting the opening game of the World Series.

When I asked to speak to Henry, she told me she didn't want to disturb him. He was either writing at the computer or else napping, she said. Or passed out in an alcoholic stupor, I figured. Ruth was having a little afternoon snort herself. A sweating glass of something or other sat on the porch floor next to her.

"Just tell him I apologize about the delay," I said. "It can't be helped. There's been a bunch of circumstances beyond my control the past several days."

"So we read," she said. I looked away.

"Tell him . . . tell him I can probably have the house prepped by next Wednesday or Thursday—depends on how much of the trim I have to burn off." I told her I should have the job wrapped up and the scaffolding down in a couple of weeks, max, as long as the weather cooperated. "I should be able to go full-steam next week," I said. "So tell him he doesn't have to keep calling me."

When she asked me how Thomas was doing, I addressed their porch railing rather than look at her. "He's all right," I said. "He's better."

She told me that when she was a girl, a neighbor of hers back in Ohio had ripped out his own eye. For religious reasons, she said, same as my brother. She'd been sitting on the couch, reading a book, when she heard the man's wife screaming. Later, she watched them lead him out the door and into an ambulance, a towel wrapped around his neck. What she always remembered was how calm he looked—how much at peace he was to have blinded himself like that. It was eerie, she said. They moved away shortly after that—the man and his wife and their two little girls. But Ruth said a month didn't go by without her thinking about him. "And I was just his neighbor. So I can't even imagine what *you're* going through," she said. "Well, I can and I can't. What I'm trying to say is that I'm sorry."

I nodded. Looked into her nervous, jumpy eyes. Compassion was the last thing I'd expected at this place.

Ruth asked me if I wanted to join her in a rye and ginger. They had beer, too, she said. Pabst Blue Ribbon, she was pretty sure. Or gin. Her body fidgeted with anticipation.

I begged off—invented some errands I had to run. I nodded over at the radio—the game. "So who's your money on?" I said.

"Oh, I'm strictly a Cincinnati fan," she said. "From *way*

back. My father used to take my brother and me to Red Legs games when we were kids. How about you?"

"Yeah, Cincinnati, I guess. Now that Boston's blown it as usual. If Clemens hadn't had that little temper tantrum during the playoffs and gotten ejected, maybe the Sox would have been playing in the Series instead of the A's. Personally, I can't stand Oakland."

"Me either," she said. "José Canseco? Yecch."

I nodded up at Rood's office window. "So what's he writing up there, anyway?" I said. "The Great American Novel?"

She shook her head. Nonfiction, she said. An exposé.

"Yeah? What's he exposing? Housepainters?"

She smiled, fiddled with a blouse button. Even two and a half sheets to the wind, she was a nervous wreck. Henry had been writing this book for eleven years now, she told me. It was hard on him; it had taken its toll. She couldn't really discuss the subject matter. It would upset Henry for her to talk about it.

It made me think of what Ma had told me about her father's autobiography: how everything had been so hush-hush that summer when he wrote that thing. How he'd hired and fired a stenographer, rented a Dictaphone, and then finally retreated to the backyard and finished it himself.

I told Ruth Rood I'd see her in a couple of days—that by the time I was through, she and her husband would be *sick* of seeing me.

"Oh, I doubt that," she said. On the radio, the crowd roared. The announcer's voice went manic. Eric Davis had just clobbered a two-run homer off of Dave Stewart. "Yippee!" Mrs. Rood said, draining her rye and ginger.

With two down and one to go, I headed over to Hollyhock Avenue to see Ray. Started thinking about that goddamned goofy Nedra Frank. She'd *stolen* that manuscript of my grandfather's, really. Cashed my check and disappeared. By now, she'd probably trashed the thing. It probably didn't even exist.

I rolled slowly up Hollyhock Avenue, pulled in front of the house, and cut the engine. Sat there, just looking up at it: the house that "Papa" had built. . . . The shrubs looked gawky and overgrown; the hedges needed a trim. It was unusual for Ray to let the yard go like that. Thomas used to say that Ray couldn't sleep unless the hedges stood at attention and the front lawn had a crewcut as short as his. The garbage barrels were out front, too—emptied the day before and still waiting to be brought around to the back. It had always been another of Ray's pet peeves: people who didn't bother putting away their trash barrels. We used to hear *lectures* on the subject.

I got out of the truck. Walked right by those friggin' garbage cans and up the flight of cement stairs to the front of the family duplex. Home Sweet Home, aka the House of Horrors. The statute of limitations was long since up on most of the crap Ray had pulled on us while we were growing up, but being back at 68 Hollyhock Avenue always made me feel pissed and small. Ten years old again, and powerless.

It was funny, kind of—the way things had worked out. Ma was gone, I owned the condo now over on Hillyndale. Over the past several years, Thomas had lived either at the hospital or in the group home, not here. The only one left at the house old Domenico Tempesta had built for his family was Ray Birdsey, a WASP from Youngstown, Ohio. No Tempesta blood in residence. No Italian blood, even. Ray hadn't wanted to rent the other side of the duplex after Little Sal, the last of the Tusia family, moved to Arizona where his daughter lived. "Why don't *you* move back in?" he asked me, after Dessa's and my divorce. "Save yourself a mortgage payment. You and him own half this place, anyway. After I kick the bucket, the whole thing'll be yours."

It would have been a smart move financially and a kind of emotional suicide. So I bought the condo instead, and the other side of the duplex on Hollyhock Avenue stayed empty. When I asked him once about renting it, Ray said he didn't need the extra income. "Yeah, well maybe *you* don't," I told him, "but I can't afford to turn my nose up at half of a $700-a-month rental income." Rather than rent, Ray went down to the Liberty Bank and took out a savings account with Thomas and me as beneficiaries. Each month, he deposited $350 into it. It was worth it, he told me. You never knew who you might get stuck with. His buddy Nickerson down at the

Boat had rented his upstairs to a bunch of pigs he couldn't get rid of, no matter what he did. Ray didn't need that kind of grief. So he paid into that account each month and lived by himself in Domenico Tempesta's sprawling, sixteen-room, two-family house.

Rather than knock, I let myself in with my key. *La chiave,* I thought. I walked through the house, front to back. I hadn't been over there for a while. The rooms looked cluttered, everything in neat piles but nothing put away. Tools, stacks of old newspapers, and a half-completed jigsaw puzzle littered the dining room table. The rugs felt gritty under my work boots. In the kitchen, the heavy stink of fried food hung in the air. Dishes and pans and cups were clean and stacked on the counter, but Ray hadn't bothered to put anything back in the cabinets. Lined up on the table were his blood pressure and diabetes medications, a stack of *Reader's Digest*s, and two piles of mail held together with elastic bands. That day's *Daily Record* was folded in quarters, heads up to the article about Thomas's committal to Hatch.

So Ray knew already. That much was over with.

I found him in the back bedroom, tangled up in his blanket, snoring away in the semidarkness. He'd begun sleeping downstairs after Ma died. His official reason was that there'd been a prowler in the neighborhood—someone had jimmied open the Anthonys' cellar door across the street. But I was pretty sure that wasn't really it. After Dessa left me, one of the toughest things I had to get used to was her empty side of the bed. I'd find myself falling asleep down on the couch in front of the TV just so's I wouldn't have to go upstairs and deal with that empty space. Not that it was something you could have ever talked about with Ray. He had to sleep downstairs with a crowbar under the bed so he could fend off burglars. Be a tough guy instead of facing whatever he was feeling about the death of his wife.

If Ray was sleeping days, then the shipyard must have him working nights again. You had to hand it to him, really. Sixty-seven years old and the guy's still working like a plowhorse. I stood there, staring at him. The midafternoon sun came through the open blinds, striping his face with light. With his mouth open and his teeth out, he looked older. Old. His hair was more white than gray now. When had all this happened?

Growing up, I had wished my stepfather dead so often, it was practically a hobby. I'd killed him over and over in my mind—driven him off cliffs, electrocuted him in the bathtub, shot him dead in hunting accidents. He'd said and done things that *still* weren't scabbed over. Had made this place a house of fear. Still, seeing him like this—white-haired and vulnerable, a snoring corpse—I was filled with an unexpected sympathy for the guy.

Which I didn't want to feel. Which I shook off.

I went back into the kitchen. Found a piece of paper and wrote him a note about Thomas. I explained what Sheffer had said about the fifteen-day paper, the security check they had to run on visitors, the upcoming hearing in front of that Review Board. "Call me if you have any questions," I scrawled at the bottom. But my guess was that he wouldn't call. My guess was that Ray had already walked away from this one.

On the way back out to the truck, I passed those garbage pails again. Then I stopped. Grabbed one handle in each hand and walked them up the front stairs and around to the backyard. Saved him a trip.

Our old backyard . . .

I put the cans down and walked past the two cement urns where Ma had always grown her parsley and basil. Fresh basil. God, I loved the smell of that stuff—the way it perfumed your fingers for the rest of the day. . . . *Dominick? Do me a favor, honey? Go out back and pick me some* basilico. *Half a dozen leaves or so. I want to put some in the sauce. . . .*

I walked up the six cement stairs to "Papa's little piece of the Old Country." That's what she always called it. According to Ma, Papa had loved to sit out here among his grapes and chicken coops and tomato and pepper plants—to sit in the sun and sip his homemade wine and remember Sicily. . . . Maybe that was why she'd heard him crying that last day as he sat up here, finishing his history. Maybe, at the end of his life, the "Great Man from Humble Beginnings" had wept for Sicily.

I remembered the way Thomas and I had played up here as kids. Saw us pogo-sticking around the yard, staging massacres with our plastic cowboys and Indians, chasing garter snakes into the stone wall. Every June, when the honeysuckle bush blossomed, we'd suck nectar from the blossoms. One small drop of elixir on your tongue per flower—that was all you got.

I walked over to the picnic table Ray and I had built one summer. The seat had rotted at one end. I ought to come over some morning and just haul the thing away to the dump for him. Maybe next spring I'd get over here and plant a garden—work the soil, bring this old yard back from the dead. Ray had let this go, too; I'd never seen the backyard so overgrown. The grapevines were all but choked off with weeds. The dead grass was knee-high. Probably hadn't been mowed once all summer. Probably *loaded* with ticks. What was the deal on Ray? . . .

I thought about what Ma had told me that time—the day she'd gone upstairs and come down again with that strongbox. With Papa's story. She'd come out here with his lunch, she told me. Had found him slumped in the chair. . . . And while she waited for help—waited for the ambulance to get here—she'd gone around picking up the pages of his life story. . . . One of these days, I was going to pursue it: find that bitch Nedra. Get my grandfather's story back if she hadn't already destroyed it. She'd told me her ex-husband was a honcho down at the state hospital. Maybe I could track her down through him. He probably had to send alimony someplace, right? And if that didn't pan out, maybe I'd go see Jerry Martineau over at the police station. Because it was *theft,* what she'd pulled, not to mention breach of contract. . . .

The summer the Old Man had died up here was the same summer Ma was pregnant with Thomas and me. Pregnant by a guy whose name I was probably *never* going to know. And what about him? Had *he* known about *us*? Why had she kept him from us? Whose son was I?

And who, for that matter, had Papa been? In my mind, I saw and felt again those legal-sized pages I had lifted out of the strongbox that morning: the first fifteen or twenty typed and duplicated with carbon paper, the rest of it written in that sprawling fountain-pen script. She'd saved her father's history for *me,* she said. Thomas could look at it, too, but Papa's story was mine. . . . And I saw Nedra Frank's Yugo sliding diagonally down the street in the middle of that snowstorm. Saw her driving away for good. Talk about shitty luck, getting mixed up with that one. Talk about "losing something in the translation."

Once all this Hatch stuff was over with, I'd track her down, even if Martineau couldn't do anything for me. Even if I had to hire a freakin' private detective. Because when you thought about it, she'd *stolen* my grandfather from me. It was a theft that went way beyond the lousy four hundred bucks I'd advanced her. . . . And maybe I'd try to find out about that stenographer, too. That Angelo guy who'd worked here that summer. Ma had said he was cousins with the Mastronunzio family. I knew a Dave Mastronunzio at Allied Plumbers. Maybe I'd start with him. Start somewhere. Maybe.

Maybe not.

twelve

Any sane man would have called it quits at that point. Would have said, "Okay, that's enough crap for one day," and driven home and crashed. But who ever said sanity ran in our family? Exhausted and antsy, I swung left and drove over to the dealership to see Leo.

Constantine Chrysler Plymouth Isuzu. "Make Gene's Boys an honest offer, they'll give you an honest deal." Yeah, sure. If honest deals were the way Diogenes "Gene" Constantine, my ex-father-in-law, made his money, then I was Luke Skywalker.

Leo was out on the lot, holding a single red carnation and helping a middle-aged redhead into a white Grand Prix. "Well, good luck with it now, Jeanette," he said. "Thanks again for the flower."

"Oh, it was nothing, Leo. You've just been so sweet. I wish I could have bought *two* new cars instead of one."

"You just give me a call if there's anything I can do for you in the future. Okay?"

Jeanette revved her engine like one of the Andrettis. "Oops, sorry," she giggled. "I'm still getting used to it."

"That's okay, Jeanette. You'll get the hang of it. You take care now."

She put the car in gear, rolling and bucking away from us. "Good riddance, Jeanette," Leo said, his mouth frozen like a ventriloquist's. "You fat-headed douche bag. I hope the engine drops out of your goddamned Grand Prix."

"Let me guess," I said. "No sale?"

"The bitch was this far from signing on the dotted line on a white-on-white LeBaron. That thing was *loaded,* Birdsey. Then I take one stinking day off to go into the city and she buys that showboat from Andy Butrymovic over at Three Rivers Pontiac. You know Butrymovic? Fuckin' weasel. Fuckin' Polack bastard."

Entering the showroom, we passed a sign-painter who was whistling and stenciling the plate-glass window for some new promotion. "So what's the flower for?" I said. "You get Miss Congeniality or something?"

He snorted. "Something like that." Snapping the stem of the carnation, he tossed it into Omar's wastebasket. Omar's the newest salesman at Constantine Motors. Black guy or Spanish or something. Now *there's* something you wouldn't have seen ten years ago, or even five: my ex-father-in-law hiring minority salesmen. You wouldn't have seen him hiring women, either. Now there were two.

"How's your brother?" Leo asked. "Angie said they checked him in down at Hatch? What's that all about?"

I told him about Thomas's commitment the night before. About the knee to the groin I'd taken and the advice I'd just gotten from Lisa Sheffer. "He gets to list five visitors," I said. "They run a security check on everyone he puts down. Then they frisk you, make you go through a metal—"

"Lisa Sheffer, Lisa Sheffer, " he said. "I *know* that name. Have a seat."

I sat down opposite him at his desk. That's a bone of contention with Leo: the fact that he's been at the dealership all these years and the Old Man still has him parked out there on the showroom floor. Dessa and Angie's cousin Peter joined the business about four or five years after Leo did, and he's already got one of the private paneled offices *off* the floor. Peter's been named Leasing Manager and leasing's the new big thing.

The veneer on Leo's desk had buckled a little and was

coming unglued at the corner. It happens with that cheap veneer shit. You should see the desk in the Old Man's office suite. It's big enough to land planes on. Leo flipped through the Rolodex on his desk. "Lisa Sheffer, Lisa Sheffer. . . . Here it is. Lisa Sheffer. She test-drove a Charger with me about six months ago. Nurse, right?"

"Psychiatric social worker."

"Little skinny broad? Short hair, no tit?" I thought about Sheffer's reprimand to me: how she was a woman, not a "gal." She must have *really* bonded with Leo.

"You know what I'd do?" Leo said. "About your brother? I'd hire a lawyer and have him start talking police brutality. Have him bring the doctor's statement and those medical pictures and everything. Maybe you could cut a deal with them—promise 'em you won't go to court if your brother gets transferred back to Settle. Then you know what I'd do? After you got him out of there? I'd turn around and sue the state's ass off anyway."

"You *would* do that. Wouldn't you, Leo?"

"You bet your left nut I would. What are they going to do? Complain that you welched on an under-the-table agreement? Better to be the screwer than the screwee." He stood up. "Hang on a minute, will you, Birdseed? I'll be right back. I gotta go check something in the service department."

In a way, selling cars was the ideal job for Leo. Professional bullshitter. He'd been bullshitting me since the summer of 1966, when I sat across the aisle from him in remedial algebra class and he got me to believe he was second cousins with Sam the Sham of Sam the Sham and the Pharaohs. Their hit song "Woolly Bully" was popular that year—the year I was fifteen. It came cranking out of my red transistor radio all summer long while I mowed lawns, solved for *x*, and lifted weights—curling and bench-pressing in an effort to transform myself into Hercules, Unchained. Leo told me that he'd been to Sam the Sham's apartment in Greenwich Village for a party and that a Playboy bunny had sat in his lap. That his uncle was a talent scout out in Hollywood. That his mother was thinking of buying him a Corvette once he passed algebra and got his license.

He was paunchy and chip-toothed back then, a middle-aged-looking sixteen-year-old who could make our fellow algebra flunkies suck their teeth just by walking into the room. Sometimes I'd watch him with a kind of grossed-out fascination as he'd pick his nose, examine what he'd come up with, and then wipe it under his desktop. He made life miserable for our teacher, shaky, old, semiretired Mrs. Palladino. Leo would raise his hand for help on some problem he couldn't have given a flying leap about solving and Palladino would come hobbling up the aisle on her bum leg. Then, right in the middle of some explanation Leo wouldn't even bother to listen to, he'd cut a fart—a "silent-but-deadly" so foul that everyone within a twenty-foot radius would start groaning and fanning their worksheets. Poor Palladino would stand there, droning on in good faith and trying, I guess, not to pass out from the stink.

Leo got away with plenty that summer, up to and including passing the course by snatching the mimeograph stencil of the final exam from the teachers' room wastebasket. But the following fall, his luck ran out. Neck Veins, the assistant principal at JFK, caught him red-handed one afternoon stretching Trojans over the heads of the athletic figurines in the main corridor trophy case. Neck Veins: I forget the guy's real name, but when he screamed, the veins in his neck would bulge out like electrical cables. Neck Veins *nailed* Leo. Had him apologize over the PA during morning announcements to all the former and present student athletes whose victories he had mocked. Then he made him run laps after school every afternoon for two months. Leo's mother, who had just become Three Rivers' first city councilwoman, dragged him once a week to a "specialist."

After all that running and counseling, Leo dropped thirty pounds and grew his hair long. By springtime, he was lead singer for this garage band called the Throbbers. Now girls liked him. Skanky girls at first, and then more and more popular ones, including Natalie Santerre, who everyone thought looked like Senta Berger and who Leo claims to this day gave him a BJ the weekend before her family moved to North Carolina. The Throbbers played the usual covers: "Wild Thing," "Good Lovin'," "Nineteenth Nervous Breakdown." Leo was a real ham; whenever they did that Question

Mark and the Mysterians song, "Ninety-six Tears," he'd drop to his knees and act like he was blowing a gasket because the girl in the song had left him. The band fell apart after a while, but by then Leo had become addicted to the attention—to standing up there on a stage. He majored in acting at UConn, dealt a little weed on the side, and was, during his junior year, stud enough to have bonked all three of Chekhov's Three Sisters over the course of a two-month rehearsal. According to Leo, that is, who you'd never mistake for a reliable source—particularly on the subject of his sex life. He played Snoopy during his junior year in *You're a Good Man, Charlie Brown.* That was the highlight of Leo's dramatic career: Snoopy. Dessa and I had been going out for about six or seven months by then. (Dessa didn't like Leo that much; she tolerated him.) When she and I drove up to see *You're a Good Man, Charlie Brown,* we brought Dessa's sister Angie along. Angie had dated my brother just before that—a two-month disaster I don't even like to think about. But anyway, for better or worse, Angie sat that night in the audience and fell in love for life. Dessa and I got to hear all the way home how adorable Leo looked, how funny he was, how Angie had laughed so hard at one point, she'd wet her pants. After Leo found out about his one-woman fan club, he asked Angie out. They went at it hot and heavy all that summer—the summer of 1971—then seemed to cool off. But the following Christmas, when Dessa and I told them we were thinking of getting engaged after graduation, *they* told *us* that Angie was pregnant. Shit, man, if Angie hadn't miscarried, that kid would be what by now? Eighteen?

That whistling sign-painter had finished his first letter on the plate glass: a blue "G," as tall as Joy. Leo came walking back across the showroom.

"Hey, I forgot to tell you," I said. "Guess who I saw down there at Hatch in the middle of everything else last night? Ralph Drinkwater."

"Drinkwater? No shit. God, I haven't seen Ralph since . . . when did we have those summer jobs?"

"Nineteen sixty-nine," I said. "The summer we landed on the moon."

"So how's he look? Ralph?"

"Not that different, really. I recognized him right off."

"Jesus, remember that bag job we pulled on him? With the cops?"

"The bag job *you* pulled on him," I said. "*You* were the one who sat there in that station and told them—"

"Oh, yeah, Birdsey, you were Mr. Innocent that night, right? Hey, not to change the subject. What do you think of this suit?" He got up from behind his desk, turned to the side, and strutted back down to that white-on-white LeBaron. *Virgins* is what Leo calls the floor models. The suit was tan, double-breasted. Looked too big for him in my book.

"I picked this up in New York yesterday when I auditioned," he said. "Armani—top of the line. I felt like celebrating because things went so well."

Leo and his auditions. For all the tryouts he's rushed to New York for over the years, I've only seen him on TV in two things—a Landlubber's Lobster commercial that ran sometime back in the mideighties and this public service thing for AIDS prevention. In the restaurant ad, Leo played a wholesome dad taking his happy family out for seafood. The thing starts with a close-up of Leo, bug-eyed and looking like he's having an orgasm. Then the camera pulls back and you see a waitress tying one of those plastic bibs around his neck. There's this motherfucking *monster* of a lobster in front of him. The rest of the family looks on, smiling like they're all high on something, even Grandma. The other ad—the public service thing—is something they still run every once in a while at two or three in the morning, usually when I'm riding the Insomnia Express. Leo plays a dad in that one, too—shooting hoops with his teenage son and talking man to man about responsibility. At the end, Leo says, "And remember, son, the safest thing of all is waiting until you're ready." Leo and Junior smile at each other, and Leo takes a hook shot. There's a close-up, nothing but net. Then Leo and the kid high-five each other. The first time I saw it, I laughed out loud. For one thing, Leo couldn't make a hook shot to save his ass. Back in high school, he made up a story about a damaged left ventricle and conned his way out of gym class for two years in a row. And for another thing, Leo talking about abstinence is like Donald Trump talking about altruism.

"So get this, Birdsey," he said. "I buy the suit, have them alter it, and I get back home around midnight. The house is dark, Angie and the kids are asleep. So I nuke myself some leftovers, flip on the tube, and there's Arsenio wearing the exact same suit I just bought. *Arsenio,* man! Recently voted one of the ten best-dressed guys in America. It's an omen."

"An omen?"

"That I'm going to get that part. How much do you think I paid for this baby, anyway?" He stroked a jacket sleeve, pivoted to the side again. "Italian silk," he said. "Go on, take a guesstimate."

"Hey, Leo," I said. "I've got one or two too many things on my mind right now. I don't particularly feel like playing *The Price Is Right* with you and your new suit."

"Go ahead. Guess!"

"I don't know. Two hundred? Two-fifty?"

He snorted. Jabbed a finger upward.

"Three-fifty?"

"Try *fourteen*-fifty, my man."

"Fourteen fifty? For a *suit?!*"

"Not *a* suit. *This* suit. Feel it!"

I rubbed the end of the sleeve between my thumb and finger. "Yeah?" I said. "What? It feels like a suit."

He picked a little imaginary lint off the jacket. "Hey, what do you know, Birdsey?" he said. "You work in overalls. By the way, did I tell you this audition's for a *movie,* not a commercial?" He sat down again and leaned back, balancing himself on the back legs of his chair. "Nothing big-budget, but it's a credential, you know? A stepping-stone. Psycho flick—probably right to video here in the States with limited release to the foreign markets. Korea, Hong Kong—places like that. They eat that slasher shit up over there."

"You already told me it was a movie," I said.

"I *didn't* already tell you. When did I tell you?"

"I don't know? At racquetball?"

"I just went to New York yesterday. We played racquetball the day *before* yesterday."

I was starting to feel a little woozy. "Oh, yeah, that's right. Angie told me, I guess. Hey, you got any coffee around here?"

"You know we got coffee. Black, right? When did you see Angie?"

"I didn't see her. I talked to her last night when I called looking for you."

"What did you want?"

"Huh? Nothing. I just wanted to tell you about my brother. Black, two sugars."

"Hey, did I tell you I'm off coffee? I been reading this book called *Fit for Life.* Angie got it for me. We're getting one of those juicer things, too. This book says caffeine's as bad for you as poison. Refined sugar, too: a real no-no. But anyways, you know what this movie's about? There's this weird broad, see? And she's both an artist and a female serial killer. First she gets screwed over by all these guys, okay? Has all these traumatic experiences. Then she snaps. Starts murdering all the guys that dumped on her and painting these weird pictures with their blood. So all of a sudden, the art critics discover her, see? She starts getting real big in the art world, only nobody knows what she's using for paint, okay? Or that she's painting pictures during the day and killing all these guys at night. I read for one of the victims—the first guy she offs—this art professor who wants to dick her in exchange for an A. I think I got a good shot at it—a callback, minimum. 'Very nice,' the casting guy said after the reading. '*Very* nice.' "

"And not that much of a stretch for you, either," I said. "Playing a sleaze."

"Hey, fuck you, Birdsey. But really, though, the signs are all there on this one, you know?" He looked around, then leaned forward across his desk. Turned his voice to a whisper. "And get this. If I get the part, there's this scene where the psycho bitch goes down on me. Just before she kills me. Don't say anything to Angie if you see her, okay? She'd go apeshit. I started doing sit-ups this morning because I'm like 99.9 percent sure I'm getting the part."

"Black, two sugars," I said.

The front legs of his chair thunked back down to earth

and he stood up. "Poison, Birdseed, I'm telling you. Live clean or die."

While I waited for him to get back, I walked around the showroom. Checked out an Isuzu truck they had parked over by the window. Thumbed through a couple of brochures. The sign-painter was on his second letter: G-O.

I was glad my father-in-law wasn't in. My *ex*-father-in-law. We'd always gotten along, Gene and me. He'd always favored me over Leo. Sometimes it was so obvious, it got embarrassing. We'd all be over at the house, some holiday or another, and Gene would invite the two Peters and Costas and me into the den for ouzo, or out for a walk through their orchards, and there Leo would be, in the other room with the kids and the women. It was sad, too, because it was an extension of the fact that the old man has always favored Dessa over Angie. That one was so obvious, it was painful. But all that changed. Ever since the divorce, if I dropped in at the dealership to see Leo and Gene was there, it'd be like I was the Invisible Man or something. Like I hadn't been the guy's son-in-law for almost sixteen years. Like *I* left *her* instead of the opposite.

I could hear Leo out by the service area, yapping with somebody instead of getting me my coffee. Leo's desk was one of four parked right out there on the showroom floor. Don't ask me why I remember this, but I do: he started working for Constantine Motors the day Reagan got inaugurated and Iran freed the hostages. Nine years and still no private office. One time, when Leo was bitching about it, he said, "If it was you, Dominick, instead of me, you probably would have been a VP by now, never mind a simple office with a door on it." And he's right. I *would* have been.

The Old Man's office suite is something else. He's even got a private bathroom in there—good-sized, too. Must go about eleven-by-eleven. It's got a red tub with gold fixtures and a hand-painted mural of the Trojan War. How's this for mature? Leo always makes sure he takes a dump in Gene's private facility whenever the Old Man's out on the lot or off someplace checking on one of his other gold mines. (Besides the dealership, Gene and Thula own a couple of strip malls—one here in Three Rivers and another up the road in

Willimantic.) The Constantines are big into those hand-painted murals, though: they've got them over at the house, too—one in the dining room and the other up in Gene and Thula's bedroom. The Aegean Sea, that one is. On the wall opposite their bed.

Leo and I ended up getting engaged to the Constantine sisters the exact same week. Dessa and I had been making plans right along, but not Leo and Angie. Theirs was your basic shotgun situation. The Old Man sent word through his daughters that he wanted to meet with Leo and me at his place of business. Give us his big "future son-in-law" speech. This was before he knew Angie and Leo had a kid on the way—before Angie dropped *that* little bomb on her father, which she did in the limo ride over to the church. Leo and I could come in together for the big talk, Gene had said; what he had to say, he could say to both of us. I remembered it whole, that summit meeting in Gene's private office. "Come in, gentlemen, come in," he called to us after we'd sat a while in his outer office. Leo thought it was all a big goof, but for me it felt like waiting for the doctor to call you in and vaccinate you. "In here," Gene said, and the next thing you know, we were in that frigging bathroom of his. He was taking a bath in his red tub. I stood there, not wanting to look at his hairy gorilla body or look him in the eye, either. Dessa wasn't pregnant or anything, but it was thanks to birth control pills, not abstinence. I kept looking at the Trojan War over the Old Man's shoulder—soldiers inside the gates, leaping from the belly of that fake horse.

"Gentlemen," Diogenes began. "My two daughters have enjoyed a good life up to this point. Their mother and I have done our best to provide them with all of life's necessities and some of its luxuries as well. And now, they've chosen to move from our home to your homes." Nervous or not, I got a silent chuckle out of that one. The Constantines live in this fourteen-room "shack" on Bayview Terrace with apple orchards and a grape arbor and a built-in swimming pool. At the time of our big bathroom summit, I was living in a ratty over-the-garage apartment on Careen Avenue with a refrigerator door I had to keep shut with electrical tape.

"Now, I don't require my daughters' husbands to be millionaires or heroes," Gene continued. "The only things I expect from you two are happy, healthy grandchildren and the knowledge that my girls are lying down each night beside God-fearing, honest men. If you can honor those requirements, then I welcome you to the family with my blessing. If you can't, then say so now and we'll part as friends."

Leo did most of the talking for both of us—gave the old man his best Eddie Haskell "yes, sir" and "no, sir" kiss-up routine until Diogenes got to the end of both his big speech and his bath. He stood up, took the helping hand Leo offered him out of the tub, and lit us all Panatela Extras. Buck-naked still. It didn't occur to the guy to put on a robe until after the three of us were all puffing away.

Neither Leo nor I said a word to each other as we walked back through the showroom and out the door, trailing cigar smoke and getting stared at by every single employee at the dealership. When we got back in Leo's Kharmann Ghia, I flopped my head back and groaned. "Well," I said, "I don't know about honest and God-fearing, but you already got the grandchildren part of the equation under way."

"Did you check out that shriveled little weenie of his?" Leo said. "Shit, man, I've seen bigger ones in a bottle of Heinz baby gherkins." Pulling out of the lot, we both broke out in that kind of laughter that almost chokes you to death. The tears fell, we laughed so hard. "If I ever get saggy tits like that, do me a favor, will you, Birdseed?" Leo managed to get out. "Take me someplace and shoot me." Speeding along the access road, laughing our fucking heads off, we rolled down our windows and chucked those stinking cigars.

I still say it's screwy when you think about it, though: the way Dessa and I derailed and Leo and Angie didn't. Well, they *did* derail, for a while—back when that dance club Leo was managing went belly up. Le Club, it was called. The owner was this coke-headed rich boy from Fairfield who got Leo fond of blow. Rik, the guy's name was—used to have a heart attack if someone accidentally put a "c" in his first name. That was the one time when I let my friendship with Leo lapse. I just couldn't stomach what the coke was doing to him—the stunts he was pulling, the way he was treating Angie. Then Rik's daddy's accountant drove up one afternoon and went over sonny boy's books. Next thing you knew, Leo was out on his ass.

While Leo was in drug rehab—which the Constantines financed—it came out that he'd knocked up one of the hostesses at Le Club. Even I didn't know about that little adventure; like I said, Leo and I didn't spend a whole lot of time together back then. The hostess—her name was Tina—had already gotten the abortion but decided to ring Angie's doorbell one afternoon for spite. Angie got a legal separation, and she and Shannon moved back to her parents' home. Then, three months after Leo got out of treatment, Angie and he were pregnant again. The old man had a shit fit; he'd been lobbying hard for a divorce. Instead, he ended up hiring Leo as a salesman at the dealership.

That was one of the few times I ever saw old Diogenes cave in on something. Angie had had to *beg* her father to give Leo that job. She argued that people can change for the better—that Leo *had* changed. That he was a wonderful father to Gene and Thula's only grandchild. That if Angie herself could forgive and forget, why couldn't the Old Man? Gene told her forgiving and forgetting was one thing and putting that hemorrhoid on the payroll was another. Then Angie delivered the clincher: if it had been *Dessa* asking, he'd say yes without blinking. *Dessa* wouldn't have to stand there and humiliate herself like this on top of everything else she'd gone through.

Which was probably true.

"What do *you* think of your sister's request?" the Old Man sat on our sofa one night and asked Dessa. Thula sat next to him, silent and sulky, her arms folded over her big belly. They'd driven over in their big New Yorker after fighting about it for a week. In sixteen years of marriage, it was the only drop-in visit Dessa's parents ever paid us.

"I guess I vote for anything that might heal things, Daddy," Dessa said. "But it's up to you. Can you handle Leo working there?"

"Can I *handle* it? Yes. Do I *want* to come into my place of business every morning and face that idiot she was foolish enough to marry? No, I do not."

I sat there and kept my mouth shut, but it wasn't easy.

Sure, Leo had his faults. Sure, he had fucked up royally. But it pissed me off when Gene called him that. We had a history, Leo and me. He had his good points, too.

"You're not doing it for him," Thula said. "You're doing it for your daughter. Your flesh and blood."

"Who says I'm doing it, *period*?" the Old Man shot back.

"Angie's got a point about Leo being a good father, though," Dessa reminded him. "He and Shannon are crazy about each other." Dessa and I were crazy about our niece, too, though being around her was a mixture of pleasure and pain for Dessa. She'd had two miscarriages by then. Having kids was the one thing Angie could do better than Dessa. Now that she and Leo were back together, she'd told her sister, she wanted another one after this second one was born. Maybe more.

"Where would *you* be, I'd like to know, if my father didn't give you a chance?" Thula asked her husband. I didn't get the full significance of it at the time, but in her quiet way, Thula was bringing out the heavy artillery in front of Dessa and me. As shrewd a businessman as Diogenes Constantine was, his original capital had come from his wife's family—a fact he never forgot and always, ultimately, respected.

So that was that. By the end of the month, Leo was one of "Gene's Boys" in the full-page newspaper ads of the *Three Rivers Daily Record*—his wide, goofy face staring up at you from the newsprint, a cartoon bubble hovering over his head that declared the Constantine Motors motto: "Make me an honest offer, I'll give you an honest deal!"

Leo came back carrying my coffee and sipping one for himself. Which was just about average for one of his self-improvement plans. "Goddamn you, Birdsey," he said. "If I didn't have to make a fresh pot and stand there smelling this stuff, I wouldn't have wanted it."

The sign-painter had three letters stenciled now: G-O-D.

"God?" I said, nodding toward the window. "You guys getting religion around here or something?"

"Nah. When he's finished, it's going to read, 'Goddamn It, Get in Here and Buy a Car Before We Go Under!' "

"That bad?"

"Welcome to the nineties." He leaned closer, lowered his voice. "The Old Man took a hit on his third-quarter numbers. He was on the phone half of yesterday with the regional manager. With United Nuclear closing down and Electric Boat talking about more layoffs, nobody's buying. Everyone's just holding on to what they've got. Hey, how old's that truck of yours, anyway?"

"Eighty-one thousand miles old," I said, "and running fine."

"We could put you in a new Dodge or an Isuzu for—"

"Uh-uh," I said. "Forget it."

"No, listen. That Isuzu five-speed is a nice little truck."

"I don't care if it's the chariot of the gods, Leo. I got a compressor that's wheezing like it's got emphysema and power-washing equipment I've got to replace in the next couple of years. Not to mention a brother who's locked up with a bunch of—"

"Hey, I hear you, Dominick. But Pop and I could put you into a—"

"Uh-uh. *No.*"

"Okay, okay," Leo said, palms up. "All I'm saying is if you change your mind, me and Pop'll fix you up."

I yawned. Took another slug of coffee. Yawned again.

"You look like shit, Birdsey," Leo said. "You been sleeping?"

"Nope."

"I didn't think so. No offense, man, but you're starting to look like a basset hound. Don't worry. You'll get him out of there. I'm telling you. Go see a lawyer." He stood up again, yanking his lapels and checking himself out in the plate glass. "See, the thing *you* don't get about these threads, Dominick, is that it's the law of the jungle. Granted, fourteen-fifty's a lot to pay for a suit. But if you want quality, you've got to pay for it."

I looked up at him. "That's not the law of the jungle. The law of the jungle is: Only the strong survive. Eat or be eaten."

"Exactly!" Leo said. "Next audition I go to, the casting director walks out in the waiting room. Who do you think he's going to notice first—all the miscellaneous assholes wearing Levi's and sweatshirts or the guy in the Armani?"

Omar walked by drinking a Diet Coke. Wearing a lime-green suit.

"Yo, Omar, get over here," Leo said. "This guy sitting here says the law of the jungle is: Eat or be eaten. What do you think?"

Omar took a swig of his soda. "Either one's fine with me," he said. "When's she getting here?"

"My man!" Leo shouted. He jumped out of his seat and high-fived the guy. He'd been the hero of the sports pages four or five years back: Omar Rodriguez and his famous buzzer-beater that had won Three Rivers the state high school championship. He'd gone on to UConn; it was during the mideighties. Played for them a couple of years. It was just before Calhoun came in as coach and UConn hit pay dirt in the NCAA. If I remembered right, Omar played a season in Europe before he packed it in. Point guard, he was.

"You hear that, Lorna?" Leo said. The saleswoman across the floor looked up from her paperwork. "Omar says, eat or be eaten. It's ladies' choice."

She looked down again, shook her head. "You guys," she said.

"Cut the crap, Leo," I mumbled. "You're embarrassing her."

"Am I embarrassing you over there, Lorna?" Leo called. "Hurting those virgin ears of yours?" Without looking up, she gave him the finger.

Leo turned back to me. "See, it's the same with selling cars, Dominick. Which is why this suit's a smart investment twice over. Joe Six-pack comes in here with his fat-assed wife and his Patriots cap, you got basically one whack at him, see? So you stand up, let him know he's dealing with class—intimidate the slob a little with how good you look. Use the upper hand to your advantage. Shoot a little spark up the little woman's thighs while you're at it, too, see, so that *she's* in your corner at decision time. Gives you a hidden advantage before you even open your mouth. You see what I'm saying? The law of the jungle."

"So who does that make you?" I said. "Cheetah?"

He adjusted his tie, yanked on his shirt cuff. "Hey, what do you know, Birdseed? Like I said, you wear bib overalls."

"And that makes you a better person than me, right, Leo?" I shot back. "The fact that you dress up for work like a high-class gigolo?"

Lorna looked over at me. I cleared my throat, looked away.

"No, Birdsey, it doesn't make me a better person. Or a worse person, either. Because we're all whores. Even what's her face—that dried-up little nun over there in India, looks like a monkey. Even the Pope. Even housepainters."

I snorted at him. "How's a housepainter a whore?"

"Would you climb up a second-story ladder and scrape paint up your nostrils for *free*? For the fucking *art* of it? You got your bod out there like the rest of us, Numb Nuts. Don't fucking kid yourself."

"All right. How's Mother Teresa a whore?"

"I couldn't tell you how," he said. "I don't know the woman personally. I just know the theory's right. That we're all playing bang-for-the-buck. Putting whatever we got out there on the open market. I'm just being *honest* about it."

A couple of racquetball games ago, Leo himself had called car sales a "whore's game." Had started blabbing about this top-secret book on the psychology of selling cars that no one in the business is ever supposed to talk about. Last winter, Gene, Costas, and Peter Jr. went to some "Meeting the Challenges of the Nineties" convention down in Miami—Leo got his nose whacked out of joint because *he* wasn't invited—and when they came back, the three of them with their Mediterranean tans renewed, they began making changes. Pushing leasing, hiring women and minorities to sell. The Old Man paid big bucks for these "consultants" to come in and work with the new sales team. Taught them how to categorize each potential victim who's outside on the lot peeking at sticker prices. They've got this system where they know before someone even walks through the door which salesperson's going to stand up smiling with his hand stuck out, and which approach they're going to use.

Minority customers is what Omar's assigned: blacks and Ricans, according to Leo. He also gets sports nuts, women in their twenties, and—get this—gay guys. The obvious ones—the ones sizing up his butt and his basket when he goes back and forth to Costas's office during the "good cop/bad cop" routine—that game they play where the Nice Sales Guy has to keep checking the numbers with the Big Bad Manager and the customer's supposed to sit there with his free cup of styro-coffee and feel sorry for the poor guy's humiliation. Isn't that weak?

The consultants even worked with Leo and the others on the kind of shit they have laying around on their desks and filing cabinets. They call it "image projection." Omar's got two or three of his trophies sitting behind him and these autographed pictures—one of him and Larry Bird and another of him with President Bush. Leo's got framed pictures of Angie and the kids. They face out toward the customers, not in at Leo. Lorna keeps magazines on her desk—*Glamour, Cosmo, People.* She's got this picture of Michael Bolton taped to her filing cabinet.

"So who does she get?" I asked Leo. "All the women in love with Michael Bolton?"

"Nope," he said. "I get them. Lorna gets professional white guys who think they can outdeal some dippy broad. Not that I should be telling you any of this, Birdseed. I could get in deep doo-doo for talking about it. But you should see these guys who buy from Lorna—they strut out of here with their bill of sale, cocky as hell, like they just fucked her or something. Not a clue in the world that two hours before they signed on the dotted line, we sold the exact same model with two or three more options for five hundred dollars less."

Leo claims he's fucked Lorna twice—once at her place and the other time in a LeBaron lease car they had to deliver in Warwick, Rhode Island. According to Leo, the two of them were sitting there in this parking lot where they'd stopped for coffee on the way to Warwick and she just started playing stroke-a-thigh with him. She was so hot for him, he says, he had to pull off somewhere on the Old Post Road and put her out of her misery. Doubtful, though. Sometimes Leo's life sounds a little too much like a porn movie to be real. "If this stuff really happened and isn't some pipe dream," I told him, flat out, the day he told me about him and Lorna, "then you're a fucking idiot. She took you back once, Leo. Twice might be pushing the envelope."

"I'm not an idiot," Leo told me, grinning. "I'm a sex addict. Me and Wade Boggs."

When I got up to go, Leo walked me back to my truck. "Body on this thing's getting some corrosion, huh?" he said, fingering the passenger's side door panel.

"Well, stop poking at it then," I said.

I got in. Started her up and backed out of the space. Gave Leo the peace sign and began driving out of the lot.

"Hey, Dominick!" he yelled. "Hold up!"

He came running toward me, that fancy suit of his fluttering in the breeze. He bent down to the window. "Hey, I was just thinking," he said. "You know that visitors' list you were telling me about? How many visitors did you say your brother gets?"

"Five."

"Well, tell him he can put me on it. If he wants to. I wouldn't mind going down there, seeing how he's doing. Saying hello. I mean, what the hell? 1969, you said? I go back a few years with Thomas, too."

I nodded—took in the gift he'd just given me. "I'll mention it to him," I said. "Thanks."

"No problem, man. Later."

See, that's the thing with Leo: he's sleazy *and* he's decent. He takes you by surprise. I drove away, one hand on the wheel, the other wiping the goddamned water out of my eyes. Leo, man. The guy's a trip.

thirteen

The Indian cemetery that abuts the sprawling Three Rivers State Hospital grounds is a modest place: a few rolling acres studded with nameless foot markers, a hundred or so gravestones. A ten-foot-high pyramid of plump, fist-sized rocks stands at the center of things. The monument commemorates Samuel, the Great Sachem of the Wequonnoc Nation, who, back in the seventeenth century, warred against the neighboring Nipmucks and Pequots and Narragansetts and cast his lot with the white settlers. Big mistake. The town of Three Rivers was incorporated in 1653 and grew steadily and legally, the law being white. Conversely, the reservation kept shrinking in acreage, the tribe's numbers dwindling.

The cemetery's oldest tombstones date back to the eighteenth century and are now so eroded and encrusted with parasites that trying to read them is a joint effort between vision and touch. Below the ground are the remains of Fletchers and Crowells, Johnsons and Grays—assimilated Indians, assimilation meaning that the dick doesn't discriminate. The newer stones mark the graves of Wequonnoc war dead: veterans of the Civil and Spanish American Wars, the World Wars, Korea. During the late 1960s, when America was once again eating its young, the Indian graveyard's final stone was erected. It honors Lonnie Peck, Ralph Drinkwater's older cousin, killed by sniper fire in the jungle near Vinh Long in 1969.

That was the summer man landed on the moon and Mary Jo Kopechne went off the bridge at Chappaquiddick and Woodstock happened. The summer I saw Dessa Constantine jockeying drinks at the Dial-Tone Lounge and fell in love for life. Home from college after our bumpy freshman year, my brother and I had jobs as seasonal laborers for the Three Rivers Public Works Department. Ralph Drinkwater, Leo, Thomas, and me: what a quartet *that* was. Our duties included clearing brush out at the reservoir, pumping the sump at the town fairgrounds, and mowing the town cemeteries, the little Indian graveyard among them. Thomas's voices had already started whispering to him by then, I think, but not so badly that you couldn't just call him high-strung or moody and then get lost in your own more important shit. We were nineteen.

A decade or so later—after the doctors had stripped Thomas of the label "manic-depressive" and declared him, instead, a paranoid schizophrenic—my brother's then most recent medication had begun to stabilize him. Had seemed like the *real* miracle this time. Dosed with two hundred daily milligrams of Thorazine, Thomas was granted a state hospital "grounds card." He was pleased and proud of this achievement; the card allowed him roaming privileges in the company of staff or family.

Dessa and I would pick him up on Sunday afternoons at the entrance to the Settle Building and wander with him past the hospital's original brick monstrosities and the Ribicoff Research Center, and then over the rear boundary and down to the Sachem River. My brother liked to watch the water, I remember—watch its movement and listen to it. He liked, sometimes, to take off his shoes and socks and wade into the cedar-tinted current. More often than not, the three of us would walk the banks and end up a quarter of a mile down, at the little Indian graveyard. Dessa and I would study the stones—the remnants of those old, buried lives—while Thomas sat on the grass, smoking cigarette after cigarette and reading his Bible. By then, he had already pretty much proclaimed himself God's right-hand man and a target of the KGB. Sooner or later, he'd get up off the ground and follow me and Dess, treating us to some Biblical interpretation or another—some prediction of coming doom based on what he'd seen in the papers or on the nightly news or in his sleep. I'd get itchy and tell him we had to go—hustle ahead of both him and Dessa and back to Settle, where I could sign him back in and leave. Check off my obligation for another week and get myself the hell out of there. "Be patient with him, Dominick," Dessa used to advise me on the drive home from those visits. "If he needs to babble, then just let him babble. Who's he hurting?" My answer to that question—*Me!* He's hurting *me!*—went unspoken. If you're the sane identical twin of a schizophrenic sibling—if natural selection has somehow allowed you to beat the odds, scoot under the fence—then the fence is the last thing you want to lean against.

At the southern end of the Indian graveyard, a packed dirt path leads away from the river, up past pines and pin oaks and cedars, and then through a grove of mountain laurel that blossoms spectacularly every June. Climbing higher and higher, you follow the path and the sound of water, jump from boulder to boulder, and come abruptly to a spot that takes your breath away. The Sachem River, suddenly visible again, rushes between two sheer rock cliffs and spills crazily over a steep gorge.

Everyone in Three Rivers calls this spot, simply, the Falls. According to history or legend or some hybrid of the two, Chief Samuel once pursued an enemy sachem to the cliff's edge and forced him to a no-win decision: either surrender and be executed or attempt the suicide leap to the opposite ledge. The enemy chief leapt, making it somehow to the other side, but breaking his leg in the process. Samuel arrived shortly after and leapt, too, intact. He quickly overtook his nemesis, bashed in his skull with a rock, and then sliced and ate a piece of his shoulder to signify to the universe who had prevailed. My tenth-grade American history teacher, Mr. LoPresto, was the one who told us about Samuel's flesh-eating, delighting in the class's squeamish reaction to the gory details.

Mr. LoPresto was a plump, middle-aged man with hips

like a woman. I hated his sarcasm, which he usually aimed at the weakest kids in our class. Hated his mannerisms and the wen on his forehead and the way he landmined his tests with trick questions. He paced when he lectured, referred to us collectively as "historians," and yanked his pants up over his little paunch every couple of steps, every few sentences. It was an embarrassment to me that Mr. LoPresto and his white-haired mother went to the same Sunday Mass as my family. They sat each week in the second pew and were always the first ones up for Communion. They seemed to *bound* up to that rail. "The body of Christ," Father Fox would say, suspending the host before Mr. LoPresto. As he prepared to receive the bread-made-flesh, you could hear Mr. LoPresto's pious "Amen!" all the way in the back of the church, where I slumped and scowled.

When Mr. LoPresto told us about Samuel's having eaten the shoulder of his enemy, he advised us not to judge the Indians by our own higher standards. *They* were indigenous savages and *we* were the product of ancient Greece and Rome and the rest of Western civilization. It was like comparing apples to oranges, monkeys to men. We sat silently and obediently, taking the notes we'd regurgitate back up to him at test time.

The Falls is and has been both a calendar picture and a trouble spot in Three Rivers. Kids cut school and party there, taking crazy risks and pushing the evidence in the town's face: smashed beer bottles, graffiti spray-painted somehow on the sheer faces of the cliffs, underpants up in the trees. I don't begrudge these kids their hormones or their illusions of immortality. I took stupid risks myself out at the Falls when I was their age—did things I'm not comfortable thinking about twenty-something years later. But I worry for them. Suicides have happened there. Accidents, murders. The year Thomas and I were third-graders, the dead body of a girl from our class was found out at the Falls. Penny Ann Drinkwater: Lonnie Peck's cousin, Ralph's twin.

Penny Ann and Ralph were the only other set of twins at River Street School. Back then, we thought of the Drinkwaters as colored kids, but they were mixed: part black, part white, part Wequonnoc Indian. They were a year older than

Thomas and me. Penny Ann should have been in fourth grade like her brother, but she'd stayed back and been assigned the seat right next to mine.

I didn't like her. She had one long eyebrow instead of two separate ones, and some mornings she smelled like pee. She ate paste, sucked on the buttons of her ratty blue sweater, chewed her crayons. To this day, I can see her big front teeth smeared hideously with waxy pigment.

The Drinkwaters were poor; we all knew that. At our school, you could usually tell who the needy kids were: most of them were in the reading groups that stumbled along and lost their place and read baby books. They stood at the chalkboard, stumped by arithmetic problems, their backs turned against the sea of waving hands of kids who knew the answers. The teachers were less patient with the poor kids than they were with the rest of us. But Penny Ann wasn't just poor; she was bad.

She stole. She stole Genevieve Wilmark's rhinestone barrettes and Calvin Cobb's glass egg and Frances Strempek's autographed photo of Annette Funicello, which was later found ripped into small pieces and hidden under the wastebasket. She snatched kids' recess snacks right out of our cloakroom, my own and Thomas's included. When something in our class was missing, it became routine for Miss Higgins to walk to the back of the class and inspect Penny Ann's sloppy desk. Penny Ann always denied any knowledge of how the stolen goods had landed in her possession. She cried frequently. Her nose ran. She was always coughing.

She disappeared the day a surprise snowstorm freed us from school early and our mothers put on their kerchiefs, boots, and winter coats and trudged through the driving snow to pick us up. The day before, Penny Ann had stood in front of me in line at the drinking fountain, turned abruptly, and told me her mother was buying her a Shetland pony as soon as she returned from a trip. Contempt for Penny Ann was acceptable at River Street School—even the nice kids sprayed her with imaginary cootie spray—and so I looked her in the eye and told her she was nothing but a big fat liar. Then I got my drink and went back to class and told Miss Higgins a lie of my own. "Penny Ann Drinkwater was eating Oreos in the hallway," I said. "She said she stole them from some kid. She was *bragging* about it."

Miss Higgins wrote a note to Miss Haas, the principal, and sent us both to the office. Miss Haas believed me, not Penny Ann, whose repeated denials turned into a combination of crying and coughing that sounded oddly like a dog's bark. Miss Haas thanked me for my information and told me to go back to class. I remember returning to Miss Higgins's room feeling satisfied that justice had been served, and then belatedly remembering that the theft of the Oreos had been pure invention on my part. Well, Penny Ann *must* have stolen someone or another's cookies at some recent point, I reassured myself. Miss Higgins announced from the front of the room that I was a good citizen for having reported a theft. Then she wrote it on the board: "Dominick Birdsey is a good citizen." The public declaration made me feel both pleased and queasy, and although I didn't meet his eye, I could feel, across the room, my brother's gaze.

For the week or so after Penny Ann disappeared during the snowstorm, the newspaper printed her picture—first on the front page, and then in the middle pages, and then not at all. At school, her empty chair, her sloppy desk with its contents protruding, became harder and harder to sit next to. Her shabby blue sweater had been balled up and jammed in there. One sleeve, threadbare and loaded with what my mother called "sweater pills," hung halfway to the floor. I asked to have my seat changed, but Miss Higgins denied the request.

Then one day Penny Ann's face was back on the front page, enlarged. GIRL'S BODY FOUND AT FALLS, the headline declared. The paper said Penny Ann's unknown killer had broken her neck and taken off all her clothes—details that both scared and baffled me. It was the middle of February. There was a foot of snow. Had making her cold been part of her torture?

In the wake of Penny Ann's unsolved murder, I began to resurrect her in my nightmares. In one dream, she was giving me a ride on her new Shetland pony when the spooked animal began galloping without warning toward the edge of the Falls. In another, she kept daring me to lick a skeleton.

In a third dream, Miss Haas announced matter-of-factly over the intercom that Penny's murderer had come to our school for a visit and was now going to kill the kindergartners. When I had these nightmares, I would scream out and my mother would come stumbling into Thomas's and my room. She'd rub my arm and tell me I was safe and let me leave the light on. Illuminated but still too afraid to sleep, I'd hang my head over the edge of the top bunk and watch my sleeping brother—listen to the evenness of his breathing, count his breaths into the hundreds—until his repose became my own.

At school, we held a penny drive in Penny Ann Drinkwater's honor. Our class was in charge, and Miss Higgins chose me and my brother to be the "bankers," an appointment that inflated me with a sense of importance. The job required us to separate and walk each morning from classroom to classroom, up and down rows, holding out the cardboard buckets into which kids dropped their nickels and dimes and pennies. Ralph Drinkwater, Penny's brother, was in Mrs. Jeffrey's class. He never gave any money, never even looked at the bucket when I passed by his desk, even when I dared to pause for a second and wait. One morning, when Thomas was collecting in Mrs. Jeffrey's room, Ralph kicked him in the leg. Thomas reported what had happened, but Ralph denied it and Mrs. Jeffrey said it had probably been an accident. That same day, out at recess, I saw Ralph trip a boy during a game of Red Rover, Red Rover. His victim had been barreling full force toward the human chain which the game obliged him to break through. When Ralph tripped him, the boy fell face first on the blacktop and skidded, and by the time the teacher on duty had been summoned, he was a bloody, shrieking mess with red teeth and a raw meat chin. I didn't squeal on Ralph the way I would have squealed on his sister. Penny Ann had been an annoyance; her brother was lethal. He, too, began to menace me in my dreams.

With the money we collected from the penny drive, the school bought a small willow tree and a plaque. By then, the air had warmed and the Pawtucket Red Sox had resumed play and even the most stubborn gray gutter ice had melted and trickled down the storm drains. Penny Ann's mother came to the tree-planting ceremony at the edge of the schoolyard. She had a single eyebrow like Penny's and straight black hair and big dark circles under her eyes that made her look like a raccoon. Earlier that week, Miss Higgins had made us write essays on what we would always remember about our dear friend Penny Ann. Unlike my brother, I usually knew what teachers were after and had written so sentimentally that I was one of the students chosen to read my tribute aloud into the microphone. My words brought tears to the eyes of the adults at the tree-planting, Penny Ann's mother and the lady reporter from the *Daily Record* and Miss Haas included. Miss Haas's tears surprised me. Our principal had a reputation for being mean and "strictly business." Beyond that, she and I had collaborated in making Penny Ann's life miserable not twenty-four hours before her abduction and murder. Together, we had made her cry. Had made her bark like a dog. But when I walked back to my metal folding chair after reading my essay, Miss Haas reached out, took my hand in her own liver-spotted hand, and squeezed it. During the ceremony, Ralph Drinkwater stood beside his mother. (No father materialized, not even talk of a father.) Ralph behaved poorly during the speechmaking, I remember, fidgeting so badly that his mother had to yank his arm twice and even swat him one in front of the entire school.

FORMER NEIGHBOR CHARGED IN GIRL'S DEATH, the newspaper announced one morning during the summer. Now the killer had a name, Joseph Monk, and a face. "This guy is pure evil," my stepfather told my mother that morning at breakfast after he'd read aloud the details of Monk's confession. "The electric chair's too good for *this* guy after what he did to that poor little kid."

Neither Ray nor my mother knew I was within earshot—in the pantry adjacent to the kitchen, making toast. Their strategy had been to avoid talking about our murdered classmate in front of Thomas and me—to shield us, I suppose, from a situation we had been facing every day at school, anyway.

"They ought to take him out somewhere and beat his head in with baseball bats," Ray continued. "Snap *his* neck just like he snapped *hers*."

"Okay, okay," my mother said. She told Ray she didn't even want to think about that poor little girl and rushed from the room in tears. Ray slapped the newspaper back down on the table and went after her.

I walked into the kitchen and picked up the newspaper. Brought it with me back into the privacy of the pantry where I stood, transfixed, staring and staring at the photo of "pure evil" being led up the police station steps. I had expected a monster—someone dirty and ugly with wild hair and crazy eyes. Someone like the crazy man who had gotten on the city bus that time and sat next to my mother and touched her leg. But Joseph Monk had short hair and black glasses, a half-smile on his lips, a plaid short-sleeve shirt.

I was still staring at Joseph Monk's ordinary looks when my toast popped up, startling me, and I saw, in the toaster's chrome face, my own face, familiar and strange. And when my brother walked sleepily, innocently, into the kitchen that morning, I remember feeling, suddenly, alone and afraid—as untwinned as Ralph Drinkwater.

After a while, Ralph disappeared from the hallways at River Street School. It wasn't a noticeable exit; I remember his absence dawning on me after the fact. He resurfaced years later during my sophomore year of high school, when he slouched into Mr. LoPresto's American history class midsemester and handed him an "add" slip.

I recognized him immediately but was surprised by his size. I was, at fifteen, a backup forward on Kennedy High's JV basketball team and already wearing shoes three sizes bigger than my stepfather's. Sometimes at supper I ate third and fourth helpings now, and drank milk in such vast quantity that my mother would watch with a combination of awe and fear. I had an inch and a half and twelve pounds on my brother. Ralph Drinkwater had seemed big and tough and intimidating at River Street School. Now he was a runt.

"Drinkwater, eh?" Mr. LoPresto said, reading the slip. "Well, that's what I always say. When you're thirsty, drink water." Several of the students rolled their eyes and groaned, but Ralph betrayed no reaction whatsoever. LoPresto assigned him the empty desk at the back of the room next to mine. On the way there, Ralph glanced at me for a half-second with what may or may not have been a flicker of recognition.

For the next several weeks, nothing much happened in American history. At the front of the room, LoPresto talked and paced and hiked up his pants; in back by the windows, Ralph slouched in his seat and sometimes dozed. Then one day, there was an unexpected showdown between the two.

Over the clank of the radiator, Mr. LoPresto was droning on and on about Manifest Destiny. Chin resting in the palm of my propped-up hand, half-stupid from too much monologue and radiator heat, I was listlessly recording notes about America's sacred, Darwinian duty to spread Democracy when, next to me, Ralph Drinkwater laughed out loud. A belly laugh, public and unmistakable.

Mr. LoPresto stopped talking and squinted back at Ralph, whose laughter was immediately interesting to him. To all of us. Ralph's outburst was the only interesting thing that had happened all period.

"Do you find something amusing, Mr. . . . uh . . ."

LoPresto grabbed for the seating chart in an effort to refresh his memory as to Ralph's existence. "If you find something comical, Mr. Go Drink Water, then maybe you'd like to share it with the rest of us. We all like a good joke, don't we, historians? Please. Tell us. What's so funny?"

There was a long pause, I remember—a standoff. Ralph's face was a smirk, but I saw small tremors in his hands. His foot was tapping the linoleum a mile a minute. As the rest of us waited, I glanced over at his notebook. He had recorded nothing about Manifest Destiny but, instead, had drawn a bizarre caricature of Mr. LoPresto. In the picture, our teacher stood stark naked, equipped with both a baseball bat–sized hard-on and a pair of breasts that rivaled Jayne Mansfield's. Ralph had sunk an ax into LoPresto's head.

"I *repeat,*" Mr. LoPresto said from the front of the room. "What's so *funny*?"

He would not have challenged most of the other boys in our class: Hank Witkiewicz, who was state wrestling champ, or Kevin Anderson, whose father was the city engineer. He probably wouldn't even have challenged me, a nonstarter in

JV basketball, a pipe fitter's stepson. But Mr. LoPresto, oblivious of Ralph's notebook illustration, had misjudged him as an easy target.

"*Nothing's* funny," Ralph finally said. LoPresto might have let it go at that—might have continued with his argument about America's holy duty to expand her territory—but Ralph's face would not stop smirking.

"No, go on," Mr. LoPresto said. He parked his big fanny atop his desk. "Tell us."

"It's that stuff you're talking about," Ralph said. "That stuff about survival of the fittest and the Indians disappearing because of progress."

I looked down at the notes which, until then, I had been recording in a kind of trance. It surprised me, I remember, that Ralph Drinkwater had been paying better attention than I had.

"Manifest Destiny, you mean?" Mr. LoPresto said. "It's *funny* to you?"

"It's bullshit."

It was shocking enough that Ralph had cursed in class, more shocking still when Mr. LoPresto repeated it.

"Bullshit?" Now our teacher was smirking, too. He smirked at Anderson and Witkiewicz and they smirked back. *"Bullshit?"*

He stood, walked halfway up Ralph's aisle, and then stopped. "Well, for your information, Mr. Go Drink Water, I hold a bachelor's degree in United States history from Fordham University and a master's degree in nineteenth-century American history from the University of Pennsylvania. I was under the impression that I knew what I was talking about, but I guess I stand corrected. What, pray tell, are *your* credentials?"

"My what?" Ralph said.

"Your *credentials*. Your *qualifications*. In other words, what makes *you* an expert?"

"I *ain't* an expert," Ralph said.

"Oh. You *ain't*?" Nervous titters from some of the girls.

"No. But I'm a full-blooded Wequonnoc Indian. So I guess not all of us 'indigenous people' have 'disappeared' like you just said we did."

Ralph had coffee-colored skin and green eyes, a modified Afro hairstyle. I was pretty sure he was only "full-blooded" for the sake of argument. Mr. LoPresto denied that he had used the term *disappeared.* He suggested that if Ralph listened more carefully, he wouldn't be so apt to misinterpret. But he *had* used that word; it was right there in front of me in my notes. Mr. LoPresto took a pink slip from his desk, wrote out Ralph's disciplinary referral, and ordered him down to the office. "Fuckin' faggot," Ralph mumbled as he rose from his seat. If Mr. LoPresto heard him, he pretended he hadn't. The classroom door slammed behind Ralph, and we waited out the sound of his boots clomping down the concrete corridor.

"Well, then, historians," Mr. LoPresto finally said. He smiled and, with a flourish, extended his hand back at Ralph's empty seat. "I guess the Indians have disappeared after all." Kevin and Hank and some of the others guffawed.

Not me. I was suddenly, powerfully, on Ralph's side—abruptly filled with an anger that set me shaking, a hot-faced shame that brought water to my eyes. Penny Ann had stolen kids' food because she was *hungry.* When Ralph had tripped that boy during Red Rover—had kicked my brother in the leg—he'd been tripping and kicking everyone who had stolen from him and lied to him and killed his sister. I had *lied* about those Oreos, knowing—even as a third-grader—that they would believe me, not Penny Ann. I had piously collected pennies on her behalf and then whitewashed her memory at the tree-planting. Had whitewashed my sin.

Rewritten history.

In my *fantasy* version of what happened next, I stood and confronted Mr. LoPresto—avenged all of the losers and nonstarters that he and his sarcasm had shat all over. Threw the motherfucker up against the wall in the name of justice and followed Ralph out of there. But in reality, I sat there. Said nothing. Wrote down whatever he said so that I could puke it back to him at test time.

Years and years later, when my marriage to Dessa was still intact but in trouble, the evening manager at Benny's hardware store called me one rainy spring night and asked me to please come and get my brother. Thomas had taken a bus from the hospital into town—he'd earned the privilege—and then had caused a disturbance, screaming and flinging items off shelves in the electrical department because everywhere he looked, he saw surveillance equipment. The store manager knew who we were—we had all gone to school together—and said he thought I'd have wanted him to call me instead of the police. When I got there, I convinced Thomas to lower his voice and to remove from his head the coat hanger hat he'd fashioned for himself. (It scrambled enemy frequencies, he told me; Soviet operatives were in pursuit.) I thanked the manager and coaxed Thomas into my truck. On the way back to the hospital, neither of us said much, letting the windshield wipers do the talking instead. And when we got back to Settle and the night nurse was escorting Thomas to his room, he turned back unexpectedly and said, "That's the trouble with survival of the fittest, isn't it, Dominick? The corpse at your feet. *That* little inconvenience." His voice, I remember, was cool and rational. To this day, what he said was a mystery to me. To this day, I can't decide if it was his craziness or his sanity talking.

After his showdown with Mr. LoPresto, Ralph Drinkwater came to history class less and less frequently, and when he did attend, it was always with a cool, indelible half-smile on his face. By second semester, he stopped coming to school altogether. In May, he quit officially. "Left: Ralph T. Drinkwater," was the succinct way the absentee sheet put it. At the end of that same school day, as my classmates and I streamed out of the building and hustled toward our buses, I saw Ralph reeling and staggering on the sidewalk across the street. "Get fucked!" I remember him screaming drunkenly, his middle finger stabbing the air. "Hey, *you*! Hey, *white boy*! Get *fucked*!"

I boarded the school bus, telling myself he hadn't been shouting it directly at me—that his condemnation was random and miscellaneous.

That he was just plastered.

Wasted.

Smashed.

fourteen

Dr. Patel had warned me she might be running late. If I saw a blue Volvo with Delaware plates in the parking lot, I could come right up. If I didn't, I'd have to wait until she got there. There was no receptionist, she said; hers was a part-time private practice.

A week and a half had passed since Thomas's transfer to Hatch. Barred from visiting my brother until the security clearance came through, I had settled for daily telephone updates from Lisa Sheffer and several over-the-phone conversations with Dr. Patel, Thomas's new psychologist. Both Sheffer and Dr. Patel had assured me my brother was holding his own. An infection at the site of his skin graft had been successfully treated with a more powerful antibiotic; his vitals were fine. Although he was generally uncommunicative with the other patients of Unit Two and troubled by the surveillance cameras that were everywhere, he was eating and sleeping satisfactorily. He had developed a rapport with Sheffer, whom he seemed to trust. And now that he'd been back on Haldol for several days, the medication was beginning to reduce his agitation. All in all, Thomas's treatment had been proceeding on course.

But that afternoon, while I was high up near the eaves at

the Roods' house, Joy had left a message which Ruth Rood shouted up to me from the ground below. Dr. Patel wanted to see me. There'd been an incident involving my brother. Could we get together later in the day?

We'd set up the appointment for five o'clock. At Dr. Patel's suggestion, I'd agreed to meet her not at Hatch but at her office in that two-story strip mall on Division Street where she shared space with a Blockbuster Video, a Chinese takeout restaurant, a locksmith, and Miss Patti's Academy of World Dance. For ten minutes, I had sat in the truck, watching people go in and out of the video store with their blue plastic boxes and catching glimpses of the little girls in leotards who leapt and tippy-toed, arms raised, past Miss Patti's upstairs window. Six- and seven-year-olds, maybe. About the age Angela would have been, if she had lived. I picked out a dark-haired kid in a yellow leotard. Made her Angela.

I still did that sometimes: snatched back my daughter's life from the children of strangers. Made *them* the parents of a dead child instead of Dessa and me. In this particular fantasy, Dessa and I were still together and Angela's drawings and school papers were stuck to our refrigerator door and her dance recital was coming up. Our lives were happy and matter-of-fact.

She died in May of 1983, three weeks and three days after her birth. I was the one who found her. Hard as it was, I've always been grateful for that much, at least: grateful that I'd spared Dessa that little bit. I'd been up past midnight the night before, correcting term papers for my students because I'd promised to get them back before the weekend. Then, in the morning, I'd turned off the alarm in my sleep and overslept. I was halfway out the door that morning when I decided, hey, screw it if I'm a little late, I'll sneak back and kiss the baby. Dessa had been up twice with her in the middle of the night. She'd mumbled the morning report while I was dressing. Said she was seizing the moment, sleeping in.

My plan was to *really* get to know Angela once school was out for the summer. Once my schedule let up. I was assistant coach in track that spring and a member of the negotiating committee for the union. And there were always my brother's needs to factor in—visits every Sunday afternoon at the bare minimum. I was planning to slow down after school let out, though. Take some time, take stock. After all, I was a father now. I'd have all of July and August to hang out with my new family. Two months of playtime with my wife and baby daughter.

Her arms were raised up stiff over the edge of the bassinet: that was the first thing I saw. Her fists were clenched. There was pink foam at her nostrils and the corners of her mouth. Her small bald head looked gray. I stood there, shaking my head, telling myself, *Uh-uh, no, this wasn't happening*. Not to *our* baby. Not to Angela. But I knew. I knew even before I picked her up and held her against me, trying to get Dessa's name out. Trying to scream for Dessa.

In the seven years since, I have tried on sleepless nights to unsee the EMTs, the doctors, the priest my in-laws called in from the Greek church, the hospital social worker—all of them performing their useless rituals. On the worst anniversaries—Angela's birthday, or her death day, or sometimes around the holidays—I still see Dessa, doubled over and wailing as the ambulance pulled out of our driveway. Or later on that morning, at the hospital, shrunken inside her clothes. Those two milk stains on the front of her shirt. . . . She didn't want to take anything to dry up, I remember; she could have, but she didn't want to. It was a kind of denial, I guess—a rejection of life's ability to be *this* bad. Later on—in the middle of the next night—I'd woken with a start and gone all over the house looking for her. Finally found her in the downstairs bathroom, standing dazed and topless in front of the medicine cabinet mirror, the milk dripping from her nipples like tears.

In those first days afterward, Dessa was a zombie and I was Management Central—the one who dealt with the coroner and the cops and all those casseroles people kept bringing to the door. The covered-dish brigade. Most of that stuff just sat in our refrigerator and went bad; we couldn't eat. A week or so later, I threw everything out, washed everyone's dishes, and went driving around town returning them. I forced myself to do it. I usually just left the stuff at the door and drove away without ringing the bell. I didn't want to talk to anyone. Hear over and over and over those empty if-there's-anything-I-can-do's.

Dessa couldn't handle going to the funeral home to make the arrangements, so her mother and my mother went with me instead. Big Gene drove us over there, in one of those luxury demonstration models from the dealership instead of his own car. One of those big showboat Chryslers. As if riding in style to the funeral parlor was going to be some kind of comfort. As if anything was. Gene stayed out in the car, I remember. He wouldn't or couldn't go in.

A lot of the funeral's a blank. I remember the pink tea roses that blanketed Angela's silver casket. Remember Dessa and her sister huddled together, propping each other up. It was brutal receiving condolences from my high school students—inarticulate enough to begin with, they were nearly tongue-tied by their teacher's baby's death. (In the weeks prior, I'd been entertaining my classes with comical stories of diaper-changing and car-seat straps and baby vomit—had turned fatherhood into a comedy routine. My world history class had organized a lottery around the baby's weight and height and birth date; the winner, Nina Frechette, came to the wake and sobbed inconsolably.)

And then there was Thomas. I clench still when I remember my brother, down in the basement of the Greek Orthodox church after the burial, eating a powdered doughnut and telling Larry Penn, a guy I used to teach with, that there was a strong possibility Angela's death had been arranged by his enemies as a warning to *him*. I forget whether it was the Colombian drug cartel or the Ayatollah who was pursuing Thomas that month, but I could have grabbed him and slammed him against the fucking wall when I overheard him say that—making our daughter's death about *him*. I remember Larry holding me back and Leo rushing over. "What's the matter, Dominick? What can I get you?"

"Just get him the fuck out of here," I said, jabbing a finger in Thomas's face, then storming into the men's room. When I came out again, hoarse and red-eyed and with a sore foot from kicking the shit out of the cinder-block wall, Leo was standing guard outside the door and everyone was carefully not looking at me. Ma came toward me and clasped my hand. Thomas had disappeared with Ray.

For a month or more, Dessa didn't want to see anybody

except her mother and sister—didn't even want to get out of bed and get dressed half the time. So I ran interference. Answered the phone and the door, did the shopping, handled the insurance and the hospital bills. My mother-in-law and Angie stayed with Dessa during the day while I was at school. Sometimes Big Gene would show up, too, in the evening. He and I would sit out in the kitchen together, talking about some new construction going up someplace in town or how the import market was killing U.S. car sales or *any* other subject, really, as long as it wasn't dead babies. When we ran out of stuff to say, we'd sit there watching TV—*Jeopardy!* or *Lifestyles of the Rich and Famous* or some baseball game. I was struck suddenly by the idiocy of sports: the importance people placed on a bunch of guys chasing a ball. But we watched, Gene and me, grateful because neither of us knew how to talk about it and both of us were afraid, I think, of the silence a turned-off TV made. The one time Gene said anything directly about Angela's death was the day it happened. We "two kids" would get over our loss, he assured me, as soon as we had another baby. We should start as soon as possible. He and Thula had lost a baby between Dessa and Angie, he said; Thula had miscarried in her second month. As if *that* was the same thing as having her—seeing and holding and changing her and *then* losing her. A lot of people did that: prescribed pregnancy as the answer to our grief. People assumed the feel and sound and smell of her was disposable. Replaceable. As if all Dessa and I had to do was erase over our daughter like videotape.

Dessa took an indefinite leave of absence from Kids, Unlimited! She resigned from the board of directors at the Child Advocacy Center where she volunteered. "I just can't *do* kids right now," she told me.

She started taking long walks with the dog. Old Sadie. Goofus. They'd be gone for hours—whole afternoons sometimes—and then Dessa would come back with bits of dead leaves in her hair, burrs and vines in her sneaker laces. Come back in a fog, most of the time. She never wanted company, other than Sadie. Never wanted me. Never said where she was going. I followed them once—trailed them down to the river, out past the Indian graveyard and up to the Falls. Dessa just sat there for over an hour, watching the water tumble over the gorge. I was worried: it's pretty desolate out there. Pretty isolated. I bought her a can of pepper spray in case some creep bothered her. Sadie *looked* more ornery than she was. If push came to shove, I didn't want to chance that damn dog turning tail. But Dessa wasn't interested in protecting herself. She'd forget to take her spray can more often than she'd remember it. She'd be gone all afternoon and there that little can would be—still sitting on the shelf over the washer and dryer, which is where she kept it.

We held on for a little over a year, Dessa and me. We never really fought. Fighting took too much energy. Fighting would have ripped the scab right off the raw truth—that either God was so hateful that He'd singled us out for this (Dessa's theory) or that there *was* no God (mine). Life didn't *have* to make sense, I'd concluded: that was the big joke. Get it? You could have a brother who stuck metal clips in his hair to deflect enemy signals from Cuba, and a biological father who, in thirty-three years, had never shown his face, and a baby dead in her bassinet . . . and none of it meant a fucking thing. Life was a whoopee cushion, a chair yanked away just as you were having a seat. What was that old army song? *We're here because we're here because we're here because we're here. . . .*

Sometimes at supper or up in bed, Dessa would try to talk about her feelings. Talk about Angela. Not at first. Later. Three or four months afterward. "Uh-huh," I'd say. "Uh-huh." She'd want me to open up, too. "What good would it do?" I told her once. "We'll talk and cry and talk some more, and then she'll still be dead." I stood up and walked out of the room—got the fuck out of there before my fucking head exploded.

On the worst nights, I'd go out to the garage and bang things. Slam things. Or else grab the keys. Get out onto the highway and crank up our '77 Celica—go eighty or ninety miles an hour, as if putting the pedal to the metal was somehow going to blow the pain out of our lives. Sometimes I'd end up out by the river myself. Drive down there and park somewhere off the road, skirt the state hospital and the Indian graveyard. Once I even climbed the rock ledge out at the Falls the way we'd done when we were kids—when a party was your buddies and a couple of joints and a bottle of Boone's Farm apple wine. I climbed it again, now, because I thought that maybe from that high-up perspective—the *long* view of things—all that crap about God's will and God's mercy might make more sense. But it never did. How could you make sense out of a coffin three feet long? Out of an empty crib in a room with moon-and-stars wallpaper, a mound of stuffed animals sitting and waiting for nobody?

Sometimes I'd wake up in bed in the middle of the night and hear Dessa in the baby's room, sobbing. One night I heard her talking to Angela—murmuring baby talk down the hall. I sat up and listened to it, telling myself that only a complete and total son of a bitch wouldn't get out of bed, go down there and hold her, comfort her. But I just couldn't do it. Couldn't quite make my feet hit the floor, no matter *what* basic human decency was ordering me to do. So I sat there and listened to her, like she was a ghost or something: the ghost of what we'd had and lost, the ghost of our life the way we'd planned it out. I've wondered a million times since then if we could have salvaged things at that point—if I'd just gotten out of bed and gone to her that night I heard her talking to the baby.

After a while, she started going to these SIDS parent support group meetings down in New Haven. Pressuring me to go, too. I went twice and then I couldn't go back. Just couldn't do it. Because that group pissed me off, if you want the truth—all those touchy-feely types connecting with their sorrow. Wallowing in it. The men were the worst—bigger crybabies than their girlfriends and wives. There was this one guy, Wade, who yapped so much about his pain that I felt like breaking his fucking jaw just to shut him up. At the second and last meeting I went to, this couple brought cake and ice cream with them. It was their dead son Kyle's first birthday that week and the mother, Doreen, wanted to acknowledge it. To celebrate. So we all sang "*Happy Birthday, Dear Ky-ul*" and said what flavor ice cream we wanted and then chowed down. . . . The Dead Babies Club. The weekly pity party. If it helped Dessa, then fine. It helped her. But it just seemed weird to me. Ghoulish. Eating birthday cake for a dead baby. I had one bite, and then I couldn't swallow any more.

Dessa was always a good planner. She saw ahead of time the wallop Angela's first birthday was going to pack and began planning accordingly. By then, she had turned her leave of absence from the day care center into a resignation. She called her parents' travel agent and went off by herself on a trip to Greece and Sicily. She'd wanted both of us to go—wanted us to use the life insurance money we'd gotten for Angela and take that trip. (Big Gene had taken out the policy on the day the baby was born; he did the same thing for Angie and Leo's kids.) I could have gotten the time off from work, I guess, but I said no. Not then. Not before the school year was over. And when she pressed me—asked me if I'd do it for *her* sake—I lost my temper. Told her I thought it was sick—taking a trip financed with death money. But the unspoken truth, the thing I couldn't say, was that I was afraid to confine myself in a ship's cabin with her. On a ship, you couldn't grab the keys and drive off. On a ship, you could make another baby. We'd made love maybe a dozen times in the year after the baby's death, always with her di aphragm in, and each time I pulled out early, anyway. The thought of that trip scared the crap out of me. "Go without me," I encouraged her. And so she called my bluff and went.

Here's how *I* celebrated Angela's first birthday: I got a vasectomy. Looked up urologists in the phone book, then looked the one I'd picked right in the eye and told him there *was* no wife to get a consent form from—that I'd come to a conscientious decision as a single man concerned about overpopulation. That was during the preliminary visit. The list of rules the nurse gave me said you were strictly forbidden to drive yourself home from the surgery. But that's what I did. Drove down to New London on a Friday afternoon, got disconnected, and drove home again. Went to bed with a book and an icepack on my scrotum. *Zen and the Art of Motorcycle Maintenance* was what I read. I'd always meant to catch up to that book. The novocaine wore off after the first couple of hours and I was grateful for the physical pain, which was nothing next to a year's worth of despair. I had finally played a little *defense,* you know? Fatherhood had fucked me over and now I'd fucked it back. Never again, I told myself. It was a zen thing: sterility and I were one.

I didn't tell anyone about it. Not Dessa, whenever she called from some port or another. Not any of my buddies at school—Sully or Jay or Frank, who'd given me a blow-by-blow account of his *own* vasectomy the year before. Not even Leo. I hadn't hung out much at Leo and Angie's all that year. Couldn't handle my larger-than-life nieces—the smell of their hair, the sounds of their voices—or the way Leo and Angie's house was land-mined with Fisher Price toys and runaway Cheerios on the kitchen floor. Couldn't stand Angie's "Dominick, can I talk to you for a minute?" and then her big speeches where she invited me to get in contact with my pain. Where she tried to appoint herself my personal shrink. As if *she* had life all figured out. As if she didn't have a husband who'd been porking other women behind her back since practically the month after they were married.

Dessa came home from the Mediterranean looking tan and rested. Looking sexy. The second night she was back, we were in the kitchen, splitting a bottle of wine and looking at the first of her trip pictures when I interrupted her in the middle of some story she was telling about someone's passport mix-up. I put my hand on her hand, my fingers in the spaces between her fingers. Leaned over and kissed her. Pushed the bangs off of her forehead. Kissed her again. I put her in my arms for the first time in a long, long time. "Hi," I said, my lips grazing her ear.

"Hi."

We went upstairs, both of us a little drunk, a little anxious. She stopped in front of the baby's room. "In here," she said. We lay down in the dark, hip to hip, our backs against the beige carpet of that empty room. The blinds were up. The moonlight outside half-lit things. Dessa reached over and started touching me where it counted and talking about Angela—saying that sometimes now she could remember little things about her without feeling like she'd just been kicked in the stomach. She said she could still smell her sometimes—smell the memory of baby powder and milky breath as distinctly as if Angela were still alive. Still feel the warm, small heft of her body—the relaxation of her muscles as she drifted off to sleep. Had I experienced anything like that?

I told her no.

She said she was glad *she* had. These returning memories comforted her. She said she felt they were gifts from God: He had taken Angela away from us, and now, in small ways, He had begun to give her back. It was something, she said, she could accept now. Something she could live with. We had made her; she had existed. She'd been more than just her death.

We were half-undressed already when Dessa sat up and undressed the rest of us. She straddled me. I reached up and cupped her breasts. Reached down and fingered her. She was already wet.

We had donated all the baby furniture to Goodwill—her stuffed animals and books and mobiles, all those shower presents. I'd been meaning for a whole year to take down the moon-and-stars wallpaper—to score and soak and strip that blue and silver paper and turn Angela's room back into an office. But on that particular night I was glad I hadn't—glad we were making love under those foil stars, that prepasted blue yonder. I'd put up that paper when Dessa was in her eighth month— when Angela was alive and kicking inside of her.

She lifted herself up and then eased down again, putting me inch by inch inside of her. For a couple of seconds, we just waited like that, completely still. "We're celebrating something," she said. She began to rock toward me, away from me, toward, away. "Celebrating my return, the return of life. I love you, Dominick." I couldn't hold back. Couldn't wait for her. Thrust three or four times and came.

At first she just smiled. Stopped. Then her mouth turned down and she started to cry. Just a few shudders at first and then out and out wailing. Crying that claimed her whole body. She lay down on top of me, her chin in the crook of my shoulder, and held on and shook us both. I felt myself go soft, get smaller—slip out of her like a guilty intruder.

"It's okay," I whispered into her ear. "I'm out of practice, that's all. Temporarily out of synch."

"I'm so scared," she said.

I thought she meant scared of getting pregnant, and so I chose that moment of intimate failure to tell her what I had done. Told her about the vasectomy. She stopped crying and, for a minute or more, everything was still. Then she started punching me—flailing away at my shoulders and my face. One shot even landed against my windpipe—started me gasping and choking. It was a kind of temporary insanity, I guess. Dessa's the nonviolent type, the kind that carries bugs outside so she won't have to kill them. But that night she gave me a gasping attack and a bloody nose. She had wanted another kid, she said. That's what she'd gone all the way to Italy and Greece to decide. That's what she'd come back wanting to tell me.

After that night, there was a couple of weeks' worth of single syllables—lots of closet-cleaning and meals that she'd cook and then not eat. One day she rented a carpet cleaner and shampooed every rug in the house. Another time, I came home and found her stripping off the wallpaper in Angela's room. Telephone calls went back and forth between her and her sister, between her and her friend Eileen from the SIDS group. Then, on a Saturday morning in July, she told me she was leaving me.

I reminded her again what I'd been saying over and over for a week: that vasectomies could sometimes be reversed. That if she needed to, we could try it.

"The vasectomy's a symptom, not the problem," she said. "The problem is your anger. What you did was just one expression of the anger you've felt through this whole thing—the blame you put on me."

I asked her how *she* knew what *I* felt inside, and she said she could feel it. That it seeped out of me like radiation. That I was practically toxic.

It was a morning for metaphors. She still loved me, she said, but our marriage had become like a game of One, Two, Three, Red Light. Every time she made a half-step's worth of progress, my anger would catch her and send her back to the starting line. "When I was away, I could feel myself getting stronger, day by day," she said. "Really, Dominick. I thought to myself that I was finally through something. That the worst of it was over. Then I got off the plane and saw you in the airport lounge, and I was back at the starting line again. I get short of breath when I'm around you. It's like you rob me of oxygen. So I'm going. I have to go because I have to protect myself. I have to breathe."

I told her I could do better. Promised her I'd go back to the support group if that was what she wanted. I begged her. Followed her all the way down the stairs and out to the car, begging. Making promises. But there all that soft luggage was, waiting in the backseat and the opened trunk of the Celica. All those tan bags she'd bought for her trip to Greece. "Come on, Sadie," she called, and that stupid dog of hers climbed in the front seat and Dessa got in and they left.

They just left.

I read for the rest of that summer. Styron. Michener. Will and Ariel Durant. I gravitated toward fat-book authors. I didn't look up. Didn't return calls. The day after Labor Day, I returned to my classroom. Made class lists and seating charts and gave the new kids my usual speech about high expectations and mutual respect. Only this time, I didn't mean any of it. It felt like I was playing a record. I distributed books. Started matching unfamiliar names to new faces. I thought I was doing okay. Then one day in late September, I cried in school. Fell apart without warning right in front of my fourth-period class. Right in the middle of some stupid, innocuous instruction about how to punctuate the bibliography for their first paper: whether to put a period or a comma after the author's name—something as safe and ordinary as that. I was at the blackboard and everything just hit me at once: I had a baby dead in the ground and a twin brother in the nuthouse and a wife who'd left me because she had to breathe. I should have left the classroom—I know I should have—but I couldn't. I just went to my desk and sat there. Started sobbing. And the kids sat there, frozen, facing me. None of us knew what to do. Neither did the vice principal after one of the kids went and got him. Fuckin' Aronson. For reasons I don't understand to this day, he called the police and they came and took me away—walked me right past a boys' gym class playing soccer and Jane Moss's art class, outside sketching the trees, and into an unmarked cruiser.

"Dominick?" I remember Jane Moss asking me, touching my sleeve. I remember the odd sensation of living in the middle of that experience and feeling, simultaneously, like it was something happening at telescopic distance. Like something I was looking at through the wrong end of a pair of binoculars.

The shrink I went to labeled what had happened an anxiety attack. Situational, he said. Understandable under the circumstances, and 100 percent fixable. I could tell he was downscaling it for me because I'd told him about Thomas—had confided that I was afraid my twin brother's craziness had begun to claim me, too. It's funny: I can remember that therapist's face—his rusty red hair—but not his name. During my second session, he said that in the weeks ahead, we'd be addressing the feelings of anger and grief and betrayal the baby's death had left me with. Later on, in a month or two, we'd probably get into the difficult work of exploring what it was like growing up as Thomas's twin. As my mother's and Ray's son.

"His *step*son," I corrected him.

"His stepson," he repeated. Made a note.

I never went back.

Never went back to teaching, either. I couldn't. How can you cry in front of a bunch of teenagers one week and then go back the next and say, "Okay, now, where were we? Turn to page sixty-seven"? I mailed my letter of resignation to the superintendent of schools and got through the worst shit and insomnia by reading. Solzhenitsyn, Steinbeck, García Márquez. All that fall and winter, I kept heating the soups and pastas Ma sent over (it was easier now that the casserole dishes came from a single source) and turning pages and turning down Leo's requests that we go for a couple of beers, go up to the Garden to see the Celtics play, go up to Sugarloaf and ski. "She's got a boyfriend, doesn't she?" I asked Leo one afternoon when he stopped by.

"How should I know?" he shrugged. "You think she checks in with me about what she does?"

"No, but she checks in with her sister," I said. "Who is he? The guy with the braid? I saw them downtown."

"He's just some asshole artist," he said. "Makes pottery

or something. It won't last. He's not Dessa's type. *You're* her type."

But it did last. I kept seeing them all over town. Kept seeing his van in the driveway out at that ramshackle farmhouse she'd rented. Saw that jazzy, psychedelic mailbox he painted with both their names on it. And so, little by little, it sunk into my thick skull that I'd lost her for good. Lost both my daughter *and* my wife, and that goofball of a dog to boot. And one night, somewhere around 3:00 A.M., I finally looked myself in the medicine cabinet mirror and admitted it to my own baggy, sleep-starved face: I'd lost her.

When springtime came around, I bought a compressor and a network of scaffolding at an estate auction. Stenciled the door of my pickup and reinvented myself as a housepainter. Premier Painting. Free estimates, fully insured. "Customer satisfaction is our highest priority." *Our:* like I wasn't the painter and the bookkeeper and the rest of the goddamned shooting match. I met Joy a year later, a month or so after my divorce decree came in the mail. We get along okay. It's not perfect, but it's all right.

When Dr. Patel's wide face appeared at the truck window, I jumped. "Oh, my goodness, I'm sorry I startled you," she said. "You were deep in thought. Forgive me."

"No, that's okay," I said, shaking my head, trying to compose myself. "I was just sitting here vegging out."

"Well, come up, come up, Mr. Vegetable," she said, a warm smile undercutting the flippancy.

On the narrow staircase up to her office, we brushed by a row of little girls hurrying from Miss Patti's to a soda machine at the bottom of the stairs. One of them, the dark-haired girl in the yellow leotard—my resurrected daughter Angela—accidentally bumped against my arm. Up close, I could see the leotard had a pattern: alternating monkeys and bunnies.

"Whoops! 'Scuse me," she said, her smile revealing missing front teeth. She and her friends descended the stairs in a flurry, a chorus of giggles.

fifteen

"Hold these, please," Dr. Patel said, handing me her briefcase and a small tape recorder. She put her key in the lock, turned it, and swung open her office door. "Come in, come in," she said, taking back her things.

Her office was a single room stripped to the essentials: small desk, two opposing easy chairs, a cube table, Kleenex for the crybabies. The walls were white and blank. The only nod toward decoration sat on the floor by the window: a cement statue two feet tall—one of those smiling Indian goddesses with the waving arms and the shit-eating grin.

"Sit down, please, Mr. Birdsey," Dr. Patel said, hurrying off her trenchcoat.

"Which chair?" I asked.

"Whichever chair you'd like."

Today, her sari was gold, green, and blue. That peacock-color blue. I've always liked the color. "I'm going to put on a pot of tea before we start," she said. "Will you join me?" My "yes" took me by surprise.

From a closet, she removed a hot plate, a jug of water, a small box of tea-making paraphernalia. I walked over and looked closer at the statue of the goddess. She was wearing a headdress with a skull and a cobra and a crescent moon.

Maybe this was what peace of mind was all about: having a poisonous snake on your head and smiling anyway.

"I see you're looking at my dancing Shiva," Dr. Patel said. "He's sweet, isn't he?"

"It's a *he*?" I said. "I thought it was a *she*."

Dr. Patel laughed. "Well, 'he' or 'she' is not as grave a matter with the gods as it is with us mere mortals," she said. "Whereas we are fixed and inflexible, they are impish, transmutable. Perhaps, for you, Shiva *is* a woman. I have—let's see—chamomile and peppermint and wildberry spice."

"Whatever," I said.

"Ah, 'whatever.' The favorite word of ambivalent American men. All day long, 'whatever, whatever.' It's passive-aggressive, don't you think?"

I told her I'd have the spice. She nodded, smiling—pleased with me. "Do you know much about Hindu beliefs, Mr. Birdsey?" she asked. "Shiva is the third god of the Supreme Spirit. The Hindu trinity. Brahma is the Creator, Vishnu is the Preserver, and Shiva is the Destroyer."

"The Destroyer?" I said. "Well, if they ever make the movie, Arnold Schwarzenegger could play the lead." The second I made the crack, I realized it was probably sacrilegious or something. I'll do that: make a wise remark when I'm nervous. When a situation's new. But Dr. Patel's soft chuckle short-circuited my apology.

"No, no, no," she said, shaking a scolding finger. "Shiva represents the *reproductive* power of destruction. The power of renovation. Which is why he's here in this room, where we dismantle and rebuild."

She sat down on the chair opposite mine, a notepad and the tape recorder in her lap. Through the partition came the faint plunking of piano music, a dance teacher's muffled command to lift and *reach,* lift and *reach.* "And of course, Shiva is a dancing god, too, so I know he's happy with my next-door neighbors. All the little tap dancers and ballerinas."

I nodded at the tape recorder. "What's that thing for?" I said. "Are you taping us or something?"

She shook her head. "I would like to *play* something for you, Mr. Birdsey. A bit later. Let's chat first."

"All right," I said. "What's going on with him, anyway? The message you left said something about an 'incident.' "

She nodded. "I believe I've told you over the telephone about your brother's preoccupation with the surveillance cameras. Have I not?"

"His fear of being watched," I said. "It's always been an issue with him."

She sighed. "With most paranoid schizophrenics, of course. But at Hatch, the cameras are a 'necessary evil.' On the one hand, the activities at a maximum-security facility certainly need to be monitored, for everyone's protection, patients and staff alike. On the other hand, many of the patients feel intimidated by them. Resentful. Which is entirely understandable."

For the past two or three days, Dr. Patel said, Thomas had grown more agitated about being watched. More and more preoccupied with the omnipresence of the cameras. He'd begun to stare and mumble at them, she said—to whisper threats and curses, engage in a one-sided dialogue. "I've tried to address the behavior in our sessions, but he has not wanted to discuss his worries. With me, he has remained rather uncommunicative. Polite and politic during some sessions, glum and nonverbal during others. Winning the trust of someone suffering from paranoid schizophrenia is a long, slow process, Mr. Birdsey. And a tenuous one. A rickety bridge."

"The incident?" I said.

"Ah, yes, the incident. This morning at breakfast, your brother apparently began shouting and throwing food at the camera mounted on the wall in the dining room. When an aide attempted to contain him, the table where he'd been sitting was overturned and—"

"Thomas turned it over?"

She nodded. "From what I understand, several of the other patients' meals landed on the floor and something of a melee followed. The guards were called and the situation was quickly brought back under control, but your brother had to be restrained and confined to the close observation room."

"Restrained how?"

"Four-point restraint. His arms and legs."

I flashed on an image from when we were kids: Ray dragging Thomas to the "bad boy seat" in the front parlor—yanking him by the wrist with one hand, the toes of Thomas's shoes skidding along the floor. One time I saw Thomas's feet lift all the way *off* the floor—saw Ray wallop him one, my brother tethered by his skinny arm, swinging back and forth and screaming.

"The restraints were removed by midmorning," Dr. Patel said. "As quickly as possible. He was back in his room by eleven." She didn't want to alarm me, she said; it was not abnormal for patients suffering paranoia to decompensate—to act out occasionally. She was telling me about the incident because I'd made it clear to both Lisa Sheffer and her that I wanted to be kept informed.

"How is he now?" I asked.

He'd been sullen for the rest of the morning, she said. Withdrawn, even with Lisa. At lunchtime, he had refused to go back to the dining hall and made do instead with a piece of fruit and some cookies. "But I'm happy to report that our session this afternoon was a productive one. This afternoon we made some progress. Now I must also tell you that I've talked to Dr. Chase, the staff psychiatrist—just before I left the Institute to come here, as a matter of fact. Dr. Chase is considering, as one of his options, increasing Thomas's dose of Haldol."

"Oh, Jesus, here we go," I said. "Take off the restraints and straitjacket him with his meds instead. That's bullshit. That's business as usual." She started to say something, but I interrupted her. "Excuse me, but I'm not interested in hearing any bogus justifications for it, okay? I've heard them all before. Your American colleagues are way ahead of you, Doctor. They've been pulling that particular stunt for years."

The smile stayed on her lips, but I thought I could read resentment in her dark eyes. "My colleagues have been pulling *what* particular stunt?" she asked.

"Overmedicating him when he freaks out. Look, the last time they upped his dosage after an episode, he was like something out of *Night of the Living Dead.* You'd go to visit him, and he'd just sit there, ramrod straight, his hands and legs twitching away like someone had plugged him into the wall socket."

"Well, Mr. Birdsey, neuroleptic medications are mostly effective in lessening delusions and hallucinations," Dr. Patel said. "They allow a reprieve from the *positive* symptoms which plague the patient. Unfortunately, the medication often enhances the *negative* symptoms: the flat affect, the Parkinson's-like tremors we so often see in—"

"Turn off his voices by turning him into one of the body snatchers. Jesus Christ, I *know* all this! I know all about Stelazine and Prolixin and all the other fun stuff. You think you can have a brother in and out of the state hospital for twenty years and not already *know* about all this chemical voodoo?"

She said nothing. Waited.

"Look, he *hates* taking Haldol, okay? Even the smaller dose. It makes him feel like shit. I don't want you guys turning him into a zombie just because he pitched a fit and turned over a table. Just because it's convenient to the staff. Upping his dosage is unacceptable."

"It's unacceptable to me, too, Mr. Birdsey," Dr. Patel said. "Please give me credit for some professional ethics. I am an *advocate* for your brother, not an enemy. Not a mad scientist."

We sat there facing each other. Her eyes, young and mischievous, belied her salt-and-pepper hair. I opened my mouth to say something, then changed my mind.

"I told Dr. Chase that, in my opinion, increasing the dosage of your brother's haloperidol—his Haldol—was probably ill advised. And certainly premature. And I'll be glad to relay your concerns to the doctor as well."

I let go a laugh. "As if *that* counts for anything. As if one of the divine gods of psychiatry would do anything except listen politely and then proceed the way they damn well wanted to, anyway."

Her smile remained constant. "That's quite a broad indictment, Mr. Birdsey," she said. "You're very angry. Aren't you?"

"Hey, I've earned the right. Believe me. But what *I* am is irrelevant. All I'm saying is that if he—"

Smiling still, she reached across and covered my hand with her own small butterscotch-colored hand. Squeezed it.

Relaxed the pressure. Squeezed again. The gesture was so unexpected, it disarmed me. Shut me up for once. "Squeeze back," she said. And I did.

"Drug treatment with schizophrenics is always a balancing act," Dr. Patel said. "As you said, a trade-off. But unless the patient is in danger of harming himself or other people, it's always best to err on the side of caution. So you and I are in agreement. Isn't that nice? And in these days of American malpractice suits, it's my guess that Dr. Chase will probably be inclined to agree as well. To listen more carefully than you'd think to the opinions of the patient's family." She gave me that mischievous look again. "Ah," she said. "The water is ready for our tea. Isn't that lovely?"

She stood and went over to the hot plate. While I waited, I looked again at her smiling statue. What had she called him? Shiva?

She handed me a small yellow cup, hand-painted with monkeys. Poured the tea from a matching monkey pot. It smelled delicious. Warmed my hands.

"It's ironic that I never drank tea when I was growing up in India," Dr. Patel said. "I acquired the habit later on when I was in my twenties. During my London days."

I wasn't sure why, exactly, but I was starting to like her in spite of myself. "Is that where you studied psychology?" I said. "In England?" This was the kind of small talk I usually had no patience for.

"Oh, no, no. When I was in London, I was earning a degree in anthropology. I got my psychology degree later on at the University of Chicago. I studied with Bettelheim. Do you know his work? Dr. Bruno Bettelheim?"

I shrugged.

"Oh, you must read him! *The Uses of Enchantment, The Informed Heart.* Splendid works."

"So you're both, then?" I said. "A psychologist *and* an anthropologist?"

She nodded. "Actually, my interest in the one field *led* to the other. They're quite interrelated, you know. The stories of the ages and the collective unconscious. Have you ever read Jung, Mr. Birdsey?"

"A long time ago. In college."

"How about Joseph Campbell? Or Claude Lévi-Strauss? Or Heinrich Zimmer?"

"I'm a housepainter," I said.

"But surely, Mr. Birdsey, you must read other things besides the side of a paint can." Her smile, her soft, nasaly voice cut against the sarcasm. "Your brother says you're an avid reader. That your house is filled with books. He was quite animated when he was telling me about you. He seems so proud of your mind."

"Yeah, right," I laughed.

"Oh, I'm serious, Mr. Birdsey. You think otherwise?"

"I think . . . I think Thomas doesn't focus much on anything or anyone beyond Thomas."

"Elaborate, please."

"Because of his disease. He *can't* think beyond himself. . . . Compared to, you know, the way he used to be."

"How did he used to be?"

"Before the illness?"

She nodded.

"Well . . . when we were kids, he used to worry about me all the time. I used to get into things, you know? Take chances. Take risks. And he'd get nervous about it. Try to talk me out of it. He was always worried about me."

"What kinds of risks did you take?"

"Oh, you know. Climb ledges we weren't supposed to climb. Jump off the garage roof. Cut through people's yards. Kid stuff. But Thomas would always hang back. Warn me I was going to get in trouble or get hurt or something. He was as big a worrywart as she was."

"Your mother?"

"Yeah."

"So when you look back, you would say that you were the more adventurous brother?"

"My mother used to call Thomas the bunny rabbit and me the spider monkey because . . . well, who cares, right? I'm going off on a tangent here."

"No, no. Continue, please. You were the spider monkey because . . . ?"

"Because I was always getting into everything. I was Curious George." She smiled. Waited. "He's a . . . a character in a kid's book. A little monkey who's always getting into—"

"Indeed, he is, Mr. Birdsey. An inquisitive little fellow. My granddaughter would have me read her *Curious George* day and night if she had her way. But go on. You were the more curious brother and Thomas was more . . . ?"

"More mellow, I guess."

"Excuse me, please. By that, do you mean more relaxed or more fearful of venturing forth?"

I looked up at her, impressed by her insight. "More fearful," I said.

She jotted something down. "The little bunny rabbit," she said.

"We were like that right from the beginning, I guess. That's what Ma used to say. Thomas would sit there in the playpen and watch me escape."

"Clarify something for me, Mr. Birdsey. Thomas was your mother's bunny rabbit because . . . ?"

"Because he was . . . soft, I guess. More affectionate. They were pretty close."

"Your mother and Thomas?"

"Yes."

"Closer than your mother and you?"

I looked away. Nodded. Watched my fingers lace and unlace themselves.

"And what about your father?"

"What about him?" I snapped back.

Dr. Patel waited.

"We never knew our father. . . . Do you mean Ray? Our *step*father?"

"Yes, your stepfather. Which of you was closer to him? Or were you equally close?"

I laughed one of those nothing's-funny laughs. "We were equally distant."

"Yes?"

"Well, not distant. You couldn't *get* much distance from Ray. He was always in your face. . . . Cautious, I guess you'd say. We were equally cautious of Ray."

"Go on."

"He would . . . he used to pick on Thomas. I mean, he'd

get on both our cases, but Thomas was the one who usually got it with both barrels. Thomas or Ma."

"And not you?"

"Uh, not so much. No."

"And how did that make you feel? To be the one of the three not getting it 'with both of the barrels'?"

"What? I don't know. . . . Good, in one way, I guess. Relieved. But not so good, either."

"Not good how?"

"It made me feel . . . it made me feel . . ."

"Yes?"

"Guilty, I guess. And, I don't know . . . *responsible.*"

"I don't understand. Responsible for . . . ?"

"For keeping them safe. They wouldn't stand up for themselves. Neither of them. So it was always me who—hey, look, *I'm* not the patient here. I thought we were talking about Thomas."

"And so we are, Mr. Birdsey. You were saying that, before his illness began to manifest itself, he used to worry about you and that since its onset—"

"It's like . . . there's nobody home at Thomas's anymore, you know? I look at him sometimes and he's like . . . this abandoned building. No one's been home at Thomas's for years."

I watched her thinking. Waited. "This just occurred to me," she said. "When your brother expresses pride in your intellect, pleasure about all the books in your house," she said, "he may be celebrating the achievements of his mirror image—the part of himself that is free of the burden of his disease. Do you think that's plausible?"

I shrugged. "Couldn't tell you."

"In a sense, as your identical twin, he is you and you are he. More than most siblings, you are each other. No?"

My old fear: that I was as weak as Thomas. That one day, I'd look in the mirror and see a crazy man: my brother, the scary guy on the city bus that day. . . . When I tuned back to Dr. Patel, she was talking about anthropology.

"And, oh, my goodness, the myths of the world are *laden* with twins," she said. "*Think* about it, Mr. Birdsey. Castor and Pollux, Romulus and Remus. It's a fascinating aspect of the collective unconscious, really. The ultimate solution to human alienation. I assure you, Mr. Birdsey, whatever burdens you bear as a twin, the untwinned world is quite envious. Your own and Thomas's duality is something we might wish to play with later on as we try to help your brother. But, as usual, I am getting ahead of myself. Going sixty-five miles per hour when I should be going forty."

Laughing at her own little joke, she pushed the tape recorder's "rewind" button and set it whirring. "This is a cassette recording of my session with your brother from this afternoon," she said. "The one I told you about. I thought it might be useful to play it for you and to hear your reactions. And perhaps, if you are willing, you can share some of *your* observations?"

I nodded. "Is this fair, though?"

"Fair? How do you mean?"

"In terms of—what do you call it? Patient confidentiality?"

The cassette clicked to an abrupt stop; the "rewind" button popped back up. "Ah, Mr. Birdsey, there you go again, worrying about my ethical intent. Listen." She depressed "play." Smiled down at the machine.

"Session with Thomas Birdsey, 2:30 P.M., 23 October 1990," Dr. Patel's voice said. *"Mr. Birdsey, you are aware I am taping our session today, are you not?"*

A muffled grunt, but unmistakably Thomas's.

"Would you speak up, please? Are you aware this is being taped?"

"Yes, I'm aware. I'm aware of plenty." He sounded put out. Put upon. But it was a relief to hear his voice.

"And I have your permission to replay the tape to the people we talked about? Your brother, Ms. Sheffer, Dr. Chase?"

There was a pause. *"Not Dr. Chase. I changed my mind about him."*

"Why is that?"

"Because it's too risky. How do I know he's not working for the Iraqis? In my line of work, you can't afford to take chances."

"Your line of work, Mr. Birdsey? What line of work is that?"

"No comment."

"I'm just trying to understand, Mr. Birdsey. Do you mean your coffee and newspaper business or something else?"

"Curiosity killed the cat, didn't it? Raid kills bugs dead. Don't check into the Roach Motel just yet, Dr. Earwig."

Another pause. *"Mr. Birdsey . . . I'm wondering if I may call you Thomas?"*

"No, you may not."

"No?"

"I'm Simon Peter."

"Simon Peter? The apostle?"

"I-eleven. Under the G-fourteen. Bingo, Mrs. Gandhi!"

There was a pause. *"Why do you refer to me as Mrs. Gandhi, Mr. Birdsey?"*

"Why? Because you dress the part."

"I do? Do you mean my sari?"

No answer.

"When you say you are Simon Peter, Mr. Birdsey, do you mean by that that you emulate him or that you feel you are his physical embodiment?"

"Who wants to know and why?"

"I do, because I'm trying to understand you. To help you if I can."

Deep, impatient sigh. Speaking in a revved-up mumble, Thomas began to murmur Scripture. *"Thou art Peter, and upon this rock I will build my church; and the gates of Hades shall not prevail against it; I will give unto thee the keys of the kingdom of Heaven; and whatsoever thou shalt bind on earth shall be bound in heaven."* Thomas stopped, came up for air. *"Are you following me, Mrs. Gandhi? I'm a fisher of souls! The keeper of the keys! It's not my idea; it's God's. How do you like* them *apples, Suzie Q?"*

"Suzie Q? Why am I Suzie Q?"

"How should I know why you're Suzie Q? Go ask Suzie Wong. Go check in with Suzie McNamara. Go shit in your hat while you're at it."

I was leaning forward, staring at the tape recorder. When I looked up at Dr. Patel, I saw that she was watching me. "Umm?" I said, raising my hand.

She stopped the tape. "What is it, Mr. Birdsey?"

"Nothing, probably. It's just that . . . I don't even know if it means anything, but that was . . . that was what my stepfather used to call my mother sometimes. Suzie Q. For a second there, he sounded like Ray."

"Was Suzie Q your mother's nickname? Her name was Susan?"

"No. Her name was Concettina. Connie. My stepfather used to call her Suzie Q when he was . . ."

"Yes?"

Suddenly, I felt overwhelmed. Shaky. Demoted back to my childhood on Hollyhock Avenue. "When he was mad at her. . . . When he was ridiculing her."

She jotted something down. "That's helpful, Mr. Birdsey. Thank you. This is exactly why I wanted to play the tape for you. You can provide insights and observations that I cannot get from reading your brother's medical records. Please feel free to interrupt the tape whenever there's something you want to tell me."

I nodded. "He's not usually like that, you know?" I said. "Thomas."

"Like what?"

"Snotty. Sarcastic. That go-shit-in-your-hat stuff."

She nodded. "It's all right, Mr. Birdsey. I hear much worse in the course of a day. After some of the things I hear, 'Go shit in your hat' sounds almost courtly to me." She put her finger on the "play" button, then took it off again. "Your stepfather?" she said. "Was he *often* derisive?"

I didn't answer at first. Then I nodded.

"Relax, Mr. Birdsey."

"I *am* relaxed." She looked unconvinced. "*Really.* I *am.*"

"Look at your hands," she said. "Listen to your breathing."

Each hand was a fist. My breathing was fast and shallow. I flexed my fingers back and forth. "Better?" she said.

"I'm fine. He sounds pretty fried, though, doesn't he? My brother? On the tape?"

"Fried?"

"He's worse, I mean. Worse than he was when he was at Shanley, right after. . . . I was hoping that when you said you'd made some progress today, I was hoping . . ." That's when I lost it. My chest heaved. My sobs came from nowhere. Dr. Patel handed me her box of tissues.

I looked away from her. Blew my nose. "I thought . . . I thought when I came in here and saw this Kleenex box that you had them on hand for, I don't know, hysterical housewives or something. Women whose husbands just dumped them. I feel like a jerk."

"Grief has no gender, Mr. Birdsey," she said.

I took another tissue. Blew my nose again. "Is that what this is? Grief?"

"Why wouldn't you grieve, Mr. Birdsey? Your twin brother is, as you said, an abandoned house. If no one is home, then someone is missing. So you grieve."

I stuffed the used tissue into my shirt pocket. Handed her back the box. "Yeah, but you'd think by now. . . . You figure you got a lid on things and then. . . ."

"Mr. Birdsey, human beings are not like—oh, those plastic containers—what are they called? The ones Americans buy at parties?"

"At parties? . . . Tupperware, you mean?"

"Yes, yes. That's it. People are not like Tupperware, with their lids on securely. Nor *should* they be, although the more I work with American men, the more I see it is their perceived ideal. Which is nonsense, really. *Very* unhealthy, Mr. Birdsey. Not something to aspire to at all. Never." She was waving that scolding finger at me again.

I looked over at her grinning statue. "Hey, do me a favor, will you?" I said. "Call me Dominick."

"Yes, yes. Very good. Dominick. Shall we go on, then?"

I nodded. Her finger hit the "play" button.

"Mr. Birdsey, tell me a little bit about yourself."

"Why? So you can sell my secrets to the Iraqis? Hand my head on a platter to the CIA?"

"I have no connections to the CIA or to the Iraqis, Mr. Birdsey. No hidden agendas whatsoever. My only agenda is to help you get better. To take away some of your pain. Some of your burden."

No response.

"You know, we have been talking to each other for sev-

eral days now, and yet I know very little about your family. Tell me about them."

Silence.

"Your mother is deceased, correct?"

Nothing.

"And you have a stepfather?"

Silence.

"And a brother?"

"A twin *brother. We're identical twins. . . . He likes to read."*

"He does?"

"You should see his house. It's filled with books. He's very, very intelligent."

I smiled and shook my head. "That's me," I said. "Joe Einstein."

"And how about you, Mr. Birdsey? Do you like to read, too?"

"I read the Bible. I'm memorizing it."

"Yes? Why is that?"

"Because of the Communists."

"I don't understand."

"If they take over, it's the first thing they'll do. Ban the Holy Word of God. So I'm memorizing it. If they ever find out, I'll be a hunted man. My life won't be worth a plugged nickel. I've seen their game plan. They don't realize it, but I have."

"So the Bible is the only thing you read? Not newspapers or magazines? Or other books?"

"I read newspapers. I don't have time for books. Or the patience. I had my concentration stolen from me, you know? Not wholly. Partially."

"Stolen?"

"When I was seventeen. Our family dentist was working secretly for the KGB. He planted a device in me that damaged my ability to concentrate. I went to college, you know. Did you know that?"

"Yes, I read it in your record."

"I couldn't concentrate. Dr. Downs, his name was. They expelled him during the Carter administration. Kept it very hush-hush."

"This is your dentist you're referring to?"

"That was his cover. They convicted him on my testimony. They wanted to execute him, but I said no. I talked to Jimmy Carter about it over the phone. He called me up and said, 'What'll we do?' and I said 'Thou shalt not kill. Period.' I'm not a hypocrite. Who are you playing this tape for, anyway?"

"You don't remember? I'm playing it for Lisa Sheffer and your brother. I'd also like to play portions to Dr. Chase if that's okay, although you said earlier you have some reservations about—"

"Do you think Muslims can't change their names? Obtain false identification? It's going to be put in a safe, isn't it? This tape?"

"A safe?"

"A safe! A vault! If you can't secure this cassette, then I'm stopping right now. If this tape got into the wrong hands, there could be major repercussions. Major *ones."*

"Relax, Mr. Birdsey. All of your medical records are safeguarded, including the tapes of our discussions. You have my word. Now, we were talking before about your brother. Is he a good brother?"

No answer.

"Mr. Birdsey? I asked you if your brother is a good brother."

"He's average."

I shook my head. Had to smile. "Now there's a rousing endorsement," I said.

"I went to his class once. When he was a teacher. I was an invited guest."

He was?

"You were?"

"My mother and I went. It was an open house at his school."

"Yes?"

"People thought I was Dominick. One of the parents came up to me and thanked me for helping her daughter."

"So you and your brother are hard to tell apart?"

"Very, very *hard. Especially now that he wears contacts. When we were younger, he had to wear glasses and I didn't.*

Then it was easy to tell us apart. We were like Clark Kent and Superman."

Yeah, right, I thought. Thomas as the Man of Steel.

"I *was going to be a teacher, like him. That's what I had decided to be. Then things took a turn."*

"A turn? What kind of turn?"

"I was called. Chosen by God. And then, almost immediately, they started pursuing me. What nobody in America seems to realize—least of all His Majesty George Herbert Walker Bush—is the similarity in their names: S-A-D-D-A-M. S-A-T-A-N. Get it? Get it? GET IT?"

"His train of thought is like channel-surfing, isn't it?" I said.

"He was nice to his students. My brother. They liked him. They respected his brains. But he quit."

"Why?"

"I don't know. Something happened."

"What was that?"

"I forget. I don't want to talk about it."

"And what does he do for a living now? Your brother?"

"I forget."

"You forget?"

"He paints houses. I tell him, 'Watch out for the radioactive paint, Dominick,' but he doesn't listen to me. What do I *know, right? I'm just the crazy brother."*

"Do you hear that, Dominick?" Dr. Patel said. "In his own way, he is *still* worrying about your safety."

"Mr. Birdsey, let's change the subject for a minute. Shall we?"

"Suit yourself. What do I care?"

"Why don't we talk a little about what happened in the dining room at breakfast today? Do you remember what happened? The problem in the dining room?"

"I didn't start it. They did."

"Who?"

His voice thinned—revved up a little. *"I'm just sick of it, that's all. They think they're such a covert operation, but they're not. They're so obvious, it's pathetic. I just wanted to let them know what amateurs they are."*

"Who?"

"How should I know? They're both after me. Either side would love to eat my flesh and drink my blood." He made a succession of weird gulping sounds.

"Are you afraid of something, Mr. Birdsey? Is that why you shouted and threw your food?"

Pause. *"Can I go now? I'm tired. When I agreed to enter this witness protection program, I didn't think I'd have to be interviewed all day long by underlings. No one said a word about interrogation. I'd prefer to speak to someone at the top."*

"Could you answer my question, please? Are you afraid?"

His voice sounded near tears. *"Personally, I think it's the CIA. They've messed with me before, you know? Beamed infrared lights on me. Sucked out my thoughts like they were sucking a milkshake up a straw. You think that's a pretty sight? Seeing your own gray matter go up a vacuum tube? Now I forget things, thanks to them. I FORGET things! I want to concentrate my efforts on the Persian Gulf—I want to be of service to God and my country—to let people know that God wants them to turn from Mammon to Him. But they distract me. They know how dangerous I am to them. Look what they did to one of yours!"*

"One of mine?"

"Rushdie! Salman Rushdie! Read the newspapers, Mrs. Gandhi! They silenced *him. Of course, that was completely different. That was heresy. When have* I *ever blasphemed? What sacrilege have* I *committed? Bush used to head the CIA, you know? Did you know that? I suppose* that's *a coincidence? I've lost 35 percent of my brain cells. They're being siphoned from me night and day, and there's not a damn thing I can do about it!"*

I looked out the window, tapped my fist against my lip. I wanted her to stop the tape, but their voices went on and on.

"Mr. Birdsey, do you feel that the CIA and President Bush are in collusion? Trying to steal your thoughts?"

"Trying and SUCCEEDING, thanks to their goddamned electric eyes. Their brain siphons."

"Why are they doing this, Mr. Birdsey? Why are they singling you out?"

"Because of what I did."

"What did you do?"

"This!" There was an unidentifiable noise on the tape, a staccato thumping sound.

"Mr. Birdsey, please stop that now. I don't want you to hurt yourself."

I looked up quizzically at the doc, then suddenly realized what the sound was. "He was whacking his stump against something, wasn't he?"

She nodded. "Against the table where we were seated. Only for a moment, Dominick. Only to make his point."

"Jesus," I mumbled. Sighed.

"I followed God's dictate! Cast off the hand that sinneth! And it humiliated *Bush. Rained on his Desert Shield parade. He hates the fact that I opened people's eyes."*

"About?"

"About the stupidity of war! About how, in his bumbling, incompetent way, Bush is going to bring about the end of the world unless I intervene. If he orders the bombing to begin, then we're done for. S-A-D-D-A-M. S-A-T-A-N. It's so OBVIOUS! Read your Bible, Suzie Q! Read about the Pharisees and the moneylenders and the serpent in the garden. Be my ever-loving guest."

"Mr. Birdsey, when your thoughts are being robbed, what does it feel like? Can you feel it happening?"

A disgusted sigh. *"Yes!"*

"Yes?"

"During the day I can. Sometimes they do it while I'm asleep."

"Does it hurt?"

"They're getting back at me."

"Does it hurt, Mr. Birdsey? Is there any pain when it happens? Any headache?"

"They can't just annihilate me—I'm too high-profile. Newsweek, Time, U.S. News & World Report. *I've been on the cover of every major news magazine in this country. You people can hide all the newspapers and magazines from me that you want to, but I know about them. I have my sources. Don't think I don't. I'm one of* People *magazine's 25 Most Intriguing People of the Year. I have a following! They can't kill me, so they have to settle for mental cruelty. Incarceration. Brain theft. He gets printouts, you know? Twice a day."*

"Who does?"

"George Bush, that's who!"

"Okay," I said, bolting out of my chair. "That's *enough*!" I walked over to the window. Dr. Patel stopped the tape. "You call that session a breakthrough?" I said. "That crap he was just talking is *progress*?"

"Progress in that he was much more verbal than he had been. Much more trusting and communicative. Which is good. May I pour you some more tea?"

I shook my head. Strapped my arms around myself.

"You're all right, Dominick?" she asked.

"It's just so *weird*. How lost he is in this fantasy bullshit. In his own ego."

"Well, Dominick, to a certain extent, that is true of us all. Just yesterday, I was on the road, hurrying to a meeting in Farmington when an elderly man pulled out from a side street. He was going twenty or twenty-five miles below the speed limit, and I caught myself wondering why this man was trying to make me late for my meeting." She laughed at her own folly.

"Yeah, but . . . *presidents* studying his thoughts? Only *he* can save the world?"

"It's narcissistic, yes. But please keep in mind that these grandiose delusions are not delusions to him. They are his reality. These mind-thefts and dangers are *happening*."

"I know that, but—"

"Do you? When you say, 'I know that,' do you mean you understand it intellectually or that you can feel the fear and frustration as he must feel it? Imagine, Dominick, how frightening his days must be. How exhausting. The weight of the world is on his shoulders. He can trust almost no one. What's interesting to me as an anthropologist—what fascinates me, really—is that he has assigned himself a task of *mythic* proportions."

I looked up. Looked over at her.

"Your brother is alone in the universe. Lost to his twin, lost to a conventional life. He is afloat in a world of evil and malignant power, his mettle tested at every turn. Thomas is, in effect, starring himself in his own hero-myth."

"Hero-myth? That's a little bit of a stretch, isn't it? Aren't you mixing up your two majors a little there?"

Her smile was sad. "It's his futile attempt to order the world. Do you have children, Dominick?"

We lost eye contact. The little girl in the yellow leotard flashed before me. "Nope."

"Well, if you did," she said, "you would most likely read them not only *Curious George* but also fables and fairy tales. Stories where humans outsmart witches, where giants and ogres are felled and good triumphs over evil. Your parents read them to you and your brother. Did they not?"

"My mother did," I said.

"Of course she did. It is the way we teach our children to cope with a world too large and chaotic for them to comprehend. A world that seems, at times, too random. Too indifferent. Of course, the religions of the world will do the same for you, whether you're a Hindu or a Christian or a Rosicrucian. They're brother and sister, really: children's fables and religious parables. I believe that both your brother's religiosity and his wholehearted belief in heroes and villains may be his brave but futile attempt to make the world orderly and logical. It's a noble struggle, in a sense, given the chaos his disease has put him up against. At least, that's one way of interpreting it."

"Noble? What's so noble about it?"

"Because he is struggling to cure himself, Dominick. To rid himself of what must be his gravest fear: chaos. If he can somehow order the world, *save* the world, then he can save himself. That was his motivation when he removed his hand in the library, was it not? To sacrifice himself? To stop the destruction that war inevitably brings? Your brother is a very sick man, Dominick, but also a very good one and, I would venture to say, in some ways, even a *noble* one. I hope that gives you some small comfort."

"Yeah, right," I scoffed. "He goes to the library and hacks off his freakin' hand. Gets the attention of every media bozo he can. . . . Yeah, it's been real comforting, Doc, I tell ya."

She said nothing. Waited. But I was finished.

If she were to work with Thomas long term, Dr. Patel told

me—and whether or not she did would be the decision of the probate judge—her eventual goals would be to help him develop better insights about his behavior and to assist in honing such life skills as money management, the conscientious performance of household tasks, the conscientious taking of the medications that could maintain him outside of the hospital setting. "The thinking now is that long-term institutionalization prepares patients for nothing except more of the same," she said. "We would dwell on his future, your brother and I, not on his past. We would, perhaps, think in terms of successful group-home placement. But, of course, that is the cart before the horse. For now, his history is what is important to my understanding of who he is. And was."

"You're a little behind the times, aren't you?" I said.

"Yes? Explain."

"His other doctors did that kind of thing for years: went over his potty training, his elementary school records. Then everybody changed their minds—decided it was all about biochemistry, the genetic cocktail."

"Oh, it is, Dominick," she said. "No question. I'm only attempting, as much as possible, to map your brother's past and present realities. To *become* him, as it were—try on his skin. And toward that end, you can be of enormous help. *If* you are willing."

"I don't know," I said. "How?"

"By continuing to listen to the tapes of your brother's sessions and sharing your insights. And by sharing your *own* remembrances of the past. I am particularly interested in your recollections of early childhood, and of the onset of the disease—the months when the schizophrenia began to manifest itself. The hows and whys of *that* time."

Nineteen sixty-nine, I thought: our work-crew summer.

"Because, as we said before, you are your brother's mirror. His healthy self. In scientific terms, you are the equivalent of a control group. And as such, it may be helpful for me to study you both as I design the shape of his therapy. If, as I say, you are willing."

I'd been suckered in before by optimism. By the bullshit of hope. I didn't know what I was or wasn't willing to do anymore. I told her I'd think about it.

"What solitary child hasn't wished for a twin, Mr. Birdsey?" she said. "Hasn't imagined that a double exists somewhere in the world? It's a hungering for human connection—another way of sheltering oneself against the storm. So who is to say that 'twinness' might not provide a key to your brother's recovery?"

A key, I thought. *Chiave.*

One thing was clear: she sounded sincere. For once, my brother hadn't been assigned someone from the hit-or-miss, take-the-money-and-run school of state-appointed psychology. For once, he had a doc who hadn't majored in indifference.

At the door, at the end of the session, she asked me what I had taught.

"What? . . . Oh. History. High school history."

"Ah," she said. "That is challenging work. And so very necessary. It is important for children to learn that they are the sum of those who have come before them. Don't you agree?"

"Yeah, well . . ."

"Why are you blushing, Mr. Birdsey?"

"I'm not blushing. I've just . . . I've been out of the classroom for over seven years. Thanks for the tea. I'll think about what you said. Call me if anything else happens."

She asked me to wait a minute. Went over to her desk and wrote down something on a slip of paper. "Here is your prescription from me, Mr. Birdsey," she said, handing me the paper. "If you are a lover of reading, read these books. They are good for the soul."

Her *prescription:* as if *I* was the patient. As if she was treating *me.*

I took the paper, glanced at it without reading it, and stuffed it into my jeans. "Thanks," I said. "Only the problem isn't my soul, Doctor. The problem is my brother's brain."

She nodded. "And toward that end, you will do as I ask? Begin to retrieve for me any childhood memories you feel may be significant? And try to recall your brother's earliest schizophrenic episodes? His initial decompensation?"

"Yeah," I said. "Okay." A step or two out into the hallway, I stopped. Turned back. "I, uh . . . you know before? When you asked me if I had any kids?"

"Yes."

"We . . . my wife and I—well, my *ex*-wife . . ."

"Yes?"

"We had a little girl." She waited, those eyes of hers smiling, still. "She . . . she died. Crib death. She was three weeks old."

"Ah," she said. "You have my sympathy. And my gratitude."

"Your gratitude? For what?"

"For sharing that information with me. I know you are a private person, Mr. Birdsey. Thank you for trusting me."

The next morning, a Saturday, Joy passed by me, her arms full of dirty laundry. "Do you want this?" she said. She was waving Dr. Patel's "prescription": the list of books I'd already forgotten about. Joy had fished it out of the pocket of my jeans. In fat, backward-slanting script, Dr. Patel had written: *The Uses of Enchantment, The Hero with a Thousand Faces, The King and the Corpse.*

"Toss it," I said, and Joy walked toward the laundry room. "Well, wait a second. Give it to me."

sixteen

1969

Ma was thrilled to have us back home from school after our first year away at college, but she didn't like the fact that Thomas had gotten so skinny. She set out to put some meat back on his bones, baking lasagnas and pies and getting up early every morning to cook us bacon and eggs and make our lunches for work. Ma packed extra sandwiches in Thomas's lunch pail and enclosed little handwritten notes about how proud she was of him—how he was one of the best sons any mother could have.

Jobs were scarce that summer, but my brother and I had landed seasonal work with the Three Rivers Public Works Department. (Ray knew the superintendent, Lou Clukey, from the VFW.) It was tough minimum-wage labor with fringe benefits like poison ivy and heat rash. But I actually *liked* working for the Three Rivers PW. It got us each a paycheck and got us out of the house during the day while Ray was home. After a year's worth of being cooped up with the books, confined in a dorm room with my brother, it felt good to catch some rays, breathe in fresh air, and work up a sweat. I liked the way you could take a scythe or a shovel and tackle a job, then look back at what you'd accomplished without waiting for some know-it-all professor's seal of approval.

The job I enjoyed most was mowing and weeding out at the town cemeteries: the ancient graveyard up in Rivertown with its crazy epitaphs, the Indian burial grounds down by the Falls, and the bigger cemeteries on Boswell Avenue and Slater Street. That first day out at Boswell Avenue, I located my grandfather's grave: a six-foot granite monument, presided over by a pair of grief-stricken cement angels. *Domenico Onofrio Tempesta (1880–1949) "The greatest griefs are silent."* His wife, *Ignazia (1897–1925),* was buried across the cemetery beneath a smaller, more modest stone. Thomas was the one who found Ma's mother's grave, halfway through the summer. "Oh, I don't know. . . . No reason, really," Ma said when I asked her why the two of them hadn't been buried together.

I was nervous, at first, about Thomas. For one thing, I was still a little freaked out about that busted typewriter bullshit. For another, he wasn't exactly the manual labor type. But I shut my mouth and kept my eyes open, and after the first week or so, I began to relax. Let down my guard.

Sometimes he'd lose track of what he was doing or drift off in a fog somewhere, but nothing out of the ordinary. He pretty much held his own. By the beginning of July, he had tanned and bulked up a little and lost his Lurch look. So college *hadn't* driven him over the edge after all, I told myself. He'd just been exhausted. He was okay. And come September, he could begin digging himself out of the academic hole he'd dug for himself with all those class cuts, the stupid asshole. The jerk.

Thomas never ate those extra sandwiches Ma packed for him. *I* ate them. Sometimes, when he didn't hand them to me outright, I'd go looking for them and find the notes Ma had written him. She knew better than to write *me* those things. One time she'd pulled that in high school, and my buddies had snatched the note away and passed it around. I'd gone home and screamed bloody murder at her. But that TLC stuff never embarrassed Thomas the way it did me. He thrived on that kind of crap.

I'll say this for Thomas: he went out and got our typewriter fixed without my bugging him about it. Without Ma or Ray catching wind of what had happened. He took the initiative, paid for the repairs out of his first paycheck from the city, and had the machine back within a week. The only problem was, he couldn't buy another carrying case. When Ma noticed it was missing, it was *me* she asked about it, not Thomas. I told her someone at school had swiped it. She stood there, looking worried, not saying anything. "It's no big deal, Ma," I assured her. "Better they took the case than the typewriter. Right?"

Ma said she couldn't believe that college boys would steal from each other.

I told her it would surprise her what college boys did.

"Is it drugs, Dominick?" she said. "Is that why he lost all that weight?"

I reached down and gave her a smooch. Told her she was a worrywart. Teased the fear out of her eyes. He's *fine,* Ma, I said. *Really.* It was just his nerves.

Each workday morning at seven-thirty, Thomas and I reported to the city barn where Lou Clukey dispatched the work crews around Three Rivers. Thomas and I were assigned this big burly foreman named Dell Weeks. Dell was a strange one. He had a shaved head, a silver tooth in front, and the filthiest mouth I'd ever heard on anyone. Dell couldn't stand Lou Clukey, who was an ex-Navy officer and a straight arrow, and you could tell the feeling was mutual. You could *feel* the tension when Dell and Lou were within twenty feet of each other. So it was no big surprise that our crew usually drew the day's dirtiest work. All morning long, we shoveled sand, cut swamp brush, pumped sewage, disinfected campground toilets. We saved the mowing jobs for afternoon.

Not counting Dell Weeks, there were four guys on our crew: Thomas, me, Leo Blood, and Ralph Drinkwater. Leo was seasonal like Thomas and me, a year ahead of us at UConn. Drinkwater was full-time. If the draft or Electric Boat didn't get him first, he ran the risk of becoming a Three Rivers Public Works "lifer" like Dell.

Drinkwater hadn't grown much since that year in high school when he'd gotten thrown out of Mr. LoPresto's class for laughing out loud at the concept that the red man had been annihilated because of the white man's natural superiority. He was still only five-six, five-seven, maybe, but he was tougher and cockier than he'd been back then. A bantamweight. He had tight, ropy muscles and walked with the trace of a strut; he even mowed lawns with an attitude. That whole summer, Drinkwater wore the exact same clothes to work. He didn't stink or anything, the way Dell sometimes did. He just never wore anything else but these same black jeans and this blue tank top. Leo and I had a twenty-dollar bet going as to when Drinkwater would finally break down and change his clothes. I had the odd calendar days and Leo had the evens, and we both waited all summer to collect.

Although I wouldn't have admitted it at the time, Drinkwater was the best worker of the four of us, focused and steady-paced, no matter how hot it got. All day long, he listened to the transistor radio he kept hitched to his belt loop—Top 40, baseball if the Red Sox had an afternoon game. He played that radio so relentlessly, I *still* know half the commercials by heart. *Come alive, you're in the Pepsi generation. . . . You've got a friend at Three Rivers Savings. . . . Come on down to Constantine Motors, where we're on the hill but on the level.* All day long, the music and talk moved with Drinkwater.

He was pretty antisocial at first. He seemed always to be watching Thomas and me. About fifty times a day, I'd look up and catch Ralph looking away from one of us. It wasn't anything new: people had always stared at Thomas and me. *Oh, look, Muriel! Twins!* But Ralph had been a twin, too. What was *he* looking at?

Riding out to a job, Thomas, Leo, and I would usually hop into the back of the truck and Ralph would ride up front with Dell. He'd talk to Dell sometimes, but he hardly ever said a word to us, even when one of us asked him something directly. Ralph's older cousin Lonnie had been killed in Nam earlier that year—had been buried in the Indian graveyard. When we were mowing out there, Ralph would steer clear of Lonnie's headstone. It was me who'd usually trim around it; we'd divide the cemetery into quadrants, and that was always my section. I'd be clipping and yanking weeds and start thinking about Lonnie—the time he got in trouble for spitting on kids at the playground, that time at the movies, in the downstairs bathroom, when he'd grabbed me by the wrist and humiliated me for his and Ralph's entertainment. *Why you hitting yourself, kid? Huh? Why you hitting yourself?* . . . It was good-sized—Lonnie's gravestone. Granite, rough-hewn on one side, polished on the other. Placed there by the VFW, it said, in honor of Lonnie's having been one of the first Three Rivers kids to fall in Vietnam. Some honor: giving up your life for our national mistake. For nothing. When Thomas and I were little kids, the big villains of the world were other kids. *Bad* kids. Troublemakers like Lonnie Peck. Now Nixon was the enemy. Nixon and those other neckless old farts who kept escalating the war over there—kept sending kids over to the jungle to get their heads blown off.

Ralph's sister's grave was out there, too. Penny Ann's. It was close by Lonnie's but not right next to it, twenty-five or thirty feet away. Hers was just a small sandstone foot marker with her initials, *P.A.D.* I'd missed it the first couple of times we were out there. Then, *bam!* It hit me whose stone it was. I kept trying to say something to Ralph about the graves. About Lonnie's at least. The death of a soldier was easier to talk about than the rape and murder of a little girl. But I didn't say anything about either one. Ralph gave me no openings. Didn't let down his guard for a second. One time during the first week, the two of us—Ralph and me—were loading tools back into the truck bed. I reminded him that we'd both been at River Street Elementary School together and then together again in Asshole LoPresto's history class at JFK. Drinkwater just looked at me, expressionless. "Remember?" I finally said. He stood there, staring at me like I was from Mars or something.

"Yeah, I remember," he said. "What about it?"

"Nothing," I sputtered. "Sorry I mentioned it. Excuse me for breathing, okay?"

When the morning was cool and the job wasn't too strenuous—or if Lou Clukey was in the vicinity—Dell would become a *working* foreman—would labor alongside us. Otherwise, he'd sit in the truck, leaning against the open driver's side door, smoking his Old Golds and finding fault.

Sometimes he'd get up off his ass and go over to my brother. Snatch Thomas's push broom or bow saw away from him and give him a little demonstration on how he *should* be doing it. Or else he'd tell Drinkwater to stop work and go show Thomas the right way to do something. It was degrading for both Thomas and Ralph—enough so that you'd have to look away. But Dell liked the flustered reaction Thomas never failed to give him and the look of contempt he'd get from Ralph. He *enjoyed* busting their balls, Thomas's especially. Dell started this joke about how he couldn't tell my brother and me apart unless we each had a shovel in our hands. Then he knew who was who, no problem. He nicknamed us the Dicky Bird brothers, Dick and Dickless.

Of the four of us, Dell came to favor Leo and me. We were the ones he always picked to stop work and drive over to Central Soda Shop for coffees, or fill up the water jugs at the town spring, or run and get him some cigs. Leo and I were the ones that Dell started addressing his stupid jokes to.

"Nigger's walking down the street leading a bull on a rope, and the bull's got this hard-on that's yea-big. Woman comes up to him and says, 'Hey, how much would it cost me to slip that foot-and-a-half of meat up my cunt?' So the nigger says, 'Well, I'll fuck you for free, lady, but I'll have to get someone to watch my bull here.' "

When Dell told his jokes, I'd usually give him a fake smile or a nervous laugh. Sometimes I'd sneak a glance over at Drinkwater. Ralph might have been a full-blooded Wequonnoc Indian like he'd claimed that day in Mr. LoPresto's class, but he was pretty dark-skinned. I'd never seen an Indian with an Afro. All summer long, Ralph's transistor radio kept singing about the dawning of the age of Aquarius and everybody smiling on their brother and loving one another, but Dell's jokes had a way of curdling those songs.

Drinkwater was always deadpan when Dell got to the punch lines of those racist jokes. He never cracked a smile, but he never gave him an argument, either—never challenged him the way he had that day in class with Mr. LoPresto. I hated those jokes of Dell's, really *hated* them, but I was too gutless to object. Not that I admitted it to myself. With thirty college credits under my belt, I was able to intellectualize my silence: eventually, people our age would be in charge and all the bigots of the world would die off. And anyway, if Drinkwater didn't say anything—he had to be at least *partly* black—then why should I? So I kept selling myself for the privilege of making those big-deal errands to the spring and the coffee shop. I smiled and kept my mouth shut and maintained my "favored worker status." Leo did the same.

That summer, Leo and I rekindled the friendship we had started a couple years before in summer school math class. The few times I've ever bothered to think about it—to analyze what it was that made us friends in the first place, way before we were brothers-in-law married to the Constantine sisters—the only thing I ever came up with was the fact that we're opposites. Always have been. At high school dances, I was your basic fade-into-the-woodwork type. The kind of guy who'd stand there all night watching the band because he was too scared to ask any girl to dance. Not Leo, though. Leo was a performer. That was back when his nickname was "Cool Jerk." Sooner or later, someone would request that song, "Cool Jerk," and Leo'd get out there in the middle of the gym floor and dance this spastic solo. Kids used to circle him four or five deep, clapping and hooting and laughing their heads off at him, and Leo's fat would flop in all directions, the sweat would fly off his face. I admired his nerve, I guess, in *some* screwy way. One time, in the middle of a schoolwide assembly—one of those slide-show yawners about people from other lands—Leo raised his hand as a volunteer and got up on stage, yanked on a grass skirt, and took a hula lesson from these visiting Hawaiians. "Cool Jerk! Cool Jerk!" everyone started chanting over the ukulele music, until Leo's hip-rolling began to look like something other than the hula, and the crowd went wild, and even the Hawaiians stopped smiling. Neck Veins, the vice principal, walked onstage, stopped the show, and told the rest of us to go back to our third-period classes. Instead of taking off his grass skirt and exiting gracefully, Leo started giving a speech about how JFK High was a dictatorship like Cuba and we should all go on strike. He was suspended for two weeks and barred from extracurricular activities.

"How can you hang around with the biggest a-hole in our entire school?" Thomas kept asking me that whole summer when Leo and I had been in remedial algebra together. Leo *was* an asshole; I knew that. But, like I said, he was also everything my brother and I were not: uninhibited, carefree, and funny as hell. Leo's colossal nerve had gotten the two of us access to all kinds of forbidden pleasures that my goody two-shoes brother would have objected to and my stepfather would have beaten me for: the X-rated Eros Drive-In out on Route 165, the racetrack at Narragansett, a liquor store on Pachaug Pond Road that gave minors the benefit of the doubt. The first time I ever got shit-faced drunk was out at the Falls in Leo's mother's Biscayne, smoking Muriel air tips and passing a jug of Bali Hai back and forth. I was fifteen.

Now, four years later—during our work-crew summer—Thomas was just as resentful of Leo's and my rekindled friendship as he'd been the first time around. "Just what I need: another dose of Leo Blood," Thomas would say if I told Thomas that Leo was coming over after supper to hang out or to pick me up. Ma liked Leo because he was a good eater. Ray said he'd learned in the Navy not to trust the Leos of the world any further than you could throw them. "Watch your rear flank with that one," Ray told me. "He's too full of himself. Guys like that will sell you right down the river."

The fact that my stepfather worked third shift meant that he was home all day and had first dibs on the mail. I had two magazine subscriptions coming to the house back then, *Newsweek* and the *Sporting News*. It always bugged me that Ray got his hands all over them before I did—bent back the pages, wrinkled up the covers, left them all over the place so's I'd have to go looking for the things. At our house, mail was Ray's property no matter whose name was on the envelope, and if you complained about it, it was *you* who was committing the federal offense.

One day in July, Thomas and I got home from work and found Ray sitting at the kitchen table, drinking a bottle of Moxie and waiting for us. "Well, well, well," he said. "If it isn't the two geniuses. Have a seat, fellas. I want to have a little chat with you guys."

Ma was waiting, too, looking ashen, twisting a dish towel in her hands. She had made sweet cucumber pickles that day, a favorite of Thomas's and mine. A row of canning jars was lined up on the counter. The kitchen smelled sweet and vinegary.

We sat. Ray turned to Thomas. "Suppose you explain *this*!" he said.

In his hand, he was crinkling Thomas's tissue-paper grade report from UConn—all those D's, F's, and Incompletes my brother had said nothing about. Ray waved it back and forth like evidence. "What's the story here, Einstein? You been taking a joy ride up there? First you flimflam me out of my hard-earned money and then you can't even bother to study?"

"Come on now, Ray," Ma said. "You said you'd give him a chance to explain."

"That's right, Suzie Q. And that's *exactly* what I want to hear. His explanation. And it better be a good one."

Thomas sat there, hands in his lap, eyes averted and brimming with tears. Like I said, Thomas never could defend himself. So Ray continued to bully him.

He himself had never been to college, Ray said, so maybe he was just stupid. But for the life of him, he couldn't figure out why he should keep throwing away his hard-earned money so that this clown sitting here across from him could make a joke out of his college education. What, exactly, was he paying for? Could either of us two Einstein college boys or our mother tell him *that*?

Thomas's whole body shook. He could explain what had happened, he said, but could he please just get a drink of water first?

No, he could *not* just get a drink of water first, Ray told him. He could tell them what the hell he'd been doing all year long instead of studying. Ray took a long sip of his Moxie and slammed the bottle back down on the table in a way that made me jump. Made all thirty of those college credits evaporate.

Thomas cleared his throat. "Well . . . ," he began. His voice was loud one second, nearly inaudible the next; he explained in a rambling way that he had had a tough time adjusting to college. A hard time sleeping. "I was always so tired. And so *nervous.* I just couldn't concentrate. . . . I kept trying and trying, but it was always so noisy there."

"It was noisy?" Ray said. *"That's* your excuse? That it was noisy?"

"Not *just* that. I felt. . . . It was a lot of things. I guess . . . I guess I was homesick."

Ma took a step toward him, then stopped. Caught herself.

"Oh, gee whiz," Ray mocked. "Mama's poor little bunny rabbit was homesick." Each time Thomas opened his mouth, he handed our stepfather more ammunition.

"I'm really sorry, Ray. I know I let you down. You, too, Ma. All I can say is that it's not going to happen again."

Ray leaned toward him. Got right in his face. "You're goddamned right it isn't, buddy boy. Not with *my* money." He turned to Ma, jabbing a finger at her. "And not with yours, either, Suzie Q, just in case you're getting any cockamamy ideas about getting another job. Maybe *you* don't know a con game when you see it, but *I* sure as hell do. This guy's going to stay home in September and *work* for a living."

Thomas was silent for several long seconds. Then he told Ray that if he had another chance, he could get things under control.

"Oh, you could, eh? *How?"*

Thomas looked over at me. "Dominick goes to the library to study," he said. "Maybe I could try that. Go study at the library with Dominick. And if some of the teachers could just give me a little extra help . . ."

I could tell by Thomas's thickening voice, by the way his words kept catching in his throat, that he was about to surrender to full-out sobbing—the kind of snorting, sore-throat wailing that Ray had been able to draw from him ever since we were kids. I wanted to save my brother from that. Didn't want him to hand Ray that satisfaction. So I put my own neck on the chopping block.

"My GPA is 3.2, Ray," I said. "Why don't you tell me what's wrong with that?"

He looked over at me. Took the bait. "Well, why don't you tell me what a goddamned GPA *is* then, Mr. Smart Ass?" Ray said, turning to me. "After all, I only went as far as my third year of high school. I only fought in two wars, that's all. I'm not a walking encyclopedia like you and Smarty Pants over there. I'm just the working stiff that puts food on the table."

I stared him down. "It's a grade point average," I said. "Four points for an A, three for a B, two for a C. I made the dean's list, Ray."

"I made the dean's list, Ray," he mimicked back. "So who does that make you? King Farouk? Does that mean my shit stinks and yours doesn't?"

"No. All it means is that I made the dean's list."

"Gee, that's great, honey," Ma said wearily. "Congratulations."

Ray told her to shut her trap and stay out of it. He put down Thomas's grade report and picked up mine, then proceeded to discredit my accomplishments one by one. B-plus in psychology? Big deal! That stuff was a bunch of happy horseshit as far as he was concerned. A-minus in probability? He didn't even know what that was, for Christ's sweet sake. He laughed with particular disdain at the A I had earned in art appreciation. "Kids your age are over there *dying* for their country, and you're sittin' in some nice little classroom, 'appreciatin' paintin's on a wall? And *I'm* paying for it? I never heard of anything so goddamned pathetic."

"So what is it you want, Ray?" I said. "You want the two of us to go over there and get our heads blown off by the Viet Cong? Is that what would make you happy?"

"Don't say that, honey," Ma said.

Ray leaned forward and took hold of me by the front of my T-shirt. Pulled me up to a standing position. "Don't you *dare* talk to me like that, buddy boy," he said. "Understand? I don't care how many A's you got on your lousy—"

"Let go of me, Ray," I said.

"You hear me? Huh?"

My T-shirt twisted a little in his grip. Cut into the back of my neck. "I said, let go of my fuckin' shirt."

"All right, you two," Ma said. "Come on now. This isn't necessary. Calm down."

"Calm down?" Ray said. He let go, shoving me backward so that I lost my balance, fell against one of the kitchen chairs. "You want me to calm down, Connie? Okay, I'll calm down. Let me show you how calm I can get."

Ray took Ma by the arm and walked her over to the counter where her pickles were. He grabbed one of the jars and flung it like a grenade against the refrigerator door. Grabbed another. It smashed on the floor in front of Thomas. A third smashed against a leg of the kitchen table. By the time he'd finished, the floor was littered with broken glass and pickles and rivers of juice—the ruins of my mother's day.

I wanted to kill the bastard. Imagined picking up one of those jagged pieces of glass and going after him with it. Sinking it into his heart. But I just stood there, terrified.

"How's *that* for calm, honey bunch?" Ray asked Ma. He was red-faced, short of breath. "How do you like *them* apples? Huh?"

Ma went for the broom and the mop, but Ray told her to stay put and to shut her big trap for once in her life. He had something to say to all three of us and all he wanted us to do was shut up and listen.

Thomas and I were *both* a couple of pantywaists, he said, and as far as he was concerned, it was all Ma's fault. We were Suzy and Betty Pinkus, the little college mama's boys, hiding behind her apron strings instead of doing what was right. Neither of us gave a good god*damn* about our country—about *anything* except ourselves. Did we think he had *wanted* to go over there and fight the Krauts? Did we think he *wanted* to put his life on the line a few years later in Korea? Men did what they *had* to do, not what they *wanted* to do. Our mother had spoiled us rotten—had treated us like a couple of crown princes. The two of us were nothing but take, take, take. We'd been like that our whole fucking lives and he was sick of it. We could go plumb to hell if we thought *he* was going to keep shelling out. He was *finished* with that bullshit.

It was futile to defend yourself when Ray went full-tilt into one of his rages. Whatever shots you got in weren't worth what he'd come back at you with—weren't worth the toll it took on Ma. The best thing you could do was cut your losses. Relax your face of any emotion. Play defense.

That was something I always understood and Thomas never did. That afternoon, my brother sat there, sobbing and apologizing, as if enough tears and "I'm sorrys" would make him love us. Or at least stop hating us. Ray railed on, backing up and slamming into him again and again, one verbal collision after another. Just witnessing it was enough to make me puke.

I headed for the back door, sloshing through pickle juice, crunching glass underneath my work boots with every step.

"Get back here! Who told you this was—?"

I slammed the door behind me.

I was in a jog by the time I got to the end of Hollyhock Avenue, clomping up the hill to Summit Street and then through the woods. I stumbled past a family having a picnic and a teenage couple swapping spit by the edge of Rosemark's Pond. Went crashing into the water, boots and work clothes and all.

Breathed deeply in and out, in and out.

Went under.

I got home sometime around midnight, I guess—well after Ray had gone to work and Thomas had gone to bed. The kitchen floor had been cleaned of glass and pickles. The supper dishes were dry on the rack, my meal Saran-wrapped on a plate in the refrigerator. I was sitting at the table, eating and reading the paper when I heard my mother on the stairs.

She smelled like the lilac dusting powder I gave her every Christmas—the only thing she ever claimed she needed. She was wearing a housecoat I'd never seen before—a colorful, flowery one. Her toenails were painted pink.

"I don't know how you boys can eat cold spaghetti like that," she said. "Why don't you let me heat that up for you?"

"It's fine," I said.

She sat down at the table across from me. "Honey?" she said. "Are you all right?"

"Yup."

"Well, you don't look all right. You look like the wreck of the *Hesperus*."

"I hate him, Ma," I said.

She shook her head. "No, you don't, Dominick."

"Yes, I do. I *hate* him."

She got up and turned her back on me, started putting away the dishes. "You hate his temper, not him. Boys don't hate their fathers."

"He's not my father."

"Yes, he is, Dominick."

"The only thing that makes him my father is some stupid piece of paper he signed. What kind of father would bully his son the way he bullied Thomas tonight? What kind of father wants his sons to go off to war and get wasted?"

"He didn't say that, Dominick. Don't put words in his mouth. He loves you boys."

"He can't stand us and you know it. He resents everything about us. He's been that way all our lives."

She shook her head again. "The thing about your father is. . . . Well, I don't want to tell tales out of school, but he didn't have it easy when he was a kid."

"Don't keep calling him my father. He's *not* my father."

"He didn't have much of a home life, Dominick. His mother was a no-good tramp. He doesn't talk about it much, but I think that when his temper goes off like that, it just all comes back at him."

"Is our *real* father alive?" I said. "Did he croak or something? Just *tell* me!"

She looked me in the eye for a second, and then looked away. Put her hand over her cleft lip. "All I'm saying, honey, is that these kinds of problems pop up in every family. Not just ours. Now do me a favor and don't walk around here with bare feet. I think I got all that glass, but sometimes you miss a piece. Just be careful, honey. Okay?"

"Who *is* he, Ma?" I said. "Who's our father?"

She stood there a while longer. Gave me a weak smile. "Well, good night," she said. "Get some sleep now. Watch out for that glass. Okay?"

seventeen

"Mr. Birdsey, tell me about your stepfather."

Silence.

"Mr. Birdsey? Did you hear me?"

"What?"

"Yesterday, near the end of our session, we were—"

"Can I have a cigarette?"

"Smoking is bad for your health, Mr. Birdsey. And for mine, too, since I'm in the room with you. I'd rather you didn't get into the habit of having cigarettes every time we sit down to talk."

"You didn't mind yesterday. You lit the first one for me."

"Yesterday was an exception. We were making some progress and—"

"I think better when I smoke. I remember *better."*

"I don't quite see how that's possible, Mr. Birdsey. Physiologically speaking. Let's move on, please. With regard to your stepfather, do you suppose—"

"Do you believe in reincarnation?"

A pause. *"Mr. Birdsey, I discuss neither my religious beliefs nor my personal life with patients. It's my policy. It's not relevant to what we're trying to accomplish."*

"Well, I want a cigarette. That's my *policy."*

"And how do you justify that in terms of your religious conviction, Mr. Birdsey? I'm curious about that. If, as the Bible says, the body is a temple, then—"

"Don't call me that."

"Excuse me?"

"Call me by my code name. Especially if this is on tape. I'm vulnerable enough already."

"Shall I call you Thomas then? You said during one of our earlier sessions that you prefer the more formal 'Mr. Birdsey,' but perhaps now that we've established a—"

"Call me by my code name, I said. Mr. Y."

"Mr. Y? Yes?"

"You secure these tapes. Right?"

"Yes, yes. This has come up several times already. The tapes are—"

"Do you really think they'd put me under house arrest and then not *watch my every move?* Not *sit there waiting for me to slip up?"*

"Whom do you mean?"

"Never mind. What you don't know can't hurt you."

"I want to assure you, Mr. Birdsey, that we are in a completely safe environment. As your doctor—your ally—I have taken all necessary precautions to assure your safety."

Pause. *"Indira Gandhi was assassinated, wasn't she?"*

"The prime minister? Yes, she was. Now, since our time together is precious, let's talk a little about—"

"Killed and cremated. Whoosh! Don't tell me the CIA didn't have a hand in that *one. . . . Maybe it has something to do with the blood vessels."*

"Excuse me?"

"Why I remember better when I smoke. It probably has to do with the way the nicotine affects the flow of blood to the brain. Not all truths are scientific. Go try and prove a miracle in some chemistry laboratory, Mrs. Gandhi. Go analyze God's DNA."

"You're quite safe here, Mr. Birdsey. Quite safe."

"Can I have a cigarette?"

On the tape, I heard the sliding open of a drawer, the flick-flick-flick of a lighter.

I had to smile. "Thomas, one; Doc Patel, nothing," I said.

She nodded. "Your brother is a talented manipulator, Dominick. I suppose it's what twenty years of institutionalization will teach you."

"Hey, if he was out in the real world, jerking people around would be a valuable skill. Right?"

"Yes? You think so? That's an interesting perspective." She was always doing that: turning some flip remark of mine into a revealing observation. You had to watch it with Dr. Patel, even if you were only the patient's brother.

We were in Lisa Sheffer's office at Hatch, not the doc's. Sheffer had arranged the powwow that morning after she'd gotten an unexpected phone call from the office of the probate court. There'd been a change of plans. The judge was reviewing my brother's case that day instead of waiting for the end of the fifteen-day observation period. The move was premature and unanticipated—"fishy," in Sheffer's words. We'd planned to meet in her office at four o'clock that afternoon to discuss the outcome—Lisa, Dr. Patel, and me. Since Sheffer was running late, the doc had suggested we listen to the tape of Thomas's latest session while we waited. My brother had mentioned several things she said she'd be interested in getting my reaction to. *But,* she'd warned me, some of what he'd said might be upsetting. I'd shrugged. Reassured her I could take it—that I'd heard it all at this point.

On the tape, Thomas exhaled.

"Mr. Birdsey, the last time we spoke, you mentioned that your stepfather was sometimes abusive to your mother. Do you remember?"

"One of these days, Alice. Pow! Right in the kisser!"

"Is he quoting your stepfather there, Dominick?" Dr. Patel asked.

I shook my head. "Jackie Gleason."

Her face went blank. She stopped the tape.

"*The Honeymooners.* It was a TV show." No lightbulb yet. "This guy—this comedian named Jackie Gleason—he used to say that to his wife. On the show. 'One of these days, Alice. Pow! Right in the kisser!' "

"Yes? Excuse me. What is the kisser?"

"The kisser? The mouth."

"Ah, the mouth. Yes, yes. And this was a comedy? About a man who struck his wife in the mouth?"

"He never actually . . . it's, uh . . . you're taking it out of context."

"I see," she said. She kept looking at me. I wasn't sure why my face felt hot.

"Was your father physically abusive to your mother, Mr. Birdsey? Or was it more in the nature of—"

"It was not a pretty picture."

"Will you elaborate, please?"

No response.

"Mr. Birdsey? What was 'unpretty' about it?"

"He used to use her like a punching bag, that's what. He'd sock her in the jaw. Kick her. Slam her against the wall. He used to make us watch."

"Us?"

"My brother and me."

"That's complete bullshit," I said.

Dr. Patel hit the "stop" button. "Yes? You're saying it never happened?"

"No!"

"One time we were sitting there eating dinner, the four of us, and Ray just reached over and elbowed her, right in the face. For no reason. Just because he felt like it, that's all. He broke her nose."

I wrapped my arms around my chest. Shook my head. "Never happened," I told the ceiling.

"You're sure?"

"My stepfather breaks my mother's nose and I wouldn't remember it?"

"He used to rape her, too. Right in front of us."

"Jesus God. Does he really—"

"You watched this, Mr. Birdsey?"

"Plenty of times. He made us."

"Let me make sure I understand. You're saying your stepfather used to rape your mother and insist that you and your brother watch?"

"He'd pull us out of bed in the middle of the night sometimes. Drag us down the hallway to their bedroom and—"

"That is complete—"

"—push her nightgown up and just attack her."

"And you and Dominick witnessed this?"

"We had to. We had to just sit there and shut up. My mother would beg him to let us leave, but he'd tell her to shut up or he'd cut our throats. And then, after he was finished with his business, he'd say, 'There, this is what the world is really like, you two. Might as well get used to it.' He was always trying to toughen us up. Sometimes he'd make us . . ."

He kept rambling. I sat there, trying not to listen. I read the wording on Sheffer's framed diploma. Studied the little area where paint was peeling off her ceiling. Picked away so thoroughly at a dried paint splatter on the knee of my jeans that I poked a hole in the cloth. Hadn't Thomas made Ma suffer enough while she was alive without bringing her back from the dead so Ray could rape her? In *front* of us, for Christ's sake? God, I hated Thomas. *Hated* him.

"Dominick?"

That's when it dawned on me: she'd stopped the tape. "Yes?"

"I said, you look pale."

"I'm all right. I'm fine."

"Perhaps that's enough for today. Maybe we could—"

I straightened my spine. Managed to look her in the eye. "Can I ask you something? Is he trying to con you with this crap or does he really think it happened?"

"I believe he thinks it happened. And you say it did *not* happen. Correct?"

"That Ray raped my mother and we had ringside seats? Gee whiz, now, let me think." I got up, walked over to the barred window. Looked out onto that sorry-ass recreation area with its rusted basketball hoop, its picnic tables that looked like they'd been gnawed on the ends. How could Sheffer work here? How could *any* of them work at this place—listening all day long to this kind of crap—and not go nuts themselves? I turned and faced her. "You know what *I* think? You want *my* opinion? I think he's bullshitting you. He knows that if he gives you a good horror story, you'll call it 'progress' and let him smoke. You said it yourself: he's a good manipulator. You're being manipulated."

"Your stepfather—"

"Look, my stepfather could be a first-class son of a bitch when he wanted to, okay? I'm the first guy to admit that. But he was a bully, not some inhuman . . . Jesus Christ, if we'd watched something like that, don't you think we'd *both* be off the deep end by now? Him *and* me?"

"You seem angry."

"Just answer me one thing, will you? Is psychology or psychiatry over in India twenty years behind the times or something?"

"Why do you ask that, Dominick?"

"Because . . . look, I don't mean to insult you, but this technique you're using is a little backward, isn't it?"

"What technique do you mean?"

"All this family history crap. It's like we've gone full circle or something."

"Full circle? In what respect?"

"When he was first hospitalized, *way* the hell back, the doctors were always sniffing around this bad childhood stuff. Did he get spanked? How was he toilet-trained? Did she and Ray fight a lot? She used to come home from those sessions with his doctors and . . . she'd have to go upstairs and lie down. I'd hear her up in their bedroom, sobbing her head off."

"Your mother? Why was that?"

More tea, Mrs. Floon?

Yes, thank you, Mrs. Calabash.

"Dominick?"

"Because . . . because they were always insinuating that somehow or another *she* had caused it. And it wasn't . . . *fair.*"

"The doctors were suggesting your mother caused Thomas's illness?"

"Which was complete crap."

"Yes, of course it was. I'm not at all implying that—"

"I mean, first of all, this kid who she's *devoted* to, who she's run interference for all his life . . . first, he cracks up and they cart him off to the loony bin. Then she comes down and visits him every single *day*—has to take the fucking *bus* down there because Ray wouldn't . . . because he was too ashamed to . . . and then the doctors have to slap this *guilt trip* on her on top of it? It wasn't *fair*!"

"Dominick, nothing about your brother's illness is 'fair.' If you look for fairness when it comes to schizophrenia, it will be a futile search. No patient or patient's family *deserves* this affliction. And I'm certainly not trying to place guilt on anyone. I'm merely investigating—"

"Investigating his past. I *know* that! That's what I'm saying. It's what the shrinks were doing twenty years ago when this whole . . . when this nightmare first started. And then, later on, his other doctors—Ehlers and Bradbury and those guys—when *they* came along, it was like, 'Oh, no, all that history stuff's irrelevant. It has nothing to do with his upbringing; it's all genetic. We don't need to figure out the past. All we have to do is focus on the future: how to control his behavior with medication, how to teach him self-management.' So, I'm just wondering why we're back to picking apart the past. Is that what they're still doing over in India?"

"I don't know, Dominick. I'm not an expert on the current psychiatric practices of my native country. I haven't lived there in over twenty-five years. Tell me. Are you uncomfortable about remembering the past?"

"Am *I*? No, I'm not *uncomfortable*. I just . . . I was just *wondering*. If it's all just about genetics and finding the right chemical cocktail so he can go live in a group home somewhere, then—"

"Genetics and long-term maintenance are *certainly* both parts of the whole treatment picture. *Integral* parts, Dominick. I'm not at all in disagreement with Dr. Ehlers and the others about that. And we're learning new things all the time. Just this year, there have been some exciting developments. The approval of Clozapine for one. Now, at the present time, it doesn't seem that your brother is likely to benefit from—"

"We've been over that. What's the other thing?"

"Excuse me?"

"You said Clozapine or Clozaril or whatever it's called for *one* thing. What's the other thing?"

"I've been wanting to talk to you about that, actually.

There's some fascinating research just coming out of the National Institute of Mental Health. A study involving twins, as a matter of fact. They've been looking at the physical differences in the brains of schizophrenics and their healthy twins. Investigating the possibility that the abnormalities they're seeing might be related to early viral infections or autoimmune disorders. I've been in touch with a Dr. Weinberger at the Institute. He's very interested in you and your brother, as a matter of fact—about the possibility of getting MRIs of you both."

"MRIs? Are those the things that—?"

"They're pictures of the body's soft tissues. Pictures of your brains, in this case. The procedure is completely noninvasive. Completely painless."

"We're not lab rats," I said.

"No, you're not, Dominick. And I am not a mad scientist. Nor, to the best of my knowledge, is Dr. Weinberger. I'm not suggesting this is something we should pursue right now. Down the road, perhaps. I only mention it to reassure you."

"Reassure me about *what*?"

"That I'm not twenty years behind the time. *Despite* the fact I am Indian by birth."

I looked away. "All I'm saying. . . . I just don't see why you're spending all this time. . . . If it's all about brain abnormalities and these MRI things, then what's all this taping and talking about ancient history supposed to accomplish?"

"I'm not sure, Dominick. I'm merely probing—trying to get a fuller picture. Let me put it this way: when he was nineteen years old, a young man walked into the woods and became lost. I have merely gone to the woods to try to find him. Others may be flying helicopters above, analyzing data—using more state-of-the-art methods. But as for me, I'm on foot. Calling out the young man's name and listening for some response. I can't give you any guarantees about what I'll find. If, indeed, I find anything helpful at all. The process is trial-and-error."

"Yeah, well, as far as I can see, it's just a big fat waste of time."

"Thank you for your opinion."

I looked up at the clock. "God, where the hell's Sheffer,

anyway? You'd think if she was going to be *this* late, she'd call or something."

"Perhaps a phone wasn't available to her. Perhaps she's on her way back now."

"Look, I don't mean to insult you. I know you mean well."

"You don't insult me, Dominick. You are merely expressing your opinion. Which is fine. Which is lovely." She smiled.

I sat back down. "All right, go ahead," I said. "Play the rest of it then."

"The tape? You're sure?"

"Go ahead."

"Mr. Birdsey, you said during our last session that your stepfather was abusive not only to your mother but to you and Dominick as well. Let's explore that a little."

"Let's not and say we did."

Another flick of the cigarette lighter. The sound of Thomas inhaling, exhaling.

"Did your stepfather hit you, Mr. Birdsey?"

"Yes."

"Frequently or infrequently?"

"Frequently."

"Infrequently," I said, correcting him.

"He used to take his belt off and hit me with it."

"Where?"

"Anywhere he felt like it. In the kitchen. Out in the garage."

"No, I mean where on your person did he strike you? Where on your body?"

"My legs, my arms, my behind. . . . One time he hit me across the face with his belt and the buckle chipped my tooth. Here. Right here. See that little chip?"

I pointed an incriminating finger at the tape recorder, Perry Mason style. "Okay, right there," I said. "Thomas chipped that tooth during a sledding accident. We were sledding over at Cow Barn Hill and Thomas hit his mouth on a metal runner."

"He never hit Dominick the way he hit me."

"No?"

"No. He always picked on Thomas Dirt."

"Thomas Dirt? Why do you refer to yourself in that manner, please?"

"I'm not *referring to myself. I'm Mr. Y."*

I felt the blood rush to my face. Felt Patel watching me. She stopped the tape. "Is that accurate, Dominick?" she asked. "Was Thomas singled out?"

I cleared my throat. "Uh . . . what?"

"When your stepfather abused or bullied your brother, were you usually spared?"

"I don't know. . . . Sometimes." I watched the fists on my knees tighten, relax, tighten. "I guess."

The old guilty relief: being the one *not* screamed at, *not* yanked by the arm or whacked in the head. "The thing is . . . the thing is, I wasn't always pushing Ray's buttons like Thomas was. I don't know. It's hard to explain. You had to be there."

"Take me there, then, Dominick. Help me to understand."

"It's no deep, dark . . . I just knew when to shut up."

"Yes?"

"And Thomas . . . he just never knew how to play *defense,* you know? I mean, you should have seen him at contact sports. He just didn't *get* it. And, in a way, it was . . . it was the same with Ray."

"Can you explain what you mean, Dominick?"

"You had to play *defense* with Ray. Know when to bluff, when to get out of his way. . . ."

"Yes, go on. This is helpful."

"When to stand up to him, too. Ray respected that: when you drew the line, fought back. When you showed him you had the balls to . . . the nerve . . . I just . . . God, why is this so *hard*?"

"Why is what so hard?"

I couldn't answer her. If I answered her, I might start to cry.

"Dominick, what are you feeling right now?"

"What am I *feeling*? I don't know. Nothing. I'm just . . ."

"Are you afraid?"

"No!"

"Angry?"

"I just . . . that's just the way it was with Ray. You just had to play *defense.*"

I suddenly saw and heard Ray—red-faced, goading, an inch or two from my face. Driving against me toward the basket he and I had bolted over the garage one Saturday morning. "*De*-fense! *De*-fense! What's the matter, sissy girl? You want to play basketball or go inside and play with your paper dollies?"

"Mr. Birdsey, why do you think your stepfather was more harsh with you than he was with your brother?"

"I don't think *why. I* know *why. He was jealous of me."*

"Yes? What made him jealous?"

"Because he realized that God had special plans for me."

I rolled my eyes. Shifted in my seat.

They were *Thomas's* paper dolls, not mine! He'd seen them at the five-and-ten—had begged Ma until she'd finally given in and bought them for him, and when Ray found them, all *three* of us were in trouble: Thomas, Ma, and me. Guilt by association. Guilty because I was his spitting image. Ray had gone bullshit when he saw those things. Ripped their heads off, their arms and legs. . . . And that hoop over the garage: it was supposed to be for both of us, but Thomas would never come out and play. And when he had to—when Ray *made* him come out—he was always missing a pass or something. Taking a ball in the face. Running back inside to Ma, crying, chased back indoors by Ray's ridicule.

"And you feel that may have made your stepfather envious? Your special relationship with God?"

"Yes!"

"Would you say Ray was a religious man?"

"Not half as religious as he thinks he is."

"Could you explain that, please?"

"PEACE BE WITH YOU! THE BODY OF CHRIST! MAY PERPETUAL LIGHT SHINE UPON YOU! Just because you're the loudest person in church, it doesn't mean you're the most holy. . . . He never even used to go to church at all when we were kids. Not until he turned Catholic."

"Yes? He converted?"

"To please my mother. They were having problems."

"Marital problems? How do you know this, Mr. Birdsey?"

"I'm Mr. Y."

"Excuse me. I stand corrected. But how did you know they were having problems?"

"Because she used to tell me. I was her best friend. She was thinking about getting a divorce. Nobody got divorces back then, but she was thinking about it."

"No, she wasn't," I said.

"No? Could she, perhaps, have been confiding in your brother about such things and you were possibly unaware? Is it possible that—"

"No."

"No?"

"She started going to see the priest for help. Then he started going, too. Then he decided to turn Catholic."

"This is true, Dominick?" the doc asked. "He converted?"

"Yes."

"How old were you and your brother at the time, please?"

"Nine, maybe? Ten? I doubt very much that she was confiding in him about—"

"That's when he started going to Mass every morning. After work. He worked third shift, and he'd get off and go right to early Mass. He was buddy-buddy with the priests. He used to do all their yard work free of charge. Change the oil in their cars. . . . As if acting like their slave was going to get him into Heaven. As if THAT was going to erase the way he treated us. He used to make Dominick and me shovel snow over at the rectory and the convent and we could never take any money for it. One time, the nuns gave us a box of ribbon candy—my brother and me—and when we got home, Ray made us turn right around and go down to the convent and give it back to them."

"That is accurate, Dominick?" Dr. Patel asked.

I nodded. Closed my eyes. "Neither of us even *liked* ribbon candy. You'd think that by this time, the statute of limitations—"

"It was my favorite kind of candy, too. Ribbon candy. . . . You know what it was? Why he had it in for me? Because it began to dawn on him that it was me *God had chosen. Not* him. *Not Mr. Mass Every Day. It made him nervous, too: that the one person he had picked on all his life was a prophet of the Lord Jesus Christ."*

"Did that make him jealous? Knowing that you had been singled out by God for something special?"

"Extremely *jealous. The thing he doesn't realize—that nobody realizes—is that it's a terrible burden."*

"What is, Mr. Birdsey? Would you explain what the burden is?"

"Knowing! Seeing things!"

"Seeing what, Mr. Birdsey?"

"What God wants. And what He doesn't want." Deep sigh. *"He doesn't WANT us to go to war against Iraq. He wants us to love one another. To honor HIM, not the almighty dollar. This country, right from the very beginning, has . . . Look at our* history*! Look at Wounded Knee! Look at slavery!"* He began to sob. *"He wants me to lead the way. To show people that their greed is . . . But how am I supposed to do that when they've got me under house arrest?"*

"When who *has you under house arrest, Mr. Birdsey?"*

"I just want to wake people up*! That's all. I'm just trying to do God's bidding. That's why I did* this."

"Did what?" I said. "What's he talking about there?"

Dr. Patel tapped a finger against her wrist.

"But nobody understands that it was a sacrifice. *Not even Dominick. He says he understands, but he doesn't. He's so mad at me."*

"I've talked to your brother several times now, Mr. Birdsey. He's concerned about you, but he's not angry."

"Then why hasn't he come to visit me?"

I closed my eyes, as if not seeing the tape recorder in front of me would make his voice go away.

"You don't remember? He can't visit you until his security clearance comes through. It's a policy here. Your brother wants very much to see you, and he will as soon as he can."

"Oh."

"You remember now?"

"I forgot."

"Mr. Birdsey?"

"What?"

"Did your stepfather ever abuse you in other ways?"

Long pause. *"Yes."*

"Would you tell me about that, please?"

Deep sigh. *"One time he made me walk on glass."*

"Yes? Continue, please."

"He broke glass all over the floor—the kitchen floor—and then he made me walk across the room. I had to get stitches. Had to walk on crutches. You should have seen the bottoms of my feet."

I held my hand up for her to stop the tape. "That was an *accident*," I said. "I remember the exact time he's talking about. Ray had one of his little temper tantrums and he threw a jar on the floor—a canning jar—and then later on Thomas accidentally stepped on one of the pieces and cut his foot. But it was an *accident*!"

"I see. How often did Ray have these 'temper tantrums'?"

"What? I don't know. Not that often. But don't you see how he's twisting it around? Thomas? Same as the sled thing. He's taking these *accidents* and—"

"You sound protective, Dominick. Do you feel protective of your stepfather?"

"No!"

"Of your family's privacy then?"

"I'm not 'protective' of anything. I'm just saying that Ray didn't bust glass all over the floor and then say, 'Okay, Thomas! Walk on this because you're Jesus' right-hand man.' I thought you *wanted* my insight. I thought that's what this was all about."

"It is."

"Then what are you accusing me for?"

"Accusing you?"

"Or . . . psychoanalyzing *me* or whatever. *I'm* not the patient."

"He used to open up my closet and urinate all over my clothes. My shoes, too. He was always doing that—pissing

into my shoes. . . . Nobody else knew about it. He said he'd kill me if I told anyone."

"Mr. Birdsey, why did your stepfather urinate on your clothes?"

A pause. *"That was nothing. That was the least of it."*

"He did worse things?"

"Much, much worse."

"What did he do that was worse?"

"He used to tie me up and then stick things up my rear end."

"Jesus! Why . . . why are you *dignifying* this? If Ray knew he was saying stuff like this, he'd—"

"What kind of things, Mr. Birdsey?"

"Sharp things. Pencils. Screwdrivers. One time he took the handle of a carving knife and—"

"All right, stop it! Stop that goddamned thing! I can't—just *stop* it!" I lurched forward and stopped the fucker myself.

We both sat there, waiting for my breathing to calm down.

"Dominick?"

"What?"

"What your brother said has upset you very much. Hasn't it?"

I laughed. "Oh, hell, no. Let's see now. My mother used to get raped and we sat around and watched. Ray used to stick screwdrivers up his butt. This is real easy to listen to, Doc. Piece of cake."

"Tell me what you're feeling right now."

I turned and faced her. "What the fuck difference does it make what *I'm* feeling? I'm not the one having these sick, perverted—"

"You seem angry. Are you angry, Dominick?"

"Am I *ANGRY*? Yeah, you could say that. I'm fucking *FURIOUS*, okay?"

"Why?"

I could feel myself letting go into the rush of it—passing the point of no return. That's the one thing I understood about Ray: that sometimes rage could feel as good as sex. Could be as welcome a release.

"Why am I *ANGRY*? I'll tell you why I'm *ANGRY,* okay? Because right now I should be over on Gillette Street finishing a paint job I should have finished three *fucking* weeks ago. But where am I? I'm in a *fucking* maximum-security nuthouse listening to my *fucking fucked-up* brother talk about . . . about . . . and she says to me, 'Why don't you ever stop thinking about him and think about me, Dominick? Put *me* first instead of your brother.' . . . Jesus fucking Christ! When is this shit going to—"

"Dominick? Who is 'she,' please?"

"Joy! My girlfriend! I've been carrying him on my shoulders my whole *fucking* life and she goes, 'Why don't you ever take care of me?' Well, I'll *tell* you why! I—"

"Dominick, please lower your voice. It's very good for you to let out this anger, but why don't you sit down and take a few deep breaths?"

"Why? What are deep breaths going to do? Make him less crazy? Make his fucking hand grow back?"

"It would just make you calm down a little and—"

"I don't *want* to calm down! You asked me why I'm angry and now I'm telling you! Do you know what it's *LIKE*? Do you have any *IDEA*? I'm fucking forty years old and I'm still—"

"Dominick, if you don't lower your voice a little, the security staff will—"

"Other people go to the library and get *BOOKS,* right? Check out *BOOKS.* But not *my STUPID FUCKING ASSHOLE BROTHER*! Not *HIM*! He goes to the library and cuts his fucking hand off for Jesus! And you want to know something? I got fucking *CONNIE CHUNG* calling me up! I got some stupid bloodsucker from New York wants to be his fucking *BOOKING* agent! And I can't—"

"Dominick?"

"You want to know what it's like for me? *Do* you? It's like . . . it's like . . . my brother has been an anchor on me my whole life. Pulling me down. Even *before* he got sick. Even *before* he goes and *loses* it in front of . . . An *anchor*! . . . And you know what I get? I get just enough rope to break the surface. To breathe. But I am never, *ever* going to. . . . You know what I used to think? I used to think that eventually—you know, sooner or later—I was going to get away from him. Cut the cord, you know? But here I am, forty years old and I'm still down at the nuthouse, running interference for my fucking . . . Treading water. It's like . . . like . . . And I *hate* him sometimes. I do. I'll admit it. I really hate him. But you know something? Here's the *really* fucked-up part. Nobody *else* better say anything—nobody *else* better even look at him cross-eyed or I'll . . . And the thing is, I think I finally *get* it, you know? I finally *get* it."

"Get what, Dominick?"

"That he's my *curse.* My *anchor.* That I'm just going to tread water for the rest of my whole life. That he *is* my whole life! My fucking, fucked-up brother. I'm just going to tread water, just breathe . . . and that's it. I'm *never* going to get away from him! Never!"

There was a knock on the door. "Not now, thank you," Dr. Patel called out.

"The other day? Last week, it was? I went to the convenience store. My girlfriend says, 'We're out of milk, Dominick. Go get some milk.' So I go to the convenience store and I put a gallon of milk on the counter and this clerk—this fat fuck with orange hair and a pierced nose—he's just . . . he was just *staring* at me like . . . like I'm . . ."

"Like you were what?"

"Like I'm *him*! *Thomas.* Which I . . . Which I probably *will* be before I'm through. I mean, we're twins, right? It's going to happen eventually, isn't it?"

"What, exactly, do you think is going to happen, Dominick?"

"He's going to pull me under. I'm going to drown."

I did her stupid breathing exercises. Laced my fingers like she instructed and rested them on my belly. Filled my stomach with air like a balloon. Breathed out in a long, steady stream. In again. Out. It felt stupid, but I did it. And by the sixth or seventh breath, it worked. Calmed me down. Brought me back.

"It frightens you, doesn't it, Dominick: the thought that you, too, could become mentally ill? How could it *not* have frightened you all these years? His brother? His twin?"

De-fense! *De*-fense!

"It's not like . . . Look, I'm not saying he *never* hit her. Ray. He did. It's just—"

The office door banged open—so loudly and abruptly that the doc and I both jumped. "Jesus!" I snapped at Sheffer. "You ever hear of knocking?"

"At my own office door?" she shot back.

She threw a stack of files on her desk. Took in the tape recorder, the warning look I caught Dr. Patel giving her, the way I guess I must have looked right about then. Sheffer looked a little whipped herself.

Her hands went into the air, palms up. "I'm sorry," she said. "Give me a couple of minutes, will you? I just need to go to the ladies' room for a second."

After the door closed behind her, Dr. Patel asked me if I was all right.

I told her I'd live.

"Which do you want first?" Sheffer asked us. "The bad news or the good?"

"The bad," I said and, simultaneously, Dr. Patel said, "The good."

Sheffer said the probate judge had decided to drop the criminal charge against my brother. The weapon thing. The bad news—*potentially* bad, anyway—was that Thomas had been released to the custody of the Psychiatric Security Review Board.

"The law-and-order guys, right?" I said. "The ones that want to lock up everyone and throw away the key?"

"Not everyone, Domenico. But the headline-grabbers do tend to have a built-in disadvantage." She looked over at Dr. Patel. "In *my* opinion, anyway."

"But Lisa," Dr. Patel said, "Mr. Birdsey's case is quite different from some of the other high-profile cases that have come before the Board. There's no criminal charge, no victim."

"Arguable," Sheffer said. "The other people in the library that day were terrified, right? Afraid for their safety? Doesn't that make *them* victims? They could argue that."

I thought of Mrs. Fenneck's appearance at my front

door—that librarian telling me how she hadn't been able to eat or sleep since. "*Who* could argue it?" I said.

"The Review Board. Or how about this: that Thomas was both perpetrator *and* victim. They could say they need to commit him long term to keep him safe from himself. Which may be a perfectly valid point. The weird part—the thing that worries me, frankly—is that they've already scheduled his hearing. Know when it is? The thirty-first."

"The thirty-first of *October*?" Dr. Patel said.

Sheffer nodded. "Trick or treat, kids."

"But that's next week, Lisa," Patel said. "His medication will have barely had time to stabilize him by then. He'll have been back on his neuroleptics less than three weeks."

"Not to mention that the fifteen-day observation period will be up *that day.*"

"Ridiculous," Dr. Patel said. "How are they proposing to use our recommendations if we don't even have time to observe him and write them up?"

Sheffer said the judge wouldn't even *listen* to her argument about postponement. "Ironic, isn't it?" she said. "I'm usually complaining about how *in*efficient the judicial system is, but in this case, it's the efficiency that scares me. Why are they being so *expedient*?"

"I'll tell you one thing," I said. "If this is some kind of bag job—if they're trying to rush this through so they can sentence him to this rathole for another whole year—I'm going to raise holy hell."

"You know, Domenico," Sheffer said. "Hatch might *be* the most appropriate place for Thomas. Or it might *not* be. That's the point: it's just too soon to call it. But I'll be honest with you: if you show up at the hearing 'raising holy hell,' that may just be your best shot at getting him out of here. At least it'll make a statement: that he's got family that cares. That his family might be willing to shoulder some of the responsibility. They might hear that, if you put it right. It all depends."

"Depends on what?"

She looked over at Dr. Patel. "I don't know. On politics, maybe. On who—if anyone—might be pulling from the opposite direction."

* * *

When I got up to go, Dr. Patel asked me if I'd wait for a minute while she returned the tape recorder to her office. She'd see me to the front entrance, she said. She'd only be a minute.

Sheffer went over to her filing cabinet. She was wearing a tan suit and little matching high heels. Dressed up like that, she looked even *more* like a pip-squeak.

"Where's your sneakers?" I asked her.

"Excuse me?"

"Your high-tops. I almost didn't recognize you in your lady lawyer disguise."

She rolled her eyes. "You've gotta dress the part for these conservative judges. Nothing wilder than Sandra Day O'Connor. You see the lengths I go to?"

"I'm starting to," I said. Caught her eye. "Thanks."

"I just hope it works," she said. "Rough session today?"

"What?"

"Your brother's session? You looked a little shell-shocked when I barged in here. Which I apologize for, by the way."

I shrugged. Looked away from her. "No problem," I mumbled.

When Dr. Patel returned, she took my arm and walked me back through Hatch's liver-colored corridors. Past the guard station, up to the metal detector at the front entrance. Under the halogen glare, her gold and tangerine–colored sari was almost too much to take.

"It was difficult for you today," she said. Gave my arm a squeeze. "And yet, I hope, productive."

I told her I was sorry.

"Yes? Sorry for what, Dominick?"

"For losing it. For screaming. All those four-letter words I was letting rip back there."

She shook her head vigorously. "Your reactions—your insights—have been very helpful to me, Dominick. Perhaps they'll prove crucial in the long run. One never knows. I think, however, that we should discontinue the practice of having you listen to the tapes of your brother's sessions."

"*Why?* I thought you said it helped."

"It does. But one brother's treatment should not put another brother at risk."

"Look, if I can help him . . . I *want* to help him. If you can learn things."

She reached for my hand. Squeezed it. "I learned something very useful today," she said.

"Yeah? What's that?"

"I learned that there are *two* young men lost in the woods. Not one. Two."

She gave me one of those half-smiles of hers—one of those noncommittal jobs. "I may never find one of the young men," she said. "He has been gone so long. The odds, I'm afraid, may be against it. But as for the other, I may have better luck. The other young man may be calling me."

eighteen

1969

The summer Thomas and I worked for the Three Rivers Public Works was also the summer of Woodstock, Chappaquiddick, and Neil Armstrong's "giant leap for mankind." Ray was so thrilled that we were about to beat the Russians to the moon that he went down to Abram's Appliance Store the week before the launch and traded in our old black-and-white Emerson TV for a new cabinet-model color Sylvania. He said he didn't care for himself, but he wanted my brother, Ma, and me to be able to see history being made on a TV where the picture didn't roll whenever it felt like it and make everyone look like a bunch of pinheads.

Ray spent that whole first week jumping out of his chair to readjust his tint and contrast buttons; none of the rest of us was allowed to adjust the color on the new set. He must have been trying to get his money's worth, I guess, because he always made the picture ridiculously bright—so vivid it seemed obscene. He'd fiddle with those little knobs until the NBC peacock's tail feathers bled into each other and the field at Yankee Stadium turned psychedelic lime green. Newscasters' complexions glowed like jack-o'-lanterns.

On the big night of the moon landing, I was on Ray's shit list because I'd made plans with Leo Blood to drive down to

Easterly Beach. "One of the biggest moments in American history and you're going to some dance hall?" he asked.

"That's the beauty of America, Ray," I said. "It's a free country."

The wisecrack was one I could afford to spend in the wake of Ray's tantrum with the pickle jars. For several days, he'd acted subdued with Ma. Indulgent, even. With Thomas, too, who had walked barefoot into the kitchen the morning after Ray's jar-smashing and stepped directly onto the one jagged shard my mother's cleanup had missed. The one-inch piece of glass had lodged itself so firmly into the heel of Thomas's foot that neither Ma nor I had wanted to extract it. Instead, we hustled Thomas to the emergency room, where an intern poked and prodded and removed the glass. Thomas passed out during his ordeal. The gash had required both inside and outside stitches. By the time we got back home, Ray had returned from work and cleaned up the blood that trailed from the kitchen through the house and down the front stairs. He waited for us at the front door, pale and shaken. "What the hell happened?" he said. The three of us let him wait for an answer until Thomas had negotiated the cement stairs with his crutches.

More than anything, the new TV was Ray's unspoken apology. And my going out on the night of the moon landing was my way of saying thanks but no thanks.

"They serve alcohol at this place you're going to?" he asked, passing me as I waited at the front door for Leo to show.

"I can't get into a place that serves alcohol," I said. "They card you at the door."

"They better," he said. "I catch you doing something you're not supposed to be doing and I'll make your ass bleed."

Like you made his foot bleed, you son of a bitch, I thought.

Leo's horn finally honked somewhere after the landing of the *Eagle* but before Armstrong's descent to the moon. He no longer drove his mother's Biscayne. Now Leo tooled around in his own car, a '66 Skylark convertible, cobalt blue, with a V-8, four on the floor, and a built-in eight-track with rear reverb speakers. He'd gotten a good deal on it because the engine leaked oil and the convertible top was stuck down, more or less permanently. He kept a case of Quaker State, a plastic sheet, and a stack of bath towels in the trunk for emergencies.

Leo drove the convertible fast and recklessly, which appealed to me, especially that night. Neil Armstrong and company may have torn through the heavens, but Leo and I were tearing down Route 22 with the Stones on the tape deck and a wall of oxygen rushing against us. I felt like I could breathe again. We drank beers all the way down there, chucking the cans out on the side of the road as we flew. Fuck Ray and fuck the moon and the astronauts, too. We were cooking.

Leo wanted to check out two clubs, the Blue Sands and a new place called the Dial-Tone Lounge. "We're gonna get us some action, tonight, Birdsey Boy," he called over to me. "I can feel it underneath the old loincloth."

"The old loincloth?" I laughed. Leo let go of the steering wheel and beat his chest. Then he grabbed the wheel again, stood up straight, and yelled like Tarzan. The Skylark weaved and wobbled onto the shoulder and back again.

In the Blue Sands parking lot, Leo handed me a bogus majority card and told me to memorize my name and birthday and to look the guy at the door right in the eye. Don't ask me why I still remember this, but I was Charles Crookshank, born January 19, 1947. "Where do you get these things, anyway?" I asked Leo.

"It's a kit. You send away."

The guy posted at the door looked like something out of *Planet of the Apes.* He studied our IDs with his flashlight, then shone the light right in our faces, pretty much killing off the idea of eye contact. "So," Leo said. "How about this moon landing stuff? Pretty wild, eh?"

The gatekeeper ignored Leo and looked at me. "You got a driver's license or some other form of identification, Mr. Crookshank?" he asked.

"Funny you should mention that," Leo intervened. "We're both from Manhattan, see? With all the buses and subways there, we just never bothered to get licenses. You don't really need them in New York."

"Wasn't that you who just drove in? In the Buick with Connecticut plates?"

"Yes, it was. Very observant," Leo laughed. "We borrowed my sister's car."

The guy took another look at Leo's fake ID and asked him when his birthday was. Leo got the day right but messed up on the month. "Hit the road, you two," the Ape Man said.

"That's fine, my man," Leo told him. "Peace, brother. And may I congratulate you on this great career you got going for yourself. There's an awful lot of guys would *love* to be at the top of the heap like you, collecting soggy dollar bills and stamping people's hands at a bar as scuzzy as this one." We had to run back to the Skylark and hop over the doors, King Kong lumbering across the parking lot after us.

At the Dial-Tone Lounge, those same phony IDs got us in, no sweat. All the tables at the Dial-Tone were numbered in neon and came equipped with telephones. The gimmick was: you could scope out some chick, then call up her table and flirt for a few minutes while she and her girlfriends checked out all the guys and tried to match the conversation to the moving lips.

There were more guys than girls at the Dial-Tone. The place was crawling with sailors from the submarine base over in Groton. Most of the squids wore tie-dye and love beads and bell-bottom jeans—by '69 it was bad for your sex life to look military—but the accents and haircuts gave them away. Leo and I managed to snag the last table, a two-seater stuck in the corner behind a couple of squids. One was a tall, skinny doofus and the other a squat fire hydrant with eyes. "Just what we needed," Leo mumbled as we sat down. "Popeye and Bluto blocking our view."

"Call *her,*" the skinny one kept goading his no-neck friend.

"Which one?"

"The one I was talking to at the bar."

"Should I?"

"Hell, yeah. Go for it, man! Her name's Cindy."

No Neck picked up the phone and dialed. "Hello? Cindy? You don't know me, but I got a message for you from Dick Hertz."

He cupped his hand over the receiver and winced in his effort not to laugh. "Whose Dick Hertz? Well, now that you mention it, Cindy, mine's killing me. Care to give it some relief?" He slammed down the receiver. Their loud guffawing and table-whacking made half the people in the place look over in our direction.

"Jesus Christ, Birdsey, these guys make *you* look suave," Leo said. "No wonder we're losing the fucking war."

No Neck's buddy stared over at us for a couple of seconds, then leaned forward and tapped Leo on the shoulder. "Excuse me, pal, but what'd you just say?"

"Huh?" Leo said.

"I asked you what you just said. To your friend here. Something about my buddy and me and the 'fucking war'?"

Leo looked bewildered. Then he laughed. "Fucking *whores,* is what I said. I said this place is full of fucking *whores.*"

"Oh. Well." He looked over at his buddy and back again. "You got *that* right. I thought you said something else."

"No problem, my man," Leo said, flashing him the peace sign. I shook my head and smiled.

Leo was all horny energy as he scanned the room. His leg was tapping a mile a minute, his knuckles rapping against the tabletop. "Table 7, over by the bar?" he said. "From left to right: C-minus, C-plus, B-minus, C. Table 18, near the door, everyone's an F except for the brunette in the white top—the one just sitting down. I'll give her a B. Nice ass, nice set of lungs, but she loses it on the schnoz."

"The nose knows," No Neck leaned toward us and said.

"She could bend over and use that thing as a dildo on her friends," his buddy added. Leo acted like Popeye and Bluto were invisible.

"Now there's a couple of A chicks right over there, Birdsey. Table 12. Those two brunettes in the minidresses. What do you say we put them out of their misery?" He picked up the phone and told me I could have the one with bangs.

It was "mine" who answered. Leo told her he and I were visiting the East Coast from L.A. and we just had to know something. "You work for Twentieth Century Fox, too, don't you? Haven't we seen you on the lot out there?"

I groaned and shook my head. "Honest to Christ, Leo," I said. "Sometimes I can't believe you."

He cupped his hand over the receiver. "You can eat shit, Birdseed. You're listening to a maestro at work. You ought to be taking notes."

He wove an elaborate story about how he and I were both Hollywood stuntmen and personal friends of Steve McQueen. Leo said he'd done some stunt work in *Bullitt* and that he'd just finished filming a new James Bond that wasn't out yet. Had she and her girlfriend seen *Butch Cassidy and the Sundance Kid*? The part where Paul Newman and Robert Redford say goodbye to each other and jump off the cliff? That was really Leo free-falling in that scene, not Rob Redford. That was what all his friends called him, by the way: Rob. He and Leo played cards together once or twice a month.

You could tell from the girls' body language and the way they were looking over at us that they were skeptical. Then the one with the bangs handed the phone to the other one, who said something snotty to Leo. He told her she could blow it out her ass.

"See, that's what I hate," he said, hanging up. "An A chick who *knows* she's an A chick. It goes to her head, like a brain disease. I'll take a good-natured B chick over an A with a bad attitude any day. Your basic B chick knows enough to be grateful."

Our waitress stood at the table, dark and slight, her long hair twisted into a braid. "You're *scoring* these women?" she said.

"No, we're *hoping* to score a couple," Leo told her, looking her up and down. "Hopefully two from the A or B division."

"Oh, well, I'm sure they'll be impressed by your sensitivity," she said. "What'll you guys have?"

In the middle of writing down our orders, one of the sailors at the next table reached over and yanked our waitress's braid. She banged her tray down, pivoted, and faced them. "Keep your hands to yourselves or I'll have you thrown out of here," she warned. "You understand?"

"Hey, sweetheart, I was just trying to get your attention,"

No Neck said. "Can we get us another pitcher? And how about some food? Can a guy get food at this dive?"

"Yeah, you can get food," she said. "What do you want?"

"How 'bout you, darlin'? Can I get an order of you sittin' on my face?"

I leaned toward them. "Hey, look," I said. "Why don't you guys ease off and let the lady do her job?"

"No, *you* look," she snapped. "I've been working here since noontime and the woman who was supposed to relieve me two hours ago *still* hasn't shown up yet. So the last thing I need is you starting a brawl in my honor, okay?"

"Okay," I said, holding up my hands, palms out in surrender. "Fine. Forgive me."

She turned back to the sailors. "We have sandwiches," she said, poker-faced. "They come with chips and a pickle. That's what we have."

"Sandwiches, eh? You got any baked Virginia ham sandwiches?"

"We have ham," the waitress told him. "I don't happen to know its point of origin."

"Hey, baby, if you're on the rag, it ain't my fault. Get me a baked Virginia ham sandwich on rye with mustard and another pitcher of whatever this panther piss is we're drinking. Scofield, you want anything to eat?"

"I'll have some of that dessert you were talking about before," he said. "Some of that pie *à la* sit-on-my-face."

"Assholes," the waitress mumbled. She was stuck between our two tables and I stood to let her by. "I'm not doing this to be a gentleman or anything," I said. "Honest."

"Just shut up," she said, pushing past me.

Leo started explaining his personal theory about how women with dirty mouths tended to be less inhibited in the sack. I wasn't really listening. I was watching our waitress—the way her order pad swayed in the back pocket of her jeans as she hustled back and forth, the way she retied the string on her apron and lifted up her braid to massage the nape of her neck. She was short—five feet, if that. Nice bod, nice face. There was something sort of gutsy about the way she was working the room. I couldn't stop watching her.

The TV above the bar was turned to the moon landing,

twenty or twenty-five people huddled around watching. Not that they could have heard anything over the music and the squawking deejay. Walter Cronkite was lip-synching everyone through the experience. The astronauts still hadn't emerged from the lunar module.

I nodded up at the TV screen. "Remember when Alan Shepard went up in space? What a big deal that was?"

"I was in sixth grade," Leo said.

"We were in fifth."

"Who's we?"

"Thomas and me. Our teacher brought in a radio and we got to sit around and listen and not do any work. After the splashdown, we all stood up at our desks and sang 'My Country 'Tis of Thee.' "

He nodded. "You know what I been noticing about you, Birdsey? Whenever you talk about something, you always say 'we.' Like you and him are joined at the hip or something." His eyes looked past me. "Whoa, mama, I'd like to be joined at the hip with *that* one."

My eyes followed his to a long-haired blonde over by the bar. I scanned the crowd for the little waitress. Found her three tables down.

"I was *into* all that astronaut shit when I was a kid," Leo said.

"You?"

"Oh, yeah. *Big* time. Gus Grissom, Wally Schirra, all those guys. I had this whole astronaut scrapbook. My main ambition in life was to go down to Cape Canaveral and shake hands with John Glenn."

"Thomas and I had astronaut lunch boxes," I said.

"Me, too. I had one of those. Thought I was hot stuff."

I told Leo I wasn't even sure *how* I felt about our landing on the moon. "I mean, shit, it *is* kind of a mind-bender—science fiction made real or something. Hooray for the guys with the slide rules. . . . But it seems so pro-Nixon. The triumph of capitalism, victory over the evil Communist empire. So what that we're napalming a whole fucking country and getting our asses kicked besides. Right?"

"God bless America," Leo said.

"My stepfather went out and sprung for a TV to celebrate. He's probably sitting home right now, getting a hard-on watching it."

"Speaking of which," Leo said. "Check out the redhead wearing that plaid thing. Table 16. I think I'm in l-o-v-e."

Just as he picked up the phone to dial, some other guy asked the redhead to dance. "Too bad, Sundance," I ribbed him. "Guess you're going to have to jump off the cliff a little faster than that."

"Jump off *this,* Birdsey," he said. "Hey, you know what Dell told me? About the astronauts? That it's all a hoax—that they're not really up there orbiting the moon. He says they're hanging out in some top-secret TV studio in New Jersey. Nixon arranged it to take the heat off of the war. Dell says he read all about it in this newspaper he gets."

"That would be the *New York Times,* right?" I laughed.

"Fucking Dell, man," Leo laughed. "I don't know *what* planet that guy's from."

A big part of that night is a blur to me. I recall dancing with some blonde in pigtails who reminded me of Ellie May Clampett. I remember the Dial-Tone passing out free champagne after Armstrong and Aldrin's moon bounce. Remember No Neck throwing a punch at someone and getting escorted out by two bouncers. Somewhere along the way, we changed waitresses.

"I'm going outside," I told Leo. It was sometime after midnight by then. "Walk the beach or something."

He had connected with the redhead after all; their slow-dancing was starting to look like foreplay. "Nice knowing you," Leo said.

Outside, the air was cool and misty and the moon had a hazy glow. Someone at the far end of the parking lot kept trying to start their car, grinding the ignition over and over and over again.

I climbed up the bank and down the other side to the ocean. The tide sounded like a flushing toilet. Clots of seaweed littered the beach.

There was nobody else around. I took off my sandals and flung them back toward the lifeguard stand. Rolled up my jeans and walked down by the water.

The cold sea air sobered me up some—washed away the

wooziness and the stink of cigarettes and the strobe light flashes from inside. Meat shows: that's all these bars were. I could still hear the thump of the music inside, but more and more faintly, the farther I walked. The surf lapping over my feet felt good. I stared back up at the moon.

I must have walked for a mile, mile and a half, just thinking about shit: how it must feel to be way up there, looking down at the earth. Not being a part of it. Taking in the place, whole. That was the thing, man. That's what was hard: we were all moon walkers, in a way. Me. Leo. Ralph Drinkwater. My brother. Even my stupid stepfather, locked in a three-against-one with Ma and Thomas and me. Even all the clowns back there at the Dial-Tone Lounge, getting loaded so they could get up the nerve to try and fuck some girl—*any* girl—tether themselves to *some*one, even for a couple of minutes in the backseat of someone's car. For a couple of seconds, everything was all clear. It all made sense. Who was that guy we'd read in my philosophy class last semester? That existentialism guy? He was right. Every one of us was alone. Even if you were someone's identical twin. I mean, why *had* Thomas gotten up in the middle of the night and run those laps around the dorm? *None* of it made any sense, man, that was why. Because the whole freaking world was absurd. Because man *was* existentially alone. . . . *Whoa, far out,* I said, teasing myself back to earth again. *Heavy, man.* I'd actually remembered something from school a whole month after the final exam. I was turning into a freaking philosopher. I reached down and picked some rocks off the beach. Chucked them, one by one, into the rolling surf. I don't know how long I stood there, pitching stones.

When I got back and went to get my sandals, I saw a silhouette up in the lifeguard's perch. Someone small. "Yoo-hoo," she called. "Do you have jumper cables?"

I told her I didn't. "Were you the one I heard a while ago? Sounds like you might have flooded her. If I were you, I'd wait a little while longer, then try again."

As I approached, I realized who it was: that little waitress from the Dial-Tone. She was sitting with her knees to her chest, wearing a sweatshirt with her hands tucked inside the sleeves.

"Not that I'm trying to rescue you or anything."

She smiled. "Hey, I really *did* appreciate you trying to get those jerks to back off," she said. "It was sweet. Thanks."

"No problem."

"I just get so tired of it, you know? Guys playing grab-ass all night. Showing their buddies what he-men they are. One of the other waitresses—one of the veterans—taught me to cop an attitude. Snap at them like you're their mother and if they don't stop it you'll send them up to their room. So that's what I do. It works."

I nodded. "Sure scared the crap out of me," I said.

She looked back toward the Dial-Tone. "God, I hate that place," she said.

"Yeah, well, if it's true Western civilization's in decline, I guess we may have hit bottom with the Dial-Tone Lounge." She laughed that pretty laugh of hers. That night out by the lifeguard stand was the first time I ever heard it.

"So what'd they do, fire you?" I said. "Or did you quit?"

"Neither. My replacement finally showed up. God, I hope I can get that stupid car started. I don't want to have to sit around until two and wait for my sleazy assistant manager to bring me home."

"Where do you live?" I said. "Maybe my buddy and I can give you a lift."

She smiled. "The guy who grades women? Thanks anyway."

"No problem."

Neither of us said anything for several seconds. I started to walk away.

"You feel like sitting up here with me?" she said. "Come on up. There's room."

"Yeah?"

She said she had a spot all warmed up for me.

I climbed the tower and squeezed in next to her. Saw the book in her lap. She's always been a big reader—even back then she was.

"Didn't your mother ever tell you not to read in the dark?" I said.

"I wasn't. I was reading by the moonlight."

"Same difference. What's so good that you're wrecking your eyesight over it?"

"Richard Brautigan," she said, handing me the paperback. "I don't really get it, but I can't stop reading it," she said. "It's mysterious. . . . It intrigues me."

I opened it up and squinted. Made out the first paragraph. Read it aloud. *"In watermelon sugar the deeds were done and done again as my life is done in watermelon sugar. I'll tell you about it because I am here and you are distant."*

"Look at his picture," she said. "He has his picture on all his book covers."

I closed the book, held it up to the moon. "Looks like Mark Twain on acid," I said. She laughed. Passed her hand through my curly hair, messed it up a little. Am I remembering it right? Was *that* all it took? I know this much: that I fell in love with her right there. Before I even jumped down from that lifeguard tower.

She was easy to talk to—that was the thing. And pretty. And smart. Funny, too. She told me she was twenty-one, a senior at Boston College majoring in early childhood education. Besides waitressing, she worked mornings at a Head Start program. "My father wanted me to work for him again this summer," she said. "In the bookkeeping department with my uncle Costas. He owns a car dealership. But I'd done that for three summers in a row. I was looking for a little change. And some independence, I guess. Can you believe I actually *wanted* to go through the interview process? Fill out applications to see if anyone besides my family would hire me? Does that make sense?"

"More sense than the fact that your father owns a dealership and you're riding around in a car that won't start," I said.

"Oh, God, Daddy would die if he knew I was out here stranded. He means well, but he's just so overprotective. What's your name?"

"*My* name? Dominick."

"Dominick," she repeated. "Italian, right?"

"Yup. Well, half."

"What's the other half?"

The whack of the funny bone. The unanswerable question. "Oh, little of this, little of that," I said. "How about you?"

"Greek," she said. "Both sides. My father's Greek-American and my mother's an immigrant. By the way, my name is Dessa."

"Dessa what?"

"Constantine."

"Constantine? As in 'Come see the Dodge boys at Constantine Motors'?" I started singing the radio jingle I'd heard a million times from Ralph Drinkwater's radio.

She laughed. Swatted me one. "I'll have to tell my father when he gets back that those ads are starting to pay off."

"I haven't bought a car yet, have I?" I said. "Where's he at?"

"What?"

"Your father. You just said, 'when he gets back.' "

"Oh. He's in Greece. He and my mother and my little sister. They go back every year to visit relatives. This is the first year I haven't gone. Have you ever been?"

Yeah, sure, I thought to myself. The jet-setting Birdseys. "Can't say that I have."

"Oh, *go* sometime if you get the chance. The Aegean's so incredible. The sense of history, the sun—the light there doesn't look anything like it does around here. And the water! You wouldn't believe the color of the water."

We sat there for a minute or so, watching the ocean, saying nothing. Ordinarily, with a girl, I would have panicked at that amount of dead airtime. But with Dessa, the silence felt comfortable.

"How old's your little sister?" I said.

"Athena? Yuck. She's seventeen."

"Athena? As in, the goddess of wisdom?"

She laughed. "More like the goddess of obnoxious behavior. She hates the name. We're supposed to call her Angie. She's such a brat! My parents let her get away with murder."

I told her I had a twin brother.

"You do? Identical or fraternal?"

"Identical."

"Oh, wow," she said. "Is that cool? Having a twin?"

I gave her a short snort. "*No.*"

"No? Why not?"

For some reason, I started telling her about our first year at UConn—Thomas keeping himself cooped up in our room, taking his frustration out on our typewriter.

She just listened. Just let me keep talking, which I couldn't quite believe I was doing so much of.

"I guess it *would* be hard, having someone *that* close to you," she said. "Especially if he's so dependent. You must never feel like you have any breathing room."

I couldn't believe someone had actually heard me. That someone, on some level, understood. I reached over and kissed her. She kissed me back. "You taste nice," she said. "Kind of salty."

Half a dozen kisses later, I was wired up and hungry for her—had gone from zero to sixty in about a minute. "Hey, hold it, cowboy," she said. She pulled my hands off of her and jumped down from the tower. Looked up at the moon. "It's strange, isn't it?" she said. "To think there are actually a couple of earthlings up there, right now, walking around? The men on the moon. It's surreal, isn't it?"

She walked slowly to the water's edge. Waded in.

I am here and you are distant, I thought, unsure if I meant Dessa, or my brother, or the astronauts up there on the moon. Unsure of what I meant.

"Hey, Dominick, come here!" she called. *"Look!"*

When I reached her, she took my hand. She was staring into the water. "God, I haven't seen this since I was a kid," she said.

"Seen what?"

"Phosphorescence. In the water. Right there!"

"Right where?" I said. "What are you talking about?"

"Those little twinkles of light along the surface of the water. You have to be quick. They only last about a second. *Look!* There's another one! See it?"

I saw ocean. Sand. Our feet in the water.

"My sister and I used to call it pixie dust. There's another one!"

I kept thinking she was pulling my leg. Kept missing it. Then, son of a bitch, there it was. Phosphorescence.

Pixie dust.

Her car started on the first try.

* * *

Later on, I rode home half-listening to Leo complain about what cock-teases redheads were. “It’s like a club,” he said. “An unwritten law.” We stopped at the Oh Boy Diner. Drank coffee, ate eggs. I didn’t mention anything about Dessa—didn’t say a thing. I didn’t want to hear any of Leo’s theories about waitresses, or girls with braids, or rich guys’ daughters. On the way back to the car, I reached into my jeans pockets and fingered the Dial-Tone Lounge matchbooks. I’d had Dessa write her number on the inside covers of two of them, not just one. The second was for security, in case I lost the first. I wasn’t taking any chances.

It was after two by the time I got home. My brother and my mother had both gone to bed; Ray lay stretched out on the couch, snoring, alone with his big night in history. The TV was still on, Walter Cronkite keeping watch at mission control. His skin glowed infrared. He babbled on and on about the moon.

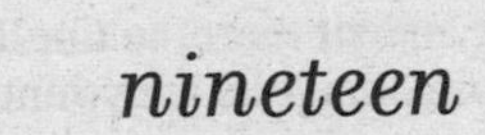

nineteen

1969

Dell Weeks never drank before noon and usually not before the middle of the week. But by Thursday or Friday, he'd start sipping from his pint bottle of Seagram's at lunch and be wasted by midafternoon.

Dell was a Jekyll and Hyde drunk. Sometimes alcohol made him everyone's best friend. "No sense killing yourself for minimum wage," he'd say, his arm around your shoulder, his sweet, boozy breath in your face. Other times he'd needle and harass—start mouthing off about "lazy spooks" and "dumb-ass college faggots" who didn't know which end of the shovel did the work. It was during one of his mean drunks that Dell started calling my brother Dickless.

If we got lucky on the afternoons he was drinking, Dell would curl up and doze in the shade of some tree or alongside or even under the city truck. He'd tell us to just get lost somewhere if we finished the job early—to leave him alone and not bother him unless we saw Lou Clukey's truck coming. At first, Leo and Thomas and I would just sit around and bullshit and Ralph Drinkwater would park someplace nearby—far enough away to be antisocial but close enough to listen in on the conversation. If one of us had remembered a deck of cards, we'd play pitch or setback. A couple of times we were so bored, we even played tag—keepaway or whatever—as if we were all nine instead of nineteen.

Sometimes when the rest of us were killing time, Ralph would take out a joint and sit there, toking away and smirking at us as if there was some joke that went over everyone's head but his. As if Thomas and Leo and I *were* the joke. It was that same smirk he used to wear in Mr. LoPresto's history class. "Nope," Ralph would say whenever we'd asked him if he wanted to join us in some cards or whatever. "Not interested." I kept waiting for him to return the invitation and pass around one of those joints of his—I'd gotten high a couple of times at school and liked it—but Ralph didn't offer and I wasn't about to beg.

"Graveball" was what eventually got Drinkwater to let down his guard and join us. One day out at the Boswell Avenue cemetery, Leo ran his mower over something that made a loud thump and then shot out sideways. It was a Wiffle ball, nicked and battered up a little, but still serviceable. Leo invented this game where you had to hit the ball with a pair of hedge clippers, then run the bases—designated gravestones. The catch was, you had to roll your lawnmower along with you from base to base.

We started off with Leo on one team and me on the other. Thomas pinch-hit and ran bases for both of us and we cooked up a bunch of rules for "ghost runners." We'd been at it for half an hour or so when Drinkwater just couldn't stand it anymore. He stood up. Ambled over. "What are you jokers playing, anyway?" he asked. He'd been pretending not to watch us.

Leo named the game on the spot. "Graveball," he said. "Wanna play?"

Even stoned, Drinkwater was great at graveball. You just wouldn't suspect how far a Wiffle ball could travel after a collision with a pair of hedge clippers. *Thwock!* That thing would go flying the width of the cemetery and into the woods. Half the time Ralph got his at-bats, we ended up having to stop and hunt for the damn ball. He could fly around the bases, too, lawnmower and all. The guy was *fast.* But anyway, it was graveball that broke the ice with Ralph.

I'd started dating Dessa by then. The Constantines lived

in a sprawling three-story house up in Hewett City, a sixteen-mile bike ride due north from Three Rivers. They had an in-ground pool out back and a tiled patio and these fancy flower gardens. The double doors in front opened to a foyer with a marble floor. Just inside the living room, with its velvet sofas and chairs—its oil paintings of Dessa and her sister—there was this massive grandfather clock. The size and workmanship of that thing—the *tone*—put to shame that sorry-ass clock down at the S&H Green Stamp store that Ma had loved, saved for, and never even gotten. Whenever I walked into the Constantines' house, I felt my own family's smallness.

Dessa's father had had a security system installed before their trip to Greece and had exacted promises from his brother Costas to call and check in on Dess. Daddy had made his daughter promise she wouldn't entertain male company alone while they were gone, especially that good-for-nothing musician who had manhandled her. Julian, his name was. She had made a mistake, Dessa told me, and her father probably wasn't going to let her forget it for the rest of her life. Mrs. Constantine assured Dessa that her father trusted *her.* It was all the hippies and lunatics running around these days that he didn't trust. Look what had just happened out in Hollywood with that poor movie director's wife. And six months pregnant, no less! Anything could happen these days, especially to a girl who was too trusting for her own good. *Anything.* Dessa should be going with them to Greece instead of working as a barmaid at that kooky dance place with the telephones. She should be relaxing and soaking up the sun and meeting some nice young Greek men.

Dessa had shared all this over the phone before my first visit, so there was something sexy and defiant about pedaling my Columbia three-speed up the U-shaped driveway and into the Constantines' backyard, into the garage where I tripped the kickstand and parked next to Dessa's mother's dormant Chrysler Newport. Sexy, too, to peel off my sweat-soaked clothes after those long bike rides, drop them onto the mosaic floor in Dessa's bathroom, and lather up under her oscillating showerhead. The first time I visited, Dessa stayed downstairs while I showered and changed. The second time, she was a talking blur in cutoffs and a bikini top on the other side of the glass doors and I had to wait out my erection before I could shut off the water and emerge. By my third visit, Dessa and I were showering together, washing away the sex we'd just made, passing the soap over each other's body in ways that fired us up all over again.

Before Dessa, I had never felt that kind of fire. Had wondered sometimes if I'd ever feel it. In *Newsweek* and on TV, they were always talking about the sexual revolution—spouting some jaw-dropping statistic about how the majority of young American males had experienced umpteen partners by the time they were my age. Maybe that had happened to Leo and every other guy, but not to me. Before Dessa, the sum total of my sexual experience had been my episode out at the Falls with Patty Katz and the time during a dorm party the semester before when a drunk girl had laughed in the dark at my confusion over her pantyhose and then stuck it inside her and said, "There. *Go.*"

Dessa was the experienced one—the one with "two serious relationships" behind her. Both the dulcimer player and the antiwar organizer had been older than she—had sometimes made her feel, she said, like a foolish little girl. And although her parents only knew about the incident with Julian—she'd called them from the Brighton police station the night he'd slammed her against the wall and broken her wrist—she'd been roughed up by both men. She told me she appreciated my inexperience. My shyness. She said she felt safe in my arms.

"That's what I hate about waitressing," she told me one afternoon. "The fact that, some nights, I just don't feel safe." The two of us were lying on her bed, listening to music and just holding on to each other. "Most guys get so hostile when they drink. I hate the way they egg each other on." She shifted around on the bed so that she could look at me. "What are you guys so *angry* about?" she said.

I rubbed my hand up and down her leg, kissed her temple, kissed the corner of her mouth. "I'm not angry," I said. "I come in peace."

"But seriously, though," she said. "Sometimes at work,

even with the bouncers and the bartenders keeping an eye on us, I just don't feel safe."

"Then quit," I told her.

"I can't quit."

"Sure you can," I told her. "How do you think *I* feel knowing that every guy at that bar is checking you out? If you quit, we could see each other on weekends. Go to the beach. Spend whole days together."

"Dominick, I have to work," she said.

"You've got your Head Start job. That's work."

She laughed. "You know what I clear at that job, Dominick? Thirty-six dollars a week. I make double that—*triple* that some nights—bringing drunken jerks their beers down at the Dial-Tone."

"Hey, it's not as if you *need* the money. Your tuition's probably, what? Seven or eight car sales down at your father's place?"

"But that's not the point. I need to prove something to myself."

I stifled a smile, swallowed a little bit of resentment. I wished *I* had the luxury of working for something other than the money. "You need to prove *what*?"

"Dominick, my father is the most generous man in the world, okay? He'd give my sister and me anything we asked for. But that's the problem. You pay a price by being on the receiving end of that. You give up your independence."

I began stroking the inside of her leg. "If I quit, it would prove *his* point, not mine," she said. She yanked her shirt up over her head, unhooked her bra. "Daddy would just love it if his little Dessa couldn't fend for herself. If she was still just Daddy's little girl. But I'm *not.* I'm my own person. Right?"

"Right," I said.

She slid out of her panties. Grabbed onto my arm. "Does any of this make sense to you?" she asked. "I mean, you're saying 'right,' but do you really get the point?"

I reached over and kissed her breast. "Yeah, I get the point, all right," I told her. "I'm pointing all over the place here."

"Oh, forget it," she sighed. "I swear, you guys are all alike."

* * *

She was a patient lover. After the first two or three jackrabbit sessions, she showed me the value of taking my time, making choices with her. "Do you like this?" she'd ask. "Does this feel good?" Then she'd take my hand in her hand, guide my fingertips and show me how and where I could return the favor. "Slower, now," she'd whisper. "That's it. Nice and slow." When she was ready, she'd draw me against her, inside of her. I learned how to pace it, how to hold on until I'd feel her whole body tense, close to the edge, and then over the edge, lost in a pleasure that was both ours and hers in private. Sometimes that privacy would worry me a little, make me feel insecure, and I'd think, maybe she's imagining it's one of those other guys. Then, as if by instinct, she'd open her eyes and smile at me and touch my face. Say something like "Hey, you?" and turn her attention to me. To *my* pleasure. Until I was caught up in a release so wild and sweet that it was hard to believe that, oh Jesus, this was real and here and happening to me, Dominick.

One time right afterward, when we were both still catching our breath, I told her I loved her. Watched her face go from peaceful to sad.

"I've heard that line before," she said.

"It's not a 'line,' Dessa. I mean it."

"Okay, *why*? *Why* do you love me?"

"Because you're you," I said, groping. "And because . . . you're a good teacher."

She smiled, jabbed me one. "I think you just like the lesson plan," she said.

On those summer nights alone together in the Constantines' big house, teasing was part of what was sexy. So was eating. Downstairs, lying on her parents' beige wall-to-wall carpeting, we'd play Greek music and drink red wine and feast: feta cheese and oily brown olives, tomatoes and basil, crusty bread from Gianacopolis Bakery. Sometimes Dessa would heat up the food her mother had frozen for her in little foil packages before the trip: spinach pie, moussaka. And afterward, more wine and fruit. Sometimes we'd read to each other, or watch TV, or Dessa would tell stories about when she and her sister Angie were kids. After she got me laughing, she'd say, "Now you tell me about *your* childhood," and I'd remember nothing but spankings and crying jags—the time Ray caught Thomas and me eating Halloween candy at church, the time he pulled over to the side of the highway and made us get out of the car because we'd been arguing with each other. We were what? Six? Seven, maybe? We got out, stood on the side of the road, and he drove off. Just drove away and left us there. And by the time he came back, Thomas and I were holding on to each other, crying our fucking heads off. . . . It wasn't *all* bad. It wasn't *always* like that. But when Dessa asked about my childhood, those were the only kinds of things I could think of. So I'd just shrug and tell her I couldn't remember that kind of stuff the way she could. Then I'd look away and change the subject. Wait for her to stop looking at me. Wait for her curiosity to pass.

Sometimes after dark, we'd swim out back in their pool. Or do other stuff out there. Or go back up to Dessa's room. Once we even made love on the floor of her parents' bedroom, Dessa on top and me looking past her shoulder, past the bottles of fancy colognes and lotions on her mother's bureau and into the mirror at the two of us, rocking, joined together. We hadn't *planned* it. It just happened. I'd gone into Thula and Gene's room to wait out Uncle Costas's surprise visit and half an hour later, when Dessa came back upstairs and found me, we just . . . *bam!* It was like we hadn't seen each other in five years or something. That's the way it was at the beginning: neither of us could keep our hands off the other. Get filled up. It felt powerful and powerless both—what we kick-started that summer in the Constantines' big empty house.

Because of our work schedules, I saw her on Monday, Tuesday, and Wednesday nights. Come eleven or midnight, I'd throw a couple cups of coffee in me and then get back on my bike—pedal like a maniac down Lakeside, across Woodlawn, and out onto Route 165. By the time I got home, Ray would be at work and Ma and Thomas would have gone to bed. I'd sit in our pathetic plastic-tiled kitchen with its corny knickknacks, its flypaper hanging from the ceiling, studded with victims, and feel embarrassed about who and what we were. Or else I'd lie in the dark in the living room on our shabby, unraveling braided rug from Sears and think, here I am, a rich girl's boyfriend, the only guy who can make her feel safe. And not just any rich girl, either. *Dessa.* And I'd feel again the small heft of her breast, my lips against her nipples—see my fingers unraveling that long black braid of hers. Exhausted but wired, I'd twist and fidget, unable to go upstairs and sleep. Unable to get filled up with her.

I thought I was playing it cool. I didn't think it showed, but it must have. At work, Leo teased me about my yawning, my dozing at lunchtime—about what I must be "ordering off the menu from my little waitress friend." At home, Ma kept asking me when she was going to be able to meet my "new gal." Thomas kept bugging me about what Dessa looked like. Possessive of what I had—reluctant to share even information about her—I volunteered the minimum. "She's short," I told him. "Brunette."

"What else?"

"That's it," I said, shrugging. "Short and brunette. She goes to Boston College."

One morning while I was shaving at the bathroom sink, Ray walked in and stood behind me, studying my sleepy face in the medicine cabinet mirror. I'd gotten in at three that same morning, had copped a grand total of three hours' sleep before I'd had to get up for work.

"What's up?" I said.

"Your mother tells me you were out late again last night," he said.

I shut up. Kept shaving.

"You and this chippy of yours being careful?" he said.

The night before, Dessa had shaken her dialpack at me like a box of Good & Plentys, then kissed me and gulped down one of the tiny tablets that kept us safe from complications. "Safety" was something I saw as her department.

"This *chippy*?" I said. Tried on a Ralph Drinkwater smirk of indifference.

Ray took a box of Trojans out of his workshirt pocket and tossed them onto the top of the toilet tank. Said nothing. I steadied the razor in my hand and shaved—tried as hard as I could to act nonchalant, to ignore his big investigation. *De*-fense! *De*-fense!

"I'm not discussing my personal life with you, Ray," I said. "It's private."

Ray let go a one-note chuckle. "Fine with me, Romeo. As far as I'm concerned, you can go out and be as private as you want. Just don't come back here telling your mother and me that you got the clap or that you knocked up some little tootsie."

I turned and faced him, half of my face lathered, the other half clean-shaven. "Atta boy, Ray," I said. "Go to it. Make love sound as ugly as possible." Then I turned back and faced the mirror.

He stood there for another several seconds, watching as I nicked myself, winced, dabbed at the blood. Then he did something totally unexpected: reached up and grabbed my arm with his leathery hand. More in a fatherly than a threatening way. For a couple of seconds, we stared at each other in the mirror. "All I'm saying, hothead, is that I remember what it's like to be your age and getting a little pussy," he said. "I was in the Navy, kiddo. I know the ropes. Just be careful where you're sticking your dipstick—that's all I'm saying. Don't let it get complicated."

I couldn't look at him. Couldn't accept this sudden father-to-son stuff. I resented him anywhere *near* what Dessa and I had put in motion. So when he walked out of the bathroom, I called his name. Reached over to the toilet tank for the box of safes. "Here," I said, tossing them back. "You forgot these."

He caught them. Threw them back again. They landed in the sink bowl, under the running water. "I didn't forget them," he said. "Who do you think I went out and bought the damn things for? The Pope? Your brother?"

After a week or so of graveball, Ralph Drinkwater *did* start passing around those joints of his. The first couple of times, it was a novelty for Leo and me, getting high on the job, working with a buzz on. Then it turned into a kind of semi-routine. While Dell was sleeping one off—and even some afternoons when he wasn't—Leo and Drinkwater and I would find something real interesting out in the woods, then circulate the wacky weed. Get wrecked on company time.

Leo kept trying to get Thomas high, too, poking the lit roach in front of his face no matter how many times my brother refused. It flustered Thomas, having to keep saying no; he'd get up on his high horse. "Just what I want to do, Leo," he told him once. "Inhale something that's going to turn me into as big a goofball as you are."

Drinkwater's dope shifted the whole dynamic. Ralph, Leo, and I turned into a trio and Thomas became the odd man out. If we had a field to mow or an acre of brush to clear, the three of us would cook up a plan to make it go faster, easier, and Thomas would plod along on his own, uninvited. At lunchtime, he'd sit by himself in a huff, hardly speaking to the rest of us. Sometimes Dell would assign Thomas a separate job altogether—send the three of us off someplace and then sit there and watch Thomas work. Criticize him. Bust his balls. Dell began to take a special interest in making Thomas's life miserable.

"Tell your brother he better watch out for Dell," Ralph said to me one afternoon. The two of us were painting picnic tables side by side down at the fairgrounds, high on hemp and paint fumes. Dell and Thomas were across the field, painting a set of bleachers.

"What do you mean, 'watch out for him'?" I said.

He shrugged. "I don't mean nothing. Just tell him."

During the first couple of weeks on the job, it was Drinkwater who'd ridden shotgun in the cab with Dell, but now Thomas sat up front. That saddens me now, but it didn't back then. I was *glad* for the reprieve—grateful to be a free agent for a change. I remember Thomas, sitting up front, craning his neck back at Leo and Ralph and me—the three of us laughing and hooting at girls on the street or sipping another joint on the way back to the city barn.

"That brother of yours is fucked *up,*" Leo said one time when he caught Thomas looking back at us.

"He's more fucked up than a soup sandwich," Ralph added. And the three of us broke into snorts and giggles, courtesy of Thomas. On another of those rides, Leo started blowing kisses to this woman in a convertible behind us. She yelled back something about us being the Three Stooges, and Ralph launched into this imitation of Curly Joe that was so dead-on and unexpected, none of us could breathe from laughing so hard. Leo made up a theme song for us: "Three Dumb Fucks," sung to the tune of "Three Blind Mice." Sometimes we'd sing that song all the way back to the barn, making up new lyrics that struck us all as hilarious. The three of us were happy as pigs in shit to be wasted and working for the Three Rivers Public Works.

But as tight as Leo, Drinkwater, and I got that summer, there was always a kind of mystery about Ralph. A question mark hanging over his circumstances. He never volunteered much. We knew he didn't live at home, but he never quite said where he *did* live. He took a ride home from Dell sometimes, but he always refused one from Leo. He was always "too busy" to hang out with us on the weekend. The only time that whole summer that Leo and I got together with Ralph was one Sunday when the three of us drove up to Fenway for a doubleheader. And even then, Ralph acted like some kind of secret agent about where he lived. We had to pick him up downtown in front of the post office, I remember. And drop him off there, too, even though we got back late in the middle of a rainstorm—the three of us soaked to the bone because of Leo's broken convertible top.

Part of what was between us was Ralph's race. You'd see it sometimes when Dell started up with his stupid jokes, or when Leo hit a nerve. Indian or mulatto or whatever he was, Drinkwater was different from us lily-white college boys who got to go back to school at the end of the summer while he stayed stuck in Three Rivers. And it wasn't like he was stupid. He was always trying to talk to us about politics or something he'd seen on the news or read about in some science article. He read a lot—as much as any college kid. He kept trying to get us to read this one book, *Soul on Ice,* by Eldridge Cleaver. He recommended that book to us so many times, it got to be a joke.

One time Leo called Ralph "Tonto," and he got pissed about it. He told Leo that Leo wasn't fit to lick the foot of a Wequonnoc Indian. Another time the three of us were toking up out at the reservoir. I was sucking away on the end of the roach and Leo said, "Jesus Christ, Birdseed, you don't have to nigger-lip the thing to death." Drinkwater and I both laughed a little when he said it, but then there was this silence that lasted about fifteen seconds longer than it should have. Ralph got up and walked off into the woods. "That was real swift of you," I told Leo. "Congratulations, man."

"Hey, shoot me, okay, Birdsey," Leo snapped back. "I can't keep track of whether he's an Indian or Afroman or *what* he is."

Another wedge between Ralph and us—between Ralph and everyone—was the death of his sister. I didn't catch on at first. Couldn't read where some of his moodiness was coming from. I knew the obvious: that Penny Ann was buried out there at the Indian cemetery. His cousin Lonnie, too. You couldn't miss Lonnie's gravestone. *"In Memory of a Modern Warrior."* In contrast, Penny Ann's stone was about the size of a dictionary. *"P.A.D."* was all it said. *"1948–1958."*

Ralph would get sulky every week when we mowed the Indian graveyard. Nothing anyone said out there struck him as funny. It was something I thought I understood. Then one day it hit me like a brick in the head: this wasn't just the place where his sister's and cousin's graves were. It was worse than that. This was the place where that sick bastard Monk had taken Penny Ann during the snowstorm. This was where they'd found her body.

Dell liked to save the Indian cemetery—the smallest of the town graveyards—for Friday afternoons. We always finished ahead of time, and more often than not, Dell would take out his Seagram's and start celebrating the weekend early. One hot afternoon, Leo got the bright idea that we should head up the path to the Falls, then climb down and go swimming in the river. I figured Drinkwater would steer clear of the place. It made me a little squeamish myself. But Ralph surprised me and followed us up the path. I don't remember Thomas being there that day. It may have been around the time he cut his foot.

There were "no trespassing" signs posted all over the place and chain-link fence on both cliff edges at the waterspill. All that stuff had been put up by the town years ago in response to Penny Ann's murder. But by the summer of '69, those "keep out" signs had all rusted and chipped. Kids had long ago bent an opening in the fence and trampled a path down to the water.

Leo went first. I followed, half-walking and half-running down the steep path. Drinkwater brought up the rear. Down by the water's edge, Leo and I shucked off our clothes and eased into the cedar-tinted water. Ralph yanked off his boots and socks, threw his wallet onto the pile. Then he waded in, still wearing his tank top and jeans. I wondered why—what all the modesty was about—but I didn't say anything. Didn't kid him about it. If I didn't really understand the *whys* of Ralph's boundaries, I at least had a sense of what they were. Unlike Leo.

"Hey, you guys! Look!" Leo called over the roar of the water. He was pointing to the middle of the river. "Holy shit! Is this what I think it is?"

Ralph and I stood watching as he dived underwater, swam to the spot where he'd been pointing, and resurfaced. "Hey! I don't believe it! It *is*!"

"What?" I yelled. Ralph and I waited, riveted.

Instead of answering, Leo dived again. Surfaced. "Yup. Just like I thought. Holy Christ!"

"What?" I said. "What the fuck you talking about?"

"It's that Mary Jo Kopechne broad. She must have floated downstream from Massachusetts. Psyche!" He broke into obnoxious guffawing that ricocheted into the treetops. "Man, I got you two *bad*!"

I shot a nervous glance over toward Ralph. "Shut up, Leo," I called to him.

"What's the matter with *you,* Birdsey?" he laughed. "You related to the Kennedys or something?"

Then Ralph went under. I waited. He resurfaced fifty feet or so up the river. Climbed the bank and disappeared back into the woods.

I swam upriver myself, wanting to distance myself from Leo. I cooled off for five or ten minutes. When I got back to the Falls, Leo called my name. He was pointing straight up.

Ralph had climbed back up the path, but instead of crawling through the opening in the fence, he was scaling the remaining ten or twelve feet of cliff wall. We watched him in silence until he was out on the unprotected side of the ledge.

From there, he started climbing the mammoth oak tree that grew right at the cliff's edge. He rose way the hell up into the branches and leaves, until he was so high up there that it made me nauseous to even look. Finally he climbed out onto a branch and just sat there, his legs dangling over the sides. He was staring down into the falling water, smirking that smirk. What struck me most was the loneliness of his position: the black Indian, the nonseasonal worker. The untwinned twin. There was something about Ralph that filled me up with sadness. Some pain that was readable just in the way he sat up there on that tree limb. But not completely readable. Something *un*readable, too.

"Hey, Drinkwater," Leo shouted up. "Let's see a dive! Come on, you chicken-shit bastard. *Jump!*"

I saw Penny Ann's body falling over the edge and down. "Shut up!" I yelled and whacked Leo one across the mouth.

"Hey! What'd you fucking do that for?"

"To shut you up, asshole." I grabbed his wrist as his fist came flying at me in retaliation. The two of us tussled, went under. I'd split his lip. Bloodied up his teeth. I got him in a hold from behind. "His *sister* died out here, you idiot," I hissed into his ear. "The guy threw her body over—"

"Whose sister? What the fuck you talking about?"

We both stopped. Looked up. Ralph was standing on the tree limb now. Rocking the branch. For a few seconds, I thought we were witnessing his suicide. Then he turned back toward the trunk, climbed limb by limb back down the tree. Got to the ground, the ledge. Squatting, he went through the fence hole and back into the woods. I swam, as far away from Leo as I could get. If I hadn't, I would have pummeled him. Uncapped his capped teeth. Rearranged his entire fucking face.

By the time Leo and I got dressed, got back to the truck and roused Dell out of his stupor, Drinkwater still hadn't shown. "Screw the bastard," Dell said. "It's quitting time. I ain't waiting around forever." He threw the truck in gear. Drove us out of the graveyard.

During the ride back to the barn, neither Leo nor I spoke. "Hey, Dominick, I'm *sorry* already!" he finally blurted out as the truck pulled back into the Public Works yard. "My mother and I didn't even *move* here until 1963, okay? So shoot me, already. I didn't even know the guy *had* a sister!"

That same night, Thomas began to lecture me on the evils of smoking marijuana. We were lying in the dark, in our bedroom, neither of us able to sleep. Nighttime hadn't done dick to cool things down, take away a little of the humidity. The air just hung there, pressing against me.

I'd planned that night to ride up to Dessa's house, but she'd called at the last minute and said she had to go to work—cover for another waitress. "If you'd stop being so stubborn and just quit that stupid job, then things like this wouldn't happen," I'd snapped at her. She'd given it right back to me. Why didn't I quit *my* stupid job? Make *my*self available when it was convenient for *her*?

"Because I'm not Daddy's little girl, that's why. Because if *I* want to go back to school next month instead of going off to Vietnam, I've got to bust my ass five days a week to pay for it. Okay, princess?"

She'd hung up in my ear. Not answered when I called her back. Between what had happened out at the Falls that day with Ralph and Leo and the argument I'd had with Dessa, I was in no mood to take any shit from Thomas.

"It's just not right, Dominick," he argued from the bottom bunk. "You guys are getting paid to work, not to smoke that stuff."

"The town gets more of their money's worth out of us working *stoned* than it does out of you working straight," I said. "*Much* more."

"That's not the point. The point is, that stuff turns you into a whole different person. Plus, you're breaking the law. What if Dell finds out what you guys are up to?"

I hung my head down over the top bunk and laughed in his face. "What if *Dell* finds out? *Dell,* who gets so cocked on the job that he has to sleep it off? *He's* going to blow the whistle on *us*?"

"Well, what if Lou Clukey gets wind of what's going on? I hate to tell you, Dominick, but you guys *reek* after you smoke that stuff. And your eyes glaze over—yours especially. I've seen guys from the other crews *stare* at the three of you when we get back to the barn sometimes. What if Lou Clukey catches on and calls the cops? That would make Ma feel great, wouldn't it? Reading your name in the arrest report? What do you think Ray would do to you?"

I told him he was being paranoid—that nobody at the barn was staring at us.

"Oh, yeah, right," he said.

"Look, everyone in this entire country's getting wasted except for little saints like you," I said. "We do our work. It's not a big deal."

"Well, fine then. Tell that to Lou Clukey."

"*Screw* Lou Clukey! I'm not afraid of him. And I'm not afraid of Ray, either." I clamped my eyes shut and rolled over toward the wall. "And screw you, too. Next time I want my conscience to be my guide, I'll call up Jiminy Fuckin' Cricket. Okay, Thomas?"

"Okay," he said. "Fine. Excuse me for worrying about my own brother."

I rolled over and hung my head back down again. "Look, no one but *me* has to worry about *me,*" I told him. "You got that? I've been taking care of myself my whole life. *You're* the one everyone around here has to worry about. Not *me.* Remember? *You're* the one who's messed up."

I was sorry as soon as I said it. I pictured him back in our dorm room, pacing and shaking in front of that smashed typewriter case. . . . Saw him sobbing at the kitchen table while Ray slammed into him about his grades. Saw him sulking at work because I wasn't willing, anymore, to stay joined at the hip.

Thomas said he wanted to know what that was supposed to mean.

"What?"

"What you just said. That I'm messed up. That everyone has to worry about me."

"It just means . . . it means you ought to take care of your *own* screwed-up life instead of butting into mine. . . . Look, just take a hit or two off a joint yourself once in a while. It's no big deal. Join the human race, for Christ's sake."

Neither of us said anything for several minutes. It was Thomas who spoke first.

"Can I ask you something?" he said.

"If it's about marijuana, no. The subject's closed."

"It isn't about that. It's about you and your girlfriend."

I rolled over in bed. Looked up at the ceiling. "What about us?"

"Are you and she . . . going to bed with each other?"

"Why? You gonna give me a big speech about premarital sex now?"

"No. I was just curious."

"What Dessa and I do is none of your business. . . . Curious about what?"

He kept me waiting for several seconds. "About what it feels like," he said.

"You *know* what it feels like. Don't tell me you never woke up in the middle of a wet dream or reached down and had a little fun with yourself. You're not *that* much of a saint, are you?"

"I didn't mean that," he said. "I meant, what it feels like to be inside of a girl."

The room was still for a while. Then I surprised myself. "It feels good," I said. "It feels unbelievably good. It's like . . . this private connection that you get to share with another person." In the morning, I would call Dessa and apologize. Maybe send her some flowers, buy her a mushy card. Or maybe I'd go down to the Dial-Tone and wait for her to get off work. "It's like . . . it's like you're magnets. Your body and her body."

I lay there, in the dark above my brother. Got hard just *thinking* about her. "When she gets excited . . . she gets wet inside."

I reached down and touched it the way Dessa touched it. Ached for her. Her want, her wetness. "She *wants* you inside of her," I said. "She gets ready, so that by the time you're in, it's like . . . it's like this . . ."

I was struck, abruptly, by the intrusion of it: my brother elbowing in on one more thing of mine. Thomas wanting another chunk of *my* life instead of going out and getting one of his own.

"Like what?" he said.

"Like *nothing*. Like none of your *business*. If you want to know what it feels like, then go find some girl and fuck her brains out. And get high first, too. That makes it even better. Now shut up and go to sleep." I flipped over onto my stomach. Sighed. Calmed back down again.

Several minutes went by. "Dominick?" he said. "Are you awake?"

I didn't answer him for a while. A minute or so. "What do you want?" I said.

"About you smoking pot? I'm just worried, that's all. I just don't want anything bad to happen to you. Because you're my brother and I love you. Okay?"

I didn't answer him—didn't even know *how* to answer. His out-of-the-blue declaration of brotherly love disarmed me. Embarrassed me. I could buddy up with whoever I wanted to for the summer, pedal up there and screw Dessa seven nights a week, but I was *never* going to be rid of Thomas. . . .

He fell asleep long before I answered him, which I did, finally, half out loud and half to myself. In the dark, in the midst of his snoring. "I love you, too," I said.

"You know what gets to me when I remember that conversation? That little talk we had in the dark, him and me? What gets me is that, back then, he was still there."

"Still there in what respect?"

"Still able . . . still able to care about someone other than himself. I guess the disease must have already started claiming his brain by then. That had to have been what that typewriter stuff was about. Right? . . . But there was still someone home in Thomas's head that summer. And I squandered it. Wasted the last weeks he had. Hindsight, right? Twenty-twenty. . . . But all I wanted to do that summer was to cut loose from him. Be one of the guys—one of the Three Dumb Fucks in the back of the city truck. Be Dessa's lover. I was just so tired of . . .

"Later on? After the disease took him to the mat, he lost that ability to care about other people. Worry about anyone besides himself. His enemies. . . . Well, he did and he didn't lose it. I mean, hey, he's always trying to save the world, right? Save civilization from spies and Communists and all that happy horseshit. He still *cares about people in some*

weird way, I guess. But he lost the ability to care about . . . well, about me, I guess. He just . . . those voices. They just drowned out everything else. . . .

"I remember the morning of my wedding. Mine and Dessa's. I got ready early and drove down to the hospital in my monkey suit—me and Leo. He was real bad then; he couldn't go to the wedding. So Leo drove me down there. Waited outside in the car and I went in by myself. In my tuxedo. And I told him, I said, 'You know, Thomas, if things were different, if you weren't so sick, you *would have been my best man.' "*

"What was his reaction?"

"Oh, I don't know. Nothing much. He was just kind of out of it—zoned on whatever they were giving him back then. Librium, I think. I forget. . . . I've got all that stuff written down—his history of medication and all that. You should see all these folders I've got on him. A whole filing cabinet full. My mother and I started it together and then, after she died, I more or less kept it up. Took over his records. . . .

"I remember the morning I drove down to Settle to tell him Ma had finally given up the fight. Ray and I went, but Ray cut out of there pretty quick. And Thomas was—I didn't know how *he was going to react. But he was . . . what? Philosophical about it, I guess. I mean, he understood. He* got *it that she was dead. It was just . . . you know what he did? He started showing me that stupid* Lives of the Saints *book of his. Comparing Ma's death to . . . talking like she was some stupid saint who'd lived five hundred years ago and been tortured by Pope What's-His-Face or whatever. Like Ma was someone out of his stupid saint book."*

"Do you want a tissue, Dominick? They're right there. Help yourself."

"I'm okay. . . . You know when I did get a rise out of him? The night I went down there after Angela was born. I went down there and handed him an 'It's a girl' cigar. Told him he was an uncle. He liked that, I remember. Uncle Thomas. Big smile on his face. . . . He, uh . . . he never even saw her. My daughter. We just hadn't gotten down there yet. I mean, three weeks? We were going *to go that weekend. Drive down there and show her to him. But then she died.*

"Mostly, I can just accept it, you know? That total absorption of his—the way his illness finally did what I'd been trying all my life to do: separate the two of us. Untwin us. *But I'll be honest with you. There have been times when I've ached to have him back again. When I've needed him bad."*

"Here. Take a tissue."

"That night the baby died? And then, a year or so later, when the bottom fell out. When . . . she says to me, 'I have to breathe, Dominick. You suck all the oxygen out of the room.' Try hearing that *from the person you love. The one person you need more than. . . . Well, anyway, I just . . . I just wanted to throw down my armor for once, my defenses, and share . . ."*

"Share what, Dominick?"

"My brother's love. I just wanted to tell him, 'I'm scared shitless, Thomas.' And hold him. Hold on to my brother for dear life. Because, you know, he's my brother. *Right? Only, by then, he wasn't Thomas anymore. By then, he was just the paunchy guy with the institutional haircut and the gray pants and shirt. Jesus' apprentice. The guy that the FBI and the KGB and the aliens all wanted to destroy.*

"You know what the funny thing is, though? I look back . . . I look back at that summer the four of us were cutting lawns and playing graveball. Playing tag. And I think . . . I think how it could have tagged any one of us. . . . Ralph. Leo. Me, especially.

"Why did it tag him and not me? His identical twin. His other half. That's what I've never been able to figure out. Why Thomas *was 'it,' not me."*

twenty

1969

Ray jerked my brother around about school until mid-August, then announced one night at the supper table that he'd help him finance one last chance. He handed a two-thousand-dollar bank check to my mother for Thomas's and my tuition bills, due that week.

"God bless you, Ray," Ma said and burst into tears. Ray loved that: being the big hero. The savior.

Thomas told Ray he wouldn't regret it, honest to God. He'd learned his lesson. From now on, he was going to stay ahead of his assignments and get to bed earlier. He'd get out of his room and take walks when he was feeling nervous. He'd go to the library and study with me. In the midst of all Thomas's suppertime resolutions, I made a silent promise of my own: he was going to make it or break it without my help. I wasn't going to hold Thomas's hand or walk him to the library or cover for him the next time he took out his frustrations on our typewriter.

I wasn't going to live with him, either. Three weeks earlier, Leo and I had driven up in secret to the university housing office and asked about the possibility of our rooming together at South Campus. Now they'd notified us that the change had gone through. Beyond that, I was planning to haul my ass up to Boston College every weekend to be with Dessa—to make sure I didn't lose out on the best thing I had going in my whole life.

The problem was wheels. If I wanted to see my girlfriend, I couldn't exactly pedal my bike up the Massachusetts Turnpike. Hitchhiking was cheap but unreliable. It could get crazy, too. I'd had a string of bad experiences bumming rides: a guy who said he had explosives in his trunk, a driver whose acid-head wife thought my head was on fire. There were all kinds of wackos out there waiting to pull over and give you a lift. I needed a car.

I'd managed to save almost eleven hundred dollars over the summer. Ray and I agreed that I'd add five hundred to the loan he was giving me to cover college costs. I was planning to use most of what was left to buy a secondhand clunker and some insurance. The rest was for living expenses. But now another thought kept spinning in my head: getting Dessa a diamond for Christmas. So what if I *was* only nineteen? I'd turn twenty over the holidays. How much surer could I be that she was the one? That I was the one for her? She'd said it herself: I was the only guy she felt safe with. In a recurring fantasy, I pummeled those other two jerks she'd gone out with—beat the shit out of them for having hurt her. From what I gathered, the dulcimer player was still living up in Boston; he could walk right back into Dessa's life. Or she could meet someone new—some faceless guy I hadn't even bothered to beat up in my daydreams. If I could buy a car for around two hundred, I reasoned, and get a part-time job once I got to school, then I could start the engagement ring fund right away. Not that I could buy her anything like that boulder her mother wore. Not in a million years. But as well off as the Constantines were, Dessa didn't really care about material stuff. Ever since her family had gotten back from Greece, she and her father had argued about several things. One of them was his focus on money. Another was me.

The Constantines had had me over for the big inspection the week after they got back from Europe. It seemed weird to wear a sports jacket and tie, walk politely through the same rooms where Dessa and I had run around buck naked.

Eating dinner was the worst of it: the five of us plunked down at their fancy dining room table. Dessa's mother kept asking me questions every time my mouth was full. I spilled lamb gravy on this new tablecloth they'd just brought back from their trip. Then Dessa's little sister, Angie, told me right there in front of everybody that I had a "nice bod." She just came out with it. Not that Angie was that little at the time, either. Seventeen was old enough to know better. Old enough to know how to bust her big sister's chops, too. Angie was an expert at that.

The worst part about that dinner, though, was Dessa's old man. Every time I looked over at him, he was watching me—just chewing and staring, swallowing and staring. I half-expected him to turn off the lights and start rolling the surveillance films—replay the evidence of me screwing his daughter all over their fancy house.

The second time I saw Diogenes Constantine was at Constantine Dodge & Chrysler Motors. I had tried *not* to go there—had told Dessa it was a bad idea—but she'd insisted. "Dominick, they have two *acres* of used cars. I'm sure Daddy'll do whatever he can for you." When we got there, her old man greeted us coolly in his office and then palmed us off on George, his buzzardy-looking nephew—one of Dessa's cousins who used to be in the business. George kept steering me to the thousand-dollar-plus models and rolling his eyes at every car I asked about. "I wouldn't *sell* you that death trap," he said about a banged-up Fairlane that was only a hundred and fifty bucks over my price range. "I wouldn't be able to sleep nights knowing my cousin was riding around in that thing." We ended the visit without a sale.

Down at work, I thumbtacked a notice on the bulletin board that I was looking for a car for around two hundred dollars. It was a desperation move. I'd already made the rounds at all the lots and junkyards around Three Rivers. I'd practically memorized the classifieds. Nothing.

Nothing was also what I'd done about telling Thomas that he and I weren't going to be roommates anymore. Before long, we'd be saying good riddance to our summer jobs and getting back to school. Thomas deserved to know. *Needed* to know. I just couldn't make myself do it.

One morning, in the midst of all this procrastination, Thomas and I were walking to work. It was already a scorcher—killer humidity, temperatures heading for the nineties. The air wasn't moving. Okay, I told myself, this is it. When we get to Stanley's Market, I'll just come out with it. Stop making it such a big deal.

But as we passed Stanley's, it was my brother who spoke, not me. "Dominick, could you do me a big favor?" he said.

"What?"

"Could you speak to Dell? Get him to stop calling me Dickless?"

Throughout the summer, I'd remained on neutral ground with Dell, basically by doing my work, keeping my mouth shut, and being the Birdsey brother he preferred. "Look, you been putting up with his bullshit all summer," I told Thomas. "We've got less than two weeks left and then Dell Weeks is ancient history. Just ignore him."

"I'm *sick* of ignoring him," he huffed. "How would you like to be called Dickless?"

"Then *you* tell the son of a bitch," I said. "Put your own foot down for once. That's exactly the point."

"All right, fine, Dominick. Thanks for nothing."

"You're welcome," I said. "Anytime."

Neither of us spoke the rest of the way there.

It was customary for the guys on the various work crews to stand around in the morning and shoot the shit while Clukey and the foremen discussed the day's jobs. Ralph and I were in the middle of an argument with a bunch of guys about whether or not Tom Seaver and Koosman could take the Mets all the way to the Series when Dell whistled through his teeth and made a "come here" gesture at me.

"Hey, Lassie, you better run," someone joked. "Timmy's calling you." All the guys laughed.

"Hey, look, I don't appreciate getting whistled at," I told Dell, approaching him. "If you want me for something, use my name."

Ignoring my protest, he tapped his finger against the bulletin board—my notice about the car. "I just seen this," he said. "You still looking?"

"Yeah, I'm still looking. I been looking all over the placc."

He told me he had a '62 Valiant parked out in his backyard that he might be interested in selling. It had been his wife's before she got MS. It was just sitting there.

"What's wrong with it?" I said.

Dell shrugged. "Battery's probably dead by now. Body's got a little rust. But the engine's fine. Thing's only got about sixty thousand miles on it. You put a little money into it, you'd have a cream puff."

"How much you asking for it?" I said.

He shrugged. "I'd have to get a little more than two hundred. Why don't you come over sometime this weekend and take a look at it. I live on Bickel Road, just past the old woolen mill. We can talk price then if you're interested."

"All right," I said. "Thanks."

"Call first, though. I'll probably be in and out. I'm in the phone book."

We were cutting brush at the reservoir that day—mosquitoes, wood ticks, horseflies zapping us every two seconds. Lou Clukey and his crew were there with the wood chipper, so we were all hauling ass, even Dell. The bugs and the heat and the constant rattle of the chipper had everyone riled up. Clukey and his guys took off just before noon, leaving us to finish the job.

The five of us were sitting at a picnic table, hunched over our lunches, when Dell looked up at Thomas. "Go up to the truck and get me my smokes there, will you, Dickless?" he said.

Thomas looked over at me, then at Dell. "Go to hell," he said.

A smile crept across Dell's face. He asked Thomas to repeat what he'd just said.

"You better not call me that anymore," he said.

Dell put down his sandwich. Rested his chin in his hand and stared at my brother like he was suddenly the most amusing thing in the whole world. "Call you what?"

"You know. And I mean it, too. I'm warning you."

When I had advised Thomas that morning to stand up for himself, I hadn't meant for him to turn it into a shootout at

Dodge City. I'd meant for him to say something to Dell in private—in the truck or something. But that was always the trouble with Thomas: you'd make an assumption that he had *some* kind of instinct about how to deal with people and then he'd prove you wrong. Show you how completely clueless he was. A showdown in front of the rest of the crew was the exact wrong way to go with Dell Weeks.

"*You're* warning *me*?" Dell laughed.

Thomas got up from the table. Just stood there, blinking.

"He's not *warning* you," I said. "He's *asking* you."

Dell held up his hand to shut me up. "Did you say you're *warning* me, there, Dickless? What are you *warning* me against?"

Thomas pouted. His bottom lip was shaking. *De-fense, Thomas! De-fense!*

"Just drop it, Dell," Drinkwater said. "It's too hot for this shit."

Dell stood up. He sucked in his gut, hiked up his pants, and ambled around the picnic table to where my brother was. At six-two or six-three, Dell had Thomas by about four inches and outweighed him by maybe fifty or sixty pounds.

"I'm waiting, Dickless," he said. "What are you warning me against?"

Thomas looked flushed. Confused. The rest of us sat there, staring stupidly.

"You gonna take me on? Is that it? You got the balls to go a few rounds with your foreman?" He reached out and gave Thomas a little shove that sent him back a step. I felt my whole body clench up.

Thomas looked over at me, then at Leo and Ralph, then back at Dell. "No, I'm not going to 'go a few rounds' with you," he said. "But if you don't stop, I'll talk to Lou Clukey. I'll tell Lou you're bothering me."

Dell glanced at the rest of us, a grin on his face. "Well, you just tell him whatever you have to tell him, Mr. Dickless Dicky Bird. You just go crying to your uncle Lou and let him know the Big Bad Wolf's been teasing you and you don't have the balls to do anything about it yourself."

Dell reached over and poked my brother in the breastbone with his knuckles. Once. Twice. Three times. "Course,

Uncle Lou might have one or two other little things on his mind. Like the new sidewalks they're pouring over on Broad Street next week. Or that big paving job up on Nestor Avenue. But I'm sure Uncle Lou will just drop whatever he's doing to come out here and give me a spanking for calling the little candy-ass fairy boy a bad little name."

"Why can't you just *stop* it?" Thomas blurted. "That's all I'm asking you to do! Just stop calling me that name!" He was shaking badly.

Dell took a step closer—got within a couple of inches of his face. He reached out and began kneading Thomas's shoulder. "Tell you what," he said. "I'll make you a deal, right here and now. You drop your drawers and show me and my witnesses here that you got the proper equipment, and I guess I'll just have to come up with a new name for you."

"Jesus H. Christ," Ralph muttered.

Dell's hand moved from my brother's shoulder to the back of his neck. Thomas flinched. "What do you say there, Dickless? You want to show us once and for all that ain't a twat between your legs?" Smirking, he began to sniff the air. He turned back to us. "You smell what I smell, boys? It's either a rotten fish or Dickless's smelly cunt."

Leo's laugh was a single nervous note.

Thomas swallowed. Said nothing.

"No deal, eh, Dickless? Well, that's just what I figured. You just plain got the wrong equipment to mess with me. I rest my case."

Dell looked over at Leo and me, his smile slackening. He seemed more miserable than triumphant. He told us to get the scythes out of the truck and start cutting down the meadow grass in the field. After we were finished, he said, we could fill the water jugs out at the spring. We could take our time, take a swim in the reservoir if we wanted to. Cool off. We'd done enough grunt work for one day. We could take it a little easy.

It was the sound of Thomas's sobbing that made us all turn in his direction. His hands were yanking at his belt buckle, fumbling with the snap of his jeans.

"*Don't!*" I yelled.

Thomas jerked his pants and underpants to his knees and

stood there, blubbering, exposed. "Are you happy *NOW*?" he screamed at Dell. "*NOW* will you just shut up and leave me alone?"

Ralph and Leo looked away. Dell stood there, smiling and shaking his head. "Pathetic," he said. "Just plain pathetic."

I hustled over to my brother, shielding him. His humiliation was my own. "Pull your goddamned pants up!" I screamed at him. "What's the matter with you?"

Ralph was the only one still seated at the picnic table. Hunched down low, he kept eating, chewing angrily, mumbling something I couldn't hear.

"Let's go, Ralph," Dell said. "Lunch is over."

"Fuck you, lunch is over!" Drinkwater snapped back. "We got six minutes left. Don't tell me lunch is over when it's not over." Ralph's arm swept across the table, sending lunch pails and thermoses flying.

Dell stood there, glaring at Ralph. Then, without saying anything, he walked over to the picnic table, bent, and lifted it—first onto its side and then up and over. Ralph lay splayed on the ground, his legs still hooked beneath the bench where he'd been sitting.

Dell squatted down next to him. "Now, unless I died and they made *you* foreman," he said, "you get that shit-brown Indian ass of yours back to work or I'll have you off this crew before you can count to ten. Come to think of it, I got a *special* job for a couple of tough guys like you and Dicky Bird over there. I got a *special* assignment for you two."

Dell put Drinkwater and my brother in the muckiest, most bug-infested part of the reservoir—an area I had overheard Lou Clukey tell him earlier we wouldn't have to tackle.

I *almost* spoke. My mouth opened and closed a couple of times, but nothing would come out. Dell's bullying felt just like Ray's and the familiar dread fell over me, settling in my gut, my arms and legs. Paralyzing me. So instead of speaking up, I grabbed a scythe, walked to the meadow he'd said to cut, and started swinging. Every blade of grass I whacked that afternoon was Dell's throat. Ray's. Every swipe I took cut down the two of them.

At the end of the day, Drinkwater and Thomas climbed up into the back of the truck with Leo and me. They were both filthy with mud, studded with scabs and bug bites. Nobody said anything for miles. Then, without warning, Ralph's boot slammed so hard against the tailgate that, for a second, I thought the truck had hit something. Dell looked back in the rearview mirror to see what the racket was. "That's right, cocksucker, you *better* watch your back," Ralph said, glaring back at Dell's reflection. "You *better* keep your eye on me from now on."

When we got back to the yard that afternoon, instead of driving right into the garage the way he usually did, Dell pulled off to the side of the road, cut the engine, and came around to the back.

"I got one thing to say about what happened out there today at lunchtime," he informed us. "I'll say it to all of you at once so there's no misunderstanding. What goes on in our crew stays in our crew. Understand? It ain't nobody's business but ours."

His eyes bounced nervously from Leo to Ralph to my brother, then landed on me.

"Oh, yeah?" I said.

"That's right. What we do is *our* business. Not Clukey's. Not anybody's on one of the other crews. My guys and I cover for each other." He nudged his chin toward my brother. "Take that stunt he pulled out there today. Pulling his pants down and crying like a little baby. They'd love a story like that around this place. But they're not going to hear about it."

"You *told* him to do it," I reminded him. "You *goaded* him into it."

He took a step toward me, glaring so hard and hatefully that I had to look away. "Or take all that dope you guys been smokin' on the job all summer long, Dicky Boy," he said. "You guys been high as kites half the summer. Having yourselves a great old time with your mary-j-uana. You think I didn't know it? You think you fooled old Dell? Well, guess what? You didn't. And if Clukey ever found out you been sucking on those funny little cigarettes, next thing you know, the cruiser and your old man would *both* be down here. But what we do is our business, nobody else's. See? Long as you guys get your work done, I don't see nothing. Understand? One hand washes the other."

The four of us sat there, dumbfounded. Then Drinkwater hopped over the side of the truck and started walking away.

"Hey, big shot!" Dell called after him. Ralph didn't answer. Didn't look back. "What about your time card, wiseguy? How'd you like to lose a day's pay?"

Without turning back, Ralph raised his arm, his middle finger, high into the air. The four of us watched his cocky gait, his exit around a hedge.

Dell got back in the truck and started her up.

"Can you believe that fucking prick?" Leo whispered to me. "He's been *spying* on us." I told him to just shut the fuck up.

Thomas quit. He didn't talk it over with me or ask me to go into Lou Clukey's office with him or anything. Dell pulled the truck into the garage, cut the engine, and Thomas just made a beeline for Clukey's office. He was in there for less than three minutes and then he was out again. And that was it.

I couldn't walk back home with him—couldn't stomach his pissing and moaning or his I-told-you-so's about the dope smoking. Nor was I about to forgive him for the way he'd degraded himself in front of the other guys. So I walked in the opposite direction, down Boswell, onto South Main, and into downtown. I ended up in front of the pinball machine at Tepper's Bus Stop. I didn't want to think about anything. I just wanted to slam those little silver balls, jerk knobs, pound buttons, grab the sides of that fucking machine and rattle it. Which I did a little too vigorously, I guess. Old Man Tepper came out from behind the counter and asked what the hell was the matter with me. What was the big idea, thinking I had the right to destroy someone else's property? What was the *matter* with me?

What was the matter with him? What was going on?

By the time I got home, Thomas had already opened his mail from the university and learned that his roommate for the 1969–70 school year was a transfer student from Waterbury named Randall Deitz.

"This is just great," he groaned, waving the letter in my face. "This is just what I needed after today. Some stupid secretary makes a mistake, and now we have a big mess to fix!" He was pacing the kitchen floor just the way he'd done in our dorm room the year before—getting riled up all out of proportion.

Ma was at the stove, making sauce for supper. "Okay, calm down, honey," she told Thomas. "Maybe it's something you can get straightened out over the phone."

"Nobody knows what they're doing at that stupid school! We'll probably have to go through this big rigmarole just to undo one person's stupid mistake."

"There's no mistake," I said.

"First they'll tell you to go to *this* office! Then when you get there, they'll say, 'Oh, no, you don't want *this* office. You want this *other* office!' "

"There's no mistake," I repeated. Thomas and Ma both looked at me, waiting for the punch line. Unable to look at my brother, I addressed Ma instead. "I'm not rooming with him. . . . I'm rooming with Leo."

I could feel, rather than see, the panic taking over my brother. He flopped back on one of the kitchen chairs and crossed his arms over his chest. He craned his neck as far away from me as it would go.

"When did you decide this, Dominick?" Ma asked me.

"I don't know. A while back. We went up to school and put in a request."

"We?" Thomas said. "You and Leo? The two of you just snuck up there behind my back and switched things on me?"

"It's not that big a deal," I said, still looking at my mother. I watched her face go pale. Saw the fear creep into her eyes. "You asked me to room with him freshman year and I *did*. . . . I've been *meaning* to say something. I just . . . I've just been so busy."

"Don't tell me," she said. "Tell your brother."

I turned to Thomas. "It'll be *good* for you, man. You'll meet new friends. How do you know this new guy—what's his name? Randall? How do you know he's not a great guy? He'll probably be a *much* better roommate than I ever was. We're too close, you and me. We get on each other's nerves."

He sat there, pouting, saying nothing. A minute or more went by.

"Well," Ma said, "why don't you two boys go upstairs and get cleaned up? Supper's going to be ready in about half an hour, soon as your father wakes up. Thomas, do you want ziti or shells? You pick."

He didn't answer her.

"I don't really have time to eat, Ma," I told her. "I'm going out."

"Who are you going out with?" Thomas said. "Your two little buddy-buddies from work?"

"No, I'm not," I said. "I'm going out with my girlfriend. Is that all right with *you*?" I was planning my escape as I spoke. Dessa was working that night at the Dial-Tone. Her shift was over at 1:00 A.M. Maybe I'd ride down there on my bike. Surprise her.

"Oh, you mean Mystery Woman?" Thomas said. "The girl you're too ashamed to have your family even meet?"

"I'm not ashamed to have you meet her. You want to meet her? Fine. You can meet her."

"Okay, when?"

"I don't know. Sometime."

His laugh was sarcastic. I stood there, watching him fiddle with the salt and pepper shakers—making little piles on the table. "Traitor," he mumbled.

"Look, Dominick, you have to eat *something*," Ma said. "I've got eggplant in the refrigerator and there's some grinder rolls left over from yesterday. Why don't I fry up some peppers and make you a couple of sandwiches? Come on. Get me the provolone."

That was Ma for you: pissed and hurt but ready to feed you, anyway. Ready to make you feel even *more* guilty.

I headed toward the upstairs bathroom, then stopped at the doorway and looked back at Thomas. "Hey, numskull?" I said. "You want first shower?" I meant it as a kind of apology, I guess—to show him I wasn't a complete bastard. Fighting over who had first shower had been a ritual of ours since we were kids.

But Thomas ignored me. He picked up the salt shaker and started talking to it. "Hello, I'm Thomas Dirt," he said. "Feel free to lie to me and walk all over me. Everyone does it. It's fun!"

It was just this side of a suicide mission: riding down to the beach in a Friday night drizzle on a bike with no light and no reflectors. The trip was an hour and a half's worth of honking horns and cars swerving away at the last second and drivers cursing me out. Although I knew damn well I wouldn't mention anything to Dessa about what had happened that day at work, I imagined myself telling her all about it. Saw the two of us at one of the back tables. Felt the sympathetic touch of her hand on my face, the compassionate kisses she'd give me. All along the way, I comforted myself with her imaginary understanding.

The place was packed. Dessa acted surprised, not happy, to see me. "It's a zoo here tonight," she said. "I won't even be able to talk to you until quitting time. God, you're soaked."

"Dance with me," I said.

"I *can't* dance with you, Dominick. I'm working."

"Just one dance."

"Dominick, *no.* I have orders to pick up. I have tables that have been waiting—"

I walked away from her explanation and grabbed a seat at the bar, ordered a beer. Later, on her break, she handed me the keys to her mother's car. When the manager wasn't looking, the bartender sold me a two-thirds-empty bottle of vodka and I headed outside. I threw my bike in the trunk and slumped down in the driver's seat to wait for her. Played the radio, swigged vodka. Watched the windows fog up. I wanted a joint. I wanted Dessa. I kept trying *not* to see my brother out there at the reservoir, bawling like an idiot, his pants down around his knees. . . . *Traitor,* he'd called me. *Hello, I'm Thomas Dirt.* Jesus, how long was I supposed to keep carrying him? When was I ever going to be able to get on with my own life? Starting in September, that was when. Fuck him. Let him sink or swim. I closed my eyes. Shifted around to get more comfortable. The vodka, the thump of the ocean, the beat of the rain on Dessa's mother's car roof made me sleepy. . . .

* * *

By the time Dessa nudged me awake again, it was after two in the morning. "Hi," she said. I yawned and stretched and kissed her. She had work stink on her: beer and booze, cigarette smoke in her hair. When I went to rub her leg, my hand ran into the tumor of tip money in her jeans pocket.

I hadn't seen her in a week. Hadn't screwed her in two. Since the Constantines' return, we'd been reduced to making out in parking lots. But that would change in a couple of weeks. Dessa was a supervisor at her dorm, which meant a single room and a double bed. If that car deal went through with Dell, then Dessa and I would be stretched out up there in Boston instead of sitting inside her mother's Chrysler-fucking-Newport.

"Guess what?" she said.

"What?"

"My father's not speaking to me. We had a fight."

"About what?" I said.

"Oh, it doesn't matter. . . . Well, yes it does. It was about you."

"Me? What about me?"

"Oh, it was my own stupid fault. I accidentally left my dialpack out on my bathroom counter. My mother saw them."

"Your birth control pills? Oh, *shit.*"

"So instead of saying something to *me,* like a *normal* mother would, she went to my father instead. He came into my room last night and said he wanted to talk to me. I was embarrassed to death, but I said, 'Look, Daddy, I'm a big girl. I can make my own decisions about things.' So then he starts in on you."

She pulled in closer to me. Put her head on my shoulder.

I asked her what he'd said.

"That he had nothing against you personally, but if all you were planning to do with your life was teach, then maybe I should think twice before I got myself pregnant and realized I'd sold myself short."

I cleared my throat. Somehow, I was feeling both drunk and hung over. "What's that supposed to mean?" I said.

"Oh, Daddy thinks I should be the wife of a doctor or a businessman or someone who owns property. I pointed out to him that *I* was training to be a teacher, too, and he said, oh, teaching was a perfectly acceptable job for a woman. Women weren't expected to provide for a family. Men were. Then, I just let loose. I couldn't help it. I was so *pissed*! I told him I judged people by who they were inside, not by their income potential. Money might be *his* god, I told him, but it wasn't mine. That made him *furious*. He told me it was a sorry day when daughters spoke to their fathers so disrespectfully—when children had that little gratitude for what had been provided them. So now we're not even speaking. And it was all . . . If my mother had just come to me about the pills instead of . . . Sometimes I *hate* him, Dominick!"

We sat there for a couple of minutes, neither of us saying anything. Then I reached over and started putting the moves on her—kissing her, stroking her a little. But I couldn't get her interested. She wouldn't shut up about her father.

"How can he possibly think that selling cars is more valid than educating kids? And how dare he dismiss *you* like that. He doesn't even *know* you, Dominick. I don't think I ever realized before how shallow my father is."

I reached down and diddled her the way she liked—the way she'd taught me—but she stopped me. "Dominick, I can't just finish a seven-hour shift and . . . well, you know. And now I'm angry all over again at Daddy. I'm sorry. I'm just not in the mood."

"What about me?" I said.

"What *about* you?"

"Well, for starters, I drove down in the pouring rain to see you. I been waiting out in this friggin' car for over four hours. Maybe I *am* in the mood."

"Dominick, what was I supposed to do? Just tell my manager, 'Oh, sorry, but my boyfriend decided to show up unexpectedly so I guess I can't work the rest of my shift'?"

"No, you didn't have to tell them that. All's you had to do was act like you were at least half-glad to see me."

"I *am* glad to see you," she said. "I'm just keyed up. You know how I get working here. And then with this thing with my father. I mean, I *am* an adult, right? I *do* get to make my own decisions. But, God, when your mother finds your birth control pills—"

"Do me a favor, will you?" I said. "Just shut up about your parents!" The car filled up with silence.

After a while, I sat up and opened the door. Got out and went into the backseat. "Hey," I said.

No response.

"Hey, you?" I tried again.

"Hey me what?"

"Come back here."

She didn't move for a minute or so. Then she climbed over the seat and into the back, flopped down next to me. Wrapped her arms across her chest, as tight as tourniquets. "As if *his* relationship with my mother is some kind of great model," she said. "You should see the way she has to ask him for household money every morning at breakfast. She tells him what she needs, accounts for every penny, and then if he's satisfied, he reaches into his wallet and counts twenty dollar bills into her hand. It's disgusting."

I fumbled at the opening of her pants, reached up inside her blouse. She wasn't wearing a bra, but there was something covering her nipples. "What's this?" I said.

"What?"

"This." I took one of her breasts in my hand, rubbed my thumb where the nipple was supposed to be.

"Band-Aids," she said. "You put them on so your nipples won't show. That's the last thing I'd need with the animals I wait on."

I pulled up her shirt, peeled off the Band-Aids. Started kissing her breasts. If she wasn't in the mood, well, I was horny enough for both of us. I shifted a little, got us both down onto the seat. I pried her legs apart with my knee, rubbed her a little.

"Hey, you know what, Dominick? I already told you, I'm just not . . ." *Shut up, shut up,* I thought, undoing myself. "I'm just too keyed up right now. I don't feel like—hey, *stop* it!"

But stopping didn't seem like an option. I'd been out in that car for hours. She owed me something. And she was right, now that I thought of it: how *dare* that rich fuck of a father tell her to aim her sights higher than me.

I started dry-humping her. Her not being wet seemed like

a kind of stubbornness. *Stupid rich girl.* I reached down and grabbed myself, rubbed it against her.

I kissed her hard. "I fuckin' love you," I said. Kissed her again. Pushed myself inside of her. She grunted a little. I heard her telling me to stop it—saying it hurt, that I was scaring her. But what *I* needed was stronger than her fear, and when she tried to get out from under me, I wouldn't let her. "I love you," I told her each time I hammered into her. "I *love* you. I *love* you. I *love* you." But my head was filled with hatred: what right did Dessa's fucking father have to assume he was better than *me*? . . . I might as well have been swinging that scythe out at the reservoir. Rattling that pinball machine down at Tepper's Bus Stop. I only realized she was trying to fight me off when she *stopped* fighting. Just lay there and took the fuck. The springs squeaked, the whole car rocked with what I needed, and then I came, cursing and clutching her, my one hand slapping the upholstery.

I was sorry before I was even soft again. Before I could even catch my breath. "Oh, Jesus," I said. "That was intense. I guess I got kind of carried away."

Dessa burst into tears. She was shuddering against my shoulders and chest.

"Hey, really. I'm sorry. I'd just been waiting out here so long. Drinking vodka and—" When I reached up to stroke the side of her face, she slapped my hand away. Punched me.

"I couldn't help it, Dessa. I'm sorry. I just wanted you so bad, I got a little wild."

"Shut up!" She punched me again. "Get off of me!"

I reached down to put myself back together again. Dessa did the same and climbed back in front.

"Is it really *that* bad?" I said. "That I went a little out of control because I wanted you so much?"

"You know what 'wanting me' like that is called, Dominick?" she said. "Rape."

"Yeah, right. It's not like you and me. . . . Look, I would never—"

"You just *did,* you jerk!" She started to cry again.

"Hey, hold on a second. That's not fair."

"I have had such a horrible week," she said. "And now *this* happens."

"Hey, you know what?" I said. "I've had a really horrible week, too. Did you ever think to ask *me* what kind of a week *I've* had?"

She started the car. "I'm going to drive you home," she said. "Then I'm going to go home myself. Take a hot bath and wash off this little 'experience' we've just had. Just do me a favor, all right? Just stay in the back and don't talk to me. Just don't say anything."

"You accuse me of raping you and I'm not even supposed to defend myself? Well, fuck that, Dessa! Fuck *you*!"

I got out of the car and slammed the door. Opened it and slammed it again. I started hoofing it away from her—out of the parking lot, onto the road. I jabbed my thumb at a passing car.

She rolled up next to me. The whirring sound of the power window was in my ear. "Come on. Let's not do this, okay? Just get in and I'll take you home. We both need to cool off and get some sleep."

"Just *go,*" I told her. "You wouldn't want a rapist in your car."

"All right, I'm sorry," she said. "That was a little strong. It's just that after my last relationship, I'm kind of—"

I started screaming at her. "I am *nothing* like that guy! Don't you *ever* . . . I am nothing like that guy at all!"

The power window went whirring up again. She gunned it. Just drove away. That's when I remembered my bike, stuck in her mother's trunk like a dead body.

I got home two hours and three rides later—relieved, for once, to be back there. I walked through the dark house and up the stairs. Dropped my clothes on the floor and climbed up into my bed.

When I rolled over, I heard crinkling paper. I lay on my back, squinting in the dark at whatever it was—trying to decide whether or not to get up and look at it. Another couple of minutes later, I had to take a leak anyway. I jumped down from the top bunk and made my way to the bathroom.

All these years later, I still remember what that note said. Can still *see* it, even—this weird version of his regular handwriting. He'd addressed it to *Dominick Birdsey, Traitor.*

Do you think it's easy having your sleep stolen every night? Do you think it's fun to feel the wings of the Holy Ghost fluttering against your throat?

Sincerely,
One Who Knows

I stood there, squinting at it in the bathroom light, trying to make it make some kind of sense. He's nuts, I told myself. Told it to the mirror in front of me. He's fucking nuts. Then I balled up his stupid note, tossed it into the toilet, and pissed on it—pushed it around and around the inside of the bowl. Flushed it away.

I stayed awake until dawn, coming up with dozens of arguments about why I *wasn't* a rapist. Why *not* being Thomas's roommate was something I deserved.

I dozed off watching the first watery gray light coming through the venetian blinds.

twenty-one

1969

It was after two the next afternoon by the time I woke up. My head ached. The room smelled sour. I reached down to scratch an itch and felt my own stiff jiz. The night before—what I'd done to Dessa—hit me like a fist in the gut.

"Hey?" I yelled down the stairs on my way to the bathroom. "Anyone home?" The silence was a relief. I needed to get on the phone with Dessa to repair the damage and didn't want anyone overhearing me.

I stuck my face in the sink and splashed cold tap water, put my mouth to the faucet to sluice out the sour taste. Pissing into the toilet, I suddenly remembered that goofy note of my brother's. *Do you think it's easy having your sleep stolen? Feeling the wings of the Holy Ghost against your throat?* What the hell was wrong with him, anyway? First that typewriter crap. Then that stunt out there at the reservoir. . . . I got halfway under the shower, then got out again and went dripping down the hall and back to our room. I stood there, staring at Thomas's unmade empty bed. What was going on?

Back in the shower, soap and hot water helped wash away the night before. Dessa and I had just had a misunderstanding, that was all—a communications misfire. She usually wanted it as much as I did. Maybe if I'd just slowed down a little. My bike in the trunk of her mother's car gave me an opening. Maybe she could drive it over and we could talk—straighten things out. Pack a picnic and go out to the Falls, maybe, if we were both feeling in the mood. Undo the crap from the night before. God, I needed a car.

I wrapped a towel around myself and went into Ma and Ray's room to use the phone. In the mirror above Ma's bureau, I started shadowboxing with Dessa's old boyfriends, letting punches fly at my own reflection. I dropped to the floor and did some push-ups. I was edgy. Couldn't stop whistling. I told myself I was feeling good—feeling "up and at 'em"—but it was nerves. The fear that I'd blown it with the best person I'd ever known in my whole stupid, sorry life.

I dialed the Constantines' number and waited. Looking around, I suddenly saw Ma and Ray's bedroom the way Dessa might see it. Her parents' room was three times this size. It had wall-to-wall carpeting, a couch, a mural painted right onto the friggin' wall. My mother and Ray had a worn linoleum floor and pull-down window shades, Ray's collection of ceremonial weapons, Ma's Holy-Roller stuff: crucifix, Mary statue, praying hands on this sorry little wooden shelf that Thomas had made in junior high shop class. The afternoon sun highlighted the dents in the wood where his hammer had missed, the nail hole he'd forgotten to wood-putty. In that same shop class, I'd made an end table with a built-in record rack to hold LPs. Mr. Foster had put it in the spring showcase where he put the best stuff. He'd placed a philodendron plant on top of it and some of his own records in the rack. My project gets put in the showcase, but what does Ma save? Put up in her bedroom? Thomas's piece-of-shit shelf.

Why wasn't Dessa answering? Where was she? . . .

I looked over at Ma's holy picture of the Resurrection—Jesus, his Technicolor heart aglow, his eyes as forlorn as a basset hound's. Some sex life they must have with that thing hanging right over their bed. . . . I flashed on the long-ago day when she'd bought that thing, down at the five-and-ten. The same day that crazy guy on the city bus started touching her. Got off the bus when we got off and chased us. . . .

I saw her sitting there on that bus seat across from us, scared to death, letting that guy's hand wander wherever it wanted. She'd acted the way she always did when anyone pushed her around: just shut up and took it. Waited for Jesus to come to her rescue. If it was true that the meek were going to inherit the earth, then Ma was going to be a Rockefeller.

I thought about a discussion our political science class had had the semester before: about whether religion was or was not "the opiate of the people." . . . I hadn't bothered going to Sunday Mass once since I'd gotten home from college for the summer. I was making a statement about who I was now—how I'd changed—so I stayed in bed every Sunday morning. It was a sore point with Ray, especially now that he'd been made a big-deal deacon down at the church. I was pretty sure it was a source of pain for Ma, too. Not that she ever said anything. Not that she'd risk *that*. . . . But, hey, it was *my* life, not theirs. Why go to church when God was just a big joke? A cheesy painting from the five-and-ten? I wasn't going to be a hypocrite about it like Ray. . . . Thomas still went every week, of course. Mr. Goody Two-shoes. Mr. Touched-by-the-Holy-Ghost. . . . I thought about Professor Barrett, my art appreciation teacher the semester before. Her and her abstract expressionism. She'd taken our class down to the Guggenheim Museum in New York. "Come *here*! Let me *show* you!" she'd said, leading me up the spiral to a wall full of drips and squibbles. She'd singled *me* out for some reason—had taken me by the arm and pulled me toward Jackson Pollock, her patron saint. "God is dead and Pollock knows it," she'd announced out of the blue one day in class, her profile lit eerily by the dust-flecked cone of light between slide projector and screen. Sondra Barrett: according to the rumor, she was hot to trot. Got it on with both famous artists and undergraduates. Had she been coming on to me that day at the museum? Could I have pursued it? If Sondra Barrett ever got a load of my mother's Jesus painting—fine art by Woolworth's—she'd probably need oxygen or something. I tried to think of me and Sondra Barrett in some loft someplace, going at it. Tried not to keep seeing that crazy guy who'd felt up my mother that day on the bus—his filthy coat, the lump on his forehead. The way he'd sniffed at my mother while he touched her. She'd done nothing, said nothing. . . . Maybe that was how Thomas and I had come into the world: maybe some miscellaneous motherfucker had jumped her in a dark alley someplace and she'd lain there. Done nothing. Maybe *that* was why our conception was some deep, dark secret.

A breeze entered the room, flapping the window shades. Some of the rips in those stupid shades had been repaired with Scotch tape gone brown. What had Dessa's old man told her—that she'd be settling for less if she hooked up with me? I felt myself blush with the truth of it. Crooked the phone between my chin and shoulder and threw a few more sucker punches. *Take* this, *you rich old fuck! I been sneaking into your house all summer long. Making your daughter scream from it. Fucked her one time on your bedroom floor, you prick, so take that!*

I heard footsteps on the stairs.

Thomas's.

Heard him close the bathroom door, take a leak, flush. I listened to his clomp-clomping back down the stairs. I realized I'd been holding my breath at the sound of his moving through the house. Suddenly, the ringing in my ear came back to me. The phone over at Dessa's: on its fortieth or fiftieth ring by now. Why wasn't she answering?

Maybe she was out at their pool. Or standing right there, watching it ring. I banged the phone back down on the receiver, then picked it up and dialed again. If she'd just goddamned answer, I could explain myself. The night before had been a case of temporary insanity, that was all. It would never happen again. She was *safe* with me.

Period.

End of subject.

I flopped back onto Ma and Ray's bed. The sheets had been stripped, the mattress's imprint of coils and springs showing through from beneath. Brown stains dotted the middle. Maybe they flipped that Jesus painting over when they were in the mood. Shit, man: Ma having sex. And not just with Ray, either. Who *was* my brother's and my biological father? Maybe he never even knew about us in the first place. Maybe she'd never had the guts to tell him he'd knocked her up. . . . I flashed on a long-ago afternoon down at the playground when Lonnie Peck told me that dirty joke. *You know what happens when your father fucks your mother?* The punch line had included a demonstration: one of Lonnie's cigarettes poking in and out of a circle he was making with his thumb and finger. Lonnie must have been in seventh or eighth grade at the time—lethally cool in the eyes of my friends and me. Lonnie's joke had simultaneously clarified for me the plumbing that went on between men and women and planted the dirty picture in my mind of Ray and my mother doing it up here in this bedroom. When I got home that afternoon, I first taunted my brother with my new knowledge and then burdened him with it, leading him into Ma and Ray's room and demonstrating the same way Lonnie had, using one of Ray's own Viceroys from the pack on his nightstand. Thomas told me I was a pig. "Maybe that's the kind of thing Gina Lollobrigida does," he said. "But not Ma." I kind of wanted to believe that myself, but I *didn't* believe it. And if *I* was going to know, then Thomas was going to know, too. I needed to inflict the knowledge on him. So I held my little demonstration closer to his face and laughed and sped up the cigarette's jabbing motion. That was the thing about us, the difference: I *knew* that the world was basically a bad place—that life stunk and God was a joke, a cheap painting you could buy at the five-and-ten. I knew it; Thomas didn't.

Pacing the room, I stopped to finger the stuff on top of Ma's chest of drawers: Avon cologne, dusting powder, jewelry box, family pictures. I'd given Ma the jewelry box for Christmas the year I was a high school freshman. When I opened it, that song "Beautiful Dreamer" plinked away underneath the small satin compartments, same as it always had. It was Thomas who'd spotted the jewelry box first, downtown in the window of the Boston Store. He told me he had decided to save up for it for Ma even *before* he'd known it played her favorite song. He seemed to marvel at the coincidence. Then a snowstorm had put shoveling money in my pocket while Thomas sat around all day watching TV, and I'd gone downtown late that afternoon and beaten him to the punch. I was always doing that to him when we were kids: letting him know which of us was smarter, stronger, faster on the draw. Maybe *that* was why he was acting so wacky these days. Maybe I'd finally made him crack. I'd had no idea "Beautiful Dreamer" was Ma's favorite song. If I'd ever thought about it at all, I would have probably guessed "Hot Diggedy, Dog Diggedy" or "Ricochet Romance," two of the tunes I remembered her singing along with the radio when we were little. In the kitchen with us, with Ray out of the house, Ma sometimes let her hair down. Risked being silly.

I don't want no ricochet romance
I don't want no ricochet love
If you're careless with your kisses
Find some other turtle dove

I snapped the jewelry box closed again. Hey, if it was true that I'd pulled a dirty trick or two on my brother, I reassured myself, it was just as true that I'd saved his ass plenty, too.

Ring, ring. . . . Answer, goddamnit! I *knew* she was home. Playing games.

One by one, I studied Ma's framed photographs: Ray, young and skinny in his Navy uniform; Thomas and me, kindergartners in bow ties and sideburned high school seniors; Billy Covington in his Superman pajamas. The largest photograph—the one in the heaviest, fanciest frame—was a brown-tinted portrait of Ma's father,, whose gravestone I'd been trimming and weeding around all summer long.

Domenico Tempesta. "Papa." *The greatest griefs are silent.*

I'd asked Ma about the significance of that gravestone inscription. However she'd answered me, it had been a non-answer.

"Did *he* have that put on there, Ma? Or did *you*?"

"What? . . . Oh, he did. He made all his own arrangements a couple years before."

"So what's it mean: '*the greatest griefs are silent*'?"

She'd never answered that question. Or the other question I'd had: why he and his wife—my grandmother—had been buried on opposite sides of the cemetery. According to the date on his stone, "Papa" had died the summer before Thomas and I were born. Had *he* known about us—that his unmarried daughter was pregnant with twins? In the framed photograph, Domenico's eyes seemed guarded and suspicious—as if he didn't quite trust whoever was taking the picture. I looked over at Jesus' eyes on the adjacent wall. Compared the two. Jesus was a sad sack; Domenico was a son of a bitch.

This is ridiculous, I thought. I'm wasting an entire Saturday afternoon listening to a fucking phone ring. Still, I couldn't quite hang up yet. She could be just getting home from someplace, throwing open the front door, and rushing to pick up. Or, if she was playing games, then fine, I'd outlast her. Sit there and let it ring until she weakened.

Ray's side of the bedroom still had that same "no trespassing" feel to it—a holdover from when we were kids. From the earliest days, Thomas and I had been warned not to wake up Ray while he was asleep. And whether he was asleep or awake or out of the house, we were forbidden to enter their bedroom by ourselves because of the sheathed knives and swords and daggers he kept on the wall. "Those things are sharp enough to lop someone's head off," he'd warned us more than once. "If I catch you in this room when you're not supposed to be, I'll wallop you into next week."

I walked over and opened his closet door. He was still a nutcase about shoes: ten or eleven pairs on the floor, spit-shined and lined up, ready for inspection. The gray work pants and shirts he wore every night to Electric Boat hung neatly from hangers, pressed and ready to go. Ray always had Ma roll up his shirtsleeves to the elbow and then iron the folded cuffs.

On the wall above Ray's bureau were the untouchable weapons, his framed service medals, and the small, blurry photo of his dead mother, a skinny hillbilly-looking woman who, my brother had once observed, looked like a young Ma Kettle. Sitting atop the bureau in their usual order were Ray's shoehorn, hairbrush (comb stuck inside the bristles), Gold Bond powder, Aqua Velva. One time as a kid, I'd tiptoed into the room while Ray was sleeping and borrowed the shoehorn. Waking up Ray during his daytime sleep would have made him hitting mad, but Billy Covington had said he needed the shoehorn to hypnotize us. He'd dared me to do it, and I had. Billy had tied the shoehorn to a string, rocking it back and forth, back and forth, in front of my brother and me the way he'd seen a man do on TV. *"You're getting sleeeepy,"* Billy droned in a strange accent. *"Veddy, veddy sleeeepy."* After the experiment flopped, the three of us had gone outside and dangled the shoehorn into the culvert until it accidentally came loose from its tether and fell in. Later that afternoon, Ray woke up, went to put on his shoes, and screamed bloody murder. Billy's mother had picked him up by then. Through tears and sharp intakes of breath, Thomas and I came clean about the hypnosis attempt and the accident. Ray didn't beat us as we'd suspected he might. Instead, he positioned me at the top of the stairs and Thomas at the bottom, then instructed us to march up and down until he told us we could stop. It had seemed silly at first. I remember stifling giggles and making secret faces at my brother as we passed each other on the middle steps. But inside of an hour, I was sweat-drenched and wobbly-legged and Thomas was crying because of the cramps in his legs. "Can't they stop now?" Ma had asked Ray, who sat on a kitchen chair he'd set up by the front door to read the *Daily Record* and supervise. Ray told her we could stop when he was good and sure we had learned our lesson about respecting other people's property. That night, while Ray was at work, Ma got out of bed and rubbed witch hazel on my charley horses. We'd spent two hours doing penance—climbing stairs.

Fuck her! I banged the phone back down on the receiver and the second I did, it rang. "Hello?" I blurted out.

I was sure it was Dessa, but it wasn't. It was Leo.

Yeah, all right, I'd go fishing with him. I didn't have anything *better* to do. Six o'clock? All right. Yeah.

When I went downstairs, Thomas was slumped in the middle of the couch, wearing a T-shirt and pajama bottoms and this stupid red and blue striped stocking cap on his head. He'd worn that thing all winter long. *In*side the dorm. Seeing that hat on his head brought everything back: that weird first year of school, his weird behavior. He was staring like a zombie at the TV.

"Where's Ma?" I said. He wouldn't answer me.

I went out to the kitchen and came back with cereal, milk, a bowl, a spoon. "Shove over," I said. Flopped down on the couch next to him. The proximity was a half-baked attempt at peacemaking.

He was watching an old Tarzan movie—Johnny Weissmuller and Brenda Joyce. When we were kids, Thomas had maintained that Johnny Weissmuller was the best Tarzan and I'd insisted Lex Barker was. I'd even half-convinced myself that Thomas and I resembled Lex Barker—that maybe *he* was our father and would come back to claim us. I was always doing that when I was little: dreaming up fantasy dads, Hollywood rescues from Ray. It was pathetic. But now, sitting there on the couch eating Cheerios, it suddenly struck me funny: Lex Barker swinging through the trees on Hollyhock Avenue and coming in for a landing in Ma's bedroom. Ma getting pregnant by Tarzan the Ape Man. Him coming back years later to get us and bring us back to where? The jungles of Africa? Hollywood, California? God, little kids are such idiots.

"Hey, Jerk Face," I said to Thomas. "I *still* say Lex Barker's a better Tarzan than this guy. Hands down. No contest."

No answer.

"So where'd you say Ma and Ray were?"

Nothing.

I reached over and clapped my hands in front of his face. "Hey, Thomas! Wake up! Where are they at?"

"Who?"

"Ma and Ray!"

"At a picnic," he said, still watching the tube.

"Ray's union picnic? That's today?"

No response.

I poured myself more cereal. I almost needed the silent treatment from Ding Dong after all the other bullshit I'd been through in the past forty-eight hours.

The Tarzan movie had been spliced in about a hundred different places; the action sort of hiccuped every couple of seconds. As usual, it was the white hunters in their freshly ironed safari clothes who'd caused the problem—whose greed had stirred up the entire sleeping jungle. Tarzan hustled Jane and Boy down a jungle path, the Zambezis in hot pursuit. Then the three of them jumped into a crystal-clear pool and swam like speedboats. I'd seen this one about a hundred times when I was a kid but had never before noticed the cut of Brenda Joyce's little jungle dress, the way she half-fondled her tits as she climbed from the glassy water.

"We will return in a moment to Big Three Matinee Theater," the announcer said.

I looked down at my brother's hand on the couch cushion next to me. His fingers and fingernails were bitten to shreds, the skin red and raw, dried blood in the cuticles. All that past year in our dorm room, he had gnawed and bitten, bitten and gnawed. In two semesters, he'd probably chewed off about five pounds of his own skin. "I think there's a Yankees game on channel ten," I said. "You want to watch it?"

No answer.

"Thomas? Hey! You want to watch the ball game?"

He put the weight of the world into the sigh he gave me. "If I wanted to watch stupid baseball, then I'd be watching it."

I let it pass. Got up and tried Dessa again. Maybe I'd have better luck on the downstairs phone. But there was still no answer.

I sat back down next to Thomas. My leg was tapping against the floor a mile a minute. "Hey, you remember that time at Ray's labor union picnic when he made us sing those stupid songs for everybody? Those war songs he taught us when we were little kids? What were those songs again?"

Thomas blinked three or four times in a row. Swiped at his nose. " 'You're a Sap, Mr. Jap' and 'Good-bye Mama, I'm Off to Yokohama,' " he said.

"Yeah, that's right! 'You're a Sap, Mr. Jap.' " I shook my head. "Fucking Ray, man. Fucking racist bastard."

I poured myself more cereal. Ate a few spoonfuls and put the bowl down on the coffee table. "Me and Dessa had a big fight last night," I said. "It was my fault."

The disclosure just slipped out—took me as much by surprise as it did Thomas. He looked over at me. "Nothing too serious, though," I said. "Nothing we can't straighten out.

You and her will really have to meet each other one of these days. I think you'd like her. She's good people. I *want* you to meet her sometime."

"I'm going to meet her tomorrow afternoon," Thomas said.

"What? . . . What are you talking about?" I felt suddenly panicky.

"She called this morning. While you were still sleeping. She thought I was you."

"Dessa? What'd she say?"

"She told me what happened last night."

I just sat there, trying to figure out how to respond. "What do you mean—what happened?" I finally said.

"She said you forgot your bike in her car. She's going someplace all day with her mother and her sister, but she said she could come over tomorrow afternoon and bring it back. She wanted to know if I was going to be around so she could meet me."

"Yeah? She say anything else?"

"No."

"How'd she sound?"

"I don't know. She sounded nice."

"Yeah? Good. Great. . . . She *is* nice. She's real nice."

I was suddenly overwhelmed with relief. Overwhelmed with sympathy for my goofy brother. "Hey, Thomas, about this roommate stuff," I said. "Leo just asked me one day, you know? It's not like this master plot against you or anything. I just . . . I figured I'd make a change. It'll be good for you *and* me. That's partly why I did it. For *you*."

He laughed at the baldness of the lie.

"Hey, *don't* believe me," I told him. "I don't give a crap. But it's the truth."

He muttered something under his voice.

"What?"

"Nothing."

Neither of us said anything for a minute or more. On TV, the Zambezis had captured Jane and Boy and tied them up. They were doing this psycho-looking dance around them. If Thomas was going to meet Dessa, he had better not embarrass me. As a matter of fact, now that I thought about it, he *wasn't* going to meet her. Not yet. I'd find some way around it. "So what's with the stocking cap?" I asked him. "What are you wearing that thing for in the middle of summer?"

But Thomas was on some other wavelength. "As if *he's* Mr. Innocent," he said.

"What? Who you talking about?" I waited. "As if *who's* Mr. Innocent?"

"Would you do me a favor?" he said.

"Depends. What is it?"

"Would you just stop playing Mr. Friendly Brother? Because it's not convincing at all. I know what all three of you are up to."

I laughed. "Who's 'all three' of us?"

"You and your two buddy-buddies. You've been plotting against me all summer. I have all the information I need."

That crazy note I'd flushed down the toilet the night before came flying back at me again. What had that thing said? "Whatever you're talking about, you're full of shit," I told him. "What are you—paranoid or something?"

"No, I'm just aware."

"Yeah? Aware of *what*?"

He yanked down the stocking cap until it nearly covered his eyes. Then he picked up the *TV Guide* and started ripping the pages into strips.

"Hey, that's the new one, asshole," I said. "What are you *doing*?"

In response, he started singing "You're a Sap, Mr. Jap." Louder and louder. Started screaming it at me.

"Cut it out!" I warned him. "Stop it!" And when he didn't stop, I grabbed him. Jumped on him and *made* him stop. He screamed loudest when I yanked that fucking hat off his head. He began fighting back with more strength than I thought he had. The two of us toppled off the back of the couch, knocked over an end table, rolled across the floor. A lamp fell; it didn't break but the shade got bent to shit. When I got on top of him and pinned his shoulders to the floor, he lunged up and spat in my face. That was it: I popped him one, in the nose. Put him in a choke hold while he was trying to get away from me. Gave him a couple of good jabs in the ribs and tightened my grip around his neck. He gagged. Went limp. "Okay, okay, okay," he said.

I let go. He coughed, cleared his throat.

We were both out of breath. Both scared, I guess. I got up and righted the coffee table, the end table lamp. Threw away the wasted *TV Guide,* vacuumed up spilt cereal, bent the lampshade back in place the best I could. Thomas just sat there on the floor, rubbing his arm over and over.

Down in the cellar, I got my fishing gear ready. Checked my tackle box, my lures. I tried and tried to untie a knot in my line, but my fingers wouldn't stop shaking. What was the *matter* with him, anyway? Writing that stupid note. Accusing us of plotting against him. If this was some kind of stupid bullshit game he was playing, he was going to be sorry he started it. I'd see to that personally. I'd had it with him. . . . But what if it *wasn't* a game? And if it wasn't, what the fuck was it? What was happening?

I went outside and stood on the cement steps, casting my line over and over across the backyard, into the honeysuckle bush. After her father retired, my mother told me, he used to spend whole days out in that little yard, sitting in his grape arbor, smoking cigars, and thinking about Sicily. He'd died out there, of a stroke, the summer Ma was pregnant with us.

No shit, man. What was wrong with him? *Something* must be wrong.

Just before Leo was due to pick me up, I went back inside the house. Thomas was still sitting on the floor where I'd left him, still rubbing his arm. The cap was back on his head. "You hurt your arm?" I asked him.

No answer.

"Is it sprained or something? You okay?"

Nothing.

Part of me wanted to deck him again and part of me wanted to reach down and pull him off the floor. "If I were you," I said, "I'd turn off the boob tube and go down to the store and get another *TV Guide.* Ray sees you wrecked the new one, he's going to go apeshit."

Thomas looked up and faced me. "You *are* me," he said.

"Come again?"

"You said *if* you were me, you'd buy a new *TV Guide.* But you *are* me."

"No, I'm not," I said. "Far from it."

"Yes, you are."

"No, I'm *not*."

Thomas's smile was private and serene. My heart thumped, wild with fear.

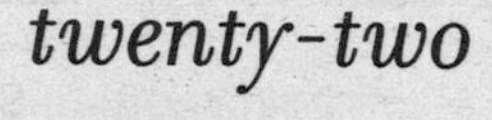

twenty-two

1969

I was outside in front, waiting on the wall, when Leo pulled up in his Skylark.

I threw my fishing gear in the backseat and got in the front. "Here," I said, tossing him one of the foil-wrapped eggplant grinders Ma had made me the night before. "Present from my mother."

"See that, Birdsey," he said. "Even the older babes love me. When you got it, you got it." Ma a babe? I had to laugh in spite of my headache, and the mess I'd made with Dessa, and the fight I'd just had with my stupid, whacked-out brother.

Leo norfed down the sandwich as he drove. Asked what was new since yesterday.

"Not much," I told him. "Just that, in a twenty-four-hour span, I managed to get my brother, my mother, and my girlfriend totally pissed at me." I skipped the part about Thomas acting like a psycho.

"Whoa, my man's three for three," Leo laughed. "What's your little honey honked off about? You forget to heat up the oven before you stuck the meat in or something?"

I shot him a look, amazed at how close he'd come to the truth. But Leo, oblivious, took another bite out of his sandwich. "I figured we could try out by the trestle bridge," he said. "Ralphie told me the bluegills were biting like mothers up there a couple nights ago. Says he caught a nice-sized trout last week, too."

"You should have asked him if he wanted to come with us," I said.

Leo took another bite. "I *did* ask him. Said he was busy, as usual. Hey, speaking of Drinkwater, look in the glove compartment."

"Drinkwater's in the glove compartment?" I said.

"Real funny, Dominick. Go ahead. *Look.*"

I did what he said. Fished through what was in there. "Yeah?" I said. "What? Glove compartment shit."

"Check out the Sucrets," he said.

Inside the tin were three joints, tightly wrapped in red rolling papers. "Ralphie just got this new stuff from a friend of his. Says he might be able to get us some if we want. What do you think, Birds? You want to go halves on a little back-to-school stash?"

I didn't. Getting wasted while you were mowing lawns was one thing; doing it while you were trying to survive a killer semester like the one I had coming up was another. I'd signed up for another poly sci course, British lit, Western civ, trig. The last thing I wanted to do was wake up from a semester-long stupor with a grade point average that looked like my brother's. Still, I picked up one of the joints, sniffing the sweetness of the weed, the scented paper. "How much?" I said. "Nickel bag? Dime bag?"

"Well, here's what I was thinking," Leo said. "If this shit's as good as Ralphie says it is, why don't we see if we can get, say, a couple of pounds."

"Couple of *pounds*?" I said.

"Shut up and listen a minute," he said. "What I was thinking was we could maybe keep a little of it and sell the rest. There's some serious dopers down at South Campus. We could unload this stuff no problem."

"Nope."

"Wait a minute, Birdsey. *Listen.* We get the stuff from Drinkwater, then jack the price up say seven or eight bucks an ounce and make a little profit. We could each clear over a hundred apiece."

"I said no."

"Why not?"

"Because I'm not interested in dealing, and Drinkwater's probably not interested in being your supplier, either. He *gave* you these jays, right? Did he say anything to you about selling?"

"No, he didn't. But that doesn't mean he wouldn't. You ever hear of capitalism?"

"And anyways, Leo, I can't be buying any two pounds of marijuana. I'm trying to finance a car. Hey, speaking of which, could you do me a favor? As long as we're going out to the bridge, could you stop at Dell's first for a couple of minutes?"

"Dell's?" he said. "Dell's *house*?"

I told him about Dell's wife's car. "He lives out near the old mill on Bickel Road," I said. "He says his house is just past there. It's right on the way—wouldn't take more than ten minutes."

"All right, Birdsey. All right. But I tell you, man, the last thing I want to do after I've been looking at Dell's ugly puss all week is go and fuckin' visit him on the weekend."

"Yeah, well, you're a trouper, Leo," I said. "A prince among men."

"Hey," he said. "What you just said? Maybe that's an omen."

"What?"

"You just said I'm a prince among men. I got this thing in the mail today from the theater department. They just announced their new schedule for this coming year. They're doing *Hamlet,* and this play by some Spanish dude—somebody-somebody Lorca—and a musical, *You're a Good Man, Charlie Brown.* And you just said it: I'm a prince among men. Maybe I'll audition for Hamlet." He rolled up the foil that Ma had wrapped his grinder in and chucked it on the floor of his car.

"Yeah, and if they do that *Charlie Brown* thing, you probably got the part of Pigpen locked up," I said. You should have seen all the crap rolling around on that car floor. Leo's cars have always been disgusting like that.

He ignored the comment, though. For someone who more or less dedicated his life to being a goof, Leo could get amazingly serious when he talked about acting. "See, they usually cast juniors and seniors for the major roles, right? But this teacher I had last semester for Shakespearean theater—this guy named Brendan? He said he really likes my work. Says I've got great projection and that I'm not afraid to—how did he put it?—'let people in.' And *he's* the one who's directing *Hamlet.* So who knows? I might have a shot at it. Check this out: 'To die, to sleep—to sleep—perchance to dream: ay, there's the rub.' "

"Rub *this,*" I said.

"Hey, you know what your problem is, Birdsey? You're like a fucking one-man cultural wasteland. You couldn't tell a Shakespearean tragedy from *What's New, Pussycat?*" He belched, wiped his mouth on his arm. "So what's your mother mad at you for?"

"She found out I'm not rooming with Thomas."

"Uh-oh. You finally lowered the boom?"

I shook my head. "I was *going* to tell him," I said. "This weekend. But the fucking housing office beat me to it."

"They called him?"

"Sent him a letter. They matched him up with some guy from Waterbury."

"Hey, look. Your brother's a big boy. How'd he take it?"

I pictured Thomas on the couch, wearing that foolish cap and shredding *TV Guide.* I didn't answer Leo.

"He's a trip, though, huh? How 'bout that stunt he pulled out at the reservoir yesterday? Dropping trou, showing Dell his dick. That was weird, man."

"He quit," I said.

"Thomas? Quit work, you mean? What'd he do that for?"

I told Leo I wanted to talk about something else—that I'd settle for any subject that wasn't my stupid brother.

"Hey, relax, Birdsey," Leo said. "It was just a little freaky, what he did. That's all I'm saying. Him taking Dell that serious. . . . I almost envy him, though. I can't wait until it's *sayonara* to that job. Fuckin' Public Works Department. But anyway, Birds, I'm telling you. I think we ought to sample a little of Ralph's reefer tonight, and if it's any good, we should make ourselves an investment. Earn a little spare change this semester."

* * *

I couldn't remember Dell's street number. We drove past the mill, then slowed down when we got to the dingy strip of row houses just past the mill. It was one of those neighborhoods with car engines in front yards and abandoned grocery store carts overturned at the curb. Most of the people hanging around outside their houses were black or Spanish—not exactly the kind of neighborhood you'd figure a racist like Dell would live in. But it was typical, according to my sociology teacher. The biggest bigots were the ones who felt most directly threatened by the "underclass." The ones who felt the most moved in on. We drove up and down, up and down, collecting dirty looks and trying to scope out Dell's car. Finally, I got out and began looking in backyards while Leo rolled along in the Skylark.

I found the Valiant Dell was selling sitting in a yard at the end of the street. It was faded red with black-and-white-checked upholstery. The body had cancer; two of the tires were bald. You could wobble the tailpipe with your foot.

"Well, it ain't going to win any beauty contests," Leo said, approaching. He squinted in at the dashboard. "What'd you say he told you this thing had for mileage?"

"Around sixty."

"Try seventy-eight and change. You seen the driver's side seat? Stuffing's coming out. Dell's wife must have done some powerful farting while she was driving around in this thing. Let's go, Birdsey. You don't want this piece of junk."

"I do if it runs okay and he lets me have it for two hundred," I said. "I could put a seat cover over it. Come on. We're already here. Let's go talk to him."

"Keep pointing out everything that's wrong with it," Leo advised me. "Make a list in your head. That's how you get them down."

The garbage out by Dell's back porch was ripe and overflowing; about a zillion flies lifted off it as we passed. The porch steps were rotting away. "This is exactly the sort of dump I expected him to live in," Leo whispered. "Dell Weeks, the guy from Scumville."

I rapped softly. Squinted through the screen door. A cat was up on the stove, licking the inside of a frying pan. Somewhere inside, a TV was blaring.

I rapped again, louder. "Wait a minute, wait a minute," someone called.

Then Ralph Drinkwater was at the door, shirtless and barefoot, as dumbstruck to see us as we were to see him. For a couple of seconds, the three of us just stood there. "What the hell are you doing here?" Leo finally said.

Ralph looked flustered. He disappeared back inside for a second and then came back again, yanking on a shirt as he pushed past us. "I was just leaving," he said. He had his shoes in his hand.

"Hey!" I called after him. "Is Dell home?"

"How the fuck should I know?" Ralph said, not bothering to look back. At the front sidewalk, he broke into a run, shirttails flying behind him.

Leo and I stood there, watching him go. I remember thinking, stupidly, that he'd just killed Dell—had come to Dell's house and murdered the bastard and then, by some quirky twist of fate, had run smack into us. What other reason did he have for being there? Why else would he be running?

"Birdsey, what day is it?" Leo said.

"What? It's . . . it's the twenty-second. Why?"

"Because you owe me twenty bucks."

"What?"

"Our bet. It's an *even*-numbered day and Ralphie's wearing something besides his blue tank top. You owe me twenty bucks."

I waited for another couple of seconds, trying to figure out what to do. Then Leo turned the screen door handle and walked in. "Hey, Dell?" he called. "You home?"

No answer.

"It's Leo and Dominick. We came to look at that car."

From down the hall, I heard Dell cough. "I thought I told you to call first."

"I would have," I said. "But we were going fishing and I just thought. . . . We can come back some other time if—"

"I'll be with youse in a couple minutes. Go out back and give 'er a look."

"We just did, asshole," Leo whispered. We stood there, waiting.

The place was a pigsty: dirty dishes and clutter everywhere you looked, tumbleweeds of cat fur all over the floor. It smelled, too—the whole place smelled like Dell. There was a half-eaten grilled cheese sandwich and a half-drunk bottle of 7-Up on the coffee table. Drinkwater's copy of *Soul on Ice* lay cover open on a stack of magazines.

"You know what I think?" I said. "I think Ralph *lives* here."

"No shit, Sherlock," Leo said. "You catch on real quick."

He walked over to a barbell on the floor, picked it up, did a couple of curls. Then he put the weight down and picked up *Soul on Ice.* "This book tells it like it *is,* man!" he said, mimicking Ralph. "I've read it 153 times now!" He tossed the book on the couch and started flipping through the magazines. "Hey, Birdsey, get over here," he whispered. He looked quickly down the hall for Dell. "Check these out!"

Mixed in with the *Rolling Stone*s and the head comics were homo magazines. On the cover of one, two guys were tonguing each other. On another, some dude was straddling a Harley, wearing just a biker jacket.

"They're queers!" Leo whispered. "Ralphie and Dell! They're queer for each other!"

"No, they're not," I said. "Dell's got a wife."

"Yeah? Where is she then? And whose magazines are these? *Hers?*"

Down the hall, a toilet flushed. "Come on," I said. "I'm going outside. I'm getting out of here."

Dell came out a minute later, calling to us from the porch. I couldn't look at him. I needed to get the fuck out of there almost as much as I needed that car.

"I jumped the battery and started her up after work yesterday," Dell said as we went around the back. "She sounded good. Here, let me start 'er up again."

"How come your wife's selling it, anyway?" I asked.

"I told you already. She's got MS. The doctor don't want her to drive no more." I followed his eyes to an upstairs window. Sure enough: a middle-aged woman, fat and sorry-looking, was at the window. She waved down at us; I waved back.

Dell backed his Galaxy out of the garage and inched it

toward the Valiant until the bumpers clunked. We put up the hoods, connected the jumper cables. When Dell's hand brushed against mine while he was checking a connection, I jerked it away. "If a queer ever tries anything funny with you," Ray had once advised my brother and me, "knee him in the nuts first and ask questions later."

Dell told me to get in the Valiant and start her up.

"So what do you think?" he said. "Sounds good, don't it?"

"Sounds all right," I said. "You mind if we take her for a test drive?"

"She ain't registered and there's no insurance. My wife let everything run out."

"This thing have any snow tires?" Leo asked.

Dell shook his head. "What you see is what you get."

The three of us stood there, staring at it. Then Dell reached inside and turned off the ignition. The yard went uncomfortably quiet.

"So, Dell," Leo said. "What's the story with Ralph?"

His eyes narrowed. "What do you mean, what's the story with him?"

"He answered the door a few minutes ago. Does he live here or something?"

"Why?"

"I don't know. I was just wondering."

Dell shoved his hands in his pockets, jingling his change. "Yeah, he lives here. Him and me and the Mrs. You got a problem with that?"

"Uh-uh," Leo said. "We just didn't know he lived here, that's all. Neither of you ever mentioned it. You two related or something?"

For several seconds, the two of them just stared at each other. "I'm white and he's a nigger," Dell finally said. "What do *you* think?"

"So, anyway," I said. "About the car."

Dell took his time finishing his staring contest with Leo. Then he turned to me. "I'll let you have it for four hundred," he said. "That's a damn good price."

I told him I couldn't afford four hundred—that I'd already told him two hundred was all I could afford.

"Two hundred bucks for *this* car? For two hundred bucks, I might as well let it stay right where it is and be a goddamned lawn ornament."

"Two-fifty, then," I said. "I can't go any higher than that." He spat on the grass. Said nothing. "Okay. Two-seventy-five then. That's it. That's my last offer."

He stood there, smiling and shaking his head.

"It's got over seventy-eight thousand miles on it, Dell. That tailpipe could go tomorrow. I'd have to get insurance, register the thing."

"Yeah?" he said. "So?"

"You said yourself it's just sitting here. I need a car."

"We all need things, Dicky Bird. *Three* seventy-five. Take it or leave it."

I shook my head. "Leave it," I said.

He shrugged. "No skin off my nose. See you Monday."

We were halfway across the lawn when Leo made a U-turn and walked back up to Dell. I followed, oblivious. "You know, it's like you were saying yesterday, Dell," Leo began. "What the guys on our crew do is nobody else's business. Right? Like us smoking a few joints. Or you getting cocked on the job two or three days a week. Or harassing my buddy's brother to the point where he's in tears. To the point where he—"

"His brother's a little dickless pansy-ass," Dell said. "Quits his job over some stupid little thing like that. I can't help it if he's—"

"Hey, you know what I could never understand, Dell?" Leo said. I had no idea where this was going. "I could never understand why you've been so interested all summer about what Dominick's brother's got inside his pants. Why'd you go on and on with that dickless stuff all summer, anyway, Dell? Huh?"

Dell looked nervous—vulnerable. "Stupid kid can't take a little bit of teasing, that ain't my problem. That's *his* problem."

"Yeah, I guess. Because what us guys on the crew do is nobody else's business, right? Not Lou Clukey's or anyone else's. Like, for example, the living arrangement you and Ralph got going out here. Lou know about you two being roommates, Dell?"

"Come on, Leo," I said, turning to go. "He doesn't want to sell me the car, fine."

But there was a smile in Leo's eyes. He stayed put. "How long's he been living here, anyways? You and Ralph been roommates for a short time or a long time?"

"We ain't 'roommates,' " Dell said. "He sleeps on the couch on and off. Since his mother took off for parts unknown."

Leo put his hands in his pockets. Scuffed at the dirt with the toe of his sneaker. "Yeah? That right? Was that while he was still a minor?"

Now there was genuine fear in Dell's eyes. "You see that house?" he said. He swallowed. Tried to smile. "That one down there? The green one? Him and his old lady used to live up there. Top floor. She was no good. White girl, but she preferred the coons to her own kind. After the little girl was killed—his sister—it got so that the mother wasn't good for anything. Drunk as a skunk half the time, screaming and fighting with all her different nigger boyfriends. Ralph was like one of those stray cats you feed once and then they won't go away."

"Come on, Leo," I said. "Let's go."

"It's *her,*" Dell said, nodding back toward the house. "My wife. She's too good-hearted for her own good. White, colored, she don't care. She'll take in any stray dog. He ate more meals over here than he did at home. And then the next thing you know—"

"Whose fag magazines are those in there?" Leo said. "The ones in your living room? They yours or his? Or do you share them?"

Dell crossed his beefy arms across his chest. Looked from me to Leo. Moved to within a few inches of my face. The truth was this: in a fight, he could have probably killed both Leo and me. "What is this, Dicky Boy?" he asked me. "Blackmail? You and Big Mouth here trying to blackmail me?"

Was the tremor in my face visible? The winner of this one was going to be the guy who didn't flinch first. "Blackmail?" I said.

"Because you and your buddy here and that pansy-ass

brother of yours are going to be three sorry little motherfuckers if you fuck with me. You got it?"

My gut was churning, but I was into it now. There was no backing away from what Leo had begun. "No, this isn't blackmail," I said. "If this was blackmail, I'd be asking you to *give* me the car. But I'm not. I just want you to sell it for what it's worth."

Just when I thought the worst was coming, he nodded. "Two-seventy-five, you said?"

I looked over at Leo. Looked back again. "I said two-fifty."

"What about you, Big Mouth?" he said, nodding over at Leo. "If your buddy and I make a little private deal here, you gonna keep your trap shut for once in your life?"

"Mum's the word, my man," Leo said. "Mum's the word."

"Okay, then, Dicky Boy. Bring the money over here Monday night. I want a bank check. Two-fifty. Make it out to Delbert Weeks."

"No problem," I said.

"No problem at all," Leo echoed. "Delbert."

"Good," he said. "Now both of youse get off my fucking property before I change my mind. And do me a favor, will you, Dicky Boy? Explain to Big Mouth here what the difference is between a white guy and a nigger, will you? He can't seem to figure it out on his own. Big Know It All he is, but that one escapes him."

He pounded back in the house, slamming the screen door behind him.

We walked back up to where Leo had parked his car. Got in. Neither of us said anything. We rode for a mile or more in silence.

Leo was the first to speak. "Unbelievable," he said. "Unfucking-believable."

"What?"

"All of it! The fact that they're queers together! The fact that we got you that car for two-fifty! Frankly, Birds, I didn't think you had it in you, but that was the sweetest victory I've ever seen. What'd you say to him? *No, Dell, if this was blackmail, I'd expect you to* give *me the car.* I wish I had that on tape, Birdseed. You're my new hero."

I told him to just shut up. Told him Ralph wasn't queer.

"Hey, really, Birds. An hour ago, I was thinking you were a pussy because you wouldn't sell a little weed on the side with me. Now, come to find out, we're a couple of what-do-you-call-its . . . *extortionists!* I'm going to buy us a couple bottles of Boone's Farm on the way out to the bridge. My treat, my man. This calls for a celebration."

"I said shut up, Leo. Okay?"

"Okay, my man. Sure thing. No sweat. Because you are my fucking *hero*."

The wine and two or three hits off of one of Ralph's joints mellowed me out a little. Out at the trestle bridge, I kept feeling something striking my line but nothing would hook itself. Leo kept talking about queers. "And how about that little fruity kid we went to Kennedy with? He graduated in your year. The guy everyone always used to pitch pennies at in the hallway?"

"Francis Freeman?" I said.

"That's the guy. Francis Freeman. He was *definitely* light in the loafers."

"God," I said. "This stuff from Ralph is strong. I am *wrecked*."

"Me, too. So, what do you think, Birds? Could you ever do it?"

"Do what?"

He took a sip on the roach. When he held out the joint for me, I shook my head. "Make it with another guy," he said, exhaling.

"Yeah, right," I said. "Bring him on."

"No, I mean it. How about if it was a matter of life or death?"

"How's something like *that* going to be a matter of life or death?" I said.

"I don't know. Suppose . . . okay, suppose this psycho-fag pulls a gun on you and says, 'Okay, I got a bullet ready for your brain, but I'll let you live if I can bugger you.' Would you do it?"

"Jesus Christ, Leo," I said, casting. "Give it a rest. Will you?"

"*Would* you?"

"That's such a stupid question, I'm not even answering it."

"All right, all right, how about some guy comes up to you and says, 'See this four-on-the-floor '69 Chevelle SS-396? How would you like to cruise up to Boston College on the weekends and visit your little honey in this mean machine? All's you gotta do is let me suck your dick once a week.' Would you do it then?"

"What are you, nuts or something?" I changed my mind about the joint—reached over for it. "Why? Would *you*?"

"Me? No way, man. I ain't no three-dollar bill." I reeled in, cast again. Leo cast. "I might consider doing it for a Mustang, though," he said. I looked over at him. "I'm kidding, Birdseed. I'm kidding, I'm kidding."

My mind floated from the Valiant I'd just bought to Drinkwater standing at the screen door at Dell's to the sound of the ringing phone over at Dessa's house. Fish or no fish, it felt better to be out here in the late afternoon sun than back at the house with my stupid, screwed-up brother. Better to fish and get stoned than wait all day long for *her* to pick up the phone. Let *her* wait now, I reasoned. Let *her* sit and wait for a call from the guy her father said wasn't good enough for her. . . . Unless she agreed with him by now, after that stupid stunt I'd pulled out in her mother's car. I'd scared her: that was the thing. Blown her trust.

I reeled in my line. Cast out as far as I could. Man, I was wasted.

"You ever have a guy hit on you?" Leo said.

"What?"

"A queer. Did a queer ever try and pick you up?"

"Man, Leo, would you get off it about queers?"

"Did you, though?"

"No. Why? Did *you*?"

"Nah. Not really. . . . Just this old guy once. Down at the beach. He came up to my blanket and asked me if I wanted to take a walk with him and let him give me a hum job."

I looked over at his dope-glazed eyes. "And what'd you say?"

"I told him no. That I was saving myself for you, Birdseed. Hey, you know what? Maybe you and me and Ralph and Dell can go on a double date sometime."

I rolled my eyes. "Maybe Dell's one. But not Ralph."

"You mark my words, Birdsey. Believe me."

"Why? What makes you such a big expert?"

"Well, for one thing, I'm a theater major, aren't I?"

"Yeah? So? What's that got to do with anything?"

"Because there are a lot of fags in theater. There's tons of 'em. You know that professor I was talking about before? The Shakespeare teacher? *He's* one."

"Yeah?" I said. "And how do you know that? He announce it in class one day?"

Leo reeled in his line. "This is hopeless," he said. "Come on. Let's go."

"No. Answer the question," I said. "You tell me your teacher's a homo. You tell me you're an expert about it. I'd just like to know how you know."

"I just do, that's all." I sat there, watching him unhook his lure. As wrecked as I was, the operation was totally interesting to me.

"Because the guy kissed me once. Okay?" I looked from Leo's fingers to his face.

"He *kissed* you? Some professor *kissed* you? That's bullshit, Leo."

"Why would I bullshit about that?" he said. "You think I go around—"

"Whereabouts? In class? Up on the stage?"

"At his apartment."

"His apartment?" I didn't know whether to believe him or not. "What were you doing at the guy's apartment?"

"It's not like I went over there by myself," he said. "There was a *bunch* of us went over there." He chugged the last of the wine. Flung the bottle against a ledge. We both paused for the satisfaction—the sound of smashing glass. "He had this cookout thing at his place at the end of the semester. For the whole class. He'd bought all this food and wine and shit, but then only about six or seven of us showed up. I got wasted—I mean, the guy had bought enough stuff for about twenty people—and before you know it . . . I don't know. I was the last one there. Me and him. . . . And he just . . ."

"Just what?"

"I told you already. He kissed me."

I sat there.

"It wasn't that big a deal, Dominick. You don't have to look at me like that. He just did it, and then the two of us laughed a little, and I said thanks but no thanks, and he said fine, fine, he was just—how did he put it?—he was giving me an option I could exercise if I felt like it. And that was that."

"That's *weird,"* I said.

"Why?" he said. "What's so weird about it? It's different in theater. . . . Hey, I swear to Christ, Birdsey, if you ever tell anyone about—"

"I just can't believe some teacher would just—"

"That's because you're so fucking naive," he said. "You were brought up in this one-horse town. You never been anywhere, man. Come on. Let's get out of here."

I stood up, reeling a little from the dope, and followed Leo down the path.

Back in the car, we decided to smoke the second joint. Leo lit the thing up and passed it over.

I was just sitting there, thinking. "It happened to my brother one time," I said.

"What?"

"Thomas. This gay guy started coming on to him once while he was hitchhiking. He was . . . he told me about it."

"Told you about what?" Leo said. He was wasted.

"This . . . this guy in a station wagon pulled over. He had out-of-state plates. Michigan, I think he said. . . . And he . . . Thomas said he looked like somebody's grandfather, this guy—white hair, one of those old-man sweaters with the patches on the sleeves, all these family snapshots magnetized to the dashboard. So he . . . he gets in the car and . . ." Leo looked so stoned, I couldn't tell if anything was registering. If he was even listening. "And the guy says how he's visiting his daughter and her family. How he'd just decided to go out and take a drive. Says he's lonely. So . . . so they're riding along. Thomas and him. He just seemed like some friendly old guy. And then, out of the blue, he says, 'You know what? You're a good-looking son of a gun. Why don't

I find someplace and pull over so the two of us can get to know each other a little better?' He said he'd pay him twenty bucks to . . ."

I sat there, remembering. That guy's hands groping me, petting me like an animal. His not listening when I told him to stop.

"Dominick, stop it! You're scaring me!" I heard Dessa say, and floated back to the Dial-Tone parking lot the night before. *"Stop it! Stop it!"* I told myself it wasn't the same thing at all: the way that old pervert had scared me in that car, on that road, and the way I'd scared Dessa the night before. How were those two things anything alike?

"And then what?" Leo said.

"Huh? What'd you say?"

"He told your brother he'd pay him twenty bucks and then what?"

I looked over at Leo. Why were there gray pants at the driver's side window?

"Evening, gentlemen," someone said.

Leo jumped. Cursed. Tried, ridiculously, to shove the joint under his seat. I was so out of it, I didn't get it at first. The officer asked to see Leo's license and registration.

"My partner and I have been observing you two gentlemen and we have probable cause to believe you may be in possession of an illegal substance." A car door slammed. A *cruiser* door. In my sideview mirror, I saw the other cop approach us.

Oh, *fuck,* I thought. We were royally fucked now.

"We're going to have to search your vehicle," the first cop said. "Would you gentlemen please get out of the car and stand over here please?"

"Absolutely, officer," Leo said. "However my friend and I can be of assistance."

twenty-three

1969

When my stepfather warned me not to trust the Leo Bloods of the world any further than I could throw them, I dismissed the advice as Ray's usual warm view of humanity. But that night, in the interrogation room of the Connecticut State Police Department, Barracks J, I saw what he meant.

Within the first minute of their examination of Leo's Skylark out at the trestle bridge, Officers Avery and Overcash had discovered both the unsmoked joint and the burning one that Leo had chucked under the seat. "Hey, how'd *that* get in there?" Leo asked stupidly about the smoldering roach. "Birdsey, you know anything about this?"

They drove us to the station in the cruiser, explaining that they'd have Leo's car towed back there, too. Riding through downtown Three Rivers, I slumped low and listed all the things our little fishing trip was probably going to cost me: my girlfriend, my tuition loan from Ray, my future teaching career. What school was going to hire a teacher with a drug charge on his record? I'd probably end up in Nam in a body bag after all. Stupid, I kept saying to myself. Stupid, stupid.

At the station, they had us sit on wooden benches with the other losers and lawbreakers they'd netted that night: an old immigrant guy who'd shot his neighbor's dog, a speed freak who'd head-butted his arresting officer. They wouldn't let Leo and me sit together. They parked him across the room and me next to this real scuzzed-out woman who was so loaded, she didn't even realize that the crotch of her pantyhose was hanging below her dress. She kept mumbling about some guy named Buddy. Behind me and Crotch Lady, a noisy air conditioner pushed out a nonstop column of damp breeze. I was scared. I was freezing. I had to take a leak.

Leo stretched, got up, and strolled over to the water fountain: Mr. Nonchalance. Did I look as stoned as he did? It dawned on me that my brother had been right when he'd told me we weren't fooling anyone at work—that anybody could just look at us and tell we'd been smoking weed on the job. Hanging around with Leo was going to get me in trouble, Thomas had warned me, and here I was at the goddamned police barracks. Stupid asshole, I thought. Loser. Jerk.

Passing by, Leo stopped in front of me and squatted. Untying and then retying his shoe, he said something ventriloquist-style which I couldn't catch because of the noise from the air conditioner and because of Crotch Lady's mumbling. *"What?"* I whispered.

"I *said*, when we go in there, let *me* do the talking. Agree with whatever I say."

"Why?" I whispered. "What are you going to say?"

"I don't know yet. I'm still thinking. Just back me up."

"Do you know a guy named Buddy Paquette?" Crotch Lady asked Leo.

"What? Yeah, sure," Leo said. "Buddy and I go way back."

"Did he ever mention me?"

"You? What's your name?"

"Marie. Marie Skeets."

"Oh, yeah. Marie Skeets. He mentioned you plenty of times." The cop at the front desk yelled at Leo to go sit down.

This was the catch: they questioned Leo and me separately. He went first. How was I supposed to corroborate whatever bullshit story he'd cooked up when I didn't even know what it was? A headache had begun to gnaw at the edges of the buzz I'd been enjoying out at the bridge. When I got up and asked the desk sergeant if I could use the bathroom, he told me to wait and ask the officers who'd be talking to me.

"How does that guy know Buddy?" Crotch Lady asked me.

"He doesn't," I said.

"He *said* he did."

"Well, he doesn't. Not that I know of, anyway."

"Oh. It's chilly in here, ain't it?"

"Yup."

"Is it January?"

I told her no—that it was August. Late August.

"Oh," she said. "Got any gum?"

Half an hour later, I passed Leo in the hallway. He looked panicked—tried mouthing something I didn't catch. "This door here," Officer Overcash said.

I got my wish: a visit to a cracked toilet in an adjoining bathroom-supply closet just off the interrogation room. The only thing was, I had to keep the door open. Had to have Officer Avery stand there while I took a wiz, aiming a sample into this plastic cup about the size of a shot glass. At first, in my nervousness, I got "stage fright." Avery and I waited and waited. Then, when I finally got past that little problem, I managed to piss all over my jeans and onto the floor. I cleaned it up with paper towels, apologizing like I'd just committed murder.

When we stepped back into the interrogation room, another cop was sitting at this enamel-topped table. He told me his name was Captain Balchunas and that I should have a seat. Balchunas was older than Avery and Overcash—grayish crewcut, red face, Santa Claus twinkle in his eye. I sat down, folding my arms across my chest. The enamel had worn off the tabletop at the exact points where I rested my elbows.

They'd decided not to bother with the formality of a tape recorder, Balchunas said. Avery and Overcash sat on either side of him, a pair of stone-faced bookends. Overcash took out a pen and a legal pad. Did *I* have any questions before they started?

"Should I . . . do I need a lawyer or anything?" I said.

"For what?" Captain Balchunas asked. "You a bigtime drug lord or something?"

"No. I just—"

"You think these officers and I are going to step on your rights? Is that it? You one of those kids who thinks all cops are fascist pigs?" He was smiling as he said it.

"No."

"What is it then?" He gave my paperwork a quick scan. "Tell me why you think you need a lawyer, Dom."

"I just . . . Never mind. Go ahead."

"See, what we're thinking is, if you cooperate with us the way your buddy just did, we can streamline this process. Probably be able to get you out of here before a lawyer even had time to get in his car and get down here. See what I'm saying?"

I didn't really see, but it sounded good. I nodded.

Captain Balchunas said he noticed I lived on Hollyhock Avenue. When he was a kid, he said, he used to hike up that road on his way to Rosemark's Pond. He and his brothers used to catch snapping turtles up there. "That pond was lousy with them—ornery sons of bitches," he said. "Some good-sized ones, too. You'd poke a stick at them and they'd latch on for dear life. Break a good-sized branch in half sometimes, neat as a pair of lopping shears." He grabbed Officer Overcash's pen and stuck it in his mouth, imitating the way the snapping turtle bit the stick. He had those really fake-looking false teeth—those grayish-green jobs. It struck me kind of funny, in spite of my nervousness. Or *because* of it, maybe: him chomping on that pen, shaking it back and forth, his jowls flapping. There was a tingling in my toes and fingertips. I was maybe 25 percent still stoned.

Balchunas stopped. Stared at me. *Kept* staring. "Why you shaking, Dom?" he asked. I looked over at Officer Avery. Shrugged. I was a little nervous, I told him.

"Nervous? Yeah?" He said they'd done a preliminary check on me and that my record was clean as a whistle. "Everyone makes mistakes, Dom," he said. "Has lapses in judgment. You just talk straight with us and we'll talk straight with you. All right?"

"All right," I said.

"Because your buddy Leon—he was *very* candid with us just now, and we were equally candid with him. And things went well. Didn't they, fellas?"

Very well, the other two agreed. I recalled the look on Leo's face in the hallway a few minutes before. If he'd been so candid and straight with them, why was he trying so hard to tell me something?

"Leon says he and you are both in college, right?" Balchunas said. "Gonna be roommates this coming year? Up at the university?"

"Yes."

"You ever have to do any research, Dom? For any of your college courses? Do some research on a subject, and then write a paper about it?"

"Yes."

"Well, that's what this is like, see? These officers and I are just doing some research, that's all. You see, Dom, you might need a lawyer if protecting your rights was an issue. Which isn't really applicable in this 'sitchy-ation.' At least we don't *think* it is. That urine we took on you isn't going to show us any surprises, is it?"

"Surprises?"

"Like that you're a heroin addict or an LSD freak or something?"

"No."

"Good," he said. "That's good. Cryst-o-mint?"

A blur waved in front of my face. A roll of Life Savers. "Uh, no . . . no thanks."

"No? You sure? Gee, your buddy Leon had three or four of these things. Said he had dry mouth. I guess being stoned affects different people different, right? One guy gets dry mouth, the other doesn't. Course, he talks a lot, too, that pal of yours. He's got quite the gift of gab."

I sat there. Said nothing. The less I said, the less likely I'd be to contradict whatever Leo had told them.

"Jesus Christ, Dom, you're shaking like a leaf," Balchunas said. "What's the matter? You got Saint Vitus' dance or something? We scaring you?"

Trying *not* to shake with them looking at me was futile. "I'm just . . . I'm all right."

"Well, just relax. I could be wrong, Dom, but I don't think you're going to get the chair on this one." He said it deadpan, then smiled.

I smiled back.

He popped himself a Life Saver.

"Gave up smoking three weeks ago, and I been sucking on these things ever since," he said. "I was a two-and-a-half-packs-a-day man. How about you, Dom? You smoke?"

I looked over at Officer Avery. Looked back. Didn't answer.

"Tobacco, I mean? Cigarettes?"

I shook my head.

"No? Good. Take my advice and don't start. I quit over two weeks ago and I'm still bringing up phlegm."

"Um . . . are you . . . are you going to arrest us?"

"Who? You guys? You and Leon? Well, let's put it this way. We're going to *try* not to. See, frankly, Dom, you and your buddy are more trouble than you're worth. Couple of gnats on the windshield, you know? To *us,* I mean. To the justice system. Not, I'm sure, to your parents. Or your girlfriend. You got a girlfriend, Dom?"

"Yes, sir." *Had* one, anyway, before this weird weekend. I saw Dessa, beneath me on the backseat of her mother's car. Punching me, pushing me away.

"I bet you do. Good-looking fella like you. She pretty?"

What did he care? What did Dessa have to do with anything?

"Yes."

"Hell, I bet she is." He leaned forward and smiled. "She big-busted, Dom? You get to bury your face in some good-sized tittie, do you?"

I looked over at Officer Avery. No expression. "Uh . . ."

"None of my business, right? Okay, Dom. I withdraw the question. Consider it withdrawn. I envy you young guys these days, though. All this 'sexual revolution' stuff I read about in the papers. When I was your age, a guy used to have to stand on his head and spit nickels just to cop a feel, and nowadays you young fellas say, 'Open your legs up,' and all she wants to know is, 'How wide, honey?' Right, Dom?"

I told myself he was just trying to piss me off—get me

mad enough to incriminate myself. If I said I wanted a lawyer, didn't they have to let me call one? Except getting a lawyer probably meant having to call Ma and Ray. Shit, if Ray found out . . .

"But like I was saying, Dom, you guys are small potatoes," Balchunas said. "You and . . . what's his name, again? Your fishing buddy? Motormouth, there?"

"Leo," I said.

"That's right. Leo. We might be able to clean this up pretty quick is what I'm saying. Your parents nice people, Dom?"

Oh, *fuck.* "Yes."

"That's what I figured. Bet they'd be a little upset if they knew about what was going on down here. Right? Here. Last chance." He was holding out the goddamned Life Savers again. "Humor an old geezer, will you? *Take* one."

I reached across and took one of his fucking mints. Put it in my mouth. Chewed it.

"How 'bout you, fellas?" he asked the other officers. "Cryst-o-mint?"

"No thanks, Captain."

"I'm good, Captain."

"Okeydoke." He turned to Overcash. "Where was I, Clayton?"

Overcash consulted his pad: cross-hatchings in the margins, a single word or two. "Small potatoes," he said.

"Oh, yeah, that's right. You see, Dom, with all the stuff going on in this town, you and Leon are what we classify as 'nuisance cases.' Frankly, prosecuting you guys is a waste of police time and resources. You see what I'm saying? Not that we *couldn't* make the charges stick if we had to. I mean, come on, Dom. These officers here caught you two dead to rights." He stopped, sniffed the air. "I can still *smell* the sweet stuff on you, for Christ's sake. You *reek* of it. So what we look for in 'sitchy-ations' like this is some kind of trade-off. Something that makes hauling you two guys in worth our while. See, what we're interested in is where you *got* the stuff. We want to know who's selling to guys like you and Leon, and who's selling to *them,* and so on and so forth all the way up the food chain. *Capisce?*"

"Yes."

"Good. That's good. So tell us about this Ralph Drinkwater character."

"Ralph?" I said. "Uh . . . what do you want to know?"

"Whatever you want to tell us."

For some reason, I started talking about Penny Ann Drinkwater's long-ago murder out at the Falls. About the tree-planting in her honor. About Ralph's showing up in my history class years later and then, again, on the work crew. I told them about graveball—how far Ralph could clobber a Wiffle ball. I was in the middle of explaining our rules on ghost runners when Balchunas interrupted me. "What's the most grass you ever saw in Ralph's possession at any one given time? What's the max?"

"Uh . . . let me think. Couple of joints, maybe? Three joints?"

"You sure? Because Leon says he's seen him with a hell of a lot more than that. Tonight, in fact. You two were over Ralph's house tonight, right? You and Leon? You're sure all you've ever seen on him was a couple of joints?"

Agree with whatever I tell them, Leo had said. But *this*? *Frame* the guy. "I'm . . . I'm not sure what Leo saw. All *I* ever saw was a couple of joints."

"How 'bout hash? Ralph ever try and sell you any hash?"

"No."

"Uppers? 'Ludes? Acid?"

"No. He never—"

"Okay. Let's change the subject. What do you recall hearing about the guy Ralph works for?"

"You mean Dell? Our foreman?"

"I mean the guy he *sells* for."

"He doesn't sell for anybody," I said. "Not that I know of, anyway."

Balchunas chuckled. "Oh, come on, now, Dom. Where you been all this time—never-never land? If Ralph's dealing, then he's getting it from someplace. Right? I thought we were going to talk straight with each other. Let's cut the bullshit. Shall we?"

How was I supposed to walk *this* particular tightrope—not bag Ralph and not bag Leo, either? Not end up bagging myself?

"We . . . we were over there looking at a car, okay? Ralph lives at our foreman's house, and our foreman has this car that he might sell. And . . . and I was out there looking at the car. And for a little while, a few minutes, Ralph and Leo were in the house, so maybe Leo saw something then. But *I* didn't. . . . He never *sold* us anything. Ralph. All's we did was get high a couple of times at work together, that's all. At lunchtime or whatever. He just, you know, lit up a joint and passed it around a couple of times."

"Just passed the joint, eh? How many times is 'a couple of times,' Dom?"

"I don't know. . . . Six or seven, maybe? Eight?"

Balchunas turned to Overcash. "You hear that, Clayton? This must be that new math they teach in school nowadays. 'A couple of times' is eight times." He turned back to me. "You remember Ralph saying anything about a guy named Roland?"

"Roland? No. Who's Roland?"

"Leon says Ralph talked to you two once about a guy named Roland. Thinks he comes from New York, maybe? Thinks he might be Ralph's connection? What do you remember about that conversation, Dom? Your buddy says you were there that time when Ralph was talking about Roland."

Leo could get in deep shit for lying to the cops like this. Could get us *both* in trouble. "I don't remember anything about any Roland. Maybe Ralph said something to Leo—I don't know. Not to me."

"You got some reason to protect this guy, Dom?"

"Protect who? Ralph? *No.*"

"No? You sure? Because your story's not matching up that good with your buddy's. Which leads me to the conclusion that one of you guys isn't being 100 percent honest."

I said nothing. This was just great: they thought *I* was bullshitting them, not Leo. Let *me* do the talking, he'd said. If I ended up having to call Ray, I was really fucked.

"You getting dry mouth, Dom? You keep swallowing. Want another mint?"

"No, thank you." Fuckin' pig bastard. He could *shove* his mints.

"So this Ralph never sold you anything, right? Just 'passed the joint.' Generous guy, huh? Just brings his stash to work and shares it." He smiled. Leaned forward—close enough for me to smell his peppermint breath, see the little pockmarks on his nose. He whispered his next question. "And how about you, Dom? You ever share anything of yours with Ralph?"

"What . . . what do you mean?"

"Well, how can I put this delicately? Your friend Leon says this Ralph's of the persuasion where—where he likes the fellas better than he likes the girls. Leon says Ralph and this foreman over on Bickel Road might have a little something funny going on. A little something more than a boss-and-worker relationship. See what I'm saying? So I guess I was just wondering out loud if you and Ralph ever made any kind of private deal. You know. He gives you something you want and you give him something he wants."

What was he asking—if Ralph and me had ever gotten queer together? Had *Leo* told him something like that? If he had, I'd beat the shit out of him. But he wouldn't say that. Would he? "If you're saying what I think you're saying, then no. No way. *Never!*"

"It's interesting, though. How you and Leon like to go over to their house, hang out with these guys on the weekend. Unusual for two normal, red-blooded American guys to want to do that. I'm not making any accusations, Dom. I'm just making an observation."

"We don't 'hang out' there. I was just looking at a *car.* Dell's wife's *car.*" I turned to Overcash. "The guy's got a *wife.*" I addressed Avery next. "They're selling her car because she's got multiple sclerosis. . . . Look, I want a lawyer. Okay?"

"What do you want a lawyer for?" Overcash asked. "Captain already told you we're just doing some research. Asking a few questions, seeing what we can eliminate."

"Yeah, well, you can give me a lie detector test if you think—"

"Hey, you want a lawyer, Dom?" Balchunas said. "We'll be glad to let you call a lawyer. But like I said, all we're trying to do is streamline this thing. Get you and your buddy out of here nice and easy. All we gotta do is iron out a few discrepancies, that's all. A few inconsistencies between what you're telling us and what Leon told us. Like this business about Ralph's contact, for instance. This Roland dude from New York."

Fuck 'em—Ralph and Leo both. I wasn't going to let any stupid cop sit there and call *me* a fag—I didn't care what kind of bullshit story Leo had given them. "He just . . . Ralph grows his own, okay? That's what he told us, anyway. He said he has a few plants out in a field someplace. Out in the woods. . . . I swear to God. That's all I know."

"Must be damn good plants, eh?" Balchunas said. "Must have a pretty high yield. Because Leo says he's seen *pounds* of the stuff. Now you're saying Ralph gets *pounds* of the stuff from 'a few plants'? I mean, even if 'a few' is nine or ten, that's still quite a yield. Wouldn't you say, Dom? This Ralph must have one hell of a green thumb."

"I never saw pounds of it. Maybe Leo did, but all I saw was a couple of joints."

"This Ralph's a Negro fella. Right?"

"What?"

"He's black? Of the Negroid persuasion?"

"I guess."

"You *guess*? Jesus, you can't even give me a straight answer about *that*?"

"He's . . . I think he's part Indian, too."

"Yeah? American Indian or India Indian?"

"American Indian. Wequonnoc, I think."

"That right? Half-black, half-Indian, huh?" Balchunas turned to Officer Overcash. "Poor guy. Probably doesn't know whether to go out and scalp his next meal or let welfare pay for it." He turned back to me. "You know what Leon says, Dom? He says Ralph reads a lot of radical literature. Black Panther stuff. Overthrow-the-government kind of stuff. You know anything about that?"

I shook my head. Was this Leo's whole big plan to get us off the hook? Trash Ralph? Slander the guy? Slander me, too, maybe, while he was at it?

"You ever seen Ralph with guns? Firearms of any kind?"

"No."

"No, huh? You sure?"

"He read . . . he's read this one book called *Soul on Ice.* That's all I ever heard him say anything about black power or power to the people or whatever."

"*Soul on Ice,* eh? I heard about that book. Right on, brother! Who wrote that one, anyway, Dom? I forget."

"Eldridge Cleaver."

"Eldridge Cleaver. Any good—that book? Would *you* recommend it?"

I told him I'd never read it.

"No? How about Roland? The guy from New York? He's a colored boy, too, right? Black Panther, maybe?"

"I already told you. I don't know anything about any Roland."

"You got a brother works on this work crew, too. Right?"

What was he dragging Thomas into it for? What had Leo said about Thomas? "My brother doesn't have anything to do with any of this," I said.

"No? Leo says your faggoty foreman takes a little bit of a special interest in him. You and your brother are twins, right?"

I nodded. Felt my heartbeat revving up. "He just likes to tease Thomas, that's all. Pick on him. He's a bully. . . . He knows he can get a rise out of him."

"Get a rise out of him, huh? Interesting way to put it. You guys *identical* twins?"

I swallowed. "Yes."

"Your brother expose himself at work last Friday, Dom? The queers on that crew get him to play show-and-tell for them, did they?"

I was going to *nail* Leo when we got out of there. What right did he have to feed Thomas's humiliation to the cops? And why? For what purpose?

"Look, you're jumping to the wrong conclusions. My brother just—"

"What'd they do—trade him a couple of joints for a look-see?"

"It was nothing like that!" I felt close to tears. I knew they were busting my balls—toying with me the way a cat bats around a mouse before he bites his fucking head off. But why my brother? Why did Leo have to drag Thomas into it? "Dell's been harassing my brother all summer," I said. "Bullying him. Calling him names. And he just . . . my brother's a little high-strung and he just . . . he freaked. They goaded him into it."

"Who goaded him into it? Ralph?"

"Dell. Really. You've got the wrong idea. He was just bullying him. Just jerking him around."

"Just jerking him around," Balchunas said.

"God, you're twisting everything I say. My brother's—"

"Look at his ears, Clayton," Balchunas said. "You're blushing, Dom. Why you covering for Ralph?"

"I'm *not* covering for him."

"He's just a generous guy who likes to bring his dope to work and share it, right?"

"I don't know what kind of a guy he is. We just work together. He's very private."

"Uh-huh. You ever let him get private with you? In exchange for some hash?"

"No!" Leo was going to pay for this, big time.

"Take it easy, Dom. This is off the record now. This is just research."

"I don't care *what* it is. I would never . . . me *or* my brother!"

"Relax, Dom. Relax. We know you're okay. We know all about that girlfriend of yours." He cupped his hands in front of his chest, fondled a pair of imaginary breasts.

"Leave my girlfriend out of this," I said. "And my brother, too. My brother never even took one stupid toke all summer long." I was fighting back tears.

"Okay, take it easy," Avery said. "Suppose we change the subject."

Balchunas's fist whacked down hard on the table. "No, let's not *change* the subject," he said. "Let's just *end* the subject and let this little twerp get his lawyer like he goddamn wants to. Because you know what?" He turned to Overcash. "You know what, Clayton? I'm starting to get a little tired of wasting our time while this little shit here keeps talking around in circles. I'm starting to think maybe this arrogant little son of a bitch might *need* to call a lawyer after all. Or call his mommy and daddy, or his buddies over on Bickel Road, or someone. Because Leon's telling us one thing and this guy's telling us another, and all we're trying to do is get the two of them out of here tonight."

"I'm *telling* the truth," I said. Turned to Avery. "I *am.*"

"You know what?" Balchunas said. "Send the other one home. I got no beef with him; he cooperated with us. That's what this little shit doesn't seem to understand."

"I *am* cooperating!" I said. "What am I supposed to do—lie about it? If I didn't hear him say anything about some Roland guy, am I supposed to just . . . ? You accuse me and my brother of all this perverted stuff we didn't even do, and I'm supposed to just—"

"Okay, okay. Let's lower the volume, all right?" Officer Avery suggested. "No sense getting all excited. How about if we put it a different way? You listening to me?"

"Yes."

"Is it *possible* Ralph might have talked to you guys about this Roland and maybe you just don't *remember* as much detail about it as Leo does? Maybe you were high at the time or thinking about your girlfriend or something? Or maybe Leo just has a better memory than you do? But maybe you remember *something*—even something vague—about Roland? Is that possible?"

"I don't . . . I'm all mixed up. . . . It's *possible,* I guess. Anything's *possible.*"

"But you're still saying Ralph never sold you any marijuana, right?" Overcash said. "Just passed the stuff, let you take some hits off it?"

"Yes."

"How about that stuff you two had tonight, then? Out at the bridge? Ralph wasn't passing the joint tonight. He wasn't even there."

"I don't . . . I guess he just gave Leo a couple of joints."

"*Gave* them or *sold* them?"

"Gave them. As far as I know. Leo never said anything about buying them."

"Was Ralph *planning* to sell you some?" Avery asked. "You know—in quantity? *Talking* to you guys about the possibility? Was this stuff a sample?"

It had been Leo's big idea that we should sell dope at school, not Ralph's. But what was I supposed to do—whack him the way he'd probably whacked me? Or had he? I didn't know anything anymore. I shook my head. "Not that I know of."

"Not that you know of, not that you know of," Balchunas mimicked. "That stuff you were smoking tonight: potent stuff, right? Little more kick to it than the stuff you guys were smoking at work. Right?"

"Look, what about my rights?" I said. "I have rights, don't I?"

He shot out of his seat. Started jabbing his finger at me. "You know who's always concerned about their rights, wiseguy? When they get backed into a corner? I'll *tell* you who. The guys who are lying between their teeth, that's who. The guys who are trying to cover something up."

"I'm *not* trying to cover anything up. I just—" He waved his hands at me in disgust. Sat back down.

"Look, Dominick," Officer Avery said. "We'd advise you of your rights if we were planning to arrest you. Which we're trying like hell *not* to do, if we can help it. Now Leon says that stuff you guys were smoking tonight was a sample. Right? That Ralph wanted you to try it and if you liked it, you guys and he might make a little arrangement? Sell for him at school?"

"I'm . . . he never said anything like that to me."

"You never heard Ralph say he wanted you guys to buy a couple of pounds from him and then turn around and—"

"*I* didn't hear him say that. No."

"But maybe he said it to your buddy Leon?" Balchunas asked. "Maybe he offered Leon that deal to the both of you? Leon ever mention any arrangement like that to you?"

"I don't know. I don't think so. Maybe."

"That's an imprecise word, Dom. 'Maybe.' In your estimation, would you classify 'maybe' as 'yes' or 'no'?"

"How much longer do I have to stay here?"

"Well, that's up to you, Dom. If 'maybe' is 'yes,' Radical Ralph *was* trying to put together a deal with you guys to sell his dope up there at the university, then you could probably get up and walk out of here in about three to five minutes.

And if 'maybe' is 'no,' he *wasn't,* then this might take a while longer. You see what I'm saying? Gets a little more complicated if 'maybe' means 'no.' Because then we've got this discrepancy between what you say and what your buddy Leon says. If 'maybe' is 'no,' then I guess we ought to have you call yourself a lawyer after all, or call your father, or call someone. Because, hey, let's face it—between what we found out in that car and what's going to show up in your urine sample, we got the goods on you, pal. And frankly, my friend, I've cooperated with you about as much as I'm willing to cooperate. We got other fish to fry out there in that waiting room. So you tell us, Dom, and you better be quick about it, too. What's 'maybe'? Is 'maybe' yes, you were aware that Ralph offered you guys a deal to sell for him? Or is 'maybe' no, he didn't?"

I just wanted to get out of there. Not get arrested. Not cry in front of them.

"Yes."

It was after midnight by the time they let us go. The benches out front where we'd been waiting were almost empty. Crotch Lady was still there, snoring open-mouthed. Avery took us around in back to where Leo's car had been towed. Unlocked the gate. Waved us off.

At first, neither of us spoke. We just rode through Three Rivers with the windows down, the radio off. Leo kept checking the rearview mirror. It was one of the few times I'd ever seen him speechless—*not* running his mouth.

"What the fuck did you tell them, anyway?" I finally said.

He started singing to himself, pounding out a tune on the steering wheel. "Who? The cops? I don't know. I told them a bunch of shit."

"Like what?"

"Why? What'd they ask you about?"

Part of me didn't even want to get into it. Didn't want to find out just how much of a weasel he could be—how low he'd go to get himself off the hook. Why had he dragged my stupid brother into it? Or told them Ralph was a queer? A radical with weapons?

"Birdsey, look back," he said. "Is that anyone?"

I turned around. "What?"

He was watching the rearview mirror as much as he was the road in front of him. "You think they're following us? The cops?" In the sideview mirror, I saw the car behind us take a right.

"Nope, false alarm," he said, exhaling. "Man, my mother would've shit a brick if she found out about this. . . . Hey, Birdsey, reach in back and get that box of eight-tracks on the seat, will you? I don't feel like talking. I just feel like mellowing out, listening to some tunes. Too bad they took that last joint Ralph gave us, right? I could go for a couple hits off of that thing. I'm all nervous still."

I reached around and got the box of tapes. Put them on the seat between us. We were riding out of Three Rivers, down Route 22. I didn't know where he was taking us. Didn't really care. I felt more pissed than nervous.

"Hey, I know," Leo said. "Let's get some eggs. That's what I could use right now. Some eggs and toast and home fries. And coffee, too. About two gallons of coffee. Enough coffee so I can piss this whole experience right out of my system."

I kept staring out the sideview mirror. "What'd you tell them?" I asked him again.

"The cops? I don't know. I partly told them the truth and partly bullshitted them a little. Mixed it up, you know? Something would come to me and I'd just . . . *use* it. Hey, not to change the subject, but you got any money on you? All's I got is three bucks. The Oh Boy's open all night, isn't it? I'll pay you back."

We rode on in silence, half a mile's worth or more. "And they *bought* it, too, you know?" Leo said. "That's the funny part. I *knew* they would. Cops are so fucking stupid." He patted his box of eight-tracks. "Put a tape in. Go ahead, Birdsey. Ladies' choice."

"What'd you say about my brother?" I said.

"What? I didn't say anything about him."

"You must have. They knew all about him pulling his pants down at work."

"Oh, yeah, that. I forgot. I was talking so fast, you know? Talking a blue streak. They were asking me all about the work crew and—"

"What did *that* have to do with anything? Why'd you drag Thomas into it? They made it sound like we were all sitting around getting queer with each other."

"I was just—okay, look. Cops *hate* queers, Birdsey. Ask my mother. Ask *anyone* in law enforcement. So, what I did was, I created this smoke screen, okay? Made it sound like Dell and Ralph were, you know, trying to get funny with us and Thomas just . . . It was a *smoke screen,* Dominick. Something to draw attention away from us getting wrecked out there by the bridge."

"So you just bag my brother—slander Ralph—so that we can weasel out of—"

"I didn't slander either of them. How'd I slander them, Dominick? Your brother started crying and he yanked his drawers down, didn't he? Did I *imagine* that? . . . You saw those queer magazines they had out there. What, did those things just fall out of the sky and land there? Wake up, man. Ralph's a flit and so's Dell, and all I did was tell them."

"So what if they are? That doesn't mean you can just—?"

"Hey, look, Dominick. I did what I *had* to do. Okay? Why don't you just shut your mouth and play a fucking tape and don't worry about it. We're both out here driving around instead of at the friggin' *state police barracks,* aren't we? They didn't *bust* us, did they? I did what I had to do, and I'm not taking any shit from you about it, either."

I said nothing for a mile or more. Heard Balchunas asking me all those embarrassing questions again. Saw him chomp that pen of his, snapping-turtle style.

"You smeared *me* while you were in there, too. Didn't you?" I said.

"No, Dominick, I *didn't* smear you. I got you *out* of that mess is what I did. But, hey, thanks a lot for the accusation. You're a real pal. You're—"

"You sure? Because one of the things they wanted to know was if I'd ever let Ralph get funny with me for some hash. Why'd they want to know *that,* Leo? What'd you do—bag all three of us? Thomas, Ralph, *and* me? Fuck over three guys for the price of one?"

"Look, Birdsey, you ought to be thanking me right now instead of accusing me of all this shit. That's all *I* got to say.

As far as I'm concerned, the subject's closed." He turned on the radio, punched several stations, snapped it off again. "And anyways, it's not my fault if the cops took what I said and twisted it around. They were just fucking with your head, you idiot. Trying to get you pissed off. It's a *technique,* asshole. Don't blame me. Cops do it all the time. Ask my mother."

"So what did you say then? What'd you tell them about this supposed hash deal?"

"All's I said was. . . . I told them Ralph made us this offer that he'd, you know, give us some hash if we'd let him go down on us. And that we *both* told him to take a flying leap. I'm telling you, Birdseed, cops *hate* queers, and they're not exactly in love with blacks, either—especially groups like the Panthers. So I stretched the truth a little and—"

"Those are total fucking lies!"

"Yeah, and they worked, too, didn't they? You want me to turn around, drop you back off at the barracks so you can tell the whole truth and nothing but the truth so help you God? Well, sorry, Dominick. I guess I ain't as much of a saint as you. I'd rather be out here than inside that station."

I stared up at the moon. Didn't answer. I didn't know what to think.

"Look, Birdsey, I had to think of something fast, okay? And on top of that, I was wrecked out of my mind. Remember? It was the best I could come up with. What was I supposed to do—sit around and wait for *you* to get us out of this mess?"

He had a point. If it was me handling it, we'd probably still be back at Barracks J, getting fingerprinted, having our mug shots taken. Not that I was willing to admit that.

"Well, I just gotta hand it to you, Leo, that's all," I said. "When you decide to slander your friends, you can be pretty goddamned merciless."

"I wasn't trying to 'slander' anybody, Dominick. It was just . . . survival of the fittest. So just do me a favor and shut up about it, will you? Let's just go eat."

Survival of the fittest: I let that hang in the air for a mile or more. Let it good and goddamn piss me off. Leo fished a tape from the box and shoved it into the player. Started singing along. *I'm your captain. Yeah yeah yeah yeah. . . .*

I reached over and yanked the fucker out of the machine. Yanked out two or three yards of tape and chucked the whole pile of spaghetti out the window. "Hey!" Leo protested. He braked hard enough to throw us both toward the dashboard. Then he changed his mind and gunned it. "What'd you do *that* for?"

"Because I wanted to, asshole."

"Yeah, well, *you're* the asshole, Birdsey. You owe me a tape."

"Survival of the fittest?" I said. "You frame the guy because he's black, or because you think he's queer, but it's okay because it's just the fucking law of the jungle?"

"Yeah, that's *right,* Dominick. It was Ralph or us, so I chose us. You mind?"

"So the big, bad, black dope peddler tries to get us poor innocent college kids to deal for him. Right? That was *your* bright idea, Leo. Remember? Not Ralph's. *Yours.* You were going to see if he'd sell us some shit and then we'd jack up the price and make a profit. Remember?"

"Did you tell them that? The cops? That it was *my* idea?"

"Geez, I don't know, Leo. Did I? I was talking so fast—I was so wrecked—I don't remember *what* I told them."

"Cut it out, Birdsey. Did you tell 'em it was my idea or not?"

"Tell them the *truth,* Leo? No, I didn't. And you know why I didn't? Because *I* don't bag my friends. Maybe I should have, though. Practiced 'survival of the fittest.' "

"Hey, how do you know he's *not* dealing, Birdsey? All that grass we smoked all summer. That's probably *exactly* what he was doing—getting us interested so he could use us in his little drug operation."

"Yeah, right, Leo. I think I saw that episode on *The Mod Squad,* too. Real life's just like TV, isn't it?"

"No shit. *Think* about it. We worked with the guy all summer long and we didn't even know until tonight that he lives over at Dell's. That he's a fucking fruitcake. How do we know he's *not* a dealer?"

"Who's Roland?" I said. "Where'd Roland come from?"

"Roland? Roland's nobody. Roland's my great-uncle from New Rochelle. I was just giving them a false lead."

"Yeah, and it's probably going to backfire in your stupid face, too. In *both* our faces since I—"

"Since you what?"

"Since I covered for you, asshole. Since I said I *might* have heard Ralph say something about this imaginary pusher friend of his. Said he *might* have been interested in having us sell for him."

"Oh, so you ain't Saint Dominick after all, huh? You bagged Ralph, too."

"Because you'd backed me into a corner, that's why. What the fuck was I supposed to do—tell the truth and let the cops nail you for possession *and* false information? I guess I just don't know how to play bag-a-buddy as good as you do, Leo. Shit, man, you're the big pro at that. You could give *Judas* a few pointers."

He spat out the window. Turned back to me. "Hey, maybe Ralph's *your* buddy, Birdsey. Maybe he's *your* big pal. But to me he's just some guy I worked with. Smoked a few jays with. Because, personally, I don't hang around with fags. Okay?"

"No? How about that drama teacher of yours? That guy you made out with?"

"Fuck you, Birdsey! I didn't 'make out' with anyone. Besides, I told you that in *confidence.* You just shut your mouth about that."

"What do you have to do to get the lead, Leo—to play Hamlet in that play this semester? You got to let this guy fuck you in the ass or something? Or is that already a done deal? Are you *already* the fuckin' prince of Denmark?"

"Shut up, Birdsey. You better shut your fucking mouth before you're sorry."

"Oh, big man. You don't like it, do you? When someone makes up shit about *you*? Asshole!"

"Don't call *me* an asshole, Birdsey. *You're* the asshole!"

"Yeah, and you're a fucking liar! You're a fucking snake in the grass!" I grabbed his box of eight-tracks, threw the whole bunch of them out the window.

He slammed on the brakes. Shoved me against the car door. I shoved him back.

"What are you, *nuts*? You turning mental like that mental case brother of yours?"

I was on him instantly—choking him, letting my fist fly. I grabbed his head in both hands—was ready to smash it into the steering wheel. Knock his teeth out. Bust his nose.

"Stop it!" he screamed. "Stop it, Dominick! What's the *matter* with you?"

It was the fear in his voice that stopped me—the way he suddenly sounded like Dessa out in the parking lot the night before. I saw blood dripping from his nose. Saw my raised fist opening, closing, opening.

"Don't you *ever* . . . !" I was out of breath. My heart was pounding so hard, it hurt. "Don't you *ever* call *me* crazy. Me *or* him, understand? *Understand?*"

"Okay. All right. Jesus."

I got out. Slammed the car door hard as I could and started walking, kicking his eight-tracks out of my way. When I turned back at about fifty yards, he was out of the car, bending over to pick up his tapes. I grabbed a rock and chucked it at his stupid Skylark. It rang out as it hit the bumper. "You dent this car, you're paying for it!" he shouted back. "My tapes, too. I'm going to play every single one of 'em tomorrow, and whatever ones don't play anymore, you're paying for! I mean it!" I heard his door slam. Heard him peel out, drive off.

Fuck *him*, I thought. Asshole. Cool Jerk. Good riddance. . . .

I walked along the dark road, my head filling up with sounds and pictures of things I didn't want to think about: Thomas, sobbing and yanking down his drawers for Dell. Dessa beneath me, crying, pushing me away. Balchunas's big face. . . .

I walked for hours—for eight or nine miles. And by the time I reached Hollyhock Avenue, my arms and neck were scabby with mosquito bites. My feet burned like I'd been walking on hot coals.

I just stood there, looking up at our house—the house my grandfather had built. I couldn't go in, no matter *how* exhausted I was. Couldn't bring myself to go up the front stairs, unlock the door, climb the inside stairs, go down the hall to mine and my brother's room. Couldn't go in there and see my sleeping brother. Something was wrong with him, whether I wanted to admit it or not.

I couldn't do it.

So I kept walking. Up the rest of Hollyhock Hill, then out through the pine grove and down to the clearing, to Rosemark's Pond.

You know what I did? I shucked off all my clothes, waded into the water, and swam. Swam until my limbs were numb, leaden. Until they couldn't kick or push aside any more water. I guess . . . I guess I was trying to wash myself clean of everything: the stink of sweat and marijuana, the stink of what we'd done to Ralph—of what I'd done to Dessa out in that parking lot. What kind of a person *was* I? If my brother was cracking, maybe I'd helped cause it. Ray wasn't the only bully at our house. . . . Survival of the fittest, I thought: whack whoever's vulnerable, show 'em who's in charge.

It didn't work, that swim. You can't swim away your sins, I learned that much. I came out of the pond feeling just as dirty as when I'd gone in. I remember standing there on the shore, naked still, panting like a bastard. Just looking at my reflection in the water.

Not looking away. Not lying to myself for once in my life.

Facing what I really was.

"And what was that?"

"What?"

"You said you stood there at the pond that morning and faced what you really were. I'm wondering what that was. What was your conclusion?"

"My conclusion? That I was a son of a bitch."

"Explain, please."

"A bastard. A bully. I think it was the first time I'd actually ever admitted it to myself. . . . At least that's how I remember it, anyway. I never know, during these sessions, whether I'm rehashing history or reinventing it."

"Well, yes, memory is selective, Dominick. An interpretation of the facts as we recall them, accurate or not. But what we select to remember can be very instructive. Don't you think?"

"He works over there, you know. At Hatch."

"Who?"

"Ralph Drinkwater. He's on the maintenance staff."

"Is he?"

"I've run into him down there. The night Thomas was admitted. He had an accident, pissed himself. And guess who shows up with the mop?"

"How did you feel when you saw Ralph?"

"How did I feel? Oh, I guess I felt . . . like a good, red-blooded American."

"Yes? Explain, please."

"Keep them damn minorities down, boys. Put 'em on the cleanup crew. Survival of the fittest."

"You're being ironic, yes?"

"You know much about American history, Doc? What we did to the Indians? The slaves?"

"I'm afraid I'm not grasping your point, Dominick."

"My point is: who the hell do you think those three white cops were going to believe that night—a couple of white kids or the dope-peddling black Indian? The radical queer? I mean, you got to hand it to Leo. It was a little over the top, maybe, but it worked. Right? I mean, stoned or not, it was a brilliant defense."

"And so, when you saw Ralph here at Hatch, you felt . . . ?"

"I don't know. There was a lot going on that night. . . . I felt bad, I guess."

"Can you be more specific, please? What does 'bad' mean?"

"Guilty. I felt guilty as sin. . . . We just fed him to the cops."

"Ah. Interesting."

"What is?"

"That's the second time you've used that word today."

"What word? 'Guilty'?"

" 'Sin.' "

"Yeah? So?"

"Do you recall the context of your other reference to sin?"

"No."

"You said that when you emerged from the pond, you realized that one cannot swim away from one's sins."

"Yeah? And?"

"I merely note that you described your swim almost as an attempt at purification. And now, this second reference to guilt and sin. I'm just struck by your religious—"

"It's just a figure of speech. 'Guilty of sin': people say it all the time."

"Are you angry?"

"No, I just . . . I think you're confusing me with the other *Birdsey brother."*

"No, no. I assure you. I know the difference between—"

"Look, Ma! Two hands!"

"Dominick, sit down, please."

"I don't want to sit down! I just . . . You know something? Let me clue you in to something. When you go to lift your kid—your beautiful little baby girl—out of the bassinet some morning and . . . and she's . . . Well, never mind. Just don't start confusing me with my one-handed Holy-Roller brother. I don't do *religion, okay? I gave up on God a long time ago. . . . I was just some stupid, mixed-up kid up there at that pond that morning. I was hot and tired and . . ."*

"Take my hands, please, Dominick. That's it. Now, look at me. That's right. Good. I want to assure you, my friend, that I do not confuse you and your brother. I am quite aware of the distinctions between you. All right?"

"I—"

"I only ask this: that, during this process, you try not to disown your insights."

"My insights? Have I had any insights yet?"

"Yes! And more will come in time. Be patient, Dominick. They're coming. Do you, by any chance, know who Bhagirath was? In Hindu legend?"

"Who?"

"Bhagirath. He brought the Ganges from heaven to earth."

"Yeah? Neat trick. What was he—a civil engineer?"

"Of sorts, I suppose. You see, Bhagirath had a mission. He needed to cleanse the honor of his ancestors because they had been cursed. Burned to cinders. So he routed the river from the feet of Brahma, the Creator, through the tangled locks of Shiva, the Destroyer, and thus to earth. It was

his gift. The holy river. And that is why orthodox Hindus bathe there: to cleanse themselves of their imperfections. To wash away their ancestors' sins."

"Uh-huh."

"Keep thinking back, Dominick. Keep remembering."

"I just . . . It's painful. I don't see the point."

"The point is this: that the stream of memory may lead you to the river of understanding. And understanding, in turn, may be a tributary to the river of forgiveness. Perhaps, Dominick, you have yet to emerge fully from the pond where you swam that morning so long ago. And perhaps, when you do, you will no longer look into the water and see the reflection of a son of a bitch."

twenty-four

1969–70

The next day, Dessa and I drove out to the Falls to talk. We made up. Made love.

On Monday morning, I quit the Public Works so I wouldn't have to face Ralph. Walked into Lou Clukey's office and told him I needed to leave earlier than I'd figured because of school. Leo had quit, too, Lou said. At least I'd come in and told him in person. On the way out of the yard, I ran right into Ralph. He acted embarrassed, not angry. If the cops were going to haul him in for questioning, they hadn't done it yet.

"Well," I said. "It's been real." I held out my hand for him to shake.

"It's been real," Ralph repeated. And he grasped and shook the dirty hand of betrayal. The white boy's hand.

The weekend before school started, Dessa came over to the house with her sister. Thomas and I were out on the front porch, shucking corn for supper. Angie plopped herself down next to my brother and started teasing him. *Flirting* with him. Then and forever engaged in a one-sided competition with her big sister, Angie had decided on the spot that if Dessa wanted me, what she wanted was the closest facsimile. It was Angie who suggested the four of us drive down to Ocean Beach to play miniature golf. On the way home, Angie and Thomas started making out in the back-seat. In a way, it was kind of funny: Thomas getting the moves slapped on him. And, if the rearview mirror didn't lie, responding. Acting normal for once in his life. Acting human. . . . It was funny, but it *wasn't* funny, either. Thomas's behavior was always a wild card. And Dessa's little sister was just plain wild.

Angie and Thomas went out the next night, and then the next. The morning before we were due back at school, I stepped out of the shower and saw Thomas standing in front of the medicine cabinet mirror, shirtless, touching the hickeys Angie Constantine had sucked into his chest and neck. "Hey, listen, loverboy," I said. "You do anything stupid—anything to mess up Dessa and me—and you're a dead man. Understand?" Thomas just stared at me, bewildered, as if sex and girls and fratricide weren't options on the planet where he came from. Then he went back to the mirror—touched his chest again, passed his fingers over his rose-colored bruises.

That night, I dreamed I was screwing Angie. "Don't tell Dessa," I kept begging her, mid-fuck. When she told me she wouldn't, I hooked my chin over her shoulder and closed my eyes and we went at it something fierce. And when I opened my eyes again, there was my brother, watching us.

During our first week as dormmates, Leo and I spoke in grudging single syllables, then in guarded, self-conscious sentences, then normally again. I threw a twenty-dollar bill on his desk, partial payment for the damaged tapes, but not all of it. Neither of us apologized. Neither of us said much at all about our near-arrest by the state police and how we'd gotten out of it and how I'd lost it and almost busted his face in. We just let it lie. Let it get layered over with classes, loud music on the turntable, guys busting into the room for a bull session or a game of poker or pitch. Leo's drama professor cast a better actor as Hamlet and gave Leo the part of Osric, court asshole, Elizabethan "Cool Jerk." Leo had five or six lines, maybe. Two or three sorry little scenes. Watching Leo in that performance—the costumer had outfitted him in checked tights, a floppy hat with a big plume—I forgave him for who he was: a buffoon, a bigmouth, a guy who couldn't be trusted any further than you could throw him.

Across campus, Thomas and his new roommate began their awkward adjustment to each other. Randall Deitz was a nice enough guy—one of those quiet, fade-into-the-woodwork types. "How's it going with my brother?" I asked him one morning when I bumped into him on the way to class. I was afraid to hear his answer.

"Fair," he said. "He's *different*."

Against the odds, Thomas's relationship with Angie Constantine continued—went into overdrive, in fact. At the same time, killer classes and a leaking radiator on that piece-of-shit car I'd bought from Dell had temporarily downshifted Dessa's and my relationship. Angie started driving up to UConn on weekends and sleeping over. (Deitz worked weekends at a pharmacy back home and was never around.) The Constantines were pissed. Big Gene threatened to fire Angie from her accountant trainee's job down at the dealership if she didn't start acting like the decent girl they'd brought her up to be. But Angie called her father's bluff. Daddy's disapproval was a big part of the appeal, see? A way to get herself noticed. In a way, she was just *using* my stupid brother. But part of me was relieved: Thomas was normal, I told myself. Normal enough to shack up on weekends, like anyone else.

One Sunday morning, Angie phoned Dessa up in Boston. This was it, she said. The real thing. She and Thomas were in love. Angie told Dess they might be getting engaged. And something else: she might be pregnant. It was okay, though. They *wanted* kids. Wanted a family as soon as possible. Dessa called me from Boston, in tears.

I waited until Angie's car had left the dorm parking lot that afternoon, then barged into my brother's room and reamed him out. He was already on academic probation, I reminded him—hanging on by a thread, and now *this*? Dessa and Angie's parents were going to go apeshit when they found out. And what about Ma and Ray? Wasn't she on the pill? Hadn't he even been using a rubber? How could he *be* so stupid? Thomas gave me that space alien look again, as if knocking up your girlfriend carried no complications whatsoever.

Then something weird happened. Thomas did something that Angie said she was never, ever going to talk about, not even to Dessa. Something that freaked her out. She broke up with him—dropped him cold—and started telling anyone who'd listen that my brother was "the weirdest guy on earth."

She *did* talk about what had happened, eventually: blabbed it all over creation, once she got started, about how my brother had bought this book called *The Lives of the Martyred Saints* and become preoccupied with the descriptions of the saints' bizarre and gory persecutions. He'd lie there naked on his bed, Angie said, and make her read aloud about the saints' beatings and amputations and flesh burnings, their being pierced with arrows, gashed with hooks. She didn't want to do it, she said—read him that stuff—but he'd *beg* her. So she'd read it, and he'd writhe and roll around, moaning and groaning. And then . . . and then he'd . . . well, you know. All by himself, on the bed, right in front of her. Without her even touching him. Angie said she'd done it twice—that he'd *pleaded* with her. He was just too weird for words. She wanted a *normal* boyfriend: someone who liked to dance and have fun and double with other couples. There was no more talk about a baby. There had never *been* a baby, Angie told Dessa. She'd just been late; she'd just miscounted, *okay*? She didn't care whether Miss Perfect believed her or not.

I introduced Angie to Leo a couple of months later. It was Angie's idea, not mine or Dessa's. I promised I'd fix her up if she stopped telling the world about my brother. The funny part is, for better or worse, it's been Angie and Leo ever since. They made it through two kids, two separations and reconciliations, Leo's drug rehab, his little flings on the side. They're an institution by now, Leo and Angie. But before that—for a month or so, way the hell back—it was Angie and my brother, hot and heavy. Hard to imagine now that it ever even happened—that it ever *could* have happened. It was one of life's stranger twists, I guess. . . . Not that things didn't get a whole lot stranger after that. Not that, by the fall of 1969, the whole fucking world wasn't falling apart, anyway.

My Lai, the antiwar protests, the cops gunning down the

Panthers. And then, one morning, a headline that hit closer to home. "Look at this, Birdsey!" Leo said, bursting into our room. He was waving a *Hartford Courant* in my face like a victory flag. "Jesus Christ! *Look!*"

COUPLE INDICTED FOR CHILD PORNOGRAPHY;
POLICE RAID YIELDS FILMS, PHOTOS

It was November by then, I think—two or three months after Leo and I had lied to the state cops about Ralph. Accompanying the newspaper article was a picture of Dell Weeks and his wheelchair-bound wife entering the same state police barracks where Leo and I had been. Originally under surveillance for suspected drug trafficking, the paper said, the Weekses' Bickel Road home had been searched in September by state police, who had unexpectedly come upon an extensive cache of child pornography. Confiscated materials included equipment for production and distribution as well as hundreds of obscene photographs and amateur eight-millimeter films featuring minors as subjects. A twenty-year-old resident of the Weekses' home, unrelated to the accused, had turned state's evidence in the continuing investigation. The witness, whose name was being withheld, was reportedly the subject of many of the confiscated photographs and films, the earliest dating back ten years.

"God, just think, Birdsey. We worked all summer long with those two slimeballs," Leo said. "We were inside their *house,* for Christ's sake."

Ten years, I thought. Which meant it would have started when Ralph was ten years old. Joseph Monk had killed his twin sister, then his mother had folded, then Dell Weeks and his wife had moved in for the kill. They'd taken him in, fed him, and used him for ten years—had killed him every time the camera rolled, every time the shutter blinked.

"Jesus, Birdsey. You know what?" Leo said. "If it wasn't for the two of us, the cops would have never even gone *into* that scummy house. You know what we did? I'll tell you what. We performed a public service, that's what. We did society a favor. They should give us an *award* or something."

* * *

On the evening of December 1, 1969, Leo and I and a couple dozen other guys from our dorm parked ourselves in front of the lounge TV and watched the first U.S. draft lottery since 1942. It was prime-time entertainment that night: some fat-assed Selective Service guy down in Washington reaching into a revolving drum and yanking out, birth date by birth date, the fates of all American guys, ages nineteen to twenty-six. Selective Service estimated that the men whose birthdays were among the first 120 or so pulled from the drum would get their "greetings" from Tricky Dick and go to war.

"Life is absurd!" my philosophy professor had declared that same morning in a lecture hall of two hundred sleepy students. "That was the conclusion of Sartre and Camus and the other existentialists living through the insanity of war-torn, bombed-out Europe." But at least World War II had had clearly defined battlefields, heroes and villains—villagers who didn't switch their allegiance at nightfall and then back again in the morning. Ray and his fellow servicemen had entered their war convinced that they were doing the right thing. That *we* were the good guys. Not us, though. Not in 1969 with Nixon in charge, and the death tolls mounting, and My Lai splattered all over the full-color pages of *Life* magazine.

Fat Ass reached into that drum 366 times, counting leap year, randomly determining which of our birthdays would send us off to active duty once our student deferments were up and which birthdays would save us from that waste of a war. Someone in the dorm had taken up a collection and we'd tapped a keg. By the time the lottery was over that night, both the guys who were celebrating and the ones who were drowning their sorrows had used the occasion to get shit-faced drunk. Leo was home free at number 266. Born at 12:03 A.M. on January 1, I was in even better shape: number 305. But my brother, born six minutes before me, at 11:57 P.M. on December 31, had drawn number 100. He and his academic probation were bobbing around in the pool most likely to be called to active duty—safe only as long as his 2-S student deferment remained intact. I fell drunk into bed that night, feeling both relieved and guilty, both saved and doomed.

Things *always* went my way, Thomas told me the next day in Leo's and my dorm room. They had gone my way since the day we were born.

The *days* we were born, I thought, but didn't say. We'd been born six minutes apart on different days. In two different years, even.

The deck had *always* been stacked in my favor, Thomas said, exasperated. He lit another cigarette. He smoked now—Trues. He'd begun smoking after Angie gave him the hook. He bummed Deitz's at first—Deitz smoked like a chimney—and then he'd started buying his own. Except Thomas didn't smoke like a guy—didn't hold the cigarette in like he was hoarding it, the way most guys do. Thomas held it pointing up and out, like a European. Like a flit. He *still* smokes that way, as a matter of fact. After all these years. I *still* hate to see the way my brother smokes.

"Never mind whether or not the deck's stacked," I told him. "If your grades are okay, you have a three-year reprieve. In three years, this fucking war'll probably be over. You been studying? You been going to class? How are your grades?"

Instead of answering me directly, he recycled the same excuses he'd used the year before: his dorm was too hot, he couldn't concentrate, his teachers asked trick questions because they were out to get him personally.

During midyear exams, Thomas withdrew himself from school.

"What do you mean, you *withdrew*?" I screamed into the phone when he called me. "Are you *nuts* or something? Are you *crazy*?" He was back home in Three Rivers by then—had packed and left campus without even telling me. "Why don't you just go and fucking *enlist,* Thomas?" I shouted. "Why don't you just *volunteer* to go over there and get blown up?"

He was a nervous wreck all through the holidays, I remember. He tried calling Angie so many times that her father threatened to notify the police. He hadn't bought anyone any Christmas presents—not even anything for Ma—which was *really* weird. Which wasn't like him at all. Thomas had always been a big Christmas guy, generous to the point where you'd open up your present and be embarrassed about what you'd gotten him. But that Christmas, nothing. Not even for Ma. He burst out crying right in the middle of opening *his* presents, I remember. Started talking about what a bad person he was and how by Christmas of the following year, he probably wouldn't even be alive and didn't deserve to be. Then Ma was crying. Ray got so disgusted with the both of them that he got up and walked out—didn't come back until late afternoon. Ho ho ho. Happy Holidays at the Birdsey house. It was typical.

On Thomas's birthday a week later, Ma made him a cake. Dessa and I were going out for New Year's Eve, so we sang "Happy Birthday" early—Ma, Dessa, and me. Ray wouldn't come away from the TV. He hadn't spoken to anybody for that whole week. Thomas stood fidgeting in front of his twenty candles. Then, when the singing stopped, instead of blowing them out, he picked them up one by one and shoved the lit ends into the frosting. The three of us just stood there, watching him, speechless. And when he'd extinguished the last candle—when the room was hazy with smoke and burnt sugar—Ma started singing "For He's a Jolly Good Fellow." As if everything was normal. As if everything was what Ma liked to call "hunky-dory." That was the night Dessa told me about Thomas and her sister: all that *Lives of the Martyred Saints* bullshit—Thomas lying there, getting off on all that ripped and burned flesh, all that suffering. Happy New Year, folks! Happy 1970! Welcome to a brand-new decade!

In mid-January, I went back to school and Thomas stayed home. Stayed up till all hours, Ma said, and then slept all day long as if he was working the night shift, same as Ray. She was trying as hard as she could to keep Ray from flying off the handle, Ma told me, but he was getting fed up. It could be months before the draft board called up Thomas, Ray said; he should be out there looking for a job instead of goofing off. He was lazy and irresponsible. The Army would knock that out of him, quick.

"Something's wrong with him, Dominick," Ma told me over the phone. "I think it's more than just nerves." He kept refusing to see the doctor, she said. But what could she do? She couldn't pick him up and carry him there if he didn't want to go. She just hoped he stayed out of Ray's way. That was all she asked for. *Prayed* for. She didn't want to bother me, but she was just sick about it. I should stay up at school and study hard, she said. She was so proud of me. I had enough to worry about. She could handle things at home. She was worried, but she could handle things.

In February, the Selective Service Board notified my brother that he'd been reclassified from 2-S to 1-A. In early March, Thomas was ordered to New Haven for his preinduction physical. Ray drove him there. Later, Ray told Ma that Thomas was mostly quiet along the way, but fidgety. He'd had to go to the toilet three different times en route. He probably hadn't said more than ten words. He'd acted "in the normal range," though, according to Ray. Ray told Thomas that the service would be good for him. Reassured him that more guys stayed stateside or got stationed in Germany or the Philippines than ended up in Nam, anyway. Whatever happened, the military would change him for the better, Ray promised. Toughen him up. Give him something to feel proud about. He'd see.

Thomas passed the vision, hearing, and coordination tests. His heart rate and blood pressure were fine. He was neither color-blind nor flat-footed.

He failed the psychiatric examination.

Ray drove him back home again.

"I don't know, Dominick," Ma said. "If you *could* manage to get home over the weekend, that would be great. I know you're busy. But he's not eating, he won't take a bath. I hear him traipsing around the house all night long. He won't even talk to me anymore, honey. Remember how he used to talk to me all the time? 'Hey, Ma, let's have one of our talks,' he always used to say. But now he hardly says anything, except all this mumbling under his breath. And when he does say something, it doesn't make any sense."

"What do you mean? What's he saying?"

"Oh, I don't know. He keeps talking about the Russians. He's got Russians on the brain. And I've been finding blood in the bathroom sink. I ask him where the blood's coming from, but he won't tell me. Maybe he'll talk to you, Dominick. Maybe he'll tell *you* what's bothering him. If you can make it home, that would be great. If you can't, you can't. I understand. But I'm worried sick about him. I used to think it was just his nerves, but I think it's more than that. I don't know what it is, honey. I'm afraid to talk to Ray."

The following Saturday, Thomas and I went to lunch at McDonald's. It was my idea: get him to take a bath, get him out of the house. He neither welcomed the idea nor resisted it wholeheartedly. Ma said he was having one of his good days.

It's stupid—the things you remember: we both got those shamrock shake things McDonald's has every year for St. Patrick's Day. Cheeseburgers and fries and green milkshakes: that's what we ate. It was crowded; we were seated near a kids' birthday party. The kids kept looking over, staring at the two identical twins eating their identical orders. I remember asking Thomas if he'd seen in the newspaper that week about Dell and Ralph and that whole mess. The trial was over. Dell had been found guilty and sentenced to fifteen years at Somers Prison; his wife had gotten six months in Niantic. They'd let Ralph off with a suspended sentence. "Weird, isn't it?" I said. "That all that stuff had been going on and here we were *working* with those guys? That that shit had been going on since you and me and Ralph were in grammar school?"

"No comment," Thomas said. He was doing something weird to his hamburger bun: picking off the crust bit by bit. Examining each little shred he pulled off.

"What are you doing that for?" I asked him.

He told me the Communists had targeted places like McDonald's.

"Yeah?" I said. "For what?"

He said it was better for me if I didn't know.

"Hey, what's going on with you, anyway?" I asked him. "Ma says you're having a hard time. She's worried about you, man. What's bothering you?"

He asked me if I knew that Dr. DiMarco, our dentist since boyhood, was a Communist agent and a member of the Manson family.

"Dr. DiMarco?" I said. When we were kids, Dr. DiMarco had given us his back issues of *Jack and Jill* magazine, serenaded us as he worked on our teeth with songs like "Mairzy Doats." It was so ridiculous, it was funny.

Dr. DiMarco had drugged him and planted tiny radio receivers in his fillings, Thomas said. It was part of an elaborate plan by the Soviets to brainwash him. They sent messages to him twenty-four hours a day. They were trying to enlist his help in blowing up the submarine base in Groton. Thomas was key to their success, he said—the "linchpin" of their entire plan—but so far he'd been able to resist. "The body of Christ," he said, placing a shred of his hamburger bun on his tongue. "Amen."

The birthday kids and their parents got up and left, taking the noise with them. In the sudden quiet, I looked around to see if anyone was listening. Watching him. Was he just yanking my chain—putting me on for some sick reason. "Dr. DiMarco?" I said. "*Our* Dr. DiMarco?"

Now something had malfunctioned, Thomas said. The radio receivers were heat-sensitive and Thomas had made himself a cup of hot cocoa and scalded the inside of his mouth. Since then, he'd begun to pick up other messages as well. He'd tried to rip out the receivers but he'd only cut the inside of his mouth.

"Yeah?" I said. "Let's see."

He opened wide and pulled at both sides of his cheeks. There were raw, purple gashes on his gums and tongue, slashes in the roof of his mouth. That's when I started to get *really* scared: when I saw how he'd mutilated himself like that—saw where that blood Ma had seen had come from.

"What . . . what do these messages say?" I asked. I was afraid to hear his answer.

He told me about a voice that had been encouraging him to hang our mother's crucifixes upside down, another that kept ordering him to go to the maternity ward at the hospital and strangle the infants. He wasn't sure whose the latter voice was, but it might have been someone from the Manson family. Maybe Charles Manson himself. He wasn't sure. "You should hear the way *he* talks," Thomas said. "It's disgusting." He took a sip of his shamrock shake. "Nothing I can repeat in public."

"Thomas?" I said.

"Then there's another voice—a religious voice. He keeps telling me to memorize the Bible. It makes sense, really. Once the Communists take over, watch out! The first thing they're going to do is burn every single Bible in the United States. Don't think they won't, either. That's why I've started memorizing it. Who else would do it if I didn't?"

I felt light-headed, robbed of oxygen. This wasn't happening, I promised myself.

"Is this . . . is this the same voice that's telling you to do the other stuff?"

"What other stuff?"

"The bad stuff."

Thomas sighed like a parent whose patience was ebbing. "I just *told* you, Dominick. It's a *religious* voice. He disapproves of everything the other voices say. They bicker all night long. It gives me headaches. Sometimes they *scream* at each other. You know who it might be? That priest that Ma used to listen to on television. On Saturday nights. Remember? He had white hair. I can see him, but I can't remember his name."

"Bishop Sheen?" I said.

"That's it. Bishop Sheen. He's our father, you know? He impregnated Ma through the television. It can be done; it's more common than anyone thinks. 'This is Bishop Fulton J. Sheen saying good night and God loves you.' . . . I don't know. It might be him, but it might not. You know that Dr. DiMarco and the Manson family have orgies, don't you? In Dr. DiMarco's office. One of them guards the door so that patients don't walk in on them accidentally. They do anything they want to each other. *Anything.* It's disgusting. That's why I'm in danger. Because I know about the link between Manson and the Communists. I shouldn't even be out here in public like this. It's a risk. I know too much—about the plan to blow up the sub base, for instance. They're very, very dangerous people, Dominick—the Communists. If they ever suspected I've begun to memorize the Bible, I'd be shot in the head. There'd be orders to shoot on sight. Listen! *'In the beginning God created the heavens and the earth; the earth was waste and void; darkness covered the abyss, and the spirit of God was stirring above the waters.'* I'm only up to chapter 2, verse 3. It's a lifetime's work. It's risky business. How's Dessa?"

"Dessa?" I said. "Dessa's . . ."

"That's why I had to break it off with her sister, you know. It was too dangerous. They might have hurt her to get at me. What was her name again?"

"Her . . . ? Angie? You mean Angie?"

He nodded. "Angie. It was just too dangerous, Dominick. Do you want the rest of my fries?"

That conversation—and the psychiatric lockup that followed it later that night, Thomas's first—occurred a full ten months after the panic attack that had made my brother trash our jointly owned typewriter in May of the previous year. In the interim, the war had escalated, man had walked on the moon, and I'd tried as hard as possible not to see what was coming—what, inch by inch, had already arrived.

On that first night of many nights when I drove my brother between the brick pillars and onto the grounds of the Three Rivers State Hospital, I went home to our shared bedroom on Hollyhock Avenue and dreamed a dream I have remembered ever since.

In it, my brother, Ralph Drinkwater, and I are together, lost somewhere in the Vietnamese jungle, wading ankle-deep in muck. A sniper, perched in a tree, raises his rifle and aims. No one sees him but me; there's no time to tell the others.

I duck, pulling Ralph down with me. There's a dull crack. A bullet rips through my brother's brain. . . .

twenty-five

"Almond, peanut butter, or crunch?" Lisa Sheffer asked.

"The usual," I said. "One of each." I fished into my wallet, slid three bucks across the desktop.

Since my brother's commitment at Hatch, I'd had five meetings with Sheffer and had bought fund-raiser candy bars for Thomas each time. It was part ritual and part thanks to Sheffer for watching out for him. Part connection between me and my brother during our state-enforced separation: a candy bar bridge, a link of chocolate, nuts, and sugar. It was the first thing Thomas asked about whenever she saw him, Sheffer said. Had she seen me? Had I bought him any candy bars?

"Make sure your daughter remembers me when she graduates from Midget Football and becomes a Dallas Cowboy cheerleader," I said.

"Oh, *please,*" Sheffer groaned. "I'd have to shoot myself."

I asked her if her daughter looked like her.

"Jesse? No, she looks like the sperm donor." I guess I must have looked at her funny. "My ex-husband," she said. "If I think of him as the sperm donor instead of the toad I was stupid enough to marry, it doesn't make me seem like such a bad judge of character." She fished a picture out of her desk and passed it over: a chubby brunette in a pink leotard.

"She's a cutie," I said. "Seven, right?"

"Seven going on thirteen. You know what she wants to do when she grows up? Wear eye shadow. That's *it*—the sum total of her future goals: wear blue eye shadow with glitter in it. Gloria Steinem would be furious with me."

I had to smile. "I met Gloria Steinem once," I said.

"Yeah? Where?"

"Down in New York. At a *Ms.* magazine party. Me and my wife."

"Really? Geez, Domenico, I wouldn't have automatically assumed you were on the guest list. What was the occasion?"

"My wife—my *ex*-wife—had started a day care program with her friend at Electric Boat. For working women, single moms. It was right after the Boat started—"

The phone rang. "Excuse me," Sheffer said.

I told myself I had to stop doing that: talking about Dessa all the time, forgetting to put the *ex* in ex-wife. It was pathetic, really: the abandoned husband who couldn't let go. You got a divorce decree and a live-in girlfriend, I reminded myself. Get *over* it.

"Yeah, but Steve, what *you're* not understanding is that I'm in the middle of a meeting," Sheffer told whoever was on the other end of the phone. I picked up the picture of her kid again. It was kind of funny: this little girlie-looking girl belonging to Sheffer, with her crewcut and her wrist tattoos.

"I'm not saying I *forbid* it, Steve. I'm not in a position to *forbid* anything. I'm just saying it's not particularly convenient right now because I have someone in the office with me." She held the phone in front of her and mouthed the word *asshole.* "Fine," she said. *"Fine.* Send him up then."

She banged the phone back down and moaned. "God forbid that clinical needs should interfere with the maintenance schedule," she said. "I've been asking for two weeks to have that light replaced." Her head nodded toward the dead fluorescent tube above my head. "Suddenly, it's now or never, meeting or no meeting."

I shook my head in sympathy. "So, anyway," I said. "You told me over the phone you wanted to talk about the hearing? Wanted to 'brainstorm' or something?"

She nodded, refocusing herself. "Okay, look. Here's the deal. The Security Review Board meets on the thirty-first. Halloween. That gives us less than a week to build our case."

"*Our* case?" I said. "I thought you were undecided about whether he should or shouldn't stay here."

She picked up a paper clip. Moved it end over end across her desk. "Well, Domenico, I had insomnia last night," she said. "And somewhere around my twelfth or thirteenth game of solitaire, I joined your team."

I looked at her. Waited.

"I really wasn't sure before—I kept going back and forth—but I've come to the conclusion that another year here at Hatch would probably do him more harm than good."

"What happened?" I said. "Did something else happen?"

She shook her head. "Nothing, really. Nothing out of the ordinary."

"Which means *what*?"

"He's been taking a little teasing here and there—at meals, at rec time. Don't worry. We're monitoring it. The trouble with Thomas—with anyone who's paranoid—is that he tends to perceive run-of-the-mill ribbing as proof of grand conspiracy. Someone says something, and he immediately sees it as part of some master plan. And, of course, when he gives someone a big reaction, it invites more of the same. But he and Dr. Patel and I are working it out. Developing some strategies he can use when someone starts teasing him."

"You know what sucks?" I said. "This security clearance bullshit. The way I can't even *see* him." I picked a candy bar up off her desk and waved it. "The way I gotta communicate with these things."

She assured me my security clearance would be coming soon. That the teasing was nothing out of the ordinary. "He's *safe*," she said.

"Oh, yeah. Safe with all the psycho-killers and pyromaniacs and God knows what else. Not to mention the goons in uniform. If he's so safe, what made you decide he needs to get out of here?"

She sighed. "Well, ironically enough, the security. The inspections, the surveillance cameras, room checks—all the routines and precautions that *keep* it safe. The bottom line is: this is a very threatening environment for a paranoid schizophrenic. People *are* always watching you. I just think he could be better served, long term, at a facility where security is less of an issue."

"But nothing else happened? He didn't freak out in the dining room again or anything?"

"He's *better,* Dominick. *Really.* His wound has healed nicely. The psycholeptics are starting to kick in. And he knows what to expect now—what the day-to-day routine is. But I'll be honest with you. He's miserable here—scared, withdrawn. It's sad. I just feel that a maximum-security forensic hospital is an inappropriate placement for him."

"Which is what I've been trying to tell everybody right along!"

She nodded. Smiled. "So, okay, you're ahead of the rest of us. Go to the head of the class. Anyway, I'm going to help you fight for his release."

Sheffer took out a legal pad and we began to plan our arguments for the Review Board: the things *she'd* say, the things *I'd* say. It was crucial that I be there to advocate for him, she said. It would show the board that Thomas had family support—a safety net to fall back on. She wanted to know if Ray was planning to attend. Given Ray and Thomas's past history, I said, I wasn't sure if it was a good idea or not. Sheffer suggested that Ray be there—sit there—but not say anything. "You'll be the spokesperson; he can be the 'extra.' Okay?"

"Okay with me," I said. "I'm not sure if it'll be okay with Ray."

"Do you want to ask him about it? Or should I?"

I looked away. "You," I said.

Together, Sheffer and I came up with a list of potential advocates for Thomas's release: former docs, staff members at Settle, people from the community who might be willing to write a letter on his behalf. We divided the list; each of us promised to approach half. "Now," Sheffer said. "We have to talk about the unit team recommendation."

There was a knock on the door. "Maintenance," Sheffer said. "Come in!"

But it was Dr. Patel's little grapefruit-sized gray head that poked around the door. I'd have preferred the janitor.

"Hello, Lisa," she said. "Hello, Dominick." She explained to me that Sheffer had mentioned I was coming in for a meeting; she wanted to see me for just a minute. Was this a convenient time? "Yeah, sure, Rubina," Sheffer said. "I've got something I should check on, anyway. I'll be back in five minutes." She closed the door behind her. It was a setup.

Doc Patel cut to the chase. "You missed your appointment yesterday," she said.

I reminded her I'd phoned and left a message with her answering service.

"Which I received," she said. "Thank you. But that is not the point. My point is: *why* did you cancel, Dominick?"

"Why?" She hated when I did that: answered her by repeating her question.

"You'd had a difficult time of it the session before and then you didn't show up yesterday. Naturally, I'm wondering if—"

"It was the weather," I said.

"Yes? The weather? Explain, please."

"They were . . . they were predicting rain on Wednesday and Thursday."

She shrugged. "My office is indoors, Dominick."

"It's the end of the outdoor season. The *painting* season. I got this house I've got to finish—big job—and with everything else that's happened, I haven't. . . . We've had frost two nights in a row now."

She shrugged again.

"Your work's not seasonal," I said. "Us lunatics keep you busy all twelve months of the year. But I can't afford to—"

She held up her hand to stop me. "You're being flip with me," she said. "That's a defense. I would prefer a more direct response."

"Look," I said. "It's not that I don't appreciate your help.

I *do* appreciate it. But I just don't have the luxury right now—if it's a decent weather day—to leave the job site and go over to your office so I can rag about my brother. Not with November almost here. Not with this client named Henry Rood who keeps calling my house every other minute."

"It's interesting," she said.

"What is?"

"That you refer to our work together as a 'luxury.' For me, a luxury is a hot bath on a weekend afternoon, or a trip to a museum, or the time to read a good novel. Not something as emotionally demanding as what you've begun. You are doing enormously difficult work, Dominick. Don't devalue it, or yourself, like that."

I got up and walked the four or five steps over to Sheffer's barred office window. Looked out at that sorry excuse for a recreation area they had out there. "I didn't mean *luxury,*" I said. "Jesus. Do you always have to take every word I say and—"

"Dominick?" she said. "Would you look at me, please?"

I looked.

Her smile was sympathetic. "I know that you were in a great deal of pain during our last session," she said. "Your recounting of Thomas's first severe decompensation—his hallucinations, his lacerating the inside of his mouth—these are such sad, frightening memories for you to have to relive. And such *vivid* memories, my goodness. The detail with which you recall those disturbing events indicates to me that you have been carrying an enormous burden for a very, very long time. So in my opinion, Dominick, the work we've been doing—unearthing these memories, dealing with their *toxicity,* if you will—this is important for your emotional health, perhaps in ways that you cannot yet assess."

"Their 'toxicity,' huh?"

She nodded. "Think of your past as a well in the ground," she said.

Jesus, here we go again, I thought: Doc Patel, Queen of the Metaphors.

"Wells are *good* things, are they not?" she said. "They give life-sustaining water, they replenish. They support. But if the underground spring that feeds the well—and by that, I mean your past, Dominick—if the spring is poisoned, *toxic* for some reason—then the water cannot sustain. Do you see the comparison I'm making?"

"Yup."

"And what is your opinion, please?"

I made her wait. "My opinion is that housepainting is how I put bread on the table," I finally said.

She nodded. "And therapy will sustain you as well, my friend. My concern yesterday when you failed to keep your appointment was that our process may have frightened you. Overwhelmed you."

"I was *painting,*" I said. "I had to *paint.*"

She reached out and patted my arm. "Very well, then. Would you like to reschedule your missed appointment or wait until next week?"

"Actually," I said. "Now that you bring it up."

I told her I'd been thinking about putting the whole process on hold for a while. Not quitting or anything, I said. Just postponing things until the dust settled a little.

"Yes? Then that's something we'll need to talk about the next time we meet. Shall we reschedule your missed appointment?"

"Let's . . . let's just hold off until Tuesday," I said. "My regular appointment."

"Which you will honor?" she said. "Rain or shine?"

I nodded. She shuffled the files in her hand. Headed for the door.

"Wait," I said. "I wanted to ask *you* something, too. How are you . . . which way are you planning to vote?"

She turned back toward me. "Vote?"

"On my brother? That team unit thing's coming up in three or four more days, right? The recommendation? Are you going to recommend he stays here, or gets transferred back to Settle, or what?"

She studied my face for a few seconds. "I'd rather not discuss it, please," she said.

"Why not?"

"Because it's premature. Our recommendation isn't due for several days, and I'm still very much in the process of observing your brother—the daily effects that time and his medication are having. And please keep in mind that our unit recommendation is only that. A recommendation. The Review Board will make the final decision."

"But which way are you leaning?"

"I'm *not* leaning," she said. "As I've just said, I'm reserving judgment." She held my gaze. "We'll talk next Tuesday, then. We have a great deal to talk about."

When she opened the office door, Ralph Drinkwater was standing there.

"Maintenance," he said.

"Yes, yes. Come in, please."

I caught the flicker of shock on Ralph's face when he saw me, replaced almost immediately by that look of indifference he'd perfected all the way back in grammar school. That you-can't-touch-*me* look. He entered the office, a stepladder hooked against his shoulder, a fluorescent light tube in his other hand.

I could tell Doc Patel hadn't made the connection—didn't realize that this was the same guy we had talked about two sessions ago: the guy who Leo Blood and I had fed to the state cops to get ourselves off the hook. It was one of those Twilight Zone moments: me, my shrink, and Ralph all standing there in Sheffer's little office.

Dr. Patel closed the door behind her. Ralph and I were alone.

"Hey, Ralph," I said. "How you doing?"

No answer.

"This . . . this office is like Grand Central Station today. Long time no see."

He unfolded the stepladder without looking at me. He'd always been good at that: making me feel invisible.

"I . . . uh . . . I saw you a couple weeks ago," I said. "That night they brought my brother in? I was gonna say something to you then, but I was pretty worked up about things. About Thomas getting admitted here. . . . Which was why I didn't say anything. Recognized you right away, though. You look good. . . . So, uh, how's it going?"

"It's going," he said. He climbed two or three steps up the ladder. Squinted at the bad fluorescent tube. Granted, it had been one of the scummier things I'd ever done in my life—

me and Leo bagging Ralph to save our own asses—but twenty years had gone by.

"So I saw in the paper where the Wequonnocs won their case, huh? Got that recognition from the federal government after all? Congratulations."

He disengaged the bad light. Didn't answer me.

"You involved with that much? Tribal politics? All those plans for the big casino out there? That resort thing?"

No answer.

"I saw . . . saw the architect's drawings in the *Record* last week. Pretty impressive. God, if that thing actually flies, it's going to be *huge*."

"It'll fly," he said.

I reached out to take the dead light tube from him, but he ignored my outstretched hand. Climbed down the ladder and leaned it against the wall instead.

"I heard you guys got foreign investors interested, right? Malaysians, is it?"

"Yes." He climbed the ladder again, new bulb in hand. He'd always been a man of few words, but this was ridiculous. This qualified as ball-busting.

He installed the new tube, then came down from the ladder and flicked the switch. The room lit up, brighter than was necessary.

He folded the ladder. Jotted something down on a form. "Hey, Ralph?" I said. "You see my brother much?"

He looked over at me, expressionless, his eyes as gray and noncommittal as the moon. "Yeah, I see him."

"Is he . . . are they treating him okay? In *your* opinion. I haven't seen him since that first night. They won't let me see him until I get some stupid security clearance."

"Well, *that* won't be a problem," he said. "Will it?"

"What do you mean?"

"Your record must be white-boy white." The two of us stood there, neither of us saying anything. I was the first to look away.

"He's okay," Ralph finally said.

"Is he?" I swallowed hard. "They teasing him a lot? Picking on him?"

"Some," he said.

"I wonder . . . I was wondering if you could do me a favor? Just until my security thing comes through?"

His eyes narrowed. One side of his mouth lifted into a smirk.

"Just . . . if I could just give you my number at home and . . . let's say you see something you think I might want to know about. *Anything.* In terms of him being mistreated or . . . This, uh . . . his social worker he has is good. I'm not saying otherwise. She's *real* good. But if, you know, you happen to see something that the medical staff wouldn't necessarily catch—if someone's bothering him or anything . . . God, this is hard."

He just stood there, expressionless.

"I know . . . I know you don't owe me any favors, Ralph. Okay? I *know* that. That was a shitty thing we did to you at the end of that summer. I *know* that, man. I've felt like crap about it ever since, for whatever it's worth to you."

"Nothin', cuz," he said. "It ain't worth nothin'."

"Okay," I said. "Too little, too late. I know. . . . But if you could just . . . If I could just give you my phone number."

I grabbed a blank sheet of paper from a pad on Sheffer's desk and scrawled my number on it. The numerals came out shaky. He looked at my outstretched hand.

"They won't let me *see* him, man. The guy's my *brother* and they're all telling me . . . If you could just keep an eye out for him. I know you're busy, man, but if you see anything. If you could just take my number and . . ."

But he wouldn't take it. I tossed the paper back onto Sheffer's desk. "Yeah, well, thanks, anyway," I said. "Thanks a heap, Ralph. Thanks for nothing."

His chin pointed toward the window. "Out there," he said.

"What?"

"You said you want to see him? He's out there now. His unit just went on their rec break."

It took a second to sink in. Slowly, hesitantly, I walked over to the barred window. There was Thomas.

He was seated by himself at the end of a picnic table bench. He looked pale, puffy. His hand—the stump—was tucked inside his jacket sleeve. He was smoking fast, inhaling every couple of seconds.

There were nine or ten of them out there, most of them just standing around and smoking, same as Thomas. Two young guys—one black, one Spanish—were kicking around a hackey sack. Neither of them looked crazy—not even dangerous. The psych aide on duty was that same guy in the cowboy hat I'd seen before. He and a few of the patients were laughing and talking, leaning against the side of the building.

No one was bothering Thomas. But no one was bothering *with* him, either. Even here at Hatch, he was the odd man out.

I turned away from the window. Caught Ralph watching me watch my brother. "God, he looks awful," I said.

Ralph said nothing.

"You read about him in the paper? What he did?"

"Yep."

When I looked back, Thomas was stubbing out his cigarette. He reached into his jacket pocket for another. Stood up and walked over to the cowboy to get it lit. But Tex was too busy holding court to acknowledge Thomas's existence and Thomas was too mousy to speak up. He just stood there, waiting, his stump tucked into the opposite armpit. Another guy approached Tex, got his cigarette lit. I *knew* that son of a bitch saw Thomas standing there—he couldn't miss. But he made him wait. Made him stand there, silently, and beg.

Goddamned bully, I thought. Don't fuck with his head. Just light his fucking cigarette.

"What's the deal on that aide out there?" I said. "The guy who thinks he's John Wayne?" But when I turned around, I saw that Ralph had left the office.

It was a relief, though—finally seeing Thomas. Even in *this* state. Even with a barred window and a security clearance between us. You look out for a guy all his life, you can't *not* look out for him.

He was paunchier around the middle, maybe seven or eight pounds heavier than he'd been. He'd always walked a lot before this, both when he was living at Settle and at Horizon House downtown. But here at Hatch, "recreation" meant smoking. Or standing there with your unlit cigarette, *waiting* to smoke. There were bags under his eyes. His head kept jerking slightly. The medication, probably. I'd noticed when he'd gotten up and walked over toward Tex that his medication shuffle was back. Thomas *hated* the way he felt when they overmedicated him. I made a mental note to call Dr. Chase. Be the squeaky wheel on his behalf again. I knew the spiel.

He was wearing gray prison-issue, white socks, and those sorry-ass brown wingtip shoes of his. Tongues out, no laces. All their shoes were like that. Sheffer had told me they take their shoelaces away so no one can use them as a weapon. A garrote. Nice place. Real peaceful environment.

The hackey sack went flying past Thomas's face. He flinched. Dropped his cigarette. The Spanish kid scooped it up and handed it back to him. Said something. Thomas didn't seem to answer him. Then the kid walks behind Thomas and chucks the hackey sack right at him. It ricocheted off his back. I flinched, same as Thomas. Tex glanced over there for half a second. Went back to his conversation with his pets.

It became a game: whip the hackey sack at Thomas. Get a reaction. The black kid snuck up behind him, hobbling around like Igor, yanking his hand up inside his sleeve. Someone else stood in front of Thomas, mimicking the way he was holding his cigarette. Tex kept ignoring the obvious. Then the hackey sack beaned him off the back of the head. "Goddamn it!" I said. *"Hey!"*

I heard a bell ring out there. Tex talked into a radio. They started lining up to come back in. A guard ran a portable metal detector up and down each guy before passing him through. Thomas was last in line. "I'm getting you out of here, Thomas," I whispered to him through the bars, the wired glass. "Hang in there, man. I'm getting you *out.*"

I paced around Sheffer's little cubicle. Sat down. Got back up again. I looked over at her desk. That's when I realized it: the slip of paper with my phone number on it was gone. Drinkwater had taken it.

Sheffer burst back into the office, all apologies. "I walk down the hall around here and crises just pop out at me. I'm like a crisis magnet, Domenico. Hey, yippee! They fixed my light."

I sat down. Should I tell her I'd seen him? Keep my mouth shut?

"Okay," she said. "Let's get back to business." She started up again about how getting Thomas out was a long shot—how she didn't want to understate that.

I tuned out. Saw him the way he'd looked a few minutes ago: standing there with his unlit cigarette. I realized Sheffer's voice had stopped. "Uh . . . what?" I said.

His case had come up for discussion at their unit meeting that morning, Sheffer repeated. They were split right down the middle on what to recommend. "As of today, anyway," she said. "But we still have six more days before our report's due."

"Aren't there five of you?" I said. "How can you be split down the middle?"

"One team member hasn't voiced an opinion yet."

"Dr. Patel," I said.

Sheffer said she couldn't go into specifics. In a week, the vote might be altogether different, anyway, she said. "You see, Domenico. It's not just a matter of getting him out of Hatch. It's where he's going to go if he does get out. Placement-wise, it's tough. With all the downsizing going on in mental health, there just aren't as many options as there were before."

"There's Settle," I said. "That's where he should have gone in the first place. Back to *Settle*."

She opened her mouth. Closed it again.

"What?" I said.

"Nothing."

"Just *say* it."

She told me the rumor flying around was that the state might be closing Settle—as early as March was what she'd heard.

"Okay, put him there until March then. That gives him, what? Five months? In five months, he might be back on track."

"Yeah, but if they're phasing *out* the population there, why would they take new admissions? Even short-term ones? That's not what they're doing."

"What about . . . what about a group home then? Couldn't

he live in a supervised group home? That's worked for him in the past."

"*Has* it?" She reminded me that he'd been living at Horizon when he stopped taking his meds and went to the library and lopped off his hand. And group homes were facing another round of cutbacks, too, she said. Staffs there were already like skeleton crews, compared to the way those homes had been supervised five or six years ago. That meant patient-residents had to be fairly self-sufficient—a category my brother didn't exactly fall into in his present state. "That leaves a place like Settle, which is on shaky ground. Or a place like Hatch, which isn't. *Or* . . ." She stopped.

"Or what?" I said.

"Or releasing him to the custody of his family."

I skipped a beat or two. Took in what she'd just said. "If . . . if that's what we have to do, then we'll do it. Because one way or the other, he's getting out of here."

She shook her head and smiled. "Just like that, eh, *paisano*? You're going to monitor his meds, supervise his hygiene, chauffeur him back and forth to therapy a couple times a day. Oh, and don't forget to safety-proof your whole place. Lock up all the knives, etcetera, etcetera."

"That's not funny," I said.

"No," she said. "It's not. How are you going to paint houses? Park him at the curb? Put a pair of overalls on him and make him your foreman?"

I told her to do me a favor and skip the sarcasm.

"But come on, Dominick," she said. "Let's do a reality check. You've got a *life*. How's your wife going to—"

"I don't have a wife," I said. "I have a girlfriend."

She shrugged. "Wife, girlfriend. You guys live together?"

I nodded.

"Well, then, how's that going to affect *her*? And you two as a couple?"

"We'll work it out," I said.

"Yeah? You sure? Is she a saint or something?"

But I suddenly saw it: Thomas moving in, Joy moving out—exiting the same as Dessa. And then what? An empty mattress to roll around on all night. My crazy brother across the table at breakfast. Even if we weren't a perfect fit—Joy and me—she was a warm body to lie next to at night. A life preserver to hold on to out in the deep. What would I have if she left? Thomas, that's what. My anchor. My shadow. Thomas and Dominick: the Birdsey twins, as it was in the beginning, is now, and ever shall be, world without end, amen.

"That's why Rubina—Dr. Patel—is riding the fence, I think," Sheffer said. "She's reluctant to put the burden of your brother back onto your shoulders. She mentioned something about that at the meeting—about how the family's best interests have to be factored in. How did she put it? That the good of the patient and his family are *intertwined.*"

I was furious. Patel had no right to take what I'd said in that private office and use it against my brother. It had been a mistake seeing her—going over to that office of hers and spilling my guts out about the past. I could take care of myself. *He* was supposed to be her patient, not me. It was *his* best interest that mattered. She was going to hear from me on this one. She was going to hear loud and clear.

"I'll talk to her," I said. "I'll get her over to our side."

Sheffer's eyes widened. "Don't you *dare* tell her I've been sharing all this information with you!" she said. "No shit, Domenico. You could get me in big trouble. Those unit meetings are confidential. And, anyway, she's a strong woman. She's going to make up her own mind; you're not going to 'talk her into' anything. But whatever she decides on the recommendation—even if we come out on opposite conclusions—I trust her judgment. I respect her. She's *fair,* Dominick."

"Yeah, well, don't respect her too much," I said.

She cocked her head. Her face was a question.

"Did you know that I'm seeing her?"

"Professionally?"

I nodded. Looked away for a second. Looked back. I hadn't even told Joy I was seeing a shrink. Why was I playing true confessions with Sheffer?

"Dr. Patel would never share information like that," she said. "But I'm *glad,* Domenico. I think it's a good thing that you're seeing her. I think it's great."

"Not if it's a conflict of interest, it isn't. Not if it keeps my brother locked up here because she's advocating for *me.*"

"What do you mean?"

"I mean, what I've been doing, basically, is going to her office over on Division Street and pissing and moaning about all the ways my brother has screwed up my life. Digging up ancient history—all this shit from our childhood and from the year he first cracked up. Dredging up all this stuff that should have just stayed buried."

"Well," she said. "That's what therapy *is*. Right?"

"But if she's recommending he be admitted here long term because it's better for *me*—because I happen to have been through the wringer—"

"She wouldn't do that, Dominick. Whatever her decision—I mean, sure, she's going to look at the big picture, yes—but she's not going to deliberately choose something that's detrimental to Thomas. He's her *patient*. She's not going to choose one of you over the other."

No? Why not? Everyone else had—our whole lives. Nobody's *ever* chosen Thomas. Not Ray, not the kids in school. Nobody except Ma.

"Dominick, you need to calm down a little. Chill out about all this. Because I'll tell you one thing. If you lose it this way at the Review Board hearing, you're not going to help anyone. Okay?"

She waited. I looked back at her. Nodded.

"And one other thing. Are you listening? Because I really need you to listen to this. This place isn't quite the hellhole you keep saying it is. We had a tag sale a while back, you know? Sold off the torture chamber and the leg irons and hot pincers. All right? Every time you say something like how this is such a 'hellhole' and a 'snake pit,' it dismisses what we try to do here all day long, day in, day out. What *I* try to do. Okay? . . . I'm in a healing profession by choice, okay? . . . And I wouldn't stay here if I didn't believe in the work this facility is doing. I'd like to think I'm not *that* much of a masochist. So don't write this place off when you haven't even walked through the wards yet. All right, Domenico?"

I nodded. "I could take him in if I had to, though," I said. "I know it wouldn't be easy, but I could do it. I've taken care of him his whole life, one way or another."

She just kept looking at me. Studying me. "How was your visit?" she finally said.

I looked over at the window. Looked back at Sheffer's face. I tried to read what she meant. "You . . . did you set that up? My seeing him out there?"

"It was the closest I could get to letting you visit him. And I figured you might want to be alone. How'd he look to you?"

I told her he looked terrible. Told her about the harassment I'd seen—about how that cowboy psych aide had made my brother invisible.

"That's Duane," she said. "Not one of my favorites, either. I'll look into it. But he's safe here, Dominick. I promise you. He's okay."

twenty-six

Beep!

"This is Dr. Batteson's office calling for Joy Hanks. Please call our office at your earliest convenience. Thanks."

Beep!

"Dominick? It's Leo. Hey, guess what? You know that part I auditioned for? The slasher flick? I *got* it! They start filming middle of next month down in Jersey. That's *film,* Birdseed. I'm going to be in a goddamned *movie*!"

As he babbled, I made a list in my head: go to the dump; get paint thinner; get Halloween candy; 11:00 A.M. meeting with Sheffer. Joy had been promising for days to get trick-or-treat stuff. She'd pulled the same thing last Halloween. Then, when the doorbell started ringing, I'd had to make a mad dash—pay double at the convenience store.

Over on the kitchen counter, Leo's voice was asking about racquetball. "Thursday or Friday, if either of them's good. You got that hearing thing for your brother tomorrow, right? Give me a ring."

Beep!

"Hello? Hello? . . . Yes, this is Ruth Rood calling for . . . Hello? Mr. Birdsey? . . . Oh. I thought I heard you pick up." She was talking in slo-mo, slurring her words. God, I'd hate to see what *her* liver looked like. "Henry and I were wondering why you weren't at the house today. You said you'd be here, so we were expecting you." Her voice dropped to a whisper. "Henry's very discouraged. He says the scaffolding in his office window is starting to make him feel like a prisoner in his own house. He can't even work, he's so despondent. Please call. *Please.*"

I picked up the phone, flipped through the Rolodex. Too bad, Morticia. I've had one or two other things on my mind—like trying to get my brother out of goddamned *actual* prison, not scaffolding prison. Henry ought to check in down at Hatch if he *really* wanted to feel "despondent."

She picked up on the first ring, her voice as sober as 7:00 A.M. "Oh," she said. "Yes. I was expecting a call back from Henry's doctor."

I skipped the apology for the no-show the day before and told her I'd try to make it over to their place that afternoon. "They're saying rain later today. What I'll do is, I'll pull the shutters off and bring 'em back after they're scraped and painted. That way I can work no matter what the weather's doing. Make up a little lost time. Tell Henry I should be ready to prime by the end of the week, Monday at the latest. He feeling okay?"

Pause. "Why do you ask?"

"You, uh, you just said you were waiting for the doctor to call back." She gave me that line again about Henry being despondent. Too much booze and too much time on his hands, that was *his* problem. "I'll try and give you half a day tomorrow," I said. "Best I can do. There's this thing I have to get to tomorrow afternoon. I'll probably work all day Saturday at your place, though. I'll let you go now in case his doctor's trying to call."

Shit. If I ever finished *that* job—ever kissed *this* painting season goodbye—then maybe there was a god after all.

What was the call for Joy? I'd forgotten already. I hit the "save" button. Hit "messages." Jotted, "JOY: Call Dr. Batteson." Who was Dr. Batteson? Not another one of those holistic guys, I hoped. The last one of those quacks she and her buddy Thad had gone to had soaked her for three hundred bucks' worth of "herbal" medicines. . . . Thad. The Duchess.

There was another one with too much time on his hands. Why couldn't she have *girl*friends like every other woman?

I dialed Leo's number. Whether I had time to play racquetball or not, the idea of smashing something against four walls was starting to appeal to me. I drummed my fingers on the countertop and waited out the kids' cutesy singing message. God, I hate that: the way some people's machines hold you hostage.

"Leo: racquetball: yes," I told the machine. "The hearing's at four o'clock tomorrow. How about early Friday morning? I can have Joy reserve us a court." I started to hang up, then stopped. "Hey, good news about your movie. I knew you when, Hollywood. Later."

I grabbed my keys. The dump, paint thinner, Halloween candy . . . what else? what else? Oh, yeah. Pick up my suit at the dry cleaner's. Had to look my best for those dipsticks on the Security Review Board the next day—had to look as sane and conservative as possible. God, I'd be glad when *that* thing was over. Which reminded me: I needed to bring my notes to that meeting with Sheffer. She wanted us to review our arguments one more time. Jesus Christ, man. This was starting to feel like *L.A. Law.* But I was going to *make* those honchos on the Review Board listen to me. I was getting him the hell out of there. . . .

Yeah, and then what? If they sprung him from Hatch and wouldn't readmit him to Settle, what were we going to do then?

I locked the door behind me. Frost again last night, damn it. These cold nights were no good for outside painting.

The truck started on the third try. Better let it run a few minutes, I figured. Painting Plus had wrapped up their outside season two weeks ago. Of course, Danny Labanara didn't have a crazy brother complicating his life every two seconds. Labanara's brother pinch-hit for him during July and August.

My eyes scanned the courtyard. The frost had browned the lawn, killed off those scraggly plants that passed for landscaping here at Condo Heaven. It was a joke the way we had to shell out to the association for groundskeeping. If I had more time or energy, I'd be all over them about that. Of course, if Dessa and I were still together, I'd still be over at our old place, doing my own goddamned yard work. Doing it *right.*

Joy had overstuffed the garbage cans again, I noticed. Why didn't she just issue *invitations* to the goddamned raccoons? *Come and get it, guys!* That was the thing about Joy: you'd tell her to do something, and she'd say okay, yeah, she'd do it, and then she *wouldn't.* She had zilch for follow-through. . . . I hadn't said anything yet to Joy about what Sheffer and I had talked about: the possibility that Thomas might land back here with us. Cross *that* bridge when I came to it, I figured. . . . Ah, screw it. I had to go to the dump, anyway. Might as well just throw the damn garbage bags in back and take 'em with me. Better than waking up at 2:00 A.M. and listening to those goddamned scavenging raccoons.

I swung bags one and two into the truck bed. Bag three busted open at the seam, midflight. Motherfucking cheap bags! I needed *this*? Scooping up the junk mail and dead salad, my eye caught something else: a blue pamphlet.

Directions for a home pregnancy test? In *our* garbage?

I sifted around a little more in the wreckage. Found a plastic tray, cardboard pieces from the ripped-up box. *Pregnancy* test?

I got in the truck. Drove toward the hardware store. Did I have those notes for the meeting with Sheffer? Had I remembered my dry-cleaning receipt? . . . How could she think she was pregnant? False alarm, maybe—missed period or something? Miraculous vasectomy reversal? I'd had myself "fixed" back when I was still with Dessa—had been shooting blanks the whole time I'd been with Joy. Not that *she* knew. I'd never told her. It was partly a not-wanting-to-get-into-it thing: the baby's death, the divorce. Partly a male ego thing, too, I guess. When we started going out, she was twenty-three and I was thirty-eight. What was I supposed to say to her? I'm fifteen years older than you, and, oh yeah, I'm sterile, too. . . .

By the time I came out of my stupor—looked around to see where I was—I'd overshot the hardware store by half a mile. I was way the hell over past the cinemas and Bedding Barn. Hey, wake up, man. Earth to Birdsey.

* * *

I sat in Sheffer's office, twiddling my thumbs and waiting as usual.

Lisa Sheffer: psychiatric social worker and queen of the unexpected emergency. I liked Sheffer—I was grateful and everything—but this whole routine was getting pretty old. Check in at the gate, get your parking pass, check in with security, go through the metal detector, get escorted down to her office by some stone-faced guard, and then just *sit* there and wait for her. I was going to say something this time—soon as she started up with some excuse.

I heard voices outside in the rec area. Went over to the window. It was those camouflage guys this morning—the Vietnam burn-outs. Unit Six. Jesus God, I was starting to recognize the different units. . . . Fucking Nam, man. Some of those guys looked like old men. Didn't recognize the aide. Where'd they get this one from—*Big Time Wrestling*?

Stay calm, I told myself. Her period was just late or something. Used to happen to Dessa some months, back when we were trying to get pregnant: we'd get our hopes up and then, bam, she'd wake up with it. She'd have just been a little late. . . . Jesus, I had to get *focused.* Had to think about the hearing. Over at the dump, I'd thrown my empty paint cans in the wrong recycling bin. "You need something in the nature of supplies this morning, Dominick?" Johnny over at Willard's had said. "Or'd you just come into the store to lean on my counter and meditate?"

Was she cheating on me—was that it? I was no picnic, either, I reminded myself, especially lately. I'd never cheated on her, though. Never cheated on Dessa, either. *Never.* It was just a false alarm, I assured myself. What's the matter, Birdsey? You don't have *enough* to worry about?

I reached over and grabbed the phone book on Sheffer's desk. Batteson, Batteson.

Russell A. Batteson, Ob-Gyn. . . .

Outside, the camouflage guys started lining up to come back in. All day long at this sorry place: herd 'em out, herd 'em back in. Some of these Vietnam casualties would have made out better if they'd just stepped on a land mine or something. . . . If that pregnancy test had come out negative, why was an ob-gyn's office calling her? What was she trying to hide from me?

Yeah, well, you haven't exactly been Mr. Open Communication, either, I reminded myself. You've committed a sin of omission or two. She was already on the pill when we started making love—had told me that first night—and so I'd just shut my mouth about the vasectomy. Kept the status quo instead of getting into any of that past history stuff. Joy didn't even know I'd been a teacher until almost a year after she'd moved in with me. Someone at work told her—Amy someone. She'd been in my homeroom.

What had Dr. Patel said that time? That my rushing into another relationship after Dessa was like applying a fresh coat over peeling paint. A *housepainting* metaphor—custom-made for the guy in the hot seat. . . . Hey, Joy never *asked* about my marriage, either. She could have asked. We'd discussed the possibility of kids a total of one time. We'd both agreed neither of us was interested. Period. End of subject. "No kids" was one of her assets. One of the big reasons why I'd asked her to move in with me.

Sheffer's entrance into the office made me jump. She was hyper—all nervous energy. Which did I want first, she said—the good news or the bad? The good, I told her.

"Your security clearance came through. You can see him."

"I can? When?"

"Today. As soon as we finish our meeting. I'll call security, and we'll meet him in the visiting room. All right?"

I nodded. Told her thanks. Gave her a jerky little smile. "What's the bad news?"

"The unit team took our vote this morning. It's not really 'bad' news. It's not good *or* bad. It's neutral."

I tilted my head. Waited.

Things had gone pretty much along the lines she thought they would, Sheffer said. Dr. Chase and Dr. Diederich had voted to recommend Thomas's retention at Hatch. She and Janet Coffey—the head nurse—had voted for his release to a nonforensic facility. "But here's the part I *didn't* see coming," she said. "Dr. Patel abstained."

"Abstained? *Why?*"

"I don't know why. I don't really get it myself. She said she was professionally obliged not to go into it."

"But that's stupid. That's just throwing her vote away." I got up. Sat down again. "So it's a hung jury then? Man, this *sucks*!"

Sheffer reminded me their team was just advisory, anyway. "Just the lowly medical professionals who have actually *worked* with the patient." The Review Board was the real jury, she said. She told me the team had decided to write up the vote as is—explain that they were split, with one abstention. So there'd be no clear recommendation either way.

"Then they'll go with what the two shrinks want, right? Aren't the doctors' opinions going to overrule yours and the nurse's?" Her finger tapped against her lip. She said if it weren't a sexist world—if male doctors didn't still sit up on Mount Olympus—then she'd say no. But, unfortunately, I was probably right.

"I'll talk to Dr. Patel," I said. "I'll get her to *un*-abstain."

Sheffer shook her head. "It's a done deal, *paisano*. I know you're disappointed, but think about it: it could have been worse. It could have been a 3-to-2 recommendation to retain him here. With the political pressure from the state and a vote like that, Hatch would have been a foregone conclusion. At least we still have one last chance to lobby for his release tomorrow. Let's *go* for it."

I snorted a little at that one. Yea, rah rah. Sheffer as head cheerleader.

She asked me if I'd gotten the letters. "All two of them," I said, handing them over. Between us, we had approached twelve people about the possibility of writing letters to the Review Board advocating my brother's release from Hatch. We'd gotten refusals from all but two. "I like this one," Sheffer said, holding up the letter from Dessa.

"I can't believe Dr. Ehlers reneged on us," I said. "First he says he'll write one. Then I go over to his office to pick it up and his receptionist says he's changed his mind. You know what I think? I think someone from the state got to him—told him *not* to write the thing."

Sheffer smiled. Told me I was starting to sound a little paranoid, like someone else she knew. I stared back at her, not laughing. "Okay, let's focus on what we've *got* instead of what we didn't get," she said. "And we still need to put the finishing touches on *your* argument. Because I think that if anyone's going to sway the Board, Domenico, it's *you* who has the best shot."

"Yeah?"

"Yeah. As long as that Sicilian temper of yours doesn't flare up."

I got up. Walked over to the window. "So what's your gut feeling on this?" I said. "You think he's going to get out of here?"

She told me we had done everything we could—that a lot of it depended on whether or not the Board was willing to check their baggage at the door and listen without prejudice. "We'll just go in there and state our case point by point—everything we've gone over. Wait and see."

"I'm worried about Thomas blowing it," I said. "Does he *have* to be there?"

She nodded. "We've been over this already. Yes, he *has* to be there, and yes, he *has* to answer their questions." She started to say something else, then caught herself.

"What?" I said. "What were you going to say just then?"

She didn't want to worry me, she said, but Thomas had been acting a little schizy that morning—a little agitated. It was probably nothing, just an off morning.

I sat back down and faced her. "You didn't answer my question before," I said.

"What was your question?"

"Do you think they're going to release him tomorrow?"

She shrugged. Told me not to bet the farm. "But, listen, Dominick. Worst-case scenario is that he stays here a year, his medication stabilizes him, he gets good treatment. By next year's annual review, not only is he much better, but the media's off his trail, too—on to 'sexier' cases, as they say."

I asked her if she wanted to know what the worst-case scenario was for me. "For me, it's that one of the other fun guys you got down here sticks him in the ribs with a homemade knife or strangles him in the shower with someone's missing shoelace." I told her I stayed up nights thinking about shit like that.

She said I'd probably seen too many Alfred Hitchcock movies.

"Yeah? Is that right, Sheffer? Tell me something then. If this place is so goddamned safe and therapeutic or whatever—if everyone's so goddamned on top of things around here—then let me ask you this." I reached over and snatched her daughter's picture off her desk, waved it at her. "Would you bring *her* down here? Let your little girl play down at Hatch for a day? Or a week? Or a whole freakin' *year,* until they were on to 'sexier' cases?"

She reached over to take the picture back.

"No, really," I said, holding it away from her still. "Come on, Sheffer. Answer the question. Would you?"

"Stop being a jerk," she said. She was getting pissed.

"What's the matter? Your maternal instinct kicking in, is it? Well, let me tell you something." I was near tears. I *was* acting like a jerk—I *knew* that. "Speaking of mothers, I promised mine—his *and* mine—I told her the day she died that I'd look out for him. Okay? That I'd make sure nothing happened to him. And that's just a little hard to do in this place. . . . She's just a little kid. Right? Your daughter? Well, listen, Sheffer. In a weird way—in ways I can't even explain to you—Thomas is still a little kid, too. To me, anyway. It's always been that way. I used to have to beat kids up in the schoolyard for messing with him—used to have to make kids pay when they made fun of him so they wouldn't do it again. We're . . . we're identical twins, okay? He's a part of me, Sheffer. So it *hurts,* okay? The thought of him being down at this place for another year and me not able to make it safe for him—beat up the bad guys for him—it's . . . it's killing me."

I handed her kid's picture back to her. She put it in her desk drawer and closed it. We sat there, looking at each other.

She picked up the phone and dialed. Told security that she and I were ready to see Thomas Birdsey.

When the guard brought him in, Thomas stood hesitantly at the door, taking me in in small, shy glimpses. There were dark raccoonlike circles under his eyes. Those jerky movements his head was making—the ones I'd noticed when I'd seen him out there in the recreation area—they were more pronounced up close. "Hey, buddy," I said. Stood up. "How you doing?"

His bottom lip trembled. He looked away. "Lousy," he said.

It was kind of ridiculous, really—they've got that visiting room set up like a boardroom: heavy upholstered chairs, this long table about ten feet long and five feet wide. Like we were a bunch of bankers or something. Sheffer invited Thomas to come in and take a seat. When she asked the guard if he could wait outside—give the three of us a little privacy—he shook his head. "You know better than that," he said. He listed the visiting rules: Thomas had to stay seated on one side of the table and Sheffer and I had to sit on the other side. No hand-shaking, hugging, or physical contact of any kind. I recognized the guard; he was one of the ones who'd been on duty that first night—not Robocop. One of the others. He pulled out a chair for Thomas and told him to sit.

Thomas clomp-clomped over to the table in his laceless wingtip shoes. I recalled the sight of those damned things riding through the metal detector the night he was admitted. They'd taken away his Bible but let him keep his wingtips.

He sat down across from us, his elbows on the table, hand and stump facing me. I tried to make myself look at it, but my eyes bounced away. "So you're lousy?" I said. "Why are you lousy, Thomas?"

Half a minute went by. "Ralph Drinkwater's a janitor here," he said.

I told him, yeah, I'd seen Ralph—both that first night and then again last week when he fixed a light in Sheffer's office. "Looks pretty much the same, doesn't he?" I said. "Hasn't even changed that much after all these years. . . . You look good, too, Thomas."

He gave me a belittling snicker.

"No, you *do.* Considering."

"Considering what?"

"Well, you know. Your hand. *This* place. . . . They treating you okay here?"

The sigh he let out sounded like defeat itself. "I'm thinking of having myself declared a corporation," he said.

"A what?"

"A corporation. It's for my protection. I've been reading about it. If I incorporate myself, I'll be safeguarded. If someone tried to sue me."

"Why would anyone want to sue you?"

He turned to Sheffer. "Can I have a cigarette?" he asked. When she shook her head, he got miffed. "Why *not*? They have ashtrays in here, don't they? Why can't I smoke if they have ashtrays?"

"Well, for one thing," she said, "I've given up smoking and I don't want to be tempted. And for another thing—"

"They don't let you walk the grounds here," he said, cutting her off midsentence. Addressing me again. "The food is disgusting."

"Yeah?" I said. "Shit on a shingle, huh?"

His hand moved to his mouth—covered it up the exact same way Ma was always covering up her cleft lip. "They served rice and beans for lunch yesterday," he said. "And wheat bread and canned pineapple. There was a dead beetle in my rice and beans."

Sheffer asked him if he'd told anyone about it—if he'd let them know so that they could get him another serving. He shook his head. "Well, if something like that happens again, how could you handle the problem?" she asked him. "What could you do for yourself to make the situation better?"

Ignoring her, he addressed me. "Remember when we used to take walks on the grounds on Sunday afternoons? You and Dessa and me?"

I nodded.

"I was thinking about that today. You two always used to stop and read the gravestones at the Indian cemetery."

"And you used to take off your shoes and socks and wade into the river," I said. He seemed to drift off when I said that. "Hey, speaking about the Indians," I said. "You hear about the Wequonnocs? They won that court case. So I guess they're going ahead with that big casino now. Over at the reservation." I'd waited two weeks to see him—talk to him—and now all I could do was make small talk. "Going to be huge, I guess, the way they're talking. Las Vegas II."

Thomas closed his eyes. His lips moved slightly. *"And he showed me a river of the water of life,"* he said. *"Clear as crystal, coming forth from the throne of God and of the Lamb."* He stopped. Scratched his neck with his stump. I looked away.

"How's your . . . ?" I said, then stopped myself, stymied by what to call it. His wound? His sacrifice? "You adjusting okay? Getting used to using your other hand?"

He asked me if I could do him a favor.

"What?"

Could I go down to the river—the spot where he and I and Dessa used to walk? Could I get a jar and fill it up with river water and bring it back to him? Behind him, the guard shook his head no.

"Why?" I said. "What do you want it for?"

"I want to wash with it," he said. "I think if I wash with the water from the river, it might help to heal my infection. Purify me. I'm unclean."

"Unclean?" I said. "What do you mean?" In the silence that followed, I forced my eyes down to his self-mutilation. The scar tissue was pink and shiny, as soft-looking as a newborn's. As soft as Angela's skin had been. I blinked hard—felt an involuntary tightening in my groin and stomach. "It looks pretty good now," I said.

"What?"

"Your . . . your wrist."

"I meant my brain," he said. "I think the water might heal my brain."

I sat there, not saying anything. Wiped the tears out of my eyes. I probably could have counted on one hand the number of times over the years when Thomas had acknowledged his sickness like that—when he hadn't taken the attitude that *he* was the reasonable one and the *rest* of us were crazy. They threw me: those out-of-nowhere moments when he seemed to have some inkling of his own sorry dilemma. That it *wasn't* the Communists or the Iraqis or the CIA, but his own brain. Those little flickers of insight were almost worse than his Loony Toon business-as-usual. You'd see for just a second or two who was trapped inside there. Who Thomas might have been.

I looked over at the guard. "What's the big deal?" I said. "If I brought him a jar of water?" The guy stood there, stiff-necked, his hands behind his back.

Sheffer said she could work on the request, but right now we needed to talk about the hearing.

"Has the war started yet?" Thomas asked me. "I keep trying to find out, and nobody will tell me. They've ordered a news blackout within a fifty-foot radius of me."

Sheffer reminded him that they had discussed Desert Shield just that morning—that she updated him about the standoff whenever he asked her about it.

"Anyways, I doubt there's even going to *be* a war," I said. "Bush and Saddam are like two kids out in the schoolyard. Each of them's just waiting for the other to back down. It's all just bluff."

Thomas scoffed. "Don't be so naive," he said.

Sheffer reminded us again that we needed to talk about the hearing.

"You see?" Thomas said. "They have orders to change the subject every time I mention the Persian Gulf. I'm at the center of a news blackout because of my mission."

"Thomas?" Sheffer said. "You remember there's a hearing tomorrow, right? That the Review Board is going to be meeting to decide—"

His exasperated sigh cut her off. "To decide if I can get out of here!" he shouted.

"That's right," Sheffer said. "Now, I'm going to be at the hearing. And Dominick and Dr. Patel. Maybe Dr. Chase. And you're going to be there, too, Thomas."

"I *know* that. You *told* me already."

"Okay. So what we need to do is go over a few more things with you so that you'll make a good impression with the Review Board. Okay?"

Thomas mumbled something about the Spanish Inquisition.

"What's one of the things they're probably going to ask you about tomorrow?" Sheffer asked. "Do you remember? The thing we were talking about yesterday and this morning?"

"My hand."

"That's right. And what are you going to say when they ask you about that?"

Thomas turned to me. "How's Ray?"

"Thomas?" Sheffer said. "Stay focused. Answer my question, please. What are you going to tell the Board about why you removed your hand?"

We waited. He put his hand to his mouth and started smoking an imaginary cigarette. "Answer her question," I said.

No comment.

"Thomas? Look, man, you want to get out of this place, don't you? Maybe go back to Settle for a while? Back to your coffee wagon?"

"*In the midst of the city street, on both sides of the river, was the tree of life,*" he said. Closed his eyes. "*Bearing twelve fruits, yielding its fruit according to each month, and the leaves for the healing of the nations.*"

"Answer her question," I said.

His eyes sprang open. "I *am* answering it!" he snapped. "I was following a Biblical dictate! I cut off my hand to heal the nations!"

I was beginning to lose it—beginning to feel that Sicilian temper Sheffer had warned me about. "Okay, listen," I said. I pointed a thumb at Sheffer. "She and I have been working real hard to try and get you out of here, okay? Because we know how miserable you are here. . . . But if you start spouting this Bible stuff at that hearing tomorrow, instead of just answering their questions directly, you're not going anywhere. You're going to stay right here at Hatch. Okay? You understand? You're just going to stay here and walk around without your shoelaces and eat beetles in your dinner or whatever."

"Uh, Dominick?" Sheffer said.

"No, hold on. Let's give it to him straight. You listening to me, Thomas? You've got to lay off that Bible bullshit and play it smart with these Review Board honchos. You understand me? If they ask you if you regret what you did in the library, you tell them, yes, you regret it, and if they say—"

"Whatever happened to Dessa, anyway?" he said.

"What? . . . You know what happened. We got a divorce. Now when they say something like—"

"Because your baby died," he said. He turned to Sheffer. "They had a baby daughter and she died. My niece. I held her once. Dominick didn't want me to hold her, but Dessa said I could."

Which was bullshit. He'd never held her—had never even seen her. I looked over at Sheffer. Looked up at the ceiling, over at the goddamned guard. "Never mind about that now," I said. "We need to talk about the hearing. *Stop* it." I could feel Sheffer looking at me—pitying the father of a dead baby. "Listen . . . listen to Ms. Sheffer, now, okay? She's going to tell you what to say and what not to say. So we can get you out of here."

"Dessa came to see me when I was in the hospital," he told Sheffer.

"Listen!"

"She loves me. I'm still her friend, whether she and Dominick are married or not."

I stood up. Sat back down and strapped my hands across my chest. This was hopeless.

"Sure, she loves you," Sheffer said. "Of course she does. She wrote a really nice letter to the Review Board about how she thinks you should be let out of here."

"I'll just tell them the truth," Thomas said. "That I had to make a holy sacrifice to prevent Armageddon." His face looked suddenly arrogant, clenched. His cheeks flushed. "It would have worked, too, if they hadn't sequestered me like this. Silenced me. They'd probably be at the peace table right now if war wasn't so profitable. When Jesus went into the temple . . . when Jesus went into the temple and . . ." His face contorted. He began to sob. "They torture me here!" he shouted.

The guard moved closer. Sheffer held up her hand.

"Who does?" I said. "Who tortures you? The voices?"

"You think putting insects in my food is the worst of it? Well, it *isn't*! They hide snakes in my bed. Stick razor blades in my coffee. Push their elbows against my throat."

"*Who* does?"

"I'm unclean, Dominick! They have keys! They rape me!"

"Okay," I said. "All right. Calm down."

"Sneak into my cell at night and rape me!" He pointed across the table at Sheffer. "She's nice—she and Dr. Gandhi—but they have no idea what goes on behind their backs. At night. No one does. I'm public enemy number one because I have the power to stop this war. But they don't *want* it stopped! They want me silenced!"

"Who does?"

"Use your head for once! Read Apocalypse!"

I stood up and started around that massive table toward him.

"Whoa, whoa, wait a minute," the guard said. "Hospital requires you keep a distance of five feet from the patients while—"

Thomas stood; I took him in my arms. He fell against me, stiff as a two-by-four.

"Sir? I'm going to have to ask you—"

Sheffer got up. Stepped between the guard and the two of us.

"Maybe if I was incorporated," Thomas sobbed. And I held him, rocked him in my arms until he was quiet. "I think if I was incorporated . . ."

I never did show up at the Roods' that afternoon. I drove around and around and ended up at the Falls, watching the spilling water, my legs dangling over the edge of the cliff. Talking to that falling water like it was the Psychiatric Security Review Board, pulling one Rolling Rock after another out of the carton. What had Dr. Patel said? Something about the river of memory, the river of understanding. . . . What if we *did* beat the odds? Get him out of there at that hearing? What then? . . . Was Joy going to leave me? Was that it? Pack her bags and run off with whoever had knocked her up? It wasn't perfect—Joy and me—it had *never* been perfect. But if she left me . . .

I drained another beer and dropped the bottle into the rushing river. Saw Penny Ann Drinkwater's dead body tumble and fall. Saw Ma in her casket over at Fitzgerald's Funeral Home. Saw Ray going up the stairs and down the hall to the spare room, his belt in hand, going after Thomas. . . .

* * *

By the time I got back to the condo, it was after eight. The lights were on. The Duchess's car was parked out in front. Why didn't that little faggot just pack his bags and come *live* with us? Why didn't we just charge him rent, for Christ's sake?

I unloaded the antifreeze, the paint thinner. Grabbed my notes for the hearing, my dry-cleaned suit. What was that on the front step?

A jack-o'-lantern, smiling out at nothing.

I considered hauling off and drop-kicking the fucker across the yard. Went inside instead.

"Hi, Dominick," Joy said.

I clunked the stuff I was holding onto the kitchen counter. "Yup."

"Hi, Dominick," the Duchess chimed in. "Want some toasted pumpkin seeds?" He was pulling a cookie sheet from the oven. I walked past him without a word. Drop-kick him, too, if he didn't stay the fuck away from me.

In the bedroom, I flopped facedown on the mattress. Rolled over. Started reading through my notes on the hearing. Joy came in and closed the door behind her.

"Okay, Dominick," she said. "I know you have a lot on your mind with that hearing thingy tomorrow. But that doesn't give you the right to walk in and be totally rude to my friends."

"Get him out of here," I said.

"Why should I? This is *my* house, too, you know? If I want to relax after work and have my friends over—"

I sent my notes flying across the bedroom, papers fluttering to the floor. Stood up. Should I tell her I'd seen her little pregnancy test? Have our little showdown right then and there? I was tempted—still buzzed enough from those beers out at the Falls to start something. But I needed to save my energy for the hearing. Get into this at a later date. I walked past her. Went into the bathroom to take a leak. When I came back in the bedroom, she hadn't moved.

"I'm sick of it," she said. "I'm sick of you being this big martyr all the time."

"Look," I said. "I know you couldn't give a flying fuck about whether he stays down there at that place and rots. I *know* that. I *accept* that. But I got an *obligation,* okay? Now, I need to go over these papers—prepare for tomorrow. Then I need to eat something. Some real food, I mean, not *toasted pumpkin seeds.* Then I need to get some sleep. So just get your little boyfriend or girlfriend or whatever he is out of here."

She stood there, hands on her hips, chin jutting out. "If you have so much to prepare, why have you been drinking?" she said. "You smell like a brewery. Is drinking beer part of your 'preparation'?"

"Get him out of here," I repeated.

"How about what *I* need? Do you ever think about what *I* need, Dominick?"

"I mean it, Joy. Get him out before I go out there and fucking *throw* him out."

She stood up, glaring at me. Walked to the door and slammed it behind her. Out in the kitchen, there was mumbling between them. Then the TV went dead. Then, in this order, I heard: back door, car doors, ignition.

"Joy?" I got off the bed, opened the door. "Joy?"

The message machine was blinking. Once, twice. I hit the button.

"Mr. Birdsey? This is Ruth Rood again. I—" I reached over and fast-forwarded. Let up my finger in the middle of Sheffer's voice.

"Okay, then. End of sermon. See you tomorrow. Get some sleep."

I went back in the bedroom, flopped back on the bed, my face to the ceiling.

"They rape me, Dominick. They come in at night and rape me!"

"This is Dr. Batteson's office calling for Joy Hanks."

I let the tears drip down the sides of my face. Let my sobbing shake the bed.

Somewhere during the night, I dreamt that Dessa was doing me, slipping my cock in and out of her mouth. She *hadn't* left me, then? We were still together? Then, the sweet rush of release. I woke up, coming.

Saw Joy's head move away. Saw Joy reach up and tuck her bangs behind her ear.

I lay there, catching my breath, letting the spasms die away.

Joy pulled tissues from the box on her nightstand. Started cleaning us up.

"Hey," I said.

"Hey," she whispered back. "Did that feel nice? I wanted to make you feel nice."

I reached over for her, but she took my hand and led it away from her. Parked it back on the mattress. Sometimes, with Joy, sex wasn't so much something we shared together, but a service she performed. She turned on the table lamp. Traced and retraced the line of my eyebrow with her finger.

"I saw him this afternoon," I said.

"Saw who?"

"My brother."

"You did? So the security thing came through? . . . How is he?"

Same as he always is, I told her. Sick. Crazy.

"Dominick?" she said. "I have something to tell you. Something big. I didn't want to say anything until I was sure, and now I *am* sure. . . . God, the last thing I wanted tonight was for us to get into a fight."

I let time go by—half a minute or more. She was leaving me, right? She was leaving me for the baby's father. What was the hum job for? Going-away present? Something to remember her by?

"What is it?" I said.

"I'm pregnant." She took my hand. "We made a baby, Dominick. You and me."

She talked about her symptoms, the home pregnancy test, what they'd told her at the doctor's. She talked and talked. At first, she didn't think she wanted it, she said, but now she did. She said she thought we'd make good parents. That maybe we could start looking at houses. . . .

I reached over and turned off the light. In those few seconds of absolute darkness—before my eyes adjusted—it felt like we were in some place more open and wide than our bedroom. Like we were falling together, somewhere in space.

"Well?" she said. "What do you think? *Say* something."

twenty-seven

The thump outside woke me up. Raccoons, I thought. Rolled over. If she'd just put the damn garbage lids on tight. . . .

We made a baby, Dominick. You and me.

They rape me!

Don't think about it now, I told myself. Don't think. Take deep breaths. *Sleep!*

1:07 A.M., according to the clock radio. Well, it was finally here: D-Day. The day of his hearing.

Joy rolled onto her side. She'd been cheating on me and now she was lying through her teeth. Hey, it wasn't like I hadn't been warned ahead of time. Miss Shoplifter. Miss Screw Her Own Uncle. Get through the hearing and *then* deal with it, I told myself. Watch her. Give her enough rope to hang herself. Hell of a way to be thinking about the woman you slept next to. . . . Come on, Dominick. *Sleep.*

I flashed on the Duchess earlier that night in our kitchen—him and his toasted pumpkin seeds. I bet that little flit knew who she'd been screwing behind my back. Whose baby it was. Joy told the Duchess everything.

Outside, another thump. Footsteps. . . . Footsteps?

I got out of bed and padded across the bedroom floor. The notes on Thomas's hearing that I'd flung earlier rustled under my feet. Outside, a voice. By the time I got to the stairs, I was running.

I threw open the front door. "Hey!"

One of them grunted as they took off. Kids. I took off after them in my bare feet and skivvies—chased those bobbing baseball caps through two or three front lawns.

Stopped. Winded. . . .

Five years ago, I'd have had one or both of them down on the ground—would have had them wishing they hadn't messed with *my* house. I stood there, my heart pounding like a jackhammer. Forty, man. Shit.

They'd wished the neighborhood Happy Halloween by egging car windows, snapping radio antennas. That jack-o'-lantern the Duchess and Joy had put out lay on our front walk in chunks, its broken mouth smiling up at the moon.

Now I was *wide* awake. Now I was up for the long haul.

Back in the house, I flopped onto the sofa, aimed the remote. Better to troll than think. Letterman was dropping dollar bills out a window. The Monkees—middle-aged, now—were hawking oldies. I surfed past CNN, the Catholic station, a couple of those 1-900 bimbos who wanted to share their "secret fantasies." . . . She manipulated me with sex—used it whenever she wanted something. She'd done that right from the beginning. . . . *The Business Beat,* Rhoda Morgenstern, VH-1. Shit, man. I had to get some *sleep.*

"Dominick?" She was up at the top of the stairs. "What's the matter?"

"Nothing."

"Are you crying?"

"No. Go back to sleep."

Later, back in our bedroom, I stumbled into my pants, groped around for my wallet and keys. "Where are you going?" her voice said. I'd figured she would have fallen back to sleep.

"Nowhere. Out."

"Why were you crying down there? Is it about your brother?" I finished lacing my work boots and started out of there. "Dominick? Are you upset about the baby?"

While I was backing the truck out the driveway, the porch light went on. The front door opened. She stood outside on the stoop, arms crossed, those muscular legs of hers visible beneath her nightgown. Don't talk to me, I thought. Don't call my name.

Those asshole punks had egged my windshield. By rights, I should have gotten out and cleaned it off. Or turned off the goddamned motor and gotten back in bed with Joy—hung on for dear life, no matter what she'd done—no matter what she was trying to pull. Instead, I flicked on the wipers. They smeared a layer of shell and egg slime between me and my visibility and I remembered too late that the fluid well was dry. Fuck it, I thought. Threw her into gear anyway. Who the fuck else was out at this time of night?

I drove through downtown, up River Avenue, to Cider Mill and Route 162. My eyes burned, my stomach hurt, from sleeplessness. Everywhere I drove, smashed pumpkins were in the road. It hadn't even been a *conscious* decision, really—me driving out there, past that shabby farmhouse of theirs. If she'd have just held on, I would have come around. Gotten over the baby. I know I would have. . . .

I pulled over. Turned the lights off but kept her idling. Walked past their jazzy mailbox, up their gravel driveway. I'd never come this far before.

The house was dark, their van parked in front of the barn. *Good Earth Potters*. I leaned against the side of it and looked up at the house. She's gone for good, I told myself. You screwed up and she cut you off, same as he cut off his hand. She amputated you. You're dead meat, Birdsey. Go home to the woman you don't love.

Except I didn't go home. I got back in the truck and hung a U at the next fork. Took a left onto the parkway. It was a relief to drive *past* the state hospital for once. The roads were slick from a mist so soft and light it seemed to hang suspended in the air around the streetlamps. I flicked on the wipers—pushed around the egg slime a little.

Driving through New London, I hung a left onto Montauk and headed for the beach. Parked, walked across the boardwalk and down into the sinking sand. At the water's edge, little waves lapped in and phosphorescence bounced and winked at the toes of my work boots. Phosphorescence, man. Pixie dust. What was there about water?

When I came off the beach again, I saw a cruiser parked next to my truck. Engine and lights off. Waiting. Just him and me in that empty thousand-car parking lot.

A window whirred as I approached. "Evening," the cop said. In the dark, he was a voice, nothing else.

"Evening."

"Out for a stroll?"

"Yup." It was like speaking to nothing. Like speaking to the goddamned mist. He started his engine when I started mine. Tailed me all the way back through town until I turned back onto I-95.

Driving over the Gold Star Bridge, I looked across the river at the halogen glow: Electric Boat, third shift. At EB, they were still building submarines around the clock—even now, with the Cold War on the respirator. *Nautilus, Polaris, Trident, Seawolf*: war and Connecticut had always had a romance going, a kind of vampire's dance. "It puts food on the table, too, doesn't it, wiseguy?" I heard Ray's voice say. "You *ate* every night while you were growing up, didn't you?"

Was that what Joy expected me to do? Be like Ray: be a father to someone else's kid and hate the kid for it? Do a number on some poor little bastard his whole life? For a second or two, I could taste the bile that must have sat in Ray's gut all those years: catch a fleeting glimpse of life from Ray's perspective.

I exited in Easterly and drove up Route 22, out by the Wequonnoc reservation. As close as I can figure, that's when I must have started dozing. . . .

In the dream, I'm my younger self, slipping and sliding on a frozen-over river. A tree's growing out of the water—a cedar, I think it is. Beneath my shoes, babies are floating by. Dozens of them. They're alive—trapped under the ice. They're those babies the nuns told us about in Sunday school—the ones that died before they were baptized and had to stay stuck in limbo on a technicality until the end of the world. I worry about those babies—wonder about them, about God. If He made the whole universe, why can't he just relax his own rule? Accept those blameless babies into Heaven? . . .

And then Ma's in the dream. Alive again, up in the cedar tree, holding a baby . . .

A movement beneath the ice distracts me and when I look down, I see my grandmother, alive, under the ice. Ignazia. . . . I recognize her from the brown-tinted photograph in my mother's album. Her wedding portrait—the only picture of her I've ever seen. We make eye contact, she and I. Her eyes beg me for something I can't understand. I run after her, slipping and sliding across the ice. "What do you want?" I shout down. "What do you want?"

When I look up again, the cedar tree's in flames. . . .

I awoke to a car horn's blare. Jesus! Jesus!

A rock ledge rushed past, headlights crisscrossed in front of me. I veered to the right and drove over an embankment, unsure how far I'd fall.

There was an ugly scraping sound beneath me, I remember—the wail of my own *Oh, no! Oh, no!* My head bounced against the roof. Barreling toward that tree, I held out my hand to stop the collision. . . .

I was out for a little while, I guess. I must have been. I remember pulling my hand back inside the busted windshield. Remember the pain, the pulsing blood.

That same cedar tree grew in a pasture, not the river. A half dozen Holsteins stood staring at me, griping from the far end they'd run to when I'd come flying over their bank. Disturbed their peace. I grabbed a paint rag, pulled the tourniquet tight with my good hand and my teeth. I got out of the truck. Sat down in that frost-dead field.

The mist had stopped—had made way for a bright, hard-edged moon. Crumbs of windshield glass glittered in the hair on my arm. In the moonlight, my blood looked black.

Up on Route 22, I saw a vision: the steady flow of gamblers in cars, driving to the Wequonnocs' casino. *"What do you want?"* I had yelled through the frozen river to my dead grandmother. *"What do you want?"*

twenty-eight

GOD BLESS AMERICA! the five-foot-tall letters proclaimed across Constantine Motors' showroom window. Translation: Prove your patriotism with your down payment. Buy a car and stick it to Saddam.

I was seated across from Leo's desk, waiting for the insurance guy to show. I'd gone right from the hospital to the phone—had kept hitting Redial Redial Redial until someone at Mutual of America finally answered. They'd tried to put me off—to give me an appointment with the claims adjuster the following week. "Look, lady," I'd said. "I make my *living* with that truck. One way or the other, someone's looking at that vehicle *today*!" So there I sat, twiddling my thumbs at Constantine Chrysler Dodge Isuzu instead of pulling those shutters over at the Roods' like I'd promised. I should have been running point by point through my arguments to the Security Board a couple more times instead of just sitting there. Me and my seventeen stitches, my Tylox high.

Omar the ex-athlete was seated at the sales desk across from Leo's, talking on the phone. "Uh-huh. Uh-huh. I understand that, Carl. But *you're* talking about some car in the abstract and *I'm* talking about this cobalt blue Dakota that

I'm looking at right out there on the lot." He was wearing a shirt, a tie, and a red, white, and blue baseball cap. "Plus, if you act now, you've got the added savings of our God Bless America promotion."

God bless America!

I cut it off to heal the nations! . . .

My stitched-up hand was starting to hurt again. My neck now, too. The doctor over in the emergency room had tried to order me one of those collar things, but I'd refused. I'd said yes to the pain pills, though—three of them in a little brown envelope and a prescription for a dozen more. I considered popping another one now but decided against it. If that claims adjuster was going to give me a hassle, I didn't want to sit there smiling at him like Goofy.

My truck, man. My livelihood. . . .

I looked over at Omar in time to catch his eyes jump away from the sight of me. Banged up, bandaged up, slumped in the chair: I must have looked about as pathetic as my truck. "Where do you want this thing towed to?" the state cop had asked me out at the accident. "Constantine Motors," I'd said—a knee-jerk response.

A wave of nausea passed through my gut. My hands started trembling, my legs. Last thing I needed right about then was to lose it in front of Omar. I cleared my throat, stood up. "Tell . . . uh . . . tell Leo I went to the can," I said.

Omar looked over like he hadn't been aware of my existence. "Huh? Yeah, sure thing." I got up and headed for the men's room.

I locked the door, looked at my face in the mirror. Night of the Living Dead looked back. Another wave of queasiness came and went; I broke out in a clammy sweat. I rested my head against the wall and listed all the things I was supposed to be able to fix: my truck, my brother's placement, the Roods' house.

We made a baby, Dominick. You and me. . . .

I saw, again, the way Joy had looked when she got to the emergency room that morning: no makeup, her hair all crazy. "Hold me," she'd said. Broke down right in front of everyone. Cried against me. In almost two years together, it was maybe the second or third time I'd seen Joy cry. Those tears meant there was *something* between us, right? That she felt something, whether she'd been screwing someone else or not. Right?

When the shaking subsided, I got up and doused my face with cold water, purposely avoiding the mirror. I walked back out into that gleaming showroom.

That's when I noticed the patriotic balloons bobbing from the business manager's platform desk: bouquets of them. Looked like a goddamned altar, that desk. In the name of the father, and the son, and the dollar bill. Leo was strolling toward me from the opposite direction with our two coffees. He was wearing that fancy Armani suit of his and one of those *God Bless America!* caps like Omar's. Every employee at the freaking dealership was wearing one of those caps, even Uncle Costas and the secretaries. They had a major theme going on, courtesy of Kuwait.

"Here you go, Birdsey," Leo said, handing me the coffee. "What time did that guy say he'd be here?"

"Ten-thirty." I squinted up at the wall clock for the umpteenth time. Ten fifty-five.

Leo sat down, put his feet up on the desk, his hands behind his head. "And your brother's thing is *when*?"

"Four this afternoon."

"What do you think? You gonna be able to spring him?"

I shrugged. Needed to change the subject. "What's with the doofy-looking hats?"

He reached up and took off his cap, tossing it onto the filing cabinet next to his desk. "It's the old man's idea. He ordered a gross for giveaways. We're having a Desert Shield rally this Saturday. Tent, hot dog roast, zero-percent down."

I rolled my eyes. "You got hat head," I said.

"What?"

"Hat head." I pointed at the ridge the cheap hat had made in his forty-dollar haircut. That's what he told me once that he pays his "stylist": forty bucks a throw.

He took a little mirror out of his desk and tried tousling away the damage. That was *Leo's* biggest problem: hat head. "Hey, if Big Gene thought it'd move cars off the lot, he'd dig up *Patton* and stick him in the window." He leaned forward, whispering. "With the economy this sucky and the Boat talking about more layoffs, nobody's buying *nothing*. September was our worst month since the gas crisis."

I'll cry for 'em later on, I thought. Checked the clock again. 11:03. Where *was* that insurance fuck?

I watched Leo's eyes follow his coworker Lorna across the sales floor. "Hey, you know what I found out yesterday?" he whispered. "About the she-bitch over there?" He drew a pen out of his desk set, plunged it in and out, in and out of the holder. "She and Omar. One of the mechanics caught 'em doin' the big nasty after hours in the back of a Caravan. The old man'd go ballistic if he found out. You know how he hates that black-on-white stuff."

Get a life, Leo, I thought. I tried swiveling my neck from side to side; it hurt more when I turned to the right than the left. It was stupid of me not to have gotten that collar.

"So, Birds," Leo said. "You got any idea how long that hearing thing's going to take this afternoon? I got an appointment at five thirty. If it starts at four, I should be back here by five thirty, shouldn't I?"

My leg pumped up and down. My fingers drummed on his desk. I told him Ray could take me. "I'll *take* you," he said. "I don't mind *taking* you. I just gotta—"

"I don't *know* how long it's going to take," I snapped. "I've never *been* to one of these things before. Okay? It'll just be simpler if Ray drives me."

"Hey, don't bite *my* head off. Wasn't *me* who fell asleep at the wheel."

In the next breath, he started yapping about his stupid movie—telling me how he was waiting for them to FedEx him the script and then the next step was blah blah blah.

I checked the clock again. Did some calculating. If that insurance idiot showed up in the next fifteen or twenty minutes, I could probably still salvage an hour or so over at the Roods'. Pull those shutters off, minimum, so I could take them back to my place and prep them. It'd be awkward with my hand bandaged up like this, but I could do it. . . . Except how was I going to get the damn things home with no truck? *Shit.*

"But don't worry, Dominick," Leo was saying. "The old man and I'll take good care of you. Put you in a Dodge or an Isuzu five-speed, no *problemo*. That Isuzu's a good little truck, actually. You wanna have a look-see while you're waiting?"

I said I doubted they'd total the pickup. We both looked out at it and Leo shook his head. "That truck is *gone,* my man," he said. "That ve-hicle is *DOA.*"

11:12. My hand was starting to hurt like it meant it. If I moved my head to the right, pain shot up my neck. Okay, here's what I'd do, I thought: I'd take another one of those painkillers right after I was through with the insurance guy, go over to Roods' and pull the shutters—see if Ray could borrow Eddie Banas's truck. Then I'd go home and get a couple hours' sleep. Set the alarm—give myself an hour to clean up and go over my notes. If my hand hurt this bad by afternoon, I'd just have to tough it out until after the hearing. Be great, otherwise: me standing before that Security Board, zoned out on narcotics.

I asked Leo if I could use his phone again. "Dial nine first," he said.

"Mutual of America. How may I direct your call?"

It was the same woman I'd talked to the other three times. She was getting a little less polite with each call. "Look, lady," I told her. "I spent half the night in the hospital, I got about a thousand things I've got to take care of today, and I'll be damned if I'm going to spend my whole day waiting for your representative to show." She told me there wasn't really anything else she could do, but that she sympathized with me. "Yeah, well, your sympathy isn't doing me a goddamn bit of good, is it?" I snapped back. Banged the phone down louder than I'd meant to. Every *God Bless America!* cap at the dealership turned its bill in my direction.

"Hey, Birdsey, chill out a little," Leo said. "No shit, you're stressing *me* out, man."

I got up. Walked to the other end of the showroom and back. Sat back down. "What time does the old man usually get here?" I said.

"Gene? What is it—Wednesday? Any time now."

"Great," I said. "Just what I need: seeing Daddy Dearest."

"Yeah, the guy's got a hell of a nerve showing up at his

own place of business, don't he?" He threw up his hands. "I'm kidding, Birdsey. I'm *kidding*."

A waxed white Firebird pulled into the dealership and coasted down to the body shop. A young guy in shades got out, walked around my truck, squatted in front of it. Strictly business, now that he'd finally managed to arrive.

"I'll be out in a couple of minutes," Leo said. "I just want to try my producer again. See if he can tell me when they're sending me my script."

The investigator aimed his camera at my wreck. It whined, shit out a Polaroid. "You the claims guy?" I said.

"That's right." When he turned around, I recognized him: one of those weight lifters at the health club. He practically lived down there. "Shawn Tudesco. Mutual of America." He held out a square, manicured hand for me to shake—withdrew it when he saw *my* bandaged hand. Down at Hardbodies, this asshole strutted around like a little bantam rooster.

"You're late," I said.

"Right again," he shot back. Which was all I was getting in the way of an apology.

He propped the Polaroid in a tuck of the pickup's mangled bumper, aimed, took another. A third. A fourth. He had one of those slicked-back Pat Riley hairstyles, a tiny red earring in one ear. Couple of times, I'd seen him leaning against the counter down there, chatting it up with Joy. Spandex Man—God's gift to women. Took steroids, was my guess.

"What's this?" he asked me.

I followed his fingers along my smeared windshield. "That? . . . It's egg."

He cocked his head to the side. "Egg?"

"Kids last night. Celebrating Halloween a day early."

"Yeah?" He just stood there. I was the first to look away.

He stretched on a pair of plastic gloves and pulled some glass crumbs from the windshield. There was a brown smear where my hand had busted through the glass, some dried drips on the hood that he bent close to look at. What was he doing? Doubling as an FBI agent or something?

Leo came out of the showroom and crossed the lot toward us, whistling. Holding his patriotic cap instead of wearing it.

"Where'd the accident happen, anyway?" the insurance guy asked.

"Route 22. Out by where the Indians are building the casino."

Leo approached, placed his hand on the small of my back. "Numb Nuts here was driving down to play some blackjack with Tonto and the boys. Didn't realize they haven't broken ground yet." He held out his hand for the investigator to shake. "Leo Blood."

"Shawn Tudesco. Mutual of America."

Leo nodded. "You work out at Hardbodies, right?" Leo said. "Weight lifter, right?"

"Yeah, that's right," he said. "You go there?"

"Me and him both. We play racquetball," Leo said. "His girlfriend works there."

"That right?" he said. "Who? Patti?"

Patti: little pot belly pushing against her leotard, Geraldine Ferraro hairdo. Joy told me once she hoped Patti got the rest of the way through menopause without driving everyone off the deep end. "Joy," I said.

"Joy? *Really?*" He looked at me for the first time—inspected me up and down like I was a dented vehicle. "I know Joy," he said.

"Everyone knows Joy," Leo chimed in. "She's world famous."

The investigator nodded at Leo, then back at me. Smiled. I took both their grins, took the pain that shot up my right arm from the fist I was making. What did *"world famous"* mean? How was I supposed to take *that* little remark?

Mutual of America squatted down and passed his fingers over one of the truck's front tires. "Rubber's good," he said. "Road slippery last night?"

I shrugged. He could read the police report if he was so goddamn curious. Behind the inspector, Leo grabbed an imaginary steering wheel and pantomimed me sleeping. Asshole. Dick-for-brains. . . . World famous as in how? She circulates? She's a slut? What made Leo the big expert on *my* girlfriend?

The investigator leaned against the truck and rocked it. It made a metal-against-metal screech. "Buddy of mine grew up out there by the Indian reservation?" he said. "Just sold his parents' farm to the tribe for *a million and a half.*" He shook his head. "They must have cash flow up the wazoo from the way they're buying up land. Getting it from some billionaire Korean investor is what I heard."

"Malaysian," I said.

"What?"

"*Malaysian* investor. It was in the paper."

"Well, they're getting big bucks from somewhere," Leo chimed in. "One of the chiefs or whatever came into the showroom the other day, him and his two assistants. Mr. VIP. Couldn't talk to anyone but the GM. Ended up paying cash on the barrelhead for this top-of-the-line New Yorker. That damn car was so loaded with extras, it did everything except wipe the guy's ass for him."

The inspector walked over to his Firebird, took out a clipboard and some forms. "It's just like what's happening down in Manhattan," he said. "The way the Japs are buying up the whole damn city, Radio City Music Hall included."

"Hey, speaking of New York," Leo said, "I was just down there this week. Had to go to a meeting with my producer."

Mr. Insurance didn't take the bait. "If that casino goes over," he said, "I hear they're putting in a resort, a golf course, the whole nine yards. And every square inch of it tax-free. That's what burns my butt."

"I'm an actor," Leo said.

The investigator got down on the ground, poked around underneath. "*You and me* pay taxes, right?" he said. "No one's giving *us* a free ride." He'd stuck a bumper sticker onto that briefcase of his: *Power lifters give good thrust.*

I fished around in my shirt pocket, felt those three pain capsules. That's when Big Gene rolled into the dealership in his silver LeBaron. He was scowling his permanent scowl, surveying the Ponderosa. He braked as he was passing us. His power window whirred down. "Hey, Gene," I said. "How's it going?"

Looking right through me, he snapped at Leo. "Where's your hat?"

"Right here, Pop," Leo said, waving it at him. "I just took it off about two seconds ago. To let my head breathe a little. I swear to God."

"Well, put it back on again! We're in the middle of a promotion!"

Hello to you, too, Gene. Nah, I got shaken up a little, but I'm all right. Thanks for asking, you prick. *She* divorced *me* remember? . . . Sometimes I didn't know how Leo stood it—working there, getting reprimanded all the time like a seven-year-old.

Leo suddenly looked older than his age, despite that classy suit, and the role in the movie, and the forty-dollar haircut. "Hey, you can say what you want to about the Indians," he said, "but it's going to go from bad to worse if the Navy cancels those *Seawolf* contracts and EB lays off as many guys as they say they might. I heard they're going to employ a couple thousand people down at that casino once it gets rolling."

"The Navy's not going to cancel those subs," Mutual of America said. "Not with this Persian Gulf situation. You watch. The Russians'll back that lunatic over there and Bush'll have no choice except to escalate. Electric Boat won't be able to crank out submarines fast enough." He totaled something on his calculator, wrote something else on his clipboard. "If Saddam keeps screwing around over in Kuwait, Bush'll kick his ass like he kicked Noriega's. Bush rules, man. He wasn't the head of the CIA for nothing."

"Hey, how old are you, anyway?" I said. Truck or no truck, I couldn't help it. Leo started jingling the change in his pockets.

Mutual of America looked up from his clipboard. "What?"

"What are you? Twenty-three? Twenty-four?"

"I'm twenty-eight," he said. "Why?"

"Because you haven't *seen* the shit that guys our age have seen."

"Like what, for instance?" Don't smirk at me, asshole.

"Like Vietnam. The *last* thing this country needs is for Bush to turn Kuwait into Vietnam II." Leo gave me a zip-the-lip gesture. But I didn't *want* to zip my lip. Mr. Weight Lifter. Mr. Hang Around Down at Health Clubs Impressing All the Women. When he laughed, the sun caught his little red earring.

"Vietnam, Vietnam, Vietnam," he said. "No offense, but it's like a broken record. Get *over* it."

I saw those camouflage washouts down at Hatch. Unit Six. Those guys whose brains Vietnam had eaten. "We *can't,*" I said. "We *can't* get over it. That's the problem."

Why was I doing this—picking a fight with the guy who was going to either make me or break me, insurance-wise? Why couldn't I just shut up?

Leo must have seen the mood I was in because he positioned himself between me and Mutual of America and started talking a mile a minute. "You were saying before about the Indians. Heh heh. . . . All's I know is, if the defense industry goes down the toilet around here, half the state'll be down at that casino, begging for jobs. Who knows? Maybe the Wequonnocs will end up scalping us and saving our sorry asses at the same time. You know what I mean?" He turned back to me. "Hey, Birdsey, didn't you say you needed to call Ray? Have him pick you up? Go up there, use my phone. Hit nine first."

I waited for a second, then started up toward the showroom. Heard fragments of Leo's conversation: "Poor guy's been under a lot of pressure . . . sick brother . . . if you can diddle the numbers a little for him."

Inside, I passed by Omar. Passed Gene's office. He looked away when I nodded at him. Fuck you, Gene! It was *your daughter* who wanted out of that marriage. Not me.

I went back into the bathroom and locked it. Waited for the shaking to pass. I didn't know how much more of this I could take. That was the scary part: Dominick, the tough guy, the *un*crazy twin. . . . I was falling apart at the seams. I reached in my pocket, fingered those three Tylox. "The Father," I said. "The Son." I opened my mouth and popped a pair of them. Decided I'd save the Holy Ghost for later.

When I got out of the bathroom, I stood behind the GOD BLESS AMERICA! window sign and dialed my stepfather's number. Watched the weight lifter through the *O* in GOD. Had he ever diddled my girlfriend was what I wanted to know.

I listened to the phone ring over at the duplex on Hollyhock Avenue. Crooked the phone against my sore neck. Outside, a sudden breeze blew that stupid cap right off Leo's head. Sent Mutual of America's Polaroids flying. The two of them went chasing after their stuff. Assholes, I thought. Idiots.

The phone clicked at Ray's end. " 'Lo?"

When I got back down there, the investigator said he'd decided to total the truck. We'd make out better that way, he told me. He said he'd try and work the numbers a little; there was a little bit of play in there, not too much. He could probably get us about five hundred dollars better than book value. That was about the best he could do.

"Fair enough," I said.

"Oh, it's better than 'fair enough,' " he said. "Say hello to Joy for me."

"I will."

"You do that."

He shook Leo's hand, got back into the Firebird, and roared out of the dealership. Leo and I stood there watching him. "You all right, Dominick?" Leo said.

I told him I'd live. Told him thanks.

He waved me away. "Thanks for what? I didn't do anything. What'd *I* do?"

twenty-nine

Leo approached my stepfather, holding out his hand. "How you doing, Mr. Birdsey?" he said. "Long time no see. Not that I'm complaining."

"Where'd you get that jazzy suit from?" Ray fired back. "You mug a Puerto Rican or something?" It was the way they always sparred with each other. Over the years, against the odds, my stepfather and Leo had come to a mutual appreciation.

Ray walked around the truck, whistling at the front end. "Congratulations," he said, turning to me. "You really outdid yourself. What's that gunk on the windshield?"

"Egg," I said.

"Egg?"

Ray braked slowly, cautiously, gliding over the speed bumps on the way out of the dealership. "You didn't say over the phone that you got hurt," he said. "What's the matter with your hand?"

I filled him in on the seventeen stitches, the pain in my neck. Those two Tylox pills had begun to kick in nicely, though. The pain was still there; I just didn't give a shit about it. Even riding with Ray was a breeze.

He turned onto the post road, accelerating steadily. "She with you when it happened?" *She*. Never her name. No love lost between Joy and Ray.

"Nope." I could feel him looking at me.

"How about insurance? Your insurance paid up?"

I nodded.

"So what are you planning to do for transportation?"

I told him I hadn't gotten that far yet—that Leo was trying to talk me into an Isuzu.

"Bullshit on that!" Ray said. He rolled the window down and spat. "Why should you buy some Jap piece of shit? So you can stuff money into the pockets of that son of a bitch father-in-law of yours?" *Ex*-father-in-law, Ray. The guy didn't even bother to speak to me anymore. "Get yourself a Chevy," he said. "Or a Ford. Ford's a good truck."

"God bless America," I mumbled.

"What?"

"Nothing."

We rode for a while in silence. At a traffic light, I felt him looking over at me again. "Why didn't you tell me over the phone that you got hurt?" he said.

"You didn't ask."

"I shouldn't have to ask," he said. "You're my kid, aren't you?" He fished into his jacket pocket, brought out a couple pieces of hard candy. "Want one?"

I told him no thanks. Asked him what he was doing with candy in his pockets with *his* diabetes. They were sugarless, he said.

I looked out the side window—watched Three Rivers go by. *You're my kid, aren't you?* Much as I hated to admit it, it was more true than untrue—by default. He was here. I'd called and he'd picked up the phone. Had come and gotten me.

"Why didn't they give you one of those collar things at the hospital? If your neck's bothering you?"

"I'm all right, Ray," I said. "I'm fine."

"Well, you don't *look* fine. You look like hell. You had any breakfast?"

I told him I wasn't hungry—that what I wanted was to get my prescription filled and then go over to Gillette Street, pull those shutters, and get back home. Grab a nap if I had time, clean up, and then get ready for the hearing. He gave me an argument, of course—how was I going to remove shutters with my neck hurting and a banged-up hand?

I closed my eyes, repeated that I'd be fine.

He couldn't help me today, he said—he had a doctor's appointment—but he could give me a hand the next day. I told him the doctor who'd stitched me up hadn't said anything about restricting myself.

"Probably figured you had the common sense to know that already," he said.

"Look, Ray," I told him, "I'll feel *better* if I get something accomplished over there, okay? I been trying to get to work on that house all week. I told these people back when we signed the contract that the job'd be done by the end of the summer, and here it is Halloween."

"Don't remind me," he said. "Goddamned foolish holiday." Did I want to know what *he* was doing for Halloween? Turning the lights out and going to bed, that's what. He'd be goddamned if he was going to keep getting up and opening the door all night, have the furnace kick on over and over. He'd stopped answering the door two, three years ago—the year some of the *parents* started holding out bags. Let 'em get their free handouts somewheres else. Whole country was going to hell in a handbasket as far as he was concerned. You could tell when even the *parents* went trick-or-treating.

In the middle of his rant, I remembered that the next day was his birthday. November the first. All Saints' Day. . . . What a bummer that had been when we were kids: after the high of Halloween, the double downer of having to go to church—a holy day of obligation—*and* having to honor the one guy I hated most in the world.

Get over it, I told myself. Ancient history. "You got a birthday coming up, don't you?" I said.

Did he? Guess he did, now that I mentioned it. Hadn't even given it a thought.

"How old you going to be, anyway?" I asked.

"Thirty-nine," he said. "Same as Jack Benny."

"No, really. Sixty-seven, right?" No answer. "You celebrating? Taking some broad out dancing or something?" He scoffed at the idea. Ma was the one who'd always been big on birthdays—Thomas, too, before he got sick. After Ma died, Dessa had taken over all that crap—baking a cake, getting a present, a card. After Dessa left, none of us bothered.

"How much work you got left over at that house of horror, anyway?" Ray asked. "Because if you want, I can give you a hand mornings. Help you knock it off."

I told him thanks anyway. He had enough to do. He should be slowing down a little, instead of taking on other people's work.

"If I didn't think I could swing it, I wouldn't offer," he snapped. "I'm still ticking like a Timex and don't you forget it." He turned the radio on. Turned it off again. If they went through with those layoffs down at the Boat, he said, he might be *looking* for work. Might be able to give me the whole goddamned day. He rolled down the window and spat again. His eye twitched. What drugstore did I want to get my prescription filled at?

I told him I didn't care. Price-Aid, I guessed.

"Price-Aid? They'll charge you an arm and a leg over there. You ought to go to Colburn's. Bob Colburn'll take good care of you."

"Fine," I said. "Let's go to Colburn's." I closed my eyes. Took a couple of deep breaths. If he wanted to go to Colburn's, what had he asked me for?

"Listen," he said. "You know what your problem is? You take on too much."

I told him I was all right.

Yeah? Well, if I was so "all right," how come I'd cracked up my truck in the middle of the night? That didn't sound too "all right" to him.

"Who said I cracked it up in the middle of the night?" I said.

"Your buddy did. Motor Mouth back there at the dealership. He took me aside just now. Says *he's* worried about you, too. You're trying to do too much—run a business all by yourself, run interference for him down there at the bughouse. And it's not like you're getting any help from that little chippy you're living with, either. Not that I can see."

I kept my mouth shut. What Joy and I had going was

none of his business. And as for Thomas, who the fuck else was going to run interference for him down at Hatch? Was *he* suddenly volunteering for the job?

"I know you been bearing the brunt of it," he said. "All that business with him down there. Carrying your own load and his load. My load, too, I guess."

I waited, listened.

"Of course, it was different when your mother was alive. *She* used to look after him. . . . I don't know. It wasn't the same—raising him and raising you. Dead ringers for each other, and you two were like night and day. . . . Used to piss me off sometimes, if you want to know the truth: the way she always doted on him. . . . I don't know. Him and me, we just never hit it off."

No kidding, Ray. I was there, remember? When I opened my eyes, I saw his knuckles gripping the steering wheel.

"But Jesus Christ, what did he have to go and cut off his *hand* for? I don't care *how* crazy he is. That's what's eating *me* up. . . . You two were lucky. You never had to go to war like I did. It *changes* you: being in a war. You come home, you don't want to talk about it, but . . . it just changes you. That's all. The things you see, the things you do, and then you come back into civilian life and . . . When I was stationed over in Italy? I seen a guy get blown apart right in front of me. Cut in half, right at the waist. . . . So every time I think of him going over there to the house and taking my knife off the wall. Taking his hand off *voluntarily*. . . . At the library, of all places. I *know* he's crazy. I *know* he can't help it. But *Jesus* . . ."

It disarmed me—Ray's verbalizing his struggle over what Thomas had done. His out-of-the-blue acknowledgment that there was something vulnerable underneath that armored exterior of his. I looked out the window because I couldn't look at him.

"Just let me give you a hand with that house, all right?" he said. "Because that's what I can handle right now. . . . That's what I can contribute."

I cleared my throat. "Yeah, well, thanks," I said. "We'll see."

We were both quiet for a while—a mile or more. "Hell of a thing, though, ain't it?" Ray finally said. "Down at the

Boat? You give 'em your whole goddamned life down at that shipyard and then they turn around and boot you out the door. Try and fuck with your pension on top of it."

I told him they weren't about to lay off an old goat like him—that the whole place would probably fall apart without him.

"Don't kid yourself, sonny boy," he said. "Us old goats is exactly who they're sending to the slaughterhouse this time. Corporate bastards. They all got a chunk of ice where their heart should be."

I shifted in my seat. "So what are you going to the doctor's for?" I said.

"What? . . . Nothing much."

"What?"

"Nothing. Little numbness in my feet, that's all. Who are you—Dr. Kildare?"

Rounding the next curve, Ray saw her before I did—a woman jogger crossing the road. He swerved, slammed on the brakes. Tylox or not, the pain knifed up my neck.

Ray cranked down his window. "Good way to get yourself killed, there, Suzie Q!" he yelled. And "Suzie Q" raised her arm high in the air. Gave him the middle-finger salute.

Hey! I thought suddenly. It's Nedra Frank!

But after we'd passed, I managed to crane my sore neck back and see that it wasn't Nedra after all. Not even that close—face-wise *or* body-wise.

"Jesus Christ, look at that!" Ray said. "You see that? That's something you never used to see a woman do—sticking her finger up like that. There's that Gloria Steinberg for you. That's *her* big contribution to society."

I was too whipped to get into it with him. . . . And besides, I thought, massaging my neck, even if it *had* been Nedra jogging along just then—even if she *did* surface someday, if I was walking along and *fell* over the bitch—it didn't mean that she had kept my grandfather's manuscript. She'd been totally whacked-out that night—irrational and pissed as hell. She'd probably skidded home in the middle of that snowstorm, gotten into her place, and trashed the damn thing. Destroyed Domenico's history, page by page. . . .

* * *

Ray poked me awake. We were in the parking lot at Colburn's Pharmacy. Did I want him to get me one of those neck collar things while I was in there?

"What? . . . Uh, no."

In the sideview mirror, I saw my brother's face—the way it used to look when we'd wake him up from his nap. Ma and me. Thomas always slept longer than I did—woke up looking lost. Looking like he'd been traveling to some other dimension. . . . I suddenly remembered that dream I'd had the night before, just before I'd crashed the truck: Ma's mother, floating under the ice, her eyes begging me for something. . . .

Colburn's front window was decorated for Halloween. . . . Was tomorrow All Souls' Day or All Saints' Day? I could never remember which was which. Couldn't remember the last time I'd even stepped inside a church, for that matter. . . . *I don't "do" religion,* I heard myself tell Doc Patel. *That's the* other *Birdsey brother.* . . . I was seriously thinking of quitting that whole thing with Patel, anyway: all that dredging up of past history. What purpose did it serve? What could you do about the past? Nothing, that's what. . . . I saw Thomas and me as kids on Halloween. Every year, two hobos with pillowcases—our everyday coats and clothes instead of costumes, our faces smudged with coal dust. Ray tolerated Halloween back then, but he was goddamned if he was going to throw away good money on plastic Dracula capes, rubber monster hands. And we could stop whining about it, too. Home by eight-thirty sharp. Church tomorrow.

Halloween, and then All Saints' Day? All Souls' Day? Ray's birthday . . .

"Ray's birthday!" Thomas would nag, weeks ahead of time.

"I know, I *know* already. Shut up about it, will you?"

How pathetic was this? Forty years old and I could still list the birthday presents my brother had bought for Ray. Coping saw; handheld spotlight; that deluxe shoeshine kit, complete with wooden-handled brushes, polishing cloths, and tins of polish. Thomas would have Ray's presents wrapped a week in advance—have those homemade "Best

Dad in the World" cards colored in and hidden away in his bottom bureau drawer.

Not me. Each November the first, I'd rush around before church, grab a couple of the candy bars I'd hauled in the night before, wrap them up in Sunday funnies from the stack of old newspapers out back. Scrawl "happy birthday" on a piece of loose-leaf paper and Scotch-tape it to the package. Shove it at him. "Here."

The funny thing—the *sad* thing, really—was that Ray never seemed to register the difference in our efforts. "Yeah, okay, thanks," he'd tell us both—embarrassed, I think, to be on the receiving end of gifts. Then he, Ma, Thomas, and I would rush out to the car and ride off to early Mass. They bookended us in the pew, Ma on one end, Ray on the other, Thomas and me in the middle. We sat in the same positions every single time. . . . Grudgingly, guiltily, that morning, I knelt, stood, genuflected—sneaking Halloween candy from my coat pocket up into my mouth. Ate candy in church, right under my stepfather's nose. Ray Birdsey, the religious convert, the heathen-turned-super-Catholic: each sugary bite I took mocked Ray and God, both. Risked their rage . . .

But it was Thomas, not me, who got caught. The year we were fifth graders—our last for trick-or-treating, by Ray's decree. An hour before Mass that morning, my brother had given Ray a transistor radio. He'd come up with the idea the previous summer and walked Mrs. Pusateri's cocker spaniel for months to save up. Ray's eyes were closed, his face hidden in his steepled hands; Ma was clutching her rosary, praying into the cupped hand that shielded her cleft lip. I slipped my brother a roll of Necco wafers. I didn't *like* Necco wafers; my generosity had cost me nothing. Sin with me, Thomas, my hand said. I placed the candy against his palm and squeezed. Be tempted. Eat candy in church like me.

It was the crunch that Ray heard. He looked up, over. That was always the trouble with Thomas: he had never mastered stealth—had never learned the art of hating Ray deeply enough to defy him successfully. Ray reached past me and confiscated the Necco wafers—held up the evidence for my mother to see. He began to stare at Thomas—would not look away. Held Thomas in his gaze from the homily all the way to the consecration. And by the time Father Frigault had turned bread into flesh, wine into the blood of Christ, my brother's whole body trembled in dread of the penance he would pay after Mass.

Ray stood for Communion and waited at the end of the pew. My mother and I rose and walked past him. Thomas rose, too, then sat again—pushed back down by Ray's relentless gaze.

"The body of Christ," Father Frigault said, suspending a Communion wafer before my face as I knelt at the rail.

"Amen," I answered, and stuck out my chocolaty tongue to receive the brittle, tasteless disk, in size and shape not *un*like a Necco wafer. With my tongue, I stuck the Eucharist to the roof of my mouth, soaked it in my sweet saliva, swallowed it. I returned to the pew and knelt beside my brother, who was whimpering now as well as trembling.

Thomas's atonement began in the parking lot, as he reached for the back door handle of our Mercury station wagon. Ray's hand shot out; he clutched my brother's wrist and began walloping him with his free hand. "Dominick," Ma said, "get in the car."

We got in, Ma in the front seat, me in the back. We waited rigidly, silently, while outside Thomas bawled apologies, wriggling like a fish on a hook. St. Anthony's parishioners passed by, some of them staring, others looking away from something that was none of their business. The Birdseys: that poor, mousy woman with the funny lip, those illegitimate twins of hers, and the ex-Navy man who'd been good enough to stand in as their father. He had *his* hands full, that poor guy. Worked down at the Boat and helped keep up the church grounds on weekends. It couldn't be easy with that wife of his, afraid of her own shadow, and those two young hellions. Whatever that one who was getting the dickens had done to make his father mad, it must have been pretty bad.

Ray was silent during the ride from St. Anthony's to Hollyhock Avenue. We all were, except for Thomas, who shuddered involuntarily.

Ray finished punishing my brother in the privacy of our home. *"You're dirt is what you are! You're garbage! Your name is mud!"* Thomas wailed and squatted on the kitchen floor in the duck-and-cover position we'd learned at school. *"A goddamned embarrassment to your mother and me! A greedy little pig!"* For the grand finale, Ray reached for his brand-new transistor radio, wound back like a pitcher, and hurled it as hard as he could against the wall. Plastic cracked, batteries flew across the room. *"There you go, piggy boy! That's for you! How do you like* them *apples?"*

That evening, Ma lit Ray's birthday cake with a shaky hand. In a wobbly voice, she led us in reluctant rounds of "Happy Birthday" and "For He's a Jolly Good Fellow." When Ray refused to blow out his candles, she leaned over and blew them out for him. Having married Ray Birdsey for better or worse, she was determined to believe in his jolly good fellowship, no matter what the evidence said. No matter what the feeling in our stomachs. "A *small* piece, please," Thomas requested. "No ice cream, please." Ray stood and left the room, his cake and ice cream untouched.

Thomas never squealed on me—never told Ray that it was I, not he, who had smuggled the candy into Mass. And I never confessed—never picked up the heavy end of what had really happened that morning. That was the irony of it, the bitter pill I've swallowed my whole life since: that *I* was the guilty one, the one who deserved Ray's wrath. But it was always Thomas he kept in his rifle sight. It was always Thomas who Ray went after.

"Here," I told my brother that night of our stepfather's happy birthday tirade. "I don't even *want* this crap. Take it." And I'd flung Milky Ways, Skybars, and Butterfingers onto his bed.

Thomas shook his head. "I don't want it, either."

"Why not?"

He burst into tears. "Because I'm dirt. Because I'm nothing but a greedy little pig."

Ray would lie in wait for him. Nail him every chance he got. But still, every Father's Day, every birthday and Christmas: "To the best dad in the whole wide world!"

Statute of limitations, I thought, sitting slumped in Ray's Galaxy at Colburn's Pharmacy, half zoned-out on Tylox. All that's ancient history. Why dig up the past? Why go sit in that office every week and tell her your big tale of woe?

* * *

When we got to the Roods' house, Ray told me he'd swing by and pick me up as soon as he got out of the doctor's. "Maybe I'll stop by the medical supply place first and get you one of those collars," he said. "Just in case you want it later. Get you a leash while I'm at it, too. And a flea collar."

I got out of the car. He warned me not to overdo it. He could help me tomorrow, he reminded me. If the Roods couldn't wait one more day, then fuck 'em.

I'd been there half an hour or more—had managed to pull most of the downstairs shutters—when Ruth Rood came to the window. She waved. I waved back.

It was awkward working with one hand; it was a royal pain in the ass. Ray was right: my coming here to work today of all days had been a stupid idea. Blood was beginning to seep through the bandage—not much, just a little. I'd probably just busted a few of the stitches. My hand hurt. And how was I going to get these damn shutters back to my place, anyway? They weren't going to fit in Ray's Galaxy and I'd forgotten to ask him about borrowing Eddie's truck. Maybe Leo could arrange a loaner at the dealership. Or maybe Labanara would let me borrow his truck. I couldn't take any more painkiller until after that hearing at four o'clock. Once the stuff I'd already taken wore off, my hand and my neck were really going to let me know they were there.

Ruth Rood came out onto the porch in her bathrobe. She just stood there, her hands wringing a dish towel the same way Ma used to do when she was nervous. Ruth looked like she wanted to say something.

"How's it going?" I said. I kept working, trying to loosen a rusted hinge screw.

"I didn't hear you drive up," she said.

I told her I'd gotten dropped off. "Had an accident last night," I said. "Totaled my truck." Her eyes said nothing. My well-being barely registered a blip on her radar.

She walked to the far end of the porch and stood there for a minute, her back to me. Was she crying? "As it turns out, this isn't a very good day for you to be here," she said.

"Henry's having a bad time right now. He's not in very good shape."

I stopped. Stared at her.

"He's depressed," she said.

Henry's not in good shape? *Henry*'s depressed? Her saying that got me so mad, so fast, that the frozen screw I'd been working on creaked and started turning. Hadn't she and Henry been running a three-week harassment campaign to get me over there? If I had a buck for every message those two had left on my machine . . .

"I'm not going to be here that much longer anyway," I said. "I just have to pull the rest of these shutters, like I told you on the phone. Should be out of here in an hour."

"It might be better if you just left now," she said. "Can . . . can you just go?"

I reminded her that I'd wrecked my truck—that I couldn't leave until my ride got there. God, I hated these people.

"All right," she said. She turned and went back inside the house.

I was *pissed*. Hand or no hand, sore neck or not, I dragged and yanked and raised my extension ladder until it rested against the second story. One-handed, I gripped the side of the ladder and started to climb. One thing about working angry: it made the adrenaline pump. Even with all the trips up and down the ladder, I got those second-story shutters off faster than I had the ones on ground level. Gimp or not, rusted screws or no rusted screws, I was cooking. Working up a sweat. Not thinking, for once, about my truck or my brother or who had knocked up my girlfriend.

By the end of an hour, it had caught up to me, though. I'd removed and stacked all the shutters on both floors. Fuck that pair up on the third story, I thought. I made my good hand a visor and squinted up at that attic window, the little tar-roofed widow's walk. Made more sense to just ring the goddamned bell and walk up through the house, anyway. Climb out onto that little porch from the attic window. But, hey, I wouldn't want to disturb poor Henry while he was depressed, now, would I? Not when poor Henry was having himself such a bad day. He should trade places with *me* if he wanted to know what a bad day was really like. Trade places with my brother. *That* would cure his depression. As far as I was concerned, old Henry was living the good life.

I walked to the sidewalk and looked all the way down Gillette. Looked the other way. No sign of Ray. Buying that friggin' neck collar was probably what was holding him up. Either that or they were way the hell behind at the doctor's office. I had to get home—go over those notes for the hearing. Whatever the holdup was, I was probably going to kiss that nap goodbye.

I sat down on the Roods' front wall. Looked back at those top floor shutters. *I can give you a hand mornings.* That'd be great: Putting up with Ray every day on the job on top of everything else. Listening to him tell me how *he* would have done something—how my way was all wrong. . . . *Just a little numbness in my feet.* That was all I needed: him up there on the ladder some day and he can't feel his feet on the rungs. What was that numbness from, anyway? The diabetes? I hadn't even asked him.

My hand was starting to throb like a bastard. Still no Ray. I reached into my shirt pocket, fished out the last of the pain pills. If I took it now, I'd be clear-headed by four o'clock. How was I supposed to go home and sleep if I was in *this* much pain? Sheffer would love that, though: me arriving for the big hearing stoned. *If anyone's going to convince the Security Board to release him, paisano, it's going to be you. . . .*

I looked back up at those third-floor shutters. Fuck it, I thought. I was just sitting around waiting, anyway. If I got that last pair of shutters down, then that'd be all of them. Maybe I'd bring 'em down to Willard's and have them dip-stripped instead of scraping them all myself. Bite the bullet. I was already losing money on this job anyway. Screw it.

I flip-flopped my thirty-foot extension ladder over to the widow's walk. It'd be easier than the second-floor windows, actually: just climb over that little railing and onto the porch up there. *This isn't really a very good day for you to be here.* She had one hell of a nerve. . . . I climbed up, up—over the railing.

From up there, I could see all the way to the end of Gillette and out to Oak Street. See a little sliver of the river, even. Still no sign of Ray. I had to get home, go over those notes for the hearing a few more times. Grab a shower; I must be getting pretty rank by now. Doctor had said not to get the bandage wet—to wear a plastic bag or something. God forbid Joy should be home to give me a hand. . . . Hurry *up,* Ray.

The left shutter came off easily: the window frame was so rotted out, I could pull the hinge screws out by hand after the first few turns. It might be a bitch to get that shutter back in there tight, but getting it off was *no* problem. I lifted it, adjusting it as best I could for the climb back over the railing, the descent.

Something moved against my hand—a leathery flutter against my wrist. "Jesus!" I muttered, letting the shutter go. It banged against the railing, bounced, fell over the side.

I was watching it break apart on the ground below when a black blur flew back up at me. For half a second I thought, stupidly, that it was part of the shutter—shrapnel or something. Then I realized what it was. Saw it up close and personal: a goddamned *bat.*

"Get out of here!" I yelled, shooing it away. Man, I hate bats; I'm scared of them. You ever want proof that there's evil in the world, go look at a bat up close.

It circled back to where it had been sleeping, hovered, looking for the protection of the missing shutter. Then it landed on the top of the sill, three feet away from my face.

I stared at it and it stared back—cocked its little walnut-sized head and studied me. When it opened its jaws and hissed, I was close enough to see the pinkish-gray inside of its mouth, its little saber teeth. My heart chugged. I broke out in a sweat. . . . This little fucker could have just wasted you, I told myself. It could be *you* busted up on the ground down there, instead of that shutter.

It kept shifting its head, staring. Watching me. I reached into my tool belt and found some glazing points—started pelting them at it. It hissed again, flapped its wings, and flew to a nearby tree. "And *stay* there!" I said. Leaned against the house for a second to let the wooziness pass.

That's when I saw him. Rood. He was standing there at the attic window, staring. Was he looking *at* me? *Past* me? It was scary, the way he kept looking. And there I was, too, my reflection in the glass superimposed over him. "What?" I said. "What do you want?" Thought: Get away from me, man. Stop *staring*.

He put the gun in his mouth. I stumbled back.

Fell.

The rush toward the ground was soundless. I could see them both—in slow motion and in a gleaming streak—my daughter and my mother. Angela spun in a kind of pirouette. She was wearing a pure white dress.

thirty

"Carry the corpse," the monkey says.

"Which corpse?"

"He's hanging from the cedar tree."

And then I see him, the rope around his neck, his naked body swaying back and forth, back and forth. I approach him slowly, and he raises his arms as if for an embrace. His severed hand has grown back.

"But he's alive," I say.

"Kill him," the monkey says. "Carry the corpse."

My heart pounds. I'm afraid not to obey. When I step onto a rock, he and I are at eye level. I look away from his pleading gaze. Lift the bag over his head and pull. He bucks, flails, twitches. Then he's still.

I cut him down from the tree. Carry him over my shoulder, stumbling toward the sound of spilling water. And when I see the water, my burden lightens and I realize it's no longer my brother's corpse I'm carrying. It's the monkey's corpse.

"Forgive me," it whispers, its lips moving against my ear. I stop, surprised that the dead can talk.

"Forgive you for what?"

The monkey sighs.

* * *

Miguel, the night nurse, pointed to the bag hanging from a pole next to my bed. "It's not you, man," he said. "It's the morphine. Lots of patients freak out on this stuff."

I held up my hands to look at them—the stitched one and the other. I had smothered my own brother—had felt life leaving him. "It seemed so real," I said.

Miguel cupped his hand under the popsicle I'd been nibbling and held it in front of me. I took another bite. "That's the kicker with hallucinations, right?" he said. "Is it real or is it Memorex? You ever do acid?"

I shook my head, awkwardly because of the neck brace.

"I dropped it a coupla times—back in my *hombre* days, before Wife Number Two got ahold of me and parked my butt in an LPN program. One time when I was tripping, I thought I was running with a pack of wild dogs. Thought I was turning *dog,* man. I could have sworn it was real. . . . Hey, you want any more of this? It's getting a little drippy."

I said no. Reached up and grabbed the chain bar suspended above my bed. Shifted my position an inch or two. "What's this for, anyway?" I said, tapping the soft cast on my shoulder.

"Tore your trapezius muscle—caught a corner of the porch roof on the way down, I guess. I was talking to one of the EMTs that brought you in? This guy that goes to my church? He was telling me about it. Said they were working on you for a good five minutes before they realized they had the wrong guy. . . . Hey, how's that catheter feel?"

"Better," I said.

"You sure?" As he lifted the blanket and sheet to have a look, I raised my head. Looked down at my swollen, stapled leg, my purple eggplant of a foot. "Jesus, what a mess," I said. Looked away and shuddered.

"Coulda been worse, man," Miguel said. "Coulda been worse."

According to Miguel, when the EMTs had arrived at 207 Gillette Street in response to Ruth Rood's hysterical 911 call, they'd found me unconscious in the front yard, adrift on a pile of broken shutters. The medics made two incorrect assumptions: that I was Henry Rood and that the tumble I'd taken was the suicide attempt Mrs. Rood had been screaming about over the phone. My left leg was splayed beneath me; my foot was cocked at a right angle to where it should have been. My fibula had separated from its ball-and-socket joint, splintered, and was poking out of my leg. They had me sedated and were readying me for transport before someone finally deciphered Ruth Rood's ranting about the attic, her husband, the gun he'd fired into his head.

I remembered the fall but not the landing. Flashes of the aftermath flickered back at me: a barking dog among the sidewalk gawkers, someone screaming bloody murder when they tried to take off my work boot. (Had the screamer been me?) I told Miguel I didn't remember the pain. "That's cause your brain acts like a circuit breaker," he said. "When it gets too intense, a switch flips you unconscious." He flipped his hand back and forth to demonstrate. "Computer this, computer that," he said. "If you want high tech, give me the human body any day."

Henry Rood had been pronounced dead on arrival at Shanley Memorial, Miguel said, although he'd probably died a second or two after he pulled the trigger. According to what Miguel's friend had told him, the back half of Rood's head was all over the wall and the floor. I arrived at Shanley shortly after Rood, I was told, in a *second* ambulance with a *second* trio of EMTs. Dr. William Spencer, chief of orthopedic surgery, was called away from a father-and-son golf tournament halfway across the state and arrived at Shanley somewhere around 6:00 P.M. It was he who made the decision that my shattered foot and ankle and the broken and dislocated bones of my lower leg required reconstructive surgery right away. That night. The operation began shortly after seven and lasted until sometime after midnight, by which time fourteen bones and bone fragments had been rejoined with screws and plastics and two curved steel plates. My leg had so much metal in it, Miguel said, it could probably conduct electricity.

I asked him how Mrs. Rood was doing—if he'd heard anything.

Miguel shrugged. "The funeral's Monday. I seen it in the paper. Hey, you better excuse me for a minute. I gotta check on your buddy over there." He tiptoed to the other side of the room and disappeared behind the drawn curtain.

When I closed my eyes, I saw Rood at the attic window, staring. He'd gone out angry, that was for sure. I'd read that someplace: when they leave that much of a mess behind, they're getting even with the cleanup crew. Ruth, probably: he must have been evening some score with his poor, pickled wife. But why had he dragged *me* into it? Gone up there and given *me* the evil eye just before he did it? I started to shake, a little at first and then uncontrollably.

"Miguel? . . . Hey, Miguel?"

His head popped out from behind the curtain. "What's the matter? You cold?" He told me he needed to check on a few things but that he could come back in a few minutes with another blanket. He left the room.

I closed my eyes and tried to unsee Rood. Wandered back, instead, to my morphine nightmare. The monkey, the cedar tree. . . . I'd strangled my own brother, for Christ's sake: morphine or no morphine, what kind of a sick son of a bitch would dream up something like *that*? A wave of nausea passed through me. I grabbed for the plastic tray on my bedstand and missed, retching bile and melted popsicle all over the front of me.

When Miguel came back, he cleaned up the mess and changed my johnny. "How you doing now?" he said. "You feel better now?"

I managed a weak smile. "Can you . . . Are you real busy?"

"What do you need, man?"

"I was . . . I was wondering if you could sit with me. Stay with me for a while. I'm just . . . I . . ."

"Yeah, all right," he said. "It's a pretty slow night. I guess I can swing that." He sat beside my bed.

"What . . . what day is it, anyway?" I asked. "I don't even know what *day* it is."

"It's Saturday," he said. He craned his neck around to see the clock in the corridor. "1:35 A.M."

"Saturday? How can it be Saturday?"

"Because yesterday was Friday, man. You been in and out

of it for a couple days now. More out than in, to tell you the truth. That first night you came in here, you were one of the most out-of-it dudes I ever seen at this place. Kept trying to get off the bed, yank out your IV. That would have been something, huh? You getting out of bed and trying to walk on *that* foot? Between the surgery and the Percoset and then the morphine drip, you were—"

It began to sink in: I had never made it to Thomas's hearing. I'd blown it for my brother. "What . . . what's the date?"

"The date? Today? November the third."

I saw Thomas, the bag over his head. I grabbed hold of the bed railings and tried to raise myself up. "I've got to use the phone," I said. "*Please.* I've got to find out what happened to him."

He looked at me as if I were hallucinating again. "What happened to who?"

"My brother. Did you hear anything? About what happened to him?"

Miguel shrugged. "I heard about your truck. I didn't hear nothing about your brother. Why? What's the matter with him?"

I told him it was too complicated to go into—that I just needed to make a call.

"Who you going to call at one-thirty in the morning, man? Look, you're a little disorientated, that's all. It happens when you been laying in bed for two, three days. You call somebody this time a night, they're gonna come down here and bust your *other* foot. You ain't thinking, man. You got to wait till morning."

Before, I might have balked. Might have jumped all over him. But I had nothing left to fight with. I felt helpless, overwhelmed. I burst into tears.

"Hey, *hombre,*" Miguel said. "Come on. Everything's going to be okay. It's the morphine." He reached over and took my hand. I could call whoever I wanted in the morning, he promised. If he was still on, he'd dial the number for me himself. He held my hand until the shaking subsided.

Miguel said he had worked a double shift the night before. Had met my family. He asked if my brother was the tall guy who'd been here with my father and my wife.

He'd visited me? Thomas? Had they released him, then?

"Did he . . . We're twins," I said. "Did he look like me?"

Miguel shrugged. "This guy was tall, a little on the stocky side. He had dark hair like you, but I wouldn't say he *looked* like you. He kept talking about how he was going to be in some movie."

I closed my eyes. "That's my friend," I said. "Leo."

Had he just said my wife had been there? I had no recollection of visitors.

"I seen that guy *some*place. I just can't remember where. Is he *really* going to be in a movie, or was he just b-s-ing me?"

"I don't know," I said. "My . . . You said my wife was here?"

He nodded, his face breaking into a grin. "Hey, if you don't mind my saying so, that's one fine-looking woman you got there. And you and her got a kid on the way, right? Beginning of May? She was telling me all about it."

Joy. It was Joy who'd been here. Not Dessa.

"Hey, just think: by the time your kid gets out of the oven, you'll be back on your feet, running around good as new. Changing diapers and everything."

I closed my eyes again. Suppressed another shudder.

"Me and my wife just had a kid last month," he said. "Our third. Plus I got a daughter from my first marriage. Blanca. Four kids in all. Blanca's nineteen already. I can't even believe it sometimes." He took out his wallet and showed me their pictures.

A kid in the oven . . .

"Hey, come on, buddy," Miguel said. "You gotta think positive. Look. That's my wife right there." His thumb tapped a stocky, long-haired brunette at the center of a family portrait. Even through the blear of my tears, I was taken by the directness of her gaze back at the camera. At me. I mumbled something about her being a nice-looking woman, too. "Yeah, and she don't take no crap from nobody, either. Me, especially. She's three-quarters French Canadian and one-quarter Wequonnoc. You don't mess with that mix. Know what I'm saying?"

I handed his pictures back. Blew my nose. Cleared my

throat. "Married to a Wequonnoc, huh?" I said. "Once the big casino goes in, you'll probably have to quit nursing to stay home and count all your money."

He laughed. "Hey, I like the way you think, man. Maybe in a few years, you might be looking at the Puerto Rican Donald Trump. Who knows, right?"

There was a lull for the next few minutes. The intermittent whir of the IV machine, the sound of snoring across the room, behind the curtain.

"She's my girlfriend," I said.

"Hmm?"

"She's my girlfriend. Joy. She's not my wife."

"Yeah? Well, if you two are having a kid together, it's the same difference. You and her got married as soon as that test said 'positive,' know what I'm saying? This your first?"

We lost eye contact. "*Her* first," I said.

"Yeah?"

"I . . . had another kid. A daughter."

"Sounds like you don't see her anymore."

I shook my head.

"That's gotta be tough, man. Not being able to see your kid. That's one thing my ex and I did right. We worked it out so I saw Blanca every weekend. It was worth it, too, because she turned out good. She's studying to be a legal secretary. . . . So where's your daughter at? She live in another state?"

"She's dead."

It stopped him for a minute. I didn't usually come clean like that—unload on people about Angela. But I was too tired to keep up the front.

"Wow, that's tough, man," Miguel said. "Ain't nothing tougher than that. . . . But, hey, now you got this new one coming, right? You gotta think positive. And I mean it—she's a very good-looking woman, your girlfriend. I wouldn't mind checking out of the hospital and going home to *that* myself, you know? I don't mean no disrespect."

"Was there . . . Did anyone else visit me?"

"Anyone else?" He shook his head. "Not on my shift. Not that I seen, anyway. Just your girlfriend and your father and that other guy—the movie star."

* * *

The Three Rivers State Hospital switchboard answered promptly at 7 A.M. and transferred my call to the security station at Hatch, Unit Two. No, the guard who answered said, they weren't authorized to give out patient information over the phone. No, he could *not* give me Lisa Sheffer's home phone number, even if it *was* an emergency. The best he could do was try to contact her and give her my message.

There was no answer at Ray's. And when I called home, all I got was the sound of my own voice, yapping about free estimates, satisfaction guaranteed. Five minutes later, the phone rang.

"Dominick?" Sheffer said. "How *are* you? When I found out what happened, I was like, 'Oh, my *god.*' "

I asked her if they'd postponed the hearing.

There was a pause. "Look, you know what?" she said. "Why don't I come see you? I think it would be better if we went over all this in person. You feeling well enough for visitors?"

"Just *tell* me," I said. "Did they postpone it or go ahead with it?"

"They went ahead."

"Where is he?"

"Where is he? Now? He's at Hatch, Dominick. Look, let me just make sure my friend can watch Jesse for an hour or so, and I'll get there as soon as I can. Okay?"

I got the phone back on the cradle, but dropped the whole damn thing trying to get it back on the nightstand. Tried unsuccessfully to grab it by the cord and pull. When I looked over at the other bed, I saw my roommate—lying on his side, awake, watching me. "You want me to get that for you?" he said.

Getting out of bed, he let go a long, rumbling fart. "Whoops. 'Scuse *me,*" he said. His slippers scuffed across the room. "One of the side effects of this diet they started me on. Gives me terrible gas."

He picked up the phone. Stood there, rocking on the balls of his feet. "Nice to see you back among the living," he said. He was about fifty or so—gray hair, beard, beer gut under his cinched bathrobe. Go back to your bed, I felt like saying. I don't want to socialize. Leave me alone.

He looked down at my uncovered leg, my foot. "Ooh, baby, that's gotta smart," he said. "How's it feel?"

I shrugged. "Not bad. I guess they got me pretty well doped up."

"Yeah, well . . . How else you gonna get through it, right? . . . They were telling me about it—the nurses—when you came in a couple days ago. Took quite a tumble, huh?"

"So I hear."

"I'm in here with a bum gut," he said. "Bleeding ulcer." He tapped his belly with his fist. "They think they got it under control, though. They just want to watch me through the weekend. I'm probably checking out on Monday."

"Uh-huh. Good." I closed my eyes. Listened to him scuff back to bed.

Why couldn't Sheffer have just told me over the phone what had happened? Because it was *bad* news, that was why. Break it gently to the poor gimp. . . .

Bleeding Ulcer over there was getting out when? Monday? How long was *I* going to be stuck in here? And how long was I going to be out of commission once I *did* get out? I needed to talk to that surgeon. Doctor . . . ? Jesus, the guy had operated on me for five hours and I couldn't even remember his name. Couldn't even picture him. And I'd probably have to wait until Monday to talk to him, too; I doubted chief surgeons showed their faces on the weekend.

Be patient, honey, I heard Ma say. *You need to be more patient with people.*

And how much was this whole fiasco going to cost me? The truck, a five-hour operation, an extended stay at Club Med here. I'd crunched some numbers back in September—just before Thomas's "big event" down at the library—and even *then* I'd figured I was probably only going to clear twenty-two, twenty-three grand for the year, give or take a few inside jobs in November and December. Of course, those jobs were shot to hell now. And what if my climbing-up-and-down-ladders days were over altogether? There was no way in hell I'd be able to afford contracting out. . . . My insurance *had* to cover falls, right? I'd have to wait until Monday for answers on that, too. Doubted I could decipher that mumbo jumbo the policy was written in. Just the *thought* of making those insurance calls exhausted me. *If you want to file a personal claim, press one. If you want to file a business claim, press two. If your entire life's going down the toilet, please stay on the line. . . .*

I pictured that house of horror over there on Gillette Street—framed in scaffolding, scraped and burned down to bare wood, waiting for primer and paint. Jesus Christ, that house was like a curse or something. Maybe I could talk Labanara into finishing the job for me. Or Thayer Kitchen over in Easterly. Kitchen did drywall, mostly, but he'd paint if he was between jobs. Whoever I got to finish it, I'd just have to pay him out of pocket. Screw it. It'd be worth taking the loss just for the privilege of not having to go back there again. . . .

I wondered how Ruth Rood was doing. Hell of a thing: goes up to the attic and there's her husband's brains all over the place. Who gets the fun job of cleaning up something like that, anyway? Not Ruth, I hoped. That son of a bitch Rood. Once she got past the shock, she'd be better off without him. Who wouldn't drink, married to *that* guy?

Better off without him: the exact words Dessa's father had used when she made her big announcement to the family that she was going ahead with the divorce. Leo told me that. It was after the dealership's annual Fourth of July picnic out at the Constantines'—after all the employees had gone home and it was just the family. We'd been separated for a couple of months by then. . . . Jesus, that hurt, though: hearing from Leo that the Old Man had said that. *Better off without him.* We'd always gotten along okay—Gene and me. We'd had a kind of mutual respect for each other. Plus, there'd been all that time we'd logged in together after the baby died, when Dessa had had to keep calling her mother, having her mother come over. Big Gene would always come, too. We'd just sit there, him and me, staring at the idiot box and waiting for time to pass. Waiting for Dessa to stop crying and realize that Angela's death wasn't, somehow, *her* fault. *Our* fault. . . . Hey, I'd wrestled with that one, too. *Still* wrestled with it sometimes: if only I'd done this, if only I'd done that. "You're like a son to me, Dominick," Gene had said to me one of those nights. One of us must have turned off the TV; guess he had to say *something*. "Like the son I never had." And I'd bought it, too—believed Big Gene, who'd made his fortune selling half-truths and false promises to car buyers. It wasn't as if I hadn't been looking for my real father my whole life. . . . But what had I expected? That he'd be loyal to *me* instead of his firstborn daughter? His pride and joy? What did I even *know* about a father's loyalty, anyway? I'd had a great role model in that particular department, whoever the guy was who'd knocked up my mother. Left her pregnant with twins. As far as fathers went, I was unclaimed freight. Me and my brother—left on the loading dock for life. Ray Birdsey's twin step-burdens. . . .

And as long as I was lying there, not bullshitting myself for once, I might as well admit it: Big Gene was right, wasn't he? She *was* better off without me. Me and all my baggage—shitty childhood, crazy brother, even that vasectomy I'd gone out and gotten. That had been it for Dessa, the last straw—my vasectomy. Getting myself sterilized without even discussing it. Going behind her back and having it done while she was away so that . . . so that . . . *Your anger poisons everything else that's good about you,* she'd said that morning she packed her bags. *I'm going because you suck all the oxygen out of the room, Dominick. Because I have to breathe. . . .* And she'd been right, hadn't she? Lying here in "time-out," benched by my big fall off the Roods' roof, I could finally *see* it. *See* what she meant. Getting myself fixed like that, cutting off even the *possibility* of kids . . . you had to be one angry motherfucker to do something like that. And what about that father's loyalty crap I was always so hung up by the balls about? What about *that,* Birdsey? What's so loyal about a father who goes over there and puts his feet in those stirrup things and has them sever his options. Sever, even, the *possibility* of another kid. That had been *real* loyal, hadn't it, Dominick? Loyal to her, to your marriage, to any kid that might have come along later. . . . That was why she'd gone away to Greece, she'd said. To decide whether or not she wanted to try again. And she'd come back knowing she *did* want to. . . . So face it, Birdsey. Own up to it. *You* did more to end your marriage than she did. She might have been the one to pack her bags because she couldn't "breathe," but it was you who ended it. *You* who'd sucked out all the oxygen. Killed off the possibility, the hope of anything ever . . . And all those reconciliation fantasies you'd been fooling yourself with—all those rides past that farmhouse where she and her boyfriend lived now. It was *sick*, man. . . . I was like some ghost haunting what she and I had had and lost, instead of just getting on with it. I'd gone out there the night I totaled the truck, come to think of it. I'd been pulling that shit for years now. For *years*. . . . Too bad I hadn't totaled *myself* along with my truck. Or maybe I had. Maybe I'd totaled myself the day I'd gone down there to that urologist's and spread my legs and said, "Here I am. Disconnect me. Cut off my options." Totaled. It was like . . . it was like Angela's death had been this huge, mangled wreck in the middle of our marriage. And Dessa . . . Dessa had gotten up and gotten on with it. Had walked away from the wreck. And I hadn't. I was road kill, man. *Road kill.*

Don't cry. De-fense! De-fense!

Well, screw it, man. I was too *tired* to play D anymore. I didn't give a crap whether Mr. Bleeding Ulcer over in the other bed heard me or not. I was exhausted. Used up. If I had to cry, then tough shit. . . .

Did Ruth Rood have family to lean on, I wondered. Some friend who'd go over there and sit with her? She wasn't a bad woman. She'd been decent to me, in spite of all the hassle about their house. . . . I saw Rood up in that window again—the way he'd stood there, staring out at me. Why me, Henry? Why'd you have to go up to that attic and stare that way at *me*? What were you doing, you bastard—inviting me along for the ride?

God, I couldn't stand much more of this—just lying there, thinking. Only what was I supposed to do? Get out of bed and walk away from it? Hop into the truck I'd totaled and *go*? Miguel had said something about being able to give me something to make me sleep, hadn't he? That's what I *wanted* to do, man: Rip Van Winkle my way through the rest of my sorry-ass life. Wake up after everyone I knew was dead and that baby Joy was pretending was mine had reached the age of majority. Wake me when it's over, man. Wake me up at checkout time. Except the only catch with sleeping was dreaming. Dead monkeys, dead brothers. Jesus. . . . So let's see, Dominick. You don't want to sleep, you don't want to stay awake. Guess that eliminated everything but the third option. The big *D*. . . . And if I chose that route, *how*? It scared me a little to think about it, but it jazzed me up a little, too. I knew one thing: I wouldn't make a mess the way Rood had. No one deserved that. So she'd slept with some guy behind my back. Gotten herself pregnant. That didn't give me the right to fuck with her head for the rest of her life.

My roommate let another one rip. "Whoops," he said. "Excuse me again." I tried to ignore him. Maybe I didn't have to go to the trouble of offing myself, after all. Maybe all's I had to do was lie here and get asphyxiated.

"Hey, you want the newspapers?" he said. "I got the *Record* and the *New York Post*. I'm through with 'em." Before I could say no, he'd swung his legs to the floor and started over.

"Thanks," I said. "I'll look at 'em later."

"Whenever you want," he said. "I don't want 'em back. Hey, no kidding, I'm sorry about all this gas. It's this diet they got me on. I can't help it."

"No problem," I said. Thought: Okay, now get back in bed and shut up. I don't *want* to be your hospital buddy. Just let me lie here and think—play with the idea of dying.

"By the way, my name's Steve," he said. "Steve Felice."

He waited. Kept looking at me. "Dominick Birdsey."

"Housepainter, right?"

I shrugged. "*Used* to be. I don't know what's going to happen now. With my leg." He just stood there, waiting. "What . . . what do you do?"

"Me? I'm a purchasing agent. Down at EB." He told me we were both in the same boat, in a way. Hell of a thing—not knowing from month to month if the next round of layoffs was going to zap you. It got to you after a while. That was how he'd gotten his ulcer—not knowing if he was going to have a job by the end of the year or not. He'd always been pretty easygoing before all this. *Relatively* easygoing, anyway. *He* thought so, anyway. But what the hell, he said. He heard the Indians were going to start hiring in the spring.

They'd need purchasing agents down there, right? Big operation like that? They'd need to *order* things. *Buy* things. Or maybe he'd go down there and try something completely different—deal blackjack, maybe, or train to manage one of the restaurants that were going in down there. That's what life was about, right? Taking chances? Shuffling the deck a little?

I told him my stepfather worked down at Electric Boat.

"Yeah," he said. "Big Ray. We been shooting the shit last couple of days, him and me. He's been here three or four times to see you."

He had?

"He's going to be glad to see you today, I tell you. You know, clear-headed—back to normal again. You been a little discombobulated. He's been worried about you."

"Has he?"

"Well, *sure* he has. He was telling me how he got over to that place where you were working just as they were loading you into the ambulance. He was supposed to pick you up over there, right? Hell of a thing to have to drive up to: your kid being loaded into an ambulance, screaming bloody murder, and you can't do a damn thing about it. *Sure* he's been worried. My two are grown up and out of the house now and I *still* worry. It never stops. You wait till yours comes along. When's the little woman due? May, is it?"

What had Joy done—stood up on a chair and made a big announcement?

"You'll see. When it's your kid, you're going to worry no matter what." Climbing back into bed, he cut another fart. "Whoops," he said. "Thar she blows again. *Pardone*."

I reached for the phone. Dialed Ray. Figured I'd give him the big medical bulletin: that I'd come back to Planet Earth. But there was still no answer over there. I dialed my own house again. This time, she answered, groggy-voiced. "It's me," I said. "I'm back from the dead."

There was a pause at the other end. "Dominick?"

"Yeah. You didn't cash in my life insurance policy yet, did you?"

She sounded relieved, I'll give her that. She kept repeating my name. She might have been crying—she's not a big crier as a rule, but she might have been. We talked for half an hour or more. Caught up. She did most of the talking. By the time I hung up, she'd filled me in on her three-day vigil at the hospital, all the ways that Ray had driven her crazy, how her morning sickness had begun to set in in earnest. She'd finally gotten through to Dr. Spencer the night before, she said.

That was the surgeon's name: Spencer, Dr. Spencer. . . .

He said they'd know more after the swelling went down—it was a waiting game until then, but he was cautiously optimistic. He was a little concerned about the amount of painkiller they'd had to give me. A necessary evil, he'd said, due to the severity of the break—*breaks*. But he didn't want me to end up drug-dependent on top of everything else I was facing. It was going to be a tough enough row to hoe. Eight to ten days in the hospital, he figured—limited physical therapy beginning on Monday. I'd probably need PT for a good six months, minimum. They still weren't sure about permanent damage; it could go either way. I might be facing more surgery—six to nine months down the line, maybe. "He said it was one of the most complicated breaks he's ever worked on," Joy said. "He might even write about it for some medical journal. He said he'd like you to sign a release so that—"

"What about Thomas?" I said. "Did you hear anything? How *he* made out?"

A sigh. A long pause. "Dominick," she said. "Why don't you worry about yourself for once instead of your brother? Maybe if you'd been taking care of yourself instead of running around like a chicken with your head cut off for the past—"

"I missed his hearing, Joy. I failed him."

"Honest to God, Dominick. *Listen* to me. You have to stop trying to be his big savior and start taking care of Dominick instead. Why do you think this happened to you, anyway? Have you stopped to think about that? The way you've been rushing down there every two seconds, losing sleep, getting all hyped up over your brother? Worry about *yourself,* Dominick. Worry about *me*. About our *baby*."

Our baby: how could she do it? Just lie through her teeth

like that? Because she was basically dishonest, that was why. Because truthfulness had never quite gotten hardwired in Joy. And I was supposed to just live out this charade with her? Act the part of the chump and pretend I was this baby's father? Become *Ray,* the substitute dad I'd hated all my life?

Joy said she'd be down to see me as soon as she got cleaned up and had something to eat. *If* she could even stand to eat. She hadn't been able to keep anything down except strawberry Slim-Fast.

"That crap?" I said. "*That's* all you're eating?"

She told me not to get on her case about it—that it was better than nothing, wasn't it? Did I need anything? Did I want her to do anything for me?

"Yeah," I said. "Call Ray. Tell him I'm better." Dead air. Five, six, seven seconds' worth. "What?"

"I just . . . Why don't *you* call him? I'm sure he'd rather hear it from you than from me." I told her yeah, all right, I'd call. Told her not to rush. To try and eat some eggs or something before she left. "Eggs?" she said. Groaned. I told her that when she got there, she got there. It wasn't like I was going anyplace.

"I love you, Dominick," she said. "I don't think I even realized how *much* I love you until the past few days." She said she hadn't meant to jump all over me about my brother. It had just been real hard, that was all. God, she felt so *sick*.

"Okay," I managed to squeak out. "I'll see you when you get here." Got off the phone quick.

Jesus, I thought. Felice over there was going to think I was the biggest sob sister ever born. And why *was* I crying, anyway? Because she'd just said she loved me? Because I couldn't say it back? I just wished I could have grabbed my keys and gotten the hell out of there. Bolted, like I always did. But I was grounded. I was *good* and stuck.

Out of the corner of my eye, I could see Bleeding Ulcer's efforts to pretend not to hear me. He got out of bed again. Walked over to the window. Whistled. . . . They were worried I'd get addicted to the painkiller? Not likely, if one of the little side effects was hallucinations like I'd had in the middle of the night. . . . Suffocated my own brother. Jesus. Doc Patel would have a field day with that one if I ever went back to *that* whole thing—*that* big waste of time. Dredging up your whole childhood as if you were dragging the bottom for a dead body. And then what? What was the point? . . .

Carry the corpse.

But he's alive.

Kill him.

Was that what Thomas had been putting up with the past twenty-one years? Talking monkey voices? Had the morphine let me peek inside my brother's brain? I couldn't remember what the voice had sounded like—only the power it had over me. I hadn't questioned it or anything—I'd just done what it said. . . . Maybe Miguel was wrong. Maybe it *wasn't* the morphine. Nothing I'd ever read said anything about an onset as late as forty, but that didn't mean anything. Maybe I was headed for the bed next to Thomas's down there after all. Twin beds for twin schizophrenics. Monkey voices, in stereo. Except I'd never let it get that far. *Never.*

"Yeah, you should have heard us here yesterday, your dad and me," Felice said. "Both of us bellyaching about the Boat." He was standing at the door now—rocking on the balls of his feet, watching the world go by.

He's not my *father,* I wanted to say. He's my *step*father. But I kept my mouth shut for a change. Give it a rest, Dominick. You've been correcting people for years and the only one who ever gave a shit about the distinction was *you.*

"Hell of a thing they're doing to the older guys like your dad, though, isn't it? Screwing around with their retirement packages like that? I mean, *I* been there seventeen years. That's bad enough. But your pop says he started in what—fifty-two? Fifty-three? Gives them almost forty years of his life and *that's* the thanks he gets?" He walked back to his bed and sat. "Big business—what the hell do they care? Your rank and file are nothing more than chess pieces to those guys: it's always been like that. You think Henry Ford gave a rat's ass about the guy on the assembly line? You think, what's his name down there in Atlanta?—Ted Turner?—you think he cares anything about the poor slob that sweeps the floors down there at CNN?" He swung his legs back onto the bed. Let go another fart. "Hey, is the TV going to bother you if I put it on for a while? Not that there's much on on a

Saturday morning, but I'm starting to get a little stir crazy in this joint. Sometimes you can catch a fishing show or bowling or something."

"Go ahead," I said.

"You fish?"

I told him I used to—that I probably hadn't dropped a line in since I'd started up my business.

"Yeah, well, when you work for yourself, you know? That's the other side of the coin. . . . I like to fish, though. Got my girlfriend into it, too, now. When we started going together, she didn't even know how to hold the pole. Now she loves it. About a month ago, she caught a trout as long as my forearm. I practically got a hernia helping her lift that Big Bertha out of the water. I got a picture of it on my desk at work—her and that fish."

"I used to fish a lot when I was a kid," I said. "My brother and me. Used to go down past the Falls and catch snapper blues."

"Really? No kidding? Whereabouts past the Falls?"

I didn't want to do this: get suckered into telling fishing stories with Gadabout Gaddis over there. "Down, uh . . . down by the Indian cemetery," I said. "There were these three white birch trees right in a row. Just past—"

"You're not going to believe this!" Felice said. "We used to go to that exact same spot. My old man and my uncle and me. I know *exactly* the place you're talking about. What the hell. We probably ran into each other down there, you and me, and we don't even remember it. Small world, huh?" He turned on the TV. "My name's Steve, by the way. Steve Felice."

"Uh-huh. You told me."

"Did I? Jesus, my mind's like a sieve in this place. Lack of stimulation, I guess it is. Makes me nuts just hanging around like this. My girlfriend says if I'm getting antsy, that's a good sign. I'm not the sit-around type, you know? Wash the car, mow the lawn—I always gotta be doing something, whether it needs it or not. You know what I mean?"

He flipped through the channels—cartoons, the Frugal Gourmet, that smug, head-up-his-ass George Will. Felice finally settled on a nature show—mountain lions stalking an antelope. *"She pounces,"* the unseen British voice said. *"She goes for the throat."*

"Oh, hey, I forgot to tell you," Felice said. "My fiancée says she knows you."

"Hmm?" I looked away from the mountain lions.

"My girlfriend. She was in here yesterday. She says she knows you from someplace. Didn't recognize you at first and then it dawned on her."

"Yeah?" The polite thing—the hospital buddy thing—would have been to ask her name, verify for him again that it was a small world. But I didn't care about being polite. Didn't give a crap *who* his girlfriend was. I closed my eyes to shut him up. . . . Maybe I *could* get ahold of Dr. Spencer on the weekend, I thought. And when was Sheffer going to get here? For someone who was coming right over, she was taking *her* sweet time.

"Yeah, it's funny," Felice said. "If you'd have told me a year ago I'd be thinking about getting married again, I'd have asked you if you'd been smokin' wacky weed. My first wife and her lawyer took no prisoners. You know what I'm saying? And I'm not just talking about the stuff she finagled away from me, either—the house, the better of the two cars. I'm talking about the *bitterness,* too. The emotional stuff. At the time of the divorce, I said to myself, Uh-uh. Never again. Not me. I even went so far as to write it down on an index card and tape it to the medicine cabinet: never again.That's exactly what I wrote down. And now, here I am, planning to get married again. In Utah, maybe. We traveled out there this past summer. You ever been out West?"

I closed my eyes.

"You know what me and her did a couple weekends ago? Went out and bought matching Western outfits together—hats, boots, jackets. It wasn't cheap, either. They don't exactly *give* that stuff away. But I don't know. We just hit it off, her and me. Which is screwy, in a way, because in a lot of ways we're like night and day. . . . But it's like if I leave the Boat. End up down there dealing blackjack. Life goes on, right? You gotta take chances or else you better check your pulse. See if you're still living."

I didn't answer him.

"You know where we met?"

I pretended I was dozing.

"At Partners. You know that little steakhouse out on Route 4? My sister and her husband call me up one night, out of the blue, ask me if I want to go out and grab a bite to eat and that's where we ended up. We were going someplace else—to the Homestead—but they were closed because of some private party. So we stood at the door and said, 'Okay, where else can we go?' and I said, 'Let's try that place, Partners.' Don't ask me why I said it, but it was *me* who suggested it. I mean, I could have named half a dozen other places, right? But I said 'Partners.' So that's where we ended up.

"And it was a Thursday night, see? They got line-dancing down there on Thursdays." He stopped, cut a fart. Sighed with relief. "If you told me a year ago that I'd meet my future wife in a line-dance, I would have told you to go get your head examined. Life's unpredictable, though—that's the beauty of it. I'm trying not to sweat the variables so much. Gives you ulcers. I started believing in fate about the time I turned fifty—realized I wasn't ever going to be master of the universe, you know? What do the kids call it? 'Go with the flow.' . . . But anyway, she says she knows you. My fiancée. 'From a past life,' she says. Kind of defies logic that we got together—we're nothing alike. Well, we're *growing* alike, I guess. My first wife, Maureen, she'd blow a gasket if she saw me in that Western outfit. But screw her, right? I'm just going with the flow."

A growl came from the wall-mounted TV, the sound of stampeding hooves. "*But the sleek antelope is not without resources of its own,*" the announcer said. . . .

A long, curving chain of people stands holding hands in a meadow. At the front of the line, Ray holds on to my foot. I'm floating in the air, tethered only by my stepfather's grip. If he lets go, if my foot falls off, I'll rise into the sky like a helium balloon. . . .

I opened my eyes. A chubby black nurse was standing beside my bed, taking my pulse. "I'm Vonette," she said. "I'm going to be your caregiver today. Okay?"

I stretched. Blinked my eyes back in focus. "Okay."

"Did you see that you have company?"

Sheffer approached the bed, a smile blinking on and off. "Oh," I said. "Hi."

"Hi." She was holding a pot of yellow chrysanthemums and a small wrapped gift. "These are for you," she said. "The little one's from Dr. Patel; the flowers are from me." She thunked the mums down on my nightstand.

We made small talk while the nurse finished checking my vitals. Away from Hatch, Sheffer looked even scrawnier. Looked a little goofy, really: bib overalls, knit hat squashed down to her eyelids. I noticed her lip right away: orangy powder covering up a purple bruise. When she caught me looking, she raised her hand to cover her mouth. Hand hiding a busted lip: same as Ma.

"I'll be back to change your bag in about half an hour or so," Vonette said. "We wouldn't want you to float out of here before your lunch arrives."

"Yeah, what is it?" I said. "Chicken à la wallpaper paste?"

She turned to Sheffer, shaking her head. "Must be on the mend," she said. "You can always tell when they start crabbing about the food."

I looked over at Steve Felice's bed. Empty, the sheets rucked up. TV off. I told Sheffer I appreciated her coming down. Told her she should have skipped the flowers.

"I wish I got carnations instead," she said. "Something that smells good. I was thinking in the elevator on the way up how chrysanthemums smell like dog urine."

I sighed. "So?"

"So-*oo* . . ."

"It's not good, is it?"

She shook her head. "It's not what you wanted." She said she should probably begin at the beginning.

When the Psychiatric Security Review Board convened at 4:00 P.M. on Halloween afternoon, Sheffer said, they were scheduled to determine the status of two prisoners. At Sheffer's request, the board flip-flopped its agenda and put Thomas second, buying more time for me to get there. Sheffer said she'd tried two or three times to call me by then, but all she kept getting was my machine.

As Sheffer, my brother, and a security guard waited outside the meeting room, Thomas became more and more agitated about my failure to show. He told Sheffer he feared the worst: that I'd been kidnapped by the Syrians. Both Bush and Assad had a lot to gain if America and Iraq went to war, he said. Since he, Thomas, was an instrument of peace, he was vulnerable and so were his loved ones. Sheffer shook her head. "You know how he gets when he starts perseverating."

I nodded. I was feeling a little queasy.

My brother had described to Sheffer the vision he saw: me, bound and gagged in some makeshift Syrian prison—my feet battered and broken by thugs with wooden bats. When she'd attempted to reason him out of it, he'd gotten testy, reminding her that identical twins communicated in ways she knew nothing about. He'd shouted for her to just shut up. "Then the guard warned him that that was enough of that kind of talk and Thomas started giving *him* an argument. 'My brother's hurt!' he kept insisting. 'I *know* he's hurt!' " She shrugged. "Which, my god, you *were*."

In an attempt to calm everyone down, Sheffer had reached to take Thomas by the hand. That's when he'd freaked—hauled off and whacked her in the face. The guard had leapt forward and put him in a choke hold, knocking Sheffer to the floor in the process. He'd let go of Thomas only after Sheffer's repeated pleas.

"He *hit* you?" I said. "That bruise on your mouth is from *Thomas*?"

"Well, so much for me trying to cover it up," she said. "I've always sucked at makeup."

"He *hit* you?"

She told me she'd tried as best she could to downplay the assault, both to the guard and to the medical secretary who came running from a nearby office. Dabbing at her lip—it was bleeding "a little"—she kept trying to get my brother refocused on the hearing. Sheffer was scared the Board might hear the commotion.

"I can't believe . . . He's never done anything like that before," I said.

"Are you sure you want to hear all this, Dominick? I can

skip the details and cut to the chase. I brought a copy of the transcript. You want me to just leave it here and—"

"No, go ahead," I told her. "Jesus, it's just . . . I can't believe he *hit* you."

She said it was her own stupid fault—that even someone *without* her training knew enough to keep their distance when a patient was in an agitated state. She'd had a moment of temporary insanity herself, she said. She was, admittedly, a wreck about things, going into the hearing.

By the time the conference room door had opened and the other patient's entourage had exited, Sheffer's lip had stopped bleeding, she said, but by then it had begun to swell. Thomas and the guard had both calmed down a little. Dr. Richard Hume, the psychiatrist who presided as the Review Board's chair, refused Sheffer's request for a postponement. Given the public's perception and the media attention that had surrounded Thomas's case, he said, the Board felt that action of some sort was preferable to stasis.

Sheffer reminded the Board that the patient's welfare needed to come before the state's concern about negative media attention. Given the publicity Thomas's case had generated, she wondered aloud if it was even possible for them to listen objectively to an argument about his being freed. "It was so *stupid* of me, Dominick," Sheffer moaned. "I'd meant to challenge them a little—play devil's advocate—but it came out wrong. I mean, there I am, moving my mouth like a ventriloquist so they won't notice my fat lip, my bloody teeth. I'm scared to death he's going to start losing it in front of them. I didn't know where the hell *you* were. I just . . . I was just so *nervous*. I committed the mortal sin of questioning their almighty judgment. It was exactly what I *shouldn't* have done."

Looks were exchanged among the Board members, Sheffer said. Dr. Hume told her that while they appreciated the "missionary zeal" with which she was advocating for her client, they needed no reminders of their obligations—to the patient *or* to the community. After that, Sheffer said, the proceedings were polite, efficient, and frosty.

Sheffer explained to the Board that the treatment team had failed to reach a consensus about Thomas's placement and therefore was not making a specific recommendation. She read aloud the two letters we'd gotten that advocated Thomas's transferral to a nonforensic facility. She assured the Board that the patient's brother was committed to his well-being and recovery and that they should not misread my absence from the hearing as indifference or tacit approval of Thomas's remaining there at Hatch. "They all just sat there, listening politely," she said. "No questions. No concerns raised. It was all so streamlined and civil. Then it was time to question Thomas directly. Here."

She handed me the transcript. "Hey, you know what?" she said. "We ran out of coffee at my house and I've got this major caffeine headache going on. I tell you what? Let me go downstairs, get a fix, and let you read through that thing. I'll come back in ten or fifteen minutes, and if you have any questions . . ."

"Read it and weep, eh?" I said.

She nodded. Backed away. "I'll see you in fifteen minutes."

I skimmed through the first part—the Board's refusal to postpone, the skirmish between Sheffer and Hume about what was good for the public versus what was good for the patient. Sheffer was right: it had been a tactical error on her part, antagonizing them like that. I slowed down when I got to my brother's interview.

The Board wanted to know, in Thomas's own words, why he'd cut off his hand.

He answered them from Scripture: "*If thy right hand offend thee, cut it off and cast it from thee.*"

So, was he saying that he had mutilated himself to atone for his sins?

No, he answered; he'd done it to atone for *America's* sins.

Which were?

"Warmongering, greed, the bloodletting of children."

And did he think he might ever feel compelled, at some point in the future, to commit any other acts of self-harm?

He wouldn't *want* to, he said, but he took his direction from the Lord God Almighty. He was God's instrument. He'd do anything that was necessary.

Anything? Including harming someone who stood in his way?

"I didn't mean to hit her," Thomas said. "I lost my temper."

What? Whom had he hit?

"Her. Lisa."

Sheffer had volunteered for the Board a version of what had happened out in the waiting room. An accident, she told them—bad judgment on her part. Thomas was upset because his brother had been detained. His arm had just flailed out and hit her accidentally, that was all.

A Board member named Mrs. Birdsall wanted to know how Thomas was getting on with the day-to-day routines at Hatch?

He said he hated it there. You were watched like a hawk. You couldn't smoke when you wanted to. He had found insects in his food, he said. He was awakened and violated repeatedly in the middle of the night. His mail was stolen.

Stolen?

Thomas said he knew for a fact that Jimmy Carter had sent him three registered letters and that each had been intercepted.

Why did Thomas feel the former president was trying to contact him?

He was attempting to invite him to join him as an envoy to the Middle East on a mission of peace, Thomas said.

And who did he think it was that was intercepting his mail?

Thomas took off on his George Bush refrain, lecturing the Board like they were the village idiots. Wasn't it obvious? War was profitable; Bush's hands were stained with the blood of the CIA. If they would all just go back and reread American history, they'd realize there was a fundamental crack in America's foundation. He ricocheted from the Trail of Tears to the Japanese-American internment camps to the conditions that ghetto children lived in today. Drive-by shootings, crack houses: it all had to do with profit, the price of crude oil. It was so obvious to him, he said. Why couldn't anyone else see it?

See what, specifically?

The conspiracy!

Thomas must have broken down at that point, because someone asked him if he needed a moment to compose himself.

Jesus had wanted us to re-create Jerusalem, he answered, and we had rebuilt Babylon instead. He went on and on. If it had been Jesse Jackson saying it instead of Thomas, he might have brought down the house. Great sermon, wrong congregation.

One of the Board members wanted to know if Thomas understood *why* he had been detained at Hatch.

Yes, he told them; he was a political prisoner. Throughout history, America had gone to war because war was profitable. Now, finally, we had arrived at the critical crossroads prophesied in the Bible—the Book of Apocalypse. As a nation, our only hope was to quit the path of greed and walk the path of spirituality instead. He, Thomas, had been tapped to lead this movement. It was God's will. Did it come as any surprise to them that the state wanted to keep him locked up? Wanted to demoralize him? He told the Security Board that the CIA paid men to wake him up each night and foul him—make him impure. That they were purposely trying to break his spirit. But his spirit *hadn't* been broken. They'd underestimated him, the same as they had underestimated the peasant-warriors in Vietnam. Thomas was on a divine mission. He was trying to do nothing less than subvert an unholy war that would call down on America and the Western world the most hideous of Biblical prophecies. George Bush was the false prophet, he warned them, and Iraq was the sleeping dragon about to wake and devour the world's children. Capitalism would kill us all.

A Board member said he'd read in my brother's report that Thomas had told the police he was inspired to his library sacrifice by voices. Was that accurate?

It was, Thomas said.

And did he always feel compelled to obey the voices he heard?

The voices of good, yes, Thomas said—he battled the voices of evil.

And he could distinguish between them?

The voice of Jesus, Thomas told them, was like no other voice.

Jesus spoke to him, then?

"Jesus speaks to everyone. *I* listen."

But not all the voices Thomas heard were benign?

"Benign? Not by a long shot."

And what did the bad voices tell him?

Thomas said he'd rather not repeat, in mixed company, what they said.

Well, then, suppose one of the voices of good—let's say the voice of Jesus Christ himself—asked Thomas to hurt someone. Kill someone, say. One of His enemies. Would Thomas feel obliged to obey?

If Jesus asked him to?

Yes. If Jesus Himself asked.

Thomas told them the question was ridiculous. Jesus would never tell him to harm anyone. Jesus had died on the cross to show the world the light.

But just for example's sake, suppose He did ask. Would Thomas obey? If it was the voice of Jesus that commanded it? If Jesus said, say, "Go back to the library and cut the throat of the woman behind the desk because she's an agent of the devil. Because you need to destroy her to save the world. To save innocent children, say." Would Thomas do it then—take his knife to the woman, if Jesus asked him to?

Jesus wouldn't ask him to do that, Thomas repeated.

But *if* He did? Would he?

If He did?

Yes, *if.*

Yes.

Sheffer returned with her styro-coffee. I handed her the transcript. "Did you finish?" she asked.

I said I'd stopped at the part where they'd gotten him to say he'd slaughter a librarian for Jesus.

"Could you *believe* that? The way they led him? I was so *pissed*!"

"So what was the final verdict?" I asked. "As if I don't already know."

By a unanimous vote, Sheffer said, the Psychiatric Security Review Board had decided to retain my brother for a period of one year, citing that he had shown himself to be potentially dangerous to himself and others. His case would be reviewed again in October of 1991 and an appropriate decision would be made at that time as to his release or his placement for a second twelve-month period.

"Detain him at Hatch?" I asked.

She nodded. She had requested a follow-up review in six months, rather than twelve, she said. Dr. Hume had reminded her that if Thomas had not been ruled Not Guilty by Reason of Insanity, he could have been convicted in the criminal court of a felony and would have faced a prison sentence of *three* years, minimally. If the Board members were erring at all in their decision, Hume told her, they were perhaps erring on the side of leniency.

"And I told him, 'That's a bunch of bull. If he went to prison, he'd be bounced out in three or four months with a suspended sentence and you know it. Six months, max.' I'm telling you, *paisano,*" she said, "my Jewish sense of justice and my Sicilian temper were both doing a hard boil by then. It was hopeless. I knew that. But I just couldn't keep my mouth shut. They're going to nail me for it, too. My supervisor's already called me to schedule 'some dialogue' on Monday about my 'emotional outburst.' "

I asked Sheffer how Thomas had taken the news.

"Like a stoic," she said. "But you know who took it hard? The news about Thomas? Your stepfather."

"He did? Ray?"

She'd called and called him after the hearing, she said—hadn't reached him until the following morning because he'd been at the hospital with me. "He started crying when I told him how the Board had voted," she said. "He had to hang up and call me back. I felt so bad for the guy."

Neither of us said anything for several seconds. Poor Ray, I thought: forty years old and we were *still* his twin nuisances. But he'd cried? For Thomas?

"I'm just so sorry, Dominick," Sheffer said. "I can't stop thinking that maybe if I'd just not lost my cool at the beginning of the hearing . . ."

I reminded her that she'd warned me over and over that it

was a long shot—that the decision had probably already been made before the Board even met that day.

"Yeah, but maybe if I had just—"

"And maybe if *I* hadn't fallen off the goddamned roof. And maybe if he just hadn't gotten schizophrenic in the first place. Don't drive yourself nuts with the ifs."

I lay there, arms across my chest, my head sunk into the pillow. I didn't have the energy to feel angry or indignant or much of anything anymore. I was spent. Broken. I realized, suddenly, how much Sheffer's visit had exhausted me.

"That morning I first met you," she said. "Remember? That first day in my office? I said to myself, 'Whew, this guy's a walking attitude problem. This guy's got chips on *both* of his shoulders.' But, I don't know, *paisano*. I somehow got sucked into your brother's case—began to see how the things that were supposed to keep him safe might end up damaging him instead. It's the first thing they tell you in the school of social work: don't get personally involved. Don't lose your objectivity. But, then, I don't know . . . Well, for whatever it's worth, I guess I just began to see *why* you were so pissed. And then *my* blood started to boil a little, too."

But that was the weird part: I *wasn't* pissed anymore. I wasn't anything.

"Do me a favor, will you?" I said.

"Sure. What?"

"Go someplace nice with your daughter today. You and her: go have some fun."

She smiled. Nodded. "Look," she said, "you *know* we'll take good care of him, right? Dr. Patel, Dr. Chase, me—the whole staff. And you have your security clearance now. You can visit him. He'll stabilize, Dominick. I *know* he will."

I smiled. Told her I'd see about getting her the Purple Heart for that bruise. She waved me off. Picked up the present from Dr. Patel and handed it to me. "Here," she said. "Aren't you going to open this?"

I unwrapped the package, lifted off the top of the box. Took the small soapstone statue out of its tissue paper nest—a four-inch version of the one in her office.

"I like her smile," Sheffer said.

"It's not a her," I told her. "It's a he. Shiva. The god of destruction."

She looked at me funny. "Destruction?"

Dr. Patel had enclosed a card. *"Dear Dominick, I give you Shiva the dancing god in hopes that you will soon be on your feet and dancing past your pain. Do you remember Shiva's message? With destruction comes renovation. Be well."*

Sheffer was on her way out the door when Joy arrived. I introduced them. Saw Joy take in Sheffer's bib overalls, her smooshed-down hat. It was a little odd—how instantly Sheffer's cocky humor evaporated in Joy's presence. She seemed almost to sink into those overalls of hers.

"Who's the hippie chick?" Joy asked.

"Thomas's social worker."

I filled Joy in on the Board meeting, Thomas's sentence down at Hatch. She looked as pretty as ever, Joy—but pale. Frail, even. Whipped. When I started telling her about Thomas's interview, she bent and kissed my forehead, my nose, my lips. "I love you, Dominick," she said. And my throat constricted. I could not say it back.

Between the stress she'd been feeling about me and the nausea from the baby, Joy said, she hadn't been able to sleep or eat or do much of anything but hug the toilet all day. I'd made her so paranoid earlier about drinking Slim-Fast that she'd called the doctor's office and talked to the nurse practitioner. He'd told her not to worry about it—that the baby took what it needed first. The fetus was her body's first priority right now, he'd said, and her body knew it. She should just take it easy and try not to worry. The nausea would pass. Little babies were tougher than she thought.

I flashed on Angela, the way she'd looked that morning—fists clenched, blood-flecked foam at her mouth. . . .

"I still can't quite believe it," Joy said. "*Me.* A *mother.*"

We talked about what was in store for the next several months—the pregnancy, my injuries, my business. Lying there, speculating about worst-case scenarios, was driving me crazy, I said. And when I dozed off, I had these hallucinations.

"Like what?" she said.

"Never mind. You don't even want to know."

Joy told me she'd packed me a bag of toiletries, and then had rushed out of the house, forgetting everything. She'd visit again that evening, she said. Was there anything else I needed? I described the place in my desk where I kept my insurance policies for the business. My health insurance policy, too. It was all together. Could she bring that stuff? It was driving me nuts, just lying there, thinking my insurance might not cover this.

Sure, she said. She'd bring it. Anything else?

I shook my head. Started to cry again, goddamn it.

Everything was going to be okay, she said. *Really.* I should try not to focus on my leg or on my brother. Why couldn't I just focus on the *baby*—the fact that I was going to be a *father*. She touched my hip cautiously, testing it like it was something hot from the oven.

Maybe none of it mattered anymore, I thought. Maybe I could just go *with* the exhaustion instead of fighting it. Give in to it. That was how people drowned, wasn't it? They just stopped fighting. Just relaxed and gave themselves over to the water. . . . Maybe that's what Thomas was doing down there at Hatch, too. He'd taken the news stoically, Sheffer said. It was funny, really: ironic. All our lives, *he'd* been the crybaby and *I'd* been the tough guy. The guy who didn't let his guard down. Cross Dominick Birdsey and he might blow up at you, might come out swinging—but you were never going to see him cry like that pansy-ass brother of his. . . . But ever since I'd fallen off Rood's roof—had come bubbling back up from hell or wherever it was that the morphine had taken me—all's I could *do* was cry. Now *I* was the crybaby and *Thomas* was the stoic. Gets locked up in maximum-security hell for a year and takes it with a stiff upper lip. I had to laugh.

"What's so funny?" Joy said.

Instead of answering her, I rubbed at the tears. Blew my nose. What had Felice said? Believe in fate? Go with the flow? Maybe *that* was the big cosmic joke: you could spend your whole life banging your head against the wall and all it boiled down to was fortune-cookie philosophy. *Go with the flow*. Which, come to think of it, was what people did when they drowned. . . .

"It's *not* going to be okay," I told Joy.

"Yes, it is."

"No, it's not. I'm never going to fix anything. And even if I could, I'm just too tired. I can't do it anymore, Joy. All's I want to do is wave the white flag. Take the damn water into my lungs."

She looked confused. "It's the drugs they're giving you," she said. "Narcotics are depressants, right? They're bringing you way down."

I saw Rood up there in his attic window. Shook my head. "I think . . . I think when I went off that roof, something else busted up besides my foot and my leg and my ankle. Something that all the surgery and physical therapy in the world aren't going to fix. . . . I'm just tired, Joy. I don't want to keep fighting anymore."

It was the medication, she said again.

"It's *not* the medication. It's *me*."

Lying around and feeling sorry for themselves never helped anybody, she told me. I should think about the *baby*.

I hadn't planned on getting into it. I'd planned on shutting my mouth—maybe until after the kid was born, or after I couldn't take it anymore. Or maybe for the rest of my life. I hadn't been sure *how* it was going to play out. But I suddenly knew I was just too tired to keep up the game. Knew right then and there that I couldn't do it.

"I know the baby's not mine," I said.

She looked more bewildered than surprised. "What do you mean, not yours? Of course it's yours, Dominick. What are you talking about?"

"It can't be. I'm sterile. I got a vasectomy back when I was married."

She blinked. Sat there. "What?"

"I never told you about it. My wife . . . Dessa and I . . . we had a kid. A little girl. Her name was Angela. She died."

"Dominick," Joy said. "Stop it. Why are you doing this?"

"I *should* have told you. I *know* I should have told you, but . . ."

I asked her if she remembered that time when we'd discussed kids—way back, right near the beginning. We'd both said we weren't interested. "So I just . . . I told myself that it wasn't even an issue. Convinced myself that I didn't have to get into it because you didn't want babies anyway. That I could just let you keep taking your birth control pills and . . . But I see now that it was the same as lying. Keeping it from you. You're not the only one who's been dishonest. We've both been lying to each other. I'm not even mad, really. God, the way I've been treating you the past couple months. . . . I mean, I *was* mad. When I first found out about it? I was ready to come out punching."

"It's this medication they're giving you," she said. "It's making you think strange."

"You remember that night you got arrested for stealing? And you were saying how, now that everything was out in the open, that it was a *good* thing, not a *bad* thing? That things were going to be better than ever between us? And I told you not to get your hopes up. Remember, Joy? I told you I was damaged goods. You remember me telling you that? . . . That's what I was talking about, I guess. The baby. What it did to my wife and me. I don't know, Joy. It damages you. When you have a baby and you get to know her for three weeks and then she . . . just *dies*. I'm not trying to make excuses. I just . . . That's what I meant when I said I was damaged goods. So I . . . I went and got a vasectomy. I can't have kids, Joy. Whoever the father of your baby is, it's not me."

She just sat there, blinking. Looking at me strange.

"And . . . and I'm not even mad. I'm sad, Joy. I'm just real sad, because . . . because I was never really going to be able to give you a fair shake. You and me, I mean. I see that now. I *used* you. I'm damaged goods. But now I'm too tired to . . . I can't fake it anymore, Joy. I can't keep playing whatever game it is we've been playing. *I can't.*"

She blinked. Laughed. "Stop it, okay? You're wrecking everything. This is *your* baby. Mine and yours. You're going to get better, and we're going to have this baby, and buy a house and . . . Who *else's* would it be, Dominick? I don't even know what you're *talking* about."

We both just sat there, looking at each other.

"Honest!" she said. "Honest to God!"

That nurse came back into the room. Vonette. "Let's see about that bag now," she said. She took a look. Took my hand and felt for the pulse. Joy backed away from the bed. She looked shell-shocked. Scared. I hadn't meant to scare her about Angela. I was sorry about that. But I couldn't keep it up. I was too tired. I just wanted to sleep.

"Where's your buddy?" Vonette asked me. "He didn't go AWOL, did he?"

What? Leo? She nodded toward Steve Felice's empty bed.

"Oh. . . . I don't know. He's probably out in the solarium."

"Your BP seems a little high, hon," Vonette said. "I'm going to come back and check it for you in another half hour or so. Okay?"

"Okay."

She turned to Joy. "All right now, hon. If you don't mind, I have to check his catheter and change his bag. I'm going to draw the curtain for a couple minutes and then you can get right back to your visit. All right?"

"All right," Joy said. She smiled. Backed up another few steps. Vonette drew the curtain between us.

I had imagined some big showdown when I lowered the boom—lifted the lid off the fact that she'd been cheating on me. But it hadn't been like that at all. I felt so sleepy.

"There now," said Vonette. "You're all set."

When she pulled the curtain back again, Joy was gone.

Ray visited later that afternoon. That evening, too. Neither of us mentioned Joy. We didn't say much at all, really—just sat and watched TV together. I dozed more than anything else. Leo and Angie came on Sunday afternoon, with a homemade poster from the kids. When Angie asked where Joy was, I shrugged. Said something about a cold.

Leo came back later by himself, carrying this three-ton fruit basket—something like a picture out of a magazine. The card said, "Best wishes for a speedy recovery. Fondly, Gene and Thula Constantine." Fondly? Since when? Leo pulled off the cellophane for me. Ate one piece of fruit after another, practicing his hook shot with the wastebasket and the cores and peels and rinds. "Okay, where is she?" he finally said.

"Who?"

"Joy. Is she *really* sick?"

I shrugged. Yawned. Grabbed the chain bar and shifted my position a little. I told Leo I appreciated his visiting, but did he mind leaving now? I was tired. I wanted to sleep.

I was dozing in and out of *60 Minutes* when something woke me up. A shadow. I opened my eyes.

He was just standing there, watching me. The Duchess.

"What do *you* want?" I said.

He handed me my Walkman from the house. And a cassette. I didn't get it.

"This is from Joy," he said. "She wants you to listen to it."

"Yeah? Why didn't *she* come up and give it to me, then? Where's *she* at?"

"In the car," he said. "She explained everything on the tape. Just listen to it."

He turned and left.

"That was a short visit," Felice said.

"What?"

"Your friend there. He didn't stay long."

"My friend?"

Hi, Dominick. I'm, uh . . . I've been trying all day to write you a letter, but nothing's coming out right. I never was a big one for putting things down on paper, so Thad said, "Why don't you just make him a tape? Tell him what you need to say on a tape." And I thought, yeah, maybe that's a good idea, because I guess I have a lot of explaining to do. . . . I don't know, Dominick. I guess if I wasn't so ashamed of myself, I would have told you everything in person.

I . . . I've been doing a lot of thinking since I saw you yesterday afternoon. I was up all last night thinking about you and me, and where I've been in my life, and where I'm going. I have to admit that you blew me away when you told me the baby couldn't be yours. I wanted it to be your baby, Do-

minick. Our baby. I just wanted it to work out for us. When you used to say to me how you couldn't give me a "happily ever after" life, I used to go to myself, yes he can. He just doesn't know it yet. But I guess I was just fooling myself. As usual.

Ever since I was little, Dominick, I've had this Carol Brady picture of myself as this nice, pretty mom with a nice house and a husband who loves me, and we have real cute kids. Things in my life got unbelievably complicated, but that was really all I ever wanted. . . . I know I told you some of the stuff about my childhood, but there's way more I never went into. It was hard. All my mom's husbands and boyfriends . . . I'd just start getting used to things and then we'd move again. And my mom would always say, "Well, this is it. I finally found what I've been looking for," and then the next thing you knew, we'd be moving again. Sometimes we moved so quick, I couldn't even hand in my schoolbooks. Last night I counted all the different schools I went to by the time I graduated from high school. I came up with nine. I never counted them before last night. Nine schools by the time I was seventeen.

The worst times were when she was between guys. Sometimes we didn't even have any food in the house and I'd be like, "Mom, you have to get a job so we can eat something," and she'd always go, "Don't worry. Something will turn up. I'll meet someone." We had this trick where we used to rip off grocery stores when there was nothing in the house. . . . We'd go in and get a cart and fill it up like we were doing a big shopping and then we'd just eat stuff out of the cart—bananas, crackers, American cheese. Then we'd pretend we forgot something in Aisle 2 or whatever and just walk out of the store and my mom would go, "Don't look back! Just keep walking!" Sometimes I'd still be hungry and she'd be rushing me out of there.

When she was between guys, she used to have to get all dressed up and go out at night. She wasn't a hooker or anything. Don't get me wrong. She just used to have to go out to bars and clubs and let men know she existed. . . . I used to think she looked so beautiful when she went out. I'd always help her get ready, help her fix her hair and zip her up in the back. It was like playing dress-up with your dolls or something, except it was your own mother. I didn't think it was weird or anything, but that time after I got arrested? And I was going to Dr. Grork? He said it was abnormal. Unhealthy. I guess I just didn't think that much about it at the time. Analyze it or whatever. It was just our life. . . .

I used to hate staying by myself all night when she went out. I don't really blame her. She couldn't help it. How was she supposed to pay some baby-sitter when we couldn't even pay for the food we were eating at the grocery store? . . . But I was always a nervous wreck when she was out like that. Thinking some killer or burglar was going to get me. I used to get so nervous that I'd pull out the hairs on my eyebrows. I did it in school all the time, too. It got to be a bad habit. I had this one witch of a fourth-grade teacher who was always yelling at me for making the skin around my eyebrows bleed. It was like this woman's personal mission in life was to get me to keep my hands away from my face. There's this school picture of me that year that I still have. I never showed it to you. It's kind of pathetic. We were living in Tustin then. (It was just before my mom met her husband Mike.) And, in the picture, you can see these red scabs where my eyebrows are supposed to be. Whenever I look at that picture, I get that same feeling in my stomach like I used to get when I'd be by myself all night, or half the night, or whatever. It's like I'm that same little girl again and nothing else in my life has ever happened. It's weird. . . . I'm not telling you all this to make you feel sorry for me, Dominick. I'm just trying to explain why I wanted so much for us to have a house, and a baby, and maybe even get married at some point. But you have to admit that I never tried to push you into it. . . .

The pregnancy just happened, Dominick. I keep thinking that you think I got pregnant just to trap you into marrying me. I'm real upset about that because that's not at all what happened. Honest to God.

I really think having this baby is gonna change me for the better, Dominick. Make me a better person. I hope it does. . . . Ever since you told me yesterday about your baby daughter that died, I can't stop thinking about her. I am so, so sorry, Dominick. That must be so heavy duty. And it explains a lot about you that I could never figure out. Why you seem so mad at the world or whatever. I just wish you had told me about her. I might have been able to help you through it.

I keep thinking about your ex-wife, too. I had a good cry over her last night—right in the middle of everything else I was thinking about. Probably because I'm gonna be a mother, too, now. . . . I never told you this, but I saw her one time. Your ex-wife. I don't even remember her name, but I knew it was her. She was at the mall with Angie. Angie and her are sisters, right? That's how I figured it out. They didn't see me, so I just . . . I followed them. I sat down in back of them at the food court and listened to their conversation. They were talking about their mother—what they should get her for her birthday—and I just sat there going, this is Dominick's ex-wife. This is the woman he was with before he was with me. . . . She seemed nice. I remember sitting there wishing that she, Angie, and I were three girlfriends out shopping together. That probably sounds kind of strange, but I never really had many girlfriends. Other women don't like me very much, I don't even really know why. Last month, Patti at work had a baby shower for Greta (the nutritionist) and I think every single woman at Hardbodies got invited except me. If I was going to stay there, which I'm not, I bet no one there would ever give me a shower. I'd be lucky if I got a card that someone bought and passed around and everyone signed. I guess when you change schools nine times before you're even out of high school, you don't get to develop many friendships. I'm twenty-five years old, Dominick, and I can't even say that I ever had one real girlfriend. Isn't that pitiful?

Anyways, your ex-wife seemed so nice. And funny. She was complaining about her mother—not mean or anything. She kind of reminded me a little of Rhoda from Mary Tyler Moore. *Not looks, just the way she was talking. . . . I know you never stopped loving her, Dominick. You never said anything, but I could always tell. It was like you always held something back from me. I know I never really measured up, and I know you never thought I was smart enough for you—intelligent enough or whatever. You never said anything, but I knew. . . . But anyway, I cried for her last night because I was thinking about how she lost her little girl. It makes me kinda scared to think about everything that might go wrong. But it also explains a lot. I just wish you had told me before. I might have helped you if you let me in a little. At least I could have tried.*

I guess I've finally gotten to the hardest part of what I have to say, Dominick, and I hope it's not too hard for you to have to listen to this on a tape. . . . It's not easy what I have to tell you. I just want you to remember one thing. My feelings for you have always been real. I may have been dishonest about a lot of things—shoplifting, etcetera—but I'm being totally honest about my feelings. I know it hasn't been good for us for a while now, but I thought at the beginning that we had something pretty special. In some ways, you made me happier than any of the other guys I've been in relationships with. I guess what I'm trying to say is that I wish the baby was yours. Because I really, really care about you. The feelings are still there, Dominick. Honest to God.

Thad is the baby's father. It's pretty complicated, but I guess I owe you an explanation, if you're even still listening. . . .

Dominick, I was never honest with you about Thad and me. To begin with, he's bisexual, not gay. I guess you've probably figured that out by now. He told Aaron about the baby yesterday, and Aaron kicked him out of their place. Another thing you never knew was that Thad and I didn't meet each other at work, like I told you we did. We've known each other for a long, long time. Do you remember me telling you about my mom's half-brother that came to live with us out in California? And how him and me were fooling around when everyone else was at work? Well, that was Thad. I was only twelve when it all started, and Thad was nineteen. He's always looked younger than his age. I was just some stupid kid; I didn't know what I was doing. Well, I sorta did and sorta didn't. But, like they say, he kind of got in my bloodstream or something. Maybe because I was so young. . . . I just never could get over him. He was in the Navy back then—I think I told you—and then he got transferred to Portsmouth. That's where he began "experimenting" with guys. Started going to these bars and stuff. He used to call me up and tell me about it—all these descriptions of what him and some guy had done together. He'd call right after I got home from school, before Mom and Phil got home from work. He'd say, "Do you want me to tell you what we did next?" And I'd go, "Yeah, tell me." Then I'd get off the phone and have dry heaves because I was so upset. It got so I couldn't eat or anything. I missed him so much. I used to beg him on the phone to send me stuff—his fingernails and things—and that was all I ever wanted to eat. It was so sick. But that's how it's always been with me and Thad. It's like a sickness.

Yours and mine isn't the first relationship this has ruined. When Denny, my second husband, found out about Thad, he went crazy. Ronnie, my first husband, never even found out. Which was good, because Ronnie could get real mean. It's just that . . . Well, do you remember after I got arrested up at the Hills?

And I was seeing Dr. Grork? He kept telling me I needed to get Thad out of my life and tell you about him. Come clean. Dr. Grork said it was a big risk, but that I really had to take it if I ever expected to really get some of the things I've always wanted. . . . But I couldn't do it. I tried to, Dominick, but I couldn't. I guess I was afraid it was gonna wreck my chance to be Carol Brady. Which is a big joke, I see now. I know he's not good for me, but I can't let go. Sometimes I hate him. You're a hundred percent better person than he'll ever be, Dominick. He's very manipulative, very controlling. That's what Dr. Grork kept telling me, and he was right. . . . It's not you, Dominick. It's me. Thad and me are like a disease.

I'm not proud of what I have to tell you next, Dominick, but I guess I need to tell you. I don't expect you to understand, or to forgive me, because I don't deserve it. I just hope you don't hate me too much. Maybe someday you can forgive me. Because I really, really broke your trust. . . .

I let him watch us, Dominick. When we made love. It happened twice. I said no for a long time, Dominick, but finally I gave in. . . . He used to beg me. He really got off on it. Thad's had a crush on you all along. The first time was just . . . I don't know. I just finally said all right. It felt weird. . . . And the second time, he set it all up, told me what he wanted me to do, which way to turn and everything. He was like a movie director or something. . . . He never taped us or anything—I didn't mean it like that. Both . . . both times it was on a Friday. He'd get there before you came home—Fridays were one of the times when you and I would get intimate. Our pattern or whatever. So . . . he hid in my closet with the door open a little. He told me that the thought of you catching him was part of the excitement. Part of the thrill.

I didn't want to do it, Dominick. It made me feel awful. I was a nervous wreck with him hiding in there. But he begged me. Got mad when he wanted to do it that second time. He said he was going to leave me. Move away and not tell me where he was going. And so I said I'd do it, but that was it. Just that one more time and no more. . . . I know it was a huge betrayal. I'm so sorry. I don't expect you to forgive me, Dominick, but at least now you can say, "Good riddance to bad rubbish. I'm glad I got rid of her. She was sick." Which I know I am.

Tomorrow, I'm giving my notice down at Hardbodies. Thad's already quit. I know you're going to be in the hospital for at least another week and I'll be out of the condo by then. Out of your hair—me and this baby. Don't worry. I'm not going to rip you off or run out with your stereo or anything. I already have enough to feel guilty about. I told Thad he can't even come over to the condo. He's staying at a motel until we leave.

We're . . . we're probably going to drive cross-country. Or else I may drive out there by myself. I'm going to stay with my mom and Herb in Anaheim at that motel they're managing. Mom said I can stay there for free until after the baby's born and then we'll see. It depends on what Herb wants. . . . I don't know what's going to happen with Thad and me. I really don't. He's still talking about starting up a catering business and having me be his bartender. I don't know. Maybe after I'm a mom, I'll have the guts to tell him to leave me alone once and for all. . . . I know he won't make a very good father like you would have. If it's a boy, I know you would have taken him to Little League, and Cub Scouts, and all those things. I can't see Thad ever doing anything like that. He's too selfish for one thing. I really wish so much this baby was yours. . . . I'm not looking forward to living with my mother again, but she can probably help take care of the baby after it's born. Especially if I go back to work, which I guess I'm gonna have to do. No kid of mine is going to have to go into Safeway and eat groceries in the aisles that we can't even pay for.

I'm not sure, but I might put in an application at Disneyland. To be a cast member. Maybe that woman is still there who told me I'd make a perfect Cinderella. I still remember her name. Mrs. Means. Maybe by some miracle, she still works there. Still remembers me. Maybe I'll end up waving at little kids in the Festival of Lights parade and they'll go, "Look! It's Cinderella!" Thad thinks I should do it. It might be a stepping stone, he says, and he could be my manager.

Dominick, I know you're going to get better, and that you'll find someone who'll make you happy, because it's what you deserve. I'm sure you hate me right now, which is totally understandable. I hate myself. But no matter what you think of me, I'll always be glad we were together for those almost two years. I was watching this program once? About Paul Newman? And someone on that show said how Paul Newman was a "real quality person," and that's what you are, Dominick. A real quality person. Just remember that we had some good times, too. Especially in the beginning. I'm so sorry I betrayed you. And that I had to lay all this on you while you're so sick. But when you told me the baby couldn't be yours, I didn't know what else to do. . . . I'm probably the last person you're gonna want to talk to once you listen to this, but if you want to get ahold of me, I'll be at the condo for a few more days and then, by the end of next week, I'll be driving out to my mother's, which the number is in that Rolodex thing of yours.

If . . . if you're worrying about AIDS or HIV because of Thad—his lifestyle or whatever—don't worry. He's very careful about things. Aaron's a fanatic about not taking any chances. So that's one less thing you have to worry about.

Dominick? I'm sorry I always acted so jealous about your brother. If I ever had a brother or sister, I'd want them to be as loyal as you are. In my personal opinion, you're fighting a losing battle, but that's your business, not mine. Don't forget to take care of yourself instead of everyone else.

I love you, babe. Just don't . . . please don't hate me. Okay?

I *didn't* hate her. I didn't even hate *him.* I just lay there, looking at my ugly purple foot, which should have hurt but didn't. I didn't feel a thing.

"You know what kills me about this show?" Felice said from across the way. "Wherever she goes, someone's always getting knocked off."

I reached up and pulled off the Walkman's earphones. I'd listened to that tape twice, hoping it would make some kind of sense, but it didn't. I wasn't outraged, though. I wasn't hurt. I wasn't anything. "I'm sorry. What'd you say?"

Felice pointed up at the wall-mounted TV. "Jessica Fletcher there. *Murder, She Wrote.* She goes shopping; there's a stiff. She goes to visit some friend of hers; there's another one. She goes off on vacation. Boom! When's the last time *you* went out someplace and ran into a corpse? She's like the Grim Reaper or something."

I'd wait until I got home, I decided. I'd have to. And I wouldn't leave any mess—something someone would have to clean up afterward. Leo, or Ray, or some poor slob on the rescue squad. . . . Because I wasn't angry like that bastard, Rood. I was just tired—just wanted to stop fighting and give in. Go with it. . . . I could hobble out to the garage, stuff rags in the cracks on the sides of the door.

Gentlemen, start your engines. That's when I remembered about the truck. I couldn't carbon monoxide myself out of existence. I'd totaled the truck.

Pills, then. They'd send me home with painkillers, right? I could take them all at once with a bottle of . . . what did I have in the house, anyway? I still had that Christmas bottle—that Scotch one of the wholesalers had given me? Booze and pills. That would do it. Rid the world of Dominick Birdsey, the loser's loser. The bad twin.

"She's like a corpse magnet," Felice said. "I tell you one thing. If you ever see Angela Lansbury coming toward you, start running the other way *quick.*"

Was the fact that the Duchess had hidden in her closet and watched us make love any more weird than the fact that my brother had hacked off his hand in the name of peace? Any more strange than the fact that the Wequonnocs were about to ascend—rise from the ashes? Any more fucked up than the fact that America was getting ready to fight another war with gung-ho kids too young to remember anything about Vietnam except *Rambo*? . . .

That was the big joke, wasn't it? The answer to the riddle: there *was* no one up there in Heaven, making sure the accounts came out right. I'd solved it, hadn't I? Cracked the code? It was all just a joke. The god inside my brother's head was just his disease. My mother had knelt every night and prayed to her own steepled hands. Your baby died because of . . . because of no particular reason at all. Your wife left you because you sucked all the oxygen out of the room, so you pretended she was the one in bed with you while you screwed your girlfriend and her boyfriend hid in the closet, watching. . . . Hell, why *couldn't* she go out there and become Cinderella? . . . Let go of my ankle, Ray. I'm ready to float away. Ready to cut my brother down from that tree and carry him to the Falls and throw him over the side. Jump in headfirst, after him. Because it didn't matter. It was all just a joke. *Riddle me this, Batman. What's the point?* And the answer was: *there was none*. Pain pills and Scotch—that was how I'd do it, because there was just no point at all. . . .

"Hey, *here* she is," Felice said.

Who? Angela Lansbury? Had she come for the corpse already? But when I looked over at him for clarification, he was staring at the doorway. Beaming.

She was wearing a turquoise suede jacket with fringe, a tan cowboy hat, tan boots. I didn't recognize her for a second or two and then, Jesus Christ, I did.

"Get over here, Annie Oakley," Felice said. "Give your old hound dog a kiss."

Instead, she approached the foot of *my* bed. "Long time no see," she said.

"Yeah," I said. "Been years, hasn't it? How's my grandfather doing?"

She lifted up a bulky plastic bag—the head of John the Baptist, except it was rectangular. "He's all yours," she said.

"Is he? And now I suppose you're going to tell me I owe you—"

"No charge beyond what you've paid me already," she said. "And by the way, you have my condolences."

She held Domenico's bulky manuscript in front of her, at arm's length, and let go. It thudded onto my bed, just missing my injured foot.

thirty-one

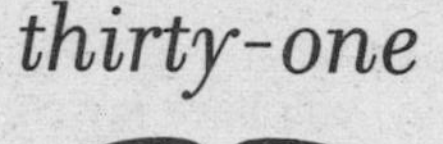

The History of Domenico Onofrio Tempesta, a Great Man from Humble Beginnings

8 *July* 1949

I, Domenico Onofrio Tempesta, was born sixty-nine years ago in the mountain village of Giuliana, Sicily, *lu giardino dello mondo*! I am the descendant of great men and many would say that when I look into the mirror, greatness looks back! Nonetheless, my life has been marred by sadness and tragedy. Now old age afflicts me with aching in my joints and rumbling bowels and weakness in my knees. But my mind remembers!

My beloved wife, Ignazia, *a buon'anima*, gave me one daughter but failed to honor me with sons. My daughter, Concettina Ipolita Tempesta, is too homely to marry (harelip) and so she stays home to be an old man's nuisance. From that red-haired girl with the rabbit's face, Tempesta blood spills wasted to the ground, like wine from a cracked jug. The proud name of Tempesta dies when I die.

If God has not blessed me with sons, He has at least given me the gift of keen memory. I tell my life story to keep alive the name Tempesta and to offer myself as a model for Italian youth to imitate! May the Sons of Mother Italy who read these words learn from them the path to prosperity and may they never be cursed, as I have been, with frightened rabbits underfoot or with skinny, goddamned monkeys!

As a boy, I grew up in the fearful shadow of Mount Etna, the great and terrible *vulcano* that brought my grandparents to ruin. Alfio and Maricchia Ciccia, my maternal grandparents, were proud landowners. Their hazelnut and almond groves were destroyed in the year 1865 when lava spewed from the western rim, choking life from the trees that had provided their livelihood. Four days later, the earth itself cracked open, killing my grandfather and his three sons. As Etna's cursed vomit cooled, it armored the Ciccia land with porous black rock. Worthless! My grandmother, crazy with grief, ended her life with poison soon after.

The only surviving member of the Ciccia family was the youngest child, Concettina. She had been playing alone in a field with her rag dolls when the lava began rushing down the hill after her. Scooping up the dollies in her arms, she ran to a nearby cedar tree to save herself from the *vulcano*. As she climbed up amidst the leaves and branches, she dropped one of her little dolls. With foolish bravery, the girl came down again, intent on saving her little friend made of rag and sawdust, but as she reached into that hateful hot stew from hell to rescue the *popa*, little Concettina burned the skin of her right hand severely, dropping once again the foolish doll, which sank back into the lava and was carried away. Somehow, Concettina held on and managed to elbow and claw and climb the tree again. From the highest branches, she screamed and screamed until it was safe to descend. For the rest of her life, Concettina wore on her right hand the reminder of her foolish attempt to rescue that worthless toy—a pink, shiny scar like a glove. As a child, I would stare at that scarred hand as I heard, over and over, the story of how little Concettina had saved her life but lost her *popi di pezza*. That damaged hand, with its more normal twin, held and fed and slapped me as I grew. Concettina, *a buon'anima*, was my beloved mother.

Orphaned at the age of eight after her own mother's self-poisoning, Mama was given to an old widow, a seamstress and lacemaker whose duty it was to dress the altar and the statuary at the little village church, including the famous Statue of the Weeping *Vergine*, famous throughout all of Sicily. The old woman taught my mother her painstaking craft and Mama herself became a skilled lacemaker. Sadly, as she grew to womanhood, she was often seized with screaming fits and strange dreams. She claimed, as well, that she could hear the voices of moths—those fluttering creatures which, she believed, were the souls of the dead who had failed to attain heavenly light. Instead, they swarmed around the counterfeit light of earthly things. The moths spoke to her—*pleaded* with her—Mama insisted, so endlessly that she sometimes had to lock herself in her room with the window bolted and the candles extinguished to be rid of their begging.

In 1874, Concettina Ciccia became the wife of my father, Giacomo Tempesta, a sulphur miner. Papa's work took him away each week from Giuliana to the mines, nine or ten kilometers into the foothills of Etna. With his fellow miners, he would travel back each Saturday to the village, where he would bathe and feast, then lie beside his wife on their finely embroidered sheets. It was on such a Saturday night in the year 1879 that my humble father became a hero.

According to the story first whispered by my mother to the village women and then repeated by those loose-tongued crones, Papa was lying awake after sharing a *passione* with his wife that was to result in my fortuitous conception! Etna had been asleep for several years, but that night Papa heard the faint first rumbling and hissing of the awakening *vulcano*. He rose from his bed and ran to the home of the buck-toothed *magistrato*, the richest man in Giuliana. There, Papa unfastened the bell from the magistrate's cow and ran through the village, ringing and shouting, awakening the citizens of Giuliana so that they could rescue themselves. Some say my mother, too, saved lives that night. She ran to the nearest tree and screamed like a siren!

For his heroism, my father received a *medaglia* from the King of Italy. It arrived by way of the *magistrato*'s official mail. Even before Papa could hold it in his hands, that goddamned buck-toothed *magistrato* bit the medal and determined it was solid gold, marking it forever with the impression of his horse-like teeth. Later, he presented the marred *medaglia* to my father at a formal *ceremonia* in the village square. At the time of this great honor, I was merely a seed in the melon of my mother's belly, but the village women agreed that the alignment of my conception with Mount Etna's eruption indicated that my destiny was to be a great and powerful man! I was now, in addition, the unborn son of a hero!

My mother presented her husband with three sons. Sons of Italy, marry wisely! Male heirs are the greatest gifts a woman can bestow! I, Domenico Onofrio Tempesta, came into this world on 11 May 1880 and my brother Pasquale was born two years later under more ordinary circumstances. My brother Vincenzo was born in 1883.

My father's heroism made him, after the village *padre* and the *magistrato*, the most respected man in our little village. As a young boy, I remember Papa leading parades and processions at holiday times and presiding with dignity at village festivals. At these times, he would take his *medaglia* from its keeping place and wear it proudly against his breast. I remember, too, that medal, with its likeness of the King on horseback and the magistrate's big teeth marks embedded in the horse's golden flank.

When I was six, the Virgin Mary herself confirmed the suspicions of the village women that, amongst the children of Giuliana, I was *speciale*!

Sent by my mother to deliver a new goose-down pillow to the *padre*, I looked for him inside the small limestone church and then out in the grotto made famous years earlier by the Statue of the Weeping *Vergine*. It was there that I—Domenico Onofrio Tempesta—witnessed a miracle! After a drought of seventy-seven years, tears were falling once again from the eyes of the statue! Of all the villagers—men, women, and children—it was I to whom the Weeping *Vergine* chose to reveal herself!

The statue cried for a week. Its precious tears were collected and applied to the sores of the afflicted, the eyes of the blind, the legs of the lame. The miracle became the subject of many theories about past sin and predictions of coming doom. News of the Weeping *Vergine* had kept the village priest at his station by the grotto day and night, saying prayers for the faithful and listening to the emergency confessions of newly repentant *siciliani*! It was only after the statue's eyes had dried and the number of pilgrims had dwindled that the *padre* was able to have a minute's peace and to interpret the meaning of the miracle. The good priest visited our home the following Sunday and told Mama and Papa that my discovery of the Virgin's tears had been a sign from Blessed Mary herself. I had been called to the priesthood, the *padre* said.

Believing, as most *siciliani* believe, that it is dangerous business for a father to educate his sons beyond himself, my father at first resisted the idea of my priestly studies. Papa had already spoken many times of my eventual work in the sulphur mines, first as his *caruso* and later as a miner myself. Papa's fellow miners shook their heads and warned him against allowing me to be sent away and taught to read and write. Yet my mother supported the priest's campaign to make me a man of God. Her status in the village had already been elevated because she had given birth to the boy to whom the *Vergine* had revealed her tears. As the mother of a priest, her standing would be raised higher still.

The *padre* wrote a letter to Rome concerning my religious calling and campaigned amongst the villagers to hand over their coins on behalf of the room, board, and travel expenses that would be required to turn me into a priest. When my father protested, my mother resumed once again her screaming fits on behalf of my education and circulated in the village the news of an ominous dream she had had. In the dream, God Almighty took the form of a black falcon and pecked out the eyes of my father for flouting His will. In the end, Papa surrendered.

And so I was sent on my seventh birthday to the convent school in Nicosia, run by the good Sisters of Humility. There, over a period of six years, I learned first the rudiments and then the subtleties of the Italian language. I learned, too, the hard and bitter lessons of jealousy and snobbery which my fellow students were happy to teach to the school's poorest but most gifted student, Domenico Onofrio Tempesta! The wealthy city boys would laugh at me as I scratched out my lessons on the cheap slate provided me. They, of course, had been handed the best supplies—quill pens, fine paper, and oceans of India ink with which to do their shoddy work! They, of course, had *famiglia* who paid the extra for confections on Saturday afternoon and musical shows and other distractions and *ricreazioni* while I had only my considerable native talents with which to entertain myself. But if I was the least well provided for amongst the boys at the convent school, I was the best loved by the good

Sisters of Humility, who marveled at my intellectual gifts and only occasionally boxed my ears or yanked my nose for small acts of temper or venial sins of pride—petty transgressions at most. I was, in truth, the sisters' favorite.

Back at home, my younger brother Pasquale took my place in the mines and became my father's *caruso*. It was Pasquale's job to carry the excavated rock up from the shaft and the makeshift stairway to the kiln at the mouth of the mines. There, the rock was melted and the *essenza di solforoso* extracted. It is the *caruso*'s lot in life to do the miner's dirty work—to work like a mule—and for that, my simple brother was well suited, just as I was well suited to the elevated and intellectual life of a boy destined for greater things.

With Papa, Pasquale, and me away from home, my youngest brother, Vincenzo, grew wild. Mama could not make him obey or help her, no matter how many blows she visited on his head or his *culo* with her big wooden cooking spoon. Vincenzo's theft of a lemon cake from the window of old *Signora* Migliaccio became a minor village scandal. "My firstborn serves God, my secondborn serves his father, and my youngest serves the devil!" Mama would lament.

When he turned ten, Vincenzo was apprenticed to Uncle Nardo, a *gumbare* of Papa's and a fat-bellied pig of a stonemason. May the carcass of that son of a bitch Nardo roast in the fires of Hell forever and ever and longer than that! On weekends, when our family reunited, my brother Pasquale was often bruised and swollen in the face because of accidents at the mine or because of his failings as Papa's *caruso*. Papa's stern hand often caught up with young Vincenzo on Sunday mornings after Uncle Nardo visited with his weekly report. Vincenzo was lazy, Nardo complained, and had fallen in with a band of young toughs who laughed and traveled together after work and committed acts of hooliganism. Sometimes my father beat both brothers, one after the other, Vincenzo for what he had done and Pasquale for what he had failed to do. My own behavior was beyond reproach, and I escaped my father's blows and received only his praise. Sons of Italy, take notice! Industry and seriousness of purpose will assure your success. Work hard! Honor *famiglia*, and follow the virtuous path!

More tomorrow if these goddamned hemorrhoids will let me sit and tell.

10 *July* 1949

At the age of sixteen, I was enrolled at the seminary school in R*oma* where I began my priestly studies. Meanwhile, at home in Giuliana, another scandal erupted that set my mother to screaming and caused my father such shame that he threatened to travel to the M*editerraneo* and throw his gold medallion into the sea as an act of contrition for having sired such a delinquent son as Vincenzo!

That season, Uncle Nardo had been hired by the *magistrato* to build an elaborate new courtyard and vineyard wall. One hot afternoon in the midst of this project, Nardo fell asleep in a shady spot after his noon meal. Vincenzo, unsupervised, seized his opportunity and scampered away from his afternoon work. The *magistrato*, who was entertaining a visiting *monsignore* from Calabria, had invited his guest to stroll the grounds of his estate. The two officials heard a strange groaning coming from the arbor and hurried to help whoever was hurt or wounded.

Shamefully, the groans had come from Vincenzo. What the *magistrato* and the *monsignore* found that afternoon among the twisting grapevines was my youngest brother, standing with his pants at his ankles and involved in a lewd act with the magistrate's spinster of a daughter who was twice my brother's age! The visiting monsignor nearly fainted from the shocking sight of that lunatic woman's head between my brother's legs. The shouting and screaming emitting from the mouth of the *magistrato* awoke Uncle Nardo, who came stumbling onto the scene before Vincenzo could even calm himself and button his britches. Nardo was fired on the spot. The *magistrato* banished both the disgraced mason and his lascivious apprentice from his property, uttering the wish that he, the *magistrato*, hoped to drown in the molten spew of Mount Etna before he laid eyes on either of those two again!

Uncle Nardo did not wait until Saturday to give Papa his weekly report about Vincenzo. Instead, he stormed the road that led from the village to the mines and shouted Papa's name into the gorge. What happened next was told to me by my brother Pasquale, who witnessed the whole thing.

Nardo told my father that he, Giacomo Tempesta, was liable for the sum of money Nardo had lost on the big job at the home of the *magistrato* as a result of Vincenzo's shameful behavior. Papa told Uncle Nardo that he could not hand over money he did not have. He promised, instead, that he would beat Vincenzo until the blood flowed and that Vincenzo would repent and reform. He would work so diligently from then on that the unfortunate incident would be bricked over by his youngest son's industry.

Uncle Fat-Belly shouted back that he had no use at all for a lazy billygoat with a frozen pipe in his pants. He demanded again the money he had lost. Again, my father assured Nardo that he could not pay such a sum as that to which Nardo laid claim.

"I see that a fancy golden *medaglia* cannot by itself make a man honorable," Nardo retorted. Those were his miserable words exactly. My brother Pasquale stood beside Papa and heard the slander himself!

To my father—to any *siciliano*!—an accusation against

one's honor is more painful than a blow to those loins that sire sons. Yet what could Papa do—perform an act of magic and make money spill from the sky? Pay off Uncle Nardo with bolts of my mother's lace?

That weekend, Papa went to the home of the *magistrato* with a jug of his best Malaga and his precious golden *medaglia*. *Signore* Big Shot had already sunk his buck teeth once into my father's *medaglia*; now Papa was going to allow him to gobble it up. By the time the wine jug was empty, my father's prized possession had been handed over to the *magistrato* so that Nardo could be reinstated as the *magistrato*'s mason. But there was a problem, still. Nardo would not take Vincenzo back! The next week, against the howls of my mother and the protests of the village *padre*, I was plucked from my priestly studies and sent back to Giuliana to work alongside Uncle Nardo in the unfinished courtyard. There, reluctantly, I began my apprenticeship under that fat-bellied son of the devil whom I soon grew to despise. I had no choice but to obey and honor the arrangement my father had made.

Young men of Sicily, remember this: a father's command is a son's law!

Over the months that I transformed myself from scholar to laborer in service to my father's honor, my hands coarsened and the muscles in my arms and chest grew strong from heavy lifting. With all my heart, I hated the trade of masonry and ached to be back among my books and words and religious icons, but that was not to be. With each stone I hoisted into place, with each tier of brick I laid, I honored my father's good name and good word. And as for the magistrate's filthy daughter, all her flirtations and lewd whisperings to me went unanswered. I upheld the good name of Tempesta and looked at stone and mortar and trowel, not at the hairy privates of that deranged pest of a *puttana* who kept lifting her skirts to entice me!

12 *July* 1949

In March of 1898, Mount Etna once again showed Sicily her wrath.

For three days and nights, steam leaked from the cracked southern rim. Next day, quiet as *la morte*. Day after that, the earth itself trembled and broke the town apart. In the hills, the section of the sulphur mine where my father and brother were working shuddered and collapsed. Pasquale, who was at the kiln when the shaking began, was spared. But Papa and eleven other miners and *carusi* perished in the mine.

Papa, Papa, I weep to remember your loving guidance! I curse the cruel earth that swallowed your life too soon!

Can talk no more today.

15 *July* 1949

As my father's eldest son, I was now the *sostegno del famiglia*. I took seriously my duties as both the family's main provider and its chief disciplinarian. I did not spare either of my brothers the beatings for which their actions or inactions cried out. With Vincenzo, especially, I was firm. His shameful behavior had cost me my priestly studies and cost the Tempesta family its ownership of our father's valuable gold *medaglia*. Though the *medaglia* had passed from my father to the *magistrato*, I, Domenico Onofrio Tempesta, was still allowed to wear it at village celebrations and at Easter and *vigilia di Natale*. I sat on the platform with the *padre* and the *magistrato* during parades with that medallion resting close to my heart—not only as the eldest son of a village hero, but also as the man to whom the Weeping *Vergine* had once shown her tears. It is not exaggeration to say that I was, even as a humble laborer, the most distinguished young man in Giuliana.

Sadly, as head of my *famiglia*, I sometimes was forced to raise a hand to my beloved mother. Mama had adjusted poorly to widowhood and to the reduced income and status my father's death had pressed upon us. Sometimes, crazy with grief, she would awaken screaming in the night or threatening that she would follow her mother's example and take poison rather than live this wretched life of toil and denial with three such terrible sons as Pasquale, Vincenzo, and me. She resumed her conversations with the moths. They comforted her, she said, and brought her news about her departed husband. Although I forbade these crazy, one-sided conversations of hers, she sometimes disobeyed me. The blows it was my sad duty to deliver for this and other reasons sometimes quieted Mama's screaming fits and sometimes began them.

In all things I learn quickly, and so my talents for masonry soon matched my talents for language and holy study. Within a matter of months, I had far surpassed that idiot Nardo in both artistry and industry and he knew it and was jealous. It is fair to say that I, Domenico Tempesta, carried most of Nardo's business on my strong and capable back. When I made that simple observation one afternoon as we worked side by side, Uncle Pig-Face laughed and cursed me and spat on my boot.

I reminded him that, in addition to being a superior mason, I was also the son of a hero and, unlike Nardo himself, an educated man. I demanded an apology.

Fat-Face laughed and let fly, instead, *sputa* from his mouth that landed on my other boot. My honor thus insulted, I was forced to spit into his *faccia di porco*. He spat back into my *faccia*. Fisticuffs followed and I delivered to Uncle Nardo the worst end of *that* bargain—a blackened eye and a nose that spouted blood like the Fountain of Trevi! Ha! I would have given him even worse, too, if he had not reached for his trowel and sunk it into the back of my left hand. I wear the small scar to this day—the mark of that son of a bitch of a stonemason who was so threatened by my natural superiority that he sought my ruin.

After that day, Nardo and I became bitter enemies and rivals. Giuliana offered little enough work for a mason and that goddamned Pig-Face spread slander about me and my craftsmanship. For the next two years, I watched work that should have been mine go, instead, to Nardo. To hell with those idiots who believed an old man's lies! That's what I say! They deserved the shoddy craftsmanship and heaving walls they no doubt received from that son of a bitch!

Sons of Italy, it was at this time that I conceived my plan to seek my *fortuna* in America! More tomorrow. That rabbit-faced daughter of mine calls me to eat my lunch and I have to stop just to shut up her voice.

16 *July* 1949

I had read much about *la 'Merica*—anything I could get my hands on, though in Giuliana, printed matter was rare and precious. America seemed a fitting place for me. I was, after all, the descendant of landowners. In that big country, I read, land went crying for ownership. America was the place for Great Men! In a land far away from earthquakes and slanderous old masons, I would fulfill my destiny!

We had *famiglia* there already. Papa's cousins, Vitaglio and Lena Buonano, had made the trip three years earlier and were rich already. My two brothers also wished to seek their destiny in the New World and to escape Mama's crazy screaming, which grew worse and worse. I therefore agreed to carry the burden of the firstborn son across the sea and allow my brothers to accompany me. In July 1901, Domenico, Pasquale, and Vincenzo Tempesta signed on as steerage passengers aboard the SS *Napolitano*.

Our dear Mama opposed our adventure, fearing that

our departure would make of her a destitute beggar-woman. She conjured pitiable pictures of herself, an old white-haired hag, forced until her dying days to survive on crusts of bread and rinds of cheese—left with only the moths to talk to. God would damn me, she warned, for forsaking my own mother. What would I have her do once we were gone? Roast rats for meat while her wicked sons bathed in honey and milk and counted their gold?

Despite Mama's protests, Pasquale, Vincenzo, and I sailed from Catania on the morning of 11 September 1901. Mama carried her objections all the way to the wagon that would transport us and our belongings from the village square to the seaport where the SS *Napolitano* was moored. As that rickety wagon rolled away, I looked back to see Mama raise her hands—one good, one scarred—and shout to God above, and to the sea on which we would travel, and to *Italia* itself that every mother's son should shrivel in the womb rather than grow and thrive only to rip out the heart of the woman who had borne him. "I bleed from the knife my sons have stuck in me!" Mama shrieked, over and over again, as the wagon pulled away. Her blood-curdling chant carried above the sound of horses' hooves and the wagon's squeaky wheels. "I bleed! I bleed!"

That was the last I ever saw of my mother. Later, she married Uncle Pig-Face just to spite me—took to her bed the man who had made it necessary for my father to surrender his gold *medaglia* to that greedy, buck-toothed *magistrato*, the man who had spit on my boots and ruined me with his lies. Until Mama's marriage to Nardo, I had dutifully sent her pretty postcards and, at Christmas-time, gifts of money and sweets. These were never acknowledged. Ha, never returned either! After that marriage, however, I stopped wasting my money. She died in 1913, but left me the legacy of her screaming, which I still hear in my memory. "I bleed! I bleed! I bleed!" Sitting in this room, talking into this goddamned machine, I hear her still!

Mama, what would you have had me do? Stay, and be supported by an old woman's lacemaking? Stay, and be starved out of work by the slanderer who polluted my father's bed? It was you, not I, who brought dishonor to the name of Giacomo Tempesta. It was *you*!

17 *July* 1949

Ours was a terrible twenty-four-day journey to *la 'Merica*, made unbearable by spoiled food, tainted water, and rolling seas. A broken propeller delayed us off the coast of Portugal for three extra days and nights of hell. Worst of all was the darkness and stink of life below, inside the belly of the big ship. Where there is sun and fresh air, there is hope, but here the sun did not shine and the air we breathed was stale and fetid. Aboveboard, bands played and the filthy rich dined off china and drank from fancy glasses. We in steerage lived like rats. Women and children sobbed, men fought each other over trifles, and everyone suffered the stench of vomit and excrement. There was a stabbing en route, and the birth of a baby, and the death of the child's mother two days later. That crying *bambino* was passed from breast to breast after that, and we prayed for its fate. All our fates. That baby cried for us all!

There were rats, too, plenty of them; nighttime was when those goddamned creatures prowled. One night I woke to find one sitting on my neck, sniffing at my mustache. I screamed out, waking even my brother Pasquale, who always slept like a dead man. After that night, I took no chances, napping as best I could while sitting or leaning against beams and walls. Day and night fell together on that hellish journey across the sea, and my mind existed in a place between sleep and vigilance.

During the voyage, my brother Vincenzo was as shamefully behaved as always—pinching women's behinds, boasting about his mischief, cheating at cards against men with bad and worsening tempers. Vincenzo was forever wandering away from Pasquale and me and getting himself in trouble, then calling for me to settle some dispute he had provoked. It is the firstborn's burden to unravel the knots that younger brothers make.

Throughout that endless and terrible journey across the ocean, I was afflicted with lice and worry—scratching and haunting myself with the cold fear of what would come to pass once we landed in this place I had risked everything to reach. For a Sicilian, home is everything. How could I have done this? Had I been bewitched into thinking that the unknown would be preferable to putting up with the petty nuisances of a stonemason who would die off in time anyway? The rumbling every few years of a distant *vulcano*? As much as I hated Etna for the damage it had visited upon my *famiglia*, the lives it had claimed, at least it was an enemy I could watch. What enemies awaited me in this *Mundo Novu* toward which we sailed? My heart was sick from thinking and worrying and pinching those goddamned lice between my fingernails!

The little rest I stole came to me in short, interrupted naps made terrible with nightmares. In my dreams, I saw flowing lava, cracking earth, screaming women stuck in fiery trees. Somewhere in the middle of one of those desperate nights, I promised myself that I would never again put myself through such a hellish journey—that I would never return home. That night I said farewell to Sicily forever. Whatever *la 'Merica* held in store for me, it was where I would stay for the rest of my days. The vow was small comfort, but comfort nonetheless.

Sometimes as the other steerage travelers slept, I crept amongst them and over them and did what was forbidden: climbed the narrow stairs to the ship's deck where the wealthier travelers strolled and where I might take into my lungs the clean salt air or watch the moon's rippling reflection against that endless sea. In the school run by the good Sisters of Humility, I had envied the rich boys their supplies of India ink. Now, here in the moonlight, was an ocean full of it through which we traveled—enough *inchiostro di china* in which to drown the whole world, let alone Domenico Tempesta. But I would not give those haughty boys at the convent school the satisfaction of dying! I was not weak. I had been the best of them—the student most loved by the good sisters—and I would prevail!

On one such night of watching the endless ocean, the moon shone brighter than usual, illuminating a small school of dolphins that jumped and swam alongside the SS *Napolitano*. I have always been a modern man who leaves superstition to ignorant old women, but the sight of those *delfini* that night—their bodies arcing toward the sky, their taut skin glistening in the moonlight—it seemed to me a powerful omen. That night, I stood smiling through my tears and was comforted. I knelt on the ship's deck to pray and, in that position, fell into the only sweet, deep sleep I enjoyed during that long and horrible journey.

I awakened next morning to the blinding sun, a mocking voice, and a kick in the ribs! When I squinted and looked up, I was peering into the arrogant face of a ship's waiter. Nearby, a well-dressed couple stood staring at me with looks of disdain. "Get back down where you belong," the haughty waiter ordered—commanding me, the son of a hero! The grandson of landowners! A man who had once been singled out by the Blessed Virgin herself!

The rich woman shook her head and chattered like a squirrel. "*Poveri si, sporchi no*," she told the rich man.*

Still half-asleep, I rose and stumbled toward the ship's hold, and the waiter and the well-dressed couple

* "Being poor is no excuse for being filthy."—NF

moved on. My dignity returned along with my consciousness. Boldly, I turned back, shouting to the three of them, "*Il mondo e fatto a scale, chi le scende e chi le sale*!"*

One day, I vowed, I would have power and money enough to spit in the faces of those who had humiliated me! In America, my destiny would be realized and I would be avenged!

* "The world is made of stairs: there are those who go up and those who go down."—NF

thirty-two

Rain drummed against the car roof. From the east, a flash of light, a low rumble. Thunder? In February?

Exit 4: Division Street and Downtown.

Should have canceled, I thought. Those stairs at Dr. Patel's were going to be a bitch to climb on crutches. Why was I even *doing* this?

Because you're looking for help, I reminded myself. For answers.

I reached over and punched the radio buttons, trying to get some news. Now that Saddam had set all the oil wells on fire, there was talk that the CIA, or the Israelis, or someone in his own ranks was going to whack the bastard.

"—held in Washington this morning, Joint Chiefs of Staff Chairman Colin Powell stated that, although allied combat operations have dramatically exceeded expectations, a ground campaign will most likely be necessary to ensure total victory against Iraqi aggression."

You hear that, Papa? Not just *meeting* our expectations; *exceeding* them. Money and power, man, just like you said. Might still makes right. God bless America.

"Meanwhile, in Kuwait, the hundreds of oil installations

ablaze since yesterday have blocked the sun, shrouding the region in eerie daytime darkness."

I pictured it like one of those Biblical epics Ma used to take us to. *Ben Hur, King of Kings*—one of those wide-screen jobs. And hey, Desert Storm *was* Biblical, in a way: fire and brimstone, slaughtered innocents. If you cocked your head and squinted a little, you could see that all those crazy prophesies of Thomas's had hit their mark. Hey, the freakin' *sun* wasn't even shining anymore. . . . You hear that, Domenico? You thought *you* were touched by God because you saw some stupid statue crying? He *trumped* you, man. Your crazy grandson's a *prophet*.

He'd surprised me these past weeks, though. Thomas. His nonreaction to the war. I'd gone down to Hatch the morning after they'd fired the first missiles, expecting to have to peel him off the ceiling. See him in restraints, or something. But he'd just sat there, clear-eyed, staring at CNN, same as everyone else. By then, he'd resigned himself to war—had become indifferent to the thing that, three months earlier, he'd cut off his friggin' *hand* to try and stop. Part of it was the Haldol, like they said, but not all of it. It was like . . . like he'd waved the white flag. Resigned his post as Chairman of Jesus's Joint Chiefs of Staff. These days, for good or bad, Thomas's fighting spirit was as gone as his right hand.

I had to face it: he was lost down there, no matter how much I rattled the cage door on his behalf. And hey, hadn't I finally gotten what I always wanted? Separation? Free agency? Be careful what you wish for. Right, Domenico?

I took a quick glimpse of myself in the rearview mirror. Thought: well, your brother may be lost, but at least you're still here. Fell three stories off that roof and lived to tell the tale. Got through that other night, too—the night you *really* hit bottom. . . .

And it *had* gotten better, hadn't it? Just like Leo and the doctors and everyone else had promised it would. Not great, not perfect. But *better*. I was down from two crutches to one. I was driving again. A Ford Escort beat walking. Right?

A heartbeat was more than *some* people had. Right, Papa, you sanctimonious son of a bitch? Right, Rood?

I signaled a right into the strip mall and pulled into a handicapped space near her door. Fished out my permit. It was one of the few perks of being a gimp: primo parking, the empty space by the door in the middle of a rainstorm. I cut the engine. Sat there for a minute or so, thinking about how much I *didn't* want to go up there. Get on with the autopsy of my life. All our lives, really—mine and Thomas's, Ma's, Ray's. Even old Domenico's, I guess. Judging from the little bit I'd read so far of the "great man from humble beginnings," I was going to have to factor that old bastard into the equation, too.

I was early, though. Better to just sit out in the car and listen to the rain drum against the roof than to go up and cool my jets in that cramped little space outside her door. I looked in the mirror at my fogged-up face. Thought, again, about that rock-bottom night—the third night after I'd gotten home from the hospital. . . .

For three days, everyone had been milling around, getting in each other's way trying to help out the poor jerk who'd totaled his truck and fallen off a roof, and whose pregnant girlfriend had bailed in the middle of it. The home health care people, Meals on Wheels, Leo and Angie, Ray: it'd been like Grand Central Station over there for three days and then, on that third night, it got quiet. I'd been set up for my first nighttime solo: phone, urinal, remote control for the TV. Water in a thermos, two Percoset doses laid out on the nightstand. The health care aide was due back at seven the next morning. All I had to do was lie there. Stay put. Watch TV, drug myself on schedule, and sleep.

But I got restless. Panicky. I couldn't stand just lying there, listening anymore to that yacking little bedside TV that Leo had gotten me. Only, when I turned the damned thing off, the silence was even worse. The absolute quiet: it spooked me. And when I closed my eyes, I saw my brother: the way his eyes had looked at me in my morphine dream, the way his body had jerked and twisted on the end of the noose. . . .

I saw Rood, up in his attic window. . . .

Saw the Duchess, standing by my hospital bed, holding

that cassette of hers. . . . She'd let him *watch* us, man. She'd let that sick fuck turn our most private, our most intimate . . . And both of those times he'd been there—each of those two nights she'd let him trespass like that—it had been *him* she was making love to. Not me. I'd just been the dupe, the means to their perverted little end. And so I lay there feeling ashamed. Dirty. Powerless to take back my fuck. . . .

I got up. Got out of bed, in spite of all the promises I had made to everyone to stay put. I gimped my way out to the kitchen. Stood there, watching the phone message blinks. Nine, ten, eleven. I'd been avoiding listening to that thing since I'd gotten home from the hospital three days before. At first I didn't even *know* why and then, finally, I realized what it was: Rood. I was afraid Rood's voice would be on there, whether he'd blown out his brains or not. *Welcome to the black hole, Dominick. I'm your tour guide, Henry Rood. . . .*

I'd been planning it right along—had spent a lot of time in the hospital getting used to the idea. Figuring out how. I figured I'd take my Percoset prescription and that Happy Holidays bottle of Scotch I'd gotten and just Kevorkian myself. Get it over with. Because it was all over anyway. Joy had fucked me over and left. Dessa sure as hell wasn't coming back. She'd sent over some stew, put a couple of get-well cards in the mail. But that was all I was going to get. Those years we'd been together were as dead, now, as our daughter. And without the hope of her ever coming back, I was already a dead man. Breathing was just a technicality.

I hobbled my way out to the spare room and got the Scotch. Got back to the kitchen. I eased myself down onto a chair, broke the seal, unscrewed the cap. Took three or four long swigs—swallowed, winced. In between slugs, I kept picking up my prescription vial. Shaking it. Listening to those capsules click around in there. Dead man's castanets, I thought. It struck me funny.

Should I leave a note? *Dear Ray, Thanks for the memories. . . . Dear Dessa, Thanks for sticking by me, for better or worse.* And what about Thomas? . . .

Hey, man, *fuck* Thomas. Wouldn't that be one of suicide's big perks—throwing the look-alike talking corpse, once and for all, off my shoulders? Getting my life sentence as my brother's keeper commuted? It was funny, though—not at all what I'd figured on: Thomas outlasting me. Winning.

I wanted to watch myself take them: watch the condemned man eat his last meal. On the way to the bathroom—the medicine cabinet mirror—I stopped.

Slipped open the door of Joy's empty closet.

I tapped the empty wire hangers, watched the way they rocked back and forth, back and forth. Betrayal didn't cut any deeper than what she had done. Let him into our bedroom—let him crouch in there like sin itself. . . . And I thought, suddenly, about Ralph Drinkwater. The way Joseph Monk had snatched his sister and his mother had self-destructed over it. The way Dell Weeks and his wife had given Ralph food and shelter for . . . for his nakedness. For dirty pictures that they could turn around and sell to strangers. That's what *that* had been about: profiting from a young boy's vulnerability—a confused kid's need to have a home. *This* was how bad human nature could get, I thought. This was the sweet little world I was checking out of.

The guy in the medicine cabinet mirror scared me a little—looked both familiar and strange. Looked nothing like Henry Rood had looked. . . . I held up my two hands, wiggled my fingers a little. Saw Thomas, whole again. Saw Ma without the split in her lip. And I could see Domenico, too—that stern face in the tinted portrait on my mother's bureau. The resemblances were scary. Undeniable. We were all, in a way, each other. . . .

Maybe we were damned or something. Cursed. Was that it? . . . Funny: I was never going to finish Papa's manuscript after all. I'd lost that damned thing, had gotten it back again, and then had put off reading it for weeks. Months, now, really. Had only just that week started reading it. I'd purposely *avoided* reading it—his "history of a great man from humble beginnings." Unfinished business. A loose end. Well, so what? Fuck it, man. Couldn't keep the Grim Reaper waiting. . . . It was strange, though. Or it was the Percoset or something. I could see their faces in my face. . . .

I couldn't do it.

Poured that little cascade of capsules down the sink instead of down my throat. Turned the water on and washed away my big suicide. I hobbled back into the bedroom. Eased myself back down on the bed.

Called Leo.

And by some miracle, it was Leo who answered. "Hello? . . . *Hello?*"

It felt like one of those dreams where you can't run, can't scream.

"Dominick? Dominick, is that you? . . . Hold on, man. I'm coming right over."

It was time. The rain had let up a little. I swung the door open and hoisted my bad leg over and onto the wet asphalt. With all the leg room they gave you in these luxury Escorts, getting in and out on a bum foot was a breeze. And pigs flew. And we were in that war over in Kuwait for all the *right* reasons. . . .

Inside, I surveyed the long, wet flight of stairs that led up to Miss Patti's Academy of World Dance on the left, Dr. Patel's office on the right. When I'd been going to see her before, I hadn't even really *noticed* those stairs—had probably barreled up the damn things two at a time. But that had been three months and a lifetime ago—back when Rood was still leaving messages on my machine and Joy's boyfriend was still hiding in the closet and I was still kidding myself about springing my brother from Hatch. Everything had changed since then. Everything. We'd gone to goddamned *war,* for Christ's sake. . . .

The stairwell walls vibrated with the pulse of African drum music. *"Let the rhythm enter your body,"* someone called out up there. *"Let it* be *your body. Faster, now! Faster!"*

Take it slow, I told myself. Damn stairs were wet, waxed. Your ankle's still weak, no matter how good you're doing down at physical therapy. You slip and fall, you'll set yourself back another couple months. You'll *really* need a shrink then.

I clutched the railing with my left hand, the crutch with my right. Started up. Those stairs were just the warm-up, I reminded myself. The *real* challenge was up at the top, door on the right. Because if I was serious about finally getting some answers, they weren't going to come without some pain. Without me opening up a vein or two.

I was a third of the way up when I heard footsteps, giggles. The door below banged open. I froze. Held my breath. "Wait a minute, girls," some merciful mother called. "Wait for that man to get up."

"It's okay," I called back over my shoulder. "They can go around me. I'll just hold on to the rail."

"No, no, you go ahead. Take your time."

I negotiated a step. Another one. What about that goddamned Americans with Disabilities act that Bush had signed, anyway? Where was the friggin' *elevator*? I could hear them all down there, watching me, waiting.

"Really," I called back. "I'll just stop. Have 'em go around me."

She must have given them the okay because the next thing I knew, they were clomping up, stampeding past me. "Easy," I mumbled. "Easy." My crutch hand was shaking so bad, the rubber tip on the bottom squeaked against the wet stair.

By the time I got to the top, I'd had to stop and let three more groups pass—one up, two down. My usual great timing: I'd managed to get there right when all the classes were changing. But, okay, I'd made it. Gotten up there.

I stood at Dr. Patel's door, my heart thumping, my shirt soaked in sweat. In three months' time, I'd forgotten the protocol—whether you knocked first or just went in.

So what are you going to do then, Birdsey? Just stand here? Make a chickenshit U-turn and climb all the way back *down* again?

Opening Dr. Patel's door was going to mean opening the front door over on Hollyhock Avenue. Opening the door on all our lives, and on Domenico's life, too. Stepping back into all that. I knew that now.

You want to go forward? Go back.

I raised my fist.

Lowered it again.

Took a breath, raised it again. Knocked.

thirty-three

20 *July* 1949

The hellish voyage aboard the SS *Napolitano* ended on the morning of 4 October 1901. As the ship sailed into New York Harbor, I gazed in near-disbelief at the beautiful *Statu di Libberta*! My heart beat rapidly. I made the sign of the cross. It was as if I was in the presence of the Weeping *Vergine* herself, only this time the tears fell from my own eyes, not those of the stone woman! I dropped to my knees in the middle of the pushing crowd, hiding as best I could my tears and thanking the Son of God and His Holy Mother that we had landed on American soil.

My young brother Vincenzo threw cold water on my reverie. "If all the women in America are of such formidable size as this one," Vincenzo said in a loud voice, pointing at that holy statue, "then they will be glad that Vincenzo Tempesta has finally arrived to satisfy their desires and fill up their big pussies!" The mood of the weary travelers was one of giddy relief, and so several of the men around us laughed at Vincenzo's shameful remark, my brother Pasquale included. Thus encouraged, Vincenzo thrust his hips forward and backward in a lewd manner. It was, of course, my duty and my burden to get off my knees and rise to my full height. I answered Vincenzo's shocking offense with the back of my hand, and gave Pasquale a poke as well. Chastened to *silenzio*, Vincenzo arrived on American soil dripping Tempesta blood from his broken lip.

My two brothers and I lived for a while in Brooklyn with our cousins and sponsors, Lena and Vitaglio, and their five young brats. I was unable to find work as a mason. Instead, I took a nighttime job as a *janitore* at the New York Public Library. (Just as well that I had found night work—my journey aboard the *Napolitano* had bedeviled my sleep forever!) Pasquale got work as a street sweeper and Vincenzo washed glasses and ran errands at a small *taverna* just down the street from my cousins' apartment, a saloon that was patronized mostly by *siciliani*.

During my free hours, I practiced English at the library with the help of discarded newspapers and magazines. In this endeavor, I was assisted by a kindly one-eyed librarian who gave me my beloved coverless dictionary, which the library was about to destroy. To destroy a book's insides because of outside defect? Sacrilege! The wastefulness of Americans disgusted me when I first arrived, but not my brothers. In their squandering ways, Pasquale and Vincenzo quickly became *'Mericano*. Each week, they paid board to our cousins and threw away the little of their salaries that was left on stage shows and glasses of beer and games of pinochle, ignoring, as usual, the good example I provided them. As for myself, I studied and saved my money with the determination of one who is destined to seize opportunity and succeed! Often, I pictured in my mind the snobbish waiter and the wealthy couple who had stared at me with disgust on board the deck of the SS *Napolitano*. . . . *The world is made of stairs; some go up and some go down*. . . . To this day, I am glad in my heart that that haughty couple heard my reply. And as for that arrogant, goddamned waiter, I hope that he tripped over his own shoelaces and fell into the ocean, headfirst, and was strangled by the tentacles of a hungry octopus!

In January of 1908, Vincenzo brought home a paper printed and distributed by the American Woolen and Textile Company of Three Rivers, Connecticut. That day at the tavern, Vincenzo reported, there had been much excitement about the paper from the saloon customers. "Read it, Domenico!" Vincenzo ordered me. "R*ead*!"

The paper said the company had just received a contract from the Government of the United States of America for the manufacture of cotton and wool for sailors' coats and uniforms. American Woolen and Textile paid a fair wage and they were hiring, the paper said. They ran a company store that sold goods to workers at low prices. They welcomed Italians to their ranks. Three Rivers, Connecticut, Vincenzo had heard that day, already had a sizable and growing population of *siciliani* and, no doubt, an eligible *siciliana* or two as well. According to Vincenzo, half a dozen customers at the *taverna* had already left Brooklyn to take jobs there.

My brother Pasquale, usually the most passive of men, was resistant to the idea of relocating. "Where is this Three Rivers, Connecticut, anyway?" he asked. "If it is in the Wild West, we could be shot in our hearts with arrows!" Pasquale, who was sometimes as dim as dust, had been watching out for Indians since we set foot in *Stati Uniti*.

That evening both of my brothers accompanied me to the New York Public Library. Both stared wide-eyed and open-mouthed as my finger traced on the page of the atlas the short distance from New York to Three Rivers. My friend, the one-eyed librarian, confirmed that the town was only a four-hour train ride away. We two whispered in English of the opportunity of working at the mills and of Pasquale's fear of being killed by wild Indians. The librarian smiled and told me to tell Pasquale that he would have to travel further than Connecticut to live the life of a cowboy! There were no savages hiding in the hills of Connecticut.

Pasquale and Vincenzo smiled, too, though neither spoke much English beyond "Please" and "Thank you" and "How much?" Vincenzo said to Pasquale in Italian, "This one-eyed hag must be negotiating with Domenico the price of spending an evening of joy in my bed."

Pasquale's laughter echoed loudly enough in the hushed, high-ceilinged room to raise the heads of several patrons and to put a frown on the face of my friend the librarian.

"Please!" I warned my brothers in Italian. "You are in a hall of great books! Act in a manner befitting the honor of the name Tempesta!"

I resumed my conversation with the librarian.

"My robust parts and my good looks are so exciting this hag," Vincenzo told Pasquale, "that she is undressing me with her one good eye. Better be careful, *bella donna*, or the big sausage hiding in my pants will stir and poke out your other eye as well!"

Now Pasquale's loud guffaws all but shook the books off the shelves. Librarians and patrons stared crossly at us from all points in the massive reading room. "I apologize for the stupidness of my brothers," I told One-Eye.

"The *stupidity* of your brothers," she corrected me. "Say it: the *stupidity*."

"Yes, yes, *grazie*, the *stupidity* of my brothers," I repeated. Then I yanked both brothers by the ear and pulled them toward the library's main entrance.

The following afternoon, a Saturday, we boarded the train from New York to Three Rivers. We liked what we saw of both the mill and the town. Wages were good, rent was cheap, and a meal downtown of steak and potatoes cost twenty-five cents less than it did in Brooklyn. More on the plate, too!

The three of us—my brothers and I—were hired as dyers in Plant Number 2 at American Woolen and Textile. We rented a room at *Signora* Saveria Siragusa's boardinghouse on Pleasant Hill. *Signora* Siragusa had herself grown up in the foothills of Sicily and was happy to share her house with us for the sum of one dollar, fifty cents apiece, to be paid each week after breakfast on Saturday mornings.

21 *July* 1949

I worked second shift at American Woolen and Textile and quickly impressed the mill bosses with my industry and seriousness of purpose. My friend the librarian had been both right and wrong. No Indians hid in the trees in Connecticut, but one of them worked alongside me at the mill. His name was Nabby Drinkwater. He was my partner at the dye vat, but he was a lazy son of a bitch and slowed me down. We were paid for piecework and Drinkwater's sluggish pace reached in and stole money from my pocket. "Faster!" I used to tell that *figliu d'una mingia*. "Work faster!"

Drinkwater tried to make me his friend—tried to get me to go to his house or out to a tavern sometimes—but I ignored his foolish talk and pretended not to understand him. *Siciliani* trust family first, then villagers, then fellow countrymen. I trusted no one else, especially not shifty dark-skinned Indians whose idleness stole money from my pocket!

I couldn't cuff Drinkwater on the head to make him work faster, but I could cuff my brother Pasquale or my brother Vincenzo. If one of my brothers was my partner at the dye vat, I calculated, we would show these *'Mericani* what hard work looked like. One Saturday, at the end of my shift, while the other workers ran home to their sleep and their amusements, I followed the boss dyer, Bryce, to the agent's glass-walled office. All that afternoon and evening, I had been rehearsing in English my reasons why it would be wise for American Woolen and Textile to pull one of my brothers away from his assigned work and put him to work with me instead. Now I knocked on the agent's door. I would have not only Bryce's ear, but the ear of the big boss, too. Flynn, the agent—the *pezzo grosso*.

Bryce and Flynn smirked when they saw me standing there. Their cigar smoke hung in the air like clouds over Mount Etna. "Who's *this* organ-grinder?" Flynn asked.

The two both smiled and stared at me. "New dyer," Bryce said. "Just hired him this week." He turned to me, asking me what I wanted, addressing me in a voice meant to scare me away.

"That Indian slows me down," I said. "I can earn a better wage if my work is not tied to his work."

"Who's he talking about?" Flynn asked.

"Nabby Drinkwater," Bryce said.

"Well, well, this is just what we need," the boss mumbled. "Some wop calling the shots around here. Call his bluff, why don't you? Teach this dago a lesson. Just don't fuck with production."

My brain raced. *Call his bluff*? *Call his bluff*? I didn't know *Call his bluff*. Goddamn crazy English language.

Bryce put his arm around my shoulder in a gesture of false friendship. He said he was glad that he had hired such a dedicated worker as I—and a genius besides. "You're so smart, maybe *you* should be boss dyer instead of me. What do you think?"

Dangerous for me if I told him what I really thought: that it was a good idea. Instead, I stood there and shut my mouth.

"So Drinkwater slows you down, eh?" Bryce said. "Well, I'll tell you what we're going to do. Starting tomorrow, we'll transfer Nabby to the finishing department. You can work all by your lonesome—do your job *and* his at your superior rate of speed. How does that sound?"

Their laughter at my expense began even before the door closed behind me. "I'll have the Indian clean the storage room and then get him the hell back in there before this arrogant wop keels over," Bryce told Flynn, *sotto voce*. "He won't know whether he's coming or going by the time an hour's up. That'll shut him up."

That morning I went home to the boardinghouse but could not sleep. Now they were out to get Domenico Tempesta. To break the man who only wanted to make good money for doing good work. Jealousy of superior men was everywhere, I realized—on both sides of the sea. Even foremen and agents were jealous of me.

The first shift without the Indian was the worst. I worked through dinner break, soaked in my own sweat, not even taking the time to look up at the other workers. Still, I knew they were laughing at me. I *lost* money that night. The second night went a little better (broke even). The third night was easier still. By the end of that week, I had conditioned myself for the two-person job they had given me to break me down. Working alone, I had increased the second-shift production of two men! After that, the snickering stopped, all right. The other dyers resented my industry. Bryce, too. But I had gotten Flynn's attention. Flynn began to regard me as a worker to watch and consult.

Gradually, I rose through the ranks from laborer to second hand. Then, in 1916, a blood vessel burst inside Bryce's brain. Good riddance to that son of a bitch. At his funeral, I approached Flynn and asked for the dead man's job. "We'll see," Flynn said. "But Jesus Christ, man, wait until he's cold." Through three long nights' worth of work, I waited for Flynn's decision. Then the good news came. Flynn called me into his office so that he and I could have "a little chat." By the time I left, I had been named American Woolen and Textile's first boss dyer of Italian heritage!

Sons of Italy, how had this great thing happened? It

had happened through hard work and seriousness of purpose. These are the keys to success in *Stati Uniti*! Industry like mine is what has made America great!

24 *July* 1949

Bad cold for third day. I told that good-for-nothing daughter of mine to cut up an onion and wrap it up in cheesecloth for me to wear on my head and draw out the mucus, but she says, "Go lie down, Papa. Take a nap."

"What I do is my business, *Signorina* Stupid-Head!" I told her back. "Do as you're told and get me my goddamned poultice!" I don't want her snooping around these words of mine. . . . Where was I? My promotion? Ah, yes.

No more piecework for Domenico Tempesta! In addition to my work at the mill, now at a fixed salary of thirty-five cents an hour, I took small masonry and repair jobs during the spring and summer months. Little by little, one penny after another penny, I saved my money rather than wasting it on pleasures like women and drink and stage shows. I made it my business to befriend an old Yankee dairy farmer named Rosemark. Rosemark's time was running out; he had property at the top of Hollyhock Hill but no sons to inherit it. He told me he had been talking to the big shots of the town of Three Rivers—Shanley, that goddamned crooked mayor, and his cronies. He wanted to make sure his wife would be provided for. I saw opportunity approaching. If Rosemark sold his land to the town, he told me, the town would divide the property into half-acre city lots. I had my eyes on these.

Too sick today, too much mucus in my head. I'll go listen to those no-good Dodgers on the radio and take a nap now, but not because that useless daughter of mine told me to. I thought of it before she said it.

26 July 1949

Neither of my brothers lasted at the mill. Soon after he was hired, Vincenzo was moved to the picking department, a demotion, and then was fired for running a small numbers game for American Woolen and Textile workers. Some of the foremen were regular players in Vincenzo's games of chance, but they acted the parts of pious saints when the police sergeant came to ask questions with Flynn, the agent, by his side. Of course, I was above suspicion during this little *investigazione*. I would never have wasted my money on gambling when good land would soon be up for sale. But my brother Vincenzo got the boot.

Vincenzo next became a greengrocer at Hurok's Market, where his good looks and foolish antics bedeviled lady customers into buying more bananas and beans than they needed. Customers of Cranston's Market, on the opposite side of the street from Hurok's, began to walk across the road just to buy their produce from my crazy brother. The Huroks were Jews—happy to put up with Vincenzo's nonsense if it meant ten pennies in their pocket instead of nine. "He's a nice boy, your brother," Mrs. Hurok told me once, when I stopped in for a pound of roasted peanuts. "He's a stupid-head," I responded, but not without some small sense of pride at her remark. Compliments about Vincenzo were as rare as hen's teeth, but perhaps, at long last, my good example had begun to sink into his stubborn *cocuzza*.

Customers would follow Vincenzo around the store, staring or calling his name—this much I witnessed myself. Vincenzo would whisper flattery into the ear of one woman, turn and sing a snatch of Verdi to another. His fruit-peddling each day was a performance!

"Hurok has increased my wage to seven dollars a week!" Vincenzo boasted one night at the boardinghouse. "It's because I'm so good for business!"

"Pfft," I said, waving my hand at him. "I make twenty-three dollars and fifty cents a week. What talent does it take to polish and pile fruit?" Still, I wrote a picture post-card to Mama, telling her of Vincenzo's modest success and my own more substantial achievements. That farmer up on Hollyhock Hill had died suddenly and I'd heard that the town was going to go ahead and buy his land and resell. I wrote to Mama that someday soon I would be a property owner just as my grandparents, the Ciccias, had been.

Bah! My pride in my brother Vincenzo was a boat that sank soon enough. Many of those women who visited him by day at Hurok's invited him to visit them after dark as well. Although my own good name was above reproach, tongue-wagging *siciliani* began to buzz like mosquitoes about my brother's life under the sheets with a regular League of Nations of willing women—not only Italians, but also Irish, Polish, Ukrainian—even that pockmarked Hungarian widow who ran the saloon on River Street. That one was not much younger than Mama and had a mustache thick enough to twirl on the ends! It was shameful but true: Vincenzo would poke his thing anywhere.

One day, that son of a bitch McNulty, monsignor of the Church of St. Mary of Jesus Christ, came to the dye room at American Woolen and Textile for the purpose of speaking to me. At his arm was Flynn, the agent—the big boss. Like my brothers and me, Flynn was a parishioner of St. Mary's. He was also a friend of the monsignor and a big contributor to the church. The monsignor reminded us of this every Sunday, nodding and smiling at Flynn, who sat with his family in the front pew reserved specially for Mr. *Pezzo Grosso*.

Flynn told me to follow him and the monsignor to his office. There he invited me with false smiles to sit, please sit, take a load off my feet, ha ha. Two thoughts entered my mind as I obeyed Flynn: either I was about to be fired or I was about to be ordered to start placing my hard-earned money in the collection basket at Sunday Mass! Damn them, I thought as I sat down. My own priestly studies in Rome no doubt had surpassed the scholarship of this fat-headed mick of a monsignor. I worked hard for my money while Flynn sat on his ass all day. Where my money went was my business.

"Now, Mr. Tempesta, I know you Eye-talian men are burdened with too much sex inside you," the monsignor began—to *me*, a man who was as chaste as he—*more* chaste, probably! From my boyhood experiences at the school in Nicosia, I knew all about the wandering hands of pious priests! "And while I understand and accept that it's a part of your nature," he continued, "I beg and entreat you to do something about that wild cur of a brother of yours."

"I have two brothers," I said. "Which brother do you mean?"

"The fruit peddler," Flynn answered for him. "That cocky little Romeo down at Hurok's Market."

An unfortunate problem had developed, the monsignor explained. A young unmarried Irish girl from a fine parish family had become pregnant by Vincenzo. She hadn't known any better; Vincenzo had taken advantage of her innocence. And while the girl's parents had no wish to see their daughter married off to the likes of my brother—they had arranged for her a proper marriage to a recent immigrant from Limerick—they nevertheless wanted to prevent further broken hearts and bastards. In defense of the good family name of Tempesta, the monsignor said, I must meet with Vincenzo and convince him to exert some self-control.

"My assistant, young Father Guglielmo, will be happy to help you at this meeting to give your orders moral weight and to hear, perhaps, your brother's confession and his recitation of the act of contrition," the monsignor said. "I would gladly attend the meeting myself, but perhaps it might be more effective if the young hooligan heard the message from one of his own kind."

One of his own kind—ha! For all of his faults, my brother was, like me, the son of a hero who had taken on a *vulcano* and received a gold *medaglia* for his effort! What were that skinny little Father Guglielmo's credentials beyond his Italian name? Who was that puny little priest to advise Tempestas?

"I'm sure Domenico here can get things under control," Flynn promised the monsignor. "He's not like most of the wops I got out on the floor. He keeps his nose clean and does his work."

Domenico Tempesta does the work of *two* men, I felt like reminding that rich *ipocrita*! Earlier that year, Flynn had had his way with Alma, a German girl—one of the spoolers. When she grew big in the belly, she was hurried away to American Woolen's sister mill in Massachusetts and married off to a sheep shearer. That goddamned monsignor should have announced *that* from his pulpit one Sunday!

I agreed, however, to honor the priest and the agent's request. Better to deliver a lecture to my stupid-headed brother Vincenzo—a rap or two on his hard *cocuzza*—than to lose my job or have to pour all my hard-earned savings into the monsignor's collection basket. In that respect, at least, the meeting in the boss's office was a relief.

That skinny priest Father Guglielmo called at the boardinghouse the following Sunday afternoon. From the way *Signora* Siragusa flapped her hands and carried on, you might have thought the Pope himself had rung the bell instead of that scrawny priest. He and I sat Vincenzo down in the *signora*'s parlor. Vincenzo, who was always the most amiable of young men if not the best behaved, lit us all cigars before we began. When Father Guglielmo took a puff or two, I thought he would die from all the coughing that followed. That one was more nervous than a dog during a thunderstorm!

"Vincenzo," I said, beginning my oration "We speak to you today because your behavior brings shame on our deceased father and our beloved mother back in the Old Country. Your boots beneath the bed muddy the name of Tempesta."

Vincenzo's face looked at me the same way it had looked when he had crawled at my feet as a baby, back in Giuliana. "My behavior?" Vincenzo said. "My boots? *Non capisco un cavalo, Domenico*!"* Then, realizing that the language he had just used was not appropriate for a priest to hear, he turned to little Guglielmo. "*Scusa, Padre. Scusa*."

"Your boots beneath the beds of women!" I said. But still, Vincenzo looked at me with innocent eyes, as if he had kept his pants on since his arrival in America. I was beginning to lose patience. "*Fungol! Fungol!*" I shouted.** From behind the kitchen door, I heard the *signora* gasp. Now it was my turn to apologize to that skinny priest.

Big smile from Vincenzo now, as if his behavior was a source of pride, not shame. But I would wipe that smile off the face of that cocky brother of mine.

"It is time for you to marry and settle down and be done with it," I said. "Or, if your inclination is to remain a bachelor, to keep in check your male urges."

Vincenzo answered with chuckles, proverbs, shrugs. "*Si hai polvere, spara*!† Eh, *padre*?" he said, addressing the priest.

I struck the arms of *Signora* Siragusa's parlor chair with enough force to raise two clouds of dust. "Fire your gunpowder, then, between the legs of one of the *signora*'s nannygoats who won't make you a baby!" I shouted.

More gasps from behind the kitchen door. Father

---

* "I don't understand a frigging thing you're saying, Domenico." (approx.)—NF

** "Fucking! Fucking!"—NF

† "If you have gunpowder, shoot!"—NF

Guglielmo blushed visibly and made the sign of the cross.

Vincenzo puffed on his cigar and laughed. "Better tell me then, big brother, which nannygoat is *your* sweetheart. I do not wish to cuckold you."

All around the boardinghouse, movement and sound stopped. Snooping ears seemed almost to burst right through the walls.

I explained to the priest—and to all the other eavesdroppers with their big ears to the wall—that what Vincenzo had just implied had been said in jest, ha ha. Then I continued, warning my brother that, as the eldest member of the proud Tempesta family of Giuliana, I was *ordering* him to model all future behavior after my own. Vincenzo laughed and answered that he much preferred to *have* virgins than to turn back into one again.

"Saint Agrippina the Virgin Martyr herself is no purer than my brother Domenico," Vincenzo joked to that pallid priest, poking him. "*You'll* probably enjoy a woman's pleasures before Domenico does, eh, *padre*?" Father Guglielmo grew paler still and crossed himself again.

I had reached the end of my patience with that hooligan of a brother. Standing, I walked over to Vincenzo and slapped him across the face.

Vincenzo raised his fists. I raised mine. We stood glaring at each other, brother against brother, each of us attempting to sustain fierce expressions. But in Vincenzo's big eyes I saw him, again, as he had been as a *bambino*. . . . I saw Mama and Papa, the village square, Mount Etna against the Sicilian sky. I could not keep my fists raised against a brother. Nor could I surrender my pride.

"Bah!" I said, dropping my hands. "As God and this priest are my witnesses, Vincenzo, from this moment forward, we cease to be brothers! You have slandered the family name and now you mock me! I forsake you! I will never speak to you again." And with that, I left the room, sending all the snoops at the boardinghouse scurrying. . . .

* * *

How to tell the sadness that followed?

Alas, my vow of *silenzio* was not difficult to keep. The following Saturday night, a Three Rivers police sergeant (goddamned mick named O'Meara) got a toothache and went home early. When he lit the lamp and entered his bedroom, first thing he saw was the plunging buttocks of my brother Vincenzo. As the sergeant stood in shock, Vincenzo groaned and rolled over, revealing to the moon and the husband his slimy thing and the smile on the face of O'Meara's faithless whore of a wife. The policeman drew his service revolver, aimed first at his screaming spouse, and then changed his mind and shot Vincenzo in the groin instead.

There was an investigation by the police department. Ha! Like one dog checking another dog for fleas! The sergeant was exonerated for having put "a greasy guinea" in his place. (That's what the Chief of Police himself said. I heard it from Golpo Abruzzi who heard it from his brother-in-law.) O'Meara's wife—that no-good *puttana 'Mericana*—flaunted herself for decades afterward, as if horns didn't poke through the cap of her goddamned murdering policeman of a husband, who was laughed at by every *siciliano* in town!

My brother Vincenzo, *a buon'anima*, died from infection nine days following the shooting. My brother Pasquale and Father Guglielmo were present at his bedside at *Signora* Siragusa's. Father Guglielmo gave Vincenzo the Eucharist and extreme unction before the end. This I saw to. This I arranged.

A crowd of sobbing young women, several nationalities, attended my brother's funeral Mass and burial at St. Mary of Jesus Christ Cemetery. This I was told by Pasquale; I witnessed none of it myself. I paid for, but refused on my honor to attend, the funeral of the brother who had mocked my chastity and spat in the face of family authority. Let saints and women forgive! A Sicilian's pride—his honor—is everything, *figli d'Italia*! What does a man have if he trades away his dignity as if it were a gold medallion?

Following Vincenzo's death, it was my duty to write once again to Mama with the sad news of the death of her youngest son. Two or three weeks later, I myself received a postal card from across the sea, this one from a representative of that illiterate idiot Uncle Nardo: "Mother died 24 June. Malaria."

With a heavy heart, I responded immediately to Nardo's news. In the good name of my mother, I demanded that that greedy Pig-Face go to the home of the *magistrato* and negotiate the return of my father's gold *medaglia* to me, the firstborn son of Giacomo and Concettina Tempesta, and the medal's rightful owner. It was the least that goddamned Nardo could do, I wrote, to atone for all the terrible hardships he had visited on the Tempestas. No answer. I wrote two times more to Nardo, but that *figliu d'una mingia* ignored each of my attempts to retrieve that which I had been cheated of by the crooked official.

As for my middle and sole remaining brother, Pasquale, he cared little about family honor, justice, or rightful ownership as long as his supper was on the table. Pasquale had always been the simplest of men. . . .

How do I tell the sad, strange fate of my brother Pasquale? No strength left today. Tomorrow, I tell. Not today.

thirty-four

Dr. Patel said it was lovely to see me again. She was just starting some tea. Did she remember correctly? Bengal Spice?

"Fine," I said. "Great. Anything." I told her I liked the colors she was wearing: red and gold and . . . what would she call that shade of yellow, anyway?

She'd call it saffron, she said.

"Saffron? Yeah? I painted someone's kitchen that color once. Looks much better on you than it did on those kitchen walls." She chuckled, thanked me for the compliment, if that was what I had just bestowed.

"You see my brother today?" I asked her.

She had, she said. Yes. Things were about the same.

"I was just thinking on the way down here how weird it is: how before the war began, it was all he could talk about. Then, when they actually started firing Scuds and 'smart bombs' at each other, it hardly registered a blip on his radar. Why do you think that is, Doc? Is it more than the medication?"

Dr. Patel said she would be happy to talk with me about my brother, but that perhaps we should arrange to do so at another time. After all, she said, we'd both set aside this hour to talk about *me*.

The teakettle rumbled. While I waited for her, I grabbed my crutch and gimped across the room. Looked out the window. I hadn't been up there since October. Now, in the dead of winter, you could see the river through the bare trees.

Dr. Patel asked me about my injuries—my progress with physical therapy.

"Actually, I'm *ahead* of schedule," I said. "No one down at the rehab center can believe how far I've come along in just three months. They told me they're going to make me their poster boy."

"Poster boy? What is 'poster boy,' please?" I'd forgotten how it was with her—how much got lost in translation. Why had I even called her? Jump-started this whole therapy thing again? Big Waste of Time and Money, Part II.

I reached down and touched the head of that statue of hers. Shiva. "Oh, by the way, I—thanks for, uh . . . for this guy here's little brother." She looked puzzled. "The present you sent over with Lisa Sheffer? When I was in the hospital?"

"Ah, yes," she said, breaking out in a smile. "You liked my little gift?"

"I did, yeah. I *do*. I was going to write you a thank-you note about fifty times."

"Well, now you've thanked me in person," she said. "Which is even better, don't you think? Have a seat, please." Placing the tea tray between us, she sat down herself. "Let's let this steep while we catch up."

She'd been reviewing my records, she said. Our last session had been on the twenty-second of October. We had never discussed ending our work together, she reminded me. I had seen her three times, canceled two appointments in a row, and then just not called anymore. If our work were to resume, she said, she would expect more of a commitment from me.

"A commitment?" I shifted in my chair. "Geez, you're not asking me to go steady, are you?"

She didn't crack a smile. Perhaps, she said, we could meet weekly for four sessions and then decide *jointly* whether or not we wished to continue the process.

"Yeah," I said. "Sure. No problem." What was she going to do if I didn't honor my "commitment"? Sic the bloodhounds? Alert the psychology police?

She removed the teapot lid and peered inside. "Not quite ready yet," she said.

We just sat there, Dr. Patel smiling, watching me lace and unlace my fingers, shift around in my seat. "I've . . . I've got him up on my bookcase."

"Excuse me?"

"Your little statue guy. I put him in the room where I read. . . . That's *one* thing you get to do when you fall off a roof and put yourself out of commission: catch up on your reading."

"Is it? I'm envious then. What have you been reading, Dominick?"

"The Bible, for one thing."

"Yes?" She looked neither pleased nor displeased.

"I . . . well, it was kind of an accident, really. I was trying to poke something else down from the top shelf with one of my crutches. *Shōgun,* I think it was. James Clavell. Thought I'd read that one again. But then I knocked this whole stack down on top of me, instead—this little avalanche of books. And there it was. Didn't even know I still *had* that damn thing. My mother had given it to me for my confirmation, way back in sixth grade. Thomas and me—we each got one. Mine's in a little better shape than his."

She smiled. "Which passages are you reading? The Old Testament or the New?"

"Old."

"Ah, the ancient stories. And are you finding them illuminating? Was your 'little avalanche' fortuitous?"

Was she busting my balls? Getting in a couple of jabs because of those canceled appointments? "I guess . . . I guess I can see why some people find them useful."

She nodded. "But I'm asking if *you've* found them useful."

"Me? Personally, you mean? No, not really. I guess I'm more interested in them from a historical perspective. Or, sociological or whatever. . . . Well, in a way, maybe. The Book of Job: I could relate to *that* one."

"Job? Yes? Why is that?"

I shrugged, shifted around in my seat for the zillionth time. "I don't know. Guy's just minding his own business, trying to do what's right, and he gets crapped all over. Becomes God's little test case."

"Is that how *you* feel? As if you are 'God's little test case'?"

I reminded her that I didn't believe in God.

"Then perhaps you can clarify for me why you—"

"*Fate's* test case, maybe. Schizophrenic brother, dead baby daughter, girlfriend who . . . But, hey, shit happens, right?"

"It does, yes," she agreed. "Sometimes irrespective of how we are conducting our lives, and sometimes not. What other Old Testament stories have you found relevant?"

I shrugged. "Look, don't get the wrong idea. It's not like the Bible fell off the bookshelf, struck me upside the head, and now, suddenly, I'm 'born again' or something. Gonna go down to the library and cut my hand off for Jesus."

She waited.

"But, uh . . . well, there's the obvious one, I guess: Cain and Abel. God creates the universe, Adam and Eve crank out a couple of kids, and *voilà.* Sibling rivalry. One brother murders the other brother."

"Yes? Continue, please."

"What? I . . . It was just a *joke*."

"Yes, I understand your tone. But explain a little further, if you will."

"I didn't mean anything *deep*. Just . . . brother troubles."

She waited. Wouldn't look away.

"I just . . . Well, I could understand why the guy was pissed. That's all."

"Why who was pissed?"

"*Cain.*"

"Yes? And why was he pissed?"

"Hey, *you're* the one with the anthropology degree. Not me."

"And *you're* the one who mentioned the Old Testament. Correct? Answer my question, please."

"Hey, Doc, I ever tell you how much I like your accent? 'Onswer the question, please.' 'Why was he peesed?' " No smile, nothing. I drummed my fingers against my knees. Let out a sigh. "I don't know. He just . . . he does his work, makes his offering like everyone else, and . . . and the only sacrifice God notices is his brother's. It's just typical."

"What is?"

"That all the credit goes to Mr. Goody Two-shoes. And what does the other one get? A big lecture about sin 'crouching at the door.' Like sin's the Big Bad Wolf or something. . . . That reminds me. I looked at a couple of those books *you* recommended. Those myth things, or fable things, or whatever. Remember? You made me a list?"

Yes, she said. She remembered.

"Someone went and got them out of the library for me. My ex-wife, actually. The Three Rivers library didn't have them, but she got them through interlibrary loan."

"Dessa's been helping you then?"

Had she remembered Dessa's name or looked it up before I got there? "She, uh . . . she brought over a couple of meals, ran a few errands." I wrapped my arms around my chest. I'd read somewhere that that was an instinct left over from caveman days: protect your heart. "Everyone's been pitching in. Even Ray."

"Your stepfather? Yes?"

"Well, he, uh . . . he's had more time on his hands. Got laid off in December. Happy holidays from the big guys down at Electric Boat. He gives that company almost forty years of his life and then, just before his pension maxes out, they hand him his walking papers. They keep promising they're going to call the old guys back, but they won't."

Dr. Patel nodded sympathetically.

"So anyway, he's had more time lately. Drove me back and forth to the doctor's the first couple of months, down to physical therapy. I even had him doing my grocery shopping for a while there. Before I started driving again. Kind of funny, isn't it?"

"What is funny, Dominick?"

"Well, if you'd told me a year ago that Ray Birdsey was going to be my chauffeur, my personal errand boy . . ." I stood up. Walked back over to the window.

"I find your terminology interesting," Dr. Patel said.

I turned and faced her. "What do you mean?"

"Your comment just now about Ray. By helping you during your time of need, has he been serving as your 'personal errand boy' or as your father? Despite his past failures, I mean. Despite biology. Fathers do that, yes? Come to their sons' aid in times of need?"

She checked the tea again, pronounced it ready. You had to watch Doc Patel—had to put up your dukes even before the tea was poured. In a couple of months, I'd kind of forgotten how to play D with her.

"Tell me," she said. "Which of the books that I recommended did you read?"

"Oh, well, I didn't . . . I just kind of skimmed them. That *Hero with a Thousand Faces* thing and . . . what's that one by the guy you studied with in Chicago?"

"Dr. Bettelheim?"

"Yeah. That Freud-meets-Little-Red-Riding-Hood thing of his."

She laughed. "Otherwise known as *The Uses of Enchantment.* And did you discover any?"

"Any . . . ?"

"Uses for enchantment?"

I shrugged. "I don't know. Cinderella's lost slipper's really about castration anxiety; the beanstalk Jack's climbing up is really his Oedipus complex. It was kind of interesting, I guess, but . . ."

"But what?" She was watching me with mischievous eyes. Had I actually *committed* to four more sessions, or had we just talked about it?

"I guess . . . I think maybe we ought to just let fairy tales be fairy tales, you know? Instead of turning them into these deep, dark . . . performing all these psychological *autopsies* on them. You know?" I sat there, not looking at her, picking away at a loose thread on my sweatshirt.

Dr. Patel told me she used to tease Dr. Bettelheim about that same thing. "I would say, 'Be careful, Bruno, or the magical little imps nestled in these ancient tales will become frightened and retreat back to the forest of antiquity.' But, of course, I could say that to him because I had such high regard for his work. It freed me to play the imp myself, you see."

I shrugged, sipped some tea. "Yeah, well, you and me

probably read that book of his on two entirely different levels. . . . It was interesting, though. Thanks."

She asked no further questions, made no observation. Just watched me sit there, unraveling the end of my sweatshirt sleeve.

"You, uh . . . you know what I started reading this morning? Speaking of autopsies? This thing my grandfather wrote. My mother's father."

"Yes? Your grandfather was an author, Dominick?"

"Huh? Oh, no. . . . This was just some private thing. His personal history, or whatever. We never knew him, Thomas and me—he died before we were even born. But, he, uh . . . he dictated this whole big long thing—his life story—how he came over here from Italy, etcetera, etcetera. Well, dictated part of it, I guess, and wrote the rest of it. Rented one of those Dictaphone things, hired a stenographer. This Italian guy who'd come over after the war. He'd worked in the courts or something."

Angelo Nardi, I thought: my chief suspect in the case of the missing father. Not that I was going to get into my theory with Doc Patel.

"He, uh . . . he died right after he finished it, I guess. According to my mother. He was up in the backyard, reading it over, and when Ma went outside to check on him, he was just sitting there, his mouth gaping open—dead, from a stroke. She said the manuscript pages were blowing all over the yard. . . . Life's a bitch, right? Works all summer long on that thing and then just keels over."

"What you're reading is a transcription of your grandfather's oral history, then?"

"Yeah, partly. Oral *and* written. I remember my mother said he fired the stenographer about halfway through. Wrote the rest himself. It was all in Italian; I had it translated. . . . It's part oral history, part written, and about seventy-five percent bullshit."

She asked me what I meant by that.

"Oh. I don't know. . . . He had a pretty good idea of himself."

"Explain, please?"

"It's . . . well, the whole thing—what I read so far, anyway—it keeps going on and on about how *great* he is. Compared to everyone else in his village, compared to his two brothers. . . . I didn't even know this thing existed until, maybe, four or five months before my mother died. I went over there to visit her one afternoon and she just gives it to me, out of the blue. This big, bulky thing she'd been keeping in a strongbox. It's over a hundred pages. . . . She was pretty sick by then—that day she gave it to me. She said I could share it with Thomas—that he could read it if he wanted to—but it was *me* she wanted to give it to."

"Her father's story? Why you?"

"I don't know, really. I didn't ask her. . . . 'The Story of a Great Man from Humble Beginnings.' I got this big idea that I was going to have it translated for her. Give it to her as a present. Have it translated and bound into a book, or whatever, so that, you know, she could read her father's history before she died."

"She had never read it?"

"No. She said she knew some Sicilian, but not enough to read it page by page. But anyway, I got this big idea. Hired a translator and everything."

"What a lovely gesture," Dr. Patel said. "Your mother must have been very pleased to receive her gift."

"She *didn't* receive it. The translation took much longer than I figured it would. And then she got worse. She went downhill pretty fast near the end. . . . And then the damn thing got lost."

"Lost? The manuscript?"

"Well, not lost, exactly. It's a long story." I was damned if I was going to get into Nedra Frank with her—the way she'd suddenly reappeared in her cowgirl outfit, at the foot of my hospital bed, like one of my morphine nightmares. *Thunk!* She'd practically *aimed* Domenico's goddamned manuscript at my busted foot.

"Just as well, though," I said. "That Ma never read it. Now that I'm finally getting around to reading the thing myself, I don't think I would have given it to her anyway."

"Why not?"

"Because . . . well, for one thing, he bad-mouthed her pretty bad in it."

"Your mother? Why do you—?"

"Right in the middle of dictating his big life story? Talking about what a great man he is—how all the 'sons of Italy' should follow his example? He starts crabbing about what a nuisance she is. Calls her 'rabbit-face.' 'Cracked jug.' Says how she's so homely, she can't get a husband. Can't give him any grandchildren the way she's supposed to. . . . Rabbit-face: what did he think? That she *wanted* to be born with that cleft lip? That it was her *fault* or something? . . . And the pitiful thing is, she *worshipped* the guy. When we were kids? Thomas and me? It was always, 'Papa said this, Papa did that.' . . . I don't know. I'm *glad* she never read it, actually. It just would have hurt her feelings, reading that shit."

"Dominick?"

"Hmm?"

"You seem very tense. Why do you think—?"

"You know what his whole reason for writing it was? Did I tell you that? So that young Italian boys could read about him and get . . . *inspired* or whatever. You can just tell what a pompous asshole he was. Keeps going on and on about how 'special' he is. What a martyr he is because of what he's had to put up with from everyone who's less perfect than he is."

"In what respect did your grandfather feel he was special?"

"In *every* respect. Intelligence-wise, morality-wise. He sees himself as God's chosen . . ."

"Why did you stop just now, Dominick? What are you thinking about?"

What I was thinking about was Thomas. God's Chosen One, Part II. But I dodged the bullet. "I don't know. I'm not that far into it—fifteen, twenty pages. I probably won't even finish it."

"Dominick? Tell me about your grandfather's 'closeness to God.' "

"Hmm? Oh, he . . . back in Italy? When he was a boy? He claims in this thing that some statue in their village started crying tears. And that he—Domenico—was the first one to see it."

"Domenico? You were named after your grandfather, then?"

I nodded. "Guilty. Anyway, I guess because of this statue thing, they earmarked him to become a priest. Took up a collection in the village, sent him away to get educated. Then things got screwed up. He had this younger brother—"

Brother problems, I thought, suddenly. We had *that* much in common, Papa and I.

"I don't know. I just don't *like* the guy very much. All his I'm-better-than-this-one, I'm-better-than-that-one crap. He's—what's the word?—grandiose. . . . But, you know, it's kind of interesting from a family history perspective or whatever. All the immigration stuff. How he established himself once he got here. It fills in some of the blanks."

"Yes? Tell me about that."

"Well, there's this one guy he mentions named Drinkwater—Nabby Drinkwater. They worked in the mill together—this Drinkwater guy and my grandfather. And it's weird because, well, because Thomas and I worked one summer with *Ralph* Drinkwater. Remember? We talked about that once: that summer when Thomas started falling apart? When we were all on that work crew. Gotta be the same family, right? Wequonnoc Indians named Drinkwater? . . . So, *that's* kind of interesting: the coincidences. Seeing how his generation and ours . . ."

Dr. Patel stared at me for a second or two more than I felt comfortable with, then jotted something down on the little pad in her lap.

"What'd I just say?" She cocked her head a little. "You just wrote down something."

"Yes, I did."

"Well? Did I just say something incredibly revealing, or am I boring you so much that you're working on your grocery list, or what? What did you write down?"

"I wrote the word *grandiose.*"

"Yeah? Why?"

"I believe I mentioned earlier that, before you came here today, I was reviewing our past sessions. And I was struck, just now, by your use of the word *grandiose.*"

"Yeah? Why? Because housepainters don't usually use three-syllable words?"

"No. Because you've used that word in here before. Do you recall the context?"

I shook my head.

"In connection with your brother. You were making the point, quite validly, that there was grandiosity in your brother's position."

"His 'position' on what?"

"His belief that God had somehow singled him out as His instrument in the prevention of conflict between the United States and Iraq. That God had 'chosen' him. And now, using the same word—grandiose—you've just told me that your maternal grandfather felt similarly 'chosen.' So, I found that interesting. Worthy of further exploration, perhaps."

I shifted in my seat. "Yeah, but . . . Thomas never even read this thing of my grandfather's. He couldn't possibly have gotten the idea from Domenico. If *that's* what you're getting at."

"I'm not 'getting at' anything, Dominick," she said. "I'm merely recording observations. Looking for patterns that we may or may not wish to examine later."

"During the big autopsy?"

"Ah," she said. "Now that's the third time you've used *that* word. May I inquire about your use of the metaphor, Dominick? If you see our work together here as an 'autopsy,' who, may I ask, is our corpse?"

"I just—"

"It's the key ingredient, is it not? The body of the deceased? So tell me: whose cadaver are we examining?"

"What . . . what are you being sarcastic for?"

"You misinterpret me. I'm neither working on my shopping list nor being sarcastic. Answer my question, please. Our cadaver is . . . ?"

"My grandfather?"

I could tell from her expression that it wasn't the answer she was looking for.

"My brother? . . . Me?"

She smiled as serenely as Shiva. "It was *your* metaphor, Dominick. Not mine. May I ask you something else, as long as we are discussing the subject of grandiosity? Do you feel the word—*grandiose*—in any way describes *you*?"

"Me?" It made me laugh. "Joe Shmoe? I don't *think* so. . . . Far as I know, Jesus never asked *me* to stop a war. No statue's ever cried tears for *my* benefit."

"And yet, earlier, you described yourself as fate's test case. Likened your trials and tribulations to those of Job, who, of course, is legendary because of the way God tested his faith. So, I was just wondering. . . . More tea?"

She told me I should keep reading—that books were mirrors, reflective in sometimes unpredictable ways. What the hell had she meant—was *I* grandiose? Where had *that* little zinger come from?

"Look," I said. "Do you think we can cut to the chase here? How much time do we have left, anyway?"

She consulted the clock, cocked strategically at an angle so that the patient couldn't read it. "About thirty-five minutes," she said.

"Because, no offense, I didn't come here just to have a *book* discussion."

She nodded. "Why *did* you come, Dominick? Tell me."

I told her about seeing Rood's face in the attic window.

About Joy's pregnancy—the way she'd tried to pass me off as the father of her kid.

About the night I'd faced myself in the medicine cabinet mirror.

Dr. Patel asked me if I had continued to have suicidal thoughts since that night—if I had continued to plan ways in which I might end my life. I shook my head. Told her that the worst despair had passed—that I'd weathered it.

"You're sure?"

I nodded. I *was* sure, too. I wasn't bullshitting her. That night had scared me enough so that I'd stepped back from the ledge and stayed there. Had started thinking, okay, maybe there *is* life beyond . . . beyond . . .

I fished Joy's cassette out of my jacket pocket, and the little cassette player I'd brought along. I told Dr. Patel about the night at the hospital when I'd awakened and found the Duchess standing there. "The gutless bastard was trying to sneak it onto my nightstand and get the hell out of there," I said. "He was pretty good at sneaking. He was an expert. Only I woke up. Ruined his little getaway. Listen to *this.*"

I hit "play." Studied her as she listened to Joy's confession.

•

When I finished, she sighed. "What your girlfriend did was a terrible betrayal," she said. "Obviously, she is a deeply troubled young woman. And yet . . ." She seemed stumped for a moment. Lost in thought. "And yet, Dominick, like you and me—like all of us, really—she is struggling. Working, I think, to develop some insight. To become a better person. Which is not to dismiss what she did—not at all. Tell me, how did you feel a moment ago—while you were listening again to her words?"

"I just . . . I don't know. I've listened to that damn tape so many times now, I don't . . . I guess I'm numb."

"Why did you want to play the tape for me instead of just telling me about it?"

"I just . . . I wanted you to hear what they *did* to me. I mean, taking the most intimate thing that two people can do together and . . . I just wanted you to hear it in her own words."

"So, you are not so much interested in exploring your feelings about Joy's betrayal. Or the failure of your relationship. You are merely giving me a tour of the museum."

"The museum? . . . I don't follow you."

"Your museum of pain. Your sanctuary of justifiable indignation."

"I, uh . . ."

"We all superintend such a place, I suppose," she said, "although some of us are more painstaking curators than others. That is the category in which I would certainly put you, Dominick. You are a meticulous steward of the pain and injustices people have visited upon you. Or, if you prefer, we could call you a scrupulous *coroner.*"

"What . . . what do you mean? Curator of my—"

"Well, let's see. There is the monument to your having suffered a shared childhood with Thomas. And the frequently revisited exhibit of your stepfather's many injustices. And, of course, the *pièce de résistance:* your shrine to your ex-wife."

"Uh . . . ?"

"And now, this most recent acquisition. This tape which you have brought for me to listen to—which, as you say, you have listened to many, many times yourself. So many times, it has made you *numb.*" She took another sip of tea, smiling benignly. "The Dominick Birdsey Museum of Injustice and Misery," she said. "Open year-round."

For the remainder of the hour, I was polite. Terse. I was damned if I was going to give her what she wanted: some truth-revealing tantrum, some anger-stoked baring of my soul so that we could dissect me the way her friend, what's-his-face, had dissected all those fairy tales. She was sneaky, really. Devious. First she tricks me into promising I'll come for four more sessions, then she whacks me between the eyes with a two-by-four.

She walked me to the door. Her advice, she said, was to keep reading my grandfather's transcripted story. Whatever I felt about him personally, he had given me a gift—something that very few ancestors who predeceased their descendants ever gave.

"Yeah?" I said. "What's that?"

"His voice on the page. His history. Indirectly or not, Dominick, your grandfather is speaking to you."

I started the Escort, backed out of the handicapped space. I was already in traffic before it dawned on me that I'd negotiated my way back down Doc Patel's long flight of stairs without panicking about falling. Without even really noticing my own descent.

Papa's voice. Thomas's voices. Joy's voice on that tape . . .

The Dominick Birdsey Museum of Misery. Fuck *her*. At the red light, waiting to get back onto the access road, I took Joy's cassette out of my pocket. Tossed the goddamned thing out the window. It felt good doing it, too.

Felt *real* good.

That's how good a curator *I* was.

Fuck *her*.

thirty-five

28 July 1949

For two nights now, no sleep. I long to forget but weep to remember those strange days when my brother Pasquale became not the simplest, but the most puzzling of men. . . . *Omertà, omertà*, the Sicilian in me whispers. *Silenzio*! In the Old Country, the code of silence is a stone dropped into a pond. Its rings expand and encircle all. *Siciliani* remember but do not speak. And yet my brain hungers to understand—to crack open a brother's secret and look inside. Pasquale, I speak not to dishonor your name, but to try one last time to understand and forgive. . . .

Mama and Papa's secondborn son was not blessed with my superior intelligence or my desire to embrace destiny. Unlike our amorous brother Vincenzo, Pasquale did not tempt women and women did not tempt him. His gifts were for simple labor and stubbornness and hearty eating. Each week, he paid *Signora* Siragusa seventy-five cents for the extra things she packed in the dinner pail he carried to the factory: a half-dozen of boiled eggs, a whole loaf of bread instead of half, a generous slab of cheese, a ring or two of the *signora*'s hot *salsiccia*.

Sometimes, the *signora* included a special treat in Pasquale's dinner pail—a jar of her pickled peppers, my brother's favorite. Pasquale's custom was to eat the peppers with his fingers—a kind of *insalata improvvisata*—and then wash the rest of the food down with gulps of the pickling brine. "That brother of yours has the appetite of three men!" the *signora* would often remark to me, always with a cackle of motherly approval. In his years at the mill, Pasquale became famous amongst the workers for those big dinners and valued by the bosses for the hard work the food fueled. Flynn, the agent, once stopped me and told me that Domenico Tempesta worked like a well-oiled machine and his brother Pasquale labored like a plowhorse!

He did not talk much, my brother. Was it his years in the sulphur mines as my father's *caruso* that made him so private and singular? His was a childhood spent underground in filth and toil, so different from my own sunny youth at the convent school, where I had been sent because of my *natura speciale* and because the statue of the *Vergine* had wept in my presence. By the age of fifteen, I had eyed the sights of Palermo and Potenza! I had swum in the *Adriatico*, stood amidst the relics of Rome! But my poor, simple brother had known only the rock and darkness of the earth's bowels, the stink of sulphur in his nose. . . .

And yet, I remember Pasquale as a happy boy. Each Sunday when our family reunited, he laughed and ran through the village and the hills with his friends, fellow *carusi*—those boys as pale as mushrooms enjoying their one day a week in the Sicilian sun. A pack of young dogs they were, with their pranks and *giuoco violento*. The village wives would scold and chase them with brooms, frowning from one side of their mouths and smiling at the boys' mischief from the other side. The leader of these naughty *carusi* was Pasquale's best friend, Filippo, whose pale, pointed face and dark eyes my memory still sees.

The terrible collapse that took Papa's life also took the life of Pasquale's beloved friend, Filippo. On that day, the happy part of Pasquale was buried in the mine forever.

It was Drinkwater, that goddamned lazy Indian, who ruined things for Pasquale at the mill. One night, he snuck whiskey into the plant and got my brother drunk. When Flynn came out of his office to investigate the source of the *agitazione*, he caught Pasquale singing and pissing into the dye vat while the spinning girls screamed and peeked between the fingers they held to their faces.

Flynn fired Pasquale but not that no-good Indian, an injustice that fills me with anger to this day. Under other circumstances, I might have protested Flynn's actions or even quit the mill in the name of *dignità di famiglia*. Ha! I would have gladly left Flynn to explain to Baxter, the mill owner's son-in-law, the loss of his two best nighttime workers. But a man who vows to seek his destiny must be ready when opportunity arrives! Earlier that week, the newspaper had reported a transaction between the city of Three Rivers and old Rosemark's widow. At long last, the old farmer's hill property would be divided into city lots and put up for sale. A road was planned, the paper said, and a street name had been chosen: Hollyhock Avenue. The lots would be sold later that spring for five, six hundred each. By then, I had saved twelve hundred dollars. I would need all of that and more if I was to become the first *Italiano* in Three Rivers, Connecticut, to own his own land. Despite the injustice done to my brother Pasquale by American Woolen and Textile, I could not afford both family honor and a home of my own.

Luckily, my brother's firing occurred during the spring. Pasquale found work immediately as a roofer for the Werman Construction Company. One night, drunk at a tavern he visited with fellow workers, Pasquale bought a monkey from a sailor who had just returned from Madagascar. No bigger than a house cat that scrawny thing was, with its orange fur, its human eyes and fingers. Pasquale named the monkey Filippo in honor of his boyhood friend and built him a cage which *Signora* Siragusa allowed Pasquale to keep on her front porch. The monkey soon became a neighborhood *attrazione* both because of its exotic species and its delicate conditon. That goddamned thing was pregnant!

Filippo quickly became Filippa. Several of the young West Side girls knitted and sewed hats and dresses for that foolish little creature. Another of *Signora* Siragusa's boarders, a piano tuner with a gold tooth (name forgotten), went so far as to write a song about her titled "*La Regina Piccola*."* This *strombazzatore* performed his song, *basso profondo*, on the boardinghouse porch all that summer. Each performance brought tears to the eyes of neighbor women. As for me, I held my hands to my ears and slammed the window shut.

In August, Filippa's baby came out of her stillborn. She cradled that dead, shriveled *bambino* for two, three whole days and, when she finally gave it up, cried tears which I saw with my own eyes! My brother Pasquale shed tears, too—cried as he had never cried for Papa or Mama or Vincenzo or even for his friend Filippo. He buried the dead baby in the backyard of the boardinghouse and held its grief-torn mother in his lap, stroking and rocking her for hours and hours and humming "The Little Queen"—not in the operatic style of that show-off of a piano tuner, but as a comforting lullaby, a sad but soothing lament. My brother hardly ever spoke and now, for that goddamned little *scimmia*, he wept and sang! Pasquale grieved as if Filippa's baby had been his own. . . .

Omertà, I tell my moving lips! *Omertà*! And yet I am an old man with stool like *zuppa* and a head burdened with

* "The Little Queen"—NF

memory. . . . I speak not to bring shame on you, Pasquale, but to understand why.

Why, Pasquale? Why? . . .

My brother began opening Filippa's cage and taking that smelly monkey of his to work with him. Each morning, the two would head off from the *signora*'s, Pasquale on foot and Filippa riding on his shoulder. Pasquale would spend his day hammering and hauling shingles and whistling, half the time with a stripe of monkey shit drying on the back of his shirt or his coat. Sometimes as my brother worked, Filippa would sit on the peaks of new and half-built buildings or in nearby trees, removing bugs from her fur and eating them without care or notice as she stared and stared at Pasquale.

When the cold weather came, Pasquale made an agreement with *Signora* Siragusa. In exchange for the privilege of allowing Filippa to come inside and live in the *signora*'s coal cellar during the winter months, Pasquale would tend the stove and carry his own bed to the basement, freeing space upstairs for another paying boarder.

That winter my brother seemed happy, living once again the underground life of the *caruso*, emerging from the *signora*'s cellar only for meals or trips to the tavern. His foolish monkey accompanied him there, buttoned up inside his coat, its scrawny head poking out of a gap between the buttons.

*La lingua non ha ossa, ma rompe il dorso!** By springtime, the Italian women began to gossip, chuckling and wondering when Pasquale Tempesta and his pretty little "wife" would be expecting another *bambino*, ha ha ha. *Signora* Siragusa herself whispered to me that she had seen Pasquale and that little furry witch holding hands and whispering into each other's ears, even kissing each other on the lips! The men talked, too. They were no bet-

* The tongue has no bones but can break a man's back!—NF

ter. Colosanto, the baker, stopped me on the street one day and asked me, with a laugh, was it true my crazy brother had taught that monkey of his how to undo his pants and "play the pipe" for him?

"Bah!" I told him, pushing past. "Go stick yours in a loaf of dough and bake it in the oven!"

Another time I was at Salvatore Tusia's barbershop, getting a shave and minding my business, when Picicci, the ice man, came in. "Hey, who's that whose whiskers you're taking off, Salvatore?" Picicci asked Tusia. Picicci was always a wise guy with a smirk on his *faccia brutta*.

Tusia told Picicci that he knew very well who I was. I was Tempesta, the dyer at American Woolen and Textile.

"Oh, it's Tempesta, is it? The monkey's uncle himself!"

Every man in that shop had a laugh on me that morning, even that goddamned barber I was paying to shave my face. I stood up half-done and told them all to go to hell in a handbasket—walked out of there with the soap still on my face and Tusia's cloth hanging from the front of me. On my way back to the boardinghouse, I wiped my face and threw that goddamned cloth down the sewer rather than give it back to Tusia. Let him pay for another one and have a laugh about that! I fixed Picicci, too. The next week, downtown, he called across the street to me and asked why my landlady, the *signora*, bought her ice from Rabinowitz the Jew instead of from a *paisano*. It was crowded in the street that day, I remember. Picicci had a line of three, four customers. I called back that Rabinowitz's prices were cheaper and that Rabinowitz didn't piss in his ice before he froze it. Two of those customers walked away from Picicci's cart and he raised his fist and cursed me and kicked his horse. If that goddamned son of a bitch was going to call me "monkey's uncle," then he was going to pay for it in his pocketbook!

But a family's honor is a heavy burden to bear if all the lifting falls to the father's firstborn son.

My brother Pasquale continued to smile and parade Filippa around the town, his ears deaf to the jokes and taunts of *paisani*. Each day when I got back from the mill, I would lie in my bed and close my eyes, make fists, grind my teeth. I could hear all of Three Rivers laughing at the name Tempesta because of Pasquale and his goddamned monkey. Once again, I was called upon to clean up the mess a brother had made.

My first thought was to sneak down to the *signora*'s cellar in the middle of the night and wring that animal's skinny neck! But I had learned in my sad dealings with Vincenzo, *a buon'anima*, the mistake of trying to force my will upon a hard-headed brother. Now I took a craftier and more practical path, one which called on my patience and my considerable talents as a planner. I refined my plan all that winter, always with old Rosemark's property in my mind.

On 13 February 1914, I purchased a quarter-acre city lot on the hilly west end of Hollyhock Avenue for the sum of three hundred and forty dollars. I was shrewd enough to realize that two brothers working steadily could build a home twice as quickly as one and that a *casa di due appartamenti** would give its owner both a roof over his head and a rental income. I was now thirty-six years old. Though I was not a billygoat with a frozen *cazzu* as my brother Vincenzo had been, I did have male urges and a strong desire to pass on the name of Tempesta to Italian-American sons! I assumed that my brother Pasquale had these urges and desires, too, no matter how much that goddamned monkey had managed to turn his head, and I wove that *supposizione* into my plan. A two-family house, after all, required two families.

I wrote to my cousins in Brooklyn, inquiring about eligible young Italian women, preferably *siciliani*. I wanted no city-born wives for my brother and me—no fancy

* Duplex house—NF

northern ideas. *Siciliani* are the simplest of women and simple women make the best wives. As a property owner, I insisted on strict requirements. They must be virgins, of course. For this reason, I had disqualified the eligible *signorini* of Three Rivers. Who could tell which ones had been soiled by Vincenzo? All of them, probably! The wives of Domenico and Pasquale Tempesta must also be pleasing to the eye and talented cooks and housekeepers. In addition, they must carry themselves with dignity and be devout and humble. And most important, the dowries their families provided must be large enough to furnish two large *appartamenti*.

God granted me an early spring that year. By March, the ground had thawed and by Easter, Pasquale and I had cleared and stumped my land and begun digging, shovelful by shovelful, the foundation for my vitrified brick duplex house.

My house would be *magnifico*—American in front and Sicilian in the back. Each apartment would have seven rooms, two floors, indoor plumbing. Nothing less than a palace for the first *siciliano* property owner in Three Rivers, Connecticut! And out back, a flight of cement stairs would lead to Sicily! I would plant honeysuckle, peach trees, a small grape arbor, a little tomato garden. There would be herbs growing in stone urns, a chicken coop, rabbit cages, and perhaps a family goat to graze the small yard and give a little milk. In the yard behind my big house, I would be home again at last!

As Pasquale and I labored side by side that summer, I spoke about all these plans and about our happy Sicilian childhood and our loving and unselfish mother. In poetic words, I talked of the beautiful renewal of life. We would be the happiest brothers alive once our new home echoed with the giggles of *bambini*—once the aromas of baking bread, simmering sauce, garlic and onions frying in olive oil floated from the open kitchen windows of the home we shared, one brother to a side. And now that I was on the subject, wasn't it about time for us to find wives?

Pasquale shrugged and shoveled. He said he could still hear Mama's screaming in his ears but that he had forgotten her face.

I told him I had recently communicated by letter and *telegramma* with Lena and Vitaglio, our Brooklyn cousins. The cousins' neighbors, the Iaccoi brothers—did Pasquale remember those two plumbers from Palermo? The Iaccoi brothers had big news. Their half-sister, Ignazia, age seventeen, would be arriving that summer from Italy along with a female *cugina*, Prosperine, age eighteen. Both girls were devout and eager to serve husbands. Good cooks, too! And beautiful in *faccia* and *figura*—plump and just ripe for picking!

All that afternoon, I talked of children and natural male urges and the joys of owning a home and a wife of one's own. At sunset, as we two walked back to the boardinghouse carrying our shovels, I made a generous proposal: Pasquale and I would take the train to Brooklyn at Christmastime, visit our cousins and the Iaccois next door, and decide whether or not we liked what we saw. It would probably make more sense to match the older bride to the older brother, and *viceversa*, but that could be decided upon at a later date. What did it matter, anyway—when both of the young women were beautiful virgins in the prime of their childbearing years? Both could equally satisfy male urges, eh? If my beloved brother were to take the Iaccois' half-sister for a wife, the couple would be welcome on the left side of the duplex. I would charge no rent for an entire year. After that, Pasquale could negotiate a year's rent, at a modest rate, of course—a sum to be decided at a later date. Why rush things, eh? Pasquale needn't worry about the dowry, either. As the eldest Tempesta brother and a property owner with a shrewd business sense, it would be my honor to take care of those negotiations for him, ha ha.

Get him a nice little bundle. If Pasquale needed some help with wedding expenses, I would be glad to assist there, too. A boss dyer, after all, made more money than a roofer. That was merely a fact of life—ha ha! And once the house was built and our young brides were hanging their bloodstained sheets on the backyard clothesline, Pasquale would want, of course, to rid himself of that foolish, goddamned monkey.

Pasquale let go a mouthful of tobacco juice and shook his head.

Pasquale Tempesta, *a buon'anima*, could sometimes be as mule-headed as his brother Domenico Tempesta was clever! I did not wish to awaken the *mulo* in him that day. Fine, fine, I told my brother, patting him on the back and wearing a smile that showed all my teeth. The monkey can live in a cage in the backyard until its natural death. But while we were on the subject, I said, Pasquale should really stop his foolish practice of bringing Filippa to work with him. People said unkind things, made ridiculous jokes. He would see soon enough: with a beautiful young wife to distract and provide pleasure for him, Pasquale would quickly have "little monkeys" of his own to play with. He would soon forget about that furry little long-tailed rat of his.

That stubborn mule of a brother threw his shovel aside with a clamor and told me he would work no more on a house where Filippa was not welcome inside.

"Inside?" I shouted. "*Inside*?"

The negotiations went on over supper and well into the night, at one point so loudly that several of the other boarders complained and *Signora* Siragusa descended the staircase in her long braids and untrussed bosom and demanded that Pasquale and I either whisper or be evicted. My brother, that stubborn jackass, sat in the *signora*'s parlor chair and shook his head like a metronome. Whatever I may or may not have promised the Iaccoi brothers, he said, he was not interested in a wife and that was that. He would break his back helping me build my house. He would even die for me. But he would not give up his little Filippa for some wife and he would work no longer on a house where his monkey was unwelcome.

When Pasquale and I rose, finally, from *Signora* Siragusa's parlor chairs in the middle of that long and difficult night, I was hot in the face and soaked with sweat. I swore and spat into the *signora*'s spittoon and then reluctantly shook my brother's hand. Ha! Should I say I shook that stubborn mule's front hoof? In exchange for his labor on my *casa di due appartamenti* until its completion, Pasquale had secured for himself two of the seven rooms on my side of the house, free of rent not for one year but for all eternity! One room would be his and Filippa's to sleep in, the other a playroom dedicated solely to that goddamned shitting monkey's *ricreazione*! But what could I do? Pay two or three lazy workers to do what my brother would break his back doing for free?

After a night's sleep, I was calm again. Already, a new plan had hatched inside my superior brain. I would continue in private my negotiations with the Iaccois, marry the beautiful cousin, and bring the beautiful half-sister to Three Rivers to stay with us. Nature would take its course. As a happily married husband, I would, as usual, be my younger brother's good example. The half-sister would surely awaken Pasquale's sleeping male urges. At long last, my stubborn brother would come to his senses.

1 *August* 1949

All that summer and fall, I worked in the mill by night and labored on my new house by day, stopping only in late afternoon to eat and sleep. Pasquale roofed houses for Werman until four o'clock each day, then worked on Hollyhock Avenue until dark—always with that goddamned monkey chattering nearby or shitting from her place on his shoulder. My brother and I ate cold suppers together in the *signora*'s kitchen before he went down to the boardinghouse cellar to sleep and I walked to the mill for work. On Sundays, Pasquale and I labored side by side on my house. These were the best days: two strong, young brothers bringing a dream to life, board by board, brick by brick. . . .

When winter froze the ground that year and stopped construction until springtime, I went with Pasquale to the taverns where the builders drank—not to waste my money on beer or whiskey, but to sit on stools and at tables and pick away at the brains of the workers. *Installatori, elettricisti*: I got those hibernating builders to talk and draw pictures on paper napkins, to share with me the details of their past victories and mistakes. All that winter, I asked, listened, and learned what I needed to know. And none of it cost me a penny!

Sometimes, after a night of dyeing wool at the mill, I would walk the long way back to *Signora* Siragusa's, up Boswell Avenue and Summit Street to Hollyhock Avenue, where the early morning sun shone on the brick and wood and stone of my half-built house. I would think of Papa's lifetime of labor in the hot, filthy sulphur mines of Giuliana and imagine him standing beside me in this clean, cold Connecticut air. I would imagine him seeing what I saw—shaking his head with pride and disbelief. But it was not Papa's blood I felt rushing inside of me as I looked at my house and my land. I felt Ciccia blood—the blood of my mother's people—landowners like me, Domenico Tempesta, who had been conceived while a volcano rumbled and readied its spew! Domenico Onofrio Tempesta, whom the *Vergine* herself had selected!

In December of that year, I received *telegramma* from the Iaccois in Brooklyn. They wondered when we Tempesta brothers would be coming to claim our brides-to-be. "Our sweet young relatives wait patiently," the message said, "but it is only a matter of time before *'Mericano* influences begin to turn their heads." The garment industry in Manhattan cried out for female laborers, the brothers wrote. It was only fair that one or both of the young women begin to bring money into the house, unless Pasquale and I were planning to act soon.

I sent back *telegramma* urging the brothers to send both girls to work, by all means, and to put half or more of their wages aside to increase the price of their dowries, which remained to be negotiated. I felt no sense of urgency. I was, after all, a boss dyer and the owner of a spectacular and half-completed *casa di due appartamenti*. I was also a man who—if the full-length hallway mirror in *Signora* Siragusa's front hallway did not lie—cut a dashing figure in a three-piece suit. What was the point of false modesty, after all? It did no harm to keep women waiting; it let them see who was the boss and who was not. Waiting was good for a woman's constitution. Good for the Iaccoi brothers, too. It would make them better appreciate the gifts Pasquale and I would bestow on their women in our own time. A little nervousness might, besides, raise the price of the dowries. I would ask for seven hundred dollars in exchange for marrying Prosperine and four hundred for Ignazia on my brother's behalf. (Of course, I would have to negotiate my reluctant brother's marriage without his knowledge.) The Iaccoi brothers would no doubt balk at the price, but I would remain firm. With all the indoor toilets being flushed in America, those two plumbers could probably afford three times as much.

In the early spring of 1915, Pasquale and I resumed our work on my *palazzo*, laying the brick tiers of the second story and hauling into place the granite windowsills, the stoops of Sicilian marble, front and back. We hammered window and door frames and joists, bricked the chimney, partitioned rooms. High into the house's second-story front wall, I laid brick diagonally in the shape of two three-foot-high T's for all of the town to see! This I did to honor my father and to raise high the proud name of Tempesta. By the fall of that year, the house's brick, stone, and wooden skeleton was complete. The roof would be on before wintertime.

Throughout that building season, other Italians in Three Rivers stopped by to visit and congratulate me on my nearly finished "palace." Pasquale and I were presented with cakes, cheeses, and jugs of homemade wine for good luck. Ha! Everyone wished to be in the good graces of a successful man.

I weep to remember what happened next. On 12 October 1915, *tragedia* struck at 66-through-68 Hollyhock Avenue!

I was mixing cement in my wheelbarrow for the front sidewalk. Pasquale was seated on the porch steps, finishing his lunch-for-three-workers. "Look, Domenico, two crows," he grunted, pointing with his chin toward the road. Monsignor McNulty and *his* little monkey, that skinny Father Guglielmo, stood staring at us in their black robes. Best to ignore them, I told myself, and continued my cement-mixing. If that old monsignor had uncovered another *bastardo* of Vincenzo's, what did that have to do with me? Vincenzo was dead and gone, *a buon'anima*. Whatever brats he had left behind were not my responsibility.

The two approached; the old priest began with compliments. The building of this impressive house, and my status as a factory boss, had made me a leader in the Italian community. Did I realize that?

Yes, I realized that, I told him. All my life I had served as a good example for others to imitate. My brother Pasquale chewed quietly on a heel of bread and nodded in agreement.

Yes, yes, yes, Domenico Tempesta was a man both respected and emulated, the monsignor agreed. He covered his words with so much sugar that the bitter thing he said next took me by complete surprise.

McNulty came close enough for me to see the veins in his cheeks, the pockmarks in his nose. "Therefore," he whispered, "yours is the greater sin—this flagrant ignoring of Sunday Mass! This failure to honor the Lord on His given day! This flying in the face of holy law." Here, Pasquale belched up liquor from his pickled peppers—a long, slow rumble that climaxed like a clap of thunder as it traveled up his throat and out. Little Father Guglielmo's eyes widened with fear at the distraction and he put a silencing finger to his lips. Attendance at church by the "Eye-talians" of the parish had fallen off, the monsignor said, and both he and God Almighty held me personally responsible. McNulty told me my failure to attend Mass on Sunday had left me with my own sins and the sins of all nonchurchgoers on my overburdened soul. I must put the Holy Spirit before a pile of bricks, confess my transgressions, and return to Mass as a communicant the following Sunday for all to see. At this juncture, Pasquale rose from the steps, walked to the side of the house, and pissed a river. Then he made a kissing sound at Filippa, and prepared to go back to his work.

At first I tried to be respectful to that dog-faced man of the cloth. I smiled and promised I would return to Sunday Mass as soon as the four doors of my house were hung, my twenty-two windows were glazed, and the roof was completed. I pointed a thumb at Pasquale, who was now climbing the ladder to the half-completed roof, Filippa riding atop one shoulder and a bundle of wooden shingles balanced on the other. "And now that Pasquale has his lunch inside of him," I joked, "he'll probably have that roof shingled by nightfall, as formidable in size as it is. It is often said that I work like a well-oiled machine and my brother works like a plowhorse. Ha ha."

Monsignor McNulty said that pride was perhaps the greatest sin of all and that my revering of worldly possessions over things spiritual was shocking and sacrilegious. He told me he hoped and prayed there would not be some terrible price for me to pay. Then he dropped his voice and made a comment about men and monkeys that made Father Guglielmo blush.

I stopped my cement-mixing. In my hand, the trowel felt like a weapon of murder. "*Vai in mona di tua sorella*!" I told him.

"Translation! Translation!" the old priest demanded of the meek but earnest Father Guglielmo.

In his stuttering fashion, the nervous young priest said that I had asked them both to please leave now.

"I told you to get the fuck out of here!" I shouted to Monsignor Dog-Face, this time in English. "I said to go home to your sister's cunt!"

Father Guglielmo put up both his hands and attempted to negotiate a peace, but the monsignor reached over and hit him on the head. Then he marched to the road, ordering Guglielmo to follow. When the little priest had joined him, McNulty pointed his finger at me and called back in a public voice meant to dishonor me and all my countrymen. A house from which a man of God was ordered to leave, he said—and ordered in terms only an Italian would be vulgar enough to use—such a house was a Godforsaken place, damned from its peak to its foundation! "You wait and see, Tempesta!" the old monsignor shouted. "You mark my words!"

As he turned his back, I scooped a clump of the wet cement onto my trowel and flung it. It landed against the monsignor's back, dripping down his cassock like monkey shit. The old and young priests scurried down the hill, McNulty screaming and striking his little assistant several more times, and kicking him once as well.

To have my house cursed by a man of God was no small thing, but Pasquale had no understanding of the seriousness of what had just occurred. Up on the roof, his laughter boomed and carried into the trees.

"Shut up your mouth and go to work!" I yelled, and flung a trowelful of the wet cement at him and Filippa. My action frightened that little monkey-whore of Pasquale's, and the creature jumped off her master's shoulder, scurrying along the peak of the roof. With a leap, she hid in the big maple tree.

Along with his formidable lunch on that horrible day, my brother Pasquale had consumed the better part of a bottle of good-luck wine from Pippo Conti, a fellow roofer who had visited that morning on his way to Sunday Mass. Pasquale was whistling and laying down a row of shingles when he heard, over the sound of his hammering, Filippa's cries for help. She was seated high in the nearby tree, plagued, suddenly, by angry bluejays. Pasquale rose and ran to the animal's defense, forgetting about the gap in the roof between himself and the tree.

He fell.

I saw it with my eyes.

Hammer in hand, he fell through the stairwells to the foundation below.

I saw it all and heard the terrible breaking of my brother's bones against the dirt floor of my cellar. When I ran to him and cradled his head in my lap, it wobbled like the head of a broken doll. "*Dio ci scampi*! *Dio ci scampi*!" I shouted, over and over. If only I had held my tongue with the old priest! If only I had not thrown cement!

Filippa, who had now rid herself of the bluejays and hurried down the tree, sat huddled on Pasquale's chest, curling the hair on his head around one small pink finger. Pasquale mouthed, rather than spoke, his last words, "Filippa . . . Filippa."

As I watched the precious gift of life leave my brother, mine was the greatest anguish possible! "Filippa . . . Filippa," his lips kept saying, and I pledged to my dying brother, on the lives of our ancestors and descendants, that I would care for his little monkey. Then Pasquale convulsed and vomited blood and his eyes took on the gaze of holy statues.

Now, I was alone. . . .

Pasquale was waked for three afternoons in the boardinghouse parlor. *Signora* Siragusa wailed for my brother as a mother wails. My position of respect in the town, as well as the scope of the tragedy, brought out most of the Italians of Three Rivers. Flynn, the mill boss, came with his wife to pay respects. Werman, who owned the construction company where Pasquale had worked, showed up with his two sons. At the celebration of the crowded funeral Mass at St. Mary of Jesus Christ Church, that dog-faced monsignor assumed a disdainful attitude that deeply offended me. After my brother was laid to rest in the ground beside Vincenzo, I sat and wrote a letter of complaint to the Pope in Rome. (Never a response.)

3 *August* 1949

Trouble with my bowels since Tuesday. Arthritis afflicts my joints. My body fails me, but not my memory!

Despite Father Guglielmo's counsel—the little priest visited me several times after Pasquale's death—I did not return to church when the snow flew. I vowed never again to cross the threshold of the house of God as long as that no-good monsignor was alive. And I am proud to write that I kept that promise!

In the wake of her master's death, Filippa, the spoiled "little queen" who had doomed my brother, sat shivering in a corner of her cage on the boardinghouse porch. Sometimes at night, through the opened window of my room, I heard her strange, chattering lamentation—the agitation of her cage as she threw herself, violently, against it.

Signora Siragusa, that most superstitious of old women, began to see *il mal occhio*—the evil eye—in the monkey's gaze. Young children and grandmothers began to look away from the creature and make the sign of the cross upon entering or leaving the boardinghouse. The *signora* insisted that I remove the creature's cage from the front to the back porch. There, the older boys spat at her and poked her with sticks as she sat, hissing and shivering. Americo Cavoli, the *signora*'s nephew, made a hobby of tormenting that godforsaken creature. I knew this went on, but what could I do? Quit my work? Interrupt my sleep to play policeman for that goddamned monkey?

As a boss dyer and property owner, I, of course, embraced modern ideas, dismissing as women's foolishness the growing suspicion of *il mal occhio*. I regarded Filippa not as a witch but as a nuisance—one more expense in a sea of financial obligations that swirled around me because of my new home and my brother's funeral expenses. On practical grounds, I began to realize how unfortunate my hasty promise to my dying brother had been. For the sake of economy, I cut back on the expensive mixture of bananas, grain, and honey that Pasquale had provided for her, feeding her now, instead, potato peels and other garbage from *Signora* Siragusa's kitchen. The *signora* began to complain about Filippa's lice and about the foul-smelling diarrhea with which the monkey's new diet had afflicted her. Winter was coming. The *signora* didn't want that unclean little she-devil living down in the coal cellar, dispensing trouble and bugs up through the heating grates. Soon, the boarders in her house would all be scratching themselves, or packing their bags, or meeting with tragedy like my poor brother! She owned a boardinghouse, not a *giardino zoologico*. I would have to do something, she warned.

That same evening, as I reached into Filippa's filthy cage to dump her nightly swill, that goddamned monkey bared her fangs and bit me savagely on the wrist. I cursed the thing, sucked my hand at the point of the wound, and made a plan.

The next Sunday morning, I paid young Cavoli a nickel to run to Hollyhock Avenue with a burlap sack, line the bottom of it with broken, discarded bricks, and lug the bag to the Sachem River Bridge. I instructed the boy to wait for me there. Cautiously, I opened Filippa's cage and leashed the balking monkey.

We two walked toward the river. At several points, I was forced to drag the creature, who seemed somehow to understand the fate that was about to befall her. And when we arrived at our destination, Filippa held fast to the bars of the footbridge railing and screamed.

I grabbed her by the scruff of her neck and young Cavoli held open the sack. Between us, we managed to force her inside the brick-weighted bag and cinch the top. Filippa had scratched and bitten us both in the struggle and now she poked and battled with unnatural strength to free herself from the bag. Somehow, we managed to lift that goddamned screaming monkey over the railing and let go.

The bag sank efficiently.

What had to be done had been done and now it was over.

Ha! That's what I thought!

thirty-six

"So he drags her to the bridge, shoves her into this bag they've weighted down, and throws her over the side. Just *drowns* her."

"Because . . . ?"

"Because it was easier to kill the damn thing than to keep his promise." I was standing by her window, watching the Sachem River rush by behind the trees. We'd had a week or so of warmer weather; the current was traveling at a pretty good clip from the late-winter thaw. "I don't know, Doc. Maybe I should stop reading the damn thing. Chuck it into the woodstove or something."

"Burn your family history, Dominick? Why would you do that?"

"Because it riles me up. . . . Last night? After I read about all that monkey stuff? I couldn't even *sleep*." I turned and faced Dr. Patel. "We resemble him, you know? Thomas and me."

"Your grandfather? Yes? You have photographs?"

I nodded. "My mother used to keep this big scrapbook—all her family pictures. God, she was always dragging that thing out. She even rescued it once." I saw Ma burst from the burning house, screaming—that scrapbook clutched to her chest.

"Rescued it?"

"We had a fire at our house. When Thomas and I were kids. . . . You know what's weird about reading that thing? The more I get into it, the less I can stand the son of a bitch—the way he treats people, the way he thinks he's better than everyone—but at the same time, I can sort of *recognize* him, you know? *Relate* to him, on *some* level."

"You're talking about more than physical resemblance then?"

"I guess. Yeah. . . . Last night? After I read how he drowned the monkey? I started thinking about how *I'd* gotten trapped by a promise, same as him. Same as Papa. . . . That was the last thing I ever said to her, you know? I ever tell you that?"

"The last thing you said to whom?"

"My mother. I promised her I'd take care of him. Keep him safe—her 'little bunny rabbit.' . . . It was the very last thing I said to her before she died." I locked my arms across my chest. Watched two boys hike along the bank of the rushing river.

"Do you think you relate to your grandfather in some respects because—?"

"Because we both welshed on our promises. Went back on our word."

Dr. Patel said she didn't see how I had arrived at that conclusion. Hadn't I campaigned tirelessly—aggressively, for better or worse—on my brother's behalf? What made me feel that I had failed to honor my word to my mother?

The question made me laugh. "Look where he *is,*" I said. "Locked in *his* cage down there. A year, minimum, with an option to renew. Rubbing elbows with every goddamn psychopath who . . . Yeah, Doc, I did a *great* job of keeping him safe for her, didn't I?"

"Dominick, we've been over this before. For you to take responsibility for circumstances beyond your control is both counterproductive and—"

"Look, you can say whatever you want to try and make me feel better or whatever, but the truth is I *blew* it for him. Fell off that freakin' roof over there, missed his hearing, and then *bam!* He ends up long term at the Hatch Hotel."

Dr. Patel shook her head. In the first place, she said, she doubted whether my appearance at Thomas's hearing would have changed a course of action that was most likely inevitable. And second, the pledge I had made to my mother while she was dying—merciful and well-intentioned as it might have been—had exacted a very high personal cost. *Too* high a cost, in her opinion. It had made me unhappy, unwell—suicidal, even, for a brief period last fall. Certainly, my mother would not have wanted me to sacrifice my *own* well-being in a futile attempt to secure the well-being of my brother.

"*That's* debatable," I mumbled.

"Yes? Why do you say that?"

I shrugged, looked away. "No reason. Never mind."

I could feel, rather than see, her watching me. Neither of us said a word.

"Dominick," she finally said. "In talking about your grandfather, you've been quite critical of what you see as his delusions of grandeur. I ask you to consider if that is, perhaps, *another* of the resemblances you share."

I let out a one-note laugh—asked her what *that* was supposed to mean.

"It means that Thomas became schizophrenic and you did not because God or fate or random selection made it so. It means that your brother is at Hatch for the next year because the state thinks that is where he best belongs. You cannot control these things, regardless of what promises you made, or to whom."

"Yeah, well, if I ever need a lawyer to help me beat a rap, I'll call you, Doc. But the truth is, I could have gotten him out of there. I *know* I could have."

She disagreed, she said.

"Okay, fine. We agree to disagree."

She stood up and walked toward the window. Stood beside me, looking out. "I've watched you stare out this window many times now," she said. "What are you always looking at so intently?"

Nothing, I told her. Just the river.

"Ah," she said. "Well, do me a favor, please. Give me a demonstration of these great powers you have to direct the course of things. Throw open the window, please, and *call* to the river. Tell it you want it to stop flowing in its present direction and reverse itself. Let me see this power of yours."

I looked into her mischievous eyes. "I suppose you're trying to make a point?"

"A little point, a little joke," she said. "Would it not be futile for you to make such a command? To assume that the river would ignore its inevitable course and bend to your wishes? You are limited, my friend, in what you can and cannot control, as are we all. If you are to become healthy, you must acknowledge the ineluctability of your brother's course. Acknowledge your limitations in directing it, Dominick. And that will free you. That will help to make you well."

I looked from her smile down to the one on Shiva's face. "So what am I *supposed* to do?" I said. "Shove him in a burlap bag? Drag him down there and throw him off the bridge?"

She reached out and touched the small of my back. Looked out at the river with me. "Is that what you'd *like* to do, Dominick?" she asked. I closed my eyes and saw, again, my morphine dream: saw and felt myself strangle my brother, cut him down from the tree, carry him toward this same damn river. "Answer my question, please," she said. "Do you sometimes want to destroy your brother?"

"No," I said, struggling to hold it together. "Yes."

She waited. Watched me crumble.

"No! Yes! No! Yes! No! Yes!"

I must have wailed for a minute or more, and when I was finally finished—was spent, doubled over from my admission—she guided me away from the window and back to my chair. Had me do some deep breathing. Waited until I was so calm, I felt drowsy.

Only when I faced my limitations regarding my brother, Dr. Patel said, could I begin to address my conflictedness about him. Free myself. Move forward.

"I *love* him," I said. "He's my *brother.* But all our lives, he's made me feel so . . ."

"Go on. He's made you feel . . . ?"

"Ashamed. *Humiliated.* Everybody whispering about what a fuckin' freak he is. Turning him into a fuckin' joke. . . . And half of you wants to *defend* him, you know? Punch their lights out when they say something. And the other half . . . the other half . . . just wants to run in the opposite direction. Get the hell away from him so you don't catch what he's got. So that none of it lands on *you.*"

"None of what?"

"The ridicule. The disease. . . . The *weakness.*"

She uncapped her pen and wrote something down. "So what you're saying is that being Thomas's brother makes you feel bifurcated."

"Bifurcated?" I looked up at her. "I couldn't tell you, Doc. I don't speak Phi Beta Kappa."

"Divided, Dominick. Separated. Simultaneously sympathetic *and* repelled."

I nodded, sighed. "And scared shitless. Don't forget scared shitless."

"Scared of what, please? Specifically."

I got up again, went back to the window. " 'Oh, look, Martha! Over there—identical twins! Are you their mother? How in the world can you tell which is which?' . . . You know what that was like, growing up? Having *that* be your big claim to fame? Hearing your whole life that you were . . . *interchangeable* or something? And after he got sick, after he started to fold from it, I just waited . . . just *waited.* All during my twenties, my thirties—just *waiting* for it to get me, too. . . . And my mother: She *expected* it! *Expected* me to look out for him, keep myself strong so that I could keep *him* safe. Be his personal guardian or something. That was my *function* in life, you know? To keep my brother safe from Ray, from the tough kids at school . . . And even *now.* You know how panicky I get coming here, sometimes? Walking up those stairs of yours? Coming to see a *shrink*? Because *I'm* not supposed to need fixing; I'm the *strong* one—the lookout. After . . . after he hacked his hand off last October? When it was on the news every two seconds? On the front page of the goddamned *New York Post,* for Christ's sake? And I . . . It's *still* like that sometimes. I'll be stopped someplace for gas or coffee or something. I'll have my guard down, and then I'll look over and catch someone staring. Just *staring* at me like . . ."

"Finish your thought, please."

"Like *I'm* the weak one. Like I'm . . ."

"Like you're Thomas."

I nodded. "I don't know. Maybe I ought to get it tattooed across my forehead or something: 'I'm the *other* one.' "

She smiled sadly, jotted something down on her pad. "That would be an unnecessary gesture, in my opinion," she said. "Despite your strong physical resemblance, your shared genetic coding, you and your brother are quite distinguishable."

"Yeah," I said. "I'm the one with *two* hands."

"Well, yes, but that is not what I meant, my friend," she said. "In some respects, you seem to me more like fraternal than identical twins. So much so that, at one point—back when I was treating Thomas—I checked his medical records to make sure you had both been tested."

"Tested for what?"

"To establish your monozygosis. And tests *had* been made, of course—two of them, if I recall. In terms of your genetic makeup, you and he *are* identical. Nevertheless, Dominick, you quite defy the hereditary odds. Not only in your fortunate avoidance of your brother's psychosis, but in other ways as well."

I nodded, poker-faced. On the inside, I was rejoicing.

"And, of course, you've worked very hard to cultivate and capitalize upon those differences, too. Dedicated your *life* to the cause, I would say. *Exhausted* yourself with the effort. So what's less clear to me is which of the differences between the two of you are genetically based and which ones you've orchestrated."

I let out a laugh. "Which ones we've *orchestrated*?"

"Not 'we,' Dominick. You, personally. You and your fear that what claimed your brother would claim you, too."

She stopped, wrote down something else. All that writing she'd been doing the last couple sessions was making me nervous. When she looked up again, I nodded down at her pad. "What are you working on there?"

On me, she said, my dilemma. My fears were becoming

clearer and clearer to her. She had just then been listing them. Did I want to hear her list?

Unsure whether I wanted to or not, I said I did.

First and foremost, she said, I was afraid that the shadow of my brother's schizophrenia would descend on me—of course I was. As an identical twin, how could I *not* fear it? Second, I seemed to be—and she would use my phrase, she said—"scared shitless" that the world would fail to recognize the distinctions between my brother and me—understand that we were two separate people. "And then there is your third apprehension," she said, "the one which I am just now beginning to better understand."

"Yeah?" I said. "What's that?"

My third apprehension, as she saw it, was that there were, perhaps, fewer distinctions between my brother and me than I would like. Than I had acknowledged.

"What do you mean?" I said.

"Well, for instance, Thomas has a very gentle nature—a sensitivity toward others that is evident even now, sometimes, years and years into his psychotic existence. And from what you've told me of your shared childhood and adolescence, his gentleness—his sweetness—was even more pronounced before the onset of his illness. 'He was the nicer one,' you've told me many, many times. By which I take it you mean that he was the more sensitive, the more vulnerable, brother. Yes?"

"Yeah. . . . Yes."

"Thomas was the twin who, in some respects, was *easier* to love?"

I looked away.

Dominick's my little spider monkey, and you're my cuddly little bunny rabbit. Come sit down next to me, bunny rabbit. Come sit in Mama's lap . . .

"Easier for *her* to love," I said.

"Your mother? Yes?"

I sat there, watching my right hand uncinch my wristwatch strap—cinch it again, uncinch it. When I looked up at Dr. Patel, she held my gaze.

"Let me ask you something," she said. "Given your brother's gentleness, his sensitivity, would it be fair to characterize Thomas as the more *feminine* of the two of you? Is that one of the distinctions you would make, Dominick?"

I shrugged. Felt myself tense at the word. *Go downstairs now, Dominick. I made you a special snack. Your brother and I are just "playing nice."*

"Maybe," I said.

"What is 'maybe,' please? Is that yes or no?"

"It's *yes*!" I snapped. She was beginning to piss me off.

"Ah. And has that been the case all your lives? In childhood as well as adulthood? That you were the more masculine brother and Thomas was the more feminine?"

"Yes."

"And was it that aspect of your brother's nature, that quality perhaps, that *made* Thomas easier for your mother to love?"

I forced myself not to look away from her face. "What's your point?" I said. "You saying he's gay or something? That he's schizophrenic because he's queer?"

She smiled. She was not saying that—no, no. That had been Dr. Freud's hypothesis, more or less, but psychotherapists had gotten quite beyond that early theory and into a realm of much greater complexity. "However, your immediate leap to that conclusion interests me, Dominick," she said. "It might be worth our while to examine why you equate sensitivity—vulnerability—with homosexuality."

I shook my head. "Oh, I get it," I said. "You think he's straight and *I'm* gay." She waited for the wiseass smirk to leave my face.

"What I suspect," she said, "is that you share some of your brother's sweetness, his gentleness and vulnerability—his weakness, as you put it—and that that has frightened you. And that, perhaps, it is the constant denial of those qualities in yourself which has exhausted you. Made you sick."

"*He's* the sick one," I reminded her. "I'm the *other* one."

"Yes, yes," she said. "The tough guy. The *not*-so-nice twin. Which doesn't necessarily make you well, Dominick. Does it? Look around, my friend. Here you are, in therapy."

She saw it over and over again in her male patients, she said—it could probably qualify as an *epidemic* among American men: this stubborn reluctance to embrace our wholeness—this stoic denial that we had come from our *mothers* as well as our fathers. It was sad, really—tragic. So wasteful of human lives, as our wars and drive-by shootings kept proving to us; all one had to do was turn on CNN or CBS News. And yet, it was comic, too—the lengths most men went to to prove that they were "tough guys." The gods must look down upon us, laughing and crying simultaneously. "My twelve-year-old grandson, Sava, stayed with me recently while his parents were away at a conference," she said. "And all during his visit, he begged and begged me to take him to a movie called *Die Hard the Second.*"

"Die Hard 2," I corrected her. "Bruce Willis." It was kind of nice, actually: this time-out. Imagining her as some kid's grandmother instead of my shrink.

"Yes, yes, that's right," she said. " 'Oh, Muti, please, please!' he kept begging me. 'I must see *Die Hard 2* or my life will be ruined!' And so, at last, I complied. Capitulated. And as I sat beside him in the darkened theater, watching all the far-fetched mayhem in front of us, I thought to myself, well, here it is: a cinematic catalog of all the things boys and men are afraid of. All the things they feel they have to shoot at and punch and kill in order to kill off their own sensitivity—deny their X chromosome, if you will." She paused, laughed at her own joke. "We were seated near the front of the theater, you understand. Sava had insisted upon it: in order for him to be happy, he had to have a large Coca-Cola, a large container of popcorn with butter, and a seat up near the front. And so, in the middle of *Die Hard the Second,* I had occasion to look back and see, in the reflected light from the movie screen, the illuminated faces of the audience members. Men and boys, mostly, staring trancelike at the screen. Letting Bruce Willy shoot and punch and kill for them everything that made them afraid. It was very instructive, really. I was enormously grateful for the experience." She shook her head and smiled. "Well, forgive my polemic, Dominick. But what are our stories if not the mirrors we hold up to our fears?"

At the end of our session, she said she thought we had covered some important ground, made some worthwhile progress. She suggested that, between now and our next visit, I should examine what *I* had been trying to shoot at and punch and kill for so long—whether or not *I* had, perhaps, denied some more gentle part of my nature, and if so, what it had cost me. "And don't get a tattoo for your forehead," she said, smiling. "It's entirely unnecessary." As proof, she held her hands in front of her. Wiggled her fingers and smiled. Our being human made us tragic and comic both, she had said; the gods both laughed and wept.

At the door, she asked me if I had any questions before we said goodbye for the week.

"My grandfather's story," I said. "Should I just stop reading it? . . . If all it's doing is getting me worked up?"

The question put a frown on her face. She was a bit puzzled by that impulse, she said; she thought my past was precisely what I was searching for. She reminded me that I had been frustrated by my mother's unwillingness to divulge our family history and now, here I was, in possession of a unique opportunity: the gift of my grandfather's posthumous voice. My *grandfather,* problematical or not. Why would I wish to avoid such a gift?

"I didn't want my grandfather," I said. "I wanted my *father.* As far as my father was concerned, she never even gave me a *name.*"

"Granted, Dominick. But one must accept what one is offered, no? It would be an ungracious thing to say to a gift-giver, 'No, no, I do not want this thing. I want another thing.' And my goodness, to have at your disposal this communiqué from the past—well, *I* see it as a rare opportunity, Dominick. Potentially, at any rate. After all, how many of our grandfathers rented a Dictaphone, hired a stenographer, and spent afternoons recalling, for their grandsons' sake—"

"It *wasn't* for my sake. Our sake. I don't think he had any idea she was pregnant."

As she understood it, Dr. Patel said, Domenico had wanted to leave something of himself for posterity. Whether or not he knew, before he died, of Thomas's and my existence, we were, in fact, just that: his descendants, his link to the future. My reading his story allowed him to achieve his goal, she said. Perhaps if I kept reading it, Domenico might, likewise, help *me* to achieve *mine.*

We had gone over our allotted time, she said. We had to stop. "But come here first." She took me by the arm and led me back to the window.

"It is all connected, Dominick," she said. "Life is not a series of isolated ponds and puddles; life is this river you see below, before you. It flows from the past through the present on its way to the future. That is *not* something I have always understood; it is something I have come to a gradual understanding of, through my work as both an anthropologist and a psychologist."

I looked out, again, at the rushing water.

"Life is a river," she repeated. "Only in the most literal sense are we born on the day we leave our mother's womb. In the larger, truer sense, we are born of the past—connected to its fluidity, both genetically and experientially." She folded her hands together as if praying to what we saw below. "So, that is *my* opinion, my friend. Should you throw your ancestry into the woodstove? Of course not. Should you keep reading it, even if it takes away your sleep? *Yes,* by all means. *Read* your grandfather's story, Dominick. Jump into the river. And if it upsets you, come in and tell me why."

On the way out of her office, I got a quick glimpse of her next appointment: big, burly guy—work boots, hooded sweatshirt. We gave each other a jerky half-nod for a hello. Another "tough guy" in therapy, I thought. A fellow member of the walking wounded.

The traffic on the way home was a bitch. I was antsy. Kept punching my way through the radio stations. "Night Moves" . . . "I Shot the Sheriff" . . . "The Boys Are Back in Town." If you cranked up the volume loud enough, it took over your whole head. You didn't have to think. But when I got back home, pulled into the driveway, and cut the engine, the silence came back, and with it, unexpectedly, the morning my mother died. . . .

It was just me and her in that hospital room when I'd made that promise—the same one she'd asked me to make my whole life. Ray and I had been up with her all night—just sitting there, watching her suffer, because there was nothing else we could do. "She could go any time," they kept saying: the doctors, nurses, the woman from hospice. The only catch was, she kept outlasting their predictions. Couple of days and nights, it had dragged on. We were all pretty whipped by then. . . .

The sun was just coming up, I remember. She'd been thrashing around for an hour or more, moaning, trying to yank off her oxygen mask. Then, right about when it was getting light out, she quieted down. Stopped fighting.

Ray had stepped out for a couple minutes—to make a phone call about work. And I leaned over toward her, started stroking her forehead. And she looked right at me—she was conscious at that point, I *know* it. . . . And I told her I loved her. Told her thanks for everything she'd done for us—all the sacrifices she had made. And then I said it: the one thing I know she'd been waiting to hear: "I'll take care of him for you, Ma. I'll make sure he's safe. You can go now."

And she *did*—just like that. By the time Ray got back, she was unconscious. Died sometime in the next hour. . . . Soon as she heard that her "little bunny rabbit" was going to be safe, she could let go.

I love you, Ma. I *hate* you. . . .

There was something Dr. Patel hadn't figured out yet. Something I was just starting to figure out myself: how much I hated my mother for putting me on guard duty my whole life. For making me their sentry. . . .

"Playing nice" they used to call it—whatever it was they'd do up there. Dress-up: was that all it was? Thomas clomping around in her high heels, twirling around in her dresses. . . . She had no friends. She was lonely. . . .

Go downstairs now, Dominick. I made you a special snack. Thomas and I are just going to "play nice."

And so I'd sit down there, eating my pudding or potato chips, staring at that television that, later on, would explode. Set the living room on fire.

On guard. Watching out for Ray. . . .

This wouldn't be any fun for you, Dominick. This is the kind of fun only your brother likes. . . . Let me know right away if Ray comes. If Ray ever found out about "playing nice," he'd get mad at all three of us. Madder than he's ever been before. . . .

It's not that she didn't love me, Doc. She *did* love me. I

knew that. She just always loved him more. Loved the exact thing about Thomas that Ray hated. Nailed him for . . . Her "sweetheart." Her "little cuddly bunny rabbit." . . .

I'll take care of him for you, Ma. I'll keep him safe. You can go now.

As if promising her would finally put me in first place, even for a minute—for one fucking minute before she died. . . . All my life, I had come in second. Number two in a two-man race. Even now I was, with her gone four years and him locked away at Hatch. Number two in our never-ending two-man struggle.

And it *hurt*. It *hurt,* Ma—being the lookout, the spider monkey—the one you never invited onto your lap. . . .

It *hurt,* Ma. It goddamned *hurt.* . . .

thirty-seven

5 *August* 1949

I left *Signora* Siragusa's boardinghouse and took residence of my vitrified brick *casa di due appartamenti* on 1 April 1916. I had been the first Italian at American Woolen and Textile Company to rise to the position of boss dyer. Now I became the first of my countrymen to own his own home in Three Rivers—a home I had built with my own two hands! I welcomed Salvatore Tusia, the barber, and his wife and children to the left-side apartment and received my first monthly rent, eleven dollars and fifty cents, paid to me in cash. I had wanted twelve a month, but Tusia brought me down in exchange for a haircut whenever I needed one and a daily shave. I made Tusia cut my hair every Friday, to make sure I got my money's worth.

I wrote to my Brooklyn cousins to say I would honor them with a two-day visit at Easter. Notify the Iaccoi brothers next door, I told them. The trip would allow me to meet, at long last, my bride-to-be, Prosperine. At this time, the Iaccois and I would establish a wedding date and finalize the dowry price. In fairness to myself, I would attach to the asking price the cost of my train ticket to and from New York and a new three-piece suit, which I would wear for the trip and also on my wedding day.

At my cousins' table that Easter Sunday, I raised my glass and made a memorable speech about the Old Country and the Tempesta family. I spoke a eulogy to Papa and Mama and made tribute to my two departed brothers. My words brought tears to the eyes of all present, except for Lena and Vitaglio's youngest brat, who was allowed to rummage beneath the dining room table, tickling ankles and pulling at the stockings of the adults. Shameful, disrespectful behavior! When that little mosquito snapped my garter in the middle of my remarks, I reached under the table and gave him what he deserved. The crying, head-bumping, and wine-spilling that followed ruined the rest of my speech. "Well," Lena smiled, "let's make the best of it and eat, then, before the macaroni gets any colder."

"Yes," I agreed, "if you and Vitaglio cannot rule your young ones any better than this, then why don't we ignore the dead and eat?"

That evening, I excused myself, rose from the table, and went next door to my meeting with the Iaccoi brothers. Finally, I would feast my eyes on my Sicilian bride.

Fluttering like two pigeons, Rocco and Nunzio Iaccoi met me in the foyer and told me repeatedly what a great honor it was to receive into their home a man who had made himself such a success. They took me to their parlor and offered me the largest of the stuffed chairs, lit me a cigar, and carried the standing ashtray across the room for my convenience. When they were sure I was comfortable, they called to their cousin Prosperine, who was waiting in the kitchen. "Uncap the *anisetta*, cousin," they sang out. "Bring three glasses."

There was a long wait and then, in the kitchen, the sound of things dropping, glass breaking. "*Scusi*," Nunzio Iaccoi said, smiling so broadly that it looked like he had a pain.

Rocco laughed and shrugged, shrugged and laughed. "In almost two years of living here, this is the first time that dear, sweet girl has broken anything," he said. "My hotheaded half-sister, Ignazia, she throws things against the wall during temper fits, and is clumsy as well, but little Prosperine is as graceful and sure-handed as any young girl I've seen."

That goddamned plumber wasn't fooling me. The girl's obvious clumsiness is a bargaining tool for me, I thought. Something to drive up the dowry price a bit.

Nunzio returned to the parlor. "The problem was nothing, ha ha," he said. "If only all our problems could be swept away with a broom, eh, Domenico? Ha ha ha." The brothers' laughter and sighs did little to conceal their nervousness.

When Prosperine emerged from the kitchen, I attempted to rise, but each of the Iaccois held me down with a hand on my shoulders. "Sit, sit," Rocco said. "No need to get up. Rest yourself."

At first, I could not look at her face but saw, instead, her tiny size. She was no taller than a girl of twelve. No bigger than Mama! My eyes dropped to the floor.

I looked up from her high-buttoned shoes to her black dress with its small waist. She'd pinned a cluster of artificial flowers there. My eyes rose past the *anisetta* in their little glasses, which she held on a small tray before her. My glance moved from her flat bosom to a cameo pinned to the high neck of her dress. When I arrived at her *faccia*, my jaw dropped.

"S*ignore* Domenico Tempesta," Nunzio said. "May I present Prosperine Tucci, your *sposa futura*!"

"When hell freezes over!" I shouted. Elbowing past the brothers, I made my way to their front door!

The thing that had made me drop all sense of propriety was the face of Prosperine. For one thing, she was far from the young girl those lying plumbers had promised me. That skinny hag was probably thirty if she was a day! Worse—far worse—her homely, scrawny face bore a shocking resemblance to Filippa, that goddamned drowned monkey that had bewitched my poor brother Pasquale!

That night, I twisted and turned on my cousins' lumpy divan as if I was back aboard the SS *Napolitano*! Had my brother Pasquale sent this skinny bitch up from the *mundo suttomari* as revenge because I had drowned his "little queen"? Had my brother Vincenzo sent her to mock, once again, my chastity? Or had Mama sent a monkey for me to marry because I had forsaken her to seek my fortune in America?

"*Meglio celibe che mal sposato*!"* I whispered to myself. Better to die without sons than to have to make them with *that*!

Somewhere in the middle of that long night in Brooklyn, a church bell rang three times. Mama, Pasquale, Vincenzo: maybe all three of them had conspired and sent this monkey-woman to me! But a gift sent is not the same as a gift accepted. I decided I would wait until daylight, board the earliest train possible, go back to my big house in Three Rivers, Connecticut, and live my life as a bachelor.

6 *August* 1949

The Iaccois and their monkey-cousin were already in Lena and Vitaglio's kitchen when I awoke the next morning. It was the brothers' angry voices that roused me from my pitiful sleep. "Ha! So here's the man whose promises mean nothing!" Rocco said as I entered the kitchen.

"Please," Lena told the Iaccois. "Let my poor cousin eat his breakfast in peace. Shouting is bad for *digestione*."

---

* "Better single than unhappily married." Translator's note: The original sentence, partially crossed out, reads "Better to die single than to have to fuck a monkey."—NF

She placed before me *frittata*, sausage and potatoes, coffee, Easter bread. Here was a woman who knew how to take care of men!

I took a sip of coffee, a mouthful of egg. I made those two goddamned plumbers wait. "A promise collapses when it is made to deceitful men," I finally said.

How dare I accuse them of deceit, Nunzio shouted. It was I, not they, who had initiated discussion about a wife—*two* wives, not one, he reminded me.

"So what do you think? That I climbed up on that roof and pushed my poor brother off? What do you two fools expect me to do? Marry *two* women and live the life of a *bigamo*?"

"Marrying one of them will do!" Rocco said. "The one you *promised* to marry. The one who has spent two years waiting for her home to be completed and now has spent the night sobbing into her pillow because you have so grievously wronged her!"

"Eat, Domenico," Lena insisted. "Eat your breakfast while it's hot and then have your argument."

As I chewed and swallowed, swallowed and chewed, I took small glimpses of Prosperine. She was seated on a chair by the window. In the morning light, she looked twenty-five, perhaps, not thirty, but she was even uglier than she had been the night before. Today she wore peasant clothes and a kerchief on that shrunken head of hers. She was smoking a pipe!

"You have falsely represented this creature," I told the brothers. "Look at her over there, smoking like a man! *She* is not beautiful! *She* is not young!"

Nunzio stuttered and resorted to proverbs. "*Gadina vecchia fa bonu brodo*,"* he insisted. And I answered him with a proverb of my own: "*Cucinala come vuoi, ma sempre cocuzza e*!"**

---

* "An old hen makes the best soup."—NF

** Roughly, "Cook squash any way you like, but it's still squash."—NF

"This woman is as pure as the Blessed Virgin," Rocco argued.

"If this one is *vergine*," I said, "it is due to lack of opportunity. No meat on her bones! No *tette*! This one would have shriveled the *cazzu* of my brother Vincenzo!" In reaction to my vulgarity, uttered in the heat of battle, my cousin Lena gave a scream and lifted her apron over her face. Not Prosperine, though. That one was as hard as nails!

"Beware, Tempesta," Nunzio Iaccoi warned. "In America, there are courts of law that make sure a man keeps his word. We have saved every letter and telegram you sent."

"Don't try to scare me, plumber!" I shouted back. "What judge with eyes in his head would sentence me to a life with that one? She belongs at the end of an organ-grinder's leash, not in the marriage bed of a man of property!"

Of course, I was a proper man and a gentleman and never would have spoken that way in the hag's presence if those two brothers hadn't pushed me to it, but now the damage was done. My eyes followed the others' eyes to Prosperine and a shiver passed through me. Without blinking or turning away, she puffed on her pipe and glared at me with the black look of *il mal occhio* itself. As I have said before, a modern man such as Domenico Tempesta leaves superstition to foolish old women. But at that moment in my cousin Lena's kitchen, I longed to clutch a *gobbo*, a red chili, a pig's tooth—anything to ward off that monkey-woman's evil eye!

My sweet cousin Lena, in an effort to end the impasse before fisticuffs broke out in her kitchen, poured coffee, passed *biscotti* and Easter bread to the Iaccois, and reminded us all that there had been, since the beginning of our negotiations, not one but *two* bridal candidates living under the Iaccois' roof. "*Scusa*, *Signorina* Prosperine," she said, addressing the other one without looking at her. "*Scusa* me a million times for saying so, but Domenico has changed his mind."

Prosperine took the pipe from her mouth and spat out the open window. "Bah!" she said, then clamped the pipe again between her teeth.

Lena turned to me and took my hand. "Domenico, before you begin your long trip home, wouldn't you at least like to meet the Iaccois' pretty sister, Ignazia?"

"Let them marry off their women to other fools!" I said back. "I'm done with Iaccoi business!"

At this, Rocco raised his fists, but Nunzio pushed them back down again. "*Aspetta un momento*!" he said, then whispered to Rocco, who ran out the kitchen door. The rest of us waited and waited for . . . for who knew what? As for my stomach, it felt like I had swallowed the anchor of the SS *Napolitano* instead of my cousin's eggs and bread and coffee!

Ten minutes later, Rocco burst back through the doorway. He had in his hands Ignazia's immigration papers and a daguerreotype of the girl. The papers established that she had been born in 1898 and thus was truly eighteen years of age. The photograph verified that she was as beautiful as the other one was homely—a girl well suited to be the wife of a property owner. A girl with some meat on her bones.

I was persuaded to return after lunch to the Iaccois' front parlor and wait for Ignazia's arrival back from her friend's home. As I waited, I stared at the picture of the girl, and fell under its spell. Her flowing hair and full lips stirred me. Her dark eyes looked directly at my eyes. Her full face whispered the promise of a *figura* as plump and lovely as Venus's.

I fell in love with that picture and fell more in love still with the flesh-and-blood girl who walked defiantly through her brothers' front door an hour later than she was expected.

"Where have you been?" her brother asked.

"I've been where I've been!" she answered boldly.

She was wearing a woolen coat dyed as red as blood. Such a striking *vermiglio* had never emerged from the vats at American Woolen and Textile, I tell you! And such a woman had never lived in the tiny village of Giuliana or in Three Rivers, Connecticut. Her hair, black and wild, ended where her buttocks began. Her wide hips were built to bracket a husband and to push forth children into the world. She had cast her spell upon me even before her coat was off! At long last, I was in love!

"Domenico Tempesta, it is my great pleasure to present to you my half-sister, Ignazia," Rocco said.

This is the one, I told myself. This is the woman I have waited for. Here before me, scowling, stands my very own wife!

But the girl gave me barely a glance. Turning to Prosperine, she asked if she had fed the company all the *braciola* from the Easter meal the day before. She was as hungry as an *elefante*, she said, and patted her belly.

"Please, Ignazia, worry later about your stomach," Nunzio said. "Sit and visit. Show a little respect for a man of property and a factory boss!"

Ignazia turned to Prosperine. "Ah, so this is your long-lost *innamorato*, eh?" she laughed.

"Bah!" the other one answered, puffing away on her pipe.

"Never mind your 'bah,'" Nunzio scolded. "Make us espresso. Quick, before I turn you out of this house!"

The Monkey slumped into the kitchen; the two brothers' faces regained their false smiles. They began to ask questions about my *casa di due appartamenti* and to repeat each of my answers to their half-sister. Ignazia tapped her shoe and sang a little song to herself instead of listening. "I'll help in the kitchen," she said.

I watched her rise and walk from the room. Bad as it was for bargaining, I could do nothing but stare at her exiting figure and then at the doorway through which she had passed.

"Ignazia's job at the shoe factory has exposed her to many bad influences," Rocco whispered after she had left the room. "She has gotten the foolish notion, for example, that, like *'Mericani*, Italian women should marry for love. Ha ha ha ha."

"You like what you see, eh, Domenico?" Nunzio noted from across the room. "If she becomes *your* wife, she'll soon forget all of these *'Mericana* ways. You'll make her *siciliana* again!"

For my part, I could do nothing but swallow and stare—finger her photograph in my hand and anticipate her reentrance from the kitchen.

The door banged open again a minute later. Ignazia was holding a heel of bread in one hand, a chicken leg in the other. "Oh, no!" she shouted, shaking her head violently. "Oh, no, no, no, no!"

"*Scusa*?" one of the brothers said.

"She just told me in the kitchen what you three old men have up your sleeves," the girl said. "I've told you over and over. I'm going to marry Padraic McGannon and that's who I am going to marry!"

"That lazy Irishman with no job?" Rocco shouted. "That redheaded mama's boy whose mouth still smells of breast milk?"

I had first laid eyes on Ignazia only moments before, but hearing her profess her intentions to marry another man sank my heart and made me want to find that goddamned Irishman and strangle him! Such was Ignazia's power over me.

"Where would you and that lazy good-for-nothing live?" Nunzio wanted to know.

Ignazia put her hands against her fleshy hips. "With his mother," she said.

"On what?"

"On something old men know nothing about, that's what. L'*amore*! *Passione*!"

Nunzio shook his head at the folly of it and Rocco made the sign of the cross. In the past few minutes, I had learned much about *passione* and *amore*. It was as if Mount Etna's hot lava now boiled within me where, before, my blood had been cool. Ignazia robbed the room of air. This I knew above all else: that she would be the wife of no one but Domenico Onofrio Tempesta!

"*Scusa*, young lady, *scusa*," I stood and began. "Your brothers and I have a long-standing agreement—one which will provide richly for you, *if* I should consent to make you my wife." Here, I drew a deep breath and expanded my chest for her to see, wholly, the man she was getting.

"If *you* consent?" she laughed. "If *you* consent? Who wants to be *your* wife, old man? Go marry some gray-haired old *nonna*!" She bit savagely into that chicken leg of hers, ripping meat from the bone, and chewing ravenously as she glared at me.

The *passione* with which Ignazia rejected the idea of marrying me only made me desire her more. This impudent girl would be my wife, whether she liked it or not!

"Young lady," I said, attempting reason. "Your brothers' honor is at stake here. I paid good money for a train ride from Connecticut to meet my *sposa futura*. Trust me when I say that agreements between Sicilian men—which you needn't bother your pretty head about—are binding!"

"How much?"

"Eh?"

"How much did you pay for your train ride?" she asked me.

I told her I had paid a dollar, fifty cents.

Brazenly, she produced a small change purse from a secret place beneath her skirts. She opened it and counted coins. "Here's your precious money, then," she shouted, flinging a handful of coins at my feet. Terrible behavior, and yet, it made me want her more—made me want to spank her for her impertinence, to ravage her, to tame her with my *ardore*! The girl made me short of breath—made me think crazy thoughts. I stood there, drunk with her, and suddenly knew my dead brother Vincenzo better than I had ever known him before.

"I am marrying Padraic McGannon and that's who I'm marrying!" she declared again, then stormed from the room.

"That one has a hellcat's disposition," I said to the brothers, "but I suppose she will do. I'll take her off your hands for a dowry of seven hundred dollars."

"Seven hundred!" Rocco shouted. "What do you think—that we two are as rich as you? This girl is a jewel—a diamond waiting to be polished. Once she is cured of this love-foolishness over that redheaded mick—"

The mention of that boy again was like a scream in my ear. "Five hundred and fifty, then. That is my final offer. The money, after all, will be used to furnish the *appartamento* where your half-sister will live like a queen. When you two visit, you yourselves will sleep on feather beds her dowry will have purchased."

"That's all very fine, Tempesta," Nunzio said, "but my brother and I are working men, not sultans. We haven't that kind of fortune to hand over to you. Two hundred, and the other one goes to live with you, too." Of those two snakes, Nunzio was the worst.

"Other one? What other one?" I said, though I knew very well who they meant.

"*That* one," Nunzio said, pointing to the Monkey-Face who had just entered the room with our coffee.

"Out of the question!" I said. "I would not think of robbing you of your housekeeper."

"Don't be foolish, Tempesta," Rocco advised. "She

cooks and helps Ignazia clean your big house, she midwifes the babies when they come along, and then, when the time is right, you marry her off to some widower in need of a clean house. As for us, finding a servant in this city is as easy as opening the door and shouting for one."

"Out of the question!" I repeated. "If you could not find this one a husband in all of New York, how can I hope to get rid of her in Connecticut? Four hundred. The other one stays here."

Nunzio shrugged and sighed. "Then I guess Ignazia becomes the wife of that redheaded Irishman after all and you, *Signore* Domenico, lose a precious prize because of your greed. I pity you and weep for your stupidity."

In the other room, the beautiful hotheaded girl was pacing the floor and arguing with herself. The door banged open. She threatened to cut out her heart if any of us stood between her and the Irishman. The door banged shut again.

"Three hundred seventy-five," I told Nunzio. "For the one girl alone."

"Three hundred," Nunzio said. "And you take Prosperine."

"Three hundred fifty and the other one stays here with you," I said. "That is my final offer."

Rocco opened his mouth to agree to my terms, but that goddamned Nunzio clamped his fat, hairy knuckles on his brother's shoulder and squeezed. "As the eldest of the family, *Signore* Domenico, I am afraid I have to refuse on my half-sister Ignazia's behalf." He walked to the front door and held it open. "*Arrivederci.*"

I stood stammering at their stoop, staring blankly at the brothers. Could this be happening? Was I about to lose that hot-blooded creature who had stirred my *ardore* like the awakened lava of Mount Etna? So be it, then! I would not be cheated out of a dowry that would furnish my home. And I was goddamned if I would be stuck with that skinny hag of a monkey besides.

The door flew open once more. Ignazia's cheeks were

flushed with emotion and the little groove of skin above her pouting lip held a small bead of sweat. "You heard him, old man," she shouted. "*Arrivederci*! Go!"

I moaned quietly, longing suddenly and illogically to step back inside and lick the clear, shimmering drop of nectar out of that little groove of hers, to taste her salt. I ached to undo her clothes and claim her. Such was the spell Ignazia had cast.

"*Arrivederci*," Nunzio Iaccoi repeated. He closed the door and slid the bolt. There I stood on that sidewalk in Brooklyn, more alone than I had ever been before.

8 *August* 1949

On the long train ride home from New York, I whimpered for what I wanted, mumbling arguments to myself and to the Iaccois that made other passengers look away and change their seats. What did I care? I closed my burning eyes and saw her face, her *figura*. I sat there with my coat on my lap, a goat with a frozen *cazzu* like my brother Vincenzo. I would have that wench! Somehow, I would have her!

Strangest of all on that strange, strange day was my behavior when the train pulled into the New London station. It was five in the afternoon. I was due at work in another four hours. "*Scusa*," I said, grabbing the conductor by his jacket sleeve. "*Scusa, signore*, but when does the next train leave here for New York?"

He checked his watch. "Hour, fifteen minutes," he said.

On a scrap of paper I wrote a note to Flynn at the mill: "Emergency of family. Back tomorrow. Tempesta." I gave a man headed for Three Rivers a whole dollar to make sure it got there. That's how crazy that girl had made me! A whole silver dollar, pressed against the palm of a stranger!

I paced back and forth inside the station, outside the station, around the station. I was no longer simply Domenico Tempesta—I was both myself and a crazy man! "What's the matter with you, eh?" I shouted inside my own head. "They could fire you for not showing up at work! You could lose your big house!"

"Let me lose it then!" the other part of me shouted back. "Let them fire their best worker and be damned!"

"But that hellcat's not worth it!"

"Shut up! I will have her, whether she's worth it or not!"

"You want her more than you want all that you've worked for? More than your dreams?"

"Si, more than my dreams!"

Such was the argument that raged in my head, worse by far than the worst headache. When the train rolled into the station, I found myself reluctant to get on it. She will bring you sorrow, I warned myself. But when the wheels started inching toward New York, toward my Ignazia, I boarded that train in a panic, found an empty seat, and collapsed into it. My head swam with fear and despair—and with relief. What was happening to me? What was happening?

Halfway there, I got up out of my seat, opened the door, and stood outside, letting the air rush around me. The wind took my hat and I barely noticed! I stared at the speeding ground below. Jumping headfirst might be better than this love-craziness, I told myself. But if I jumped, I would never see her again, never have that girl. I would lose her to that redheaded mick whose throat I would gladly slit if I knew what he looked like.

It was Ignazia herself who answered their front door. Her eye was blackened, her face swollen on one side.

"*What*? You again?" she shouted. "Look what I got because of you! Go away!" She spat on the stoop where I stood.

Then Nunzio was behind her, smiling like a fox with a mouthful of feathers. "*Signore* Domenico," he said. "What a surprise!"

"I'll pay *you*," I told him, still staring at Ignazia. "I'll give you four hundred for her."

"No!" she screamed. "I'll take poison! I'll cut out my heart!"

Now Rocco appeared in the doorway, too. "Five hundred," Nunzio said coolly, as if every day a suitor appeared at his door, offering to reverse the dowry process. "And you take the other one."

"I'll jump from the bridge!" Ignazia bellowed. "I'll cut out my liver!"

"Five hundred," I repeated, as if in a trance. "And I take the other one."

Nunzio Iaccoi shook my hand and pulled me inside. Rocco uncorked the wine for celebration. Both brothers' heads snapped back as they drained their glasses in single gulps, then poured some more. As for myself, nausea prevented me from doing more than wetting my lips on behalf of my good fortune. Ignazia continued screaming and wailing from the side room. Prosperine smoked in the doorway and glared.

9 *August* 1949

Ignazia and I were married in Brooklyn on 12 May 1916, civil ceremony. Prosperine and my cousin Vitaglio witnessed. On the train ride back to Connecticut, there were not three seats together. Ignazia wanted to sit with Prosperine, not me.

From my seat across the aisle and down, I could see all of Monkey-Face but only the blue velvet wedding hat of my new wife. Ignazia's hat was decorated with red strawberries that shook with the motion of the train. She would love me once she saw my home, I told myself. She would love me.

As for the other one, I would get her work at the mill. If I was stuck with her, she would at least bring money into my house.

We arrived home after dark at 66-through-68 Hollyhock Avenue. I told Ignazia to wait at the doorway, then hurried from room to room, lighting the lamps. Then I took her hand and led her through the house, the other one trailing after us like a dark shadow.

When we had gotten to the last room upstairs, I took my new wife to the window and showed her the backyard garden—my little bit of Sicily. There was a full moon that night, I remember; everything shone to its full advantage. "This is your new home, Ignazia," I said. "How do you like it?"

Her shrug pierced my heart.

From a drawer, I took the embroidered sheets *Signora* Siragusa had sent over for a wedding present. "Use these," I said. At last, I would enjoy the flesh of her who had tangled up my dreams and turned my sensible nature to porridge. At last, I would have opportunity to relieve this *passione* that had gripped me and made me crazy.

She and Prosperine dressed the bed while I waited outside in my backyard garden, smoking and watching the fireflies. Through the open window, I could see them up there—the homely one combing out the other's long hair. I could hear them, too—Ignazia's sobs and Prosperine's consoling mumbles.

In our bed, I held her face and kissed her. "In time, this life with me will make you happy," I said. She turned away. Tears dropped from her eyes onto my hands.

While I did my business, I watched her downturned mouth, her eyes that gazed at the ceiling like statue's eyes. Afterwards, I examined the embroidered sheets.

She had not bled. "*Vergine*?" I asked.

Fear flashed in her eyes. "Si, *vergine*," she said. "Don't hit! Don't hit!"

Her love with the redhead had been pure, she told me. Some women didn't bleed the first time, that was all. If I had doubts, I should send her back to Brooklyn.

She looked so beautiful. In her dark eyes, I thought I saw the truth. I beat her anyway, to teach her a lesson in case she was lying. I could not risk the dishonor of having a treacherous wife.

The next day, when I woke for my shift and went to the kitchen, Ignazia was not there. Prosperine was peeling potatoes for my supper. "Where is she, eh?" I asked. "A man wants his *wife* to cook his meals. Not a monkey."

Prosperine dropped the potato but held the knife and walked over to me. "If you raise your hand to her again, Tempesta," she whispered, "I'll cut off your balls while you sleep."

My first thought was to strike that scrawny monkey, but she held the point of her knife no more than a potato's length away from me, down there. She looked and sounded crazy enough to carry out her threat. What, after all, did I know about this witch-cousin of those goddamned Iaccoi brothers, except that they had bargained desperately to be rid of her?

I turned and laughed to cover my fear. "If you ever dare raise a knife to me, you skinny bitch, you'll get the worst end of it!"

She raised the knife higher, as high as my heart. "That's what a dead man once thought, too," she said. She spat on the floor.

"I mean what I say. Stay out of my business. I'll break your arm if I have to."

"I mean what I say, too," she answered. "Hurt her again and I'll make you a woman!"

When I returned to work that week, everyone congratulated me on my marriage and shook my hand until it was ready to fall off. Twice I fell asleep on my shift, once at the desk and once while standing against the wall as I supervised the wool-dyeing. From Flynn, my boss, I shut up and took the teasing about the *passione* of newlyweds, but not from those workers beneath me. When Drinkwater, that goddamned Indian, joked that my new wife kept me from getting sleep anywhere but on the job, I sent him home and docked him half a night's pay. I sent home two giddy spinning girls, too. After that, they shut up their faces about what went on in my home!

The truth was that I could not sleep from thinking what that crazy *mingia* Prosperine might do. Finally, I solved the problem when I began the practice of pulling the heavy oak bureau in front of the bedroom door before retiring each morning. "I have to get in there to clean!" Ignazia protested. "To put away laundry! To wash the floor!"

"Do your work when I'm not here," I told her.

"When you're not here, I sleep! It's nighttime."

"Change your habits then."

Only with the protection of that heavy bureau could I manage to get some rest, though still I slept poorly and with much interruption. Once I dreamed I saw Prosperine leaping from the maple tree into the open bedroom window, that goddamned peeling knife of hers clenched between her teeth. Bluejays flew behind her, hundreds of them. They flew inside, pecking at me and fluttering, circling around and around the bedroom. . . . Was this to be the lot in life of a man so *speciale* that he had once seen the Virgin's tears? Was I to be boss-dyer at work and a monkey's quarry inside my own *casa di due appartamenti*—the house I had built with my own two hands?

11 *August* 1949

One afternoon in the fall, I met *Signora* Siragusa on the street. "Domenico, you naughty fellow," she chuckled. "I saw your little wife at Hurok's Market yesterday. Already she's got a little belly, eh? What's the matter with you that you couldn't wait?"

Next morning, I came home from the plant and lifted Ignazia's gown while she slept in our bed. I saw.

I saw, as well, that the scowl Ignazia wore in my presence was gone when she slept. Was this the peace of mind she had had as a child in Sicily? In the arms of that redheaded Irishman? When her eyes opened and she saw me, her frowning returned.

"What's this, eh?" I asked, my hand patting her belly.

For her answer, she burst into tears.

"Eh?" I repeated.

"What do you think it is with that thing of yours always poking inside of me?"

"When is it coming?" I asked her.

"How should I know?" she shrugged, pushing and hurrying herself out of the bed. "Those predictions are never exact. Maybe February. Maybe March. . . . What are you staring at me for?"

"Are you glad about it?" I asked.

She shrugged again, pulling on her dress. She twisted her braid into a knot and pinned it at the base of her neck. "These days, I take what comes. What other choice have you left me?"

I brought Ignazia to Pedacci, who was a shoemaker on the East Side and *presidente* of *Figli d'Italia*. Pedacci could tell boy or girl by having the mother walk up and down on the sidewalk in front of his store.

He stood in his doorway while Ignazia walked back and forth, back and forth, three, four times. Each time she got back to the front of the store, she stopped, but Pedacci waved his hand for her to walk some more.

Our request for a prediction had interrupted Pedacci's game of pinochle in the back room. The other card players—Colosanto (the baker) and Golpo Abruzzi (brass factory)—watched Ignazia walk, too. From all that walking and watching, Ignazia became red-faced. She stopped and motioned me to her side, complaining in a voice loud enough for Pedacci and the others to hear. "All this staring! What am I—a statue in the museum?"

"Don't be disrespectful," I warned her. "If Pedacci says walk, then walk!"

A couple more trips to the stop sign and back, Pedacci rubbing his chin, squinting his eyes. Then he put up his hand to stop her.

My wife's pregnancy was extremely difficult to predict, he whispered to me—one of the most difficult he had ever seen. The baby did not hang in the usual way. Tuscan women sometimes carried their children in this manner. Was Ignazia by any chance from Tuscany?

"No, no," I told him. "*Siciliana.*"

Well, he said, with this one, it would be necessary to lift the *tette* to decide. Strictly for the purpose of accurate prediction. I understood, didn't I?

"Of course, D*on* Pedacci, of course," I said. "I am a modern man, after all, not some jealous, unschooled peasant from the Old Country. Let me just tell my wife."

I approached Ignazia cautiously. That woman's temper could sometimes blow like the shift whistle at American Woolen and Textile and it would not do for her to show me her usual disrespect in front of these men.

"It will be necessary for you to step inside for a minute with *Signore* Pedacci," I whispered. "To make an accurate prediction, it is necessary for him to lift the *tette*."

"W*hat*?" she shouted. "M*ine*? No, no, no, no! Go tell that old goat to lift his own wife's *tette*!"

"Please to keep down your voice," I said, more firmly this second time. "The poor man is a widower."

"Tell him to go feel the *melanzana* at the fruit market then and to keep his dirty hands off of me! I won't be handled like a pair of shoes in his shop!"

I took my wife's wrist, gave it a little twist to show her I meant business. "Show some proper obedience to your husband," I warned her. "Do as I say."

"Bah!" she said. But the twisting put fear in her eyes and she obeyed.

They were inside for four, five minutes. "Congratulations, Domenico!" Pedacci said when he emerged again. "A son!"

Ignazia stood behind him. The news had brought no joy to her face. Tears, it brought, and a frown I still see this morning, sitting in this garden, so many years later. Ignazia was, from the beginning, a wife to break a man's heart.

"Come in back for a little drink," Pedacci said. "Golpo and Colosanto and I want to toast your *bambino*." He turned to Ignazia. "Just a small drink, *Signora* Tempesta. Then I'll send him back out again. Sit down, ha ha. Tell my customers to come back in an hour, hour and a half."

Ignazia locked her jaw and blew air out of her nose. She did not sit.

In Pedacci's back room, I had a little drink and then another one and then Pedacci and the others invited me to play some cards. Was it a crime for a man who broke his back with factory work year in, year out, to sit with a *paisano* or two and have a simple game of cards? My wife thought so! I had just been dealt a beautiful hand when Abruzzi laughed and nodded his head toward the doorway.

There she stood.

I stood up and walked over to her. "What's the matter with you, eh?" I whispered.

"*Mi scappa la pippi*!" she whispered back. Her feet did a little dance. Her hands made fists.

"Don't speak such vulgarity in the presence of other men! Where's your dignity? Hold it until we get home."

"I can't hold it!" she protested. The other three smiled at their cards. Pedacci began to whistle.

"Piss on yourself then, woman," I said. "And piss on your disobedience, too!"

She banged the door. Behind it, out in the shop, I could hear her shouting at the shoes.

"That's telling her," Abruzzi said. "A king is a peasant in a castle where the woman rules."

"Si," Pedacci nodded and agreed. "Women, like horses, have to have their spirits broken or else they'll make bad wives. Eh, Domenico?"

"Si, *signore, si*," I said. "Breaking their spirit is the only way."

When I came back out into the shoe shop—not more than two, three games later—Ignazia was nowhere. That goddamned Abruzzi made a joke that my poor wife had either defied me or floated out the door from her "little problem."

When I got home, Ignazia was in the kitchen, soaking her blistered feet in warm water and salts. Her eyes were red. She had run the three miles back home.

The other one was at the sink, washing out Ignazia's dress and underclothes. "Go to your room," I told Prosperine. "I want to speak to my wife alone."

But the Monkey just stood there, staring defiantly at me and wringing out Ignazia's underclothes as if it was my neck in her hands.

"Go!" I commanded, clapping at her. "Hurry!"

She left the room slowly, watching me as she entered the pantry.

I began sweetly, as sweet as sugar. "So, you're growing a boy inside you, eh? In a little while, you and I will have a son."

"May God help any son who grows up as inhuman as you are," she said.

"*Inumano*? Why am I *inumano*?"

The water in the basin sloshed and jumped over the sides. Her whole body shook from her sobbing.

"There, there," I told her from across the room. "It's the child that brings on this nervous condition of yours."

Then Prosperine came out of the pantry again with two big onions. She began slicing them, staring not at the job but at me. She used a knife far too big for the job of onion-slicing. *Chop chop chop. Hack hack hack.* She worked and watched, eyeing me, butchering onions with her big knife.

On the night of 2 December 1916, I was at work, busy supervising the dyeing of wool for pea jackets, U.S. Navy. Earlier that week there had been problems on first shift—two bad dye runs that the second shift boss (goddamned French Canadian named Pelletier) had let get by him. The mistake had cost money to American Woolen and Textile, and Pelletier had been demoted. *Janitore* he was now, third shift.

"Have the Top Wop supervise the next runs," Baxter, the owner's son-in-law, had ordered Flynn. "If the Top Wop's in charge, it'll get done right." It was Flynn who told me what Baxter had said. "He doesn't mean anything when he calls you a wop," he said. "Take it as a compliment. Just make sure you don't fuck up any of the dye runs."

I lost sleep that week and, in my sleeplessness, thought about my first work in America. It had been years now since I'd swept the main lobby of the New York Public Library or scrubbed men's and women's filth from those long rows of toilets, but as I lay awake, the stink and ache of that miserable work came back to me—the look of all those self-important New Yorkers walking past a lowly *janitore*, congratulating themselves and thinking how much better they were than I was. I had traveled far, had seized opportunity and been rewarded for my seriousness of purpose. But one misstep could turn me from a boss back to a toilet scrubber.

On that same night of 2 December, I was reexamining and rematching samples with a magnifying glass and a special lamp I had bought for better illumination—making sure one more time before approving the run. Flynn called out my name.

"Eh?" When I looked up, I saw Prosperine walking toward me with Flynn.

"Better come with me," she said. "It's her time."

"What? How could it be her time already?"

She looked over at Flynn, who looked away. "Her water burst," she whispered. "The pains have started. Maybe a problem, maybe not."

"What kind of problem?"

She shrugged.

"You left her alone then?"

The Monkey shook her head. "*Signora* Tusia from next door is with her."

I looked from the Monkey's face to Flynn's, and then back again. I saw Baxter watching us through the glass wall of his office. "Go home," I said. "Let women fix women's problems. What do you think—that I can drop everything and run? Stop interrupting a man at his workplace."

Prosperine ignored the order. "She needs *dottore*," she said. "*Signora* Tusia thinks so, too. Better fetch him on your way home."

I leaned my face close to her face. "Doctors reach into the pockets of honest workers," I said. "Go home and midwife her instead of walking around town. Earn your keep for once, you lazy *mingia*." If I didn't get her out of there, I might end up *janitore*.

I walked back to my samples. Flynn stood staring at me. Baxter, too.

"*Figliu d'una mingia*!" her voice screamed. "You'll save a penny and lose your wife!"

My workers stopped their tasks to stare at that skinny bitch who dared to raise her voice to me that way. What could I do but grab her by the collar and coat sleeve and throw her out of that goddamned mill? I had work to do! The earnings of a *janitore* could not support a home such as mine—could not feed and clothe a wife and son, let alone a goddamned monkey with murder in her eye!

For the rest of that shift, I could not concentrate. I looked again and again at the clock. Had my son come into the world by now? Should I beat Prosperine for her public defiance? Should I fetch Quintiliani, the Italian *dottore*, on my way home from my shift? Each hour that went by was a week. But the dyeing went successfully. Baxter was right: if you wanted the job done right, put Domenico Tempesta in charge—even on the nights when his head was full of worry!

At dawn, I left the mill and hurried to the home of Quintiliani. His housekeeper said he was still out from the middle of the night, boy with burst appendix. She said my hired girl had come looking for him earlier and that she'd sent her on to Yates, the Yankee *dottore*.

When I got home, Yates's roadster was parked in front of the *casa di due appartamenti*. My heart boomed inside my chest like a drum in a parade. I opened the front door and followed Ignazia's screams to the back of the house.

She was lying on the kitchen table, wrapped in blankets and shivering. Tusia's wife wiped at her face and neck and hair. Yates was working on her down there.

Prosperine was the first to notice me. "*Figliu d'una mingia*," she mumbled under her breath.

Then Ignazia saw me. "Out! Get out, you!" she shouted. "See what your filthy business has brought down on me!"

The Yankee *dottore* told me to wait in the front room—that he and I needed to talk but not at this crucial time.

"Oh! Oh! Oh!" Ignazia wailed.

"*Avanzata*!" Prosperine commanded my wife. "*Avanzata*!"

I went into the pantry, not the front room as the Yankee *dottore* had told me to do. Who was he to tell me where to go inside my own house?

"Come on, Mrs. Tempesta! Don't stop! Come on, now!"

"Good, Ignazia, very good, keep going," Tusia's wife encouraged. Their directions, Ignazia's screaming and shouting, became a quiet murmur in the distance.

It was on the sideboard, next to the pump. . . .

A small bundle, wrapped hastily in a bloody sheet. I knew what it was before I lifted the cloth.

Blue feet, he had, and blue fingers. Black eyelashes. Black hair on his head, still wet from the birth. His thing was a little button. So perfect, he was, but blue.

I leaned closer. Smelled his smell. Touched his lips. He was neither cold nor warm. His soul was still in the pantry. . . .

I used what was there—soapy dishwater, olive oil shaken from the bottle into my hand. A worker's hand it was—rough and used, stained with blue dye. Not the smooth white hand of a priest. Not a hand worthy of touching *perfezione*. I used what was there.

With my thumb, I traced an oily cross on his forehead, one on each small eyelid as well. With my cupped hand, I dribbled the water onto his tiny head. "I baptize thee, in the name of the Father, and the Son, and the Holy Spirit." I whispered it in English, not Italian, for this dead, unnamed son of mine was *'Mericano*. His *futura* would have been a great one, but he had no life.

Was it sacrament or sacrilege, what I did? *Battesimo* performed by a man who had soiled a *monsignore* with a trowelful of wet cement and caused the death of a brother? Had I saved my son's soul or damned it to hell in that pantry? That was the question I asked myself a thousand sleepless nights after that impromptu baptism . . . the question I have asked a silent God ever since.

Always from Him, *silenzio*. . . .

I kissed my son's small hand, covered him again with the cloth. Picked him up and held him close to me.

"Aieeh!" Ignazia wailed and then the second one bleated its complaints to the world. From the pantry doorway, I held the dead firstborn and watched Yates cut the cord of the one that lived.

"Girl!" Prosperine croaked.

"*Capiddi russo*!" Tusia's wife announced.

"She's a redhead, all right," the Yankee *dottore* said. "She's got a harelip, too." Ignazia strained to see her. "Oh oh oh," she whimpered, staring at that squalling thing, hungry for her, with love in her eyes.

"*Bambina mia* . . ."

I held my son tighter.

"*Bambina mia*," Ignazia kept chanting. "*Bambina mia*." She kept kissing its face, its head, its tiny broken mouth. At that moment it was clear to me: she had not been *vergine* when she married me. She had opened her legs not only to her husband but to that Irishman she loved. Her belly had filled up with not one but *two bambini*. And now it was clear: she had no love for the dead boy that had been mine. She loved only the flawed, living girl—the child of that goddamned redheaded mick.

After he had finished with Ignazia, the *dottore* came out into my cold, brown garden. We needed to talk, he said.

Talk then, I told him. I was still holding the dead boy.

Why didn't I give that poor child to the women inside so that they could clean it up? He was going to have to take him to the city coroner when he left. It was the procedure in cases such as these. Ignazia and I would get him back for the burial. He presumed I was going to call a priest, right?

No coroner, I told him. No priest.

"Well, what you do about the religious business is your own decision, Mr. Tempesta, but the law's the law concerning the coroner. Say, you should look on the bright side of things. You were lucky this time."

"Lucky?" I asked. Was he mocking me? Spitting on my loss?

"What I'm saying is, you could have lost the both of them, and your wife to boot. This little fella here had breached. He was blocking the birth canal. It was a tricky business making things come out as well as they did. Don't worry about that harelip of hers. There's no cleft palate, far as I can tell. She'll be okay. She won't talk funny."

He waited before he said the rest.

"Mr. Tempesta, your wife could have died last night. Her heart's weak. Had the fever when she was a girl, she says. Sometimes disease leaves the heart damaged, see? The two births put that ticker of hers under a terrible strain." He talked in a loud, slow voice, as if I was deaf or stupid. "Another tricky delivery like this one could kill her, understand? Even a normal delivery—a single birth with no complications. To be on the safe side, you and her have to stop practicing intercourse. Either that, or I can fix her before I leave."

I cupped my hand to the top of the boy's head, looked out at nothing.

"Do you understand what I'm saying, Mr. Tempesta? I better say it plain. Either I fix her or you have to stop fucking her."

I closed my eyes, caressed the top of the boy's cold head. "No need to talk gutter talk," I said. "No need to speak filth in the company of my son."

"Say, look now, don't get uppity with me. I'm just telling you, that's all. Knock that chip off your shoulder, why don't you? Count your blessings." He stood and put his hands out for the boy, but I did not hand him over.

Whatever tears I have shed, I have shed them in the privacy of this garden. Never in the house itself. Never in front of women. Even in the middle of winter nights, it is here where I have always come to cry.

Later that day, Yates came back with the coroner, a policeman, and Baxter from the mill. Baxter did the talking. "You're a valued worker, Domenico," he said. It was the first time he had ever called me by my name—first time he had called me anything but Top Wop. "And I can certainly appreciate your sadness. I have children, too, you know—I know what it's like. But damn it, man! The company looks bad if something like this makes it into the papers, see? We don't like trouble. We can't keep lawbreakers on the payroll, it's as simple as that. Don't bring trouble down on your head, man. The child's dead. Give it up."

I was suddenly cold and hungry . . . and so tired that I was afraid I might weep in the presence of the four of them. The small weight I clutched to my chest was suddenly an armload of brick.

I saw Tusia's wife looking out her kitchen window. Saw the sadness in her eyes. She was a good woman, Tusia's wife. Her love for her husband and children was sweet and pure. Undirtied. She had stayed with Ignazia all night and through the morning. It was to her that I pointed—to Tusia's wife.

"Have *Signora* Tusia come out," I said. "You others go wait in front."

The *signora* came out of the house and up into the garden. "May God bless this child," she whispered, taking him from me. Tears fell from her eyes. "And may God bless you, too, Domenico, and show you His mercy."

"Save your prayers, *signora*," I told her. "God spends none of His mercy on Tempesta."

For the rest of that afternoon I sat like a stone in my garden—too tired, even, to stand up and go inside.

Sometime near dark, Prosperine came outside with a bowl of hot farina.

"Is she asleep?" I asked.

"They're both asleep," she said. "In my room in the back. Go on, eat. Put something in your stomach before you go to work."

I took a bite of the cereal. Its warmth inside my mouth was a comfort. "To hell with work," I heard my voice say. "I hope that goddamned mill goes up in flames and all the bosses with it! Give me a match and kerosene and I'll do the job myself!"

The Monkey stood in the cold, her breath a thing I could see. "It should have been the girl who died," she said, finally. "Bad enough to be born female. Worse to be born female and have the rabbit's lip. Hers will be a hard life."

I squinted up at her, studied her in what was left of the day's light. She was wearing her nightgown and long coat. Her hair was down—black braids, as skinny as knitting needles. "It's cold," she said. "Come inside."

"Ignazia is glad it's the girl who lived," I said. "My wife cares only about that one with its rabbit-face and orange hair."

"It's what she has to do," Prosperine said. "Or else the grief would kill her. She'd die in her bed from the loss of the boy."

"Bah!" I said.

"Give her time, Tempesta. Let her heal."

I stood up and went inside.

Got myself dressed.

Walked to work.

12 *August* 1949

The next morning was Saturday. When I got back to the house, I sat in the kitchen, eating and listening to Ignazia coo and sing to the baby from behind the Monkey's half-opened bedroom door. I rose and stood in the doorway. When Ignazia saw me, she told me to come and see. "Do you want to hold her?" she asked.

I shook my head. Stared at it. Lying in the sheets, it stuck out its tongue. Waved its fist at me. "Maybe this one will grow up to be a boxer," I said.

Ignazia smiled at my little joke, and then began to cry. "What do you think of Concettina for her name?" she said.

"Concettina?" I said. "That was my mother's name."

"*Si*. I remember. It's a pretty name."

"Concettina," I repeated.

"You need to get some rest, Domenico," she told me. "Then you have to go and see the priest. Arrange for the boy's burial Mass and for Concettina's *battesimo*."

I shook my head. "No priest," I said. "No *battesimo*."

Tears came into my wife's eyes. For the boy, there had been no time, she said, but she wanted to make sure this child was cleansed of sin.

I stood up. This child was *made* from sin, I wanted to shout at her. Domenico Tempesta was too wise to be a fool! But all I said was, "No *battesimo*."

All that day I slept the sleep of the dead, and when I woke again, it was nighttime. I went downstairs. Prosperine sat at the kitchen table with a glass and a jug of my wine from the cellar. "She and the baby have just gone to sleep," she said. "Sit down. Pour yourself some wine."

"I don't want wine," I said. "I just woke up."

"Pour me some more then," she ordered, as if *she* were master of my house and I were the servant.

Usually, that one snuck around with a burglar's silence—a word here, a grunt there. But on that strange night, wine and circumstance unhinged the Monkey's tongue. For hours we sat in that kitchen. She drank and smoked her pipe and talked, rapping her empty glass against the tabletop when she wanted more. Half a jug she drank that night, maybe more.

That was the night she told me her story. The night the Monkey drank my wine and revealed to me the truth of what she was—what they both were. . . .

thirty-eight

I closed the door on the pounding rain, the wind. It was blowing like a son of a bitch out there. The newspaper was sopping wet. Goddamn it. I'd *told* that delivery kid: when it's raining, put the paper *inside* the screen door.

I tried the TV again: static and snow. The cable wasn't coming back until this storm was over.

So I had three options: go out in a downpour, read a wet newspaper, or read some more of the Old Man's history. I flopped back down on the couch and reached for the water-logged *Daily Record*.

100,000 DEFY GORBACHEV, FLOOD RED SQUARE—ASK END OF SOVIET REGIME. From the looks of things over there, the "Evil Empire" was on the respirator. I thought about all those submarines Ray and the boys had built in preparation for the Soviet attack, all those bomb shelters people had sunk into their backyards. *Duck and cover!* they had taught us back in grade school. *If the Russians drop the bomb* . . . And so all us Mickey Mouseketeers had grown up ready for the end of the world, the big meltdown, courtesy of the Communists. . . . Weird the way everything was shifting, changing. Breaking up. They'd sledgehammered the Berlin Wall. The Ayatollah had keeled over. Saddam had been driven back to his bunker. Jesus, if we weren't careful, we were going to run out of bad guys. . . .

IDENTIFY L.A.P.D. BEATING VICTIM.

Except for ourselves, maybe. Except for the bad guy in the mirror. . . .

The victim looked up at me from the front page of the wet, limp *Daily Record*. He was black, of course; it was always a black man. He had a name now—Rodney King—and a battered, lopsided face, a slit for an eye. . . . Hey, man, in a way, I was *glad* the cable was out—grateful for the *reprieve*. For three days now, they'd been showing that grainy video. The cops hammering this guy—kicking him, clubbing him, zapping him with their stun guns. They'd hog-tied him, busted his legs, his jaw, his eye socket. Had paralyzed the left side of his face. Over and over and over, they'd shown it: America's *real* home videos. And the repetition had already begun to lull me, numb me—make me feel the blows a little *less* each time they savaged him. . . .

Except Rodney King wasn't cutting anybody any slack. He'd looked directly into that camera's lens and now, on page one, he met me, face to battered face, eye to bruised and busted eye. And won. . . . *I* blinked first. *I* was the one who had to look away.

I put the paper down, got up, paced around the living room. . . . It had been the second straight day of hard rain with more expected tomorrow. If this kept up, all the stores downtown would be bailing the Sachem River out of their basements. . . .

Oppression, man: the "haves" kicking the "have-nots" in the teeth, kicking them while they were down. Might was right, eh, Domenico? You had to rough her up a little. Show her who owned who—who was the boss in *your* house. Right, Big Man? . . . Well, at least that monkey-faced little housekeeper had restored a little of the balance of power over there on Hollyhock Avenue. The power of the peeling knife. *Touch her again and I'll make you a woman. . . .*

God, I was tired. Wired up and exhausted, both. Unable to sleep the night before, I had reached under the bed for the Old Man's story. Stupid move, Birdsey, no matter what your shrink says. . . . *Run away from your past, Dominick? I thought the past was what you were looking for.* . . . But Dr. Patel was right. I needed to face him whether I wanted to or not. Needed to hear his voice because . . . because that goddamned manuscript *existed*. Because before she died, Ma had come down the stairs lugging that strongbox. *This is for you, honey.* . . . Because I'd fallen off that roof and landed in a hospital room with Nedra Frank's fiancé. Weird how I'd mourned the loss of that thing—Domenico's story—and then it had come back to me.

How much of it did you know, Ma? Did you know you were a twin, too? Did Papa ever tell you about your dead baby brother? . . .

DOMENICO ONOFRIO TEMPESTA, 1880–1949
"THE GREATEST GRIEFS ARE SILENT."

I pictured his gravestone out there at the Boswell Avenue Cemetery. And hers—my grandmother's—that small, forgotten stone that Thomas and I hadn't even known about until the summer we'd worked for the Public Works. It was way the hell over on the other side of the cemetery from his, I remember. Why hadn't they been buried together? Why hadn't Ma ever taken us to see her *mother's* grave? . . . And that ornate granite monstrosity of *his:* seven or eight feet tall, those cement angels, their faces contorted in pain over his passing. Ma had said he'd made his own burial arrangements ahead of time. It figured. Who else would have chosen something that grand-scale but the "great man from humble beginnings"? . . . *The greatest griefs are silent.* So why'd you hire a stenographer then, Papa? Hire him, fire him. . . . Why'd you rent a fucking Dictaphone to be your confidante? Why did you have to burden *me*?

He hadn't been working on any "guide for Italian youth," that much I'd figured out. That had only been the "official" excuse for whatever the hell it was he was trying to do. And what *was* that? Stroke his ego a little more before he kicked off? Exonerate himself for being such a prick? . . . It was weird: when we were kids, Ma would take us out to the cemetery with her, decorate *his* grave, and not even mention her mother's. . . . How old had she been when her mother died? I couldn't remember the dates. I had to get out there to the cemetery one of these days—look for that stone, check Ignazia's dates.

I saw, again, the way she had looked in that weird dream. Ignazia, my drowned grandmother. Halloween night, it was—the night I'd totaled my truck. In the dream, I was standing on the ice, looking down at all those lost limbo babies floating beneath me. And then . . . what was the word for *grandmother*? *Nonna?* Why did you come to me, *Nonna*? What did you want? . . .

She'd drowned, Ma said—had fallen through the ice at Rosemark's Pond. Had she been skating? Taking a shortcut over thin ice? I had never really gotten the details.

The greatest griefs are silent. . . .

In that dream, Ignazia's eyes had looked up at me from beneath the ice—she had found me, had looked me right in the eye. What were you trying to tell me, *Nonna*? What?

Keep reading your grandfather's history, Dominick. . . .

But all it ever did was confuse me. Make me feel worse. . . .

Life is a river, Dominick. . . .

Well, fuck it. You could drown in a river. . . . I saw myself going down to the Falls. Throwing the Old Man's manuscript over the edge. Watching it flutter, page by page, into the water. I saw Domenico's story float away.

The thing was I *hated* the son of a bitch—the way he'd treated his daughter. His wife. Wouldn't even leave work to get the goddamned doctor. . . . The "big man from humble beginnings." The "chosen one" who'd been conceived the night a volcano blew—who'd seen some stupid statue cry. . . . He'd *paid* for it, though—all that arrogance of his. I saw him up there in his garden, clutching his stillborn son, refusing to hand him over. Even when they brought in the big boys—the cops, his boss from the mill. . . . Well, we had that much in common, Domenico and me. We both knew what *that* felt like: holding your dead child in your arms. Facing just how powerless you were. . . .

Stop it, Dominick. Don't go there. *Do* something.

I picked up the paper again—flipped to the local news. WEQUONNOCS PRAY TO ANCESTORS, BREAK GROUND AT CASINO

SITE. Good, I thought. More power to 'em. I hoped they madc millions down there. Hoped they emptied the pockets of every friggin' paleface whose ancestor-oppressors had screwed them over and left them for dead.

And then I noticed him: front and center in the oversized picture they'd run with the article. Ralph Drinkwater, whooping and hopping around, in full Indian dress. He was into it, I guess. And, hey, why not? If that casino took off like everyone said it was going to, it'd probably make him a millionaire. He'd be able to tell Hatch Forensic Institute to take its mops and brooms and toilet brushes and shove 'em. Ralph Drinkwater: part black, part Indian, and dancing up a storm. . . .

Life had hog-tied *Ralph,* that was for sure—had kicked *Ralph* in the head more than once. We'd all taken a crack at him: the teachers at school, Dell Weeks and his wife, me sitting there that night in the police interrogation room. And here he still was, dancing and celebrating. Praying to his ancestors.

His name was Swift Wolf, according to the caption, not Ralph Drinkwater. He was the tribal pipe-keeper of the Wequonnoc Nation, not the screwed-up little boy who'd posed for all those dirty pictures. . . . I saw Ralph at his desk in Mrs. Jeffrey's class, a fourth-grader, looking away while I passed the cardboard collection bucket so that wc could "honor" his strangled sister. Saw him later, in Mr. LoPresto's history class, smirking in self-defense while LoPresto declared that the Wequonnocs had been annihilated, every last one of them wiped out in the name of progress. Manifest Destiny. He'd been true to himself—had tried to claim his heritage all along. His blackness, his Wequonnoc blood. "Read *Soul on Ice*!" he kept telling us that summer we worked together. "That book tells it like it is!" And Leo and I had laughed—turned it into a joke. . . . Well, good for you, Ralph. Enjoy the last laugh, man. I hope you make millions down there. . . .

Maybe the world really was changing, I thought. The Berlin Wall was down, the Russians hadn't blown us up after all, and the Indians were rising up from the ashes. . . .

* * *

I don't know how long I dozed. Long enough for it to turn from day to night. "Yeah, yeah, wait a minute," I told the ringing telephone. Went stumbling in the dark toward it, trying to wake up.

Just what I need, I thought: me tripping over something and falling—racking up my foot all over again. I reached for the receiver. "Yup?"

"Birdsey?"

"Maybe. Who's this?"

"Is this Dominick Birdsey or isn't it?" I knew the voice but couldn't place it. I waited.

"You wrote your number down. Asked me to call if I saw anything."

Drinkwater? Ralph was calling me? "Hey, man, I was just looking at your picture in the—" Then, it hit me: something was wrong with my brother.

"And I don't want to get caught in the middle of anything," he was saying. "Understand? That's the last thing I need right now. You keep my name out of it."

"What is it?" I said. "What's happened to him?" I was standing there, getting the shakes, same as always when I got a call about Thomas.

"Get him tested," Ralph said.

"Tested? Tested for *what*?"

"HIV."

thirty-nine

12 *August* 1949

That was the night the Monkey told me her story . . . the night my enemy drank my wine and revealed to me the truth of what she was—what they both were.

"Once, many years ago," the Monkey began, "I witnessed some very strange magic. It changed my life. And now, what I saw that day long ago has come back to me with the birth of the two . . . and because the one that lived is cursed with the rabbit's lip." She was whispering—confiding to me in the manner of a criminal. "The magic I speak of involved rabbits," she said.

At the time, she told me, she was a girl of fourteen, living in her native seaside village of Pescara.

"Pescara?" I interrupted. "I thought you were *siciliana*."

"You thought that because it's what those two plumbers wanted you to think. You thought I was their cousin, too. I am not."

"Don't be stupid, woman," I said. "Why would they have sponsored a creature as homely as you, taken on the burden of marrying you off to boot, if not because of *obbligo di famiglia*?"

"Why does anyone do such things?" she said, and

stroked her thumb against her fingers. "Lying was profitable for those two plumbers, that's why. They played you for a fool, Tempesta."

I leaned toward her and grabbed her arm, demanding that she explain herself.

"I begin at the beginning," she said. "But not with you squeezing my arm like it's a chicken's neck. And not with an empty glass, either. Let go of me and pour the wine! And don't be cheap about it."

Her father was a poor macaroni-maker cursed with bad luck, she said. Typhoid had taken his wife and son and left him with three daughters to raise. Prosperine was the oldest of these, forced by circumstance both to serve as mother to the other two and to make macaroni all day long. *Ripetizione rapida* was everything in that work, she said, and those repeated movements lived still in her hands. Sometimes when her mind wandered, she told me, she *still* caught her fingers making macaroni. Even now, even here, an ocean away from her sisters and the life she had been forced to leave.

As soon as each was able, the sisters were put to work at the wheels and mills and bowls in the macaroni shop. They began each morning before dawn, their father turning semolina into dough, his three daughters pressing, cutting, and shaping the strings and strips with their knives and machines, their thumbs and fingers. Flour would fly in the air, the Monkey said, making a paste in their mouths as they breathed and dusting their hair and skin, turning each sister into a pale, gray-haired *nonna* by the time the sun had climbed to its full height in the sky.

In Pescara, she said, the noon hour was her favorite time of day. While her papa took his nap and the macaroni sat drying on racks and trays, Anna and Teodolina and she were free to roam through the busy square. Often, they were joined on these daily walks by another motherless girl, a fishmonger's daughter named Violetta

D'Annunzio. She was younger than the Monkey—closer in age to Teodolina. A saucy thing, she was! Violetta's friends, the three sisters, were plain, but she herself was beautiful. She had dark eyes and hair and skin like cream. Her eyebrows grew in an upturned direction that gave her the tortured look of saints.

Like young girls everywhere, the four friends laughed and ran through the village, touching and coveting the expensive merchandise that their poor fathers could never have afforded. They amused themselves with whatever was new that day in the marketplace—jugglers, puppet shows, some rich woman's new finery. When nothing was new, they satisfied their restlessness by mocking and giggling at the poor village *eccentrici*, those unfortunate villagers who were defective or crazy.

A favorite target of the girls was Ciccolina, a bow-legged old butcher-woman burdened with a hunchback and breasts that hung from her like two big sacks of semolina. Ciccolina mumbled to herself and cursed the girls when they teased her from across the road, swiping at the air with her walking stick. Half-blind from cataracts, the old woman was afflicted with an ugly tumor that stuck out on her forehead—a knob the size of a baby's fist that had darkened to the color of an eggplant. That hideous lump both repelled Prosperine and drew her to the old woman like a magnet. *Don't look at it! Don't look!* the Monkey would counsel herself, even as she stared in horror.

Each morning from the window of her father's shop, Prosperine watched Ciccolina hobble to the village square, dragging behind her a small cart weighted down with coops. Inside were scrawny hares and half-bald hens. These doomed creatures the old woman sometimes sold to customers, who would make their choices, and then stand and watch as their dinner was strangled, beheaded, plucked, skinned. The old woman used a rusty cleaver and a rusty knife for the job, and a scarred, bloodstained cutting board that she balanced against her knees. Her untrussed *tette*—those two big sacks of semolina—rested on the board as she worked.

There were rumors that Ciccolina was a witch as well as a butcher and that, for the price of a few coins, she could be hired to perform small acts of revenge. People said she could both cure and inflict *il mal occhio*. Superstitious mothers shielded their children from the old woman's milky-eyed gaze and guilty men crossed the street rather than walk past the *strega*. The old hunchback was said to have caused the customs officer's haughty wife to go bald and to have curdled the milk of a farmer's cows for an entire summer. According to rumor, that poor devil of a farmer had tripped over Ciccolina's cages and stumbled to the ground, drawing laughter from other villagers. Humiliated, he had stood and slapped the old woman for what, in fact, had been his own clumsiness. His cows' milk began to go bad the very next day.

Prosperine's sisters would not go near Ciccolina, but the risk of dark magic thrilled both the Monkey and her daring friend Violetta. Young and stupid girls, they wanted both to bow to the possibility of evil and to laugh in its face. And so, from across the road, they hid behind the awning of the *trattoria*, calling and chanting to the old witch.

Finocchio, finocchio!
Non dami il mal occhio!

In other ways, the Monkey said, she was the shyest and most sensible of the four girls, but in the teasing of the old *strega*, she was the loudest and most cruel, because that was what Violetta loved. Once, Prosperine dared to call out to the poor old eccentric that she must be the smartest person in all of Pescara since she had grown that second purple brain on her forehead. Ciccolina spun in the direction of the insult, squinting and demanding to know who had said it. Prosperine shouted back that it was she, Befana, the good witch of the Epiphany. "Be a nice little girl now!" she called to the old hag. "Or I will leave coal in your shoes instead of sweetmeats!" From behind the safety of the awning, Violetta screamed with delight at her friend's brazen disrespect and Prosperine laughed so hard that her throat hurt.

She stopped her story for a minute to sip more of my wine and I watched her closely as she smiled and remembered. . . . That Monkey's smile was a rare thing in my house, and soon enough into her remembrances of the past, it was replaced again by her more familiar scowl. "That was before I knew that young girls, like litters of cats and rabbits, grow toward separation," she continued. "Before I realized that fathers could sell away their eldest daughters. More wine, Tempesta. Pour!"

"Never mind about fathers," I said, refilling her glass. That night, it was as if I were the bartender and she were the paying customer! "Tell me why you lied about your birthplace. Tell me how those two plumbers played me for a fool! I ask you for the time of day, you tell me how to build a clock!"

"Shut up, then," she said. "Shut up and listen. Tonight I feel like talking and will talk!"

As the four friends grew toward womanhood, Prosperine, her sisters, and Violetta began walking not just through the square but also down to the docks to peek at the fishermen. There, Violetta sometimes cast her nets for the men's *attenzione*, encouraging the saucy remarks the men threw her way and making bold remarks back at the handsomest of them—even the married ones! Though she was the youngest of the four, Violetta knew things the other girls did not and was happy to school the macaroni-maker's daughters about the exchanges between women and men. Once, walking back from the docks, the girls saw a stallion mount a white mare in a rich man's field.

"Look," the innocent Teodolina said. "Those two *cavalli* are doing a dance."

"Si," Violetta said, "the dance that puts a baby inside the mother. All men like *that* dance!" Then she had her pupils draw nearer and squat to the ground, the better to see the stallion's thing slamming in and out of the mare, whose flank shook with each thrust, who stood and took whatever he gave her.

"*Aspetti un momento*!" I told the Monkey, stopping her. "I tell you to explain how those plumbers from Brooklyn played me for a fool and you talk about *fungol* between two horses in the Old Country. Make sense, woman, or else put the cork back in the wine jug and shut up your mouth and go to bed."

"I tell you my story the way I want to tell it," she said back. "Or else I don't tell it at all. Which shall it be, Tempesta? Eh?" I sighed and poured myself some of the wine and waited. She was *pezzo grosso* that night—that skinny bitch.

Having attracted the fishermen's *attenzione*, Violetta, Anna, and Teodolina began the practice of grooming themselves before they took their noonday strolls. Teodolina and Anna rubbed olive oil into each other's hair and skin to rid themselves of the accumulated flour which had settled on them all morning and which made them look like old women; the anointing turned them back into flirtatious girls. As for the Monkey, she wanted none of primping and preening. With a face like hers, what good would a little olive oil do? But Violetta, who spent each morning cutting fish for her father, wanted the dried scales and flecks of flesh cleaned from her long dark hair. She kept two tortoiseshell brushes in her apron and always insisted that Prosperine do the brushing—only Prosperine knew how to do it right, she insisted. Some days Violetta snitched a lemon or two from a fruit cart on her way to the macaroni shop. She would cut the fruit and wash her hands with the juice to take away the stink of fish. Sometimes, too, she rubbed lemon against her neck and squeezed the juice between her pretty breasts. Violetta's naughtiness would have shocked the older people and sometimes shocked the three sisters, too!

In the summer of the year when Violetta was fifteen, the village *padre* selected her for the honor of crowning the statue of the Blessed Virgin at the Feast of the Assumption. The custom of Pescara dictated that the heavy statue of the Holy Mother be carted by horse and carriage from the church down to the shore at low tide. There, the waters of the *Adriatico* would lap at the Virgin's feet and the sea would be made safe for sailors for the year to come. After ceremonial blessings by the village priest, the statue would then be hoisted by the men of Pescara, sailors and others, and carried in a procession back to the village, through the square, and up the steps of the church. There, parishioners would leave their offerings to the Holy Mother and say prayers, entreating the *Vergine* to keep their families safe. At the climax of the festivities, the fortunate village girl chosen to crown the Blessed Virgin would emerge from the crowd, dressed in ceremonial bridal gown and veil, and climb the ladder to place a crown of flowers and periwinkles on the top of the statue's head. The priest's selection of Violetta for this important honor was a shock to the townspeople and a sweet victory for the quartet of friends! Usually a rich girl was chosen.

It was during the men's holy procession through the village that Violetta first saw, from behind the lace of her bridal veil, the face and figure of a blond, lynx-eyed devil named Gallante Selvi. Selvi was a famous stained-glass artist from *Milano*. He had traveled to Pescara that summer to visit *famiglia*, bathe in the *Adriatico*, and draw inspiration from the spectacular Pescaran sunshine. The Monkey's eyes spotted Gallante Selvi, too, that morning. From the start, she knew that son of a bitch would bring trouble.

As Violetta slowly climbed the steps with the Virgin's crown, the faithfully devoted dropped their heads in submission and made the sign of the cross. Not Gallante Selvi. The Monkey watched as that dog stroked his waxed mustache, took a little sip from a silver flask, and eyed Violetta. Violetta, who should have been concentrating on the Blessed Virgin, got to the top step of the ladder and turned to have another peek at Selvi. It was then that she lost her balance and fell, crashing onto the offerings below and demolishing several of the more fragile gifts. But even in the midst of her terrible humiliation, Violetta was distracted with her staring after Gallante Selvi. From the start, her *passione* for that no-good glass painter was a sickness and a consumption, the Monkey said.

Selvi entered the macaroni shop the very next morning in the midst of the bustle of pasta-making. "Fetch your father," he commanded Prosperine, as if he were the king of Italy himself. The Monkey's sisters stopped their work to stare at him. Not Prosperine! She was not hypnotized like the others by those pretty looks of his. She told him to come back later, after the dough had been kneaded and cut but before her father's nap. But the great Gallante Selvi would have none of waiting. Like Garibaldi commanding his troops, he ordered Prosperine to do as he said or he would reach across the counter and twist off her nose!

Selvi told Prosperine's father that several townspeople had advised him to seek out the macaroni-maker with the shortage of money and the surplus of daughters. He would be leaving Pescara soon, he said, to begin an important commission in the city of Torino. An earthquake there had loosened from its frame an ancient stained-glass triptych at the Cathedral of the Virgin Martyrs and sent it shattering to the ground. What worse tragedy than the loss of great art? But who better than he, Gallante Selvi, to replace it? He would be a year or more designing and executing the new triptych, which would honor *Santa Lucia*, who had gouged out her eyes in an effort to fend off a rapist—who had made herself horrible to look at so that she might remain pure. On and on and on, that puffed-up painter talked until her father finally interrupted.

"*Scusa, signore,*" he said. "I mean no disrespect, but what does all this have to do with me and my surplus of daughters?"

Gallante Selvi told the Monkey's father that he had been staying during his visit with his old *madrina*, who had grown feeble now and needed a housekeeper. He wished to arrange for one before he left. Did the macaroni-maker think he could spare one of his unmarried daughters? The commission in Torino was a generous one. He could make it worth his while.

Although the three sisters stood side by side, Papa looked only at Prosperine. "Come into the other room, *Signore* Selvi, come in and sit," he told the *artiste*, and Prosperine's knees knocked together from what the two men might be planning.

By the time Gallante Selvi left the shop, the Monkey had been hired to sweep and gather firewood for the painter's old godmother, and to feed her goats and chickens and help with a small business she maintained. In exchange, she would be provided a place to eat and sleep. Her father had received a small first payment and would get the balance at Christmastime, when Gallante Selvi returned to Pescara. Prosperine's father told her he was sorry to lose a good daughter and macaroni-maker, but that he could not afford to pass up the money Gallante Selvi had offered him. Business had been worse than ever that year, he said, and such opportunity did not often walk through the door of the macaroni shop.

Prosperine dropped to her knees and begged her father to void the agreement he had made. In her mind, she saw Teodolina, Anna, and Violetta strolling through the village without her. Who would keep those silly girls in line as they paraded themselves on the docks? Who would comb the fish scales out of Violetta's hair? Only *she* could do it properly! "Why choose *me*?" she sobbed.

"Because you are the homeliest and most responsible," he answered. "My selecting you is a compliment to your seriousness and your domestic abilities."

"If this is my reward, then I fart on such flattery!" she shouted back.

Her father reached back and let fly his open hand against her face. He had hit the girl before, but never this hard.

"You'll see your sisters every day in the square if you like," he told her later, after she had quieted again and her face had swollen up like macaroni in the pot. "The old woman's business brings her into town each day. You know who she is: the butcher-woman who sits in that little space near the church, across from the *trattoria*. The poor hunchback."

"Ciccolina?" Prosperine screamed. "You've given me away to that crazy witch?" When she heard this terrible news, the Monkey wailed loudly enough for Heaven to hear. She hugged her father's knees, calling on the saints and the apostles to end her life and save her from this terrible fate. Now what she dreaded most was not separation from the others, but that ugly witch's vengeance. Surely Ciccolina would recognize the mocking voice of the girl who had so often insulted her! Surely Prosperine would die from this arrangement her father had made, or go bald, or discover that her blood had curdled!

But her father showed her no mercy.

When Violetta D'Annunzio heard of Prosperine's fate,

she shed fat tears and hugged her friend and volunteered to walk with her the next morning to the *strega*'s house near the woods and to carry her basket of belongings, the better to give her a sad and proper goodbye.

Along the road the next day, the Monkey's steps were slow and heavy, but Violetta seemed, almost, to race toward their destination. How much longer did that haughty painter say he was staying in Pescara? she asked Prosperine. What had his voice sounded like the day he had entered her father's shop? Were those eyes of his green or blue?

As Ciccolina's thatched roof came into sight between the trees, Violetta insisted that they stop first and wash their dirty feet in a nearby stream in case the old woman had visitors. Violetta produced the familiar tortoiseshell brushes and insisted, too, that her friend brush her long hair one last time. On that day, Violetta was wearing her prettiest blouse—the one that Prosperine herself had sewn, embroidering the bodice with wildflowers and cutting the neckline an inch or two below the *clavicola*. As Violetta bent over, the Monkey brushed and peeked inside that blouse at her friend's pretty *tette*. Her tears fell into her friend's long brown hair.

I drank some wine and laughed at her. "What does one girl care about peeking at another girl's 'pretty *tette*'?" I asked. "You sound like a man!"

She stood and went to leave the room.

"Where are you going, eh?" I said.

"To bed," she said. "Where no one laughs at me and calls me *uomo*."

"Stay," I said. I pulled her by her sleeve back to the chair. "Sit and finish your story, *Signorina* Hothead. Finish my jug of wine, too, what the hell! Don't walk away now that I'm interested."

"Interested?" she asked. Her eyes were stupid from the wine.

"Si," I said. "I want to find out what happened to you and the witch. . . . Tell me more about your friend's 'pretty *tette*.' "

She sat. "If you're interested," she said, "then show some respect. Keep your mouth shut while I speak. Now where was I?" I told her where and she went on.

Just as Violetta and Prosperine reached the clearing where Ciccolina lived, the Monkey said, they stopped, suddenly, and gasped. There, in the adjacent field, stood Gallante Selvi, barefooted, his hair crazy, his body covered only by a nightshirt too short and flimsy to serve the cause of decency. The girls stood frozen for several minutes and watched as the *artiste* painted the air with invisible brushes, arguing with himself, bending to scribble on a tablet on the ground. "*Demente!*" the Monkey whispered, but Violetta was too mesmerized to hear.

"Ah, so here you are, you lazy girl," Selvi said when he eyed his employee. "Lucky for you my work has put me in a good mood, or else I'd slap you for your tardiness."

Prosperine told him she was not late—that she had arrived earlier than expected. (This was because of Violetta's eager pace along the road!) She looked to Violetta to confirm what she had said, but that naughty girl was paying no attention to words. She was too busy watching the place where Gallante Selvi's nightshirt ended and his privacy began.

Oblivious, Selvi began babbling about his work—about a vision that had come to him as he woke from a dream that morning. "This will be my masterpiece—my legacy to all of Italy!" he boasted. Then he turned to Violetta, noticing her for the first time.

As Selvi looked her up and down, Violetta blushed and turned away. "And what wind carries you here, pretty one?" he asked. "I don't remember bargaining with the macaroni-maker for *two* housekeepers for *Zia* Ciccolina."

"Sir," Violetta said in a squeaky voice. "I'm just escorting my friend."

"Sir," Gallante Selvi repeated, "I'm just escorting my friend." He put his hands against his hips and wiggled girlishly as he mimicked her words. Shameless, he was, that one! Those *coglioni* of his flopped back and forth beneath his nightshirt.

Then, without warning, Selvi snatched Prosperine by the hand. She let out a little scream. "See her tragic story with me, little housekeeper!" he said, dragging the Monkey through the field, pointing here and there at nothing. "See my vision! In the first panel, on the left, Lucia the Innocent prays piously! Opposite that, on the right, she's a saint in Heaven, the holy patroness of sight. In the middle—the largest window—she rips her eyes from her head! Embraces her debasement! Blood streams down her face! Her tormentor recoils as the angels bear witness! Oh, such a tragedy to make you weep, the story of the brave little saint! I will paint my Lucia so that her *sacrificio*, depicted there before you in *vetro colorito*, will make you drop to your knees and howl with grief for that saintly girl!"

Here, that *figliu d'una mingia* of a crazy artist stopped abruptly and jerked his head back at Violetta. He circled her, making the sign of the cross and staring rudely. His breath blew against her face. "I have seen you before?" he asked.

Violetta was too afraid to answer.

"Sir," Prosperine said. "You saw her in the village at the Feast of the Assumption, but her face was veiled. She was the clumsy girl who crowned the Holy Mother and fell off the ladder."

He ignored the Monkey and spoke directly to Violetta. "You are the one. Yes?"

"Which one is that, *signore*?" Violetta squeaked out.

"The one delivered to me by divine intervention."

"Delivered, sir?"

"The saints have sent you to me, have they not, *Santa Lucia*?" He reached over and fingered her hair, kneaded her cheeks as if they were bread dough. "Such eyes! Such facial bones! *Perfezione*! . . . Have the saints willed you to me, Lucia? Has Heaven itself commissioned my work?" As he stared and touched and circled her, red blotches appeared on Violetta's face and neck. The girl was breaking out in hives!

"I must begin sketching you immediately—capture you in case you are a spirit who will dissipate."

"A spirit, *signore*?" Violetta asked. With the sailors on the docks, my friend had a voice as loud as the fire bell that shouted to all Pescara. But with Gallante Selvi, she could only squeak like a mouse.

"Come with me," he said, taking her hand in his. "Come down to the sea this instant. I must study your face in brilliant light—must let the sun be my *collaboratore*! Inspiration is a fickle mistress, after all—keep her waiting and she may desert you for another!"

He leaned forward and kissed Violetta's eyelids—made, with his thumb, the sign of the cross on her forehead. Reaching behind her, he gave her *cula* a little squeeze, as if she were a melon instead of a "saint." "My sweet Virgin Martyr," he whispered, sniffing the air around her. From the start, Selvi acted like the dog he was in Violetta's presence. "My Lucia, who has been sent to me by the saints themselves!"

"Her name is Violetta D'Annunzio," the Monkey said. "Her father sells fish."

"Shut up and go inside to your work!" he ordered, without looking away from Violetta. "Catch up on all you've missed by being late!"

"I was *not* late, sir," the Monkey reminded him again. "Violetta has to walk home now and make the *baccala*. And as for you, sir, you should put on your pants."

"*Scusa*, Lucia," that *figliu d'una mingia* said to the fishmonger's daughter. He took her hand and kissed each finger. "*Un minuto, un minuto.*" He approached the Monkey and boxed her ears so hard that they rang like the church bells at Easter. He yanked her nose, too, and gave her a shove toward the old woman's house. Then he turned back to her best friend and dropped to his knees.

"*Santa Lucia*, my blind patroness of vision, help me see! Help me see!" That crazy *artiste* was begging Violetta, praying to her as if she was a statue! Then he got up and took her hand again, leading her past Ciccolina's goats and chickens. Over an embankment the two of them ran, that crazy painter hurrying Violetta toward the sound of the sea.

Prosperine stood staring at the place where they had disappeared, tears falling from her eyes. Should she run for Violetta's father? For her own? She listened for Violetta's screams, her cries for help that did not come. And when she looked back at the hut again, the old hunchback was out in the yard, standing stooped among her chickens, beckoning her.

Prosperine pulled a handkerchief from her sleeve and blew her nose. I had assumed that hard little stone incapable of tears. She had shed none over Ignazia's troubles the day and night before—no tears for the death of my infant son. She took a gulp of wine. Another. A third. She was talking like a husband who wears the horns! But I held my tongue and waited. Then she blew her nose again, pushed the cloth back into her sleeve, and sighed. Continued.

If the old witch recognized Prosperine as her tormenter from the village square, she said nothing, took no revenge. Compared with macaroni-making, the work was easy. Ciccolina demanded little and taught the girl much: how to peel back a rabbit's skin in a single, untorn sheet, how to make a soothing bath of almond water, how to fashion a pipe from clay and smoke. It was from

Ciccolina that the Monkey learned the comfort and pleasure of tobacco.

Each morning, she walked beside the old woman, dragging her butcher cart to the village square. The days there were long and hot and Ciccolina had few buyers for those skinny animals. Some days, only Pomaricci the schoolmaster—Ciccolina's most faithful but most despised customer—bought meat. At noontime, Prosperine watched her sisters stroll through the square, waving quickly from the other side of the road, pretending to be deaf when she called for them to come and sit and visit. Her own sisters, whom she had loved and looked after, now forsook her because she kept company with the old *strega*. As for Prosperine's father, he never once left the macaroni shop and walked to the square to visit his daughter or ask how she was surviving.

Having discovered in Violetta D'Annunzio the *faccia* of *Santa Lucia*, the Virgin Martyr, Gallante Selvi changed his plans and announced that he would stay in Pescara through September. Each morning, he met Violetta at the old woman's cottage and walked her down to the sea. There, he draped her in linen or lace or sackcloth—drawing and painting her in pose after penitent pose.

In town, word spread that that clumsy girl who had crowned the Holy Mother at the Feast of the Assumption and made a shambles of things—that fishmonger's daughter!—would now be immortalized as *Santa Lucia*, the Virgin Martyr, in a stained-glass masterpiece at a grand cathedral in the great city of Torino. Gallante Selvi had traveled all the way to Pescara to find her, the gossips said—because only a sun-kissed Pescaran girl would do for such a work of art! It was rumored that *Santa Lucia* herself had appeared in a vision to the *artiste* and had led him to Violetta. All day long, the Monkey sat in the square and heard the buzzing about her friend.

D'Annunzio the fishmonger at first forbade his daughter's posing for the *artiste*—not out of moral concern but because the mackeral were running. There were hundreds of those silver fish to clean, salt, and sell. Why pay for a helper when a daughter's help was free? But Violetta's *passione* for Gallante Selvi was so crazy that she defied her father and went anyway, and before D'Annunzio could manage the time to go after her, his business began to improve dramatically. Suddenly, everyone in Pescara wanted to buy their fish from the father of *Santa Lucia*!

Sometimes in the morning, Violetta and Prosperine would meet each other on the village road, the beautiful girl rushing toward the sea for her day of posing, her homely friend trudging in the opposite direction, accompanied by the hunchback and her half-starved chickens and rabbits. Sometimes, too, Violetta and the Monkey passed each other again in late afternoon, each now traveling the other way. At first, when they confronted one another on the road, they waved or nodded. After a while, though, Violetta looked away and did not speak. Her silence drove a stick through Prosperine's heart. The Monkey knew that more than painting and posing went on in Ciccolina's house while the old woman and she were away in the square—that Gallante Selvi and her pretty friend were doing the stallion's dance. It was Prosperine, after all, who had scrubbed Violetta's blood from the painter's sheets. Sometimes, after they passed each other on the road, Prosperine would look back and peek at her friend. Violetta looked more beautiful than ever, her skin now darkened to gold, her hair wild and tangled by the wind and salt air of the *Adriatico*.

"She was more beautiful then than now," she said.

I sat up in my chair. "Than *now*?"

The Monkey jumped a little, as if she suddenly remembered she was talking not to the air, but to Tempesta. "I . . . I meant more beautiful then than I would imagine her to be," she said. "If she had lived. But who is to say, eh? She died so long ago. Violetta lies buried in the Old Country."

Prosperine stared at me. I stared back and held my tongue. "Go on," I said. "Go on with your story."

It was at those times when she saw Violetta on the road that Prosperine felt most miserable about her own new life. Alone with the old woman, she was neither happy nor unhappy and, little by little, the aching for her father and sisters went away. Freed from all that macaroni-making, she realized how much she had hated it—the *ripetizione*, the soreness each day in her back and legs and fingers. If she had stayed there, she might have turned hunchback like the old woman. Who knew? Perhaps that would be the fate of the sisters who had forsaken her? God punished such betrayals, did He not?

Prosperine was free on Sundays to attend Mass in the village, and it had been her habit to go until one morning when Ciccolina had a dizzy spell. The Monkey stayed to help her. That was the day the old woman first called her *figlia mia* and hinted about someday passing on potent gifts. As the old woman said this, she pulled Prosperine near to her and patted her face. The Monkey no longer feared her, or any power she might have to do harm. As Ciccolina smiled and touched Prosperine's face, the Monkey realized the *strega* was more blind than she had known. She studied her white chin whiskers, her big nose pockmarked like a lemon, her brown teeth more crooked than the cobblestones in the village square. Nothing about Ciccolina repelled the girl anymore—not those two filmy eyes with yellow *caccola* in the corners, not even the purple lump on the old woman's forehead. The Monkey dared herself to touch that thing, then watched her fingers move slowly toward it. Against it. The warmth of that knob surprised her. . . . *Figlia mia*, that was what Ciccolina started calling her.

By the middle of September, small crowds had begun gathering near the water's edge to watch Gallante Selvi draw and paint his pictures of Pescara's stained-glass *celebrità*. Townspeople and travelers went to stare and pray. The old nuns who had once taught Violetta—who had so often slapped and scolded her for misbehaving—now became afflicted with a convenient loss of memory. "Such a sweet girl she always was," they sighed. "So obedient and smart. So pious."

Often, the leader of the oglers was the village priest who had selected Violetta for the crowning at the Feast of the Assumption. He now took full credit for Gallante Selvi's choice of Violetta as his model. Prosperine had forgotten that priest's given name—*Padre Pomposo* is what she had called him back then and that was the only name she remembered now. He was a lover of *stravaganza* and self-promotion, that one! Did he not have a fine eye for spiritual beauty? Was there not some divine connection between himself and Selvi's stained-glass project? He began to talk of organizing a religious festival once Gallante Selvi's masterpiece was finished and, perhaps, a holy pilgrimage to Torino once the triptych had been installed in the great cathedral. And as for Violetta, she could do no wrong. In a month's time, the girl who had pestered street vendors and fishermen and pulled the backbones from a million fish had been transformed into the queen of all Pescara!

One afternoon Violetta and Gallante stopped their work and rode to the village square to shop and flaunt themselves and eat *gelato* at the *trattoria*—the very same café whose awning Violetta and Prosperine had once hidden behind, taunting the old woman whom the Monkey had somehow come to love. Now, from her spot across the street among Ciccolina's coops and cages, Prosperine glared at Violetta. She hated her fancy new clothes and shoes, her fancy new ways. She knew her secrets.

As she stared, Prosperine saw Violetta whisper something to the *artiste*. Then he looked over at the Monkey and scowled. "What are you looking at, butcher-girl, eh?" he called across from the little porch. That day, Ciccolina had been too sick to go to the market and the Monkey sat alone. "Is my *madrina* teaching you the fine art of *il mal occhio*? Should I hold up *mano cornuto* to ward off your curses?"

He laughed when he said it—had meant it as a joke. But the waiter and several others who overheard his remark eyed Prosperine suspiciously. She reddened with anger at the slander, and at Violetta's haughty smile! The Monkey stared and stared at her former friend until that smile fell off her face.

When this fine gentleman and lady—ha!—rose to leave, Violetta staggered against the table, complaining of shooting pains in her legs. "Is this *your* doing?" she screamed to Prosperine across the road. "Do you send pains to afflict me because of your jealousy?"

"Bah!" the Monkey called back. "Stop your new friend's visits between your legs, '*Santa Lucia*,' and those pains will go away!"

Violetta gasped and hobbled in shame toward their carriage. Gallante Selvi pointed at Prosperine and warned her he would beat her when she returned to his *madrina*'s hut that evening.

"What a disgusting accusation!" someone said.

"Sacrilege!" another villager agreed.

"Who does that butcher-girl think she is?"

"She's a strange one—that little witch."

In the days that followed, Prosperine was stared at, whispered about, spat upon. Even her own sisters held their noses in the air and did not speak to her. At home, Gallante Selvi tried to make good on his promise to beat her, but the old woman stood between them and forbade it. Selvi settled for growling and shoving, threatening her whenever his godmother could not hear.

But within a month of her public humiliation, the

Monkey was avenged! On the first of October, Selvi quit Pescara like a thief in the night. A porter at the train station said the *artiste* had taken with him two trunks, two portfolios of the drawings and paintings he had made of Violetta, and Violetta herself! She had bid no one goodbye, not even her father!

Afraid of losing business, D'Annunzio spread the story that *Padre Pomposo* had secretly married Gallante Selvi and his daughter before their departure, but the following Sunday the priest denied it from the *pulpito*. After that, Violetta's father tried a different approach, denouncing his immoral daughter on the streets in the same loud voice he used to hawk fish. His business fell off nonetheless and before the month was finished, a drunken man punctured D'Annunzio's lung in a tavern brawl and killed him. Gallante Selvi and Violetta were located in Torino and notified of the tragedy, but Violetta did not return to bury her father. Everyone agreed that Pescara's once-celebrated *Santa Lucia* had broken both the third and ninth commandments and would, no doubt, spend eternity in Hell.

By November, the village tongues had tired of speaking the name *Violetta* and gone on to other sinners. It was during that same month, Prosperine said, that she witnessed the strange magic involving the rabbits.

"Ah, at last the rabbits!" I said. "I was afraid I would die of old age before you got to those magical *conigli* of yours."

The Monkey lit her pipe and puffed on it, took a sip of wine, said nothing more for two, three minutes. I shut up and waited. Then she sighed and continued her story. "There were three of us who saw it," she said. "The hunchback herself, Pomaricci the schoolmaster, and I."

Pomaricci was a miserly man, tall and bony but with a little potbelly in the front. His teeth were long and yellow like a horse's, and his mouth emitted a foul smell. Ciccolina could hardly see, but knew by the stink of his breath when Pomaricci had come for fresh meat.

Every day he bought a rabbit or a chicken for his dinner and never forgot to complain to the old woman that her prices were too high, her animals too skinny. Sometimes he poked his fingers through the poor creatures' cages, more to bother them than to feel the meat on their bones. "One of these days, I'll starve to death or go bankrupt from trading with you, old woman," Pomaricci would complain to Ciccolina. Then he would turn to Prosperine and smile, revealing small bits of meat stuck between those yellow teeth from the evening before.

Ciccolina would answer that even paupers needed to eat, so for him she chose starvation. "At last I would be rid of your complaining," she told him.

Here, the Monkey's voice became a dog's growl in the throat. She drew her chair closer to mine, as if we were two criminals not wanting to be overheard.

That day, Pomaricci did his usual complaining and poking of fingers through Ciccolina's cages. Finally, he sighed and opened one and pulled his dinner out by the ears. "How much do you want for this half-dead bag of bones?" he asked.

Ciccolina lifted the rabbit and named her price.

"What? You rob me, old woman!" Pomaricci protested. "For that price, I should get twice the meat that this puny creature will yield." But as always, he opened his shabby change purse and prepared to pay what she had asked.

Ciccolina had been ill that day—afflicted as she sometimes was with dizziness and *mal di capo*. On the walk into town, she had fallen twice against the cart and once in the road. She had been angry all day. "Twice the meat, eh?" she snapped back at that *spilorcio*, Pomaricci.

"If twice the meat will shut up your face, then twice the meat you shall have!"

She slammed the frightened rabbit against the cutting board and directed Prosperine to hold down the animal by its thumping back feet. The Monkey obeyed and the old woman's big cleaver flashed in the air and came down hard, slicing the creature exactly in half and narrowly missing her assistant's right hand and her own left breast.

The magic Prosperine saw that day was this: the rabbit, split clean, shed not one drop of blood. Instead, each half grew another half—became, before the girl's eyes and the schoolmaster's eyes, two whole, living rabbits where only the one had been!

"Here! Take them both and be gone with you!" Ciccolina shouted at the schoolmaster. "I hope you choke on the bones!" She held the twitching twins by the ears in front of the schoolmaster. There they rocked back and forth, two furry *pendoli*.

Struck dumb, Pomaricci dropped the coins from his hand and stumbled backward and away from his strange bounty. At a short distance, he turned and ran, screaming about dinner and the devil's work.

Ciccolina grabbed Prosperine by the arm. With her thumb, she traced the cross of Jesus Christ on the Monkey's forehead."*Benedicia*!" the old woman whispered. "Say it quickly! *Benedicia*! And make the sign of the cross!"

The stunned girl did as she was told, but in a kind of trance. Was she dreaming? Had she really seen what she had seen? Her disbelieving eyes could not look away from those two rabbits that had been one.

That evening, the church bell rang for Pomaricci, who had died of apoplexy. As for the old *strega* and the macaroni-maker's eldest daughter, they celebrated! Ciccolina ordered Prosperine to kill and dress the two rabbits. At first, the girl thought she would not be able to slaughter and skin those magical creatures, much less fry them and chew the cooked flesh off their bones. But she did! The two ate fried rabbit, and *zucca* from the old woman's garden, and bread sopped in tomato gravy. A feast, it was! Enough so that Prosperine thought her stomach would burst like *palloncino*. In truth, it was the most delicious food she had ever tasted!

"I know it sounds crazy, Tempesta," Prosperine told me that night. "But I swear at the feet of Jesus Himself that it happened the way I say! I saw what I saw! I know this much is true!"

Here, the Monkey drew so close to me that the smells of her wine and tobacco mingled with the warm, wet breath that pushed against my face. She clasped my knee and began to whisper, as if this next was only between her and me.

"What did I see that day, Tempesta?" she asked. "A mortal sin? A miracle? The question came back to me yesterday when I midwifed your wife's twins—the boy who came out dead and the girl who came out with the rabbit's lip. What does it mean, Tempesta? Tell me. What does it mean?"

"Foolish woman," I said, and pulled my chair back a little from that crazy fool. "It means only that you should have thrown your superstitions and *allucinazioni* into the sea on the way to the New Country. *Mal occhio* and miracles—bah! You talk the stuff of idiots and ignorant peasants."

"Be careful what you mock, Tempesta," she warned, pointing her bony finger at me. "Where there is no shadow, there is no light. Heaven help the heretic!"

We sat there in silence, the Monkey and I, the word *heretic* falling hard like a rock onto my soul. And I felt, again, my dead child in my arms. Saw my thumb trace the oily cross on his forehead. If my son had been baptized by the hands of a heretic, then his was a lost and unprotected soul. I had cast him not into Heaven but Hell.

"Better shut up now about heresy and go to bed," I told the Monkey. "Ignazia will need you before the sun comes up and your head will be bigger than this house."

She stood and waited, blocking the moon in the window. There was something she was waiting to say.

"What?" I asked impatiently. "What do you want now?"

"I know what the *dottore* told you," she said.

"The *dottore* told me many things," I answered. "How should I know what you're talking about?"

"I know that if another baby comes, it could kill her," she said. "It could stop her heart."

"What of it?" I said. "That is private business between a husband and his wife. Keep your nose out of it."

"Come to me when you need to," she said.

"Eh?"

"Remember the promise I made you when we arrived here. If you hurt her, I'll make you pay. When you need to, come to me and be done with it."

At first, I did not understand what she was saying, and when I *did* understand, the thought of it repulsed me. "I have no wish," I said, "to fuck a monkey."

"And I have no wish," she said back, "to be fucked by a fool. Still, I'll do it for her sake. What do I care, if it will keep her safe? It means nothing to me. Stay away from her, I warn you. Just remember, Tempesta. I killed a man."

I laughed in her face. "A poor schoolmaster dies of apoplexy and you claim responsibility for yourself and your old witch-friend. Ha! That was God's work, woman, not yours. If there is a heretic in this kitchen, it is *you*!"

"I claim no responsibility for Pomaricci's death," she said. "I do not say he died because of the magic. I do not say he didn't."

She picked up her empty wineglass, then banged it back down against the table, cracking it. "Gallante Selvi is the man I killed," she said. "That bastard of a stained-glass painter."

"You said he left Pescara," I protested.

"I told you he left," she said. "I tell you now he came back!"

My heart raced; my hands were moist with sweat. "Sit, then," I told her. "Sit and tell me the rest."

After she had seen the witch's magical twinning of the rabbits, Prosperine devoted herself entirely to the old *strega*, whom she now both feared and loved. She begged Ciccolina to teach her the powers, but for weeks the old woman put her off with nods and smiles, pretending not to hear. Then, as the season of the Epiphany approached, the old hunchback began to hint that the time was drawing near—that midnight on Christmas Eve was the hour when mothers gave their daughters the gift of secrets.

And that was when she taught her—on the last Christmas Eve of her life, before it was too late. At midnight, as the church bells rang in the village to celebrate the birth of the Christ child, Ciccolina began Prosperine's lessons: how to diagnose and cure *il mal occhio*. The girl begged her to teach her the other, too—how to *inflict* the evil eye, cause suffering on those who had wronged her. She had enemies, after all: those villagers who had spat on her in the square and called her "little witch"; a father who had betrayed her for Gallante Selvi's money; and, most of all, Gallante Selvi himself—he who had turned her friend Violetta against her and kidnapped her from her village! But Ciccolina refused to teach the Monkey the art of revenge. Maybe the old woman suspected she would use bad power against her godson. Maybe not. The world was already too full of bad intent, Ciccolina told her—already too full of prideful people wanting to take over God's work for Him.

On that Christmas Eve, Ciccolina took from inside her shawl a necklace of red chilis which she had strung and dried the summer before. "Wear this," she ordered Prosperine. "The point of the *corno* bursts the evil eye and protects you."

She told the girl to take out olive oil and to draw three bowls of Holy Water from the cistern that *Padre Pomposo* had blessed on his visit the summer before. Into the night, the Monkey repeated the incantations that Ciccolina spoke, practiced the reading of the oil on the water. When the old woman was satisfied that the gift had been transferred, she spat into her hand and told the girl to close her eyes. She rubbed the wet from her mouth into the skin of each eyelid. "*Che puozze schiatta*!" she murmured—over and over she said it, not to Prosperine but to the darkness. Then she had the girl rub the hump on her back for good luck."*Benedicia*!" she said. "Use what you know against evil."

She died the next month, beside the Monkey, on the bed where the two slept each night. Prosperine suspected it as soon as she woke in the morning. She jumped from that mattress of husks and feathers, trying to call and shake the old *strega* back to life. When she was sure she was gone, she poured Holy Water into a bowl, placed it beside the body, and sprinkled the oil on top. The beads did not spread but held firm on the surface, which meant that Ciccolina's soul rested peacefully. The Monkey thumb-shut the old woman's eyes and kissed her hands, her face, even the purple lump on her forehead. The butcher-woman had been kind to her, like a *madre*, and Prosperine had come to love even her ugly parts.

The notary sent word to Gallante Selvi about Ciccolina's death and the painter sent back instructions that Prosperine was to continue to maintain his godmother's house and butcher business. He would return to Pescara after the solstice to pay her father for her services and to paint his colored glass in the summer light of Pescara. Nowhere else in all of Italy was the illumination so perfect for his work in *vetro colorito*. The visit would, as well, allow his little wife to enjoy a homecoming with her many admirers.

His little wife! If he was not lying about the marriage, then he was a bigger *figliu d'una minga* than the Monkey had imagined. And Violetta D'Annunzio was a bigger fool!

At this, I held up my hand to stop *Signorina* Monkey-Face. "*Aspetti un momento*!" I said. "Is this a riddle you tell?"

"This is *truth* I tell!" she protested. "Why do you say 'riddle'?"

"It's a puzzle to me to understand how your pretty friend had been a fool to trade her life of fish-cleaning and giggling at sailors for a life as a rich artist's wife and model. Ha! What did you expect—that Selvi would have immortalized *you* in a work of holy art? Married *you*? And what's this about your killing the poor man? How did you kill him—burst the blood vessels in his brain with *il mal occhio*?"

Her fist banged the table, made me jump back. "I killed him with his own art," she croaked.

"What? Quit this fantasy, woman. My chianti has turned you lunatic."

"Your chianti has made me talk truth to a fool," she snapped back. "You would be wise to keep quiet while I'm in the mood to tell my secrets."

"All right, then, talk!" I said. "Talk until the sun comes up. Talk until your tongue falls out of your mouth. How did you kill this poor painter? Tell me! Talk!"

Gallante Selvi made a grand show of his return to Pescara. He and Violetta arrived at the square in a caravan of three horse-drawn carriages and one horse-drawn cart. The first carriage held the couple themselves and their fancy luggage. In the second were the finished pieces of Selvi's precious "masterpiece," to be pieced and soldered together later in Torino. The third carriage held Selvi's crates of supplies. In the open cart sat the small kiln the artist used to bake his paintings onto glass. Each small glass section of the masterpiece-to-be was wrapped in buntings and blankets to guard against breakage. Ha! Violetta, too, was wrapped in packaging—a fur-trimmed red *bolero* with gold *aigletti*, a fancy fur toque on her head. She would have seemed quite the lady if she had not looked so shrunken and miserable in her fine new clothes.

Naturally, their showy arrival at midday drew a crowd. Selvi was always happy to act the *strombazzatore*. He stood and made a speech about beauty and art. He and Violetta had returned, he said, to mourn at the graves of his beloved *madrina* and Violetta's beloved *padre*, and so that he could capture in *chiaroscuro* for the *Santa Lucia* triptych the rich blue shades of the *Adriatico* as it looked only off the Pescaran coast. He described the terrible inconvenience of being so far from the glassworks at Torino and from his trusted glazier who bound together the pieces of his art with ribs of lead. But he had willingly taken on the trouble of doing his own firing and glazing to be in Pescara. His palette would not be limited by mere geography, he told the crowd. Only the hues found in Pescara would do for the cloak and the eyes of *Santa Lucia*, the Virgin Martyr!

Here he took Violetta's gloved hand and kissed it and the village women sighed. All but the Monkey! She spat on the ground at the lies of that *faccia brutta*.

Selvi and the Monkey's father decided that she should stay at Ciccolina's house and cook and clean for the *artiste* and his "fine lady" of a wife while they visited. As usual, the macaroni-maker ignored Prosperine's protests and told her that a complaining daughter was a howling dog begging to be beaten.

On their first day in Pescara, Violetta and Selvi were polite and affectionate with each other—putting on a show for the benefit of *Padre Pomposo* and the other important visitors to Ciccolina's little cottage. But that night, through the wall, Prosperine heard the first of the couple's fighting and fisticuffs.

The next morning, Selvi complained that the cornmeal Prosperine had cooked for his breakfast had no grit and was swill for pigs. He threw the cereal against the wall, barely missing the Monkey's head, and then left to walk the seacoast.

Violetta came into the little kitchen, hiding her swollen eye with her hand. She told Prosperine that she should forget about their past friendship. That was long ago, she said, and many things had changed. Prosperine would do well to remember who was the servant and who was mistress.

"Smell your hands, *Signora Aristocratica*," the Monkey retorted. "No doubt they still stink from fish."

A scowl overtook Violetta's swollen and bruised face. "Prepare me a warm bath and then leave me," she said. Prosperine did the first thing but not the second. From the doorway, she stood watching as Violetta disrobed, exposing the pretty pink flesh that that son of a bitch Selvi had marred with welts and bruises. Violetta flinched when she turned and saw the Monkey. "Get out! Get out!" she screamed. "I won't stand for this disobedience!" But Prosperine approached instead.

Violetta grabbed her nightgown and clutched it to herself. So many injuries, she could not cover them all. Prosperine's heart ached to see the damage Selvi had done. "This would not have happened," she told Violetta, "if you had not let him make you his *puttana*."

"How dare you call me names!" Violetta shouted back. "You, who let that old hag turn you into a witch-woman!"

"Bah!" Prosperine answered. "*Puta*!"

"Bah!" Violetta answered back. "*Strega*!"

"*Puta*!"

"*Strega*!"

"*Puta*!"

"*Strega*!" Violetta reached out and slapped the Monkey across the face.

When Prosperine raised her hand to slap back, Violetta shrank with such fear in her eyes that her friend's hand dropped down again. Gallante Selvi's cringing wife was nothing like the saucy girl who had paraded on the docks for the fishermen and explained the "dancing" horses to Prosperine and her sisters. The *artiste* had beaten all that out of her. Now Violetta seemed as doomed as the rabbits outside in the old woman's cages—as tethered to her fate as Ciccolina's goat.

The two women collapsed into each other's arms, rocking back and forth and weeping. For the rest of that morning, Violetta told what her year had been. One beating after another, *umiliazione* upon *umiliazione*. Once, when she had refused Selvi in their bed, he accused her of being unfaithful—of being more slippery than the surfaces on which he painted. "Unfaithful with whom?" she had demanded, and Selvi had named half the drunks he'd invited into their *appartamento*, describing in detail the squalid acts she supposedly had performed on each. Then, as if she were guilty of those deeds of which he had wrongly accused her, he dragged her to the washing basin and held her head down in the water so long she was sure she would drown. Another time, when she had fidgeted too much while posing as *Santa Lucia*, he had thrown her against the wall and knocked her unconscious. Her left shoulder never worked right after that. "And he has a friend, Rodolpho, a dirty pig of a *fotografo*," Violetta whispered, amidst her sobs and pauses. "Twice Gallante made me pose for that filthy man—ordered me to take off my clothes and spread my legs and worse while that other one took pictures. The second time, I begged him no. I was in the middle of miscarriage, Prosperine! That night, Gallante accused me of enjoying what he had made me do for that photographer and burned me on the back and legs. What kind of man makes his wife do such things and burns her besides? I tell you, Prosperine, I made a tragic mistake the day I left Pescara. Many times I have thought about ending my life to be rid of him. How much worse could Hell be than marriage to that monster who paints the saints but is himself the devil?"

When Violetta had no more terrible stories left to tell, no more tears inside her head, Prosperine bathed her in almond water and rubbed olive oil onto those bruises and scars. Then she dressed her and brushed her hair as she had done before. Violetta still had the tortoiseshell brushes—that much was the same. She told Prosperine her touch was medicine and the Monkey put her to bed in clean clothes and watched her sleep.

That afternoon in the village square, Prosperine killed and dressed many rabbits—a busy day. Never had butchering satisfied her more. Each head she hacked off, each body she watched twitch and bleed, belonged to that son of a bitch Gallante Selvi. He would suffer for what he had done to her friend. She promised herself that much. He would pay with his life.

But it was not so easy. What could she do? Stick a knife in his heart while half of Pescara watched him paint the glass? Behead him in the village square with his *madrina*'s big cleaver? He deserved such a fate, but she would not live the rest of her life in a dark cell. Not with her beloved friend returned to Pescara—not with Violetta to care for and protect.

At first she tried to inflict *il mal occhio*. Although Ciccolina had refused to teach her the art of vengeance, she hoped that, since she knew how to cure and diagnose the evil eye, she might also have the power to gaze with it, too—to give devils what they deserved when God Himself was too busy to do the job. For the next two, three days, she stared at Gallante Selvi with hatred in her soul. Stared at him while he slept and ate, painted and soldered. Glared back in defiance when he yelled out his list of complaints about her work: her sweeping raised dust and made him sneeze, her scowling face made his eyes hurt, the cornmeal she boiled for his breakfast each morning had no salt or grit.

But her staring did no good. The longer and harder she watched Gallante Selvi with wicked intent, the more powerful and healthy he seemed to become. At night, Violetta's begging and sobbing would wake her from troubled sleep. In the morning, the suffering wife would tell Prosperine her latest shame, show off her new bruises—teeth marks, once, on her leg, as if she had married a vicious dog instead of a man! But he was a *dead* dog, that one. That much the Monkey promised herself. And when she first whispered the word *murder* to Violetta, Violetta did not stop her. She listened quietly, her hands fidgeting. Fear and hope were in her eyes.

The triptych—Gallante's unfinished "masterpiece"—was not going well. He was a perfectionist when he worked, always painting small studies on glass squares before adding even a fingernail or a fold to the half-completed work. When these efforts displeased him, he would throw them against the wall or kick the goat or yank his wife's long hair or slap her face. He would melt lead cable, soldering one finished piece of glass to another, and then hate what he had joined, pulling the pieces apart and smashing a day's or several days' work against the iron kiln. All of his attempts to capture with paint on glass the gloomy *azzurro* of the sea were failures to his critical eye. Over and over, he mixed his pigments and lead powders and tried the results on squares of milky glass. He wrote down his recipes and waited like an expectant father for the paint to bake itself onto the glass inside the kiln. Always, when he yanked it out again and held the result to the sun, he saw that it was wrong and flung the hot glass, shouting terrible curses: "I shit on the Virgin Mary!" he would say, or "May Jesus Christ fuck your sister!"

Prosperine was expected after these tantrums to drop her work and sweep up his mess. Selvi liked the freedom of working barefooted and warned her that he would beat her blind if he cut his feet. And so, whenever she heard the smashing, she had to grab her broom and run. Each day she added new breakage, spilled paint pots, and jumbles of lead wire to the pile out past where the goats were kept. Then one morning, a kid chewed through its rope and helped himself to some of Selvi's wreckage. Later that day, Prosperine watched the creature vomit up glass and wire. Before the sun set, that poor goat convulsed and bled and died from what was inside him. Then she knew how she would kill Gallante Selvi.

They prepared for days, Violetta and she, whispering secretly when Gallante was near and hurrying to their preparations when he left. They decided they would do the job on Sunday—the only day of the week when Prosperine was not obliged to go to the square and butcher. She collected Selvi's discards of colored glass, broke the shards into chips and crumbs, and ground these to a fine powder. *Crunch crunch crunch*—she could still hear the sound of the glass between the mortar and pestle, she said. In a pot on the stove, she soaked and boiled scraps of the cable he used for glazing. Little by little, they would poison him with lead and cut up his insides with glass. They worked when he went to the tavern to drink, or to the ocean to swim. If they could only get him to swallow the food they tainted, they would be rid of his tyranny. By Saturday Prosperine and Violetta had many handfuls of fine, glittering powder.

"Tomorrow morning, his cornmeal will have grit, all right," Prosperine whispered to Violetta. "More grit than he bargained for!" But she would take no chances: on that day, she would cook for his afternoon meal some special *braciola* rolled with ground veal and walnuts and more of their special powdered glass. For dinner, she would roast him a chicken stuffed with cornbread and *pignoli* and plenty more of that powder! By nighttime or the day after, he would be as dead as Ciccolina's little goat. That *bastardo* would die from his own *digestione*!

Prosperine sat still in the chair and closed her eyes. Was she telling the truth? Telling a story to frighten me? Had she fallen into *torpore* from all that wine? Why had she stopped her story at this inconvenient place?

"Wake up," I said, and shook her sleeve. Her eyes popped open.

"Tempesta," she growled. "It *worked*!"

That next morning, Gallante Selvi ate his breakfast with no complaints—two bowls of the gritty mush made with extra salt and grit and the lead-poisoned water. Violetta and Prosperine busied themselves, holding their breath until the last spoonful had been swallowed—until they heard the sound of Selvi's satisfied belch. An hour later, he was already complaining of thirst and nausea and a strange taste that would not leave his mouth. If he could only shit, he said, he'd feel better.

"One of Ciccolina's laxatives will fix you," Prosperine told him. "It tastes vile but it does the job." She brewed him a tea of lemon-weed and fennel and lead water, with a big pinch of something extra. "Your *madrina* taught me this recipe," she said, handing Selvi the tea. "The gravel in it will loosen you up. Drink it quick, not slow. Two cups of the stuff are better than one."

He swallowed it gratefully in long gulps that made his *pomo d'Adamo* go up and down, up and down. "*Grazi, signorina*! *Grazi*!" he told Prosperine, wiping his mouth and lying back on his bed. On that last day of his life, Gallante Selvi was the politest of gentlemen!

By noontime, he was whimpering and moaning and pulling up his shirt so that Violetta and his servant-girl could watch the strange movements of his stomach. He complained that his insides felt hot, his head felt dizzy. His hands could not make fists. "A good big meal will settle that stomach of yours," Prosperine told him. She helped him off the bed and to the table. But when she placed the plate of *braciola* in front of him, Selvi coughed a milky vomit onto the uneaten food.

While he slept fitfully, Violetta paced the floor and the field outside, sobbing and muttering to herself. Prosperine stuffed and roasted Selvi's special chicken.

But he never ate that bird. By late afternoon, he awoke with stomach pains that made him scream. An hour later, he was shitting bloody stool. As night fell, he slept so quietly, they had to put a goose feather to his nose to see the breathing.

Somewhere in the nighttime, his thrashing began. Strings of blood and drool came out of his mouth. His stench was foul, his eyes wild. A few times, he tried to speak—to pray, perhaps—but his lips only made movement without sound. By the candlelight, his green eyes seemed lit with the suffering of his painted saints!

Toward the end, Violetta could not look. She cried and said they had done a terrible thing—a thing that would damn them both in the afterlife. "You were damned in this one!" Prosperine reminded her. "Remember the evil he did—the evil he would have *kept* doing if we hadn't stopped him! We did what we had to do!" Still, the Monkey took no pleasure in Gallante Selvi's dying and death. All during that night, water poured out of the sky and she wondered if the rain was the old witch's tears.

Gallante Selvi stopped breathing in the hour before the sun. Prosperine washed the blood away from both ends of him and Violetta combed his hair, crying and kissing his yellow curls. She kept begging that poisoned devil to forgive her and, finally, Prosperine had to slap her and cover the body with Ciccolina's quilt to make her stop.

The Monkey told Violetta that to sit and do nothing—to fail to go for priest or *dottore*—would cast suspicion.

But Violetta was afraid to stay alone with him—afraid Selvi might come alive again and strangle her, or that his unholy soul would suck the air from her mouth. She stayed outside while Prosperine walked to the village.

In town, the Monkey knocked on the door of the more *stupido* of Pescara's two *dottori*—the one whose errors had killed more patients. "Hurry, please, while he is still alive," she said. Together they rushed to wake up P*adre* P*omposo*.

Through all the examination and prayer that followed, Violetta wailed her sorrow—a diva's performance, or else real tears, Prosperine never knew which. That lazy *dottore* made a poke here, a prod there. "A*ppendice*," he said. "The poor man died of burst *appendice*." Then he went to the kitchen while the *padre* gave that son of a bitch the Rites of the Dead.

P*adre* P*omposo*—that lover of pageantry and *stravaganza*—advised Violetta that she must arrange a funeral befitting the great religious *artiste* her beloved husband had been. With her permission, he said, he would contact Panetta, the *impresario di pompe funebri*, as soon as he returned to the village. Panetta would collect the body, prepare it, and transport it to the church where all of Pescara would come to mourn. Prosperine's eyes tried to warn Violetta, "No, no!" They needed a fast burial. But Violetta's eyes looked only at the priest, as if his foolish *ceremonia* could save her husband's soul and hers. P*adre* P*omposo* spoke on and on about holy music and special candles, a *processione*, perhaps, on Wednesday or Thursday morning, from the ocean where the genius had worked to the church where the High Mass would be celebrated.

Prosperine made her tongue click and shook her head in a futile attempt to capture the *attenzione* of her friend and accomplice. The *padre* looked at her, then back to Violetta. Perhaps, he said, if he could have a moment of privacy with the widow . . .

Then, a shock! A thing those murdering women had not planned on—the thing that ruined them! Banished by the priest from the room where the funeral arrangements were being made, Prosperine reentered the kitchen. At the table, that stupid *dottore* sat devouring the roasted chicken she had stuffed with bread and glass!

"*Scusi, Signorina*," he told the Monkey, waving a half-gnawed leg. "I hope your pretty *padrona* won't mind that I had a little something for my stomach in exchange for my troubles. Do you have, maybe, a bottle of *vino* to help wash down this bird?" In front of him was a pile of bones and a spoon. The bird's carcass was half empty of the tainted stuffing!

Panetta the undertaker and his man came that afternoon to haul away the body. Violetta hugged Prosperine, sobbing, as the wagon drove away. That stupid *dottore* had not seemed sick when he left. He hadn't eaten nearly as much of the ground glass as Gallante had. Perhaps things would be fine.

But that greedy fool was sick by the time the wagon had returned to the village! Sick for the rest of that day, too, and through the night. When he moved his bowels the next morning, he screamed from the pain of it. His wife carried his business outside and studied it in the sunlight. The bloody *cacca* floating inside the chamber pot glittered and told on Selvi's widow and her murdering friend!

The *dottore* and his wife carried their smelly evidence to the *magistrato* and, together, the three visited Panetta the undertaker. Then the four went to the church to cut open Gallante Selvi's *stomaco*.

It was Prosperine's father who told all this to her, as he stood in his apron at Ciccolina's doorway. His hair was dusty from macaroni flour, his eyes jumped with fear for his estranged daughter. Panetta the undertaker's wife was Papa's *cugina*. She had run to the macaroni shop and tipped him off and Papa had beaten his mule half to death to get to Prosperine before the *polizia* arrived. "Take this, whatever you have done, and run away," he said. He put two fistfuls of coins into his daughter's upturned apron, then hugged her hard enough to break her bones. That was the last she ever saw of her papa, but ever since, she had been comforted by her memory of him standing there in Ciccolina's doorway: He had felt a father's love for her all along, and even before his arms had let go of her that day, she had forgiven him for having sold her away.

They ran! Through the woods and then down to the docks—ran to those fishermen who had lusted after Violetta. They employed the charms of the beautiful one and the money of the ugly one and got away from Pescara. They did what they had to do. It was the only way.

From boat to boat, down the coast, they traveled. Prosperine had never before been out of Pescara, but now they sailed past Bari and Brindisi, and across the *stretto* at Messina. And that was how Prosperine became *siciliana*—she had gone there to hide from murder!

For a while, the two women lived in Catania, lost among the workers on a wealthy man's olive farm. They were safe there until the farmer's *capomastro* became curious about what was beneath Violetta's skirts and his suspicious wife began questioning where two young *signorini* had traveled from and why. On the same night of that jealous wife's *interrogazione*, Prosperine and Violetta stole money and escaped again, this time by train to Palermo.

Those were terrible months in that busy city where people came and went. Violetta found work as a servant at a busy inn, and Prosperine toiled as a laundress there. Although the Monkey could hide in the back with the hot water and soiled linens, Violetta was obliged to serve meals to travelers. Her heart stopped a little each time the door of the inn opened. Prosperine, too, was afraid—forever mistaking people in the streets for traveling Pescarans! Women and men and *bambini* all seemed to look at her with familiar faces—with eyes that knew what she had done. She was homesick. She longed to see the *Adriatico*, the Pescaran square, her papa, her sisters Anna and Teodolina. But a bigger part of her longed to be safe—to buy safety for herself and her friend Violetta. They could not be caught! They had to get further away!

One of Violetta's regular supper customers was a fine and proper *legale*. On nights when the inn was quiet, he invited her to sit with him and talk and join him in a cognac. He was well traveled, this gentleman; three times, he told her, he had visited *la 'Merica*. And it warmed his heart to think of the number of poor *siciliani* he had helped sail to that Land of Dreams.

Had he ever aided any poor souls, Violetta asked cautiously, who were, perhaps, in trouble with the law?

The *legale* leaned closer to the murderous widow and whispered *si*, he had from time to time assisted fellow citizens whose criminal records had needed a little whitewashing. He had a friend, he said, an *ufficiale di passaporti*. Together they sometimes made the dead come alive again, equipping them with traveling papers besides! They asked no questions of prospective emigrants, he said, except the one question they needed to know: how much was a *fugitiva* able to pay?

In the weeks that followed, Violetta began to grant her friend the *legale* certain favors. In exchange, he sent secret word back to a certain Pescaran macaroni-maker that the two fugitives were alive and well and needed money. Then they waited and waited—almost a year, long enough so that Prosperine was sure her father had disowned her for the shame she had brought on his head.

One day a young sailor came to the inn. He asked to see the laundress and was brought out back to her scrubbing tubs. Without speaking a word, he took out *fo-*

tografia, holding it before himself and looking back and forth, back and forth, from the Monkey's face to the likeness in his hand. Prosperine's hands shook the water in the tub while she washed and waited. She thought, of course, that he was *agente di polizia*, but he was not. Here stood her sister Teodolina's new husband. Her younger sister had married and it was her own brother-in-law who stood before her! The sailor handed her a leather purse. Inside was money from her father, the amount the *legale* needed for passage and counterfeit passports, and for the fugitives' sponsorship once they got to America, plus a little more. Prosperine's father had sold his macaroni shop—had sacrificed his livelihood for the daughter he had first rented away to an old witch, and then to her brute of a godson.

"And so, Tempesta, I became Prosperine Tucci, a girl five years my junior who had died of *consunzione* and whose mother had been sister to those stinking Iaccoi brothers—those goddamned plumbers who tricked you. They made a nice profit from their lies, Tempesta, and made you a tool as well. And here we sit, you and me, each a curse for the other."

I reached over and grabbed her wrist. "What is your real name then, eh?" I said. "If Prosperine is a name stolen from a dead girl?"

"*Bought*, not stolen," she said. "Paid for with a father's sacrifice. My other name doesn't matter. I am *myself*, Tempesta—the woman who watches what you do. That's all you need to know."

"And are you planning to feed *me* glass to tear up *my* insides? Stab *me* some night with your butcher knife?"

"I have no wish to watch another man die—to be twice damned," she said. "Gallante Selvi was the devil himself. You're only a bully and a fool. Keep your hands off her and you'll be safe from me."

She stood, teetering, and then made her way to the

bathroom. That one who had never drunk spirits in my house before had, that night, drunk nearly half of the jug. Now, from behind the door, I heard that witch turn her wine back to water. I heard her moan, too, and wondered if she had begun to sober herself—to realize that she had told too much.

When she came out again, I stood in front of her, blocking her way to her room. "Your friend," I said. "Violetta D'Annunzio. What became of her?"

Fear crossed the Monkey's face and left just as quickly. "Eh? Violetta? She stayed . . . stayed in Palermo. . . . She changed her mind and married that *legale.*"

"Eh?"

"He fell in love with her and turned her into a gentlewoman. Now she's happy."

"Happy to be dead?" I said.

"Eh?"

"Before, you told me she died. You said she was buried in the Old Country."

The fear and confusion in her eyes spoke louder than her words. "She *is* buried there. I said she was happy *before* she died. . . . Maybe I misspoke, but that's what I meant."

"Ah," I said. "And has her second husband maintained good health?"

The Monkey's eyes could not look at me. "The *legale*? He was grief-stricken, poor man."

"S*i*?"

"S*i*, *si*. He wrote to me with the sad news when I lived with the plumbers. Influenza is what took her, poor thing. She had a sad life."

"Before, you said your father's money had paid for 'our' escape. Did Violetta come to this country or not?"

"I said 'my' escape."

"You said 'our' escape. N*ostro*. I heard the word come out of your mouth."

"You heard wrong then," she said. "*Mia, no nostra*. You must have potatoes in your ears."

Now she looked at me and I looked at her. We stood there, watching each other, neither of us looking away. That's when I saw the Monkey's lip tremble. And then, in the other room, the baby cried.

I held her gaze ten, fifteen seconds more. "You'd better go," I finally said. "Your friend Violetta needs you."

Her drunken, frightened eyes jumped from my face to the bedroom door, then back again. "My friend Violetta is buried in Palermo," she said—a little too loudly. "I just told you. It is a sin to mock the souls of the dead."

I took her arm and whispered some advice into her ear. "You're a fine one," I said, "to talk to me about sins against the dead!"

forty

Sheffer was late, as usual. Why was one o'clock always 1:10 or 1:15 with that woman? Why was 11 A.M. always 11:20, with some excuse attached?

Okay, cool your jets, Birdsey, I told myself. You bite her head off as soon as she walks in the door, you won't get what you need.

Get him tested. . . . Keep my name out of it.

Drinkwater's phone call had kept me up all night. Just my brother's paranoid delusions—right, Sheffer? He's "perfectly safe" all right. Except for one minor detail: he might be infected. Someone down here at this fucking place might have given him AIDS.

I'll take care of him for you, Ma. I promise. You can go now, Ma. . . .

Face it, Birdsey: you were asleep at the wheel. You let them lull you. Cut back your visits, stopped calling to check on him. . . . And when you *did* visit, you only half-listened to his horror stories: how they were poisoning him, programming him, coming into his cell in the middle of the night. . . . Oh Jesus, don't let him have HIV on top of everything else. Don't let that test be positive. . . .

I knew one thing: I was getting him examined independently, whether they liked it or not. I didn't trust *any* of these clowns anymore. I wasn't taking *anyone's* word.

Okay, chill out. Think about something else. . . . I reached over, snagged the newspaper on Sheffer's desk.

POST–GULF WAR OIL PRICES DROPPING. . . . *How can we kill people for the sake of cheap oil, Dominick? How can we justify* that*?* . . . KING BEATING: TAPES SHOW L.A.P.D. "LEVITY." . . . *He's safe here, Dominick. Unit Two's the best.* Sheffer had said it so often, so convincingly, that I'd bought the line. And now look what had happened.

What *might* have happened, I reminded myself. His test could come back negative.

I saw my sorry-ass reflection in Sheffer's computer monitor. Saw, whether I liked it or not, my grandfather. . . . Why the hell had I picked up Domenico's history the night before—read the one goddamned thing *guaranteed* to extend my insomnia—make me feel even worse? . . . A painter vomits and shits himself to death, a rabbit gets hacked in half and *doubles* itself. . . . So your wife and her friend were fugitives, Old Man? My grandmother was a murderer? Is *that* what's wrong with us?

And what about his other suspicion—that Ma was really the Irishman's daughter? If *that* was true, then Domenico wasn't even my grandfather, right? Mine *or* Thomas's. We beat the rap. . . . Only it didn't wash. How could she have given birth to twins with different fathers? If I *wasn't* his grandson, why had I grown to look like those sepia-tinted pictures of him—those pictures Ma had gone back into the burning house to save?

One thing was coming clear: the reason why he'd treated Ma like crap. "Rabbit-face," "cracked jug": if you disowned your own daughter—convinced yourself she was somebody else's—then you could make her your personal whipping girl, right? Punish her for her mother's sins. . . . Right, Old Man? Was *that* why you went down to that store where she worked and made her eat a cigarette? Shoved her face into a plate of fried eggs? . . . My guess was that "Papa" had shoved his daughter around *plenty.* He'd beaten his wife, hadn't he? His own mother back in Sicily? Why would he have spared a harelipped daughter he didn't even claim?

No *wonder* Ma was afraid of her own shadow. No *wonder* she'd never been able to stand up to Ray. . . . She'd let history repeat itself when she married Ray Birdsey, that much was clear. *I tell you one thing, buddy boy! If you were* my *flesh and blood . . . No kid of mine would ever . . .* That prick had spent a lifetime disclaiming us.

BOMBING OF IRAQ "NEAR-APOCALYPTIC." *"A United Nations report says the U.S.–led allied bombing campaign had wrought 'near-apocalyptic' results upon the infrastructure of what had been, until January of 1991, a rather highly urbanized and mechanized society. Now, most means of modern life support have been destroyed or rendered tenuous. Iraq has been relegated to a preindustrial age, but with all the disabilities of postindustrial dependency on an intensive use of energy and technology. In terms of human casualties . . ."*

Desert Storm, Rodney King: the front page told the same old story, over and over and over. Might made right—whoever had the "smart" bombs, the billy clubs. . . . Duck and cover, Thomas! You want mercy? Forget about God. God's a picture from the five-and-ten hanging up on Ma's bedroom wall. Pray to the oppressor, man. . . . *I'm sorry, Ray. I won't do it again. I'm sorry. . . .* The never-ending soundtrack from Hollyhock Avenue. The both of them over there—my mother, my brother—crying and begging the tyrant for mercy. . . . HEAVY RAINS EXPECTED THROUGH WEEKEND. . . .

Well, I tell you what, Ma: I may have been asleep at the wheel for the past couple of months, but I'm *wide* awake now. I'm getting him out of here if I have to drive up to Hartford and pound on the governor's front door. If I have to *torch* this fucking place.

SINGER ERIC CLAPTON'S SON, 4, DIES IN FALL. . . .

Sheffer's door swung open. "Hey, *paisano.* Sorry I'm late," she said. "You wouldn't *believe* the day I've had. First thing this morning, my daughter says—"

I held up my hand to shut her up. "I want my brother tested for HIV," I said.

She stopped in her tracks. "Any, uh . . . any particular reason?"

I'd promised Drinkwater three times during our five-minute phone conversation the night before that I'd keep his name out of it. So I shrugged back at her. Just to be on the safe side, I said. Whenever I visited Thomas, he complained about sexual assaults.

"We've gone over all this," she said. "Remember? Those are delusions. Homosexual panics." She sat down at her desk. "When he starts off on that track, the best way to handle him is—"

"I don't want him handled," I said. "I want him tested."

"The wards are monitored day and night, Dominick. If there's any prison rape going on, it's in his head. Let it go."

I told her I could make the request through Dr. Chase if she preferred. Or through her supervisor. What was her name again?

"Dr. Farber," Sheffer said. She and Farber had a meeting scheduled for later that afternoon. If I really insisted, she could broach the subject with her then—let me know in the next couple of days what Farber had said.

"If the meeting's this afternoon, why can't you let me know later this afternoon?"

She clenched up a little. They had just added three new patients to her caseload, she said; her monthlies were two days overdue; her daughter had woken up that morning with an ear infection. If she could get back to me later that day, she would *do* that. If she couldn't, I would just have to wait. She was dancing as fast as she could. "And anyway," she said, "I already *know* what Dr. Farber's going to say. If they started letting patients' families call the shots on medical testing, it would open up the floodgates."

My brain ricocheted like a pinball; I was forming the idea as I spoke. "You been . . . you been following that mess out in Los Angeles, Sheffer? The way the cops beat that black guy to a pulp out there? . . . You seen the videotape of that?"

"Yeah," she said. I watched her try to figure out where I was going.

"Pretty brutal, huh? Man, they *savaged* that guy." My adrenaline was pumping; my sneakers were tapping against the floor, a thousand beats a minute. "Public's probably not in much of a mood to tolerate brutality-in-uniform right now, huh?"

She waited.

"Remember . . . you remember that night last October when they checked my brother in down here? The way that guard roughed *me* up? You witnessed that, didn't you? Popped your head out the door right in the middle of things?"

Sheffer's face looked neutral—official. She neither confirmed nor denied.

"I followed your advice, by the way. Remember? You told me to have myself examined. And I did. Went down to the clinic. Had them take pictures and everything. That was good advice you gave me, Sheffer. To get things documented. Get proof."

She glanced up at the intercom on her wall. "What's your point?" she said.

"I just made my point, *paisana,*" I said. "Tell Dr. Farber I want Thomas tested."

At about five that afternoon, I received a call from the office of Dr. Richard Hume. Hume was Farber's supervisor's supervisor, if I had the food chain right. It was Hume who'd chaired the Security Board hearing that had sentenced my brother. His secretary asked me if I'd please hold. You had to love the power boys: *they* called *you,* then made you sit and wait for the privilege of talking to them.

When Hume came on the line, he chatted with me like we were a couple of cronies down at the Elks Lodge. He was *glad* I'd raised my concern with Ms. Sheffer, he said. Inmates' families were an integral part of the treatment team at Hatch; it was right there in black and white in the hospital's mission statement. His feeling on *this* particular request, however—my request for an HIV test for my brother—was that it was unwarranted at this particular point in time. The Institute tested patients periodically, but on their own schedule. Dr. Hume said he hoped I could see things from the hospital's position: that it was neither cost-effective nor a wise precedent for the administration to—

"*I'll* pay for it," I said. "I want it done by someone who's not in-house, anyway. Not on the payroll down there. I'll make all the arrangements and pick up the tab. Just tell me when I can bring someone in."

Dr. Hume said I didn't understand. If they allowed patients' families to dictate medical testing schedules, it could become a procedural nightmare. Thomas had been tested when he entered the hospital last October, he said. His next test would be—"

"Who's *your* boss?" I said.

There was a pause on the other end. "Excuse me?"

"Who do *you* answer to? Because I ain't going away. Me *or* my pictures."

There was a pause. "Which pictures are those, Mr. Birdsey?"

I couldn't tell if he was in the dark about what I'd told Sheffer or just pretending he was. Couldn't second-guess what Sheffer might have passed on. But I decided to go for broke. "The photographs of my black-and-blue groin," I said. "My scrotum swollen up like a basketball. One of your goons down there roughed me up the night I checked my brother in. Kneed me a couple of good ones south of the equator. 'Rodney Kinged' me a little, I guess you could say. In front of witnesses."

I hadn't thought any of this out yet—had just leapt without a net. But I was in it now. We were *all* in it—Sheffer, this talking head on the phone, my brother and me. "Got myself examined the day after it happened," I said. "I wanted everything documented, you know what I'm saying? And now, Jesus, with all this stuff out there in L.A. The way people are feeling right now. . . . I just . . . I kind of figured you might *want* to okay that test for my brother. Spare yourself Excedrin headache number seven, you know?"

No comment on the other end.

"I mean, how's one little test going to cause any 'procedural nightmares,' right? If everything checks out okay, I just go away. Me *and* my complaint."

Hume asked me if there was any particular reason why I felt an HIV test might be warranted. Drinkwater's face flashed before me. *Keep my name out of it.*

"My brother talks all the time about guys breaking into his cell at night," I said. "It's probably his paranoia—I realize that. I just want to—what do you call it?—err on the side of caution. Don't *you*?"

I waited out his big speech about State of Connecticut

policy and Hatch's unswerving concern for patients' well-being. Thanked him for the call. Told him I'd be contacting my attorney.

There was dead air for several seconds. "Well, you do what you have to do, Mr. Birdsey," he finally said. "And we'll do the same. Because unless I'm reading you incorrectly, what you're doing here is attempting to bribe me. And if you think—"

"Hey, look, Big Shot," I said. "All I'm trying to do is defend a guy who can't defend *himself*. A guy who doesn't belong anywhere *near* that happy little funhouse you run down there. All I want to do is make sure no one down there has been *butt-fucking* my brother."

He hung up in my ear.

I stood there, my heart pounding like a son of a bitch. *Goddamn it, Birdsey! That was exactly the way* not *to*—I lobbed the fucking phone across the room. Watched it bounce against the refrigerator door and clatter back across the floor. Land at my feet.

Well, asshole, I told myself. *You just did* something. *For better or worse, you just put* something *in motion.*

A couple of beers later, Hume's secretary called back. The test I'd requested for my brother had been scheduled for Monday afternoon of the following week. Thomas's physical would be conducted by hospital personnel, his blood screened by a representative of the Haynes Pathobiology Laboratory.

I tried to think past the beer buzz I'd started. Hume was doing an about-face? Giving me a reasonable facsimile of what I wanted? The victory spooked me. "Why'd he change his mind?" I said.

The secretary said she knew nothing about it; she was merely passing along a message from "the boss."

"Then put 'the boss' back on," I said. "I'll ask him myself."

A minute or more later, she came back on the line. Dr. Hume had stepped away from his desk, she said. When I told her I'd hold until he "stepped back," it was, oh, wait a minute. His attaché case wasn't there. He must have already left for the day.

"Then give him a message," I said. "Tell him I'm bringing my *own* doctor for my brother's test."

Why had he caved in? Was he running scared about something? I'd go over to the clinic first thing in the morning—try and talk to that Chinese doctor, Dr. Yup—the one who'd had friends killed in Tiananmen Square. She'd called what that guard had done to me "oppression." I wanted Dr. Yup to examine my brother.

Sheffer called the next afternoon, sounding shell-shocked. "Dominick?" she said. "Can you meet me later on today? Something's come up."

"Is he hurt?" I said. "Did someone hurt him?"

Uh-uh, she said; there was no new incident. But when I told her I could be down at Hatch in half an hour, she hesitated. Asked me if we could meet someplace else—someplace outside of Three Rivers, maybe. Her shift was over at four-thirty, she said. How about that little coffee place up across from the university? The Sugar Shack—did I know where that was? She could get there by, say, five-fifteen?

Why was she suggesting someplace a half-hour drive away? I told her I'd be there. Asked her again if my brother was all right.

Nothing bad had happened to him that day, she said. Beyond that, she wasn't sure of anything anymore. She'd explain when she got there.

The coffee I'd bought her when I got to the doughnut shop was stone cold by the time she finally walked in. She sat and gulped it anyway. She looked like hell.

"How's your daughter?" I said.

Her eyes narrowed. "Jesse? Why? What do you mean?"

"Her ear infection?"

"Oh. Better. The doctor put her on Amoxicillin. Thanks for asking." She fished out a pack of cigarettes. "Can you smoke here?" she said. "Is that a sin at this place?" I pushed the little tinfoil ashtray over to her side of the table.

I told her I was pretty sure I knew what she was going to tell me—that I'd figured it out on the drive up there. "He's positive, right? They got nervous and jumped the gun on the test. He's got it."

She shook her head. I was right about their jumping the gun, she said; they'd done blood work on Thomas that afternoon. But the results weren't in yet. They wouldn't know anything until Monday morning.

"So they'll already *have* the results by the time he's examined officially. Right?"

She nodded. Picked up her coffee cup and started shredding it. "Dominick?" she said. "What I'm going to tell you may not even *be* about Thomas, okay? Not directly, anyway. And maybe not even *in*directly. Just remember that." Her face contorted a little, the same way Dessa's did when she was struggling not to cry. She took a long drag off her cigarette. Exhaled. It was killing me, but I sat there and waited. Kept my mouth shut for once in my life.

She asked me if I recalled a conversation we had had several months back about one of the psych aides down at Hatch—a guy named Duane Taylor. I'd commented about him the day I'd stood at her office window and watched Thomas out on recreation break. It was before my security clearance had come through—before I'd won the right to visit my brother face-to-face. Did I remember?

I saw Thomas standing out in that rec area, waiting to get his cigarette lit while Duane Taylor entertained his pets. Ignored my brother's existence. "Dude with the cowboy hat, right?" I said. Sheffer nodded.

There'd been an assault at Hatch a week ago, she said. On the night shift. The administration had kept it so hushed up that most of the staff hadn't even heard about it. "Which is pretty impressive, given *our* grapevine," she said. "But this was *top* secret."

"Who got assaulted?" I said.

"Duane Taylor. He was attacked from behind in the men's bathroom in Unit Four—garroted with a wire and left for dead."

I waited. Sheffer looked up—met my eyes. "Taylor works *days,*" she said.

He'd been rushed to Shanley Memorial and then helicoptered to Hartford Hospital. It had been touch and go for several days, but things were starting to look better for him. They weren't sure yet about permanent damage: oxygen deprivation to the brain.

She took another drag. Gave her cigarette a dirty look and stubbed it out, half smoked. "I gave these things up on Jesse's last birthday," she said. "She wanted two things: for us to go to Disney World and for me to stop smoking. I couldn't exactly swing the Magic Kingdom, so I got her a Carvel cake and a Rainbow Brite doll and let her flush my cigarettes down the toilet to the tune of 'Happy Birthday.' A whole carton of them. And now, tonight, I'm going to go pick her up smelling like cigarettes." She started to cry, then stopped herself with a laugh, a shrug. "Oh, well, my credibility's shot to hell, anyway. Right?"

"Did my *brother* assault the cowboy? Is *that* what you're telling me?"

She shook her head. "Oh, god, no, Dominick. Is that what you . . . ? *No.*"

The guy who'd strangled Taylor confessed that same night, she said. A patient in one of the other units—she couldn't tell me his name. It was probably all going to come out in the papers, anyway, though. Unless the hospital could keep it hushed up, there was going to be so much garbage flying around, people would have to duck. The "official version" of Taylor's assault—the one the administration was now circulating—was that the vendetta had started over a pint of tequila. Taylor and a friend of his—a guard named Edward Morrison—had apparently been running a black market business. Alcohol and cigarettes. Pills. "That much the hospital's willing to cop to," Sheffer said. "According to the version the hospital's floating, Taylor had collected money for the tequila and then reneged. But it *wasn't* about booze. It was about sex. . . . Well, power. Rape."

The word made me tense up. "What's this got to do with Thomas?" I said.

She rested her chin against her propped-up hand. Looked at me with defeated eyes. "Hopefully, nothing," she said. "From what I heard today, it was mostly the younger kids that Taylor went after—guys in their twenties. But I don't really know the whole story yet, Dominick. I don't think I know anything anymore." For the next several seconds, we sat there, saying nothing, Sheffer's cigarette smoke swirling around us.

"Let me ask you something," she said. "How many times over the past several months would you estimate I've reassured you about your brother's safety? Twenty-five times, maybe? Thirty? Now multiply that number by my caseload. Twenty-five or thirty reassurances times forty prisoners' families. . . . God, I just can't believe how naive I've been. How *stupid*." She thrust her tiny, shaking hand across the table. Grabbed my hand and shook it. "How do you do?" she said. "I'm Lisa of Sunnybrook Farm."

She drew cigarette after cigarette out of her pack—snapped each in half, throwing the refuse into her mangled coffee cup. "Guess what else I found out today?" she said. "Through the grapevine, of course—not through our ever-responsible leadership. I found out that as much as a quarter of the population at Hatch may be HIV-positive. That we've got an *epidemic* down there, Dominick, and the administration's just been looking the other way. Sitting on the statistics. Can't have any bad PR now, can we?"

Dr. Yup accompanied me to Hatch on Monday afternoon, examined my brother, and drew blood samples which she transported personally to the testing lab her clinic used. The results of both the hospital's and Dr. Yup's tests were the same: Thomas was HIV-negative. But Dr. Yup's report also cited the presence of anal warts, contusions, and other indicators of rectal penetration.

As a result, my brother was wanted for questioning in the ongoing state police investigation of Duane Taylor and Edward Morrison. I asked to be in attendance during these interviews and was, at first, denied. But Thomas dug his heels in and insisted to both the police and the hospital administration that he would speak to no one unless his brother was there. The cops met his condition. During the four interviews that followed, I sat by Thomas's side.

This was weird: one of his inquisitors—the head of the investigation, actually—was State Police Captain Ronald

Avery. I recognized him immediately: one of the two cops who'd caught Leo and me smoking reefer out by the trestle bridge that night and hauled us in for questioning. Avery had been young back then—dark-haired and lean, probably not even thirty. He'd been the most decent of the three cops who'd grilled us that night. Now his hair was gray, his body droopy. Looked like he was maybe four or five years away from retirement. But he'd held onto his decency—his sense of fair play. He was patient with Thomas throughout the interviews—as nonthreatening as possible, given what the cops needed to find out.

Thomas's account of his involvement with Morrison and Taylor kept changing. Morrison had assaulted him but Taylor never had, my brother said. Then he claimed *both* had. Then, neither. During the last interview, Thomas insisted that Taylor had smuggled him out of Hatch one night and flown him in secret to Washington, D.C., for a meeting with the CIA. Vice President and Mrs. Quayle had attended. The Quayles had been involved in Taylor's cover-up from the beginning and were also behind the lacing of Sudafed with cyanide that had killed those people out in Seattle. Now that he was letting *that* cat out of the bag, Thomas told Captain Avery, he was probably a walking dead man.

As I sat there listening to Thomas, exchanging looks with Avery and Dr. Chase, the hospital liaison, I thought about something Dr. Patel had said several months before. *Two brothers are lost in the woods. One of them may be lost forever.*

But lost or not, Thomas could still walk. Could still be sprung from Hatch.

The second unexpected phone call I received from Ralph Drinkwater came a few weeks before the story about Morrison and Taylor hit the papers. "I have something for you," he told me. "Something you might be able to use."

"Use how?" I said.

"That's up to you. Just keep my name out of it. You coming to see him in the next couple days?"

I told him I could get down there by midafternoon the next day.

"That works," he said. He told me I should park at the far end of the visitors' lot. Leave my car unlocked.

What was this—Watergate? Drinkwater as Deep Throat? Why was he *doing* this?

After my visit with Thomas the next afternoon, I got back in the Escort. Looked in the glove compartment, under the seats. Nothing. But on the drive home, I thought of the sun visor. And when I flipped it down, a piece of paper fell into my lap: a memo from Dr. Richard Hume to a Dr. Hervé Garcia, stamped "Confidential."

He was a cynical bastard, Hume. That much was obvious. Whatever his reasons had been for entering the healing profession, he'd lost *his* way in the woods, too. In the memo, he advised Garcia against Hatch's "trumpeting these numbers to Hartford" but asked, rhetorically, whether "John and Joan Q. Public" wouldn't silently approve of the HIV stats if they ever *were* released—the "weeding out of the population," courtesy of AIDS.

Social Darwinism, I thought. Mr. LoPresto rides again. Jesus. I was beginning to understand, I thought, how Drinkwater fit into all this. Future casino millionaire or not, Ralph still needed to take a whack at the oppressor. He was *still* looking for justice.

Well, for whatever reason Ralph had stuck that stolen memo under my visor, I *had* him now: Hume. If I played it right, that confiscated memo was the key that could spring the lock. Get my brother out of there. *La chiave,* I thought. Here it is, Ma. This is what we've been waiting for.

The first two attorneys I talked to declined to represent me on ethical grounds. The third one didn't seem to understand what I needed. "We'll sue as a group," he said. "The families of the infected inmates. They might pay *millions* to make this go away."

"My brother's not infected," I reminded him.

He nodded. I'd be an "unofficial" member of the families' group, he said. A silent partner. The terms could be discreetly hammered out beforehand. He wouldn't be representing me *per se,* but because I'd provided the memo, he'd make sure I ended up sitting just as pretty as the rest of them.

I stood up, shaking my head. "You know something?" I

said. "You're like every sleazy lawyer joke I ever heard rolled into one. Go fuck yourself." For emphasis, I kicked his wastebasket on the way out of there, sent his trash flying every which way but loose.

"Constantine Motors. Leo Blood speaking. How may I help you?"

I asked him if he still had that fancy suit of his.

"My Armani? I'm wearing it as we speak, Mr. Birdseed. Why do you ask?"

"Because I need an actor in a fancy suit."

He was resistant at first: Leo, who had taken stupid risks his whole life. Who'd *thrived* on asshole stunts like the one I was proposing. It was illegal, wasn't it? Posing as an attorney? What if this Dr. Hume recognized his picture from the car ads?

"Oh, yeah," I said. "Like you're some big celebrity."

"Well, what about Gene? If he ever found out about a bag job like this, he'd fire my ass on the spot, son-in-law or no son-in-law."

"Best thing that could happen to you," I said. "Come on, Leo. You don't have to *say* you're an attorney; you just have to *imply* you're one. This is the role of a lifetime."

"I don't know, Dominick. I'd *like* to help you out, but—"

"Look, I *need* you, man," I said. "Tommy needs you. This is our only shot."

It was the first day of April when we finally "communicated directly" with Hume. I'd made three appointments by then; his secretary had called at the last minute and canceled every one of them. "Fuck it," Leo said after he stood us up the third time. "Let's ambush the prick." By then, I think he'd convinced himself he *had* passed the bar exam.

We waited across the highway from the state hospital's main entrance. "I just hope it doesn't backfire on Thomas," I said.

Life had backfired on Thomas, Leo reminded me. All we were trying to do was start a little *forward* motion for the guy.

When Hume's silver Mercedes left the grounds, I started

the car, pulled into traffic behind him. Tailed the lead-footed bastard down the John Mason Parkway, onto 395, and then to I-95. "This asshole related to the Andrettis or something?" Leo said.

"I just hope we're not making a mistake," I said.

Leo told me to stop thinking and just follow the bastard.

Hume exited the highway in Old Saybrook, drove along Route 1 for a couple of miles, and then pulled into the parking lot of some little seafood restaurant. Soon as he got out of the car, the doors of a red Cherokee parked a couple of cars away swung open. A young couple approached Hume—early twenties, maybe. The girl was a dead ringer—*had* to be his daughter. There were hugs and kisses, a slap on the back for what looked like the boyfriend. "So how's Yale treating you two?" I heard Hume ask.

I told Leo this was a bad idea—that we should just go. We could catch up with him at Hatch. He couldn't *keep* canceling appointments.

"Look, Dominick," Leo said. "I been wearing this stupid suit to work three days in a row now. Even *I'm* getting sick of it. Come on. It's showtime."

Briefcase in one hand, the other outstretched toward Hume, Leo led the way. "Dr. Hume? Excuse me, sir. If we could have a minute?" He introduced himself as Arthur verSteeg. Pumped Hume's daughter's hand, the boyfriend's. "Arthur verSteeg. Pleasure to meet you. Arthur verSteeg. And this is my friend Dominick Birdsey."

That was when the smile dropped off of Hume's face. He told the two Yalies to go inside and order him a Glenlivet on the rocks.

He stood there, scanning the memo for a couple of seconds, scowling. Then he ripped it up. Sent the pieces fluttering into the breeze coming off Long Island Sound.

"Go ahead, there, Doctor," Leo said. "Do your thing. We got *plenty* of copies."

"What is it you're after?" Hume said. "Money?"

"Justice," I said. "The only thing I want from you is—"

Attorney verSteeg cut me off. "Why don't you let *me* handle this, Mr. Birdsey?"

* * *

On April 11, 1991, the Psychiatric Security Review Board, meeting in executive session, reversed its decision of the previous October and transferred Thomas to the custody of his family, effective at once. The Board strongly advised, however, that Thomas be placed immediately in a fully staffed, fully secured nonforensic psychiatric hospital.

"Well, congratulations," Sheffer said, shaking my hand in the hallway outside the conference room. "I don't know how you did it—and hey, I don't *want* to know how—but it worked. You got him out of here."

I nodded, not smiling. "Be careful what you wish for. Right?"

Sheffer warned me that after six months in maximum security, freedom was going to be a shock to my brother's system. That as tough as it had been for him at Hatch, there had been a kind of safety in all that surveillance, regimentation, and predictability. He was apt to feel unmoored, unsafe—*too* free. And it had happened so abruptly; she'd never *seen* such expediency. There'd been no time to prepare Thomas, emotionally, for his release.

Or to get him placed.

She was doing some "fancy footwork," she said. Settle, Thomas's old stomping ground, was out of the question. With the facility definitely closing later that year, they weren't admitting any new patients. They were transferring people *out* of Settle. No exceptions. Her second choice, Middletown, was still a possibility. She had a call in to admissions there; she'd try to get me an answer by the end of the day. *All* of them, she said—she, Dr. Chase, Dr. Patel, the nurses—advised against Thomas's staying with me. It just wasn't safe, she said.

"Hey, my cooking's not *that* bad," I told her.

Sheffer didn't return my smile. "Dominick, I'm going to say something to you that you're probably not going to appreciate. But I'll say it anyway."

"Now there's a surprise," I told her.

"You're *arrogant,* Dominick. You're a real good guy and everything. I know you're trying hard to do what's best for him. But . . . well, I just hope your arrogance doesn't end up putting him at risk. Just be careful."

It was *arrogant* for a guy to want to keep his brother safe? If I hadn't managed a little *arrogance,* he'd still be stuck down there indefinitely. But I didn't want to get into it with her—it wasn't the time or the place. So I smiled, thanked her for all she'd done. Hugged her back when she held out her arms to me.

If Sheffer thought *I* was arrogant, she ought to read that thing of my grandfather's.

When I walked with Thomas through Hatch's front security gate and out into the sunlight, he stopped at the top of the stairs and squinted. Looked up at the sky, the swaying trees. He moved a step or two closer. Slipped his stump into the pocket of his jacket.

"Well," I said, "you're a free man."

"I'm a walking target," he said.

Dr. Chase had changed his medication the week before the hearing—some new psycholeptic the FDA had just approved. If there was going to be any improvement, it would take a couple more weeks to kick in. But I was hoping to avoid having to hear who was after Thomas now—hoping to savor one afternoon's worth of victory. It was only later that I realized how scared he must have been walking out of there—how terrifying all that sudden open space would be to someone who saw the enemy behind every tree, every steering wheel.

"You want to go over to my place and watch some TV?" I said. "Stop over and see Ray? . . . You hungry? Want to get something at McDonald's or someplace?"

He wanted to go to the Falls, he said.

"The Falls? . . . Yeah, all right. Sure. You're a free man now. You can do whatever you damn want to. We got the whole afternoon to celebrate."

"Celebrate what?" he said.

"Your *freedom,*" I said.

He snickered. Mumbled something I didn't catch.

"What'd you say?"

But he didn't answer me.

* * *

I pulled into the little six-car lot adjacent to the Indian cemetery. Together, we passed the graves on the way to the path that led up to the Falls.

"Remember her?" Thomas asked. He had stopped—was pointing at Penny Ann Drinkwater's small stone.

I nodded. Saw Penny Ann's body going over the Falls, the way it had in my nightmares. Saw Eric Clapton's son dropping from the sky like Icarus. . . .

"You, uh . . . you seen much of her brother while you were down there?"

"Who?"

"Ralph Drinkwater. Her brother." The guy that got you out of there, I thought. The guy who gave me the ammunition I needed to make you safe again. "He's on the maintenance crew. Remember? You told me you saw him once down there."

"Down where?"

"At *Hatch*."

He looked over at me. Looked me in the eye. "We're cousins," he said.

What was he talking about? "We're *brothers,* man."

"*Her* cousins," he said. He nodded toward Penny Ann's gravestone.

"Yeah, whatever," I said. "Come on. Let's go check out the river."

•

We trudged up the dirt-packed path at the far end of the graveyard. It was a muddy mess from that two-day deluge we'd had. Thomas was out of shape—winded from the sloping incline. A breeze tossed the boughs of the pine trees, the bare branches of the pin oaks. My emotions were all over the place.

When we got to the mountain laurel grove, I told Thomas something I'd never told anyone before, not even Dessa: that we were standing at my favorite spot. "Another couple of months and these bushes'll *explode* with flowers," I said. "Early June, it happens. I'll bring you back here. I come out every year."

Thomas told me that mountain laurel leaves were poisonous. Had he mentioned that there'd been several attempts to poison him while he was at Hatch? He was pretty sure the Republicans were behind it.

I didn't answer him. Some celebration, I thought. Started hiking again toward the sound of spilling water.

When we got to the clearing—the waterspill—we stood there, side by side, watching the river drop over the edge and down. It was roaring something fierce that day—spring thaw, plus all that rain we'd had. I looked over at Thomas, studied his grooved, joyless face. It showed, out there in the sunlight: all the wear and tear of the past six months, the twenty-odd years before that. He looked older than forty-one. *Old.* Part of me was scared to death about what the next weeks and months were going to entail. But another part of me was happy, in partial disbelief, still. He's *here,* I remember thinking. He's with me, Ma. I got him out of there.

And now what?

Turning to me, Thomas said something I couldn't hear over the roar of the water. I cupped my hand against my ear and leaned closer. "What?"

"I *said,* this is a holy place."

I nodded. Stiffened a little. The Holy Roller rides again, I thought. But as I looked into his eyes, I felt my annoyance turning into something else. Pity, maybe? Relief? Love? I couldn't say, exactly. I started to cry. Like I said, my emotions were all over the map.

Thomas asked me if I believed in God.

I didn't answer him at first. Groped around for some response that wouldn't trigger one of his Jesus speeches. Then I said something I hadn't planned on at all.

"I *wish* I did."

He took a step closer to me. Reached over and put his arm around me. In my peripheral vision, I could see his stump.

"The Lord Jesus Christ is your savior, Dominick," he said. "Trust me. I enflesh the word of God."

"You do, huh?" I said. "Well, whattaya know?" With the sleeve of my jacket, I wiped the tears out of my eyes. Took a step or two away from his embrace.

Neither of us said anything else for a while—two or three

minutes, maybe. It was me who finally broke the silence. "Know what someone told me once?" I said. "That this river is life—that all it's doing is flowing from the past into the future and passing us along the way. . . . Kind of puts things in perspective, doesn't it?"

He kept looking at me. Said nothing.

"Hey, speaking of the past," I said. "You know what I've been reading? Papa's life story. Our grandfather. . . . He dictated this whole long thing before he died. In Italian. I had it translated. . . . Ma gave it to me. To both of us."

"Papa," Thomas repeated.

"You remember the way she'd go on and on about him? Papa this, Papa that. . . . Turns out, though, that he wasn't quite the big superhero she made him out to be. He was, I don't know . . . he was *mean*. Some of this stuff I'm reading is really—"

"Can we walk down to the water?" Thomas asked.

"What?" It miffed me a little, him interrupting me—not giving a shit about it.

He wanted to take his shoes and socks off, he said. Wade into the river.

The water was too cold right now, I said. I'd take him back there again when it got warmer and he could wade as much as he wanted. In June, maybe, when the mountain laurel came out. "Come on," I said. "You hungry? I'm getting hungry."

I'd planned just to grab some stuff at the drive-thru. Going out in public was something I figured I'd reintroduce him to gradually. And restaurants were always a wild card with Thomas—even *before* Hatch. But when we pulled into the parking lot at McDonald's, who pulls in right behind us, honking, but Leo. He jabbed his finger, pointing to the parking space next to his.

Leo talked too loud. Shook Thomas's hand a little too vigorously. He insisted we join him inside—that we let him treat us both to lunch. Since our victory against Dr. Hume, Leo had begun calling himself Victor Sifuentes, after that guy on *L.A. Law*. Righter of legal wrongs in his designer suits. He didn't really get it; it was all play-acting for Leo. But this was partly his celebration, too, I thought. So we went inside.

The whole friggin' place was decorated in *Little Mermaid.* The bright lights and colors, the jostling into the crowded line: it made my brother edgy. He kept squinting, blinking his eyes. At the register, Leo and I gave the woman our orders and I turned to Thomas. "You know what you want?" I asked him. He just kept staring up at the menu board, dazed.

"He'll have a Big Mac and a shake," I told the cashier. "What kind of shake you want, Thomas? Chocolate?"

He said he wanted a Happy Meal.

"Thomas," I said. "Those things are just for little kids."

"Oh, that's okay," the counter woman butted in. "He can get one if he wants. Anyone can buy them."

I told her thanks, but he *didn't* want one.

"Yes, I *do,*" he insisted.

"Come on, Birdsey," Leo said. "If my man here wants a Happy Meal, then that's what I'm buying him. What kind you want, Thomas? They got hamburger, cheeseburger, McNuggets."

"McNuggets," Thomas said. "And black coffee for my drink."

The cashier told us Happy Meals didn't come with coffee. Just soda or milk.

"Get him a coffee if he wants a coffee," Leo told her. "Charge me extra for it."

When she went to get our stuff, Leo recited lines from some movie: something about a chicken salad sandwich, hold the bread, hold the chicken between your legs. Shut up, I felt like telling him. It had been a mistake to come here. I'd wanted to take things slow, keep everything nice and simple. I felt scared. Felt like screaming at someone.

"I have to go to the bathroom," Thomas said.

"Oh. Okay. I'll go with you," I said. "Leo can get our stuff."

Thomas said I didn't need to go with him.

"I know I don't," I said. "I have to go, too, okay? You mind?"

He complicated things, of course: locked himself in a stall for about ten minutes. Made me stand there, a nervous wreck, calling to him every thirty seconds or so. "You all right? . . . You still alive in there?" Guys kept going in and out, sneaking looks. I felt just like I'd felt on that school field trip when he'd locked himself in the bus toilet. Felt what I'd felt that first year in college, in our dorm: Thomas and Dominick, the Birdsey weirdos.

"Jesus, I thought maybe you fell in or something," Leo said. He'd picked out a booth by the front window, but Thomas balked. Said he'd be a sitting duck in that spot.

"Stop it," I told him. "Just sit down. No one's after you." He scoffed at that.

Leo started getting up, gathering our stuff together. "Sit down," I said. "This seat's fine. He's got to—"

"What's the big deal?" Leo said. "There's a glare here anyway. Come on."

When we were repositioned over by the restrooms, Thomas told Leo that he'd worked at this McDonald's once.

"Not this one," I said. "You worked at the other one—the one on Crescent Street."

"No, I didn't," he said.

"Yes, you did." *You freaked out there, remember? You trashed the drive-thru speaker because aliens were calling to you. Remember?*

"No, I *didn't,*" he insisted. "I worked at this one."

"All right, fine," I said. "It was this one. *I'm* screwed up."

Halfway through his meal, Thomas decided he had to go to the bathroom again. This time, I let him go himself.

"Listen," I told Leo. "I know you meant well, but he's got to be trained how to function *normally* in public. Someone who's forty-one years old shouldn't be getting a kiddie meal. Shouldn't be allowed to play Hide-in-the-Back-of-the-Restaurant-Because-They're-Out-to-Get-Me."

Leo filled his mouth with fries. "Hey, you know what my daughter said to me the other day, Dominick?" he said. " 'Take a chill pill, Dad.' And now let me pass on those words of wisdom to you, okay? Re-*lax.* Take a chill pill, man. He's doing fine."

"Yeah, *right,*" I said. I reached inside Thomas's Happy Meal and pulled out his complimentary Little Mermaid figurine. Waved it in Leo's face like evidence.

* * *

Thomas and I were sitting in my living room watching *The People's Court* when Sheffer called. "Okay, I got him a placement," she said. "It's a little complicated, though. Middletown can take him, but they don't have a bed until Friday."

"All right," I said. "He can stay here until Friday."

Sheffer said she had a better idea. She'd called down at Hope House, one of Thomas's old group homes. They'd agreed to bend the rules a little—take him for the interim. "They're short-staffed, but I really feel it's better than having him stay with you."

"Why?"

"What are you going to do, Dominick—strap him into his bed? Stay up all night like a sentry?"

You go downstairs now, Dominick. This wouldn't be any fun for you. Run up and tell us if Ray is coming. . . .

All right, I said. I didn't really have a problem with him going to Hope House for a couple of days. For one thing, it was close. For another, he'd *liked* it down there once upon a time—had done better at that place than anywhere else.

I was *already* feeling a little over my head, I admitted to myself after I got off the phone. That stupid trip to McDonald's had done a number on me. And if he was over at the group home, it'd give me time to get him some of the things he'd need for Middletown: new jeans, underwear, shampoo and shit. Maybe I'd get him some sneakers so's he didn't have to keep clomping around in those stupid wingtip shoes.

I made us some supper and then drove him over there. Checked him in. The nighttime superviser cataloged aloud the personal belongings Thomas had wanted to bring: "Shoes, Bible, religious book, other religious book . . ." Oblivious of the admission process, Thomas sat there thumbing through his old favorite: *Lives of the Martyred Saints*.

I left him watching TV in the rec room, slumped in a stuffed chair. On the wall above his head, a cloth banner proclaimed Hope Springs Eternal at HOPE HOUSE!

"See you tomorrow," I said. Bent down and kissed the top of his head, for some reason. I went home, got about halfway through a beer, and started dozing. Slept the sleep of the dead. . . .

The telephone startled me awake.

Missing? . . . What did she mean, missing?

He had to have left the premises somewhere after 2:00 A.M., the woman said, which was when they'd done their last bed check. The police were on their way.

Ray was already awake when I called. I swung by the house and picked him up on my way down there. The director kept throwing her hands into the air, insisting that this was the kind of thing that resulted from underfunding. Before all the cutbacks, she said, things like this just plain didn't *happen*.

Jerry Martineau was one of the cops who showed up. Ray and I gave them a list of the places where Thomas might have gone—places where he'd hidden in the past when his paranoia closed in. Martineau said he was optimistic. He'd only been missing for a couple of hours at most. In another fifteen, twenty minutes, the sun would be up in earnest—they'd be getting a nice, early start. They could probably get reinforcements by mid-morning, if necessary. He'd call in some off-duty guys if he had to. They'd find him for us.

I nodded back at Martineau—let him spoon-feed me a little optimism. But I knew Thomas was dead. Had felt his dead weight since I'd swung my legs out of bed after that phone call. It was like I was dragging around some dead part of myself.

Ray and I drove out to the Falls, parked at the Indian graveyard, and tramped up the path. It was my idea.

"Thomas? . . . *Hey, Thomas!*" Over and over, we called his name into the thundering water, the fog that hovered over the river below.

Ray said something I couldn't hear.

"What?"

"I said, let's hike down there. Walk the bank. We can walk down as far as the footbridge, then cross over. Walk the other side back again."

I shook my head. Realized I didn't *want* to be the one to find him.

We walked back down the path, got back into the Escort. I was fishing through my pockets, trying to find my keys, when Ray started up.

"I *know* I rode him too hard when he was a kid," Ray said. "I *know* I did." His eyes were panicky, pleading. "But she namby-pambied him all the time; I was just trying to toughen him for the world." He threw open the door and got out again. Circled around and around the car. "Jesus," he kept mumbling. "*Jesus.*"

They found his shoes and socks first—on the bank a couple hundred yards or so past the waterspill. Then, a little before noon, two guys from the rescue squad found his body, in waist-deep water, caught up in the branches of a fallen tree. He'd floated about half a mile or so down, they figured. The rocks had banged him up pretty bad; there were scratches all over his face from that tree. Ray told me. He was the one who went down and identified the body. The water was rushing around and over him, someone told him; the current was still pretty wild from all that rain. Later, the coroner's report would estimate the time of drowning at somewhere around 4:00 A.M.—right about the time my phone had rung. "Accidental," he'd ruled, in spite of the shoes and socks. Whether Thomas had jumped or fallen in, none of us could really say.

It was nighttime by the time all the necessary paperwork had been gotten through. Ray and I sat at the kitchen table over on Hollyhock Avenue and drank from the same bottle of Scotch we'd cracked open the night Ma died, four years earlier. We were both pretty quiet at first, both exhausted. But the second round gave us our tongues.

"They tried to *tell* me to take it slow," I said. "His social worker, the doctors. They said he'd feel unprotected after six months down there. But *I* knew better than any of them, of course. *I* was the big expert. . . . You know what it is? I'm *arrogant.* That's *my* problem. If I wasn't so goddamned arrogant, he'd probably be alive right now. He'd be okay."

Ray reminded me that Thomas hadn't been okay since he was nineteen years old.

"Yeah?" I said. "Well, that doesn't make me feel any *less* like shit."

Ray said he wished to hell he had gone down and seen him at Hatch—had made the effort. But after that stunt he'd pulled over at the library—Jesus Christ, cut off his own *hand*—well, that had been the last straw for him. "I'd had it," he said. "But not *you*. You fought that kid's battles his whole life." Ray's big, rough hand—hardened by work, by war—reached across the table. Hovered above my shoulder for a second or two and then clamped on. Squeezed. As if we were father and son after all. As if, now that Thomas was dead, I could forget the way Ray had treated him. . . .

I stood up from the table, reeling a little from the Scotch. From my stepfather's alien touch. "I'm cocked," I said.

"Stay here tonight, then," he said. "Bunk up in your old room."

If I'd been sober, I would have refused. Would have gone home instead of up those stairs and down the hall to the left—to the Dominick and Thomas Museum.

I flopped face down on the bottom bunk—Thomas's bed. Ray came in with a set of sheets. "Just put 'em on the bureau," I said. "I'll get 'em in a few minutes."

"Okay," he said. "Get some sleep. It's over now."

The hell it is, I thought. Numb as I was from Scotch and loss and exhaustion, I knew *that* was a crock of shit.

Somewhere in the middle of that night, I dreamt I was Thomas—that it was *Dominick* who had drowned, not me. I heard a lock tumble, a metallic squeak. The door of my prison cell gaped open. "Oh, hi, Ma," I said. "Guess what? Dominick died."

I awoke in the morning on the top bunk—*my* bunk. The sheets were still on the bureau where Ray had left them. I had no recollection of having climbed up there. The bedroom was flooded with light. I lay still, staring up at the ceiling—at the brown water stain over by the window that had been there since we were kids.

And as I lay there, a memory came back—the earliest memory I've ever had. I was four again. It was so vivid, so real. . . .

I'm supposed to be lying down, taking my afternoon nap because I'm a big boy. I'm all by myself. No Thomas. Before my Thomas got sick, we took our naps together on the big bed in the spare room. Ma would lie between us, telling us stories about two best friends, a little bunny rabbit named Thomas and a little monkey named Dominick, who always gets into things.

Now Ma's too busy to tell stories. She has to take Thomas's temperature and bring him medicine and ginger ale. She gave me some books and told me to look at the pictures until I felt sleepy. I know the letters in the books: m *is for* Ma, t *is for* Thomas. *I hate the pages where I scribbled on the pictures. Ma asked me who did it and I told her Thomas did. Thomas is a bad, bad, bad, bad boy.*

My Thomas has to live in the spare room now. I can draw pictures for him, but I can't have them back. I can call to him through the door, but he can't answer me because his throat hurts and because he needs rest. Yesterday he answered me in a tiny, tiny voice. Did he shrink? Is he a little tiny Thomas now? "What does Thomas look like?" I asked Ma. She says he looks the same, except he has red dots on his neck and on the tips of his elbows and something the doctor called a strawberry tongue.

I like strawberry Jell-O better than green Jell-O. When I lick the top, Ma says, "Don't do that! Only bad boys do that." One day yesterday I stuck my tongue out in the mirror. No strawberries.

And I am MAD at my Thomas. I had to get a shot and it hurt. I wanted Ma to take me to get my shot, but Ray took me. He told me the needle wouldn't hurt but it did *hurt. When I cried, Ray squeezed my arm and said, "What's the matter with you? Are you a tough guy or a sissy?" When Thomas and I both cry, Ray says, "Wah, wah, wah, it's the little sissy girls." That makes us cry more.*

Ma says last night Thomas got the shakes so bad that his teeth chattered. "Show me!" I said and she made her teeth go click click click. Thomas gets to drink all the ginger ale he wants AND there's a bowl of Jell-O downstairs in the refrigerator that's only for him, not me. When I go downstairs, I'm going to lick it. My Thomas is a bad, bad boy.

When you're big, you don't have *to take naps. You can stay up late and watch the Friday night fights and drink highballs. When I'm big, I'm going to fill up the whole bath-*

tub with ginger ale and jump in and drink it and not even get sick.

When Ma was a little girl, she got scarlet fever like Thomas. She had to stay in bed all day long and bang a pot on the wall for Mrs. Tusia next door if she needed help because her father was sleeping. . . . Little boys and girls used to die from scarlet fever, Ma says. Or they got better but grew weak hearts.

I'm not supposed to get off this bed until after my nap. If I get up, Ma is going to tell Ray. Naps make me mad. They're dumb. I'm rolling and rolling up in my bedspread. I'm a hot dog and my blanket is a hot dog bun. . . . Now I stand up and my bed's a GIANT TRAMPOLINE! I jump! And jump! All the way up to Heaven where Mrs. Tusia lives. . . . She died. She was old. Some men came and carried her down the steps and drove her away. But I won't let those men take my Thomas. I'll shoot them. Pow! Pow! Pow! Ma says Thomas can come out of the spare room in one week, but I don't know when that is. I think maybe he's dead. The man on Ma's opera records is dead and he can sing. "Ladies and gentlemen, Enrico Caruso!" They used to be Papa's records. Papa is in Heaven, too.

Why can't *I see Thomas? Why* can't *I touch the drawings he's touched? This nap is making me hot. And thirsty, too. I'm thirsty for some ice cold Canada Dry ginger ale.*

"Ma! . . . Ma-aa?"

"What?"

"Can I get up now?"

"After your nap. Now go to sleep!"

The brown stain on the ceiling turns into that monster. It's going to come alive and fly down the hallway and bang the door down and eat my brother. Unless I shoot it.

My bedroom rug is a giant lake. The flowers in it are stones. They lead to the edge. . . . I can make it. I do *make it.*

I'm at the doorway. Sometimes Ma says *she's going to tell Ray when I'm bad and then she doesn't tell him. The hallway is a boiling river. You can't swim in it. You have to fly over it in your airplane, the Song Bird. "Hang on, Thomas. I will save you!" I'm Sky King. This isn't my hand; it's my radio.*

I fly the Song Bird over the boiling river to Thomas's door. Stare at it. Listen.

I put my fingers on the big diamond doorknob. It twists, clicks open. I enter the room. . . .

It's dark in here. The shades are pulled down. It smells bad. The fan from Ma and Ray's room is in the window, blowing a breeze. I walk over to the bed. Stare at my Thomas. I say his name over the whirr of the fan. "Thomas? Thomas Birdsey! . . . THOMAS JOSEPH BIRDSEY!"

Thomas's mouth is closed. I want to see his strawberry tongue. Is he asleep or dead? . . .

He sighs.

I move closer. His shirt is off. I see the bones beneath his skin. His hands are raised above his head, palms out, as if some cowboy had said, "Stick 'em up!" and then shot him anyway.

Chattering teeth, a strawberry tongue. . . . Suddenly, I know something I never knew before. Thomas and I are not one person. There are two of us.

I move closer, bend down to his ear, and whisper my name.

He twitches. Swats at the sound.

"Dominick!"

We are different people.

Thomas is sick and I am not.

He's asleep. I'm awake.

I can save myself.

forty-one

13 *August* 1949

My wife and I never discussed what the *dottore* had said—that another birth could stop her heart. Ignazia moved her clothes downstairs into Prosperine's bedroom and I made no move to claim that which rightfully belongs to a husband.

After the night of Prosperine's story, I refused to eat the food cooked in my own home. I had a little meeting with *Signora* Siragusa, my former landlady. She agreed to make my meals for four dollars a week and an extra fifty cents to still that wagging tongue in her mouth. Each evening on the way to work, I walked past the *signora*'s and picked up my dinner pail. Each morning, at the end of my shift, I stopped there again to leave the pail and eat my breakfast in the *signora*'s kitchen. The third meal I skipped or bought downtown—'*Mericana* food with no taste, everything drowning in that yellow glue they call gravy. Bread that tasted more like cotton than bread.

Ignazia was insulted that I would not eat what she cooked. This she told me with her frowns and banging pot lids and her sighs sent up to Heaven—never with her words. We shared no words, either, about all that Prosperine had told, though I was sure those two whispered plenty about it behind my back. If I had been their fool before that night, I was their fool no longer. The Monkey's drunken *confessione* had made me dangerous to them both.

If I had been *'Mericano*, I might have run squealing to the police and repeated what Prosperine had revealed. Maybe the law would have taken that crazy monkey out of my house and sent her back across the ocean. But a Sicilian knows to keep his eyes open and his mouth shut. I wanted no more scandal brought down on the name of Tempesta—no fingers pointing at my *casa di due appartamenti* as the place where murdering women had gone to hide. Sometimes I told myself Ignazia was *not* Violetta D'Annunzio, that hellcat who had fouled herself with men and tricked a husband into swallowing glass. Maybe Violetta had paid the price for her sins and been put in the ground in Palermo, as Prosperine had said. But this I could only make myself believe for an hour or an afternoon and then, again, I would know the terrible truth.

In the first weeks of her life, Ignazia's harelipped baby suffered from *colica* and cried during night and day. Ignazia cried, too, and was plagued with female problems. Tusia's wife told my wife all problems would go away—that mother and child would be at peace—once the girl was baptized.

"No *battesimo*," I told Ignazia. She had come upstairs to my bedroom—to the room where she had once slept by my side—to ask my permission.

"Why not?" she said. "So that my suffering can continue? So that both my babies can be lost to God's mercy?"

I had said nothing to Ignazia about the boy's purification in the pantry on the morning of his birth and death. My fear was that my action may have angered God—a boy christened with dishwater by a father who had thrown cement at a priest, forsaken Jesus Christ. . . . If I had harmed the soul of my own son with blasphemous *battesimo*, I would not then send the redhead's daughter into Heaven.

"I once ordered two priests off this property," I told Ignazia. "I will not be *ipocrita* now and go crawling back to them on my knees."

"Then I'll bring her to them," she said. I shook my head and told her she would do what I told her to do.

"What kind of selfish father would keep the gates of Heaven locked against his own child?" she shouted. "Yours is a wicked sin!"

"Better shut up your mouth about *my* sins!" I told her. "Worry, instead, about your own—the ones you committed here with that no-good redheaded mick in New York and the ones you committed back in the Old Country."

She turned her face away from mine and hurried out of the room. But I followed her down the stairwell and through the downstairs to the back room. She was face down on the bed, sobbing against the pillows. From the doorway, I warned her—made it clear that if she defied me and had the girl baptized in secret, she would pay a high price. "If I discover such a plan," I told her, "you and your scrawny friend will live to regret it."

In spite of all I knew, now, about Ignazia—in spite of the fear and hatred that stood between us—my *passione* for her was stronger than ever. My eyes could never stop following her around a room. Her face and *figura* were a constant torment. A hundred times a day, I kissed her mouth, unpinned her hair, ripped away her buttons, and had what was mine, but these actions I took only in my *immaginazione*. . . . Sometimes I would torture myself by thinking of those filthy pictures the *fotografo* had taken of her back in the Old Country—see those photographs being passed around from man to man. I would shudder at this, my fingers twitching with the desire to slit the throats of those faceless men. My wife in the hands of every man except her lawful husband! But mixed with the torture of knowing that those photographs existed was the excitement of what they had captured. To have unspent lust for a murderous wife was a terrible thing—a living Hell!

Sometimes in my dreams she loved me—submitted to me with obedience and desire as a good Sicilian wife surrenders herself to her husband. I would wake from these reveries in a rush of joy and excitement. Then sadness would overtake me and I would clean myself, wipe away the spilt milk of desire that made children but could make none for me. Once, too, I had a very strange and terrible dream in which Ignazia shared her *passione* with my dead brother Vincenzo, while I sat on the bed and combed her long hair. In that dream, I was happy, not jealous, and woke only slowly to the humiliation of the story my dream had told me. I could almost hear Vincenzo laughing at me from Hell.

Sometimes my longing for my wife's flesh would reach me at work and become an ache so strong that it distracted me. Even the giggles of the homely little spinning girls could excite me . . . even Nabby Drinkwater's boastful talk of his pleasures at the whorehouse on Bickel Road.

One morning, my hunger led me past the *signora*'s and down to that place on Bickel Road where the fat Hungarian woman kept her whores and house cats. The inside of that place reeked of cabbage and cat piss. I paid and she called to a skinny servant girl who was busy polishing the staircase railing. "This way," the girl said, and I followed her up the stairs. I thought she was taking me to a whore, but when I entered the room, she closed the door behind us. She was no more than fourteen, fifteen . . . did not yet have the meat of a grown woman on her bones. While I did what I did, she looked the same as she had looked polishing that banister. I left that house with a promise that I had gone there for the first and last time. But I went there again and again, each time worrying that I would run into Drinkwater—that that goddamned Indian who worked beneath me would know that I shared his weakness for the flesh. That the devil that had claimed my brother Vincenzo had claimed me, too.

I always had the same girl. Always, after I finished my business, I made her put on her clothes and leave quickly. I would stare at the wall while she dressed herself, my shame taking over once my *ardore* had been spent. Then I would rise from that cheap bed, button myself, and walk back to my house where I lived with two murderous women and a redhaired baby whose mouth was split and whose soul remained stained with original sin.

One day, a little after the war was over, I read in the newspaper that that dog-faced Monsignor McNulty had keeled over and died from a bad heart. The paper said little Father Guglielmo had been named acting pastor of St. Mary of Jesus Christ Church—the church's first *pastore Italiano*. I was happy for both McNulty's death and Guglielmo's promotion. I had never had quarrel with *Padre* Guglielmo—he had only been the other one's whipped dog. In my mind, I wished him well.

Not a week later, when I went to the boardinghouse for my breakfast, I found Guglielmo waiting for me in *Signora* Siragusa's kitchen. The old *signora* fluttered around in a sweat, making special cakes and *frittata* and frying dough in her finest olive oil, as if the Pope himself had dropped in. "It's good to see you again, my friend," Guglielmo said. "It's been a while now, hasn't it? How's your wife these days?"

I told him my wife was fed and cared for.

"And your child? A daughter, isn't it? Why, she must be walking by now."

I nodded. Ambush, I thought. But I told myself I was too clever to be taken in by such *imboscata* as this. *Signora* Siragusa could put all the sugar she wanted on that fried dough of hers, but I was not about to let that redhead's daughter be baptized.

Two years had passed since the girl's birth. The war against the Germans had been fought and won and American Woolen and Textile had dyed all the wool for the sailors' coats. Tusia's wife and *Signora* Siragusa had both spoken to me about my refusal to let the child be christened. Even Tusia himself had had the nerve to lecture me one morning while I sat in his barber's chair getting my free shave. (Tusia thought he was a big shot now—*pezzo grosso* in both Knights of Columbus and Sons of Italy.) "*Scusa*, Salvatore," I told him, right in the middle of his big speech. "You better mind your own business before I decide to raise your rent." That shut him up, all right. For the rest of my shave, the only sound in the shop was the voice of Caruso coming out of Tusia's Victrola.

In the years I had been away from the church, Father Guglielmo's face had broadened a little and his hair had turned to silver. Now he held out his hand for me to shake it. *Signora* Siragusa stopped her bustling to watch. The three of us waited to see what that hand of mine would do.

I shook Guglielmo's hand. Like I said, I had never had a quarrel with that little priest who had once sat out in the parlor at the *signora*'s and tried to help me talk sense into my brother Vincenzo. More than just the color of Guglielmo's hair had changed. He smoked *sigaretti* now, one after another, and he no longer carried himself like a man afraid of the world. He asked about my health and my work and called me by my first name. I congratulated him on his appointment as *pastore* and said I hoped the old monsignor had gone to Hell where he belonged.

Signora Siragusa gasped and slapped at me with her dishcloth, but Guglielmo thanked me for my good wishes. "May I sit and join you for breakfast and have a little talk?" he asked me.

"Oh, *si*, *padre*, of course you can sit with him!" the old *signora* answered for me. "Sit! Sit and rest yourself! I hope you brought your appetite."

"Talk about what?" I asked. "If it's a baby's *battesimo* you want to talk about, then save your breath."

The priest shook his head. "I want to talk about masonry," he said.

"Masonry? What about masonry?"

He asked the *signora* if we might have a word or two alone. She poured our coffee, put plates before us, then hurried out of the room. Guglielmo and I said nothing more until she left.

I had guessed he was talking in priestly metaphor—that he would now begin a big speech about *battesimo*, how each "brick" in place was a stairway to God. But he surprised me. He spoke of *real* bricks, *real* mortar. St. Mary of Jesus Christ Church would soon break ground for a new parochial school, he said. A parish school had long been his dream, but Monsignor McNulty had consistently opposed the idea as too costly and too much of a headache. The Catholic schoolchildren of Three Rivers had always, by necessity, had to board in New London and separate from their families during the week. Now the archbishop had listened to Guglielmo's plan and approved it. An architect and builder from Hartford had been hired. But the archbishop had warned the little priest of the trouble he would call on himself if the project failed or became too costly for the church.

What he needed, Guglielmo said, was a knowledgeable and thrifty parishioner to supervise the construction and represent the interests of the parish. "I have no knowledge in these areas myself," he said. "And the school, successful or not, will stand as testimony to my stewardship. If my pastorate is to be permanent, Domenico, then the new school must be sound, inside and out. I come to ask your help."

I took a bite of *frittata*, chewed and chewed it. Took another bite. "How much does this job pay?" I asked.

Pays nothing, he told me. I would have to donate my time and talent. But the school would open in two years, maybe three—in plenty of time for my little daughter to attend. "That's all I can offer for compensation, Domenico," he said. "I appeal to the father in you, not the businessman."

"Fathers are breadwinners," I said. "Working for nothing puts nothing on the table."

"And yet," he said, "we have the miracle of the loaves and fishes to guide us." He told me he asked no more of me than an hour or so each day. Perhaps I could inspect the building site in the morning on my way home from the mill, or in the late afternoon when I had risen from my sleep. He just needed someone to keep an eye on the daily progress of things. "As Jesus is steward of us all, I seek a steward for this school where children will be taught His holy word," he told me.

For some crazy reason, his talk about the loaves and fishes made me think of Prosperine's story: how the witch had made two rabbits from one and killed off the schoolteacher. My head was mixed up with magic and miracles.

I finished my breakfast and stood. "Too busy," I told him.

"Too busy or too angry, still?"

I looked at his face, then looked away. He asked me to sit back down again, to give him just a minute more of my time. So I sat.

"The day your brother fell from the roof was a terrible day for us all," he said. "For you. For me. For the monsignor, too. From his deathbed, he spoke with regret about that day and prayed to God for forgiveness for having mocked your poor brother. I, too, have regretted my weakness on that day—my failure to intervene, to act as God would have wanted me to. . . . Look at me, please, Domenico. Let my eyes see your eyes."

It was hard to look, but I looked.

"Here in this kitchen, I hold out the olive branch. It is long overdue, but it is offered in good faith. Let bygones be bygones. Let anger be buried in the ground. Forgive me, Domenico. I appeal to you as a brother would appeal."

His mention of brothers made me look away again. "I have no brothers," I said. "The police shot one and a monsignor's curse pushed the other off the roof. And as for your school, there are plenty of other bricklayers in the parish. There's Riccordino or Di Prima. There's that Polack who lives on—"

He placed his hand on my hand to stop me. "You once told me," he said, "that you had to leave a life of priestly study and learn the trade of masonry because of family obligation."

"Si," I said. "I left my books, left the seminary school in Rome, to clean up my brother Vincenzo's mess. There was no choice. It was what my father ordered."

"Everything that happens is a part of God's plan," Guglielmo said. "Your beautiful home on Hollyhock Avenue would not stand today if you had no knowledge of brick. Why not let a religious school become the bridge between your early spiritual training and the masonry you learned in obedience to your father?"

When I closed my eyes against tears, I saw Papa and Sicily and my life as it had been. . . . Saw again the eyes of the Weeping *Vergine* who had, long ago, beckoned me to be a priest and save souls. Among all the children of Italy, it was I to whom the Holy Mother had revealed her sadness. . . . And now . . . and now I lived an ocean away and dyed wool instead of saving souls. Now I practiced a priest's celibacy in my own home and walked to Bickel Road to fuck a skinny whore because a baby inside my wife would kill her. Sitting in that kitchen across from Guglielmo, I saw how far my life had strayed from the life I had meant to live, and I wiped away the water in my eyes.

"I *could* ask Di Prima or Riccordino to help me, Domenico," Guglielmo continued. "I *will* ask one of them if you refuse. But it is *you* I have chosen to come to first. It is *you* whose guidance I seek."

We talked for over an hour that morning—never once about the girl's baptism, but only about buildings and bricks. We ate more of the *signora*'s cooking and drank more of her coffee, then cleared the table and had a look at the blueprints Guglielmo had brought along. By the time we left that kitchen, I had agreed to help him. Passing through the parlor on my way out the front door of the boardinghouse, Guglielmo and I took all of *Signora* Siragusa's hugs and kisses and God-blessings; she had been sitting and praying her rosary all the time we were in the other room. Praying for *me*, she said—the son she always wished was her own, even though she had four sons already.

Guglielmo was right to trust my guidance the most—and lucky to have me. Di Prima laid brick crooked—what help would he have been? And Riccordino was *pazzu*. Without Domenico Tempesta watching, those Yankee builders from Hartford would have robbed the church blind and built a school that the wind would knock over. As for that poor priest, he didn't know what a joist was for or which part of a trowel scooped the cement! But I knew, all right. Those Yankee builders would do the job right and they would not overcharge the church for a single nail as long as Domenico Onofrio Tempesta was watching.

My supervision of the construction meant daily inspections and then a visit to the rectory or the building site with Guglielmo. One afternoon, a Saturday, he took out his pocket watch during our meeting and said he had to go next door to hear confessions. Did I, perhaps, wish to join him there?

I shook my head. "I'm beyond all that," I said.

"Beyond absolution, Domenico? No, no—never beyond God's forgiveness. Jesus loves all His flock, even the lamb that strays." He said he often prayed that peace would come to my home—that he hoped his prayers would someday light a candle in my heart.

I told him to save his prayers and candles for lambs whose houses had not been cursed by an unholy *monsignore*.

"But your home can be a peaceful one," he said. "The key to serenity is forgiveness."

I stood and watched him walk toward that church where sinners waited for him, but I did not follow him there. He knew nothing of women—murderous or otherwise. He knew as little about my home as he did about building a brick schoolhouse.

But all that next week—at home, at American Woolen, even in the upstairs room on Bickel Road—I thought about what that priest had said—that he had prayed for peace to come to 66-through-68 Hollyhock Avenue. That peace was possible.

I was the first one inside the church the following Saturday. I got there early, hoping to go in quickly and leave. I didn't want to make confession—none of that. Too busy. I wanted only to ask Guglielmo a question or two, the kind of questions I could not ask from across his desk at the rectory, or walking along the periphery of the new school's foundation. Like pebbles inside my shoe, these questions plagued me. The further I went, the more they let me know they were there.

Guglielmo was late getting to the church that afternoon. Someone else came in—DiGangi, it was, I remember. Street sweeper. Then another man and his wife, a group of schoolgirls. The door creaked open again and again. We all sat in the pews and waited.

Father Guglielmo came in through the back of the church and lit the lights. He cleared his throat as he passed me but did not look or say hello. He went inside the confessional and closed the door. The others stood and formed a line. Not me. Let this line of sinners pour out their guts to him, I told myself. I'm not here to confess. I'm here only to ask my two questions.

For hours, sinners came and went. A few I recognized. Many I did not. I had stayed away from that church for six years. By four o'clock, the church was empty again, except for Guglielmo and me. He sat in his box, waiting. I sat in the pew, telling myself to stand, to walk in there, kneel, and ask Guglielmo my questions. But finally, when I did stand, I turned and walked the other way, slowly at first and then faster, up the aisle and out through the vestibule. I pushed open the heavy wooden doors—escaped into the cool air. I was out of breath, even though I had wasted the afternoon just sitting.

That next week, all through our meetings about the school, I waited for Guglielmo to bring up my presence inside the church the Saturday before—to ask me why I had gone to confession but not confessed. No doubt he would have known my voice, would have been waiting to hear what sins the supervisor of his beloved school had on his soul. I had my answers ready for him—I was busy, he had been late. I didn't want to confess anything, anyway—what was on my soul was *my* business. But he did not mention my being there. Maybe he hadn't seen me after all. I kept my mouth shut and so did Guglielmo.

At work one night, Nabby Drinkwater—that goddamned Indian who worked for me—kept dropping the bolts of wool. "What's the matter with you?" I asked him.

"I don't know," he said. "My arm's numb."

Then his eyes rolled up into the back of his head and he dropped dead. Died just like that—answering my question one minute, dead the next.

I had never had much use for Drinkwater. He was lazy, sneaky—his mischief with the bottle had cost my brother Pasquale his job at the mill. But he had worked under me, now, for over ten years. On the nights when he *felt* like working, that skinny Indian could do his share and more. He was forty-two and I was forty-two. Right to his knees, he had dropped, right in front of my eyes. I caught him before he fell, before his face hit the concrete floor. I did that much for the son of a bitch.

There was just a small turnout for his funeral—half a dozen workers from the mill (none of the bosses) and a couple of men I didn't know. He had a colored wife and four half-colored children—two sons, two daughters. Drinkwater had never talked much about family. I was pallbearer. The wife had asked the mill agent to ask me. What could I say—no? . . . There was no man of God at the grave, only someone in a shabby suit who did the talking. I didn't know if Indians could go to Heaven, but if they could, I was pretty sure Drinkwater hadn't gotten there. For one thing, he broke continually the ninth and tenth commandments (coveting wives and goods). He'd been a drinker, in trouble with the police from time to time. He had known his way to Bickel Road. He had bragged about it sometimes on dinner break—to the other men, never to me. Me, he respected. . . . He'd never been the best worker at the mill, but never the worst, either. One of the owner's sons or sons-in-law—one of those sons of bitches—could have come to his funeral, shown him a little respect at the end. A little thanks for all those nights that he'd done his work. But as soon as a man keeled over, American Woolen and Textile forgot he had ever lived and breathed.

The next Saturday afternoon, I went back to the church—this time not at the beginning of confession but near the end. I waited until it was just Guglielmo and me. But before I could get myself off the pew, he turned off his little light and came out of the confessional.

"Oh, Domenico," he whispered. "I thought everyone had gone. Have you come to make confession?"

"No *confessione*," I said. "I came to ask two questions."

"About the school?"

I looked away. "Not the school," I said. "No."

He waited but I said no more. "All right, then. Better come in." He went back inside the confessional and closed the door. Lit his light again.

Inside the box, I knelt facing his shadow behind the screen. My hands trembled in front of my face. Guglielmo said nothing. I said nothing. Finally, he told me that since we were inside the confessional, maybe I should ask my questions within the context of the traditional confession. That would signal God to listen, he said, and ensure the sanctity of whatever it was that I had to say. "All right?" he asked me.

"All right," I said. Then I said nothing.

He began for me. "Bless me, Father, for I have sinned. . . ."

"Bless me, Father, for I have sinned," I repeated. "But never as much as I have been sinned against!"

The shadow put a finger to its lip. "To prepare yourself for the Eucharist, Domenico—to be truly penitent—you must examine only your own soul. Leave other sinners to examine theirs. You must try to practice humility."

"Humility?" I said. "Believe me, Father, a man who lives with two murdering women learns to be humble in a thousand different ways."

"Murdering?" he said. "Why murdering?"

"Never mind that," I told him. "That's the business of my home, not the church."

Silenzia. And then Guglielmo asked if I understood what he had said about the sanctity of the confessional. "Whatever you say or ask here is between you and the Almighty Father," he whispered. "I am only acting as His representative."

"*Scusa*, Father," I said. "Where do your people come from? In the Old Country?"

"From Tivoli," he said. "Not far from Rome."

"Ah, *Roma*," I said. "I lived in Rome once. I saw how Romans live. In Rome, people say what's on their minds—they shout their troubles from the steps of the Colosseum if they like and no one even takes notice. But

I am *siciliano*. The code of silence runs through my veins. For your people it is different. Southerners—*siciliani*—honor the word of God and *omertà* equally."

"Why have you entered the confessional, Domenico, if not to confess?"

"I told you already. I wish to have two questions answered—questions that rob me of my sleep. . . . And maybe I come to bring a little peace to my home—to undo the curse your boss left me."

"My 'boss,' Domenico, is the Lord Almighty."

"You know who I mean: that old fart of a monsignor."

Guglielmo began twice to say something and twice changed his mind and stopped. When he spoke the third time, he advised me that to form a covenant with God, I must break my covenant with *omertà*, the code of silence. "God is looking for a sign of your faith in Him above all else, Domenico," he whispered. "Only after you have given it can you be set free of the shackles that you yourself have forged."

"That I have forged?" I said. I meant to whisper but forgot. "You were there that day he called a curse upon my home. 'A house where priests are ordered to leave is damned from the peak to the foundation.' His exact words stay in my ears. You were there—you heard! And fifteen minutes later, my brother fell to his death. A year after that, I marry a wife who whored with other men but with her lawful husband is as chaste as the good Sisters of Humility! That goddamned Irish priest was the blacksmith who forged my shackles. And if there's justice, he burns in Hell for it!"

Father Guglielmo's shadow made the sign of the cross and asked me to speak more softly. "It does you no good, Domenico, to enter God's house and malign one of His children," he told me. "But for the moment, let us walk another path. You said certain questions keep you from sleeping. What questions? Tell me your doubts and let me try to help you."

I pushed aside the curtain and looked out into the church to make sure we were still alone. I wanted no big ears to hear my business.

"I wonder . . ." I whispered. "I worry sometimes that I may have damned the souls of my brother . . . and my son."

"Damned them?" he said. "Damned them how?"

I poked my head again outside the confessional. Still no one there.

"Father, you remember that my brother Pasquale had a certain peculiar weakness."

"A weakness?" Guglielmo said. "Do you mean a physical weakness or a spiritual one?"

"I mean . . ."

"What is it, Domenico? Tell me."

"*Padre*, is it a terrible sin for a man to refuse a wife and take his pleasure from a monkey?"

At first there was no response from the priest. And when he did speak again, he brought me back to the subject of damnation. "Why, exactly, do you worry that you've sent your brother's soul to Hell, Domenico?"

"You were there! I threw the cement! If I had not lost my temper, I would not have angered the old priest and he would not have cursed my house. Then Pasquale would not have fallen." Here, my voice cracked a little, but I continued. "After my brother Vincenzo was shot by that policeman, you stood by his bed at the boardinghouse and administered the sacraments to that rascal—prepared him for his journey beyond life. But poor Pasquale . . . I *tried* to interest him in a wife, *padre*. Believe me! In that respect, I am clearly blameless. But all Pasquale ever wanted was that hairy creature of his. The devil himself must have sent that monkey up from Hell or Madagascar! To others, I denied there was anything unnatural between them, but privately . . . the way those two would stare at each other . . . Who knows what went on down there in the *signora*'s cellar? *Pompino*! *Ditalino*!

For all I know, that brother of mine got down on his knees and found a way to fit his thing inside her 'coin of no value'!"

"Shhh," Guglielmo said. "Shhh. Lower your voice, please, Domenico. And remember as you select your words that we are in God's house."

"*Scusa, padre,*" I said. "*Scusa*, please. At the mill, bad words float in the air along with the woolen fibers. Sometimes I forget. *Scusa*, again, *signore*. *Scusa*, to you, too, God. Forgive me."

"Go on, please, Domenico," he said. "Unburden yourself."

"In all other ways, my brother Pasquale was a decent man—nothing at all like that hooligan Vincenzo. Quiet and shy. Eager to help. Oh, he had a stubborn streak, all right; he sometimes drank a little more than he needed to. Even without alcoholic spirits, he was . . . he was never quite right—never all there. Even as a boy. He would laugh at the strangest times. Maybe it was his early work in the sulphur mines, who knows? He was my father's *caruso* and Papa was all the time hitting him on the head for something. Maybe that's what shook up his brains. . . . But he was never sneaky or mean-spirited, my brother Pasquale. Never *perverso*, either, until that she-devil of a goddamned monkey got ahold of his balls!"

"Domenico."

"*Scusa, padre, scusa*. I beg your pardon. There I go again, ha ha. . . . I tried to stop what was going on—tried to arrange for a wife to distract Pasquale. Really, God cannot fault me on that score. . . . Oh, to have not one but *two* brothers who bring such shame down on a father's name! What a heavy cross for an eldest son to bear! But at least Vincenzo did his funny business with humans. To share such a *passione* with a monkey and then to die without absolution. I'm not saying I'm blameless, *padre*. If only I had not thrown the cement. If only . . ."

"Domenico, did you ever witness your brother and the

monkey . . . perform these perverse acts?" Guglielmo whispered. "Did Pasquale ever boast or confide in you about them? Are you speculating about this or was there proof?"

"Pasquale talked about almost nothing," I said. "You could work with him for a whole day and hear nothing come out of him except a belch after dinner. He was a private man. . . . As for proof, one morning when I went down to the cellar to wake him up—that was my habit when we lived at the boardinghouse: to get him up for work when I came home to go to bed. One time I saw . . . I saw . . . *Scusa, padre,* but I have never spoken about what I saw that morning."

"Tell me, Domenico. What you say is between you and God, Who loves all sinners."

"Pasquale was asleep on his cot and smiling. That monkey was sitting on his belly and playing . . . playing with the buttons on his pants."

"But Domenico, if that is the only thing—"

"*Scusa, padre,* let me finish." This next part I whispered, I was so ashamed. "Pasquale had *cazzu duro*. The monkey was . . . exciting him."

Father Guglielmo cleared his throat. Once, twice. A third time. Then, for a minute or more, he was as silent as Pasquale himself. "And that was your only proof?" he asked.

"That, and the whispers of every *Italiano* in Three Rivers, Connecticut. One day in the street, Colosanto the baker asked me if it was true my brother's little monkey played the pipe for him!"

"Gossip is the devil's work, Domenico," the priest said.

"*Si, padre,* but when it came to my brother and that monkey, plenty of my countrymen are ready to help Satan with the job!"

"But surely, Domenico, what you saw in the *signora*'s cellar is by itself no proof of sin. It is a natural thing for a man to become . . . aroused in his sleep."

"Si, *padre*, it is a natural thing."

"But, of course, less natural if it happens when a monkey plays with his buttons."

"Si, *padre*. Far less natural when *that* happens."

He was quiet for several seconds and in the silence, behind the screen that separated us, I could almost hear the moving gears in his brain. "Nevertheless, Domenico," he sighed, "your brother, most likely, was entirely innocent of the immoral acts you put on his head. He may well have died without a trace of mortal sin on his soul. You yourself have said what a good man Pasquale was—how generous, how giving to a brother trying to reach his dream."

"Si, *padre*," I whispered, "but what was he dreaming that morning while the monkey made the pipe in his pants? What was he giving to *that* filthy creature?"

"You must remember, Domenico, that Pasquale was a child of God. Let that comfort you. Perhaps . . . perhaps he merely loved another of God's creatures in the manner of St. Francis. To suggest otherwise, based only on what you saw, is—"

"All over town they were laughing at him!" I interrupted. "At *both* of us! Crude jokes! Filthy talk about the two of them making a baby together. . . . Was St. Francis's brother ever called 'monkey's uncle' and laughed out of a barbershop?"

"The things people said don't make your brother—"

"Even that goddamned monsignor accused him of it—that so-called man of God! Never mind cement—I should have thrown a rock at the head of that son of a bitch! If Pasquale is in Hell, then that priest must be in a worse place."

"D*omenico*!" Father Guglielmo said. "I remind you again that the late monsignor's sins and his salvation are between God and him. Your brother's, too. To wish damnation on one and assign damnation to the other is to presume yourself capable of doing God's work for

Him. Humble yourself, man! Pray for humility. If you seek absolution, you must put yourself in a state of grace."

"I seek answers to my two questions," I reminded him. "My question about Pasquale and my question about the dead boy."

"Ask me your questions, then. Ask them directly."

"Did I damn my brother to Hell by throwing the cement?"

"You did not, no, because you have no power to do so. Only God has the power to damn or save sinners. What is your other question?"

"The child who died at birth when the girl was born? The boy born to my wife and me . . ." Here I had to stop.

"What a day of conflict that must have been for you and Ignazia," Guglielmo finally said. "Death and life—joy and sadness—together."

"No joy," I said. "What joy is there in holding your dead son and watching your wife bear the fruit of her sins with another man? Where's the joy in learning your wife is another man's *puttana*?"

"Such harsh words," Guglielmo said. "Such serious accusations. To call your wife first a murderer and now a whore . . ."

"That's my business," I reminded him. "My question is not about Ignazia. It is about the boy who died."

"Ask it, then, Domenico."

I told him the story of that terrible night: how Prosperine had come to get me at the mill and how I had refused to leave to fetch the *dottore*. Told how I had discovered the boy in the pantry while Ignazia was birthing the girl—how I, who had first ordered a priest off my property and forsaken the church, had then baptized my dead son with dirty dishwater and cooking oil. Later that day, I said, I had called God a monster.

"What is the question you wish to ask, Domenico?"

"I fear . . ." I whispered, "I fear that I have damned my

son's soul forever with sacrilegious baptism. That is the worry that robs me of sleep, even when exhaustion is deep inside my bones. Have I banished my own flesh and blood from Heaven by baptizing him with dishwater in my godless house?"

Father Guglielmo leaned closer to the screen. His lips brushed against it as he whispered. "In what you did, you were acting as God's agent, just as I act here today as His agent in the pardoning of your sins. The condition of your soul at the time you performed the baptism was not at issue. Do you see the distinction between serving God and assuming you can take over His work for Him?"

I said nothing.

"Let me answer your question directly," he said. "You did *not* damn your son's soul. Your action delivered the child from limbo and placed him into the arms of Jesus Christ, his Savior, Who will keep him safe for all eternity. The boy's baptism was valid."

At these words, my breath caught and I leaned my head against the wall of the confessional.

He asked me if I had ever told Ignazia about the baptism I had performed in the pantry that morning.

"I told no one," I said. "Until now. Until here."

"You must go home and let your wife know the child was baptized. It will comfort her to hear that her son is with God—that her dead child is safe with Jesus. Then you must bring the boy's sister to—"

I began to weep. I couldn't help it, could not have stopped, even if the whole church had suddenly filled up with people watching me. The sobbing and bellowing that came out of me that late afternoon must have nearly shaken the holy statues off their pedestals. I had no pride that day, only shame.

Father Guglielmo left the confession box and stood holding open the curtain for me. "Come out," he said.

He led me to a nearby pew where I sat and wailed into my own hands and into my coat sleeve, into my handkerchief, into Guglielmo's handkerchief. The *padre* sat and waited, his hand clamped onto my shoulder.

When I could speak again, I broke for good from Sicily—smashed *omertà* into a million pieces and let out my life. Fast and crazy I talked, with no order, no sense. "Slow down," he kept telling me, but I could not slow down. My arms flew, my fists drummed against the wooden pew. I shouted one minute, whispered the next. I told him how the Weeping *Vergine* had revealed herself to me as a child and how my father had yanked me from my religious studies so that I could clean up my brother Vincenzo's dirty business. "That's what set me on a path of sin!" I shouted. "And now that young boy from Giuliana whom the Holy Mother once visited is a man who visits the whorehouse on Bickel Road." I told how I had beaten Ignazia on our wedding night and how that goddamned *magistrato* in Giuliana had beaten me out of my father's gold *medaglia*. I described the screams of my brother's monkey when I threw it over the bridge and my mother's screams on the day my brothers and I left her behind in Sicily. Was it a sin, I asked the priest, to have wanted a better life? Bad enough I had to carry two brothers on my back to America, but a mother, too? A mother who then turned around and took to her bed the very same man who had slandered me and sent my father to ruin? I told Guglielmo that the thought of suicide had tempted me during my journey to *la 'Merica* and that my wife and her friend had murdered a stained-glass *artiste* back in the Old Country. I retold the Monkey's crazy story about the witch Ciccolina and her blasphemous black art—the making of two rabbits from one. Was it not a sin, I asked him, to harbor murdering women? I told how that goddamned Prosperine had threatened to cut off my balls if I didn't keep my hands off my wife. My own wife, whom I had married in good faith and given a home like a palace! My own wife!

For an hour—maybe more, I don't know—I confessed

my sins and listed the sins that others had committed against me. It shot out of me like a poison—like the molten rock that rumbles and groans and spills out of Etna! Over and over, I was interrupted by Guglielmo's questions as he puzzled to keep straight names and locations and to remind me over and over that absolution required me to confess my *own* trespasses, not to dwell on the trespasses of others.

By the time I stopped, my voice was hoarse from tears and talking. Afternoon had become evening and a fatigue stronger than I had ever felt before had crept inside my bones. The church was quiet and still, I remember, except for the seeping of steam from the radiators, the flickering red lights from the votive candles at the side altar. I remember I was struck by that stillness.

Guglielmo spoke.

The key to peace within my soul, he said, was to cast aside my bitterness and resentment. "In His last hour, while Jesus was dying on the cross, He looked to Heaven and said, 'Forgive them, Father, for they know not what they do.' You must imitate Jesus each day, Domenico, forgiving all those you feel have wronged you. You must pardon the late monsignor his anger, your brother Vincenzo his lust, the ice man his mockery, the *magistrato* his coveting of your father's medal. You must even forgive your housekeeper her threats and murderous recipes. . . . But most of all, Domenico, you must forgive your wife."

"Forgive that woman whose life is a lie?" I protested. "She told me she was *vergine*! She helped kill a husband! I can't even trust the food she cooks!"

"Dwell on her good qualities, Domenico, not her sins," he said. "Forgive her and she will show you the kindness she saves in her heart and has not yet spent. And if you look into your own heart, you will find your love for the daughter you and she created. If you will allow the girl to be baptized, then—"

"I have already buried the child Ignazia and I created,"

I reminded him. "She made the girl from her whoring with a no-good Irish redhead. There was no blood on the wedding sheets! She carried mine and the other one's child in her belly together! That's probably why my son died. Too crowded in there!"

Father Guglielmo sighed. "Your wife is not an alley cat, Domenico," he said. "It is not possible that two children sharing the womb could have different fathers."

"The girl has the other one's red hair and is *labbro leporino*!" I reminded him. "God has marked the child twice because of her mother's sins!"

"Domenico, each child on the face of this earth is perfection—the living proof of God's love." Guglielmo said the baby's harelip proved only that we were not meant to fully understand the wisdom of God's choices and that the child's red hair proved only that Ignazia or I had had a redheaded ancestor. "Or, perhaps," he said, "God is testing your faith. Put aside your doubts, my friend, and embrace this child. She is *yours*. Love the daughter with whom Jesus has blessed you as you love the son He has recalled to Heaven. Allow me to baptize the girl, Domenico—to cleanse her of original sin. Accept God's will and your home will fill with the blessings of the Holy Spirit."

I told him I could never love that daughter who was not my daughter, although in fairness to myself, I provided well for her and her mother. "They live in a house that has food on the table, don't they? And heat in wintertime? And indoor plumbing?"

"They live in a house where forgiveness is withheld," he answered back.

"On a cold day in January, it's better to be warm than to be forgiven."

"And best to be both," he said back. "Domenico, you must listen to me. Forgiveness is the rich loam from which love can grow. And it is love, not grudge-tending, that will make your home a godly place." He asked me if

I wished to be relieved of my sorrow or if I wanted to continue to bear it.

I told him I wanted peace in my home and in my heart and to sleep when I was tired.

"Then bring your wife and daughter to Mass tomorrow morning," Guglielmo said. "Receive the Eucharist. And the following Sunday morning, bring Ignazia and the child and her sponsors to the sacristy so that I might make your daughter a child of God like her brother in Heaven. On that day, invite me to dinner at your home. I will come and *bless* your house 'from peak to foundation,' and thank God for whatever food your women put on the table in front of me. I will eat whatever they have prepared, invite you to share it with me, and thank God for the bounty He has provided."

My penance, he said, was twofold. First, I must pray the rosary each day for a month, beginning that very day. When I recited the Lord's Prayer, I was to reflect on the words "as we forgive those who trespass against us." When I prayed the Hail Mary, I was to dwell on the phrase "blessed is the fruit of thy womb." I was to remember that the Holy Mother lived in all women—in Ignazia and Prosperine and in the Bickel Road whores, too, each and every one of them, God save their souls.

The second part of my penance was an unusual one, Guglielmo said—one which would oblige me to use my good mind, my gift for language, and the early religious education which God had bestowed upon me. I was to record with paper and pen everything I had spoken about that afternoon. "You must write down the story of your life," Guglielmo said. "Not in the jumbled way it has come out of you this afternoon, but in an orderly fashion. Begin at the beginning, put the middle in the middle, and discuss your present life at the end. Leave *omertà* and come to God. Write down your memories, Domenico, and as you do so, reflect on the Lord's wish that you forgive those who have sinned against you as

He forgives all sinners. In this way, you will untie the knots of anger and pride that bind you and make you suffer. You will imitate Jesus and begin to find humility."

I told him my English was not so good—that I could read it better than I could write it down. Guglielmo told me that God understood all languages, not just English. I could write my reflection in the language of the Mother Country if I wished—either the scholarly Italian I had learned at school in Rome or the Sicilian dialect I had spoken as a child. What was important, Guglielmo said, was not *how* I wrote it but that I completed my penance in good faith.

I protested that I was a busy man—I worked ten hours a day, maintained a home, and made sure those crooked builders he'd hired weren't robbing him blind. I asked him how many other confessors that day had been given not one but *two* forms of penance.

"Never mind about other sinners," he reminded me. "Their penance is their business and your penance is yours. Pray the rosary with humility and find time each day to contemplate and reflect in writing. And when you have finished your history, your meditation, let me read the thoughts you have put down. I will work with you, Domenico. Reflection will help you to prevent further transgression. The peace you long for will come to you and your home. You will sleep peacefully at night and when your time comes, you will sleep in eternal peace. God gives you the free will to do as I say or not to do it. The decision is yours. Now, it is late. Let me hear you make a good Act of Contrition."

I could not remember how to begin.

"O, my God, I am heartily sorry . . ." Guglielmo coaxed.

"O, my God, I am heartily sorry . . ." I repeated. Stopped.

"For having offended Thee."

"For having offended Thee."

"And I detest all my sins because . . ."

"Because . . ."

"Because I dread the loss of Heaven and the pains of Hell, but most of all . . ."

"But most of all . . . but most of all . . . because they offend *Thee*, my God, Who art all good and deserving of all my love. I firmly resolve with the help of Thy grace to confess my sins, to do penance, and . . . and I forget the rest."

"And to amend my life."

"And to amend my life."

"Amen."

"Amen."

When I got home from the church that night, I walked into the kitchen. The baby was sleeping by the stove in her cradle. Ignazia and Prosperine were at the table, eating their supper. Minestrone, it was—I still remember. Minestrone and bread still warm from the oven. Real bread—not that American cotton I had been buying downtown. The soup had fogged up the kitchen windows.

I sat down with the two of them. "Get me a little of that stuff," I told Prosperine. "It smells pretty good."

She looked at Ignazia and Ignazia looked back at her. Then Ignazia's chin shook a little bit—she was holding back her tears. It was she who got up and got the soup. And the three of us sat there and ate. Soup and bread. It was the first meal I'd eaten at my house since the night Prosperine had drunk my wine and told her crazy story. It was good soup, too—just right. My wife, may she rest in peace, could always take a little of this, a little of that, and make good *zuppa*.

15 *August* 1949

The child was baptized Concettina Pasqualina, in honor of Mama and my brother Pasquale. Tusia and his wife were *gombare* and *madrina*. Just as he promised, Father Guglielmo came after the christening and blessed my house. He went from room to room (even the bathroom at the top of the stairs), mumbling his prayers in Latin and sprinkling holy water from the small vessel he had brought. He blessed the cellar last of all, stood right on the spot where Pasquale had landed and lifted the monsignor's curse. Then he came back upstairs to the dining room table and ate what Ignazia, Prosperine, and S*ignora* Tusia had cooked—*antipasto*, *pisci*, *cavatelli*, *vitella* with roasted potatoes. Nothing but the best and plenty of it. I had bought the veal from Hurok myself. "He's busy in the back," his son had told me. "I can help you, Mr. Tempesta." But I made him get the old man. "Give me the best veal in the store," I told Hurok. "The stuff you sell to the big shots." He told me the best would cost me more. I told him to worry about the meat and let me worry about the price. It was good veal, I remember. You could cut through it like butter. And it *should* have been tender, too. M*adonna*! That thieving Jew charged me thirty-five cents a pound!

I opened a savings account for Concettina at the Dime Bank of Three Rivers (twenty-five dollars) and let Ignazia order a child's buggy from Sears and Roebuck's book. There were two of them on the same page—one cheaper, the other better built but overpriced. "Which should I get?" Ignazia asked.

"Get the sturdy one," I said. "What do you think? That I want the thing falling apart on the street with the girl in it? Use your head for once!"

That *carrozza* from Sears and Roebuck helped take away some of Ignazia's shyness around the 'M*ericana* women on Hollyhock Avenue. Concettina had red hair and a homely lip, but she was blessed with a sweet and shy *disposizione* that sometimes reminded me of my brother Pasquale. Neighborhood ladies would stop for a little visit with the child and talk about their own children with Ignazia. These little visits led to cups of tea in other women's parlors and walks into town for shopping. Ignazia reported every little conversation to me. This one said this! That one told her that! I allowed and encouraged these exchanges. It gave Ignazia practice in speaking English and got her away from the influence of that other one. The more comfortable my wife became with decent women, the more she would free herself from that crazy friend of hers who smoked a pipe and was beneath her.

She and Prosperine still shared the back bedroom together, but now Ignazia began to let the other one know who was the woman of the house and who was the servant. One morning, when I got home from work, I walked in the front door and heard Ignazia and Prosperine in the middle of an argument. I followed their voices through the house to the back bedroom. "What's the matter?" I asked my wife.

"Nothing's the matter," she said, glaring at Prosperine. "I only wish that some people knew their place, that's all. When I give her money and tell her to walk to the market and buy a pound of cheese, I mean now, not when she feels like it."

I grabbed Prosperine by the arm and walked her over to Ignazia. The two of them looked away from each other. "This is my wife and the *padrona* of this house," I reminded the Monkey. "We give you a place to sleep at night because you do what she says to do in the daytime. If she tells you 'Go and get me some cheese,' then go and get it. If she says 'Lick the dirt off my shoes,' then lick it. Or else you might find yourself sleeping outside in the cold. Understand?"

The Monkey scowled, said nothing. I squeezed her arm a little tighter. "Understand?" I asked again.

"All right, Domenico, let her go," Ignazia said. "This is our business, not yours."

"Anything that goes on inside this house is my business," I told her. "*Anything*. And if this one doesn't like it, she can pack her bag and get out of my hair." At this, I tightened my grasp around the Monkey's arm and walked her through the house to the front. Then I opened the door and gave her a little shove. "Go fetch the cheese," I said. "Or I'll beat you so hard, you'll see double again, and this time without the help of a witch's magic!"

When the Monkey reached the sidewalk, she stopped and turned back to me. "He who spits into the sky gets it back again!" she shouted in Italian.

Italian was the language I shouted back at her, too. "Threaten me until the chickens piss, you skinny bitch," I yelled back. I would have yelled more, too, but noticed two of Ignazia's '*Mericana* lady friends across the street. They had interrupted their little chat to stare. Idle women are always ready to mind other people's business.

"Trouble with your hired girl, Mr. Tempesta?" one of them called.

"No trouble I can't handle, ha ha," I called back.

Those meddling *mignotti* nodded their heads in sympathy and went back to their conversation about nothing. I closed the door and vowed I would fix this little problem whose real name I did not know but who called herself Prosperine Tucci. Once and for all, I would get that goddamned leech off my ass.

It was *Signora* Siragusa's aches and pains that got Prosperine out of my house. Arthritis had begun to bow the old woman's legs and knot her fingers so badly that she could no longer run the boardinghouse without help. The *signora* and I made a little arrangement. Prosperine would cook and clean there in exchange for a bed in the attic and a dollar a day, which the *signora* paid directly to me on Saturday mornings. At last I would get back some of the money I had spent feeding and clothing her, and a little compensation for putting up with her, too. (I gave Prosperine a dollar a week for tobacco and other necessities and kept five.)

Now I only had to look at Prosperine's ugly face on Sunday, her day off. Ignazia and the child and I would go off to Mass and Prosperine would walk over from Pleasant Hill and let herself in with the key. (That murdering *pagana* never went to church. Why bother? She knew where *her* soul was going after this life!) By the time Ignazia and I returned to the *casa di due appartamenti,* there she would be, sitting at my kitchen table, her stockings rolled down to her skinny ankles. Puffing on her pipe and helping herself to a glass of wine from the jug I kept under the sink. She never lifted a finger to help my wife with the afternoon meal. She just sat there like a little queen. Ha! That one was more like a pimple on the *culo*.

At first, Ignazia had balked at the extra work Prosperine's leaving had put on her. She was lonely without her friend, she said. But even Ignazia saw that things were better with the other one gone during the week. Concettina began to smile at me and to talk—sometimes so many words strung together that she was almost making a speech! She was a pretty girl, except for that rabbit's mouth of hers, and that hair as orange as a pumpkin. Some nights before I went to work, I rocked her on my knee and sang to her the little songs my mother had sung long ago to my brothers and me. When I sang, I sometimes saw a glimpse of Mama's eyes in the girl's eyes. Guglielmo could have been right about the red hair—my mother's people had been from the North. It was not something Ignazia and I ever talked about. . . . Strange how those little melodies would travel back to me from the Old Country whenever I sat the girl on my lap. Some nights I'd go to work and sing them in my head all through my shift.

Ignazia liked to peek at us from the doorway when I sang to Concettina. Once or twice I even caught that wife of mine with a smile on her face. Sometimes, when she bathed the girl, I heard the two of them singing Mama's songs together. They had both learned them from listening to me—my mother's songs from my wife's and the child's mouths. A little thing like that could give me peace for an hour or an afternoon—could convince me that Violetta d'Annunzio had been put in the ground in Palermo—was suffering the torments of Hell—and that Ignazia was only my Ignazia.

I tried to complete the penance that had been assigned me—to sit and write about my life as Guglielmo had advised, but always I was too busy. A page here, a page there, with a week or two in between. I did not like to bring up the old stuff—Papa's death at the mine, Uncle Nardo's control over my fate, the loss of my father's gold medal. . . . What was the good of reliving all of that? I bought a strongbox and locked up those few pages I had written—a *siciliano* knows better than to leave things like that lying around.

Sometimes after Mass or after a meeting about the new school, Guglielmo would ask me how my project was coming and I'd shrug and maybe fib a little and say I had written more than I had. What harm was there in that? I was a busy man, after all. Once I told the *padre* I was halfway to the present in the examination of my life. "That's wonderful, Domenico," he said. "Let me know when you're ready and the two of us will examine it together."

When the new school was finished, the archbishop came down from Hartford for the dedication. I invited my cousins Vitaglio and Lena up from Brooklyn. They came on the train to New London with their brats, the seven of them loaded down with bags and packages and luggage for their overnight stay. My house was like Grand Central Station that Saturday night! Lena and Ignazia cooking and yakking away in the kitchen, Lena's *bambini* squealing and chasing each other and Concettina from room to room. . . . Vitaglio and I played *bocce* ball up in the backyard and got a little drunk on the homemade wine he had brought up from the city. At bedtime, Vitaglio kissed Lena goodnight and I kissed Ignazia. Then he and I went upstairs to bed. Before he got between the covers, Vitaglio went down on his knees to pray.

"What are you asking God for?" I joked. "A million dollars? Two million?"

"I'm not asking Him for anything," he said. "I'm thanking Him for good food and wine, good health and *famiglia*."

He got up off the floor and into bed, sighed, and went immediately to sleep. I reached over and extinguished the lamp, then lay there in the dark. The ceiling above me looked as black and vast as the Atlantic Ocean had looked on those long nights of crossing to America. I felt again the despair I had felt during those endless nights of passage. I thought about all that had happened since—what I had accomplished and what had come to me. Tears dripped down the sides of my face and into my ears. Lying beside me, Lena's husband snored away. I was not much for praying—had given up all that after I left the seminary school to become a mason. But somewhere in the middle of that night, I rose from bed and went down on my knees. I thanked God for the same things Vitaglio had thanked him for—health, home, *famiglia*—and for helping me rid myself of the Monkey, too.

Next day, it seemed like every Catholic in Connecticut was there at St. Mary of Jesus Christ Church to witness the dedication of the new school! After the Mass and the ribbon-cutting, there was a special banquet and speeches in the church hall downstairs. (Guglielmo wanted me and Ignazia to sit at the head table, so that's where we sat, right next to Shanley, the mayor.) This *pezzo grosso* gave a speech, that *pezzo grosso* gave one. Someone read a *telegramma* from no less a dignitary than the Governor of the State of Connecticut! Father Guglielmo was the last to speak.

"Stand up, Domenico," he said. "Stand up, please." So I stood. Every eye in that hall was upon me.

Without the help of Domenico Tempesta, Guglielmo said, the new parish school would not have been built. "We are forever grateful to this man." Then four of the children from the new school came forward, giggling in spite of the looks the nuns gave them. They handed red roses to Ignazia and gave me a little box. "Open it, my good friend! Open it!" Guglielmo told me. He was giggling like those foolish schoolgirls!

Inside the box was a red ribbon tied to a *medaglia* (silver-plated, not gold). Stamped onto one side was the cross of Jesus Christ and the Lamp of Knowledge. Engraved on the other side were these words: "To Domenico Tempesta, With Sincere Appreciation from the Students of St. Mary of Jesus Christ School." That's what it said.

The archbishop stood and came forward. He took the medal from the box, lifted it over my head, and hung it around my neck. Then everyone stood up, gave me *ovazione in piedi*. Vitaglio and Lena, the Tusias, even some of the workers from American Woolen who had come—all of them off their chairs and onto their feet. Their hand-clapping made so much noise, I thought maybe the church would fall down!

Ignazia stood up, too. And the girl. Ignazia was holding that bouquet of roses they'd given her. The week before, I had handed her eight dollars to get herself a little something extra for the dedication ceremony. She'd bought material for a new dress for Concettina and a velvet hat for herself—bright red one, same color as those roses and the ribbon around my neck! I turned and looked at my wife. She was the prettiest woman in that crowded hall . . . standing there, clapping and blushing, wearing her new red hat. Then she put the flowers on the table and took the girl's hands—made Concettina's little hands clap, too.

"Papa! Papa!" Concettina said. "Hooray for Papa!"

I was all right until I heard that. Then I had to blow my nose and leave the hall for a few minutes. "Speech, Mr. Tempesta!" people called from the crowd as I tried to get out of there for a minute or two. "Make a speech! Make a speech!"

But all I could do was thank them and wave and blow my nose.

forty-two

Ray and I sat side by side in the wood-paneled office of Fitzgerald's Funeral Home, banging out the details: closed casket, no calling hours, private burial.

"Funeral Mass?" the undertaker asked. He had an overly helpful manner, seriously bad false teeth. The Fitzgeralds had retired since Ma's death—had sold this guy their business and their name.

"Funeral Mass?" I repeated. Ray's yes and my no came out simultaneously.

"He was *religious,*" Ray said.

"He was crazy," I snapped back. "It's *over.*"

It was False Teeth who brokered the compromise: priest at the graveside, a simple private service. The only other sticking point was what to do afterward. "Most people have a little something," the undertaker said. "But you don't *have* to go that route. You do whatever you're comfortable with."

"It'll be around noon by the time it's over," I pointed out to Ray. "People will *expect* something." I told him I'd order some food from Franco's, go over to Hollyhock Avenue early and help him set up stuff—that over at my place, even a small crowd would be packed in like sardines. Ray gave grudging approval to the plan and I sat there thinking, hey, he *grew up* in that house. Our grandfather *built* that place. Why *shouldn't* we have it there?

When I got home, I made a list: people who'd been decent to Thomas over the years—had treated him like a human being. The names and phone numbers fit on an index card. That was hard, making those calls—asking one more thing from the few people who'd already "anted up" on Thomas's behalf. I saved the two hardest calls for last.

"You have reached Ralph Drinkwater, tribal pipe-keeper of the Wequonnoc Nation. If this is Tribal Council business . . ."

I closed my eyes, stammered the particulars to Ralph's machine: 11:00 A.M., Boswell Avenue Cemetery, a twenty-minute service. "No big deal if you can't make it," I said. "It's just that . . . Well, if you *want* to come . . ." Hanging up, I asked myself what the hell I was shaking for. I'd just been talking to a goddamned answering machine.

But I wasn't lucky enough to get the machine when I called Dessa. *He* answered. The potter. "Eleven?" he said. "Okay, I'll tell her. Anything else we can do?"

I closed my eyes. Thought: yeah, stop saying *we*. "Uh-uh. Thanks. Nope."

There was a three- or four-second pause where "Goodbye" should have been. Dan the Man was the first to break the silence. "I . . . I lost one of *my* brothers," he said. "Six years ago now. Motorcycle accident."

He'd lost *one* of his brothers? I wasn't even *whole* anymore.

"My brother Jeff," he said. "He and I were pretty tight, too." I closed my eyes. Promised myself this would be over in another ten seconds. "Gone for good: it's tough, man. Out of the five of us, Jeff was the only one who'd ever pick up the phone, find out if you were still breathing. . . . Well, you hang in there. That's all I'm trying to say. You want her to call you back when she gets home?"

No need, I said. She could if she wanted to.

After I hung up, I ripped up that index card list of names and numbers. Tore the pieces into smaller pieces. At least that part was over. Halfway across the kitchen, I stopped, doubled over by it.

Gone for good.

If your twin was dead, were you still a twin?

It was sunny the morning of the funeral—warm for April, but windy. Someone had planted red and white tulips in front of the headstone. Dessa, maybe? I knew she came out to the cemetery pretty regularly to visit Angela's grave, across the street in the children's section. Not me. For me, that cemetery was like a land-mine field. Angela, Ma, my grandparents. And now my brother, too.

"JESUS, MEEK AND HUMBLE, MAKE MY HEART
LIKE UNTO THINE."
CONCETTINA TEMPESTA BIRDSEY, 1916–1987
RAYMOND ALVAH BIRDSEY, 1923–
THOMAS JOSEPH BIRDSEY, 1949–

The headstone was midsized, salt and pepper granite. Ray and Ma had bought the plot right after she got sick, I remember. She'd called me afterward. Said they figured I might marry again—that I'd probably want to make my *own* arrangements—but she needed to have Thomas taken care of. She was going to have Thomas buried with *her*.

The wind kept swaying those tulips, bending them one way, then the other way, ding-donging the heads together. A late frost would zap those mothers.

False Teeth had said six pallbearers was the usual but that we could make do with four. That's what we did: made do. Ray, me, Leo, and Mr. Anthony from across the street. The casket was heavier than I thought it'd be. Toward the end, Thomas had outweighed me by fifty or sixty pounds. All that starchy food and sedative. All that sitting around down at Hatch.

Most everyone I'd invited showed up. Leo and Angie (minus the kids), Jerry Martineau, the Anthonys. . . . Sam and Vera Jacobs came. The Jacobses—husband and wife cooks down at Settle—had always been good to my brother. Cards on his birthday and Christmas, that kind of thing. Thomas had kept them all. I found twenty or thirty of them, dated and bound together with an elastic in a box with his other stuff. So I'd put the Jacobses on my list. If he'd kept those cards, they must have meant something. Right?

Dessa was a no-show. Dessa and Ralph Drinkwater. Well, I told myself, what goes around comes around. Here's your personal history coming back to kick you in the teeth, Dominick. You betrayed both of them. Gave him up that night at the state police barracks. Gave your grieving wife up every night you'd wake up and hear her sobbing down the hall and just *lie* there. *Not* get out of bed. *Not* go to her, because it hurt too much. . . . Survival of the fittest, Birdsey: this was what it got you down the line.

The priest was goofy—not one of the regulars over at St. Mary's, but someone they'd had to dig up from Danielson. I felt bad for Ray. He'd been volunteering over at St. Anthony's for more than twenty years—plumbing, electrical work, yard work every spring and fall. But not *one* of those three priests could wiggle out of his "previous commitment." . . . Father LaVie, this guy's name was. He reminded me of someone—I couldn't quite think of who. He'd sounded young over the phone, but then, in person, he *wasn't* young. Late fifties, maybe? Early sixties? Shows up at the cemetery wearing sandals instead of shoes and socks. What was *that* all about? Trying to play Jesus or something? Like I said, it was warm for April, but it wasn't *that* warm.

It hurt, though, whether I deserved it or not: Dessa's not being there. All during the service, I kept waiting for her late arrival—kept picturing in my head how I'd gesture her over next to me when she got there. Hold her hand, maybe. Because our history was *more* than just the crash-and-burn ending. And because Thomas had loved her, too. "Dessa's my very, very, VERY best friend," he used to say. He told me that lots of times. . . . A car door slammed in the middle of things, and I thought, *here* she is. *Here's* Dess. But it was Lisa Sheffer, hustling down the hill, her trenchcoat flapping behind her. Good old Sheffer, late as usual.

Father LaVie. Father Life. . . . He performed that hocus-pocus they do with the incense, fed us the usual about ashes to ashes and dust to dust. Read us some Scripture. Anything special you'd like? he had asked me over the phone. No, I'd said. Whatever he thought might be appropriate. And what he'd come up with was that same psalm I'd heard Thomas recite a hundred times. "*The Lord is my shepherd; I shall not want. In verdant pastures He gives me repose; beside restful waters he leads me. . . .*"

Father LaVie had asked me about Ma. Breast cancer, I'd said. Told him how she used to worry herself sick about what was going to happen to Thomas after she died. "They were close?" Father LaVie had asked. "Like two peas in a pod," I'd said. Two peas in a pod, two coffins in the ground. Mrs. Calabash and Mrs. Floon. . . .

Near the end of the service, Father LaVie closed his prayer book and put his hand on Thomas's casket. Made us a Walt Disney ending: Thomas and Ma, reunited in Heaven, all of their burdens lifted. He smiled over at me, and I smiled back, thinking: George Carlin. *That's* who he reminds me of. . . . Thinking: Free at last! Free at last! They're "playing nice" in Heaven!

You go downstairs now, Dominick. Tell us if Ray comes. I made a special treat for you in the refrigerator. . . .

I looked over at Ray. He was scowling, pulling on the tips of his pallbearer's gloves. My teammate, my accomplice.

What goes on in this house is nobody else's business. You hear me?

Aye aye, Admiral! Yes, sir! . . . My eyes found Doc Patel's eyes. She gave me a nod, a half-smile. Can you read it on my face, Doc? That worst day—the one I've edited out of all our little powwows? Can you see our secret, Doc?

Go downstairs, Dominick. Watch out for Ray. This wouldn't be any fun for you.

Yes, Ma! Sure thing, Ma! Will you love me then, Ma?

And she was right, too. It *wouldn't* have been any fun up there. It was *stupid,* what they did. Ladies' hats, ladies' gloves, those tea parties up there. The older we got, the more their "playing nice" humiliated me. . . .

More tea, Mrs. Calabash?

Yes, thank you, Mrs. Floon.

I *hated* them being up there. *Hated* being their stupid lookout, eating whatever bribe she had put in the refrigerator that day. Listening for Ray, watching out for the Big Bad

Wolf. I *hated* it, Ma. I wanted you to stay downstairs. To love us *both*. . . .

I remembered everything about that day: the weather (gray and drizzly), the clothes I was wearing (dungarees, *Old Yeller* sweatshirt). Our supper—beef stew—was simmering on the stove; the kitchen windows dripped with moisture from the bubbling pot. Ma had left me pudding that day: butterscotch pudding and whipped cream in a squirt can. We'd been begging her for weeks to buy that canned cream. . . . We were fifth-graders now. It was *humiliating*. He was too *old* to "play nice."

I made five of them, Dominick—four for our dessert and an extra one just for you. Not too much cream, now. One nice-sized squirt and that's it. Save the rest for supper.

I lined them up on the counter, assembly-line style, and squirted: five puddings, five leaning towers of whipped cream. I ate them one after another—ate so fast, it gagged me. Why *shouldn't* I? What was *she* going to do about it? Tell Ray? Squeal on me to Ray? I looked in the toaster at my cream-slopped face. *He's got hydrophobie, son. You got to shoot Old Yeller because he's got hydrophobie. . . .*

I heard them laughing up there. *Why, Mrs. Calabash, these crumpets are absolutely divine.* Shut up! Shut up! Shut up!

The sugar canister caught my eye. I reached over, removed the lid, and knocked the canister onto its side. Dry rivulets spilled onto the counter, then onto the floor. A white sugar waterfall. I flicked my wrist, made sugar fly. Crunched sugar under my shoe.

More tea, Mrs. Floon?

Yes, thank you, Mrs. Calabash.

I picked up the flour canister next. Plop, plop-plop-plop onto the floor. A fog of flour swirled at my feet. It felt good, making this much of a mess. It felt like justice. Snatching the can of cream, I shook it until it blurred before me. Began at one end of the counter and finished at the other. *Thomasisabigstupidfuckfacejerk.* The spout bubbled, gurgled; the empty can hissed. I lobbed it, as hard as I could, against the refrigerator.

"Dominick?"

I didn't answer her.

"Dominick?" The clatter had interrupted their little game; she'd come to the top of the stairs. "Dominick?"

"What?"

"What's going on down there?"

"Nothing."

"What was that noise I just heard?"

"*Nothing.* I just dropped something."

"Did anything break?"

"No."

For several seconds, silence. Then her footsteps retreated back to the spare room. *Mrs. Floon, these crumpets are simply delirious! You* must *give me the recipe!* The door squeaked shut again.

I walked the length of the counter, my fist pounding through the whipped cream message. Pow! Pow! Pow! Fuck! Face! Fuck! Face! Whipped cream flew everywhere. I spotted our supper on the stove, pulled open the drawer and got the ladle. Ladled stew—our supper—onto the floor, onto the flour and sugar. Mixed up the mess with the toe of my sneaker. Stomped on it. Skidded through it. My head banged; my heart pounded. I felt powerful. As powerful as Hercules, Unchained. She'd cry when she saw it. They both would. Ma would be mad *and* scared. . . .

I turned back to survey the wreckage I'd made and there he was: Ray.

He was standing at the entranceway from the dining room. There'd been no car driving up the driveway, no warning. I had no idea how long he'd been watching me.

He didn't yell. He just kept staring at me, studying me. We waited.

I felt weak-kneed, dazed. Relieved for my brother. Ray had finally caught me, red-handed, standing in my own evidence. It's over, I thought; now he knows: *I'm* the bad twin. *I'm* the troublemaker. Not Thomas. *Me.*

He looked scared, not angry. And that scared *me.* "Where's . . . where's your mother?" he asked.

I touched my face. Felt whipped cream in my eyebrow, my hair.

"Answer me."

Why wasn't he screaming? Walloping me? Was the mess I had made somehow invisible? "It was an accident," I said. "I'm going to clean it up."

"Where's your mother?" he asked me again.

He'd had car trouble that day—*that* was why I hadn't heard him. He'd gotten a lift home, been dropped off in front. I stood there, the failed sentry.

I wanted to keep them safe from him; I wanted them caught. Ray stood there, waiting. "Upstairs," I said.

"Upstairs where?"

"In the spare room. They're playing their stupid game. They always play it there."

"O Gentlest Heart of Jesus, have mercy on the soul of Thy departed servant, Thomas," Father LaVie said. "Be not severe in Thy judgment but let some drops of Thy Precious Blood fall upon the devouring flames. O Merciful Savior, send Thy Angels to conduct Thy departed servant, Thomas, to a place of light, and peace. May his soul, and the souls of all the faithfully departed, through the mercy of God, rest in peace."

"Amen," we all said. "Amen."

The noon siren blew. False Teeth stepped forward. "This concludes our graveside service, but at this point in time, the family of Thomas Birdsey would like to invite you to the home of Mr. Raymond Birdsey, 68 Hollyhock Avenue, for a luncheon and a continuation of fellowship and remembrance of the deceased."

I had driven over to Ray's that morning like I'd promised—had vacuumed, set everything up. He was already up and out of the house. No note, nothing. He'd brought metal folding chairs down from the attic—that was it. The guy from Franco's delivered the food while I was there: Fiesta Party Platters number 4, 6, and 7, enough to feed a turnout six or seven times what we were going to get. I realized, as soon as I saw those trays, how ridiculously I'd overordered. . . .

Ray and I stood a moment longer at the coffin than the others. Neither of us spoke. From the corner of my eye, I saw Ray's fist reach out, hang in the air above Thomas's casket, knock softly against it. Once, twice, three times. Then he walked away.

I couldn't think of any profound farewells for my brother. How do you say goodbye to a polished box? To the half of yourself that's about to be covered over with dirt? *I'm sorry, Thomas. I was mean because I was jealous. I'm sorry.*

Back by the cars, people shook my hand, hugged me. Told me I'd been a good brother—that now I could take care of myself. As if, now, everything was over. As if his being put in the ground meant I *wasn't* going to keep carrying his corpse. Angie said she had talked to Dessa that morning—that Dess had *said* she was coming. I shrugged, smiled. "Guess she remembered she had to wash her hair or something."

Father LaVie approached me. Father George Carlin. I thanked him, slipped him the fifty bucks I'd remembered to put in my pocket that morning. Two twenties and a ten, curled up as tight as a joint. From my nervousness. From my hands needing to do *something* during that service. I should have put the money in an envelope or something. Should have uncurled it, at least. "I hope it wasn't too much trouble for you to get here," I said.

"No trouble at all," he told me. "No trouble whatsoever. We men of leisure have flexible schedules, you know."

"Yeah?" I said. "You retired?" Which, asking him, was a big mistake. He was one of those needy guys—one of those ask-him-one-question-and-he-volunteers-his-whole-life-story types. *Semi*retired, he said; he'd just recently relocated in Connecticut after twenty-three years out in Saginaw, Michigan. Great Lakes country. God's country. Had I ever been out in that neck of the woods?

I hadn't been, I said. No. What was Three Rivers? Godless country?

"I'm a cancer survivor," he said.

"Yeah? No kidding?" My eyes darted around for Leo—for anyone who might get this priest away from me.

It had been exactly a year ago—a year *to the day*—since the doctors had found a tumor in his groin, he said. Malignant, inoperable, the size of an orange. They'd advised him to get his things in order. Had given him six months to a year. So he'd resigned his parish and come home to be with his mother, who was eighty eight but sharp as a tack.

People were always doing that, I thought: comparing tumors to citrus fruit.

But then, he said, a miracle. A medical mystery. He'd refused chemo, special diets, etcetera, etcetera; he'd accepted his disease as God's will. But to everyone's surprise, his tumor had started shrinking all on its own—had gotten smaller and smaller with each examination. Had diminished, in nine months' time, down to nothing at all. It had baffled all the test-takers and technicians, he said. "But doctors are Doubting Thomases. There's mystery in the world. Either you accept that or you don't."

"Huh," I said. "Wow." Where the fuck was Leo?

Cancer had *enhanced* his life, Father LaVie said—had challenged his complacency. Had, as a "for instance," made him much more sympathetic to AIDS sufferers, and to the poor, and to the oppressed. To people who fought against bigotry. To bigots.

"They got bigots out in God's country?" I said.

He laughed. "Indeed they do. I'm afraid bigotry is everywhere." But back to his cancer, he said. It had *clarified* things for him. Humbled him. Reminded him that the Good Lord's challenges—hard as they were sometimes to bear—were also opportunities. "I'd lived an entire adult life of religious contemplation," he said, "and it *still* did that for me."

Shut up, I'd wanted to scream at him. Shut up! Shut up! Shut up!

Ray was already in the limo, tapping his foot, itching to get the hell out of there. He slid over; I got in. False Teeth closed my door for me. Part of the package, I guess: chauffeur service to and from, with the Grim Reaper at the wheel.

We rolled through the cemetery. Passed my grandfather's ornate tombstone, a groundskeeper on a tractor, a guy sitting in his Jeep with the motor running. We rode through the iron gates and back onto Boswell Avenue.

"I wonder who planted those tulips," I said, half to myself, half to Ray. "What do you want to bet it was Dessa?"

"It was me," Ray said.

Neither of us said anything for several seconds. "When'd you do that?"

"This morning." Which explained where he'd been when I'd gone over there to help him get the house ready.

"Yeah, well. . . . I just hope we don't get another frost."

He put his hands on his knees, turned away from me, and looked out the side window. In the silence that followed, it dawned on me who the guy in the Jeep had been: Ralph Drinkwater. Ralph had shown up after all—had stayed apart from things but been there. I looked out the window on my side. Wiped the wet out of my eyes.

"We get another frost, I'll just go over there and plant some more," Ray said.

False Teeth drove us through Three Rivers instead of skirting around it on the parkway. We passed the construction site for the new casino, the state hospital, the McDonald's where, four days earlier, Thomas had gotten his Happy Meal. We rode over the Sachem River Bridge and through the middle of town.

"Remember when I used to take you kids there?" Ray said.

"Hmm?" I glanced past him and out the window on his side. We were passing a computer store that had been, once upon a time, the Paradise Bakery. After church on Sunday, Ray would drop Ma back at the house so she could start Sunday dinner. Then he'd drive Thomas and me to the Paradise Bakery and buy us crullers. Then he'd take us to Wequonnoc Park.

"The park, too," I said. "We'd go to the bakery first and then over to the park."

He nodded. If I had blinked, I would have missed his smile. "You always wanted to play on the monkey bars and he always wanted to play on the seesaw," Ray said. "I used to have to referee the two of you. Make you take turns."

What I remembered about those seesaw rides was the way Thomas would get mad at me, midride, and evacuate. Send me crashing back down to the ground. . . . It was sort of what his death felt like: fed up, fucked up, Thomas had just jumped off the goddamned seesaw. Had banged me back down to the ground where I sat, jarred. Stopped cold.

The Paradise Bakery, Wequonnoc Park. . . . Was that how Ray was getting through this? Remembering all the fatherly things he had done? Denying the rest of it? Denying, even, that worst day—the day he and I had destroyed Mrs. Calabash and Mrs. Floon?

They're upstairs.

Upstairs where?

In the spare room. They're playing their stupid game. They always play it there.

He'd sloshed through the mess on the kitchen floor as if it wasn't even there. Tracked soupy, floury footprints from the back of the house to the front. He tiptoed, I remember. Up the stairs, down the hallway toward the spare room. Had he suspected something about them? Why else would he have tiptoed? . . .

He banged open the door. Raided them like the vice squad. From down below, I heard screaming, wailing—Ma's tea set getting smashed against the wall. It was Thomas he went after, not Ma. *A goddamned girl! . . . No son of mine!* Ma's arm got broken because she stood in his way—came between his rage and Thomas.

"Run, honey! Run!" I remember her shrieking. All three of us screamed and wailed—my brother and mother upstairs and me below. Then Thomas was at the top of the landing, heading down toward me. *Run! Run!*

Ray caught him halfway down. Grabbed him by the back of his shirt, lifting him, choking him, batting him in the head. *Now get down there! Get down these fucking stairs!*

They lost their balance. Toppled the rest of the way together, landing in a pile at the bottom. *I'm sorry, Ray! Don't hurt me! Don't hurt me, Ray!*

Thomas lay flat on his back, pinned beneath him, and I watched Ray grab him by the wrists, wave Thomas's white-gloved hands in front of his face. *These are what little girls wear! You understand! What are you—a goddamned little girl?* He kept snapping his wrists—making Thomas slap himself in the face with his own white-gloved hands. Over and over, again and again and again.

I wanted to scream at him to *leave my brother alone*! Wanted to kick Ray and punch him and yank him away from Thomas. But I was afraid—paralyzed by his anger.

Ray got up, out of breath, and pulled Thomas, bucking and screaming, toward the front hall closet. He yanked open the door and shoved him in there. Thomas landed hard in a pile of boots, rubbers, umbrellas. Ray slammed the door. Locked it. Shouted over Thomas's screaming that he had better think long and hard about what he'd been doing up there. *And when I get good and goddamned ready to let you out, you'd better walk out like a goddamned boy! You understand me?* He gave the door a kick, then went out to the parlor to cool off and watch TV.

Jesus, he kept muttering, over and over. *Jesus, Jesus. . . .*

At the top of the stairs, Ma's wailing quieted to a whimper. She was clutching her broken arm as she came down, sideways, her shoulder blades scraping against the stairway wall. "What's this?" she asked me in a tiny, quivering voice, and I followed her eyes to the footprints—the mess that Ray and I had tracked from the kitchen through the whole downstairs. Ma followed the footprints out to the kitchen. When she saw the mess I had made, she turned back and looked for me—looked me in the eye. She just stood there, looking at me. Her fist went slowly to her mouth; her whole body was trembling.

They had to take a cab to the hospital because Ray's car was on the fritz. They were gone for hours. Ray's orders to me when they left were to clean up the kitchen, clean the footprints off of the rug, and *not* let my brother out.

I began as soon as they rode away. Sopped the soupy mess off the floor with towels, washed it with Spic and Span. Mopped, washed again, mopped, scrubbed and vacuumed the living room rug. There were cream splatters everywhere—no matter how many times I wiped the kitchen walls and counters. After my third mopping, the floor still felt sticky beneath my feet.

They were gone for hours—gone so long that, illogically or not, I was afraid that Ray had kidnapped our mother. That they were gone for good. Had left us.

Thomas screamed at first—*Let . . . me . . . out . . . of . . . here! PLEASE . . . let . . . me . . . out!* Then he whimpered.

Then he got so quiet that I thought he might have died in there—that Ray might have killed him. From the other side of the door, I sat and spoke to him, sang to him. And when I ran out of songs, words, I read aloud from that week's *TV Guide*. "Donna and Mary Stone organize a mother-and-daughter fashion show. . . . Luke and Kate plan a surprise birthday party for Grandpa Amos. . . . Frontier scout Flint McCullough is kidnapped by hostile Comanches."

Thomas wouldn't answer me. He wouldn't say a thing.

They came back a little after ten. They had a pizza. Ma's arm was in a cast. When Ray unlocked the closet, Thomas emerged, staggering like a drunk, his eyes dazed, his face still swollen from crying. "Can I go to bed now?" was all he said.

"Don't you want some pizza pie?" Ray asked him.

"No, thank you."

Was *that* the night that triggered it—set into motion whatever had blossomed in Thomas's brain? Biochemistry, biogenetics: none of the articles I'd read—none of the experts I had listened to—had ever been able to explain why Thomas had gotten the disease and I hadn't. Had *we* given it to him—my mother and Ray and me? . . .

"Lot of traffic today, huh?" False Teeth said. He kept taking glimpses at me in his rearview mirror. Waiting for an answer.

"Uh, what?" I said. "Traffic? Yeah."

"Of course, from what I hear, we ain't seen nothing yet." He glanced at the road, then back in the rearview. "You want to see traffic? Wait'll that casino opens up. This town'll be bumper to bumper."

Ray shifted in his seat. Folded his arms across his chest and sighed. . . .

Ma had gone upstairs to tuck Thomas in, to go to bed herself, and Ray and I had sat at the kitchen table, eating pizza pie.

"She fell," he said.

"What?"

"Your mother. She tripped and fell on the stairs bringing laundry down. Landed the wrong way. You understand?"

I looked at him. Waited.

"What goes on in this house is nobody else's business," he said. He wasn't looking at me. He was looking at the top of the table. "You understand me?" he asked again.

I nodded.

"All right then," he said. "Good. Things just got a little out of hand tonight, that's all. Just forget about it. This kind of thing happens in every family."

Did it? I tried to picture the kids in my class being dragged, kicking and screaming, down the stairs. Ladling soup onto the kitchen floor.

"And if those two ever play that game again—if you ever get wind of *that* again. Well . . ." He stood up. Went over to the sink. "But they're *not* going to play it anymore. It's not going to ever come up again. . . . But *if* it does, you come to me. Okay?"

I asked Ray if I could go to bed, please.

"Okay?"

"Okay," I said. Sure, Ray. I'll sacrifice them to you. Survival of the fittest.

"Good," he said, nodding his approval. He lit a cigarette. "Good. Because you and I are on a team, all right? We're buddies, you and me. We stick together. Right?"

I nodded. Looked at the hand he was offering. Shook it.

And I climbed the stairs knowing, somehow, that in my two-man struggle, Thomas would always win: that Ma would always *love* him more than she loved me. That Ray would always *hate* him more than he hated me. Like it or not, we *were* two teams. Thomas and Ma versus Ray and me. Survival of the fittest. . . .

And now, here we sat in the back of the undertaker's limousine. The winning team—the victors in our good suits, riding away from the cemetery. No fingerprints. No autopsies. They were *both* in the ground now. Mrs. Calabash and Mrs. Floon. . . .

Back at Hollyhock Avenue, people milled around the kitchen, the living room, talking in hushed voices. What *was* that—respect for the dead? Fear that normal speaking voices might wake him up again? Across the room, I watched Sheffer and Dr. Patel approach Ray—introduce themselves, engage him in a little polite conversation. *They* did most of the work; Ray just stood there, nodding at whatever they said. He couldn't look at them. Far as I knew, he had never returned any of their phone calls. He'd never visited Thomas once down at Hatch; I knew *that* for a fact. In seven months, not once, because believe me, I checked the log book every goddamned time. So *let* him stand there and squirm a little. *Let* him feel guilty about it. It couldn't happen to a more deserving guy.

Jerry Martineau came over, handed me a manila envelope. "What's this?" I said.

"Look."

I had to smile when I opened it: an old picture of our high school basketball team. Martineau said he'd gone looking for it that morning—that he wanted *me* to have it. It was a candid shot taken in the middle of some game. Our senior year, I figured—my muttonchop sideburns era. The first string was out on the court, passing by in a blur, but for some reason, the photographer had focused on Martineau and me, warming the bench as usual.

"Hey, how come Coach doesn't have Havlicek and West in the game?" I said.

Martineau laughed. Reminded me that we *did* get in the game sometimes: usually the last thirty seconds of every lopsided victory. "Look at what a beanpole I was back then," he said. "I remember I used to come home from practice, eat two or three sandwiches, and *then* sit down and eat a big dinner. Snack all night. Those were the days, eh, Dominick? Other day, Karen buys me a pair of dress pants, size thirty-eight waist. Isn't that sad? And to be honest with you, *they're* a little snug. . . . But *look*."

I followed his finger to a spot near the top of the picture. "What?" I said.

Then I saw him: my brother. He was seated in the middle of the Pep Squad section, his mouth wide open in mid-yell. My *real* brother, I thought. *Un*sick Thomas. . . .

More tea, Mrs. Calabash?

Yes, thank you, Mrs. Floon.

A hand clamped onto my shoulder. "Hey, Dominick?"

Leo whispered. "You think Pop's got any hootch in the house? Some of these old geezers'd probably appreciate a drink."

"Oh," I said. "Right." I looked around for Ray, but he'd left the room. "There's some glasses in that cabinet there," I said. "Get those out. I'll go see what he's got."

Jesus, I hadn't even thought about booze. But Leo was right. Most guys like a drink when they come back from a cemetery—a chaser to help them swallow down the sight of a casket over an open grave.

Old Grand Dad, Canadian Club, Cutty Sark: I walked back to the living room cradling the bottles. Leo was wiping down the last of the glasses with his handkerchief. "Don't worry," he whispered. "I only blew my nose on this thing once today."

I just looked at him.

"I'm *kidding,* Birdsey. It's a *joke.*"

Sam Jacobs and Mr. Anthony saw us setting things up and approached, magnetized by the booze. "Ice?" Leo asked me.

Out in the kitchen, Angie, Vera Jacobs, and Mrs. Anthony were bustling around like June Taylor dancers. I had to smile. Men had booze; women had food to fix.

"We've got everything under control, sweetheart," Mrs. Anthony told me. "You just go out there and relax. We'll be ready in five minutes."

She was wearing one of my mother's aprons—that faded, flowered, snaps-at-the-shoulder smock thing you'd always see on Ma when you went over there. It was strange seeing Ma's apron again.

The room darkened. I saw Thomas hanging from that tree—the noose. Felt his dead weight fall as I cut him down, slung him over my shoulders.

Angie stood there, in front of me, staring. "Uh . . . what'd you say?"

"Serving spoons?" she repeated. "Do you have any idea where your mom would have kept her serving spoons?"

I stood there, stupefied. Serving spoons?

"They're in the hutch." Ray walked past me and yanked open a middle drawer—handed Angie a bouquet of big spoons.

"I, uh . . . Ray? I put some liquor out."

He ignored me. Walked over by the windows and stood there—his back to the women and me. *"Ray?* You hear me? I put out a bottle of rye and some—"

"Put out whatever you want," he snapped.

Fuck *you,* I thought. This is *your* victory party, too, you bastard. You were the team captain. Remember?

"Dominick?" Angie said. "Are you all right?"

"Yeah," I said. "Sure." I yanked opened the freezer, banged ice cubes into a bowl.

Back in the living room, the men were standing around in a half-circle, kibbitzing. "Pension-wise, we probably should've stuck it out a couple more years," Sam Jacobs was saying. "But it gets to you, you know? It's like working at a goddamned ghost town down there. And once they close the Settle building, *forget* about it."

I tried to follow the conversation, but my mind kept floating away. *You get cancer, it's like a wakeup call. . . . Not too much cream, now, Dominick. One nice-sized squirt and that's it. Save the rest for supper. . . . Nobody else's business . . .*

"Of course, it's a whole different operation down there now," Sam said. "Everything's premixed, prepackaged. If you can open up a foil bag, you're a *cook,* for Christ's sake."

Leo handed me a Scotch. "Drink this and shut up about it," he said. Ray walked in from the kitchen. Walked over to us.

"Hey, Pop, you limping a little there?" Leo asked him. "What's the matter with your foot?"

Nothing was the matter with it, Ray said. It was just lettin' him know it was there, that was all. If Leo wanted to climb into the ring and go a few rounds, Ray would be glad to knock him on his ass, free of charge. Foot or no foot.

"Macho Camacho," Leo laughed. "What are you drinking, Pop?"

"Nothin'," Ray said. "Milk of magnesia."

"Down in Boca Raton?" Sam Jacobs was saying. "Where my son is? They ain't even heard the *word* recession."

Leo reminded everyone that it wasn't over in Three Rivers until the fat lady sang—that if all the predictions were true about the casino, the Wequonnocs were probably going to end up saving the scalps of every goddamned paleface that Electric Boat laid off.

"That's a bunch of bullshit!" Mr. Anthony chimed in. "They must be smoking something funny in their peace pipe down there if they think New Yorkers are gonna come all the way up here to the boondocks when they got Atlantic City." He told us not to get him started on the Indians. "Any of *you* guys slaughter their ancestors?" he said. "I know *I* didn't. Why the hell should *you and me* have to pay taxes if *they're* getting a free ride?"

Benign old Mr. Anthony: what was he so hot under the collar for?

"Because for two or three centuries, we fucked over their ancestors," I said.

Everyone stopped, looked at me. No one gave me an argument, though. The dead guy's poor twin brother. I probably could have gotten away with saying anything that day.

Then Mrs. Anthony was at the kitchen door. "Okay, everybody! Come and eat! Dominick, honey? Ray? Why don't you fellas start?"

The others put down their drinks and drifted out to the kitchen. "You all right, Dominick?" Leo asked me.

I shrugged.

"Come on. Let's go get something to eat."

"In a minute," I said. "You go in."

I was thinking about Ralph: how he *had* and *hadn't* shown up for Thomas's funeral. How, back when we were on that work crew, he had climbed up into that tree—had stood on that branch that lurched out over the waterspill, rocking it, flirting with his sister's fall. . . . He'd been getting fucked by white guys his whole life, and still, he'd stuck his *neck* out for my brother down there. Down at Hatch. He could have shut his mouth, looked the other way, ignored that memo. . . . Why *shouldn't* he cash in, now, down at that casino? I hope Ralph ended up *rolling* in untaxed revenue.

I drained my drink. Poured myself another one. Stood there, on the verge of tears.

"Here," Sheffer said. "*Mangia.*"

She handed me a plate of food. Invited me to come and

sit with Doc Patel and her, over on the stairs. So I followed her over there. The three of us sat and ate.

"This is difficult, yes, Dominick?" Dr. Patel said.

"I can handle it," I said. "Thanks for coming. Both of you. I know you're busy."

"Has it sunk in yet?" Sheffer asked me.

I shrugged. Told her it had and it hadn't. "Yesterday? I called up the monument place about getting the date put on his headstone? And the woman asked me if I could stop by next Tuesday afternoon to sign the paperwork—if that would work? And I go, 'Yeah, that'll work.' And then I catch myself thinking about how close that place is to the hospital—about how maybe, while I'm down that way, I can swing by and visit him."

Dr. Patel smiled. "Grief is a gradual process," she said. "Two steps forward, one step back." The three of us sat there, nodding.

With everyone feeding their faces, the house got quiet again. *Too* quiet. I looked across the room at Ray. He was sitting by himself, not eating, just waiting for everyone to get the hell out of there. There was a grayish cast to his face; man, he looked like shit.

I figured folks would leave after they'd eaten, but they didn't. Everyone sat around, stood around, hovering *around* the subject of Thomas's death without actually landing there. Mr. and Mrs. Anthony told stories about my brother and me: the time I'd pogo-sticked into their prize rosebush and then tried to repair the broken stems with masking tape. The time they'd taken us for ice cream and Thomas's scoop had fallen off the cone and right into Mrs. Anthony's open purse.

"Oh, and they *always* found some excuse to visit me on Saturday morning when I did my baking," Mrs. Anthony said. "This guy here was Mr. Chocolate Chip and his brother was Mr. Oatmeal Raisin. That was the only way I could tell them apart." She had us reversed, but who was counting?

Mr. Anthony told the story of the day our TV exploded. In my own memory, Mr. Anthony's efforts to rescue my mother as she burst from our burning house had been a day late and a dollar short. Ma had already saved *herself* by the time he yanked her coat off, threw it on the ground, and started doing the Mexican hat dance on top of it. But in Mr. Anthony's version, my mother was a flaming shish kebab and he was Indiana Jones. To hear Mr. Anthony tell it, he had saved the day. "Now, you were away that weekend as I recall, weren't you, Ray?" he said.

Everyone turned and faced my stepfather. My teammate. He nodded. "Bad picture tube was what it was," he said. "At first they said they couldn't do anything about it, but I raised holy hell. Got it replaced free of charge—upgraded to a cabinet model, too. Got the house cleaned and painted on top of it."

Jesus Christ, I thought. The three of us could have died in that fire, but all Ray remembered was the new picture tube. How *he'd* been the hero.

I couldn't take any more of this bullshit. This rewritten history. I got up, went out to the kitchen to check on coffee that didn't need checking. Went outside to breathe. I stood on the back porch for a while, rocking back and forth on the balls of my feet. I saw Thomas, standing next to me out at the Falls that day—the afternoon I'd sprung him out of Hatch. *The Lord is your savior, Dominick. Trust me. I enflesh the word of God. . . .*

Upstairs where?

In the spare room. Playing their stupid game. They always play it there.

I would carry him my whole life after that night—shoulder the weight of him because of the way I'd betrayed him. Because of what I had and hadn't done. But what now? Where did I go from here?

Leo poked his head out the door. "Hey, asshole?" he said. "You want company?"

"No, thanks."

"Another drink?"

"Nope."

He nodded. "Angie just tried calling her sister. No answer."

"Uh-huh."

Seconds passed; neither of us spoke. "All right, man," he finally said. "You come back in when you're ready."

"Yup."

I walked up the cement stairs to the backyard—the place where my grandfather had finally retreated that summer. He'd wheeled his rented Dictaphone onto the porch for pickup, fired the stenographer. Abandoned his bullshit "guide for Italian youth" and gotten, at long last, down to business. Began, in earnest, the penance that priest had given him all those years before. . . . He'd started that thing when Ma was still a little girl. Finished it the day he died. Had made it a real buzzer-beater. . . . How old was Ma by then? That summer he wrote his *confessione*? Thirty-three, maybe? Thirty-four? She was a spinster in her father's eyes. A "cracked jug" who had failed to give him grandsons. All those secrets they kept. He'd had no idea she was carrying my brother and me. . . . He'd cried out here as he wrote that thing, Ma had told me. She'd wanted to go to him, to comfort him, but she knew better than to disturb him out here in his "little bit of Sicily." Knew better than to fuck with *omertà*. . . .

I thought about Angelo Nardi, the stenographer that Papa had hired that summer. Had hired, and then fired, and then tried unsuccessfully to hire back again. Angelo Nardi, who might or might not be our long lost father. Who else had been coming over here on a regular basis? "Dashing," she had called him. He used to sit out in the kitchen with her. She'd make him coffee. . . . What had Angelo, the recent immigrant, made of my Papa's strange conflicting need to both speak and hold his tongue? What had he thought of Papa's timid, housebound daughter? Had he figured she'd be an easy lay along the way to something better—someone so naive that he could get in and out again before she'd even figured out what was going on? Or that, maybe, she deserved a little tenderness—a little something in her life other than service to Papa? Had it been an act of mercy? . . . In the shower that morning, getting ready for Thomas's funeral, I'd made Angelo a merciful man. A kind man, not a creep. And I'd stood there, hot water sluicing over me, fantasizing about Angelo's long-awaited return. . . . Saw him showing up at the cemetery later that morning—the father I had always waited for. I saw a dignified man, conservative suit and tie, snowy white hair. "I had to come, Dominick. I regret that I've missed your brother's life, but I could not miss any more of yours. Forgive me, Dominick. I'm here for you now." And I did—stood in that shower and forgave him immediately, on the spot. . . .

Up there in my grandfather's backyard, I let the tears come in earnest. Stood there and cried the way Papa had gone out there when he needed to cry. . . . When I was a kid, I had waited for the Rifleman, Sky King . . . a whole parade of "real" fathers to rescue me from Ray. And there I was—forty-one years old, an untwinned twin, now—and *still* looking for him. My old man. My perfect mystery dad.

How pathetic was *that,* Dr. Patel? What hope was there for *this* guy?

I saw Domenico out there, a younger man, clutching the dead son he had baptized with dishwater and olive oil. Saw my mother's infant brother—her dead soul mate, her twin. . . . Dead babies, dead brothers. Dead marriages. What sense did any of it make?

By the time I got back inside, Martineau had already left and Sheffer and Dr. Patel were putting on their coats. Doc Patel took me aside for a second. "See you Tuesday?" she whispered.

"See you Tuesday."

I stood at the front door, watching the two of them walk down the stairs. They both turned around when they reached the front sidewalk. Waved. I waved back. Dessa passed them, on her way up.

Dessa, on the stairs, coming toward me. . . . Dess.

She looked upset: her about-to-cry face. Something had happened. She was carrying a pie. As she reached me, she put her free arm around me and squeezed. I closed my eyes and hugged her back. She was the first to pull away.

"I was already in the car, leaving for the service," she said. "And then I remembered *this.*" The pie, she meant; it levitated between us. When she'd gone back inside to get it, she said, the phone was ringing. "I wasn't even going to answer it, Dominick, but then I just had a feeling. . . . It was my mother. She sounded dazed. She had just fallen."

"Thula? She all right?"

I reached over, pushed away her tears. She nodded. "I'm sorry, Dominick. I couldn't find Daddy. I knew Angie would be at the service. I didn't know what to do. . . . We thought she might have broken her ankle, but it was just a bad sprain. It took forever to get it X-rayed. At lunchtime, that whole staff over there just picks up and . . ."

"Take it easy," I said. "You're here now." I handed her my handkerchief. "Here."

"My mother has a housekeeper, but of course, nobody can clean her house like *she* can. She's been having dizzy spells for weeks now and not bothering to tell anyone. She was up on a stool, cleaning light fixtures, and she started getting dizzy. . . . I *loved* Thomas, Dominick. I really wanted to be there."

I brought her inside, took her pie out to the kitchen. When I got back to the living room, she was filling in Angie and Leo on Thula's tumble.

I just stood there and looked at her. White blouse, black pants and jacket, red scarf. Her hair had a little more silver in it than the last time I'd seen her. God, she was beautiful. . . . She'd *planned* to come; it was just circumstances. I could take her out to the cemetery later on if she wanted. It would be better that way, actually—taking her out there. Just us.

I looked over at Leo. Realized he'd been standing there, watching me watch my wife. Neither of us looked away from each other. *You see,* my eyes told him. *This* is how strong it is—*this* is how much I still love her.

"Hey, here she is," Ray said.

He was on the staircase, coming down. Leo was right—he *was* limping a little. I could see it now. "How's my little girl?" he said.

Dessa smiled. Walked toward him. "Hi, Ray."

Dessa had never been crazy about Ray, but she'd always been good to him. Decent. "He's just insecure, Dominick," she'd tell me when I bitched about him. "He's not a *monster.*"

"Yes, he is," I'd tell her. "Trust me."

Now I stood there, watching him reach the bottom of the

stairs. Watching the two of them embrace. At the front door, she'd given me a one-armed hug with a pie in her hand. But now she just stood there, letting Ray hang on for dear life. Okay, I thought. That's enough. Time's up.

Then Ray was crying. *Sobbing*. In front of witnesses. . . . I'd never seen him cry like that. Not even when Ma died. Never. *Defense!* I wanted to shout at him—remind him what *he'd* taught *me*. *Defense!*

I got the fuck out of there. Had to head for the kitchen before my head exploded. My heart raced; I started to shake the way I shook when Thomas and I were kids—when Ray was gearing up for one of his tirades.

And then, suddenly, I knew something: that it hadn't been an accident out there. That Thomas had faced the Falls that morning and made a deliberate decision. For one crystal-clear second or two, I *was* my brother. Saying: *Okay, that's enough. I've had it. It's over.* And I stepped forward, just like Thomas had. Pushed open the door that led back into the living room. Launched into wherever my free fall was about to take me.

"It's his guilt," I announced. "That's why he's crying. He bullied him to death. We *both* did."

I wasn't screaming or anything; I was that undertaker out at the cemetery: *The family of Thomas Birdsey wishes to announce that his brother and stepfather are as guilty as sin.* Everyone turned and looked at me: the Jacobses, Mr. and Mrs. Anthony, Leo and Angie. Free fall was probably going to hurt like hell when I hit bottom, but goddamn if the ride down wasn't a rush.

"Isn't that right, Ray?" I asked him. I took a step toward him; he and Dessa let each other go. "We were teammates, you and me. Remember? The Birdsey wars. A fight to the finish."

I'd stopped his blubbering cold. He stood there, glaring at me with the kind of contempt he'd usually reserved for Thomas. *What goes on in this house stays in this house!* And I glared back, thinking, *Fuck you, Ray. Fuck the way she had to run around the house closing all the windows when you were about to blow, and that bullshit story about how she broke her arm falling down the stairs, and that bullshit that all the doctors were spouting about how schizophrenia had nothing at all to do with the way he was treated when he was a kid. Fuck our family secrets, Ray. Welcome to the big showdown.*

"Dominick?" Dessa said. And I turned to *her*. Pleaded my case to *her*.

"You want to know how many times he visited him while he was down there? At Hatch? I'll *tell* you how many. Zero. Zip."

I took a step closer to her—to both of them.

"Kind of funny, in a way, isn't it? The big veteran of not just *one* war, but *two*. The guy who was always trying to toughen us up for the big bad world out there." I turned to Ray; he was looking over my shoulder instead of facing me eye to eye. "You were fucking *fearless* against the Axis powers. Weren't you, Ray? Kicked the Koreans' butts, right? But, shit, man, that one-handed spook down at the forensic hospital: you were scared to death of *that* guy, weren't you? . . . Hey! Look at me, Ray. I'm *talking* to you."

And he did look. I'll give him that much: he met my gaze and held it.

"I'd go down there, go through all that rigmarole—the metal detector, the escort down to the visiting room, all that maximum-security bullshit. Because, after all, he was such a fucking danger to society, right? . . . And he'd come in—they'd escort him into the visiting room—and he'd sit down, tell me what his day had been like. What he'd had for lunch. Who was trying to assassinate him that particular afternoon. And then, oh, usually within five minutes of our visit, he'd go, 'How's Ray doing? Why doesn't Ray ever visit me? Is Ray mad at me?' "

Ray closed his eyes. Swallowed. Stood there and took it.

"I ran out of excuses for you, buddy," I said. "There's only so far one teammate can fake it for another, you know? . . . In seven months, Ray? Not *once* in seven months? Not even at Christmastime? Not so much as peace on earth, good will toward lunatics?"

When he opened his eyes again, tears spilled out, down his sagging gray cheeks. I heard Leo start to say something, but my hands flew up in the direction of his voice, stopping him. My eyes found Leo's.

"I'm not saying *I* was any kind of hero. Believe me. I made my brother's life miserable when we were kids. Miserable. . . . It's what I used to live for, I was so jealous of him. His goodness. His sweetness. He was as sweet as Ma. . . . But that stump, man. That goddamned stump. That was *my* penance. . . . I'd sit there in that visitors' room—and god, that place stunk; you'd get out of there and the smell of Hatch Forensic Institute would be on you for the rest of the day. In your clothes, in the upholstery of your car . . . I'd sit there, across from him, and say to myself, *Don't look at it, Dominick! Look at his eyes. Just look at his eyes.* But I couldn't help it. I always had to look at it because . . . because we'd *helped* him hack off that goddamned hand of his. Didn't we, Ray? You and me? We were a team, right?"

"Hey, Dominick?" Leo said. "Why don't you and me go for a little—"

"All those bad guys who were always after him: Noriega, the Ayatollah, the CIA. *We* were Noriega. Right, Ray? *We* were those Cuban assassins who were out to whack him the way they'd whacked JFK. It *wasn't* just his brain. His biochemistry. . . . It was *us,* Ray. We killed them both. Mrs. Calabash and Mrs. Floon. . . . We won, Ray. It's V-J Day. This is our victory party."

"I did the best I could for that kid," he said. "For both of you. . . . My conscience is clear. I don't even know what the hell you're talking about."

I had to laugh. "*Really,* Ray? Your conscience is *clear*?" I caught sight of Mrs. Anthony's bloodless face, her frightened eyes. "You want to hear some *other* stories about when we were kids, Mrs. Anthony? *I'll* tell you some stories. Let's see. There was the time Raymondo the Great here taped up Thomas's hands with duct tape. Bound his hands together at the wrist, like he was a friggin' prisoner of war. You know why? You know what his big offense was? He was chewing on his sleeves." I held up my own hands—put on a demonstration two or three inches from her face. "I can still see him, crying into his supper—putting his face down into his plate like a dog so he could eat. Like a fuckin' *dog*. Right, Ray? You and your conscience remember *that* night? . . .

"And then, let's see now, there was the time he caught

him eating Halloween candy in church. Remember *that* fun day, Ray? Hey, let's reopen that particular case because here's some new evidence for you, buddy. You ready? You listening, Ray? *I* was the one who filled my pockets up before we left for church that day. *I* passed the candy to *him,* Ray. *I'd* been stuffing my face all during Mass. Right in *front* of you, man. You had the wrong twin, bud. You were *always* nailing the wrong guy."

"You want to know what the probate judge said the day I adopted you two?" Ray said. It was me he addressed—looked me right in the eye; I'll give the son of a bitch that much. "He said I was a good man, that's what. That there probably wasn't one man in a thousand who'd take on what I was taking on. Not *one* of you, but *two*. *Two* of you. . . . I'm not saying I didn't make mistakes. That I couldn't have done things different. But you can march down to that goddamned courthouse and *read* those words if you want to, buddy boy! March 19, 1955. Probate Court of Three Rivers, Connecticut. Because His Honor Judge Harold T. Adams told his secretary he wanted it written right into the court record! That I was a good man. That not one man in a thousand—"

Let . . . me . . . out . . . of . . . here! PLEASE . . . let . . . me . . . out!

"Yeah, well, Judge Harold T. Adams . . ." Now *I* was crying; now it was *me* sobbing in front of the whole frigging world. "Judge Harold T. Adams would have been real proud of you that night you locked him in the coat closet. Wouldn't he, Ray? . . . That night she came downstairs with her arm wobbling at the wrong angle. *That* was quite a night. Eh, Ray? Your conscience clear about that one, too?"

He told me I could go to hell. Retreated through the living room. *Slam!* The kitchen. *Slam!* His car started, peeled out, jack-rabbited down Hollyhock Avenue.

I looked around the room, caught my breath, searched from face to bewildered face. "Uh, okay, who wants more coffee?" I said. "Leo? Mr. Anthony? Mrs. Anthony?"

Leo, Angie, Dessa, and I were the last ones there. Just like old times, I thought: the way the four of us, back when we were newlyweds, used to go over to each other's apartments on Friday nights. Play cards, listen to music, drink beer. The others started picking up plates, half-empty drink glasses. I went out to the kitchen, opened Ray's refrigerator. Opened four of his beers. "No, thanks," they all said.

"Come on. I already opened them. Have a beer."

"No, really."

Nobody but me wanted one. I couldn't *give* a beer away.

Angie said she and Leo had to leave—had to pick up the kids. Shannon was at softball practice, Amber was at her friend's. "Bring 'em back over," I said. "There's enough leftovers to feed about *fifty* kids. I haven't seen those two in months." They exchanged a look. Angie stumbled through some half-baked excuse about why they couldn't. Leo said he'd call me the next day, and they left.

I sat down at the kitchen table, amidst all the uneaten desserts. Started shredding the label off my beer bottle. Dessa was standing at the sink, wiping dishes. "*You* seen the kids lately?" I asked. "Amber and Shannon?"

She said she'd taken them to the mall the Saturday before.

"I *never* see them anymore. What is it? Is it their schedules or is it me?"

I sat there, waiting, pick-pick-picking at that label. "It's your brother," she said.

"My *brother*? What about my brother?"

She came over and sat at the table, sat across from me. "Last fall? When he cut off his hand? Amber kind of freaked out about it. She kept seeing *you* do it. To *your* hand. And it just . . . it kept getting worse and worse. Leo hasn't wanted to say anything to you. He knew you'd feel bad."

"What got worse and worse? What do you mean?"

"Amber started developing all these phobias: afraid to go to sleep, afraid to ride the school bus. It'll be like midnight, one or two in the morning some nights, and she's still awake. And then when she finally *does* get to sleep, she keeps waking up again. Two or three times a night, sometimes. They're taking her to a specialist now."

I closed my eyes—waited out the urge to cry for them both: my niece, my brother.

"Give her some time, Dominick. She'll come around. The kids love you. You know that. It's just that for now . . ."

I held my beer bottle over a perfectly good plate of cream puffs. Flattened them, one by one, watched the pudding ooze out and off the edge of the plate. "Schizophrenia," I said. "The gift that keeps on giving."

Dessa asked me where I thought Ray had driven off to.

I shrugged. Told her I didn't particularly give a damn *where* he went.

"You know what his worst offense has always been?" she said. I looked at her. Waited. "Not being your real father."

She stood up and went back to the sink.

I told her she was wrong—that that *wasn't* the worst of it. Not by a long shot.

"Yes it is," she said. "You'd forgive him for all the rest of it before you'd forgive him for that."

She stayed. Helped me with the rest of the cleanup. "Really," I kept telling her. "You don't have to do this." She ignored me, of course; whether she admitted it or not, Dessa could be as stubborn as her mother. But I was glad she stayed. I was grateful.

"I have to use the bathroom," she said. "Then I have to go."

Back to their peeling farmhouse with that jazzy mailbox, I thought. Back to him.

I was looking through Ma's photo album when she came back down the stairs. I'd taken it out of the china closet to shove Jerry Martineau's basketball picture in there and then gotten lost in the old photographs. And when I patted the sofa, she surprised me. Sat down beside me.

We leafed through the book together: Thomas and me with Mamie Eisenhower; Domenico in a two-piece bathing suit at Ocean Beach. . . . I opened my mouth to tell Dessa about how I'd been reading the Old Man's "history," and then changed my mind. I was whipped; it was complicated. She'd already had enough of Dominick and Company.

"I'm worried about you," she said. I kept turning pages. Thomas and me in Junior Midshipmen; Thomas, Ray, and me at the New York World's Fair . . .

I told her I'd be okay—that, in some ways, Thomas's death felt like a reprieve. That I wasn't sorry I'd nailed Ray in front of witnesses.

"Well, you're bound to have all kinds of conflicting emotions right now, Dominick," she said. "You really need to *talk* to someone."

I asked her if she was volunteering for the job.

"You know what I mean. A counselor. A therapist."

I told her I was way ahead of her. Filled her in on Dr. Patel.

She nodded. Reached over and took my hand. "What made you start going?"

I flipped another page of Ma's book. Shrugged. "Him being locked up at Hatch, I guess. That maximum-security stuff: it was eating me alive. I guess it was like that front hall closet all over again. . . . At first, I was just going there to fill her in on his history. Give her some background on our happy little childhood here at Happy Valley. And then . . . I don't know, things just shifted. She said to me one afternoon that Thomas and I were like two guys lost in the woods or something. She said she thought she could help me get out of the woods. So we started working on *my* shit."

"And how's it going?" she asked.

I shrugged. "She was here earlier; you missed her. She's pretty terrific, actually. Doesn't take much shit off of me. . . . We been . . . we been working on anger management. I don't think she'd have been too thrilled at my little showdown with Ray."

Dessa said that at least, these days, my anger seemed to be hitting the target I was aiming for. I looked over at her. Studied her face. Nodded.

"I'm *glad* you're seeing someone," she said. "You and Thomas had a pretty complex relationship. You've spent an enormous amount of emotional energy on Thomas. Your whole life. Now, you're going to have to take all of that energy and . . . *re*invest it, I guess. It's bound to be a complicated process."

"Sounds like shrink talk," I said. "What are you trying to do? Cut Doc Patel out of the action?"

She was serious, she said. She'd hate to see me deal with

Thomas's death by not dealing with it—have my anger boomerang back in a hundred other ways. Or dodge the pain—quit the process when the going got tough.

"*When* it gets tough?" I said. "You saying it gets *more* brutal than this?"

She shook her head. "What I'm saying, Slugger, is that it's a big step for you—therapy. I'm proud of you."

Slugger: she hadn't called me that in years. I asked her how *she* was doing.

She looked away. Looked back again. Fair, she said.

"Yeah? Just fair? What's the matter?"

Oh, Thomas's death, mainly, she said. She'd really loved my brother. He'd had to struggle so hard. She was grieving, too. And now her mother—those dizzy spells.

"Everything else all right?" I said. "Anything else bothering you?" Tell me you and him are on the skids, I thought. Tell me it's gone bad between you two.

"You've got enough on your mind, Dominick," she said. "You don't need to hear about my stuff on top of it."

"No, tell me. What?"

Sadie, she said. Sadie wasn't doing too great.

"Goofus? Why? What's the matter with her?"

"She's *old*. Her heart's bad, her kidneys. The vet said I should start thinking about the next step—whether or not I want her put to sleep."

I thought about the day I'd given her Sadie. Her twenty-fifth birthday, it was. I saw myself opening the pantry door of our old apartment, that damn puppy making a beeline right to her. Licking her bare feet. Big red bow I'd put on her. I remembered that day whole.

The two of us just sat there, neither one of us saying anything.

"And something else," she finally said.

What else what? Where were we?

"Did you read that thing in the papers last week? About Eric Clapton's little boy? God, this is so stupid."

"Little dude who fell out the window, right?" I said. "Fell from a skyscraper?"

She got up. Walked over to the window. "Hey, it's not like *I* was their close personal friend. *You* were always the big

Clapton fan. Not me. . . . But I can't stop thinking about that poor little boy. Conor, his name was. I've even dreamt about him."

"It's Angela," I said. She looked over at me. "Tell me the dream."

"No, never mind, Dominick. This is stupid. Compared to everything *you've* been through? My god."

"*Tell* me," I said.

In Dessa's dream, the boy kneels on the windowsill, waving down at them—the crowd that's gathered on the sidewalk below. They hold their breath every time he moves. He doesn't understand how dangerous it is, what can happen. "Eric Clapton's there," Dessa said. "And the boy's mother, the police. But somehow it's *me* who's responsible. I keep promising everyone that I'll catch him if he falls. . . . And I *know* I'm not going to be able to do it, but I keep *promising*. Everyone's counting on me. And then he slips. He starts to fall. . . ."

"It wasn't your fault," I said. "It wasn't *anybody's* fault. She just died."

She turned back to me. Nodded. "Maybe Thomas just couldn't take it anymore, Dominick. . . . Maybe he was just *ready* to stop fighting."

I got up and walked over to her. Put my arms around her. She leaned her face against my chest. For a minute or more, we just stood there, holding each other. "Come on," I said. "Sit down."

Thomas and me in Davy Crockett pajamas. In our high school caps and gowns. . . . Domenico and Ma, hand in hand on the front steps. . . . Dessa and me on our wedding day. "Hey, who are these two hippie freaks?" I said. "They look vaguely familiar." I could feel, rather than see, her smile.

"Oh, my poor mother," Dessa sighed. "Married on the beach instead of in the Greek church. Me in that thirty-nine-dollar peasant dress instead of something with seed pearls and a ten-foot train. Now I see what she meant. And you wearing those sandals. You don't want to *know* how much grief I took about that."

Sandals, I thought. Father LaVie.

Dessa said it amazed her to think how self-assured she

had been at that point in her life—how confident she was that if she just *planned* a future, that that would be the future she would have. "Look how young we were," she said. "No wonder."

"Better watch it, you two," I told the scraggly wedding couple. "Life's going to rear up, kick you in the ass."

I flipped the page. Our honeymoon in Puerto Rico, the two of us as godparents at Shannon's christening. We were in the thick of it at that point, I remember: all that fertility counseling. "So," I said. "How's Dan the Man?"

She talked about how busy he was—about some major buyer out in Santa Fe or something. "Dominick?" she said. "Do you ever talk about us? You and your therapist? Or is that considered ancient history?"

I smiled. "My therapist's got an anthropology degree," I said. "Ancient history's exactly what she's into." I turned a couple more pages of the album.

"Yeah, I talk about us," I finally said. "How it was my anger that made me march down there and get that stupid vasectomy. How beneath all this *anger* I've got is . . . is all this *fear.* Believe me—ancient history's *exactly* what she wants me to muck around in. She says if I want any kind of a future, I gotta go back and face all that fear. Renovate the past or whatever. She's big on that word: renovation. . . . I probably ought to go down to town hall and get a freakin' building permit, I got so much *renovating* to do."

Dessa reached over and stroked my arm.

"I been . . . I've been reading this thing my grandfather wrote? Ma's father? His autobiography, or whatever. It was all in Italian. I had it translated."

"Papa," Dessa said. "He was your mother's hero."

"He was a prick," I said. "A bully. You think *I'm* angry?"

She stayed another half hour or so. I made us tea; she cut us each a piece of her chocolate pie. At the door, I thanked her for coming, for cleaning up the kitchen.

"I love you," I said. "I know you don't want me to, but I can't help it."

She nodded. Smiled. Told me to keep going to see Dr. Patel.

"I can . . . if you want me to, I can drive you over to the cemetery some time. Visit his grave. Ma's. . . . Maybe visit the baby's grave, too, if you wanted to."

She nodded. Smiled the saddest smile I'd ever seen. She'd driven out to Angela's grave that morning, she said. She liked visiting her; she usually went there once or twice a week. Someone had just planted flowers for her, she said. Angie, maybe. Or her father—she'd forgotten to ask.

Red and white tulips, she said. They were so beautiful, they had made her cry.

forty-three

16 *August* 1949

After that victorious banquet in the church basement, everyone wanted the help of Domenico Tempesta for this thing, that thing.

"Tempesta, we need your advice. . . ."

"Tempesta, we're forming a new group on such and such. . . ." "Tempesta, can't you do us one small favor? If *you* do it, it gets done right."

I became a member of Elks and Knights of Columbus and an elected officer in Sons of Italy. I helped the Republicans downtown register Italian voters and was named to the city planning commission (first Italian in Three Rivers history). I was so busy, I had to have a telephone brought into my house. That thing rang off the hook. Always there was someone on the other end who needed my help. "Hello, Domenico? . . . Good afternoon, Mr. Tempesta." My mouth got tired from saying hello back to everyone who called needing something. Not just Italians calling, either. Now even Shanley, that crooked Irish mayor, knew that my first name was Domenico and my telephone number was 817.

"How are you coming on your personal reflection?" Father Guglielmo asked me one morning after church.

Ignazia, the girl, and I went faithfully to the nine o'clock Mass now and sat in the second pew. (I passed the basket and kept an eye on the other collectors for Guglielmo—made sure no one put "itchy fingers" on the church's money. One of that priest's problems was that he trusted everybody.)

I laughed at Guglielmo's question and told him I barely had time for a few hours' sleep each day—no time at all to sit and write about forty-five years of living. I assured him his worrying was unnecessary. He should bother the parishioners with bigger sins on their souls than I had on mine. My family and I were at peace.

I thought it was true. . . . I had stopped visiting the girl Hattie on Bickel Road. I was much too busy for that now—and too well known by the big shots in Three Rivers to be spotted at that place! Running from this meeting to that one gave me a rest from thinking too much about my wife's flesh, though if anything, Ignazia's contentment had made her a little plumper and more desirable.

My work on the planning commission led to a little private friendship with Mrs. Josephine Reynolds, a stenographer who worked at City Hall and took the minutes at our meetings. Josie was not much next to Ignazia. A little too skinny on the top. Like every other '*Mericana*, she made coffee that tasted weak as dishwater. But she knew how to comfort a busy man and knew how to keep quiet about it, too. She lived up the road in Willimantic. I got up there when I could, not too often. Gave her a little friendship when I was able. I would not have looked twice at her if my wife hadn't had a bad heart.

I *thought* peace had come to my home. I *wanted* to think that—wanted to believe Guglielmo's blessing had broken the other one's curse. But underneath the surface, trouble ate away inside my house like termites in the cellar. Quietly, that goddamned termite named Prosperine was practicing her treachery—destroying what little peace we had enjoyed at 66-through-68 Hollyhock Avenue.

17 *August* 1949

Trouble came back to my house one Sunday after church.

When we got home from Mass that day, Ignazia lit a fire under the macaroni pot and went to change out of her church dress. I was at the kitchen table, reading the newspaper. Concettina sat beside me, singing and scribbling little pictures on the funny papers. The Monkey opened the back door and came into the kitchen, pouting as always. That woman never spoke to me unless I spoke to her. And on that day, I wanted to speak to her, all right. That day I had things on my mind.

The afternoon before, when I'd gone to *Signora* Siragusa's to collect the Monkey's weekly wages, the old woman had counted four dollars into my hand instead of six. Twice that week, she reported, Prosperine had claimed she was sick and stayed up in the attic. The *signora* was sick, too, she said: sick of doing her own work and Prosperine's work as well. She complained, furthermore, that none of the boarders liked Prosperine. She never smiled or held up her side of a conversation. Two or three times the old woman had been awakened in the middle of the night by the sound of footsteps on the attic stairs. If she found that food or silverware was missing, the *signora* warned me, she would deduct that cost from the woman's wage as well. And if Prosperine was sneaking down to meet one of the bachelors on the second floor, she would have to leave the boardinghouse. The *signora* wanted no stink of scandal in the place she ran. What if Father Guglielmo found out? What if the police came? Here, old *Signora* Loose-Tongue pulled me close and spoke her suspicion: maybe Prosperine's sickness was the beginning of a baby inside of her. She herself had wanted to sleep away the day during four of her seven pregnancies.

The thought of one of *Signora* Siragusa's bachelors being blind or foolish enough to put his thing inside of that skinny bitch made me laugh. That crazy *mignotta* would probably castrate the poor man! Or poison him the next day! But I did not laugh about the two dollars missing from the palm of my hand. I told the *signora* I would straighten things out.

"Eh?" I said now, even before Prosperine took off her coat that day in my kitchen. "What's this I hear about you not doing your work over at the *signora*'s?"

"I do my work," she said.

"Yesterday, I got four dollars instead of six. She doesn't pay you to sit up in her attic and sleep."

"I was sick," she said. "Sick as a dog."

"Sick from what?"

She said nothing.

"When I'm sick, I go to work anyway," I told her. "I work sick."

"That's what *you* do. I do something else. I'm lucky I don't die of pneumonia at that place. The wind whistles through the open spaces in the roof. She won't let me leave the door open and get a little heat up there. Not even a crack. She's as stingy with her coal as you are."

"If it's so cold up there, then go downstairs and warm yourself by doing honest labor. Then you'll sleep through the night, all right, no matter what the wind is doing. And stop scowling at the boarders, while you're at it. You're ugly enough without making that puss. The *signora* has had several complaints about your bad *disposizione*. And what's this about you sneaking downstairs in the night like a common burglar."

"Who sneaks downstairs like a burglar?"

"She says you do. She hears you on the stairs." I reached over and cupped my hands over Concettina's ears. "She thinks you're up to some funny business with the men in her house."

"Bah!" the Monkey said. "The only funny business I'm up to is using the toilet. Or trying to warm my bones."

"That had *better* be the reason," I warned her. "I sent you over there to work, not to play the bachelors' pipes. I better not come up short next week or I'll wring your skinny neck for you." I let go of Concettina's ears and scooted her out of the room.

"Why should I work like a mule to line *your* pockets?" Prosperine answered back.

"Because I fed you and put up with you in my house for almost two years. Who knows where you would be right now if it wasn't for my generosity? Probably out on the streets in New York, that's where."

"*Generoso*? *You*?" she laughed. "You're tighter than the paper on the wall."

Ignazia came into the room and saw the two of us glaring at each other. She rattled pots and walked between us. "Prosperine, grate this cheese for me," she ordered. "Domenico, go down to the canning closet and get me a jar of peaches." I rose slowly, staring all the while at the Monkey to show her I meant business. At the cellar door, I warned her that she and I would finish our little talk after we ate.

"Talk until you lose your voice, then," she said. "But when I'm sick, I'm sick."

All during that meal, we said nothing. The only sounds were forks and spoons against dishes. Even Concettina was quiet. Each time I looked up from my plate to glare at Prosperine, I saw her glaring back at me. If that one *had* mastered the dark art of *il mal occhio* from her witch-friend back in Pescara, she might have burst my brain and popped the eyeballs out of my head with the looks she gave me that day.

It was my custom each Sunday morning to take my silver *medaglia* from its red velvet box and wear it to Mass.

I would keep it on until after the afternoon meal, at which time I would go upstairs, get out of my good suit, unfasten my garters, and take my Sunday afternoon nap. So the silver *medaglia* was still around my neck that afternoon as we finished our long, silent meal. Ignazia and Prosperine got up and began to clear the dishes. I pointed to the Monkey's chair and told her to sit back down. "Keep the child in the kitchen with you," I told Ignazia.

Prosperine sighed and sat. As I began my remarks, she tapped her fingers restlessly against the table, refusing to look at me; that one always knew how to show flagrant disrespect! I lifted the silver *medaglia* over my head, reached across the table, and swung it in front of her ugly face. "Take a good, long look," I said. "Do you know why this was presented to me?"

She said nothing.

"It was given in recognition of hard work and superior efforts—for doing more than expected always, for never doing less—for laboring whether I was sick or well."

Her hands made fists on the table. Deep sigh of *impazienza*. Still, she refused to look me in the eye.

"Why do you think they begged Tempesta to sit on the planning commission for this city? Why do you think the mayor knows my name and telephone number? This *medaglia* is a victory not just for me but for every *Italiano* who has immigrated to *la 'Merica*. You must take a lesson from my example and begin to do some work over there that will make you proud. And smile at the boarders while you're doing it, goddamn it!"

She looked from the swaying medal up to my face, back to the medal, back to my face. "Go swallow your fancy *medaglia* and shit it out the other end," she said. Then her head reared back, snapped forward, and the spittle flew from her mouth onto my *medaglia*.

The filth from her mouth slid from the silver face of my *medaglia*—from the very *crucifisso* of Jesus Christ and the Lamp of Knowledge and plop! onto the tablecloth. I rose and took hold of her scrawny arm, twisting it a little as I pulled her to her feet.

"Now you have gone too far," I said. "Apologize to me or I'll twist until I hear the bone snap. Say your apology loud as you can, and then get the hell out of my house and stay out."

Ignazia rushed back into the room. "Stop it, Domenico!" she said. "Let her go before someone gets hurt. I'll have none of this manhandling going on in my house."

"Shut up and stay out of this!" I warned. "This *mona* spat her filth out onto my silver *medaglia*." Concettina hid behind her mother's skirts and began to whimper. I gave the other one's arm a good jerk to show her I meant business. "Apologize!" I ordered her again. "Do it quickly if you know what's good for you."

Ignazia grabbed a table napkin and wiped my medal clean. "Do as he says now," Ignazia told her. "What difference does it make?"

But that stubborn bitch wouldn't apologize. Far from it. Instead, she reached down and sank her teeth into the meat of my hand that held her!

Crying out in pain, I let go of her and when I got hold again, it was by the coil of braids at the back of her neck. She tried to run out of there, but I tethered her and yanked her back by those braids of hers. I swatted her a couple of times in the face, to let her know who she had fooled with. That goddamned *mignotta* had broken the skin!

Ignazia's hands tried to slap and pull me away from the other one. Concettina cried. Her mother cried. But not that crazy bitch that had caused all the trouble in the first place! That one continued to put up a fight. Her hand swung up and banged me on the nose. Her other hand reached for the bread knife on the table. I grabbed hold of her and slammed her face into the wall. Slammed it again. She dropped that knife, all right.

Behind me there was screaming. When I looked back,

I saw my wife and child, sunk to the floor and cowering. Mother and daughter, screaming bloody murder.

"*Bruto! Bruto!*" my wife shrieked. "What kind of monster beats poor, defenseless women and terrifies his own child?"

I pointed down at Prosperine. "You want someone to blame? Blame this one down there on the floor who bites and spits like an animal!" Prosperine, on her hands and knees, was coughing and retching, as dazed as a beaten dog.

Ignazia got up and helped her skinny friend to her feet. The Monkey groaned and stumbled, reached out for the chair to steady herself. When she turned and faced me, I saw I had knocked one of her front teeth clear away and loosened the other one. It hung there, soaked in red, half in her mouth and half outside of it. That monkey's biting days were over. Her face looked like it had been hit with a ripe tomato.

"*Bruto!*" my wife screamed at me. "Get out! Leave us alone!" She was shaking, shuddering, but would not shut up her mouth.

"Silence yourself!" I ordered her. "Every neighbor on this street will hear you!"

"Let them hear!" Ignazia shouted back. "Let them hear that my *pezzo grosso* of a husband helps the whole world, and then comes home and knocks the teeth out of the heads of innocent women!"

"*Innuccenti?*" I shouted. "*Innuccenti?* Ha! She was going for the knife!" I waved my hand in front of Ignazia's eyes to show her where the Monkey's bite had broken the skin, but that hysterical wife of mine thought I moved to strike her, too. She dropped to her knees, flinching, wailing, and covering her head with her hands. "Don't hit me, please! I beg of you, Domenico! Don't hit! Don't hit me!"

"She had it coming!" I shouted. I told Ignazia to get up off the floor—that I would never harm her.

She screamed that I had harmed her the night I married her and brought her to this prison of a house. She sobbed and shouted that she hated me and cursed a million times the day she had become my wife!

I had not struck her once since that first night—had provided nothing but the best for her and for the child, too. But Ignazia appreciated none of it.

I started to leave the room. I meant to get the hell out of there and go upstairs to smoke and calm myself. But I wanted that troublemaking bitch out of my house by the time I came downstairs again. I went back to the dining room and made that clear to them both. And when I left the room the second time, I gave the door a good, hard slam.

But it was a dull sound I heard, not a slam. Something had stopped that. For a second, there was a horrible, terrible silence. And then the shrieking began. The girl's little hand had been gripping the door frame. I had slammed the door on Concettina's five little fingers!

Orribile! Terribile! But it was too late—could not be undone. It had been *accidente*, but above the child's screaming and Ignazia's howls of protest, I could not even speak my regret. Could not get near the child to see what damage the Monkey's defiance had made come to pass. So I stormed upstairs, slammed my bedroom door, and pulled the bureau in front of it.

All over the house, doors slammed, women and children wailed.

Ten, fifteen minutes later, from the upstairs hallway window, I watched the three of them, hunched forward, escaping down the street. Ignazia led the way. That fancy baby carriage I had let her buy was piled high with their belongings. The girl's hand was bundled in white bandages. Prosperine held the child's other hand and held a cloth to her own mouth. They marched away from my house with such determination that their feet were a blur. Those two knew how to run away, all right! They had had plenty of practice in the Old Country. But they would not go far.

I knew where they were headed, if they were not running next door to Tusia's wife. Where else in town would they go except to *Signora* Siragusa's? . . . I didn't chase after my wife. Better to let her go than to make a scene that every last *'Mericano* on Hollyhock Avenue could watch from the window. Each morning at breakfast, Ignazia told me what household expenses she needed money for that day and I counted out what she needed. Nothing extra. She could not have had more than a few dollars in coin. Let her stay away, I thought. She'll be back. She'll be back on her hands and knees as soon as she sees how far she gets without Tempesta.

That night, alone in my house, I tried to scrub away Prosperine's blood from the dining room. I got most of it out of the rug, but it had dried fast to the wallpaper and the tablecloth—had left brown stains as permanent as the dye we used at the mill. I pulled that cloth from the table and burned it in the ash barrel up in the backyard. Then I came back inside and moved the sideboard over from the other wall so that it covered the stained wallpaper.

I rang and rang my friend Josephine's telephone number but there was no answer. No one to comfort a poor man who only wanted a little peace and quiet in his own home on Sunday after church—a man who was no brute but had a monkey on his back.

All night long, I lay in my bed, unable to sleep, though I needed my rest for the next night's work. Had the child's fingers been broken, or only bruised? Had Ignazia meant what she said—that she had cursed a million times the day she had married me? If I went to see Father Guglielmo, I knew what he would say. He would tell me to forgive Prosperine for nearly biting off my hand—for reaching for a knife she was probably getting ready to stick through my heart. Forgive them both, he would say, and beg their forgiveness! Humble yourself, Domenico! Write it all down for penance!

I got out of bed, took the strongbox out of the upstairs closet, and brought it down to the kitchen table. I took out the pages I had written already, read them over, and tried to continue my reflection. But it was no use. I was shaken, still, by the remembered sound of Concettina's screaming. I saw that other one's teeth marks on the hand that held the pen. Saw her filthy mucus sliding down the face of my silver *medaglia*. . . . I was not finished with that one yet. Once and for all, I would rid myself of that murdering *mingia* that had stolen the name of a dead girl and come to America to ruin my life!

By midweek, I was fed up with my wife's little game of hide-and-seek. After work that morning, I walked over to *Signora* Siragusa's to reclaim my *famiglia*.

The old *signora* tried to scold me for what I had done to Prosperine and her teeth, but I pushed away the knotty finger that the old *nonna* shook in front of my face. "Better keep still, old woman," I warned her. "Your complaining was the thing that started the trouble in my house. Go upstairs and tell my wife to gather her things. I order her to come home now."

Signora Siragusa sighed and made the sign of the cross, then hobbled up the staircase. A few minutes later, she came back down again. "She told you to go away," the *signora* reported. "She said she'd rather rip out her heart than look at you again."

The workday had begun; the boardinghouse tenants had all gone off to their jobs. There was no one around to hear Tempesta business. I walked past the *signora* and called up the stairwell to my wife.

"Better come down now, *Violetta*! . . . Before there is trouble, *Violetta*!"

Violetta? The *signora* stared at me with a puzzled look and I stared back at her until she shook her head and went off to her kitchen. My wife appeared at the top of the stairs. Came down five, six steps and stopped. The girl came, too—hiding behind her mother's skirts.

Ignazia's face was pale, her eyes as big as a deer's eyes. Her hand reached behind her, holding on to the girl as if she would protect her from me.

"Fingers broken?" I asked.

Ignazia shook her head. "No thanks to you!" she said.

"You are my wife," I reminded Ignazia. "Get your things and come home where you belong. I am tired of this foolishness."

She shook her head once more, held the child closer still.

I told her I tolerated no defiance from my workers at the woolen plant and I would tolerate no more from her, either. Ignazia said I could drop to my knees and beg, but she would never go back to a home where women and children were not safe from monsters.

"The girl's hand was hurt accidentally," I reminded her. "And as for that skinny friend of yours, it is *she* who is the monster in my house. That crazy bitch has always been between us—has always made trouble for you and me. But now that's finished. I forbid her from entering my home ever again. And tell her for me that I mean business when I say it. Now, go get your things. If I have to, I'll take hold of your ear and pull you all the way up Hollyhock Avenue."

Trembling, she told me I would not touch her ear or any other part of her. She and Prosperine had talked through the night, she said. They were leaving town.

"And going where?" I laughed. "Back to New York with two 'brothers' who couldn't wait to sell you off? Back with that penniless mama's boy of a redhead who still drinks from his mother's tit?"

I needn't worry about her, she said. She had found her way in the world before and she could do it again.

"You'll come back in a week with your tail between your legs," I said. "Until then, tell me what I am supposed to do for meals and clean clothes?"

"What do I care what you do? Have that *puttana* 'Mericana from downtown do your dirty work for all I care—that *segretaria* with the blond hair and the fat *cula*!" Ignazia's knowledge of my little private business with Josephine Reynolds shocked me. And yet, as that defiant wife of mine threw my friendship with the secretary into my face, I softened to her. I thought I saw in her eyes the indignation of a jealous wife—a wife who wanted her husband to herself.

"It is *you* I love," I said. "*You* I have always wanted. But when a wife denies her husband what he needs, he has to go somewhere else. That secretary means nothing. Come back to our bed again and I'll tell her to go to hell."

Fat tears fell from her eyes. Concettina stared, wide-eyed. "You go to hell, you brute!" Ignazia said. "You'd put me in a coffin to satisfy your own dirty pleasure! Fill me up with your pig snot so that I might bear you another child and die!" With that, she turned, picked up the girl, and pounded back up the stairs. Concettina peeked down at me from over her mother's shoulder.

Next afternoon, I was awakened from my daytime sleep by the ringing of the front bell. I put on my pants and went down the stairs, and when I opened the front door, *Signora* Siragusa was on the other side. She looked ancient and shrunken—a little afraid. She had some news, she said. Like beggars, Ignazia and Prosperine had been pestering her boarders and had finally managed to borrow money from one of them. (The *signora* herself had refused them, she said; she told Ignazia that wives should stay at home and put up with their husbands.) Now the two women were inquiring about trolley rides to the railroad station in New London. They were planning to take the Saturday evening train bound for New York.

I myself took the trolley to New London on Saturday—the early one, not the one that would carry the two fugitives later that evening. Lucky for me, they had planned their escape on a day when I would miss no work at the mill.

I got to the train station three hours early. The wait gave me more than enough time to buy a steak dinner and to walk around and think and finally to chat with the young policeman on duty at the station. I told him I was there to pick up my cousins who were visiting from Providence. They were arriving on the train headed for New York, I said, but I had mixed up the arrival time, ha ha. I learned all about his family and his police work and even had time to treat Officer *Stupido* to two cups of coffee and a plate of pork chops. By the time I looked up and saw Ignazia, Prosperine, and the girl coming through the front door of the station, that *agente di polizia* and I were the best of friends.

"*Scusa*," I told him. "I see the wife of a friend of mine across the floor. She looks troubled about something. Would you wait here, please, while I see if there's a little problem? I don't want to alarm her if it's nothing."

He shrugged and said he was going nowhere until ten o'clock. "Just wave me over if you need me," he said. "I'll keep an eye out."

I approached them as they crossed the crowded lobby, heading with their bags toward the outside platform. "Better come home now, Ignazia!" I called out.

They pivoted toward the sound of my voice. Prosperine muttered a curse.

"My friend, the police officer over there by the ticket window, is waiting for a sign from me," I said. Their frightened eyes followed my finger to the policeman, who tipped his cap and waited. "Come with me or you'll give me no choice. I'll have to call him over here."

"Call him over then," Ignazia said. "Call him over and tell him what you do to women and children." But the trembling in her voice gave her away. The child shook in her arms. "Papa?"

Waiting for their arrival, I had filled my pockets with

sweets. I walked closer to the girl and spoke softly to her, handing her chocolates and peppermints. I whispered next to the girl's mother. "Maybe I'll tell that police officer instead about life in the Old Country—about a dead *artiste* and a fishmonger's daughter named Violetta."

Outside on the track, a whistle blew. The train rumbled in from Rhode Island. All around us, travelers picked up bags and packages, hugged loved ones, and headed for the back door of the station.

Prosperine snatched my wife's hand and pulled her toward the others. "F*retta*!" she commanded. "F*retta*, before it's too late! If we don't get on now, we'll never be rid of him."

Ignazia let the other one lead her for a few steps, then stopped and looked over her shoulder at the policeman. Her face was pale, twisted with fear.

"My friend the policeman and I have a little arrangement," I said. "The minute I give him the signal, he comes over to see what the trouble is. Come home with me, Ignazia, and there *is* no trouble. Get on that train and you'll end up in a jail cell back in Pescara. You will never see the child again if I speak up. I promise you that. Better make your decision now."

"Don't listen to his bluffing!" Prosperine barked at her. She grabbed Concettina's hand and pulled her toward the train. "New York is a big place! F*retta*!"

Ignazia moved to follow the Monkey and the child, then stopped to watch my waving arm, the policeman's nod on the opposite side of the station floor. She dropped the packages she was holding and clasped her head with both hands. "Fishmongers? Dead men? I don't even know what that crazy talk means!" she cried.

The Monkey locked her jaw, pulled at her arm. Concettina cried for her mother.

"It means," I said, "that a painter died before his time from swallowing glass and lead."

"No! Stop it, now!" Ignazia begged me. "Stop it!"

Outside, a whistle screamed. The Monkey got out the door, still holding on to the child, running now toward the train. Ignazia grabbed the bags and ran after them.

I signaled to that policeman to hurry. In a loud voice, I called to them as they pushed past others to board the train. "I'm talking about two murdering women who escaped from their sin and ran to America with false passports!"

Travelers clogging the steps up to the train turned back to stare and whisper.

"Look, Violetta!" I called. "Here comes the policeman! He's coming to get you."

Ignazia's head snapped back. She gave a little gasp. "Don't listen!" Prosperine shouted. "*Fretta!*"

"Yes, hurry, Violetta!" I called to my wife. "Hurry and get on that train. By the time you arrive in New York, I promise you, the authorities will be waiting for you at Grand Central Station. I swear it. Easier to deport you from New York—to take the child away and ship you back to Pescara where they hunger to punish a murderous wife!"

The train's wheels began slowly to roll. Prosperine, clutching child and baggage, stepped up onto the train. The whistle blew again. Ignazia was sobbing, running alongside. "*Fretta!*" Prosperine screamed. "Step up! Step up!"

The conductor warned Ignazia either to climb aboard that second or get away from the train. Prosperine reached out her hand. Ignazia took the Monkey's hand and climbed up. Then she snatched the child back in her arms and jumped down again.

"I cannot! I cannot!" Ignazia screamed to the other one, backing away. "He will take away my daughter! I cannot!"

Prosperine shook her fist at me, shouted filth.

"Better shut up and escape while you can, you toothless bitch!" I shouted back to her, running alongside the train to make sure she heard. "Better disappear from my sight or I will make sure you spend your days and nights in prison while you wait to die and go to Hell where you belong!"

Ignazia stood on the platform, rocking the child in her arms and sobbing, moaning as the other one rode away. "I cannot! I cannot! I cannot!"

I held up my hand and stopped the approaching policeman.

My wife, the girl, and I went back home.

forty-four

I spent the next several weeks tying up loose ends on Thomas's stuff, checking in with Doc Patel, and watching too much baseball. The Red Sox, mostly: bunch of bigger hopeless cases than I was. In between innings, I was trying to figure out my future.

Wake up, Birdsey, I kept telling myself. *It's May. Every other painter in town's already out there.* Then I'd reach for the remote and locate a game, list my excuses. It was like those grief books said: you didn't get over a brother's death right away—an identical twin's, especially. . . . Going up and down on ladders all day was going to put a lot of stress on my foot and ankle again. I'd paid good money for workmen's comp insurance; might as well use it until it ran out.

Truth was, I'd never loved housepainting. I'd fallen into it running away from teaching. Guys who'd started after me, younger painters, were contracting a lot of their jobs now. Danny Jankowski employed four guys, two of them full-time. He'd called me a while back, said he heard I might be bailing and wondered if I wanted to sell my power-washing equipment. The vultures were already swarming.

But painting houses wasn't *unsatisfying* work. You had your good karma jobs, your decent clients. It felt pretty good when you drove away on that last day, paid in full, having restored a little color to someone's shit-brown life.

But this was part of the trouble: I still saw Henry Rood's face up there in that window. Still felt myself falling. Jankowski had said he'd need an answer about the power washer by the end of the week. That'd been two weeks ago.

"Indecision was Hamlet's fatal flaw, Dominick," Doc Patel said one afternoon.

"Oh, man," I groaned. "Don't tell me you have a Ph.D. in Shakespeare, too?"

Since our last appointment, she'd put a new toy on the table: a thick green liquid encased in a rectangle of glass. I reached over and picked it up, made it make waves. "To paint or not to paint," I mumbled. "That is the question." But when I looked up, the good doctor was shaking her head.

"To be or not to be," she said. "To get on with your life or create your own version of your brother's imprisonment. To drown or not to drown."

She was hitting below the belt, I thought. Ten minutes earlier, I'd described for her the latest exchange dream I'd had. In this one, Dominick had died and I, Thomas, was at the wheel of the hearse, driving his body around in search of some elusive cemetery.

"Have you called the State Board of Education yet?"

I jockeyed that wave-making toy of hers back and forth, back and forth. "Nope."

"Why not?"

I shrugged. In the session before, she had informed me that my shrugging in response to difficult questions was a hostile, not a helpful, response—a passive-aggressive habit I should work on. Officially, Dr. Patel was neutral on the subject of what I should do with the rest of my life, but you could tell she was rooting for my return to teaching. You could read it between the lines. It had been *my* idea, initially; I'd mentioned it as a possibility two or three appointments back. But since then, I'd begun to actually *notice* high school kids again. At the mall, at fast-food places. They'd gotten coarser, more desperate or something. All that gang stuff kids were into now, all that bad language. The week before I'd stood in line at Subway behind two girls in Raiders jackets. "That fuckin' bitch gets in *my* face about him, I'll bust her fuckin' nose," one of them told the other. "Who the fuck she think *she* is?" She was beautiful, this kid. Hispanic. These delicate, china doll features. . . . I pictured myself standing in a classroom in front of her and her friend—trying to teach those two about the relevance of history.

"Dominick?"

"What?"

"Why *haven't* you called?"

I started to shrug but stopped myself. "I don't know. I been busy."

"Yes? Doing what?"

Watching CNN, C–SPAN. Watching baseball history in the making. The week before, I'd seen Rickey Henderson steal his 939th base and Nolan Ryan pitch his seventh career no-hitter on the same frickin' day. Not that I dared mention baseball to Doc Patel. "Those books you've been having me read?" I said. "About the grieving process? Couple of them said that it's natural to lose focus for a while. Feel a little spaced out or whatever. That it's to be *expected*." She nodded, said nothing. "What? Why are you smiling?"

"Am I smiling?" she asked.

I clunked her stupid wave-maker back onto the table. "I *meant* to call. I keep . . . I keep thinking about it after it's too late."

"Too late?"

"After hours, I mean. It'll dawn on me that I forgot and I'll look up at the clock and it'll be like fifteen minutes after they close." She gave me one of those who's-zooming-who looks and waited. "I guess I should write myself a note. That's what I'll do: write a note and leave it by the phone. . . . Maybe if they closed their offices at five instead of four-thirty, like the *rest* of the free world." Lose the snotty tone, Birdsey, I advised myself. She'll dismantle you for it. There's precedent.

Flipping through her notes, Dr. Patel reminded me that, two sessions ago, I had dictated a list of goals for myself. "Do you remember, Dominick? You told me that it would make you feel better to *act* on several things instead of continuing to vacillate. You felt that your indecision was depressing you. . . . Ah, yes, here it is. Shall we review your list?"

As if I had a choice.

"Number one," she said. "Call the State Board of Education to inquire about my teaching license. Number two, make a final decision about my business. Number three, acknowledge sympathy cards and gifts. Number four, clear the air with Ray." She asked me if I'd called back the "gentleman" who was interested in buying my equipment.

"How can I call him back when I haven't decided?" I said.

"To let him know that you are still mulling over his inquiry."

I told her Jankowski was interested in my power washer, not my mulling patterns. "Anyways, he's probably gone elsewhere by now." I shifted in my chair. What was I supposed to do? Rush into a decision about my frickin' livelihood just to please *her*?

"What about the sympathy cards?"

"Hmm?"

"Have you written back to the people who—"

"Yeah, I did that." Which was a lie. Every time I sat at my kitchen table, I'd just stare at that stack of sympathy and it would short-circuit whatever promises I'd made. I hadn't even *opened* most of those cards yet. "I started, anyway. I'm about halfway done."

Doc Patel nodded in misplaced approval. It would energize me, she said, to begin to cross things off my list. Depression was, in some ways, a crisis of energy. I had heard her say that before; we were in reruns.

"I'll have them finished next time I come in," I said. "Definitely. Not a problem." I would, too; I'd keep the TV off and start them that night.

Doc Patel closed her pad. "What about your grandfather's history, Dominick?"

"What about it?" I couldn't remember having put Domenico's life story on my list.

"Well, we haven't chatted about that for a while. The last time we discussed it, you were telling me how painful it was to read it. Do you remember? We discussed whether it was better for you to finish the history or just stop."

She waited. I couldn't speak.

"Do you remember what your decision was?"

I nodded. "I said I wanted to finish it. Get it over with. Get it behind me. . . . I don't remember putting it on my list though."

"You didn't. But I thought that as long as we were on the subject of procrastination and its connection to this depression you're feeling, it might be—"

"I'm *almost* finished with it."

"That was what you told me the last time—that you had about fifteen pages left."

"Look," I said. "The reason I'm depressed is because my brother died. Not because of some stupid things on a list. . . . We were *twins,* okay? It *hurts.*"

She nodded. "Understandable. But right now we're talking about—"

"Why'd you even *give* me those books to read—all those photocopied articles about how bereavement's a *process,* about the special needs of a grieving twin if . . . if you expect me to just be over it in fifteen minutes?"

"I don't expect you to be over it in fifteen minutes."

"I mean, he's locked up in psycho-prison for seven months. Then he gets out and drowns—kills himself, most likely—and I'm supposed to just go, 'Oh well, that's over with. Onward and upward. Time to make some major career change.' "

Dr. Patel said she most certainly understood that bereavement was a complicated process—that its movement was both forward and backward, a series of small steps over time, and not always manageable or predictable. She granted me, as well, that the circumstances surrounding Thomas's death and the fact that we were identical twins and had had a complicated relationship further entangled matters. She acknowledged my pain, she said; she neither slighted nor underestimated it. An important part of her job was to listen to my testament about Thomas's death and to explore with me my complex responses to it. But as my advocate for a mentally healthy life as a *surviving* twin—and, she said, she wished to emphasize that fact: that she was my *advocate,* not my adversary—she could not in good conscience take money for our therapy sessions and then allow me to immobilize myself under the guise of grief. *Yes,* grieving was a painful process. *Yes,* one negotiated one's losses through a series of steps. But one *lived* in the meantime. One accommodated the reality of death while living life. Dreams or no dreams, I was *not* Thomas, she said. I was Dominick. My heart beat; I drew breath. I needed to face not only my brother's death but my own life as well.

She consulted her list again. *My* list. "Have you called Ray yet?"

Bingo. The $64,000 question. All the rest had just been warmups.

In my first appointment after Thomas's funeral, I'd told her about my public tirade against my stepfather—how, after she and Sheffer had left the house on Hollyhock Avenue that day, I'd fired on Ray. Had taken him down in front of witnesses. That session had been a marathon; she'd canceled her last appointment and we'd gone on for an hour and a half longer than my scheduled time. By the end of that particular fun fest, most of the remaining Birdsey family secrets had fallen like dominoes: Thomas and my mother "playing nice" upstairs; my giving them up to Ray that afternoon when he'd come home unexpectedly. Before that session was over, I'd screamed and sobbed and chanted exactly the way my brother had chanted that night. *Let . . . me . . . out . . . of . . . here! PLEASE . . . let . . . me . . . out!* When we were done, Doc Patel had walked me down the stairs and out to my car, praising me for my big breakthrough—for having lifted the burden of all those secrets and begun, in earnest, my healing process.

And I'd *felt* unburdened, too. I'd driven away from her office feeling battle-weary but free. But it had turned out to be a pretty quick buzz; it had lasted only about as long as the ride home. Granted, I'd taken the scenic route—had driven past the old homestead on Hollyhock Avenue, out past Dessa's. But by the time I pulled up to my cookie-cutter condo that night—my sorry-ass home sweet home—the despair had already set in. Most of the anger was gone, granted, but hopelessness had seeped into the spaces. Hopelessness, exhaustion. I'd felt tired ever since. . . .

Because what good's confession without penance—right, Father Guglielmo? Right, Father LaVie? Getting your head shrunk could only take you so far, and then it came time to drop to your knees and humble yourself. Ask forgiveness of God the Father. Or, in my case, God the Stepfather. And, goddamnit, my knees just didn't seem to bend that way.

So I'd been avoiding Ray. Not answering the messages he kept leaving on my machine. Not going over there. I couldn't "clear the air" with him, whether or not I had put it on my list of goals. Whether or not he'd gone out there that morning of the funeral and planted those tulips for my mother, my brother . . . and my baby daughter. He'd been decorating Angela's grave all along, I'd found out. Almost eight years. But I *still* couldn't forgive him. Couldn't let bygones be bygones, surrender to the statute of limitations. And anyway, how could I let Ray be my old man when I was still waiting for the real thing? Still waiting for my *real* old man to show up and save the day?

"Dominick?"

"What?"

"My goodness, you're distracted today. I asked you if you had called your stepfather yet."

I answered her by not answering.

"When do you think you'll be ready to take that step?" she said. "What is your deadline, please?"

I shrugged.

At the doorway to her outer office, I thanked her, told her I'd see her on Friday—our standard *adios*. But the good doctor threw me a curveball. She was canceling our Friday appointment, she said. I should call her once I had accomplished the things on my list. She would look forward to speaking with me at that point.

I stood there, smiling, as embarrassed as I was pissed. "What is this? 'Tough love' or something?"

She said she supposed it was. Wished me good luck and closed the door.

* * *

Answering the sympathy cards wasn't *that* bad, once I started. *Not* opening them had been worse. I'd gotten a card from the crew down at Sherwin-Williams, a couple of notes from teachers at the school where I had taught. Ruth Rood sent her condolences. She was retiring at the end of the semester, she said. Putting her house on the market. She and her sister were planning to do some traveling. I had never even acknowledged her husband's bullet to the brain. Her sympathy card made no mention of him, either.

I wrote all the insides first. Depersonalized it as much as possible. Turned it into an assembly line. *Thank you for your kindness at this difficult time. Much appreciated. . . . Thank you for your kindness at this difficult time. Much appreciated. . . .* My ex-in-laws had sent this oversized gold foil job, Mass cards from the Greek church inside. I'd have to remember to tell Ray at some point: Thomas had gotten his church service after all. Servic*es*. Six Greek Masses. The Constantines had sent flowers to the funeral home, too—an arrangement twice the size of Ray's and mine. Big Gene's signature was on the sympathy card, not just Thula's. I wondered how Thula was doing since her tumble off the stool that day. I'd have to ask Leo. Dizziness could mean a lot of things. . . . It was funny, really. Whenever I saw Big Gene down at the dealership, he could barely acknowledge my existence. Then my brother dies, and he's the king of condolences. . . . That big flower arrangement had probably been turned into a tax write-off. The Mass cards, too, for all I knew. *Thank you for your kindness at this difficult time. Much appreciated.*

Mrs. Fenneck sent me a card—the librarian who'd called 911 that day and then shown up at the condo. Asking for forgiveness or dispensation or whatever the hell it was she'd wanted me to dispense that day. "My husband passed away a month ago," she wrote now. "I pray for your loss and ask you to pray for mine. I'm glad your brother has finally found peace." Well, peace be with you, too, Mrs. Fenneck. Peace on earth, good will toward widows and librarians. *Thank you for your kindness at this difficult time. Much appreciated.*

I didn't recognize the address on the card at the bottom

of the pile, but I sure as hell knew the handwriting. It turned out not to be a sympathy card; it was a birth announcement. Tyffanie Rose. Six pounds, seven ounces. Eighteen inches long.

California hadn't worked out for them, Joy wrote. They had moved back East again—to Portsmouth, New Hampshire, where Thad had once been stationed. He was working as a masseur at a "wellness" clinic now; she was waitressing at a Mexican restaurant. Things weren't going that great between them. It was pretty complicated. She had some decisions to make. Tyffanie was an easy baby, though—six weeks old and already sleeping through the night. "I've screwed up almost everything in my whole life, Dominick," Joy wrote. "Tyffanie's the one thing I managed to do right."

She'd enclosed a picture—one of those shots they take in the hospital that prove once and for all that we're related to the apes. Tyffanie Rose: dopey name, cutesy spelling. Typical. I studied the wrinkly little twerp, wished her good luck. She was going to need it with those two washouts for parents. . . . What were you supposed to *do* with pictures like that, anyway? Throw 'em out? Stuff 'em in a drawer someplace? Little Miss Monkey Face there had nothing at all to do with me, despite the fact that her mother had tried to trick me into thinking I was her father. Toss it, I told myself. I got up, got halfway over to the wastebasket, and then changed my mind. Shoved her into my shirt pocket because I couldn't think what else to do. Sat back down to my assembly line.

I stamped all the cards I'd written, put the stack over by the phone. "Call State Department of Education!" I scrawled on one of the extras. Put it on the top of the pile to remind myself.

I went into the living room and flopped onto the couch. Reached for the remote. I'd mail the cards first thing in the morning. Emily Post and Dr. Patel would both be happier than pigs in shit. At least I'd accomplished that much—could cross *one* thing off my list.

Seinfeld . . . *The Simpsons* . . . the Sox. Boston was playing New York that night. Clemens was on the mound.

Butter-butt. Big overpaid baby. Baseball's nothing but a three-hour waste of time. . . . Yeah, but the sympathy cards are done, I reminded myself; you've *earned* seven or eight innings' worth of down time. . . .

By the time I woke up, the late news was on: Rajiv Gandhi burning on a funeral pyre, Queen Elizabeth knighting Norman Schwarzkopf for having done such a bang-up job of killing Iraqis. And then, something closer to the bone: Duane Taylor being led down the courthouse steps.

He'd been arraigned that morning on 115 counts, the reporter said. The charges ranged from the aggravated sexual assault of eleven mentally unstable patients to racketeering—the consistent, methodical, and ongoing use of a state facility in the conducting of criminal activities. From the look of things, Taylor had fully recovered from his garroting, but there was nothing left of that cocky attitude I'd seen down at Hatch: him out there in that recreation yard in his cowboy hat, the big man who held the cigarette lighter and the ring of keys. He could get life if convicted, the reporter said, but the case was tricky—reliant on unreliable witnesses. When Dr. Yup had examined my brother, she'd found inconclusive evidence. But I was goddamned if I was giving Taylor the benefit of the doubt. Burn in hell, I told that hollow-cheeked motherfucker as they led him, handcuffed, into the backseat of a cruiser. Die forever.

I deadened the set, killed the lights in the kitchen. Went into my bedroom thinking I'd never get to sleep—not with a dozing session already under my belt and freakin' Duane Taylor on my mind. I brushed my teeth, washed my face, and flopped belly-down onto my bed. Lay there in the dark, thinking about those things still on my list: call Jankowski about the power washer, call the State Board of Ed.

Doc Patel was right, I knew that: grief or no grief, I had to get on with it.

Call Ray.

Finish my grandfather's book. . . .

I reached under my bed and felt for it in the dark: Domenico's manuscript. "The History of Domenico Onofrio Tempesta, a Great Man from Humble Beginnings." Once I finished that thing, I'd have a fuckin' bonfire out in the backyard. Good riddance, you pompous motherfucker.

Mother fucker. "Motherfucker," I said. In the dark, out loud.

Faced, for the first time, why I had not been able to bring myself to finish Domenico's story.

Because I was afraid, that was why.

Afraid that, by the end, he might have spoken the truth. Spelled it out in black and white. . . . Was *that* why she'd never been able to tell us? Had he taken advantage of his harelipped daughter's weakness, her innocence? . . . Was our father *not* the dashing stenographer but our own grandfather?

I lay there at the entrance of the black hole, feeling its pull. . . . Was that it, Ma? Had you been too weak to say no to him? Had Thomas and I been conceived in evil?

Sometime later on that night—after the shaking had subsided, after I was able to move voluntarily again—I rolled over in the dark. I heard a soft crinkling under me and reached over, turned on the light. Fished inside my shirt pocket. . . .

I squinted at her—Tyffanie Rose. Little Miss Monkey Face. I brought the picture to my lips and kissed it.

I put it over on my nightstand for safekeeping and turned the light off again. Lay there smiling, for some reason, in the dark.

The following morning, I drove to the post office and mailed those cards. Drove down to the beach and stood there, watching the waves, the seagulls. On my way home again, I drove right past the exit for Three Rivers. Drove all the way up to Hartford and pulled, spur of the moment, into that Cinema 1-through-500 place off of I-84. Sat there, in the dark, watching Bruce Willis and his testosterone save the free world. Again. Balls to the walls, man. Might made right. . . . Bomb those Iraqis. Hog-tie the black man, beat him with billy clubs. Make a fist and show your wife who's the boss. . . .

I drove home again. Faced the phone.

Beep. "Dominick? It's Leo. Hey, I was wondering if you

were ready to let me beat your ass in some racquetball yet? Or are you still pussying around about that foot of yours? That excuse is getting old, Birdsey. Let me know."

Beep. "This is your old man calling. You home yet? Give me a jingle, will ya?" Will do, Ray. Mind if I wait until hell freezes over first?

Beep. "Hey, Dominick. This is Lisa Sheffer. Just wanted to let you know I've been thinking about you. . . . Just wondering, basically, how you're doing. So call me. Okay?"

Beep. "Ray Birdsey. Four-fifteen P.M. You home yet?"

I'm canceling our Friday appointment, Dominick. Call me after you've accomplished the things on your list. . . .

Jankowski's wife told me she'd ask him, but she doubted he was still interested. He'd bought a power washer on Monday from some outfit in Cumberland, Rhode Island.

The third woman they referred me to at the State Department of Education was able to answer my questions about reinstatement. I'd need to take a refresher course, she said, and then take a test, and then have three classroom observations by a state-trained evaluator.

Forget about it, I told myself. The writing's on the wall. You're a housepainter.

Domenico's manuscript stayed under the bed.

I'd call Ray the *next* day, I told myself. I'd already accomplished *plenty*. I turned the TV on, turned it off again. Reached over for the Rolodex.

Shea, Sherwin-Williams, Sheffer . . .

She'd been thinking about me a lot, she said. I had been *such* a good brother. She just wanted to make sure I wasn't beating myself up about things.

I thanked her—told her I hadn't KO'd myself *just* yet. I decided to skip the counterargument I *could* have given her about what a good brother I'd been.

She wanted to know what else was new—what I'd been up to.

Not much, I said. I was trying to decide whether or not to sell my business.

"Really?" she said. "You don't feel like painting houses anymore?"

"I don't feel like falling off roofs anymore."

Somewhere during the conversation, I figured out something: *Sheffer* felt guilty. She'd been beating her*self* up. It had been her idea to put Thomas in Hope House, the place he'd wandered away from that night. When they'd sprung him so unexpectedly from Hatch, Sheffer had made an issue of how the group home would be a much safer temporary environment for him than my place.

"Look, Lisa," I said. "I want you to know something, okay? Nobody's blaming you for anything. You did everything you could for him and *then* some—up to and including getting whacked in the face at that hearing. We'd *all* be a bunch of geniuses if we had hindsight ahead of time."

She said Dr. Patel had told her basically the same thing. She'd started seeing Dr. Patel, by the way. Professionally. Not to be nosy, but was *I* still seeing her?

"Uh, yeah," I said. "Off and on." So much for confidentiality.

Sheffer advised me to discuss my decision about the painting business with Dr. Patel—that she might be able to help me "objectify" my options. Social worker talk.

"I *have* talked about it with her," I said.

"And?"

"She thinks I should pack it in. Go back to teaching." Sheffer said she could picture me in front of a high school class.

I could, too—that was the problem: I kept seeing those two little tough cookies I'd stood behind at Subway. Kept remembering those students' faces that day I'd cried in front of them. That day I'd left my classroom and never gone back. Diana Montague, Randy Cleveland, Josie Tarbox. Those kids must all be in their midtwenties by now. Out of college, into adult lives. Kids of their own, now, some of them. "Yeah, well," I told Sheffer. "I may sell the business, I may not. I'm still weighing my options. But anyway, I'm grateful for everything you did for my brother. I mean it, Lisa. Thanks."

"Hey, you know what?" she said. "Would you like to get together sometime? Come over for dinner? I can make you my Jewish-Italian specialty: spaghetti and matzoh balls?" I started stammering something about appreciating the invitation *but*—

"I'm not asking you *out*," she said. "If that's what you think. I'm asking you *over*."

"Oh," I said. "Well. . . ."

"I'm not hitting on you, *paisano*. Honest. I'm gay, Dominick."

"Oh. Right. I didn't think . . . I mean, I don't have a problem with . . . You *are*?"

She suggested we start over. "Hello, Dominick? This is Lisa Sheffer. You want to come over some night for supper? Meet my daughter and my partner, Monica?"

I didn't know what else to say, so I said okay. Asked her what I could bring.

"Bottle of chianti and a bottle of Mogen David," she said. "We'll mix 'em."

"They were so much alike," I said. "In some ways, *they* were more like identical twins than he and I were."

"Thomas and your mother? Yes? Explain, please."

Over the phone, I'd told her what I had and hadn't accomplished on my list. She'd given me bonus points for having made dinner plans with Sheffer—for having "engaged outwardly" instead of continuing my "love affair with inertia." Her Majesty had granted me a two o'clock appointment.

"I don't know. They were both so gentle. So defenseless. . . . Every year she'd go to parent-teacher conferences and come back and we'd be like, 'What did she say? What did the teacher say?' And every year, one teacher after the next, it'd be the same thing: how smart *I* was, how sweet *he* was. That was always the word they used: Thomas was so 'sweet.' And he was, too. He just *was*. But . . ."

"Yes? Go on."

"He was *weak*. Just like she was. . . . I had to take care of both of them. And I think . . ."

She waited several seconds. "You think what, Dominick?"

"I think . . . oh, man, this is hard . . . I think that was why she loved him more. Because both of them were so goddamned powerless. . . . It was like they were soul mates or something."

Dr. Patel sipped her tea. Waited.

"Do you think . . . ?" I stopped, stymied by how to put it. My hands started to shake.

"What is it, Dominick? Ask me."

"No, I was just thinking yesterday that maybe *that's* how she got pregnant. . . . I mean, it would explain a lot. Wouldn't it?"

Doc Patel said she wasn't following me.

"She was always so scared to death of everything. So powerless. So I was thinking: maybe she got raped."

"Raped by . . . ?"

"I don't know. By some stranger. Maybe our father was just some miscellaneous son of a bitch who grabbed her, pulled her into a dark alley someplace, and . . ."

I stood up, went over by the window. Rocked back and forth on my heels.

"It's not like she would have fought back or anything. I *know* she wouldn't have. She probably didn't even know what sex was until . . . She probably wouldn't even have known what he was doing."

"No? You think not?"

I looked out the window. The river was moving fast. The trees were budding. In another week or two, those unfolding leaves would obscure Doc Patel's view of the water. I turned back and faced her. "This one time? We were pretty young, Thomas and me—seven or eight, maybe. And we were on the city bus: the three of us."

"Your mother, Thomas, and you?"

I nodded. "We'd gone to the movies, I remember, and then over to the five-and-ten for sodas. And we were on our way back home, okay? On the bus. And . . . and this crazy guy gets on. Walks down the aisle and sits across from us. . . . Across from Thomas and me. He pushes in right next to my mother."

"Go on, please, Dominick. You're safe here. Let it go."

"And he starts . . . feeling her. Touching her. *Sniffing* at her."

"Be yourself on the bus for a moment. Are you afraid?"

"Yes."

"Angry?"

"Yes!"

"What does your mother do, Dominick? The man is touching her and she—"

"Nothing! That's what she does: nothing! She just sits there because she's so . . . so *weak* and . . ."

Dr. Patel handed me the Kleenex box. "She doesn't scream? She doesn't get up and tell the bus driver?"

"No! And I *hated* that! . . . She was always so *afraid*."

"On the bus. At home with Ray."

"It wasn't *fair*! I was just a *kid*!"

"What wasn't fair, Dominick?"

"I had to defend all three of us. Myself, and *him*, and *her*. And even then . . . even when I did . . ." I was sobbing now; I couldn't help it.

"And even then, although you protected her *and* your brother—fought *both* of their battles for them—even then, she loved your brother more than you?"

My head jerked up and down, up and down. I couldn't speak. Couldn't stop wailing at the truth.

The boys have the muscles! The coaches have the brains!
The girls have the sexy legs so let's play the game!

Sheffer's daughter, Jesse, shook her pom-poms like she meant it. She'd befriended me even before I'd gotten both feet in the door. Within the first half-hour of my visit, I'd been brought down to the basement to see her gerbils, up to her room to see her Barbies. Now I was out on the driveway so I could see her Midget Football cheerleader moves. Sheffer and Monica stood flanking me while Jesse turned cartwheels. "My theory is that Olivia Newton-John went into labor the same day and they mixed up our babies in the nursery," Sheffer said, under her breath. "There's just no other explanation."

Monica was a rugged six-footer from Kittery. She and another woman ran a small home-repair business. Womyn's Work, they called themselves.

"So how's business?" I asked her, my chin pointing toward her pickup, parked in the driveway. Jesse had fallen, midcheer, and scraped her knee. She and her mom had gone inside for a Band-Aid. Monica held her arm out and gave a thumbs-down.

"Couple of years ago? When we started up? We figured

that in *this* economy, everyone's just holding on to what they've got—fixing things up instead of building new. But it's been leaner than we figured it'd be. My partner and I are good—we're *damn* good—but you've got to get past people's biases."

"Like what?" I said.

"Like, that you need a penis in order to swing a hammer or knock down a wall." She laughed. "No offense, there, *hombre*. Lisa says you're a housepainter?"

"Technically," I said. "Maybe not much longer."

"That's what Lisa said." She and her business partner were trying to diversify a little, she told me—pick up some landscaping work, *maybe* some painting jobs. They were going to decide at the end of the season whether or not they could keep the boat afloat. "If not, I can always go back to my paying job," she said. "Systems analyst. *Bor*-ing."

After dinner, Jesse had to give me *two* goodnight hugs before Monica piggybacked her up to bed, Sheffer trailing behind them with a stack of laundry. Monica came back down first.

"Jesse's a cutie," I said. "Miss Cheerleader, huh?"

"Miss Pain in the Butt, usually," Monica said. "But she's a good kid. Throws a baseball like a girl, though."

I smiled. Asked her how she and Lisa had met.

At the women's shelter over in Easterly, she said. She'd done some pro bono carpentry work for them the year before and ended up on their Board of Directors.

"Yeah? Is Lisa on the board, too?" I said.

Monica averted her eyes. "Nope. Hey, you want a beer?"

We went out to the kitchen. Shot the shit about the highs and lows of owning your own business. "Hey," I said. "If I do decide to sell my painting equipment, would you be interested?" Monica said it depended on what it was, what kind of condition it was in, and how I felt about the installment plan. If they *did* start a painting sideline, they damn sure weren't going to be able to afford new equipment.

I liked her. Liked being there that night. I had a much better time than I'd figured I would. It was after eleven by the time I even looked at my watch.

Sheffer walked me out to my car. She told me that when

she was thirteen, her oldest brother had died of leukemia. "He was eight years older than me," she said. "My hero, in a lot of ways. But, god, I can't even *imagine* what it would be like to lose your twin."

"It's like . . . it's like losing part of who *you* are. I don't know. In a lot of ways, we were pretty different. Which was fine with me. Just the way I wanted it. But all my life, I've been . . . I've been *half* of something, you know? Something special—something kind of unique—even *with* all the complications. *Wow, look. Twins.* . . . And now, that specialness—that wholeness—it just doesn't exist anymore. So it's weird. Takes some getting used to. . . . Not that it was ever easy: being his brother. Even *before* he got sick. Doc Patel says I'm grieving for him—for Thomas—and for that, too. That wholeness."

Sheffer reached over and took my hand.

"She says I've got to get used to my new status. Survivor. Solitary twin."

I asked Sheffer if she remembered the day they released him from Hatch. How she had tried to warn me not to let my arrogance get in the way of my brother's safety.

"Oh, Dominick," she said. "Sometimes I run my mouth when I have no—"

"No, you were right," I said. "I *was* arrogant. You think I didn't get off on that little power arrangement we'd always had? Being the *strong* one? The twin who *didn't* get the disease? . . . That's something else Doc and I are working on—what to do with all this arrogance I've got left over. All this righteous indignation. It's just sort of sitting there, parked and not doing anything. Like me, I guess."

Sheffer took me in her arms and held me. Rocked me back and forth a little. It felt good to be held like that—held by someone who'd turned into my friend.

"I'll be all right," I said. "Hey, by the way, I like your girlfriend. She may be buying my compressor."

I was whipped when I got home. Left the kitchen lights off and headed straight to bed. Went out—*bam!*—like that.

But somewhere in the middle of the night, I woke up thirsty. Fumbled my way out to the kitchen for a glass of juice. The answering machine light was blinking red against the shiny surfaces of the toaster, the door of the microwave. Blink, blink, pause. Blink, blink, pause. I hadn't noticed it before. I hit "play" and stood there.

The first caller was Joy. Had I gotten her note a while back? The picture she'd sent of Tyffanie? Was I at all interested in seeing the baby in person? If I was, I should give her a call. Maybe we could each drive halfway or something. She said her number slowly, then said it again.

The second message was from a Dr. Azzi. "Your father's surgeon," he said.

The operation had gone well; no surprises. He'd amputated just a little above the knee, which was what he'd figured. He was sorry he had missed me at the hospital but would be in touch the next morning. When he'd left the hospital at eight that evening, my father was still groggy but resting comfortably.

Above the knee? Amputated? What the hell was he talking about?

Dr. Azzi's answering service told me he wasn't to be called unless it was a medical emergency but that he sometimes called in for his messages before he retired for the evening. The woman said she'd tell him I had called.

Was *that* why Ray had kept calling me? Was *that* what that limp had been about?

Amputated. . . .

And maybe I'd have *known* what was going on if I'd just had the decency to call him back.

He'd planted tulips at Angela's grave.

Bullied my brother and me our whole lives.

I had *humiliated* him that day of Thomas's funeral.

He'd busted my mother's arm. . . .

Somewhere in the middle of the night, I went into the bedroom. Flopped onto the bed and reached under there.

Pulled out Domenico's manuscript.

I sat up. Opened it.

I would finish it, this time, no matter what the fuck it revealed. No matter who it told me I was. . . .

forty-five

17 *August* 1949

And so, by digging that poor *bastardo* of a stained-glass painter out of his grave, I got what I wanted. I had my wife back and I had rid myself of that crazy goddamned Monkey. I had shown both of them the folly of fucking with Tempesta.

I made a new rule. Ignazia could sleep downstairs in the back bedroom during weeknights but was now expected to visit me upstairs in my bed on Saturday and Sunday. A little comfort once or twice a week in exchange for all I provided for her and the child wasn't much to ask, I reminded her; in marriage, a wife gave as well as took. With a little care and common sense, she could perform her duty to me without putting a baby inside of herself. And if an accident resulted, then maybe it was God's will. Maybe her heart was stronger than that '*Mericano* doctor had said. You'll probably end up an old gray-haired *nonna* with a dozen grandchildren trailing after you, I told her. God Almighty blessed family life. God provided.

She threatened to go to my friend Father Guglielmo and tell him about my new rule. "If you want me to keep your secrets about the Old Country," I said, "then you had better keep the ones at this house, too. No squealing inside the confessional. And no squealing, either, to *Signora* Tusia on the other side of the house or to that *dottore* who scared you away from me in the first place." Furthermore, I said, I wanted no more idle chitter-chatter with her '*Mericana* lady friends in the neighborhood. "They'll look at that long face of yours and think you're worse off than you are. Those women would like nothing better than to see trouble in an Italian home. '*Mericani* are nice to your face and call you 'dirty wop' behind your back. They want us all to fail. They wait for that to happen."

That overpriced Sears and Roebuck baby carriage stood idle in the front hallway. Ignazia obeyed my new rules, and the child grew, and our lives went on.

Around Three Rivers, I became busier than ever: zoning board, committee member for this, officer for that. I no longer saw Josephine Reynolds. Too busy. I advised families just over from the Old Country and *paisani* from the mill eager to move from the row houses owned by American Woolen and Textile to homes of their own. If I had charged for all the free advice I gave, I would have been a millionaire! This was the price I paid for being shrewd with my money and successful in life. Half of the town wanted directions from Domenico Tempesta about how to live life!

In the spring of 1924, I was voted *Il Presidente* of Sons of Italy. (Picture in the newspaper, page two. That burned me up a little. Graziadio had been *presidente* the year before and they'd put his fat puss on page one.) At American Woolen and Textile, some troublemakers came up from New Haven and there was talk of organizing a union for dyers. I didn't like the looks of those goddamned outsiders; they put ideas in my workers' heads. When Domenico Tempesta spoke out against the union, the plan fell apart. The agent, Baxter, bought me a bottle of whiskey and had the butcher deliver a dressed turkey to my home. (The meat was tough.) He had had a talk with his father-in-law, Baxter said; there was a plan in a year or two to promote me from dye house boss to nighttime supervisor of Plant Number 2.

The politicians were talking to me, too—Democrats *and* Republicans. Shanley, the mayor, called me on the telephone one afternoon and invited me to his office. He sat me across from his fancy oak desk and lit me a cigar almost as long as my forearm. It was going to be an uphill battle to get reelected in November, he said. He needed every vote he could get. The Italians in town had always had poor voter turnout. He wondered if I might help to turn that around. "You're highly respected in this community, Domenico," Shanley said. "And, of course, if you agree to work for us, maybe we could sweeten the deal."

I held my hat in my hand and looked as much as I could like the *immigrante stupido* he thought I was. "How you say 'sweeten the deal,' your excellency?" I asked. Crooked politicians who wanted something had to be willing to give a little something, too.

"Oh, we'll just keep that open for now," Shanley said. "An appointment, maybe. A favor granted here and there. George B. Shanley doesn't forget his friends or his friendly constituencies. It's like having money in the bank." I told him I would think about his request.

Walking home from that goddamned Democrat's office, I remembered the haughty couple aboard the SS *Napolitano*—those two who had stood and watched the waiter kick me awake. I thought, too, about what I had shouted to the three of them as I stumbled back below to steerage: *Some go up the steps and some go down*. And it had proven true! I had come to this country and made something of myself. *Paisani* listened to me when I gave them advice and now *'Mericano* politicians kissed my ass. Everyone wanted Domenico Tempesta for a friend. I was regarded as a man of dignity and worth throughout Three Rivers, Connecticut.

Throughout the town, yes, but not inside my own home. There, my wife cooked, cleaned, and opened her legs to me on Saturday and Sunday nights as I ordered. In her duties, she was obedient. I had scared the defiance out of her. Yet she submitted to me just as the girl Hattie on Bickel Road had submitted—with *distrazione, indifferenza* . . . with contempt written in her eyes. And always, when I awoke in the morning, she was gone from my bed, escaped back downstairs to her sewing in the back bedroom or her scrubbing in the kitchen or to her duties to the growing girl—that split-lipped reminder that my unloving wife had known how to love a no-good redhead back in Brooklyn.

Ignazia no longer took walks into town to stare into the store windows and shop for my dinner. Now she learned how to use the telephone and called in her order to Hurok's. Her face and ears would blush with shame as she shouted into the receiver, repeating again and again the names of items and brands until Hurok or his wife understood what it was she wanted, or until she slammed down the receiver and cried. She withdrew further from *'Mericano* ways; she had learned nothing but the rudiments of English, preferring instead to chitter-chatter with that scrawny accomplice of hers. But the Monkey's banishment had silenced her. Her pronunciation of English was hopeless. Even her Italian was limited by the intellect of her gender and by the dialect of her native village. I brought Italian newspapers into our home, *La Sicilia, La Nave*. Myself, I read them from front to back, but Ignazia was indifferent now even to news of the Old Country. More and more, she was alone.

"Tell that wife of yours to come next door and visit me, Domenico," *Signora* Tusia said one day at the front gate. "You would think that partition between our apartments was the Atlantic Ocean!" But Ignazia was no longer interested in visiting. Not interested, either, in attending banquets or social events as the wife of the most respected *Italiano* in Three Rivers, Connecticut. She had not even attended my installation as *presidente* of *Figli d'Italia*. At first she had said she was going and then, that evening, she wouldn't go. She shook her head no so often that I stopped asking her to accompany me. She stayed inside, moping and cleaning and playing with her red-haired, rabbit-faced daughter. After a while, Ignazia would not even answer the telephone when it rang. She would not answer the doorbell. Her daughter and her daily chores became the only two things in her life.

One night, before I went off to work, Ignazia put stewed chicken and polenta and a bowl of escarole and lentils in front of me for my supper. I ate and ate and when I put the last forkful of polenta into my mouth, my tooth bit down on something hard. I spat a little gray nugget into my hand.

Ignazia was in the bedroom, singing a song to Concettina, and making the girl's little dollies dance before her eyes. That wife of mine treated her husband like a dog and her daughter like a princess.

"What's this?" I said.

She squinted. "Looks like a little pebble."

"It was in my food."

"In the lentils?" She shrugged. "Sometimes a stone sneaks in."

"Not in the lentils," I said. "In the polenta."

Another shrug. "Probably a little chip from the millstone when they ground the corn." She held out her hand. "Give it to me. I'll throw it away for you. Lucky you didn't break a tooth."

I snapped my hand closed on the pebble. "Don't bother," I told her. "I'll throw it away." Instead, I wrapped it inside my handkerchief and put it in my pocket. Ignazia had shown me no love, I told myself, but no real hatred, either. I provided her and the child everything they needed. She would be a fool to fool with my life.

That night at work, I kept poking my hand inside my pocket to feel the tiny pebble, roll it between my thumb and finger. Was it a stone or a small piece of glass? Glass is clear, I told myself. This shard is cloudy. Still . . .

What else had she given me to swallow? Earlier that week, I had been plagued with foul gas; the Saturday before, I'd gone to bed with upset stomach. I had blamed it on bad wine, but maybe it had not been the wine. By the middle of my shift that night at the mill, I had convinced myself that my wife was poisoning me—getting ready to do me in as she had done in her last husband, Gallante Selvi, *a buon'anima*. Should I go home and beat the truth out of her? Should I go in the morning to see Father Guglielmo? Confide my suspicion to the priest and seek his advice? . . . No, that would not do. Domenico Tempesta was a man who *gave* advice now. Guglielmo would probably tell me to forgive my wife as Jesus forgave—to keep swallowing her tainted food and, for penance, to write down the recipes! I promised myself that if murder was what my wife was up to, I would make her pay. But I needed proof.

When my pocket watch said 2 A.M., I went to the office and told Baxter that I had a bad toothache and needed to go home. I didn't like leaving work—had only done it twice before in sixteen years of service to American Woolen and Textile. But if that sneaky bitch was trying to poison me, I had to act quickly. Hunt for proof while she slept. Catch her before she knew I suspected anything. . . .

When I got home, I took off my shoes at the front door and lit the oil lamp, adjusting it to its dimmest glow. Tiptoeing through the house in stocking feet, I entered the kitchen. As quietly as a thief, I opened drawers, poked inside bins, felt with my fingers along the highest shelves. I was looking for glass powder or solder wire or whatever other murderous ingredients she might be using against me.

She was in the back bedroom; I heard her groan in her sleep. I stopped and waited, then began hunting and poking again. She groaned a second time.

Then a voice spoke—not my wife's.

If that goddamned mick of a monsignor had never visited me that morning years before—if his insults had not angered me enough to throw the wet cement at him—then 66-through-68 Hollyhock Avenue would never have borne the curse that Guglielmo and all the holy water in the world had not been able to dissolve! If McNulty had not trespassed against me, I would never have seen what I saw that night when I snuck home like a burglar and entered my own house in stocking feet. On that terrible night, that godforsaken monsignor must have laughed from Hell in anticipation of what I was about to discover. That night, the curse that McNulty had put on my *casa di due appartamenti* bore its most bitter fruit. . . .

I made the lamp bright—stood for a moment at that bedroom door, then threw it open. I smelled her before I saw her—the stink of her pipe tobacco.

At first, my brain could not understand what my eyes showed me: the two of them, clinging to each other like monkeys. . . . Ignazia, I weep to this day for the sins that cast you into Hell, for the shame you brought upon my good name.

They screamed when they saw me, scrambling from the bed. "Oh, no! Oh, no! Oh, no!" Ignazia shrieked. Prosperine clutched the sheet in front of herself and grabbed Ignazia's sewing scissors.

That goddamned smelly Monkey was wild-eyed with hatred and fear. She inched her way toward the door, scissors raised and ready to hack me dead, and thus escaped from the room, first, and then from the house. Lucky for her and lucky for me, too, I realized later. If I had understood the perversion I saw—if I had been able to act immediately upon what I had interrupted—I might have strangled her on the spot. Might have ended up in the newspaper as the shamed husband whose wife . . .

I weep. It shames me to tell it, but I must let it out. . . .

Ignazia made a run from me, too—not out the back door like the other one, but upstairs to the girl's room. I caught her halfway up the stairs. "Don't hurt Concettina!" she begged. "Kill me if you want, but don't harm an innocent child!"

I told her to shut up her mouth, to let me think. My head was nearly ready to explode! Ignazia dropped to her knees, cowering at my feet like a scared rabbit. She sobbed, choking, begging me not to take her life—not to send her off to Hell and make Concettina a motherless child.

I must have stared for a minute or more, my mind racing to decide what to do—how to respond to the depravity I had seen in my back bedroom and could not stop seeing. What other husband in the world has ever faced what I faced that night?

Forgive even that, P*adre* Guglielmo? Is that what you would have told me? Forgive even *that*? . . .

"Get up!" I ordered her. Grabbed her hair and *pulled* her up. "You are the wife of Domenico Tempesta, not filth on the floor. Get into the bathroom and clean yourself. Wash away the stink of that she-devil." Ignazia would burn in Hell, all right—but not before I was finished with her.

That night I reclaimed what was rightfully mine—took what I had a right to take, did the things only a *man* can do to a woman. And when Ignazia's screams threatened to carry through the walls to Tusia's *appartamento*, I held my elbow to her throat and shut her up and took some more of what belonged to me. To me, not that goddamned Monkey! For the rest of that night, I reclaimed what was mine!

Next morning, I went to S*ignora* Siragusa's to see if the Monkey was hiding there. The *signora* said she had not seen her; it was the sorrow in the old woman's eyes I believed more than the words coming out of her mouth. She grabbed my arm and held it. Whatever new trouble there was in my house, the *signora* said, she only hoped I would not make worse trouble—would not act the brute. "Bah!" I said, and walked out the front door without closing it. Let that meddlesome old woman's coal heat the outside. What did I care? My business was *my* business.

I didn't go home. I went to the junkyard to see Yeitz, the ragpicker. He had been trying to sell me a police dog for over a month. I handed him three dollars and he handed me the rope and the dog. "Never had a better watchdog than this fella right here," Yeitz told me. "Good hunter, too. He can be a mean son of a bitch, though. He'd just as soon tear a rat apart as let it live."

Back at my house, I pulled from my pocket the underclothes that toothless Monkey had left behind and stuck them in front of the dog's nose. He sniffed and sniffed, then led me through backyards, over the top of Pleasant Hill, and into the woods. At the clearing, I saw that I had been led to the north side of Rosemark's Pond by a route I had never walked before. That goddamned dog began to bark and lunge toward old Rosemark's fishing shack on the far end of the pond. I jerked the rope almost hard enough to break his goddamned neck. Then I got him the hell out of there. Now I knew what I needed to know. In a short time, I would have my *vendetta*. However she had gotten back to Three Rivers, that filthy Monkey would regret that she had done it. I would make her sorry she had fucked with the thing that belonged to Domenico Onofrio Tempesta. She would pay the price!

Back at home, I nailed the back door and downstairs windows shut and drove an iron stake into the front yard. With the heaviest chain I had, I tied that damn dog to the stake. No one was going in or out of my front door unless I wanted it. Ignazia was terrified of the dog—afraid of its barking and lunging at her and the girl as they peeked out the windows. This was just the dog I wanted—just the animal to guard a faithless *fica* of a wife whose husband worked at night.

Upon my orders, Ignazia slept upstairs now. We were husband and wife again, as God had intended. I had never stopped wanting her in that way; my *passione* for her had survived even her vile betrayal. Sometimes, in the middle of my relief, I would see again what I had seen that crazy night: the Monkey and my wife, clutching each other in sin and perversion. I would finish my business in anger, then, sometimes striking her if she cried, and then I would get off of her—wait until her sobbing stopped, until her breathing said she was falling asleep. Then I would lean to her and whisper in her ear. "Maybe I've put a baby inside of you, eh? . . . Maybe I've just planted the seed that will burst your heart and send you to Hell where you belong."

Love and hatred: I bore the burden of them both for having loved a faithless wife, and so we each imprisoned the other. . . .

And as for that other depraved and toothless *mona*, I fixed her wagon!

"Why, Domenico, my friend! To what do I owe the pleasure, sir?" Shanley said, rising from behind his big *pezzo grosso* of a mayor's desk to shake my hand. It was the morning after the police dog had led me to the shack by Rosemark's Pond.

I told Shanley I had been seriously considering his request that I help recruit Italian voters for him before the next election.

"Splendid news!" he said. "Well worth exploring! Sit down, sir! Sit!"

"I'm *considering* it," I repeated. "But first, there is a little matter I'd like your help with."

"Anything, Domenico," that crooked *bastardo* told me, and he smiled a smile that showed his gold back teeth. "Anything at all, my good friend."

I told him about the crazy woman from the Old Country who had once worked inside my home and who now plagued my family. I explained that my wife and I had been good enough to take in this poor creature when we were married, but that, in her craziness, she had turned against us. We had put up as best we could with her eccentricities, I told the mayor—her mumbled curses, her petty thefts. But then she had threatened to hurt our precious little daughter. "Pathetic as she is," I told the mayor, "we have had to put her out of our house."

"Of course you did," Shanley insisted. "What choice did you have, poor man?"

After that, I told the mayor, this poor wretch had gone completely mad. For a while, she had run away to who-knew-where? But now she had come back. The night before, I told him, I had seen her peeking in the window. My dog and I had tracked her scent to a shack near old man Rosemark's Pond, on the other side of Pleasant Hill. I worked nights, I said. I was afraid of what she might do to my wife or my child when I wasn't there to protect them. "She's crazy, but she's sneaky, too," I said.

"She's crazy like a fox," the mayor agreed. He picked up the telephone and began dialing the Chief of Police. "Why, you've done the town a service by bringing this public menace to my attention, my friend," Shanley told me. "I'll have her picked up and put behind bars before the noon whistle blows. I'll make sure Chief Confrey makes it his top priority."

"*Scusa*," I said, raising my hand to stop him. The mayor stopped, hung up the telephone. "I was thinking . . . if she spends a few days in jail, then the problem is fixed for a few days. If she's put away in the crazy hospital where she belongs, then my poor wife and child can walk the streets again. That woman is lunatic. One time she even claimed she was a witch!"

"You're absolutely right!" Shanley said, slapping the top of his desk. "You're a shrewd man, my friend. And a practical one, too. If she has to be locked up, we might as well put her on the state's dole instead of on the city's. Ha ha." He called for his secretary to bring him the telephone number of Three Rivers State Hospital.

I waited and listened as Shanley talked on the telephone with one person, then another person. "The *mayor* of this fair city, *that's* who's calling, you goddamned jackass!" he shouted into the telephone. Then Dr. Henry Settle, the *pezzo grosso* of that godforsaken asylum, got on the line.

They talked about this, about that, and then Shanley finally got down to business. He cupped his hand over the receiver and turned to me.

"Does she have any relatives in town? If she won't sign herself in, they'll need a relative to do it for her—a blood relation to sign her in and sign her back out again if she gets cured."

I told him it would be a miracle if that addle-brained cousin of mine ever got cured—that if my poor auntie back in the Old Country could see that daughter of hers now, she would cry a river of tears. Shanley gave me a wink.

I met the police and the *dottore* at the asylum. They took her out of the paddy wagon, bucking and straining against the straitjacket they had forced her into. When the Monkey saw me, she screamed every curse in the devil's book!

After I had signed my name to the papers they wanted me to sign, I took my cap off my head and clutched it in my hand, playing once again the part of the humble immigrant. "*Scusai*," I whispered to the guard in charge. "May I have a moment in private to say goodbye to my poor cousin?" The idiot shrugged and moved across the room. I leaned close to Prosperine, pretending to give my *cugina* a goodbye kiss. But instead, I put my lips to her ear. "There's more than one way to fuck the monkey that fucks with Domenico Tempesta!" I whispered. Then

I lurched back and spat in her face the way she had spat on my *medaglia*. I left her tugging and lunging, screaming the most filthy oaths and curses of the Italian language. I had fixed that one for good!

I never saw the Monkey again. For all I know, she's still living down at that place for lunatics. Still eating and drawing breath, and paying the price she paid for fucking with Tempesta. I was never notified otherwise, but if she is dead, then I spit on her grave. . . .

For twenty-six years now—through all the tragedy and grief that has followed—through all my hard work and success and sleepless hours—I have always had that small satisfaction, at least: the memory of that moment when I won my battle against the Monkey, when I used my God-given cleverness to punish that she-devil for the sins she had committed against Domenico Tempesta.

In September of that year, the archbishop in Hartford made Father Guglielmo a monsignor and transferred him to a parish in Bridgeport. There was a High Mass for Guglielmo in honor of his installation and a banquet afterward. I received a fancy engraved invitation but could not afford the time for a trip to Bridgeport. I was too busy canvassing the West Side and the neighborhoods near the mill, knocking on doors and turning *paisani* into Democrats for Mayor Shanley.

In October, *Signora* Siragusa died in her sleep and I helped her sons carry her coffin to the grave. I wept for the old *signora* as if she had been my own mother—as if her flesh and bone had been mine. You see, Guglielmo? I still had tears inside my head. The troubles that God and the Monkey had given me had not completely hardened the heart of Tempesta! The *signora*'s sons were, of course, grateful to have a dignitary such as myself to help them bear their mother's coffin.

The following month, Shanley lost the election in

spite of my efforts on his behalf. Lost *because* of my efforts, that ungrateful goddamned son of a bitch told his two cronies, Rector and O'Brien, right in front of my face. The four of us sat there in his office the morning after, those three micks puffing away on their cigars. Shanley offered me no smoke. I was no longer good enough for one of his stinking cheap panatelas.

"You want to know how we lost it, boys?" Shanley said. "We lost it on account of three wops named Sacco, Vanzetti, and Tempesta. First, our friend here spends over half a grand registering every goddamned dago in this town that breathes and a few that don't. Then, two days before the election, he decides to spout off his mouth to the newspaper about how those goddamned murdering son-of-a-bitching anarchists up there in Massachusetts are poor, innocent victims. 'Does Mayor Shanley share your sentiments about this case, Mr. Tempesta?' 'Oh, yes. The mayor strongly supports all Italian-Americans.' As if I had to wipe the ass of every goddamned guinea in this town. It wouldn't have been so bad if all those wops we paid a dollar apiece to register had been smart enough to figure out that it was a package deal—that they had to register *and* vote in the goddamned election! Well, the swamp Yankees voted, all right, didn't they, boys? They came out with a vengeance so they could keep us all safe from wops and anarchists, and *that's* why Flint Peterson is the goddamned mayor-elect! *That's* how he did it, boys: with the help of our friend the organ-grinder here!"

I rose from my chair and took my hat from the rack. I told him I had worked my ass off for him and would not now sit there and be his scapegoat.

"Oh, no?" Shanley said. "Then whose '*skeppa goata*' are you?"

After all the work I had done for that son of a bitch, he sat there mocking my English, mocking me! "Go piss in your hats, the three of you," I told him and his goons. I'd had a bellyful of those swindlers and their dirty politics. I slammed that office door so hard, I thought the glass was going to fall out!

18 *August* 1949

It was 10 January 1925. A Tuesday, it was. Tuesday or Wednesday? I can't remember now. But I must remember. . . .

That month, the Navy had given American Woolen a rush job. The summer before, they had given us a smaller order than usual for wool for pea jackets. Then, suddenly, halfway through the winter, they need enough dyed wool for ten thousand new jackets. The Navy was always that way—no planning and then they needed everything in a hurry! For a week, I had been working double shifts, getting by on three, four hours' sleep. I was exhausted. I got home a little after eight in the morning.

Bitter cold that day, I remember. January had been warmer than usual, and then, suddenly, below zero. I was worried that Ignazia hadn't put enough coal in the stove—worried that the pipes might freeze.

The dog was the first sign that something was wrong. He lay on his side, stomach collapsed, dead in his own bloody vomit. Poisoned. I pushed him a little with my foot but he didn't budge. He was stuck stiff to the ground; he'd been dead for a while.

When I opened the door and went inside, a bird flew past my eyes! A sparrow, it was. I should have known then: a bird in the house is no good. I am not a superstitious man, but some signs cannot be ignored.

The fireplace in the parlor was stone cold. The radiators, too. The kitchen stove. I stood staring at the closed door of the back bedroom.

I put my hand on the cold knob but was afraid to open

it—afraid of what I would see. I stood there, looking at my own breath. She never closed that door during the daytime. Never.

That goddamned bird flew in circles around the parlor, its wings skidding against the walls, its body crashing repeatedly into the mirror above the mantelpiece.

"Ignazia!" I called at the closed door. "Eh! Ignazia!" No answer.

I went upstairs. "Ignazia? . . . Concettina?"

Our bed was neatly made. Nothing overturned, nothing unusual. Her clothes and things were in the closet, in the drawers. I went to the girl's room. Everything there, too. . . .

I went down to the cellar, started the furnace again. It took a while to get going. If the pipes froze, there'd be hell to pay. I stayed down there twenty minutes, half an hour, shoveling coal and watching it catch and burn. Twice, I thought I heard footsteps above my head, but when I stopped shoveling, it was quiet up there.

When I went upstairs again, that sparrow was dead on the parlor floor. I picked it up in my hand and carried it to the kitchen. Wrapped the goddamned thing in newspaper and threw it in the garbage. You would have thought a *flock* of sparrows had gotten inside, from all the feathers, blood, and shit it left. That one little bird with its crushable bones.

I still remember that: the mess that thing left in dying.

C*onfessione* is good for the soul, eh? That's what Guglielmo used to tell me. I lost track of him after he moved to Bridgeport. I couldn't say, even, if he is dead or alive. . . . "Do your penance, Domenico. Reflect on your life and be *umile*. Write it down. . . . Be humble, Domenico. To be human is to be humble. What choice is there, really? Let none of us attempt God's work."

But I was never too good at *confessione*. . . .

The police pulled her body from the bottom of Rosemark's Pond. I was there; I saw her come out of the water. She had fallen through the ice and drowned in the middle of the night, the coroner said. Before the bitter cold had set in. He could tell from the body's bloating.

I thought she had taken the girl to her death as well. There was evidence: their footprints, helter-skelter, in the snow that covered the ice. Those footprints told of a struggle between them. Now both the son and daughter she had birthed on my kitchen table were gone. She had killed a husband, and now, God help her, a daughter, too. She had hated me enough to do it. She had despaired enough to drown the one she loved the most.

But Concettina was alive, hiding in the shack, half-frozen but still breathing. That's how they found her—the police; her whimpering led them to her. And when I picked her up and held that half-dead girl in my arms, her bones felt almost as small and frail as that sparrow's bones. And I held her against me, against the cold, against what her mother had done. And now I loved her.

Next day, the story of Ignazia's drowning was in the newspaper, front page. It was after that, a week or so after I buried her, that the other details began to spread, began to fuel the fires of imagination. The poisoned dog, the footprints of both the woman and the girl. . . . All my life—even back in the Old Country—townsmen and townswomen have been happy to throw mud and gossip, to celebrate the bad fortune of my *famiglia*. Ignazia's fate became a guessing game for the people of the town. The Italians of Three Rivers—my ungrateful *paisani*—speculated that God or that crazy housekeeper I had had locked up "down below" had been at the bottom of things. For months afterward, for years, a rumor survived that Ignazia had been stolen in the night by a strange man, then killed and thrown through the ice. . . .

But there had been no strange man. No kidnapping. No evidence of that kind of struggle. Only the footprints of my wife and the girl, the black hole at the center of the pond. And as for Concettina, she was mute about that night—told nothing to me, nothing to the police. To this day, we have never spoken about it. . . . She was only eight years old the night her mother tried to take her with her to Hell to punish Tempesta. But she did not take her. I don't know what Concettina remembers.

After Ignazia's death, Italian ladies rang my bell and stood in the doorway with sympathy and hope in their eyes, food in their hands. Beside them stood unmarried daughters, spinster sisters, young widows who volunteered to clean my big house and care for my poor motherless daughter. "No, thank you . . . no, thank you." I refused them all. Each night when I went to work, I brought the child to the apartment next door where she slept in the care of Tusia's family. Tusia's Jennie left high school to launder and cook and sweep for me. I wanted no more of women in my life. No more wives. I was done with all that. . . . And by the time Jennie Tusia fell in love, married that sailor from Georgia, my daughter was old enough to take over. To take care of her father's house—that poor, harelipped girl that no other man wanted.

She's not a bad girl. She cooks, she cleans, she is quiet. Her *silenzia* honors her father. Concettina has Sicilian blood in her veins. She knows how to keep her secrets.

Well, here you have it, Guglielmo. This was what you wanted, eh?

Confession. Penance. Humility. . . .

May God Almighty save my soul!

forty-six

Thomas and I float below the Falls, easing down the Sachem River on inner tubes. From the banks, people wave to us. Strangers, people we know. Our mother is there, and behind her, in the shadows, a little girl. She steps forward, into the sun. It's Penny Ann Drinkwater, alive again, a third-grader still. She calls to us, points downriver. From the woods behind her, a siren blares. . . .

I lunged at the ringing. Knocked the damn phone to the floor, cradle and all. Hauled it by the cord back onto the bed. "Hello?"

Dr. Azzi said he was sorry to be calling this early but that, schedule-wise, he was looking at the day from hell. He was about to leave for the hospital. We could meet in the fourth-floor lounge in an hour, after he'd checked on Ray. Otherwise, we'd have to wait until the end of the day.

The red digital blur on the bureau said . . . 6:11? "Yeah, sure. I can be there. So you . . . you had to amputate?"

You didn't want to fool around with gangrene, he said. He'd see me at about seven-fifteen.

I hung up, flopped back down on the bed. Closed my burning eyes. Okay, I told myself. Grab a shower, get over there. Fourth floor, right? . . . When I swung my legs over and onto the floor, my feet crinkled paper.

In the covers, all around the bed, lay the ruined pages of my grandfather's manuscript. I had finished Domenico's "history" somewhere in the middle of the night. For all its ugly revelations, it had provided none of the answers I'd both sought and dreaded. Only more questions, more suspicions, and one bleak revelation I had *not* gone looking for: that my grandmother, in her despair, had tried to take my mother with her. That when Ma was an eight-year-old girl, she had had to fight her mother for her life. . . . Confessions, penance, family secrets: in a fit of frustration and freedom, I had gotten to the last page of Papa's history and wept. Had yanked the pages from their binder, balled them up, ripped them. Had made confetti of all my grandfather's excuses, his sorry excuse of a life.

I stumbled toward the bathroom, my bare feet padding through the wasted pages. *She cooks, she cleans, she knows how to keep secrets.* . . . I stepped into the shower and made the water hot, hotter, as hot as I could stand it. . . . He'd died a failure: that much was clear. All that confession, all that eleventh-hour contrition: too little, too late. . . . Humble yourself, they'd told him his whole life, but he'd never quite gotten the hang of it. He'd held grudges, played God with people's lives. He'd had that strange woman thrown into the asylum and had just let her rot in there. . . . Rot. Gangrene. *This is your old man calling. You home yet? Give me a jingle, will ya?*

I showered, shampooed. Stood there and let the water run over me. And when I finally stepped out, I faced myself, dripping wet and naked.

Don't *be* him, Dominick, I told my eyes. Don't *be* him, don't *be* him. . . .

"There's wet gangrene and dry gangrene," Dr. Azzi said. "Wet's worse, of course, because it means the bacteria's set in. Which was the case with your dad. That was why we had to amputate as soon as possible. If we'd let it go, the infection would have started galloping through him. Shutting him down, system by system. Questions?"

"It's . . . it's definitely his diabetes that caused it?"

He nodded. "Compromising the blood flow to the extremities. And, of course, he was doing a pretty good job of ignoring the symptoms, too. He's like my father: last of the tough guys. What else can I tell you?"

"Is, uh . . . I'm sorry. It's a lot to take in all at once. The gangrene is the actual infection, right?"

Dr. Azzi shook his head. "Look, let me back up a little. See, I had no idea you were coming at this cold. I just assumed your dad was keeping you posted."

He would have been, I thought, if I'd bothered to answer any of those phone messages. Whatever the outcome on Ray, I was pretty sure I'd just flunked some litmus test for basic human decency. "Gangrene's dead tissue," Dr. Azzi said. "It's the *breeding ground* for infection. His foot wasn't getting the oxygen and nutrients it needed. Wasn't getting any nourishment, in other words. Human tissue's like any other living thing. You starve it long enough, it dies."

Dr. Azzi detailed what the next months would be like: intensive therapy at the hospital for a week or so. Then a transfer to a subacute rehab center—a nursing home—so that Ray could learn how to walk again. Then crutches for a while, an artificial leg later on if Ray chose to go that route. Some insurance covered prosthetics, some didn't. The goal, of course, was to get him back home again. Ray had made it clear to him that he didn't want to be stuck long term in some convalescent home. "He lives alone, right?"

"Right," I said.

"Stairs?"

I nodded. "Outside and in."

At the end of our meeting, we stood, shook hands. "He's going to have a tough row to hoe, no doubt about it," Dr. Azzi said. "But he'll adapt. He was lucky, really. Remind him of that."

I asked if I could see Ray. Sure thing, he said, but he had just had a shot; he'd probably be out for most of the morning. But I was welcome to go in and take a peek.

I went down the hall, found Ray's room. *Pass at your own risk,* I thought.

He was breathing hard through his mouth. There was

dried crud on the front of his hospital johnny, a thin ribbon of blood floating in the fluid just above his IV insertion. He looked so small and gray.

Acute therapy, subacute. Wet and dry gangrene. How could I have missed the fear in his voice? . . . *This is your old man calling. You home yet?* . . . Past history or not, who else did he have?

Look at it, I told myself. Do your penance. Face it.

And so I willed my eyes down from Ray's gray face to his rising and falling chest, then down to the bottom of the bed. My stomach lurched a little. I faced the flatness where his right leg was supposed to be. . . . Remembered my brother's shiny pink scar tissue—his grafted, upholstered stump. Somewhere along the way, I'd heard that when they amputated, they didn't use some high-tech laser procedure; they just used a saw. Sawed through muscle and bone and then just threw the dead leg . . . where? In a Dumpster or something? Jesus.

He'll need to stay at a rehabilitation center for a while—a nursing home—so that he can learn how to walk again. Jesus, he was going to go off the deep end, grounded like this. Always puttering with this or that—Ray couldn't sit still to save himself.

The woman who entered made me jump. She was chubby, Asian. We exchanged nods. "I, uh . . . Dr. Azzi said I could see him. I know it's not visiting—"

"That's fine," she said. She fitted a blood pressure cuff above Ray's wrist, pumped her little black bulb. Read her gauge, pumped some more. *Corrie* something, *R.N.* In the old days, nurses wore white uniforms, not UConn sweatshirts.

"Uh, there's a little bit of blood in his IV tube," I said. "Are you aware of that?"

She squinted, leaned toward it. "Not a problem," she said. She positioned a thermometer under Ray's tongue and closed his mouth, held his jaw shut. Ray slept on, oblivious. Whatever was in that shot they'd given him had really knocked him out. The box beeped. She pulled the thermometer and jotted the results. I asked how he was doing.

"Temp's down a little, his BP's good," she said. "Are you his son?"

I stood there, unable to answer her. When she lifted the sheet to check his dressing, my eyes jumped away.

"Looking good," she said. "Looking good." She let the sheet fall again, tucking it around him. He'd probably sleep most of the morning, she said, but I was welcome to stay. I shook my head. Told her I'd stay just a little longer, then come back in the afternoon.

"Sure," she said. "I'll leave you guys alone, then."

I stood there for a while, watching him sleep.

Reached out. Reached toward his hand. Passed a finger over the hills and valleys his knuckles made.

Like any other living thing. You starve something long enough, it dies. Dr. Azzi was more right than he realized. . . .

Thomas's drowning out at the Falls had only been the *official* cause of death; he'd died down at Hatch, cut off from hope, from family. My brother had starved to death. . . . And my grandmother: she'd died in prison, too. The Old Man had installed that guard dog—had kept her captive in that goddamned, godforsaken house of his. Had raped her on weekends because she was "his." And so, in despair, she'd done what she'd done before. Run. Escaped. Dragged her daughter out to that pond and . . .

Papa was a wonderful man, Dominick. Why was that, Ma? Because he looked good in comparison? Because over on Hollyhock Avenue, everything was relative? . . .

I have to go because you suck all the oxygen out of the room, Dessa had told me that morning she left. *I have to breathe, Dominick.*

I stood there, touching Ray's hand, and finally *getting it*. . . . Dessa hadn't stopped loving me, caring about me. About us. But she'd needed to save herself. Had needed to amputate me from her life because . . . I was starving her. Infecting her. Because if she'd stayed, I would have begun shutting her down, system by system.

Well, good for you, Dess, I thought. I'm *glad* you got out alive. And my tears fell fast, splashing against Ray's bed railing, sinking into his sheets.

I got home around noon—left a message for Dr. Patel that I needed to see her as soon as possible. I heated up some soup, flipped through *Newsweek* without anything really registering. When I went to wash the dishes, I realized I'd just washed them.

Domenico's ruined manuscript was in there: lying all over the bedroom where I'd left it. Okay, I told myself, you finished it and then you trashed it. So it's trash. Right? Go in there and get rid of it.

I grabbed a garbage bag and went into the bedroom.

Stuffing page after ruined page of the Old Man's "history" into the plastic bag, I thought about Ma—what she had told me about the day her father died. He'd just finished it: his long-in-the-making *confessione,* his failed act of contrition. . . . She'd heard him crying out there—had wanted to go to him, to comfort him, but it was against the rules. He would have been too angry, and it was his anger that had ruled that house. . . . I sat back on the bed. Saw her out there, harvesting Papa's story. She must have felt her whole life shift that day, I thought. Her father was dead; her sons were growing inside of her. . . .

She had been brave after all. Brave enough to go on—to raise us as best she could. And earlier: the sober girl in those photographs, standing next to her father in a starched pinafore, her fist to her face to cover her disfigured mouth. A brave eight-year-old girl, dragged that night into the bitter cold by a mother who'd been starved of hope. Made crazy from despair. . . . There'd been evidence of a struggle out there, the Old Man had written. A story told in footprints. But that brave, serious girl had kept her mother's terrible secret—had said nothing to the police, or to her father. It was the footprints that had told. In her anger or her crazy despair, Ignazia had meant to take her with her—take her daughter's life. But Ma had struggled. Had saved herself. Had hidden in the shack and survived the night and then gone home and lived with her father. . . .

Had she loved Papa as much as she'd always claimed? Hated him? Had my brother and I been conceived in evil? . . . "The History of Domenico Onofrio Tempesta" had turned out to be just another hall of mirrors, just one more maze inside the maze. Because by the end of his story, the Old Man had confessed everything and nothing. Like father, like daughter, I thought. They had *both* known how to keep their secrets. . . .

I reached down, pulled a page from the garbage bag. Flattened it and read. *"I have always had that small satisfaction, at least: the memory of that moment when I won my battle against the Monkey, when I used my God-given cleverness to punish that she-devil for the sins she had committed against Domenico Tempesta. . . ."*

I shook my head at his hopelessness, his isolation out there on that last day of his life. Domenico had starved to death, too.

"I'm not saying it's impossible, Dominick," Dr. Patel said. "I'm saying it's highly improbable. You're not retarded. You don't suffer from hemophilia or any of the other myriad complications. If you are, as you fear, the product of incest, you seem to have come away remarkably unscathed."

Unscathed? I reminded her that my brother had been a schizophrenic, that my daughter had died in the fourth week of her life.

A specious argument, she said. As far as she knew, there was no scientific evidence linking father-daughter incest to either schizophrenia or SIDS. I was welcome to research the topic, of course, but she doubted I would find anything. That left me with what she saw as a somewhat neurotic fear and one vague remark in my grandfather's book: that my mother had known how to keep secrets. It could mean anything, she said. Secrets her mother told her, secret recipes. And, of course, the terrible secret that the mother who had given her life had tried, that night, to take it away.

Father-daughter incest: Dr. Patel's giving it a name, a label, somehow confined it. Put a cage around it and made me feel safer. What had she just accused me of? A "somewhat neurotic" fear?

From what I'd told her, she said, my grandfather had been a terribly unhappy and misguided man—cruel, self-serving, paranoid, perhaps—although she was always reluctant to diagnose the dead. But none of what I had told her meant, necessarily, that he had raped his daughter and fathered my brother and me.

"Then I'm exactly where I was *before* I read the damn thing," I said.

"And where is that, my friend?"

"Fucked up. . . . Fatherless."

She said she begged to differ on a couple of counts. First of all, I was certainly *not* fatherless, provided I was willing to think beyond sperm and egg. If one defined one's father as the male elder who attended one's passage from childhood to adulthood, then my father was lying in a hospital bed over at Shanley Memorial, recovering from surgery. Whatever Ray's parental shortcomings had been, whatever trauma he had caused me and my brother, his presence in my life had been a constant. He had borne witness.

Nor did she feel that the completion of my grandfather's history had left me exactly where I had been. "Indulge the anthropologist in me, please, Dominick," she said. "Let's think for a moment of the manuscript not as a mystery with a maddeningly inconclusive ending, but as a parable. Parables instruct. One reaches the end of an allegory and confronts the lesson it offers. And so I ask you: what does your grandfather's story teach you?"

"What does it *teach* me?" I shifted in my seat. Looked away. "I don't know. Watch out for thin ice? Steer clear of monkeys?"

She clapped her hands together like a fed-up schoolteacher. "Seriously, please!"

Our eyes met. I leaned forward. "That I should stop feeling so goddamned sinned against," I said. "That I have to let go of grudges."

She smiled. Nodded. Clapped again, this time in applause.

Intentionally or not, Dr. Patel said, my grandfather had given me a valuable gift: the parable of his failure. And I should not forget who had been the conduit of that story. It had come to me by way of a mother who, Dr. Patel suspected, had loved me deeply—a woman who, despite her meekness, had been quite courageous. In fighting for her life out there at the pond that night, she had made possible mine and Thomas's lives. She had made mistakes along the way—yes, yes, there was no denying it—but she had nevertheless raised her two sons in good faith. Had done her best. And it was to me, personally, that she had bequeathed her father's story.

"Use your gift, Dominick," Dr. Patel said. "Learn from it. Let it set you free."

"Is he finished yet?" the dietary aide asked me, a little huffy this time. She'd been in twice before to collect Ray's untouched lunch tray. At the nurses' station, they'd told me he'd woken up around eleven, been given another shot of morphine, and then drifted back to Dreamland.

"He's still out," I told the aide. "Go ahead. Just take it." It was three-thirty. Who the hell had been prescribing his painkillers, anyway—Dr. Kevorkian?

I watched the aide attempt the impossible: balancing Ray's tray atop her already overflowing cart. It slid clattering to the floor, and the two of us bent to sop up soup, reconstruct his sandwich, locate a runaway apple. By the time I looked back at Ray again, his eyes were open. "Who are you?" he said.

I told him I was Dominick. Asked him how he was feeling.

"Who?"

"Dominick," I said. "Connie's son. One of the twins."

"Oh," he said. "I thought you were the hall monitor."

The hall monitor? I asked him if he knew where he was. He surveyed the room, studied the hallway outside and then looked back at me. "The hospital?"

I nodded. Reminded him he'd had an operation the day before. He asked me when the football game was starting.

Football game? I glanced up at the ceiling-mounted TV. I'd been watching it without sound while I waited for him to wake up. "There's no football on now, Ray," I said. "It's May. Baseball season. Basketball playoffs."

He leaned forward, looking down at his amputation without any observable understanding of loss. "Has Edna been here to see me?" he asked.

"Edna?" I said. "Who's Edna?"

"Edna," he said. "You know. My *sister*." He shook his head, disgusted. "What's this?" He had picked up the tethered TV remote.

"Changes the channels," I said. "On your TV up there. Go ahead, try it. The blue button, not the red one. The red one calls the nurse." He pressed the red button, *then* the blue. Held his thumb down on it. Channels whizzed by: soap operas, CNN, the Maytag repairman. He stopped when he got to Oprah.

"Yes?" a staticky voice said. "How may I help you?"

"Oh," I said. "He . . . we just pushed the wrong button. Sorry."

Click.

"What time is the football game starting?" Ray asked again. When I reminded him that it wasn't football season, he interrupted me to lead a cheer.

Strawberry shortcake! Huckleberry pie!
V-I-C-T-O-R-Y!
Can we do it? Yes, yes, yes!
We are the students of the B-G-S!

I glanced out into the hall. Up at Oprah. "What's the, uh . . . what's BGS?"

"The BGS!" he said. "The BGS! The Broadway Grammar School! What are you, slow or something?"

"I don't know. I guess there probably is a God. There *has* to be."

Dessa dangled the tea bag in and out of her cup. Looked up at me.

"He's not merciful, though. That's a crock. He's more into *irony* than mercy. He's a *gotcha!* kind of god. A practical jokester. Because this is just too perfect to chalk up to random coincidence."

Dessa said she wasn't following me.

"Well, think about it," I said. "First my brother dies. Then my stepfather loses an appendage, starts talking crazy. Stump II: the Sequel. It's perfect."

Dessa said she was pretty sure that God dealt in challenges, not practical jokes.

We were seated at a back table in the hospital cafeteria. An hour earlier, I'd held open the elevator door for hurrying footsteps that had turned out to be my ex-wife's. Now, with the exception of the white-haired woman at the cash register and a couple of whispering candy stripers two tables over, we had the place to ourselves.

"And anyway," she said, "didn't they say he was probably just disoriented from the pain medication? Didn't you just tell me that *you* woke up disoriented after *your* surgery?" A few minutes earlier, I'd alluded to my strange morphine dream without going into the details: suffocating my brother as he hung from that tree, cutting him down and lugging him to the river. Kind of funny, in a way: in *my* morphine hallucination, I'd been a murderer. Ray had become head cheerleader in his.

Neither of us said anything for a minute or so. I finished my coffee. Began unraveling the Styrofoam cup, apple-peel style. We both sat there, watching the long, continuous spiral. "You still go to church?" I said.

It was weird I was asking, she said. She hadn't been—had stayed away for years—but she'd just started going again.

"Yeah? Why's that?"

"Oh, I don't know," she said. "Because of this place, partly."

When I'd run into her on the elevator, I'd assumed that something else was wrong with her mother, but Dessa had said no—she'd started volunteering in the children's hospice. "You should see some of these kids I'm working with, Dominick," she said now. "They're so sick, so brave. They all seem like miracles to me."

She told me about a six-year-old girl with a brain tumor and a giggle so infectious that she could start a whole room laughing. About the AIDS babies with their string of infections, their need to be held and rocked. About Nicky, a seven-year-old boy with an enzyme disorder that had gradually robbed him of speech, balance, the ability, even, to swallow. Nicky was her favorite, she said. "You should see the way music lights up his eyes. And lights. Remember those lava lamps everyone used to get stoned and stare at? Nicky will just stare and stare at one of those things, as if it makes sense—explains something to him that the rest of us don't get. He's got such beautiful brown eyes, Dominick. That's one of the places where *I* see God, I think. In Nicky's eyes." She laughed, embarrassed suddenly. "It's hard to explain. I must sound so New Age."

I poked my foot against her foot. "Well, there's probably still hope," I said. "You haven't bought any Yanni tapes yet, have you?"

The AIDS kids had the hardest struggle, she said. They didn't want to eat, because eating made them sicker. So on top of everything else the poor little guys were contending with, there was the real danger of malnutrition.

Starve something long enough and it dies, I thought.

"So what do you do for these kids?"

She said she read to them, rocked them. Did a little pet therapy.

"Pet therapy?" I said. "What's pet therapy?"

The kids really responded to animals, she said. There was a cool dog named Marshmallow that visited once a week. They had fish. And rabbits—Zeke and Zack. "We've got to be really careful because of infection—there's all kinds of restrictions and regulations—but the kids love animals so much."

Mostly she just held the kids, she said. That was probably the most useful thing she did. "Kids this sick want physical closeness more than anything else. They just want to be held."

"You sure this is good for you?" I asked. "You sure this doesn't cost you too much?"

She smiled, shook her head. She knew it sounded depressing, she said, but it wasn't. That was the miracle. It made her happy to be around these kids—to be a part of their precious days. She felt more at peace with herself than she had in years.

I smiled. Said I thought she'd kept her promise after all.

"What promise?"

"Clapton's kid? The little dude who fell from the window? I think you caught him after all." I watched her confusion turn into remembrance of that dream she had told me about. Watched her eyes fill up with tears.

Did she want to go up? Say hello to Ray?

She checked her watch. She'd like to, she said, but she was running late—meeting Dan for dinner. But, okay, she'd just stop in and say hello. She couldn't stay, though.

Riding the elevator back to the fourth floor, I realized that she'd just mentioned her boyfriend's name without me wanting to punch a wall. Progress of some kind, I figured. All that therapy had been good for *some*thing. "So how's Sadie?" I said.

"Oh. Dominick . . ." She reached for me. "She died." Her hand fell back to her side. "I had to have her put to sleep. I'm sorry. I should have called you."

I shrugged. Told her it was okay—she'd been *her* dog, not mine.

"She was *our* dog," she said.

The elevator stopped on the third floor, opened its doors to nobody, then closed again. We continued up. "She died peacefully, Dominick." She took a step toward me. Leaned, a little, against me.

When we got to Ray's room, he was sitting up, having himself a nurse-assisted sip of juice. "Brought you some company," I said.

"Hi, Ray," Dessa said. He stared at her blankly.

"You remember who this is?" I asked him.

He took another sip of his juice. Gave us a grin so slight I almost missed it. "Hot Lips Houlihan," he said.

By the third day after his surgery, Ray was lucid again. His "craziness" had been caused by the painkillers, just like they'd said. Twelve days after the amputation of his right leg, Ray was deemed steady enough on crutches to be transferred to a subacute rehabilitation center.

Rivercrest Convalescent Home had cheerful wallpaper, a cheery staff, and an earnest daily schedule of physical therapy, occupational therapy, and sing-alongs. Each day I visited, I ran a gauntlet of wheelchair-bound "sentries"—old geezers who spent their whole day parked at the front entrance, watching the ebb and flow of visitors, employees, and delivery men. Hoping, I guess, for news of life beyond the parking lot. Some of them I got to know by name: Daphne, the vamp of the group in her Technicolor housecoats; Maizie, who always asked me coming and going if I was her son, Harold; Warren, whose universal greeting was "Hello, Cap'n Peacock!"

Sitting among the sentries, slumped and wizened, was a nameless old woman I came to think of as Princess Evil Eye. Everyone down there made a big deal about the Princess; pushing one hundred, she was Rivercrest's oldest resident. She and I never exchanged words, the way I did with the rest of them, but she seemed, always, to train her beady eyes on me when I entered the home—to follow my progress down the corridor to Ray's room. I know this because sometimes I stopped and looked back and it freaked me out a little: the way she'd watch me. . . . "The Crew" I called them. Daphne, Warren, the Princess. The welcoming committee at the way station between life and whatever the hell was coming after it. Rivercrest was purgatory, with wheelchairs.

Ray was sullen and quiet his first week or so, and what his social worker called "semicooperative" after that. At the end of a two-week campaign to enlist him in her programs and special activities, the recreation director abandoned him as a project and let him stay in his room and sulk. He wavered in his decision about whether or not to get an artificial leg. "If I was a horse, they'd just take me out and shoot me," he said one day.

"Your father's depressed," they told me. They said he sometimes cried in private in his room. It was to be expected. These things took time.

I began visiting him almost every day. Began taking his dirty laundry home after Laundry Services lost his favorite shirt. He didn't have that much; I had the time. By then, I had sold my painting equipment to Sheffer's buddy or partner or whatever's the politically correct way to say it these days. I'd gone up to Hartford and taken that test for my teaching reinstatement. Signed up for that refresher course you had to take. I still wasn't sure if I wanted to go back to the classroom, but I figured I'd get my ducks lined up, just in case. I had until the end of the summer before I'd become "economically challenged." Sometimes schools needed teachers at the last minute. By then, Ray would be home and, hopefully, self-sufficient again.

I brought him the New York and Boston papers when I visited—the *Post,* the *Herald.* Brought him a hamburger from The Prime Steer once or twice a week because all of Rivercrest's meat was "like shoe leather." Because they even screwed up meat loaf. "Jesus, what'd you do this again for?" he'd say, when I'd hand him his take-out food. "Don't waste your money. I don't even have an appetite." Then he'd dig in—devour the damn thing in six or seven minutes flat.

The staff thought getting out for a couple of hours might lift Ray's spirits a little, so I took a lesson from the physical therapist on how to help him in and out of the car, what to do when he needed to get to the toilet. We were both nervous the first time. I took him for a drive around Three Rivers, out past the big casino construction. "Jesus Christ Almighty," he said. "This thing's going to be huge. Well, what the hell. More power to 'em." His position on the Wequonnocs surprised me a little; it seemed to me that he'd spent a lifetime begrudging anyone good fortune.

For our second jaunt, we went to Friendly's for lunch. When I asked him where he'd like to go for field trip number three, his answer surprised me.

"How about the movies?" he said.

"The movies? Yeah?" Ray had been on record since back when Thomas and I were kids: movies were nothing but a waste of time and money.

I held the *Daily Record*'s entertainment ads in front of him. Figured he'd probably pick *Dances with Wolves,* which I'd already suffered through once. *Naked Gun* and some Arnold Schwarzenegger thing were both playing over at Center Cinema.

"How about this thing?" he said, his finger tapping against an ad for *The Little Mermaid.*

"That's a Disney cartoon, Ray," I said. "It's a kids' movie."

He knew goddamned well what it was, he said. They ran ads for it every five seconds on the TV, didn't they? What did *I* want to see, then? What the hell had I even asked him for?

"Okay, okay," I said. "*The Little Mermaid.* We're there."

In the theater lobby, people stared at his crutches, his

flapping pant leg—kids *and* adults. By the time he'd finished up in the men's room, the movie had already started. I was a nervous wreck helping him down the sloping aisle in the dark. But after we'd gotten seated, after my heartbeat had gone back to normal and I'd recovered enough to pick up the gist of the story, I saw the logic of Ray's choice. He'd needed to see a story about a feisty mermaid who wanted what she couldn't have—wanted legs—and then had gotten both what she wished for and what she hadn't. At one point, I looked over at Ray, studying his movie-lit profile: locked jaw, scowl. What I was looking at, I realized, was his courage.

"Well, how'd you like it?" I asked him on our way back to Rivercrest. "Not bad," was his emotionless two-word review. Back at the home, the wheelchair brigade was stationed at the front door as usual. "Excuse me. Are you, by any chance, my son, Harold?" Maizie asked me, right on cue.

Ray answered before I could. "His name's Dominick Birdsey!" he snapped. "He's *my* kid!" Heading down the hallway, not quite out of earshot, he mumbled something about "old coots" and "goddamned nuisances."

Somewhere during that first month at Rivercrest, Ray made a couple of friends: Stony, a retired roofer who'd once fought Willie Pep in the Golden Gloves, and Norman, who'd fought in World War II at Bataan. Back in the old days, Norman claimed—when he was a kid working at his father's horse-drawn lunch wagon in downtown Three Rivers—he had served Mae West a piece of rhubarb pie. Free of charge. She was passing through town in vaudeville. There was a lot of kidding back and forth about that. What else had he served her? What had *she* served *him*? Maybe that new one—what'd she call herself? Madonna? Maybe *she* liked a little of Norman's rhubarb pie, too.

Norman, Stony, and Ray: "the Three Musketeers," someone on the staff dubbed them. They ate their meals together in the dining room. Played pinochle in Stony's room. (Only Stony's radio could pull in that Big Band station from New Haven.) "Your father's doing much, much better," the social worker told me. Ray decided he might as well try that fake leg. See how it felt. What the hell—his insurance paid for it. No sense them getting a free ride.

We watched baseball sometimes, Ray and me. Played a little cribbage. Usually the TV did more talking than we did. One day, he started complaining about the crummy shaves the orderlies gave him. They had to use electric razors—there was some kind of house rule about it—but an electric razor never shaved him right.

"Shave yourself," I said.

He told me he couldn't—his hands shook. He held them up to demonstrate. "You'd probably come in here someday, find my head on the floor. Why don't *you* shave me?"

I resisted at first—let it drop the first couple of times he mentioned it—but he kept it up. "All right, all right," I finally said, wheeling him into the cramped little bathroom adjacent to his room. "We'll *try* it."

It felt weird that first time—unnatural—lathering him up, holding him by the chin and scraping the stubble off his neck, his slack cheeks. We'd never touched one another much in our family, Ray and me least of all. But I got used to it. After the first couple times, it didn't seem so strange. Probably more than anything else, it was shaving Ray that broke down the final barriers between us. . . .

Because getting shaved made him talkative. Made him open up. I learned more about Ray during those shaves than I had ever known before. He'd lost both his father and his older brother to influenza in 1923, the same year he was born. At least he'd been raised to *believe* they were his father and brother. When he was ten years old, the woman Ray had always been told was his mother took sick with rheumatic fever. On her deathbed, she let out the truth: that she was really his *grand*mother. That his "sister" Edna had given birth to him.

As I listened, I thought about that framed photograph he kept on his bureau back at the house on Hollyhock Avenue: pictured the woman Thomas and I had laughed at behind his back—had called Ma Kettle. Now she had a name: Edna.

After it was just the two of them—just Edna and him—they drifted from place to place. Someone would hire Edna as a housekeeper, everything would be hunky-dory for a while and then, the next thing Ray knew, they'd have to move again. . . . She'd *meant* well enough, he said; she wasn't a *bad* person. But she was weak. "Weak to temptation. In plain English, she was a tramp, I guess. And a drunk."

The worst of it came when Edna got them a room above one of the taverns downtown. "Tavern row," they called it—plenty to pick from. Edna would make the rounds—bring home riffraff, one plug-ugly drunk after another. One night he'd been awakened right out of a sound sleep by some guy sitting there, trying to start something funny with him. After that, he'd slept with a ball-peen hammer in his bed. "It would have been okay if the others had lived," he said. "But it had come down to just her and me."

He'd gotten out as soon as he could, he said—had quit school and joined the Navy. Edna had had to sign a paper. "At first she wouldn't sign it," he said. "I was always working odd jobs, see? Bringing in a little money." But she'd signed it, finally, one night when she was "good and soused" and he'd gotten the hell out of there. He'd only gone back to Youngstown once since then, and that was to bury her. December of 1945, it was; he remembered because he'd just gotten out of the Navy. Had just bought his black DeSoto. Drove it all the way out to Ohio and back without a spare tire. Edna had died from liver problems, he said—from drink. Forty-one years old and she'd looked about *sixty*-one, lying there in that coffin. Other than that one trip, he'd left Ohio behind him at seventeen and never looked back.

In the war, he'd been stationed in France and then, later on, in Italy. *It-ly,* he pronounced it. The Italians were good people, he said—*hospitable* people, even in the middle of war. When he got out, he sold vacuum cleaners for a while. He'd dated a gal up in Framingham, Massachusetts, but it hadn't worked out. Olga, her name was. Ukrainian gal. Too bossy. When Korea started up, Ray had reenlisted. He didn't have to go—not by any means. He was only a couple of years from the cutoff age for enlisted men by that time. But he'd always felt a duty to his country, right or wrong. He didn't even question right or wrong. That was for the big shots and the politicians to decide. And besides that, he still had the fight left in him. Plenty of "piss and vinegar" that he might as well spend on the North Koreans as on the guy at the barstool next to him, or the jerk that had just cut in front of him while he was driving along, minding his own business.

"Then, after I got out of that one, that was when the job with Fuller Brush came along. It was just a stopgap thing until I could get something better. But that was how I met your mother, of course. Lets me in over there at the house, and I start unpacking my samples, and all of a sudden she bursts into tears. Just burst right into tears. At first, I didn't know what the hell had happened. I thought she'd hurt herself or something.

"She had her hands full with you two, of course. Both of you had earaches that first day I stopped in, I remember; you'd both been running her ragged. And, of course, she was all alone. She'd lost her father the year before—was just barely scraping by on what he had left her. I kind of felt sorry for her. She was in way over her head. . . .

"Course, I was kind of sweet on her, too. She had some nice curves to her. And that mouth of hers—that never bothered me. 'Just as kissable as anyone else's,' I used to tell her. I knew right away she was a good woman. Kind of shy, maybe, but I didn't mind that. I'd come to like Italians, see? Because of my experiences in the war. . . . She was nothing like Edna—your mother. She'd just made a mistake, that was all. Anyone can make a mistake. You think *I* was an angel when I was in the Navy? I'd stuck my dipstick into plenty of places I shouldn't have. Plus, I kind of got a kick out of you kids. 'Double trouble,' I used to call the two of you. You were both a couple of hellions."

His presence in your life has been a constant, I heard Doc Patel tell me. *He has been there, borne witness.*

"I know I made mistakes with you two," he said. "With him, especially. That day of the funeral, there? Afterward—back at the house? You weren't accusing me of anything that I hadn't already accused myself of. . . . I just never understood that kid. Me and him, we were like oil and water. . . . I hadn't grown up with a father, see? All I knew was that it was a tough world out there. I figured that was the one thing

I could do for you two: toughen you up a little, so that you could take whatever sucker punches life was going to throw at you. . . . 'They're just little boys, Ray,' she used to say to me all the time. But I didn't see it. I was pigheaded about it, I guess. And, of course, I knew neither of you two liked me that much. Had me pegged as the bad guy all the time. The guy who wrecked everyone's fun. Sometimes you three would be laughing at something, and I'd walk into the room, and *bam!* three long faces."

"It was your temper," I said. "We were afraid of you."

He nodded. "I have a bad temper. I know I do. It was because of what I'd come from. I was mad at the world, I guess. . . . But Jesus, I'd get so mad at her when she tried to run interference for him all the time. That used to drive me up the ever-loving wall. . . . And, of course, that day I come home and found the two of them up there, him in that foolish hat, those high-heel shoes . . .

"I failed him—I know that. Probably failed the both of you. Right?"

I couldn't answer him. Jesus, he'd been brutal to us. But he'd *been* there. . . . He'd told Ma her mouth was just as kissable as anyone else's.

"Things get clearer when you're older," he said. "Of course, by then it's too late."

I'd finished shaving him. Wheeled him out of his bathroom and over by the bed. I sat down next to him. "It wasn't just you," I said. "We were all a little screwed up, Ma included."

"She had her quirks like everyone else," he said. "But she was a good woman."

My heart thumped in my chest. I almost couldn't get it out.

Almost couldn't ask it.

"Before?" I said. "When you said that neither of you were angels? Did you . . . did she ever tell you who he was? Our father?"

We looked each other in the eye. I waited, not even breathing. My whole life rode on his answer.

"We never talked about that kind of stuff," he finally said. "Had kind of an unspoken deal, I guess. All that was water under the bridge. . . . We just let the past lie, her and me."

forty-seven

Leo's racquet scooped low for the shot. *Thwock!* The ball skidded up the back wall, arced high across the court, and grazed the front wall six inches from the floor.

"And I *am,*" he shouted, "the *King* of Racquetball!"

"Nice shot," I conceded. "Okay, that's it. Your game."

He'd just whipped me three in a row—something he'd never been able to do before. Soaked with sweat, out of breath, we headed for the rain room.

"Hey, Birds," Leo called over, midshampoo. "You got time for a beer?"

I told him I didn't—that I had to get dressed and get out of there.

"Yeah? What for? You got a hot date or something?"

I cut the water, grabbed my towel. "Hot date with Ray's social worker," I said. "We've got to go over his Medicare stuff."

It was a lie. Joy had called, out of the blue, the night before. She was in Three Rivers visiting friends, she'd said; she wondered if she could come over and see me before she went back. Just to say hello, show me the baby. I'd said no at first. What was the point? But she'd kept pushing: we hadn't seen each other in almost a year, there was so much that she wanted to tell me about. Had I gotten the picture she'd sent of Tyffanie?

That hospital mug shot: for some stupid reason, I'd stuck it on my refrigerator door. Joy promised she wouldn't stay long. A fifteen-minute visit and she'd be on her way.

"Must be a bummer, huh?" Leo said. "All that convalescent-home bullshit?"

"It's doable," I said. "Especially now that Ray's mellowed out a little." If I had told Leo about Joy, I would have gotten a lecture about how I didn't owe that bitch anything. How, after what she'd tried to pull, I should have just told her to go to hell and hung up on her. I *knew* it was stupid, meeting her; I didn't need Leo to point that out. But fifteen minutes was all she'd asked for. You could live through anything for fifteen minutes.

"Hey," I said. "Let me see your deodorant, will you? I was in a rush getting over here. Forgot all my shit." The truth was that I'd been distracted—nervous about Joy's visit.

"Geez, I don't know, Birdsey," Leo said. "I'm not sure I want to make that big a commitment to you yet." His Dry Idea came flying at me. "Hey, Dominick. Guess what I heard today? From Irene?"

When I looked over at him, he was pulling up a pair of jazzy boxer shorts. "Whoo-ee," I said. "Where's my sunglasses? When'd you start wearing those things?"

"Since I read what jockeys do to your sperm count," he said. "But listen to me. I'm serious. She said that Big Gene told her—"

"Who said?"

"*Irene*. Their *accountant*. She says Gene told her he's thinking about retiring at the end of the year. Doing some traveling with Thula. I think that tumble she took over at the house kind of scared them a little. Forced them to reevaluate things or whatever. . . . End of *this* year, Birdsey. Nobody knows yet."

"I don't believe it," I said. "They're not going to have to *carry* him out of there?"

I laced up my sneakers, went over to the mirror to calm my hair down a little. I'd forgotten my hairbrush back at the house, too. If I'd known that seeing her was going to get me this bent out of shape, I'd have stuck to my guns. I raked my fingers through my hair. That was all she was getting: a quick finger-comb. I didn't even owe her *that* much.

"Hey, Dominick?" Leo said. He had that anxious look on his face that he gets sometimes. I was pretty sure I knew what was coming. "Let's say he *does* pack it in. I mean, I'll believe it when I see it, too, but let's *say* he does. . . . You think I'd have a shot at General Manager?"

Poor Leo: he was the Rodney Dangerfield of Constantine Motors. All those years down at that place, and all he'd ever really wanted was a little respect from his father-in-law. That, and his own office—a desk parked *off* the showroom floor. But, sure as hell, the partnership was going to bypass him and name Costas's son, Peter, as General Manager. Big Gene would kick Leo in the balls one more time. Break his daughter Angie's heart by breaking her husband's agates. No doubt about it.

"I think you got a shot at it if the partners have half a brain among them," I said.

"You think I could handle it?"

I looked at his face in the mirror, behind my face. My answer was important. "You kidding me?" I said. "You'd do a *great* job." That was the thing with Leo: for all his bullshit, all his bluster, he'd always registered a little low in the self-esteem department. He should have left that dealership years ago.

He nodded, pleased with my answer. "Yeah, my time has come, I think. I've had their best sales the last four months in a row. Did I tell you that?" He knotted his tie, banged his locker door shut. "I'm freakin' forty-three years old, man. I'm the father of his *grand*children."

"Hey, speaking of which," I said. "What the fuck you worrying about your sperm count for?"

"I don't know," he said. "Us sex machines just worry about shit like that."

We left the gym, headed toward our cars. I was easing out of the parking lot, stewing again about Joy's visit, when Leo tooted, motioning me to wait. I braked, rolled down my window. He pulled up beside me. "Hey, I heard something else today," he said. "I'm not supposed to say anything. Angie would kill me. It's about her sister."

My hands gripped the steering wheel a little tighter. I waited.

"She and Danny? They're splitting up."

I just sat there, nodding, unable to think.

"It's not another woman or anything. It's one of those stay-friends-but-go-their-separate-ways deals. He wants to move back to Santa Fe and she wants to stay here."

"It's definite?"

"Far as I know. At first she was going with him, but then she did an about-face. Hey, don't call her or anything, Dominick. Okay? Angie would murder me. The Old Man and the Old Lady don't even know about it yet."

I said I wouldn't say anything.

"So anyway, about that other thing? You really think I got a shot at it?"

"What? . . . Yeah. Absolutely."

"You think I could handle it, though? Right? Be honest. It's not like I majored in business or anything."

"You majored in acting," I said. "That's *better* training for that place. And anyway, you had their best sales the last four months in a row, you just swept me in racquetball. You're fuckin' *invincible,* Leo."

He grinned. Nodded in agreement. "I'm fuckin' *invincible.*"

Driving home, I wondered why the news about Dessa wasn't elating me. I'd been waiting for years to hear what Leo had just said. For *years* . . . She'd probably stay out there at that farmhouse, I figured. Or sell it, maybe. If she was going to sell, she'd better get that damn place repainted. Subtract five or six thousand from the asking price if she didn't. It figured, though, didn't it? Now that I'd just sold all my equipment, she'd probably want to get it painted. . . . But maybe she'd stay there. Live by herself for a while. I wondered what she'd do about that jazzy mailbox of theirs: paint over it? Leave it as is? *Constantine-Mixx, happily ever after.* . . . Much as I'd always wanted to hate Dan the Man, I'd never quite gotten the hang of it. From all reports, he was a nice enough guy—even Leo admitted it. He'd been decent to me that day on the phone, after my brother died. I had to give him that much. . . . But she wasn't going to come back to me. Life didn't work that way. You couldn't just pick up where you'd left off. For my own mental health, I might as well nip that little fantasy right in the bud. You see that, Doc? Aren't you proud of me? . . . It must have been hard for her, though, these last couple of months: deciding whether to go or stay. I wondered if it had anything to do with those kids over there. Those sick kids at the hospital. . . .

Joy was parked in front of the condo, already waiting for me. Fifteen minutes early. I drove right past her without even seeing her. I'd been looking for her Toyota, I guess—had had my head filled up with Dessa. I was out of the car, halfway to the house, when she called my name. Got out of this battle-scarred white Civic hatchback.

She opened the back door, fiddled with the car seat. Lifted the baby out and into her arms. Joy with a kid: if I wasn't standing there, watching it with my own eyes . . .

The two of them came toward me.

Go away, I felt like shouting at her. *Stay the fuck away from me.*

Joy was nervous—laughing, tearing up a little. She looked awful. "It's so good to see you, Dominick," she said. She was too dressed up or something. Wearing too much makeup. In the sunlight, you could see where it ended, under her chin.

"This is Tyffanie," she said. Was she sick or something? She almost looked sick.

The baby was already bigger than Angela. Well, older, too. My eyes bounced from the top of her head to her pierced ear to her little fingers. I couldn't look at her face-on.

"Here," I said. "Let me help you with this paraphernalia. Your traveling-light days are over, huh?" I grabbed the baby seat she'd been lugging, lifted the diaper bag strap off her shoulder. "Oh, yeah," I said. "That's right. What am I doing?" Put everything back down again. Unlocked the door with my shaky key.

"Same old place," Joy said, when she walked in. In baby talk, she told Tyffanie that this was where Mommy used to live. Joy, who liked to talk dirty during sex—who'd come out with stuff that embarrassed *me* sometimes. Now she was talking *baby* talk.

When she'd asked me over the phone the night before what was new, I'd told her about my brother's death, about selling my business. I'd skipped the news about Ray. There'd never been any love lost between those two: Ray and Joy. She mentioned Thomas now, again—told me how sorry she was. But life had to be a little easier now. Right?

Six months before, that remark would have pissed me off. Would have put me right on the defensive. But I let it go. It was and it wasn't easier, I said. Had she had lunch yet? Did she want a sandwich?

That would be *great,* she said. The baby needed to be changed. Could she use the couch?

"Go ahead," I said. "You don't have to ask first. God."

Out in the kitchen, I got plates, Sprites, sandwich stuff. Funny how I could look at that kid's picture on my refrigerator fifty times a day but couldn't face her in person. . . . Jesus, Joy looked bad. All that makeup: it was like she was trying too hard or something. "Turkey breast okay?" I called in.

"Sure. *Great*. Mustard, not mayo, if you've got it."

I'd already gotten the mustard out. What did she think—ten, eleven months and I would have forgotten she hated mayonnaise? . . . Weird: her asking permission to use the couch to change the baby. She'd *ordered* that damn thing. Out of a catalog. We'd had a fight about it the day it arrived. I'd flipped it upside down and wobbled the frame for her—had given her a demonstration about cheap construction, a lecture about why it was stupid to buy a twelve-hundred-dollar piece of furniture based on some pretty picture in a magazine. It was no wonder she'd run up all that debt that time: her eyes were bigger than her head. We'd always been a mismatch, her and me.

We ate at the kitchen table, the baby sitting between us in her yellow plastic seat. Whenever Joy talked baby talk to her, Tyffanie's arms flailed. She looked nothing like that hospital picture anymore. She had her mother's looks.

"Do you want to hold her?" Joy asked me. I said no, thanks, that was okay.

"Where's that smile?" she asked Tyffanie. "Can you give Dominick a smile?" She looked over at me. "Do you want to be Dominick or *Uncle* Dominick?"

"Whatever," I said. I was nothing to this kid.

She leaned toward Tyffanie. "Don't you love the way babies smell?" she said. Their foreheads touched; Joy took a whiff. "Smell her, Dominick. Go ahead." She slid the seat across the table toward me.

"That's okay," I said. Leaned back a little.

When she asked the baby if Uncle Dominick could "pwease smell her," Tyffanie broke out in a grin so sweet and pure you could have put it on baby food jars. She was beautiful, really. Like mother, like daughter. Six weeks old and she already knew how to flirt.

I took a bite of my sandwich. Checked the wall clock. If they were only staying for fifteen minutes, Joy had better start eating. "So?" I said.

"So," Joy repeated.

She bullshitted me for a while about how great everything was. Portsmouth was great, Tyffanie was great. She didn't mention the asshole. If everything was so perfect, why'd she look so bad? Why were her eyes so jumpy-looking? *The wreck of the Hesperus,* I thought—that phrase my mother used to use.

Joy said she hadn't really understood the meaning of life until Tyffanie had come along, but now she understood it perfectly. Well, great, I felt like saying. Make sure you share the news with Plato and Kierkegaard and all those other philosophers who'd banged their heads against the wall, trying to figure things out.

She asked me again if I wanted to hold Tyffanie. I said no thanks.

"Oh, go ahead, Dominick," she insisted. "Pick her up. She's *great* with strangers."

I shook my head. Took another bite of sandwich. This visit had been a mistake.

"Not that you're a stranger," she said. "I didn't mean that. Hey, if I had been a better liar, you would have been this little girl's daddy. Right?"

I just looked at her. She looked away, looked back at me

again. "I am so sorry about the way I hurt you, Dominick," she said. "I'm sorry about everything. You never should have gotten mixed up with a loser like me."

I didn't take my cue—tell her she *wasn't* a loser. Tell her that all was forgiven now that she was a mommy. Now that she'd cracked the code on the meaning of life. Fifteen minutes, she'd promised, but she'd already been there twenty-five. Hadn't even touched her damn sandwich yet. *Eat!* I wanted to scream at her. *Eat and leave!*

"So why'd you get her ears pierced?" I said.

Because she was just so pretty, Joy said. Because Tyffanie was Mommy's pretty little girl. It was just cartilage there, she said. She'd checked with the pediatrician first; Tyffanie hadn't felt a thing. She would never, ever do anything to hurt Tyffanie. "Your parents had you *circumcised,*" she said. "I know *that* for a fact. Did *that* hurt *you*?"

Tyffanie made her lips into an O—made spit bubbles, nonsense noises. Joy laughed and mimicked her. Abruptly, she stood and snatched her out of her seat, dangling her in front of me. "Here!" she said. "Hold her, Dominick! She's *great*!"

The baby, legs ajerk, hung suspended between us.

They stayed another half hour or so. After they drove away, I found Tyffanie's pacifier—her "binky," Joy had called it. It was on the kitchen floor. So what? I told myself. She can pull into a convenience store someplace and get another one for seventy-nine cents. When I went into the living room, I saw that she'd forgotten the changing blanket, too. It was folded up neatly on the arm of the couch. I picked it up. Saw the envelope she'd hidden under it. Opened it like it was a letter bomb—which, in a way, it was.

It's four in the morning. Tyffanie's still asleep. I have awful news. . . .

She hoped she was going to find the courage to tell me what she had to tell me in person, she wrote; she was putting it down on paper in case she lost her nerve.

She was HIV-positive.

She'd found out during Tyffanie's pregnancy—during what *should have been* one of the happiest times of her life.

Thad's lifestyle had finally caught up with him—with both of them. *He wasn't as careful as he always claimed with his little "other relationships." It shows you how much he ever really cared about me, right?*

The baby had been tested three times—twice out in California and once here, up in New Hampshire. By some miracle, she seemed to be free of the virus. *They're pretty sure, anyway; she has to keep being tested up to her eighteenth month. Then they'll be sure. But three different doctors have said they thought she'll be fine. That it would have shown up by now.* She hung on to that: the possibility that she hadn't screwed up things for Tyffanie. Some days it was the only thing that had kept her from going off the deep end.

Thad's never even seen her. Great father, huh? Almost as good as mine was.

The Duchess had taken off for Mexico during Joy's seventh month, according to her letter. He and this other guy were chasing after some new "cure" that the U.S. wouldn't approve. Thad had full-blown AIDS. He told her he needed whatever money he had for his own treatments, and they'd had a big fight. What had she ever seen in that self-centered scumbag, anyway? Because that was what he was—scum. He had wrecked her entire life, and she wasn't just talking about HIV.

She'd driven east by herself, just her and the baby, after a big blowout with her mother and her mother's "subhuman" husband. The trip had been hard; she'd had to stop all the time for Tyffanie, sometimes in places she wasn't too comfortable about stopping in. She'd spent way more of her money than she'd planned to. But she was glad she'd done it—come back east. She was moving back to Three Rivers at the end of the month. That was partly what this visit had been about—setting things up, finding a place to stay. She'd rented a little third-floor apartment over on Coleman Court. She was moving in on August first. She'd already gotten a waitressing job—down at Denny's, Monday through Wednesday nights to start. It was just temporary. She'd look for a job with benefits when she got back. Her landlady was going to take care of Tyffanie on the nights she worked. This woman had some major "issues"—she weighed over three hundred pounds, for one thing—but she was a *licensed* day care provider. She was great with kids from what Joy could see. That was all that counted.

Tyffanie and I were the only two people in the world that meant anything to her, she wrote. She loved me. She still loved me. *I realized that even before Thad and I were halfway to California—realized that I'd made another one of my huge mistakes.* But for my sake, she wished I had never even walked up to the membership desk at Hardbodies that day. Because if we hadn't met, she wouldn't have had the chance to wreck my life.

You have to get tested, Dominick. I feel so ashamed. I'm sorrier than you'll ever know. . . .

I stood there, numb. Thought, in succession, these things: Were we *both* going to die, then—Thomas *and* me? . . . Where did you even *get* an AIDS test? . . . If I died, who was going to shave Ray?

I have absolutely no right in the world to ask you this, Dominick. But I don't have a choice. I'm desperate. I know I'm going to be too afraid to ask you this when I see you.

If your HIV test is negative—if you don't have the virus—would you please, please, please consider taking Tyffanie? Only if I get real sick. If it turns into AIDS. Maybe it will never even come to that. Not everyone who has HIV comes down with AIDS. Maybe there'll be a cure. I know I have no right to ask, but I'm scared to death that Tyffanie is going to end up with strangers. Bad people. There were so many of them out there, she said. Joy didn't want her mother raising the baby. She was fifty-one years old. She had never wanted her *own* kids. *I have to know that Tyffanie has a chance in life, Dominick. Maybe it's what God wants. He took your own little daughter away from you. Maybe he wants me to die so you can have my little girl. . . .*

I let the letter fall. Got to the bathroom and gave up my lunch.

I drove up to Farmington that Friday. Paid my twenty bucks. They assigned me a confidential number, drew my blood. The woman at the window told me I had to let three business days pass and then call the lab at the end of the third day.

Which was Wednesday in my case, she said. The test results usually came back around three, so I should call between four and five-thirty.

I couldn't eat, couldn't sleep. Couldn't tell anyone. Leo would tell Angie and she'd tell Dessa. What could Dr. Patel say that would make any difference?

I visited Ray as usual. Brought him his clean laundry, shaved him, chatted with him and his buddies. One afternoon, passing the wheelchair "sentries," I locked eyes with that shriveled-up human skeleton who sat out there. Princess Evil Eye. She was staring at me something fierce that day—like she knew what was up, what I was waiting to hear about. But this time I stood there and stared back at her. Gave it back to her. . . . It made no sense, really; it was pathetic. Little kids were dying every day from cancer, car accidents, AIDS. The other day in the paper, they'd run a story about a seventeen-year-old boy who'd put up a yearlong fight waiting for a bone marrow match he'd never gotten. But there she sat: a geriatric nuisance, a vegetable with a beating heart. They must have to bathe her, shovel food into her, wipe up whatever came out the other end. What a waste, I thought. What a fucked-up universe. *She* gets to hang on to life and, meanwhile, over there at that children's hospice . . .

"Something bothering you?" Ray asked me.

"Huh? No. Why?"

"I don't know. It just seems like something's eating you." I waved away the remark—told him I was fine. What was he, a shrink now?

Was something eating me?

The nights were bad; that was when the worst panics fell over me. I slept in fits and starts, sitting bolt upright from noises I thought I heard, from dreams. One night the phone rang at 2:00 A.M. I couldn't answer it. I was sure it would be Joy. Whatever my test said, I wasn't doing it—cleaning up *her* mess for her. She had no right to even ask. I was *nobody's* father.

Tuesday night—the night before I was due to call for my test results: that was when I hit bottom. Crying jags, the shakes. I went out for a drive to calm down and ran right through a red light at Broad and Benson. No one was coming the other way, thank God, but they could have been. That was the point: someone *could have been* coming. I guess I was a little screwy by then from all that sleep deprivation.

I admired the irony of it, in a way: the way God had waited all those years and then had finally gotten around to me after all. Had finally zapped me for being the son of a bitch brother. I'd never figured that out: why God had given Thomas schizophrenia and not me. But now I thought I glimpsed the master plan. The Lord Almighty had been saving me for something else. The AIDS virus: the disease you couldn't win against no matter how well you played defense. And He *was* a jokester, too: that little scare He'd given me when I thought Thomas had the disease. But that had turned out to be a false alarm. Previews of coming attractions. He'd been saving the HIV card to play on *me*. . . .

I kept thinking about that goofy priest—the one at my brother's burial service. The guy in the sandals. Father LaVie, who'd beaten cancer. The *padre* with the amazing shrinking tumor. . . . They'd imported him from somewhere else because all the priests at St. Anthony's were busy that day. He'd told me where he'd driven in from, but I'd forgotten. I opened the phone book to the list of towns. *Danbury, Danielson*. . . . That was it. He'd said he was pinch-hitting at a rectory up in Danielson.

It was Father LaVie who answered. Sure he remembered me, he said. And how about this for a coincidence: he'd just read an article that day about twins who survived their siblings and had started thinking about me. How difficult it must be to mourn a twin. So how was I? What could he do for me?

I rambled on, in no particular order, about Ray's gangrene, Angela, the weight my brother had put on me. About what a bully my grandfather had been and how I'd bullied Thomas all our lives because I was insecure in my mother's love. About Joy's visit, her news. "Every time I take a step forward, I get clobbered," I told him. "God must really hate me."

Father LaVie promised me that there was meaning to be mined from suffering—that God was merciful, whether we understood His ways or not. This is pap, I thought—Hallmark greeting card theology. But when I hung up, I felt calmer. Better. Whatever that test result was going to say, it was beyond my control. All I could do now was hang on. Pray for a merciful, not an ironic, god.

On Wednesday afternoon, I called the test center. Got busy signals until four-forty-five. The woman had me repeat my number. "Okay, just a second," she said.

I closed my eyes. Gripped the receiver. I had it: I knew I did. I'd gotten the virus to pay for the sins I'd committed against my brother, my mother, my wife. . . .

The phone clunked. "Okay," she said. "It's here. Non-reactive."

"Non-reactive?"

That was good, she said. That was what I wanted. Non-reactive.

I walked around the condo. Took deep breaths. Dropped to the floor and did push-ups. Go to some bar and get shit-faced, I told myself. Go celebrate life.

I grabbed the keys, got in the car. It took me to the hospital.

I passed sleeping children, fretting children, empty cribs. Passed those two rabbits that Dessa had told me about. Pet therapy, she'd called it. "You wanna play?" a bald-headed girl asked me. She sat before a TV screen, playing Nintendo. "I'll let you. There's two controls."

"Can't now," I said. "Maybe later."

Dessa was in a room off to the left, seated in a rocker, holding and rocking a sprawled boy in feet pajamas. A big bruiser. The two of them, sitting, rocking, made a kind of *pietà*.

"Hi," Dessa said. "What are you doing here?"

Bob Marley was playing from a kiddie tape recorder: *One heart, one love . . .*

The boy was staring at a strange lamp on the table next to them. One of those fiberoptic things—hundreds of strands, a small, fragile tip of light at each end. I squinted at it and it became the night sky in miniature—the heavens themselves.

"I heard . . . I heard there were kids at this place that need holding," I said.

Dessa nodded. "This is Nicky," she said. "My leg's asleep. I could use a break."

He had black hair, bushy eyebrows, huge brown eyes. "Hey, Nicky," I said. Reached down and took him from her. Lifted him into my arms.

All my life, I had imagined the scenario in which my father would, at last, reveal himself to me. As a kid, I'd cooked up cowboy dads, pilot fathers who made emergency landings on Hollyhock Avenue, hopped from their planes, and rescued us from Ray. Later, I had cast gym teachers, shop teachers, the man who owned the hobby shop downtown, and even benign Mr. Anthony across the street as potential fathers: the *real* thing, as opposed to the intruder who had married my mother and installed himself at our house to make us miserable. I was thirty-six years old and *still* fantasizing when the doctors told Ma that her cancer would kill her. Over the months I watched her wither, I'd kept romanticizing her death—shaping it, as usual, to my own selfish need. She would pull me close and deliver me to my father, I thought—whisper his name into my ear and then go peacefully, having delivered us both. . . . By then, I had managed to gain, then lose, my grandfather's "history"—had lost it permanently, I thought. My suspicion at the time had rested on Angelo Nardi, the dashing Italian stenographer my grandfather had hired to help him write his story, his "guide for Italian youth." They'd been friends, she said. She made him coffee, helped him with his English. She'd hardly ever gone out. Who else could it have been? . . . Later on, after Domenico's manuscript had come back to me—had dropped *thunk!* onto my hospital bed—I'd begun the history in hopes that I would find my father within its pages. Hesitantly, with growing difficulty, I had let Domenico's voice fill up my head—had struggled with the ugliness and dread of what I became surer and surer his sorry story would reveal. . . . But in the end, Domenico had left me nothing more than a legacy of riddles and monkeys, cryptic remarks about secret-keeping that neither confirmed nor denied what I had come to fear: that he had taken evil advantage of the harelipped daughter he assumed no other man would want. That he had needed to punish, even in her death, the troubled wife he had always wanted but never really had.

But in a lifetime of fantasizing—of waiting for my real father to appear—I could not have imagined that I would find him in the exact same place—in the exact same *booth*—where, ten months earlier, my brother had sat across from me and warned me that, should America launch a holy war against the Nation of Islam, God's vengeance would be swift and terrible. That he, Thomas, was fasting in preparation for a sacrifice he hoped would short-circuit a Holy War and rescue the children of God. . . . And the last person I had ever expected would deliver me from the pain and confusion of a withheld identity was the man who, I had always felt, had stepped in and stolen my true father's place. In the end, it was Ray who delivered me—Ray who took me, finally, into his arms and held me and brought me home to the man I had spent a lifetime looking for.

"So how's it feel, overall?" I asked him.

"Feels all right. It's chafing a little. I probably overdid it."

It was Ray's first foray into the world on his brand-new leg. Things had gone well for a change—better than expected. We'd gone to Benny's for some batteries. Had stopped back at Hollyhock Avenue to check things out—make sure everything was secure. Now we were at Friendly's having lunch. Celebrating his new leg.

"Well, they said they can make some minor adjustments after you've taken it for a couple of test runs," I reminded him. "Make sure you tell them about that chafing."

"Okay, Dad," he quipped. Our waitress approached with menus.

"Hi, guys. My name's Kristin. How are you two doing today?"

"None of your business," Ray said. He cracked a smile. He was feeling his oats.

"None of my business, huh? Okay, you old grouch. What can I get for you, then?"

I recognized her. She'd been a fledgling that day when she'd waited on my brother and me—a trainee. Thomas had treated her to a sample of his religious manifesto and she'd stood there, order pad in hand, speechless. Now, ten months later, the Gulf War had been fought and filed away, my brother was dead, and Kristin here was an old pro at handling cranky customers.

Ray ordered the potpie; I got one of those "supermelt" things. Kristin asked us if we wanted our coffees right away. If we thought the hurricane everyone was talking about was actually going to come up as far as Connecticut. "Pfft," Ray said. "Hurricane *Bob*. Doesn't sound too scary to me. They just play these things up on the television to jack up their ratings."

Kristin told us she and her boyfriend were going out after work to get candles, masking tape for the windows, junk food. She came from Minnesota, she said. This was her first hurricane. She was "psyched."

After she was out of earshot, Ray muttered that she wouldn't be so "psyched" if her roof blew off.

"Sure she would," I said. "She's young, she's got a landlord to worry about the roof. All she's got to do is screw her boyfriend by candlelight and pass the potato chips."

"Sounds like a good life," Ray said. "What the hell are you and I doing wrong?"

I asked him if he'd been following the news about Russia. "Looks like the Communists may be on the ropes over there, huh?" I said. "How do you feel about *that*?"

"How do I *feel* about it?" He said he didn't feel anything. Why? What was he supposed to feel?

I reminded him that he'd gone to war to stop the Communists over in Korea. That he'd worked almost forty years building nuclear subs, just in case the Russians decided to drop the bomb.

"That was all politics," he said. "I just went to work every day and did my job. . . . You mark my words, though. Day after tomorrow, all those TV guys that are ballyhooing this Hurricane Bob thing will be going 'Hurricane? What hurricane?' "

I sat there, baffled by his nonreaction to the teetering of the Soviet empire.

Our food came. The restaurant emptied out as we ate. Neither of us said too much more and, in the silence, my mind drifted to the phone conversation I'd had that morning with Joy. I *couldn't* promise her something like that, I'd told her. She'd be all right; they were coming out with new drugs all the time. How about that AZT stuff I'd just read about? Had she heard about that?

I'd try to help her out as much as I could, I'd said—help both of them out—but my *own* life was still up in the air. I couldn't commit to something as big as that—I just *couldn't.* She had to get a grip; there were support services available for people in her situation. It was just a matter of finding out how to access them. I hadn't meant for it to come out like a speech—like my lecture that time about couch-buying. But that was what Joy accused me of doing: giving her a speech when all she needed was some peace of mind—a promise that her daughter would be taken care of by someone she trusted. Not shipped off to some foster home with perverts or people who only wanted the money. She'd cried more than spoken during that conversation—had finally hung up in my face.

"I been thinking about something," Ray said. "It's been bothering me."

"Oh, yeah?" I said. I took a sip of coffee. I thought we were talking about his leg.

"Do you remember a conversation we had a couple of weeks ago? About your father? . . . How I said she never told me who he was?"

I nodded. Held my breath.

He had had a similar kind of thing pulled on him, he said—the way his family had tricked him into thinking Edna was his sister instead of his mother. That was what he'd been thinking about ever since that conversation we'd had. Our situations were different, of course, but similar in other ways. It had pulled the rug out from under him when he'd found out the truth, he said; he'd had a *right* to know who his own mother was, for Christ's sake. Having the wool pulled over his eyes like that—well, in one way or another, he'd paid for that the rest of his life. He'd always felt inferior to other people, he said. Ashamed. And *mad*—mad at the whole world. Not that my situation and his were the same. Well, in a way they were. They were the same but they were different.

"What . . . what are you saying?" My heart raced; my breathing went shallow. Now that the moment was finally here, I was afraid to know.

"I had promised her, you see? Your mother. . . . She only told me a couple months before she passed away. I didn't know anything about it before then. We didn't talk about that kind of thing. I was just as much in the dark as you were. But after she got sick, it weighed on her. She needed to tell someone, so she told me. Made me promise not to say anything. But I don't know. It's different now. There's money involved. . . . She couldn't have seen that coming."

What was he talking about?

"She was kind of ashamed of it, you see? Of what she'd done. Of course, nowadays, they have babies out of wedlock all the time, all colors of the rainbow, and nobody even thinks anything about it. But it was different back then. For the Italians, especially. People didn't like them, see? They resented them. They'd come over here in droves, up from New York to work in the factories. . . . People used to say they were smelly, greasy, all sexed-up—the same kind of thing you hear about the coloreds." He looked around, hastily, for blacks. "The Italians needed someone to feel better than, I guess. Lots of them were prejudiced as hell when it came to the coloreds. The Indians, too. Her father, for instance. He would have murdered her if he'd known."

I was listening without really hearing him. He'd just mentioned Domenico. He was about to tell me that my grandfather was my father.

"She told me she'd always worried that if you two found out—well, not so much your brother as *you*—that . . . that you'd hate her for it. Or hate yourself. But I don't know. Things are different now. You have a *right* to know, same as I had a right. To know about Edna, I mean. And now with that thing down there."

I closed my eyes. This was it, then. Just *say* it.

"He died four or five months after you two were born. Never knew a thing about you. . . . She was kind of naive, of course—in the dark about a lot of things. She told me she didn't even figure out she was pregnant until she was almost halfway along. Back then, there was no TV, of course. That kind of subject didn't get paraded around the way it does now."

Ray was wrong. Domenico had died *before* Thomas and I were born—had had his stroke in August. She had delivered Thomas and me four months *after* his death.

"He got killed over in Korea," Ray said.

I looked up at him. "What?"

"He'd been stationed over in Europe. Germany, I think she said. And then, when MacArthur went into Korea, he got shipped right over. Didn't even get to come home first. Got killed right at the beginning, I guess—during the landing at Inchon."

Was this right? My father was . . . ?

"She read about it in the paper. That was how she found out he'd been killed. Got in touch with some gal she knew—one of his cousins or something—and I guess she filled her in a little more on what had happened. But he never got home. Your father. Never even knew anything about you two guys, she said."

"But why . . . how come she . . . ?"

"He was a colored fella. Well, part colored, I guess. Heinz fifty-seven varieties. But you know how it is. You got some colored blood in you, you're considered colored, no matter what. Least that's the way it was back then. People didn't mix the way they do now. Or have babies out of wedlock, either. . . . Her father would have killed her, Dominick. You see? He probably would have disowned her. Course, the funny thing is, *he* was the one who introduced them. Your mother and Henry. That was his name. Henry. *Your* grandfather knew *his* father."

They'd worked together at the mill, Ray said. After Henry's father died, Connie's father had more or less kept up with the family. Had sent the mother a little money from time to time because the kids were still young. It was unusual for her father to do that, Connie had said. "Her old man was pretty tight with his dough, I guess. But he helped Henry's family out here and there. For some reason. He really ruled the roost, you know—your grandfather. Over at the house. What *he* said *went*.

"He worked at the store where they traded, you see?

Henry. So she got to know him that way. Saw him every week when she did the shopping. That was how it started—because her father had known his father and because she saw him all the time at the store. They were just friends at first, for a long time. For years, I guess. He used to sneak over to the house and visit her. Her father worked nights, you see? Then, I don't know, I guess one thing just led to another. They were human, same as everyone else. And like I said, she was kind of naive—didn't know too much even by the time *I* come along. Kind of in the dark, still, even after she'd had two babies. . . . Her father would have killed her, you see? If he knew she'd fallen in with a colored guy? If he had lived, he probably would have put her out of the house. Sent her over there to live with his folks."

"You guys save any room for dessert today?" Kristin asked. Man, I jumped. "Oops, sorry. Did I scare you?"

"No," I said. "No thanks. We're right in the middle of something."

"Oh. Sorry. I can take this whenever you're ready. Or if you want, you can—"

"Thanks," I said. "I'll take care of it. Thank you."

We finished our coffee. Sat there, for a few minutes, in silence. Then Ray reached across the table and patted my hand. "Don't worry about it," he said. "It's like I always say. Mongrels make damn good dogs."

"Henry what?" I said.

"Hmm?"

"Henry what?"

"Drinkwater."

I drove out to the Indian graveyard first. Walked right up to him. *Henry Joseph Drinkwater 1919–1950. In service to his country* . . . I stood there, unable to feel much of anything. He was just a carved rock. A name and two dates. Up the path, over the rise, I could hear the Sachem River, the never-ending spill of the Falls.

At a pay phone, I looked up the address of the Wequonnoc Tribal Council office. Drove up to a dilapidated two-story house with trash in the yard. Following the sign, I climbed the fire escape stairs to the second-floor office. The door was locked; the inside empty. RELOCATED TO WEQUONNOC BOULEVARD, WEQUONNOC RESERVATION (ROUTE 22), the hand-lettered sign said.

I drove down to the reservation—past the bulldozers and cement mixers, the land that had been cleared and stumped. The coming casino. The tribe's new headquarters sat at the end of a rutted road, the beginning of the woods—an impressive three-story building made of cedar and glass. Brand new, it was. Drilling and hammering echoed inside.

I entered. Asked an electrician if he knew where I could find Ralph Drinkwater.

"Ralphie? Yeah, sure. Second floor, all the way down. I *think* he's still here. That suite that looks right out onto the back."

He was hand-sanding a Sheetrock seam, lovingly, it looked like to me. I stood there, undetected, and studied him. He'd sand a little, blow on it, pass his fingers across it, sand a little more. RALPH DRINKWATER, TRIBAL PIPE-KEEPER, the plaque on the door said.

The office was handsome. Huge. Cathedral ceiling with exposed beams, floor-to-ceiling stone fireplace that faced an entire wall of glass. Jesus, what a life he'd had. His sister gets murdered, his mother goes off the deep end. And then that scummy business out at Dell Weeks's house—posing for dirty pictures just so's he'd have a place to stay. But he had declared who he was all the way through: *Well,* I'm *Wequonnoc Indian. So I guess not* all *of us got annihilated. . . . You guys ought to read* Soul on Ice*! Really! That book tells it like it is!* . . . He'd been crapped on his whole life—had scrubbed toilets down at the psycho-prison for a living . . . and had still managed to be a good man. To rise up out of the ashes. And now, he'd arrived at this big, beautiful room. This big, brand-new building. He'd come, at long, long last, into his own.

"This going to be your office?" I said.

He pivoted, spooked a little by my voice. Stared at me for three or four seconds more than was comfortable. The dust he'd raised from sanding gave him a frosted look.

"What can I do for you?" he said.

I told him I wasn't sure—that I had just needed to find

him, talk to him if he had a minute. "I found something out this afternoon," I said.

"What's that?"

"That my father's name was Drinkwater."

I watched the surprise flicker in his eyes. Watched them narrow with well-earned distrust. He nodded, leaned against the wall for a couple seconds. Then he turned his back to me and faced his wall of glass. Faced the woods. A crow flying past was the only thing that moved.

"This afternoon?" he said. He turned around again. Looked at me. "What do you mean—you just found out *this afternoon*?"

I started to shake; I couldn't help it. I walked a few steps over to the raised hearth of his big fireplace and sat. Told him about my conversation with Ray.

He had known all along we were cousins, he said; he'd thought I'd known all along, too. That I'd wanted it kept a deep, dark secret.

"Well, I *didn't,*" I said. "I've been in the dark until two o'clock this afternoon. I'm just . . . I'm trying to figure it all out. And I need *help,* man. . . . I need some *help*."

He nodded. Came over and sat down on the hearth next to me. The two of us looked straight ahead, out at the tangle of trees.

My father and his father were brothers, Ralph said. His aunt Minnie had told him one time, way back before she moved to California. Before his sister died. "Do you ever see two little boys at your school named Thomas and Dominick?" Minnie had asked him. "They're twins, same as you and Penny. They're your cousins."

There were four children who'd lived, Ralph said: Henry, Minnie, Lillian, and Asa, in that order. Asa was his father. "Ace," everybody'd called him—the youngest and wildest of the bunch. Their parents were mixed: their mother, Dulce, was Creole and Portuguese; her maiden name was Ramos. Their father, Nabby Drinkwater, was Wequonnoc, African, and Sioux.

Every one of the kids but Minnie had died young, he said; Lillian of encephalitis, Henry in the Korean War, and Ace from driving drunk. He'd never married their mother; Ralph and Penny Ann were three years old when he flipped his car over and killed himself. Minnie was seventy-two or -three now—a widow, retired from a job with a packing company out in San Ysidro. He'd gone out to see her once—had hitch-hiked most of the way. They wrote back and forth. Minnie was considering moving back to Three Rivers, once the casino got under way. Did I remember his cousin Lonnie Peck, who'd died in Nam? Lonnie was Minnie's son. She had four other kids—two boys, two girls—all well, all with families. Minnie's son Max was a gaffer at Columbia Pictures. Ralph had seen his name at the end of a couple of movies—right there in the credits at the end. Maxwell Peck, his cousin. "Yours, too, I guess," he said.

Ralph had hated my brother and me when the four of us all went to River Street School, he said—Thomas and me, him and his sister. He'd hated the way everyone always lumped us together—two sets of twins, one black, the other white and therefore better. And then? After Penny Ann got murdered? That day I read that speech about her at the tree ceremony? He'd wanted to kill me that day, he said—pick up a rock and bash my skull in with it. "I thought you knew," he said. "I thought you wanted to deny your own father. Your Wequonnoc and African blood." The first time he'd run across the word *hypocrite,* he said, he'd thought immediately of Thomas and me: the Birdsey twins, who lived a lie.

And later on? That morning when the two of us showed up on Dell Weeks's work crew? Man, he'd wanted to bust my head in that day, too. Mine and my brother's. Six different public works crews and they'd stuck us with *his.* He was as good as we were—as smart, if not smarter. But there we were, his big shot "white" hypocrite relatives, home from college and rubbing his face in how much further you could get in life if you lied about who you were. If you kept it a deep, dark secret.

It had been our mother's secret, I told Ralph. Not Thomas's and mine.

"Your brother knew," Ralph said. "How come he knew and you didn't?"

"He *didn't* know," I said. "She kept it from us both."

But Ralph said he and Thomas had talked about it once—

during that summer on the work crew. That *Thomas* had brought it up: how they were cousins. "I remember that conversation," he said. "He said your mother told him."

"He *couldn't* have known," I said. "She wouldn't have told him and not me." And as I said it, it came flying back at me—hit me right between the eyes: that day I'd finally sprung him out of Hatch. That trip we'd taken out to the Falls. Thomas had stopped in front of Penny Ann Drinkwater's grave. *Remember her?* he'd said. *We're cousins.* And I'd dismissed it as more of his crazy talk. . . .

He'd known.

She'd given *Thomas* his father but had withheld him from me. . . .

Ralph and I talked for a few minutes more, me trying to take it all in. Trying not to sink into the unfairness of it: Ma's same old fucking favoritism.

"So . . . how do you become a Wequonnoc?" I said. "What do you do?"

Ralph misunderstood the question. He started talking about Department of the Interior requirements and notarized genealogy reports, about the way the tribe planned to disburse income once the gaming revenue started coming in. "They used to tell me in school that the Wequonnocs had all been wiped out," he said. "But now that everyone's picked up the scent of money, you'd be surprised how many cousins I got."

"I don't give a shit about the money," I said. "I'm telling you, I didn't know. I found out two hours ago. I'm just trying to figure out who the fuck I am."

He looked over at me. Studied my face for the truth. We just sat there, looking at each other. Then he got up and walked over to a big, plastic-shrouded desk parked in the middle of the massive room. He lifted the plastic, opened a drawer, and took something out of it. "Here," he said, tossing something at me. "Catch!"

I plucked it from the air and looked at it: a simple, smooth gray rock.

"Found it on the reservation the other day," Ralph said. "Way the hell out, sitting all by itself at the edge of a stream. What shape is it?"

I looked at it again. Closed my fingers around it. "It's oval," I said.

He nodded. "When a Wequonnoc baby's born, the women take the cord and form it into a circle. Cinch it, so that it has no beginning or end. Then they burn it in thanks to the Great Creator."

I looked at him. Waited.

"Wequonnocs pray to roundness," he said. "Wholeness. The cycles of the moon, the seasons. We thank the Great Creator for the new life and for the life it sprang from. The past and the future, cinched together. The roundness of things."

I palmed the rock. Squeezed it, released it, squeezed, released. "The roundness of things," I said.

"You want to know how to be Wequonnoc?" he said. "There. That's your first lesson."

I looked out Dr. Patel's office window. Watched the wind toss the trees, ripple the surface of the rushing river. It had been pouring most of the morning, gusting more and more like it meant it. The forecasters had been warning that, by the time Hurricane Bob arrived at midday, it could reach speeds of ninety or a hundred miles an hour. But when I'd called and asked the doc if she wanted to cancel our 10:00 A.M. appointment because of the weather, she'd said no, not unless I wanted to.

"You were saying?" she asked me now.

"No, I was just telling you, I'm having a hard time with it. I mean, I'm trying real hard not to fall back into my same old thing—the anger, the jealousy. It's pretty pathetic to be jealous of a *dead* brother, right? Pissed at your mother when she's been in the ground for almost five years? But I don't know. It's hard. . . . I mean, *I* was the one who kept asking her. *I* was the one who needed to know who he was. She *knew* how much I needed to know. . . . Did she hate me or something? Was that why she wouldn't tell me?"

Dr. Patel shook her head. We could only second-guess as to her reasoning, of course, but had it occurred to me that my mother might have withheld the information out of some sense of maternal protectiveness? Out of love, perhaps, not hate?

"How do you figure *that*?"

She reminded me that Ma had lived her entire life accommodating the needs of angry men. "First her father, then her husband, and then one of her sons."

"Me, you mean?"

She nodded. "Thomas had a very different nature. Yes? He seemed to have developed a temperament much like your mother's. I have long suspected, Dominick, that what you perceived as your mother's greater love for your brother may have been merely a greater sense of compatibility. Maybe she told Thomas about his and your conception because she knew he would not react in anger. Maybe she felt she didn't need to protect him from his own rage the way she needed to protect you from yours."

"Protect me?" I said. "I don't get it."

"Well, let's say that you had gone to her at age thirteen, or sixteen, or seventeen, and demanded to know who your father was. And suppose she had—"

"I *did* go to her," I said. "It was like she was deaf or something."

"Let me finish," she said. "Suppose you had asked her for the information and she had given it to you. Said to you, her angry young son, 'Dominick, your father was half Native and half African American.' How do you think you would have reacted?"

I said I had no idea.

"Well, think about it. Might you have been confused?"

I told her I was pretty damn confused now. That I was halfway through my life and had just found out who I was.

"Your confusion is understandable," she said. "But at age forty-one, you have resources to draw on, a greater understanding of the world, a whole catalog of human desires and shortcomings that would not have been at your disposal back then. If you had found out the truth at sixteen or seventeen, don't you think you might have reacted with your characteristic anger?"

"I don't know," I said. "Maybe. But that doesn't—"

"And do you think you might have turned some of that anger on her? Or on her soul mate, perhaps? Your brother?"

"Maybe."

"And back onto yourself, perhaps? Is it possible that the knowledge you sought, delivered at the wrong time and with no real support to help you fathom it, might have made you somewhat *self*-destructive?"

"Self-destructive, how?"

"Well, in the socially sanctioned ways American boys are self-destructive, I suppose. With alcohol, perhaps? Or drugs? Behind the wheel of a car? All of the above?"

"But even so. That *still* doesn't give her the right to keep it from me."

"Don't misunderstand me, my friend. I'm neither condoning nor validating your mother's decision. I certainly agree that you had every right to know who your father was. I'm merely trying to present an alternate theory as to how she may have been thinking. *Why* she might have kept the knowledge from you."

She stood. Walked over to the window where I was. Placed her hand on my shoulder and looked out, beside me, at the gathering storm. "I don't for a moment accept *your* theory, by the way," she said. "That she withheld the information from you because she hated you or wanted to punish you—to make your life miserable, for some reason. You don't really believe that. Do you?"

I took a deep breath, exhaled slowly. "No."

"Well, then, we're making progress."

"Are we?"

"Oh, I think so, yes. I've been watching your hands as we've talked. Three times, now, I've observed one hand undo the opposite fist. Are you aware of that, Dominick—that you've been prying your fists apart? It's a healthy sign, I think. Come, sit down."

In ancient myths, she said—in stories from cultures as far-flung as the Eskimos and the ancient Greeks—orphaned sons leave home in search of their fathers. In search of the self-truths that will allow them to return home restored, completed. "In these stories, knowledge eludes the lost child," she said. "And fate throws trial and tribulation onto his path—hurls at him conundrums he must solve, hardships he must conquer. But if the orphan endures, then finally, at long last, he stumbles from the wilderness into the light, holding the precious elixir of truth. And we rejoice! At last, he has *earned* his parentage, Dominick—his place in the world. And for his trouble, he has gained understanding and peace. Has earned his father's kingdom, if you will. The universe is his!"

"And everyone lives happily ever after," I said.

"Sometimes," she said. "Sometimes not. I mention it because it is one way to interpret the recent turn of events: perhaps in order to find your father, you had to earn the right to him."

I sat there, hands in my pockets, my right hand fingering the oval rock.

"Now," she said. "Our time is up. We should both go home before this tempest that's descending blows the two of us away."

This tempest, I thought. Tempesta, Drinkwater, Birdsey . . . I started home and then changed my mind. Drove over to Rivercrest, instead. I wanted to check in on Ray.

He was pissed that I'd come. "Jesus, get the hell home, will you? What's the matter with you, driving around with a hurricane coming? I'm okay. I'm fine. Go home."

On my way out, I stopped in the front foyer to zip up my slicker, watch the deluge I was getting ready to run out into. The sentries were all at their stations—Daphne, Warren, and the rest of them. They were all hopped up about the hurricane; it was the liveliest I'd ever seen them. That's when it dawned on me: she was missing. The oldest of these oldies but goodies. Princess Evil Eye.

"Where's the Queen Mother today?" I asked Warren.

"Huh?"

"Your other buddy, there. The old gal."

"You mean Prosperine? They took her to the hospital early this morning. Pneumonia."

Prosperine?

"Probably on her way out, if you ask me. She wouldn't eat or drink anything, they said. Getting ready, I guess."

I sat slumped in the living room, glancing back and forth from the window to the TV. I'd filled the bathtub, put out candles and flashlights, taped the windows. It was hard: facing a hurricane alone.

I flipped the remote back and forth, back and forth, from the Weather Channel to CNN: live feeds of Hurricane Bob, file footage of Gorbachev. He was under house arrest in the Crimea, they said. Details were sketchy. Tanks had started rolling into Moscow to answer the swelling resistance. . . .

How could she *possibly* be alive? I wondered. There had to be other Prosperines in the world, right? The world didn't work this way.

I got up and looked out the window. A tree branch flew past, someone's rain gutter clattered end over end down the street. . . . She wasn't even *coherent,* for Christ's sake. She'd just sat there in that foyer every day like a diapered vegetable. How could she *possibly* have recognized me?

Then it dawned on me. She *hadn't* recognized me. She'd recognized my grandfather.

The coup leaders invoked a news blackout. The wind moaned. The power flickered and died. Hurricane Bob had just about arrived—had turned daytime as dark as night.

That's it, I thought. She's dying over there. She might not live past the storm. I put on my slicker, pulled up the hood. Stepped into the wind and pelting rain. In the fifteen steps from the house to the car, I got soaking wet. *Stay home, stay home,* every TV reporter and news anchor had warned. I started the car.

The streets were empty, the windshield wipers almost useless, even at manic speed. Sirens screamed in the distance. I negotiated around fallen limbs, past flying shingles. A couple times, I thought my car would blow right off the road.

But I made it. I got there.

The lights were dimmer than usual; walking down the corridor, I could hear and feel the backup generators cranking. Room 414A, the security guard told me. I took the stairs. Climbed the first flight, the second. I passed three, and then stopped. Stood there between the third and fourth floors. I thought for a minute. Turned and went back down to three. The floor where Dessa worked. The kids' hospice.

It was quiet there. Just a skeleton crew: the kids, three or four of the parents. Dessa wasn't there.

An aide stared at me as I emptied board games out of a cardboard box. "I, uh . . . I'm a friend of Dessa's. Dessa Constantine? I just . . . I just need to borrow these guys for a few minutes." I opened the cage, pulled out those two rabbits, one at a time, and put them into the box.

"You can't just take them," she said. "They belong to the hospice."

"Uh huh," I nodded. "I know. I'm just borrowing them. I'll bring them right back. This is kind of . . . kind of an emergency."

I kept backing up, backing out of there. A rabbit emergency: she must have thought I was nuts. Hurricane blowing outside, rabbit-napper on the floor. I don't know what that woman thought.

ALBRIZIO, PROSPERINE. DO NOT RESUSCITATE. Prosperine Albrizio? Prosperine Tucci? It didn't really matter who she was. What mattered was that I got to her in time.

I entered the room. Placed the box I was holding on the floor. I stood before her.

"I need . . . I need you to forgive me," I said. Her breathing was wheezy; her filmy eyes were slits. She betrayed no sign of consciousness. Did she even know anyone was in the room with her?

"Can you forgive me?" I asked. "Make me whole again?"

I reached down. Grabbed the two rabbits by the scruffs of their necks and held them up—held them before the dying woman. One of them kicked the air and then was still. Back and forth, back and forth, they rocked before the Monkey.

She moaned softly. Closed her eyes. Wind and rain beat against the building.

I dropped one of the rabbits back into the box. Held the other one, still, before her. And when she opened her eyes again, the two rabbits had become one.

She watched it swing, pendulum-like, before her—watched the reversal of the dark magic she had witnessed long, long ago. "Forgive me," I whispered.

Her shaking, ancient hand came out from beneath the

sheet. Reached out, caressed the rabbit's fur. I watched the hand move back—touch, first, her forehead, then her heart, her left shoulder, her right.

Her eyes closed again. I dropped the rabbit back into the box. Picked it up and left.

I did not look back.

forty-eight

There's more, of course. The coiled umbilical cord never really begins or ends.

Hurricane Bob blew through Three Rivers and out to sea. In Moscow, the coup leaders faltered, Gorbachev was freed, and the neck of Soviet Communism was snapped. *Duck and cover!* they had taught us back in grade school. *The Communists may blow us to smithereens!* And we Cold War children had maintained the position until the day we saw Yeltsin climb to the top of a tank and face down oppression. Until we heard a hundred thousand resisters roar.

Prosperine Albrizio had been in the third-to-last wave of psychiatric patients disgorged from the Settle Building before it closed its doors in March of 1992. No records survived, or existed, of a Prosperine Tucci. Nor did I find any evidence that Prosperine Albrizio and my brother Thomas had ever known each other in their long stays at Settle—that Thomas had, perhaps, drawn her a cup of coffee from his cart or that the old woman had hobbled past him one day in the dining hall, imagining herself in the presence of her nemesis, our grandfather, who had imprisoned her. If it even *was* Prosperine Albrizio whom Domenico had imprisoned. If Prosperine Albrizio had been Prosperine Tucci. . . .

In February of 1994, at the conclusion of a three-month trial, Dr. Richard Hume and four other physician-administrators were cleared of charges of negligence related to the spread of AIDS and HIV at Hatch Forensic Institute. Hatch's 127 remaining inmates were transferred to Middletown, and the forensic hospital—the last operating facility of Three Rivers State Hospital—ceased to exist. Oddly enough, the abandoned state hospital grounds, once part of the sacred hunting and fishing lands of the Wequonnoc Nation, may again revert to the tribe, annexed for the purpose of expansion. Tribal officials and the Governor of Connecticut are deep in negotiations.

Electric Boat, manufacturer of nuclear submarines—and for the second half of the twentieth century, the economic backbone of the region—has, in the post–Cold War era, laid off workers to a small fraction of its former payroll. "The ghost yard," people now call the once-booming shipyard where my brother and I long ago witnessed the launching of the *Nautilus* and posed for a picture with the First Lady of the United States of America. But if the defense industry has dwindled here in eastern Connecticut, the gaming industry has thrived. The Wequonnoc Moon Casino and Resort opened in September of '92 and has exceeded by far even the most optimistic predictions about its impact on economic revival. In the six years of Wequonnoc Moon's existence, expansion has never stopped and the complex of casinos and hotels rises, now, like an emerald Oz out of the sleeping woods off Route 22. The resort, which has both its champions and its detractors, employs seventy-five thousand. Cars and buses stream there night and day, nonstop, and the planning committee is looking into the feasibility of ferrying gamblers up the Sachem River from New York and delivering them from Boston by way of a high-speed, state-of-the-art private railroad. We 415 members of the Wequonnoc Nation are millionaires.

Dessa and I began dating again in the fall of 1993, although we'd been seeing each other regularly at the children's hospice. She called me one afternoon, out of the blue. "I have an extra ticket for tonight's UConn women's game," she said. "Angie and I usually go together, but she's busy."

"*Women's* basketball?" I said, disdainfully. But of course, I accepted. Sat there, for the first several minutes, like a male chauvinist pain-in-the-ass. "When are they gonna start slam-dunking? . . . Who's the coach—Frankie Avalon?"

"Oh, shut up, Dominick," Dessa said, elbowing me. "*Go, Jamelle!*"

By the end of that season, I knew all the players' names and positions and could give lectures on the strengths and weaknesses of each women's team in the Big East. In '95, Dessa and I traveled out to Minneapolis together to watch Lobo and Company win the national championship.

I proposed to Dessa later that spring. We were up at the Cape—Truro—walking Long Nook Beach. Mid-May, it was: bright sun, blue sky—a picture-book kind of day. I hadn't planned it out—didn't have a ring in my pocket or anything. I just put my arms around her, kissed her forehead, and asked her if she'd be willing to take another chance.

She didn't smile. She looked kind of scared, actually, and I thought, *You're an idiot, Birdsey. You promised her right from the beginning that you wouldn't pressure her.*

She said she was pretty sure it wasn't a good idea. She'd come to like living by herself. She'd think about it, though.

I told her I could withdraw the offer altogether if she wanted. No, she said. She asked for a week.

We left the beach, went back to the hotel, had some wine. Went out to dinner. Neither of us mentioned what I'd asked her back on the beach, but it sat there between us, as big as a Buick in the living room. Me and Dessa and this Buick of a remarriage proposal I'd probably just screwed up everything by making. I'd just laid it on her without any preliminaries, any planning: do you want to sign on again? Take your chances again with the guy who almost suffocated you? Hey, if I was her, *I* would have said no. . . .

After dinner, we ended up at this arcade place. Dessa beat my butt at Skee-ball; I beat hers at mini-golf. It was a nice night, it had been a nice weekend, but we were both quiet. Distracted. I kept wishing I'd just kept my mouth shut.

We got back to the hotel. Got into our separate Rob and Laura Petrie beds. After the news, we started watching this old black-and-white Italian movie called *The Bicycle Thief.* Dessa said she couldn't believe I'd never heard of it—that it was probably the saddest movie she'd ever seen. "Yeah?" I said. "Wow." I fell asleep ten minutes into the thing.

It was her crying that woke me up, her shaking my bed—which she was sitting on. "Hey?" I said. Squinted over at the TV, the rolling credits. "What is it? The movie?"

She shook her head. Put the table lamp on. Our slit-eyes adjusted to the light.

"All right," she said.

"All right what?"

"Let's try again."

I tried to read her face. "Yeah? You sure? Because we could always—"

"I still love you," she said. "And I'm not afraid of you anymore. So, okay."

"Yes?"

"Yes."

We kept it small, simple. Leo and Angie stood up for us, same as the first time.

And by the way, Leo *did* get the General Manager's job down at Constantine Motors. Big Gene was against it, of course, but Thula and her two daughters flexed a little feminist muscle and voted the promotion through. And here's the funny part. When Leo, king of the bullshitters, got the top spot? The corner office? What does he do but go legit. Gets rid of all the bells and whistles—the bogus giveaways, the jockeying around with trade-in numbers. Plays it straight on all the TV ads, too, which he stars in, of course. "It's the nineties, Birdseed," he told me. "People are tired of getting jerked around." And the formula works, too, I guess. Isuzu just named him Regional Manager of the Year. His sales have been up eleven months in a row.

So, apparently, is his sperm count, thanks to those boxer shorts he started wearing. Their third kid's going to be a boy, according to the amnio. Angie says she and Leo are old enough to be the chaperones at their Lamaze classes. Little Leo, they're going to call him. He's due the end of October.

A month after Wequonnoc Moon opened, Aunt Minnie

rolled her Winnebago back east from California. She's one of the Tribal Council Elders now: Princess Laughing Woman. She tells racy jokes, loves to dance, and makes a three-alarm chili that'll clean your clock out in the very first bite. Minnie knew my mother; she helped me fill in some of the blanks. "I'm not saying there weren't problems," she told me. "But those two were *crazy* about each other—Connie and Henry. He used to talk to me about her all the time. You and your brother came from real love."

Ralph and I warmed to each other, over time. We had, after all, a shared history, common blood. We had something else in common, too, which we talked about once: both of us understood the singular loneliness of the solitary twin. One night—it was after a General Council meeting—Ralph and I stopped back at his office for a drink. I asked him, flat out, if he could forgive me for the way I'd betrayed him that time, long ago, in the interrogation room of the state police barracks. He thought about it, took a slow sip of Chivas, and said he guessed he already had. It's something to see Ralph in action—to watch him calm the waters at those stormy Tribal Council meetings. He's fair, even-keeled—one of the best leaders we've got. It was Ralph who led the fight to get that desk off the casino floor—the one where gambling addicts had been able to sit down and sign away the titles to their cars, the deeds to their homes. He is, and always has been, an ethical man. My cousin. Ralph.

Ray got used to his artificial leg without much of a problem—got home again to Hollyhock Avenue. He was doing great for a while there, had three or four good years, and then had a stroke. It was a bad one—landed him back at Rivercrest. His buddy Norman had passed away by then, but Stony was still alive and kicking. The stroke paralyzed Ray's right side. He couldn't talk. Couldn't walk without assistance or swallow anything that hadn't been pureed into this pukelike consistency first. He's come part of the way back since then. We got him set up in a little three-room unit out at Father Fox Boulevard, that elderly housing place the parish opened last year. I could have afforded more, but that was what he wanted. I check in on him just about every day, call him on the days I can't get there. He's happy enough.

The house at "66-through-68 Hollyhock Avenue" stood vacant for a while. I went back and forth about what to do with it and then, one night, Dessa and I went over to Sheffer's house for dinner. We've gotten friendly with them: Sheffer and Monica. We got to talking about how there'd never been a battered women's shelter in Three Rivers—how, whenever an emergency came up, women had to escape with their kids and get all the way down to Easterly. The first of the casino money had started coming in by then. One thing led to another; Sheffer and I courted the zoning board and three or four state agencies. Made a case. Next thing you know, Domenico's brick *casa di due appartamenti* had become the Concettina T. Birdsey Women and Family Shelter. Monica's company, Womyn's Work, did the remodeling. They found a way to reroute the staircases and knocked down the dividing wall between the two apartments—made it one.

Joy died in March of '97. That was a tough one—draining for everyone, me and Dessa included. She'd put up a good battle. She and Dessa got to be friends during that last year or so. The first time we went to see her at Shanley, Joy told Dess about that time she'd spotted her and Angie at the mall and followed them to the food court. Had sat down near them and listened to their conversation and wished she was Dessa's friend. And then, in that last year, she became Dessa's friend after all.

Dessa and Tyffanie took to each other, right from the start—even before all those UConn women's basketball games Dessa started taking her to. Long before she started living with us. At six, Tyffanie already knows all the players, has most of their autographs. The other afternoon, out in the driveway, she made her first basket. Regulation height that thing is out there and *swish:* I couldn't believe it.

The adoption went through last January, a couple days after my birthday. Joy had signed all the paperwork two or three months before she died. She'd cried and laughed, both, signing those papers; God, she was so weak by then. She told me she'd finally gotten what she always wanted: for me to be that little girl's father.

I stopped seeing Dr. Patel at about the time we took Tyff.

During our last session together, I told her about the most recent of my Thomas dreams: those unconscious exchanges in which I fell asleep and became my brother.

"I have a theory about those dreams," Dr. Patel said. "Shall I share it with you?"

"Oh, yeah," I said. "Like I could stop you?"

"I think," she said, "that you may be attempting to incorporate in yourself what was good about your brother. His kindness, his gentleness. Perhaps you wish to be yourself *and* Thomas. Which would be lovely, don't you think? Your strength and your brother's sweetness, together?"

I nodded, smiled. "You know what?" I said. "I think I'm finished here."

"I think you're finished, too," she said.

And we both teared up a little, hugged each other. I looked at that knee-high statue of hers, standing over by the window: Dr. Patel's smiling, dancing Shiva. And I went over and snatched up that damn thing, grabbed Doc, and waltzed the three of us in circles around her office.

We Wequonnoc-Italians celebrate wholeness—the roundness of things.

I was forty-one years old the year I lost my brother and found my fathers—the one who had died years before and the one who'd been there all along. In the years since, I have become a wealthy man, a little girl's father, and the husband, once again, of the woman I always loved but thought I had lost for good. Renovate your life, the old myths say, and the universe is yours.

I teach American history now, at the Wequonnoc School—a different kind of history than Mr. LoPresto used to teach. My students balk at tests, complain that I give too much work, and learn, I like to think, what I have learned: that power, wrongly used, defeats the oppressor as well as the oppressed. More than anyone, it was my maternal grandfather, Domenico Onofrio Tempesta, who taught me that. I have come, finally, to a kind of gratitude for Papa's legacy—that troublesome document by which he tried and failed so miserably to prove his "greatness" to "Italian youth." God—life—can be both merciful *and* ironic, I have come to believe. Papa approached his true worth only when he rolled that rented Dictaphone equipment onto the porch, sent home the stenographer, and retreated to the backyard to face his failures. Until he had humbled himself. Papa, I treasure your gift.

I am not a smart man, particularly, but one day, at long last, I stumbled from the dark woods of my own, and my family's, and my country's past, holding in my hands these truths: that love grows from the rich loam of forgiveness; that mongrels make good dogs; that the evidence of God exists in the roundness of things.

This much, at least, I've figured out. I know this much is true.

A List of Sources Consulted

Baker, Russell. *Growing Up*. New York: New American Library, 1982.

Barron, D. S. "Once There Were Two: Twins Are Bound Together Forever, Even When One of Them Dies—Stories from the Lone Twin Network." *Health,* September 1996, pp. 84–90.

Bettelheim, Bruno. *The Uses of Enchantment: The Meaning and Importance of Fairy Tales*. New York: Vintage Books, 1989.

Burlingham, Dorothy. *Twins: A Study of Three Pairs of Identical Twins*. New York: International Universities Press, 1952.

Campbell, Joseph. *The Hero with a Thousand Faces*. Princeton: Princeton University Press/Bollingen, 1972.

Cohen, David Steven, ed. *America: The Dream of My Life—Selections from the Federal Writers' Project's New Jersey Ethnic Survey*. New Brunswick, N.J.: Rutgers University Press, 1990.

D'Annunzio, Gabriele. *Tales of My Native Town,* trans. Rafael Mantelline. Garden City, N.J.: Doubleday, Page and Co., 1920.

DeSio, Paul. *Ricordiamo: The Italian-Americans of Norwich*. Norwich, Conn.: Columbus Book Committee, 1992.

DiStasi, Lawrence. *Mal Occhio (Evil Eye): The Underside of Vision*. San Francisco: North Point Press, 1981.

Dittmar, Trudy. "Cows, Arrogance, the Nature of Things" in *The Pushcart Prize XXI: Best of the Small Presses,* ed. Bill Henderson. Wainscott, N.Y.: Pushcart Press, 1996. (Originally published in *North American Review*.)

Donahue, Bruce. *Case Study: The Pequot War, 1636–1638*. Norwich, Conn.: Norwich Free Academy History Department, 1996.

Gottesman, Irving L., James Shields, and Paul Meehl. *Schizophrenia and Genetics: A Twin Study Vantage Point*. New York: Academic Press, 1972.

Hagedorn, Judy W., and Janet Kizziar. *Gemini: The Psychology and*

Phenomenon of Twins. Anderson, S.C.: Droke House/Hallux, 1974.

Holy Bible—Saint Joseph "New Catholic Edition." New York: Catholic Book Publishing Company, 1962.

Keefe, Richard S.E., and Philip D. Harvey. *Understanding Schizophrenia: A Guide to the New Research on Causes and Treatment*. New York: Free Press, 1994.

Kelly, Sean, and Rosemary Rogers. *Saints Preserve Us!* New York: Random House, 1993.

Kleinfelder, Rita Lang. *When We Were Young: A Baby-Boomer Yearbook*. New York: Prentice Hall, 1993.

Koch, Helen. *Twins and Twin Relations*. Chicago: University of Chicago Press, 1966.

Lang, Joel. "Reversals of Fortune." *Northeast: The Hartford Courant Magazine* 14 August 1994, pp. 12–19.

Leick, Nini, and Marianne Davidsen-Nielsen. *Healing Pain: Attachment, Loss, and Grief Therapy*. London: Tavistock/Routledge, 1991.

Levi-Strauss, Claude. *Myth and Meaning*. New York: Schocken Books, 1979.

Lytton, Hugh. *Parent-Child Interaction: The Socialization Process Observed in Twin and Singleton Families*. New York: Plenum Press, 1980.

Morrison, Joan, and Charlotte Fox Zabusky. *American Mosaic: The Immigrant Experience in the Words of Those Who Lived It*. Pittsburgh: University of Pittsburgh Press, 1980.

Pearson, Carol S. *The Hero Within: Six Archetypes We Live By*. San Francisco: HarperCollins, 1986.

Rutherford, Jonathan. *Men's Silences: Predicaments in Masculinity*. London: Routledge, 1992.

Schave, Barbara, and Janet Ciriello. *Identity and Intimacy in Twins*. New York: Praeger, 1983.

Scheinfeld, Amram. *Twins and Supertwins*. Philadelphia: J.B. Lippincott, 1967.

Stave, Bruce, John F. Sutherland, with Aldo Salerno. *From the Old Country: An Oral History of European Migration to America*. New York: Twayne Publishers, 1994.

Talese, Gay. *Unto the Sons*. New York: Alfred A. Knopf, 1992.

Van Dusen, Albert E. *Connecticut: A Fully Illustrated History of the State from the Seventeenth Century to the Present*. New York: Random House, 1961.

Waldman, Hillary, Daniel P. Jones, David Lightman, and Kenton Robinson. "Return of the Natives: the Northeast's Indians Rise Again," an eight-part series in the *Hartford Courant* 22–30 May 1994.

Wright, Lawrence. "A Reporter at Large: Double Mystery." *The New Yorker* 7 August 1995, pp. 44–62.

Zimmer, Heinrich. *The King and the Corpse: Tales of the Soul's Conquest of Evil,* ed. Joseph Campbell. Princeton: Princeton University Press/Bollingen, 1993.

Readers wishing to learn more about or to assist people with schizophrenia and other serious mental illnesses may contact or make charitable contributions to:

The National Alliance for the Mentally Ill
200 North Glebe Road, Suite 1015
Arlington, VA 22203-3754
Telephone: (703) 524-7600
www.nami.org